PART I

CHAPTER 1

THE FLAMES STUNG. SEARED. BUT HE'D BEEN TO HELL BEFORE.

The fire was everywhere; a world seen through a lens of rippling red glass. It steamed the seawater at shore's edge, gorged on thatch and flesh, even stained the night sky. Blood. Not his. It flaked off, brittle as beetle wings, and joined the swirl of cinders.

At least the drums were silent.

Boom. Boom. Boom-boom-boom.

It'd been an incessant litany in his head for days, gnawing away at his sanity.

Hiro shaded his face with a hand as he pushed through the burning village. He shied away from a buckling hut, lifted his greatsword as if its steel would shield him. Heat robbed him of breath, a thief stealing his last coin. Coughing, he peered through the inferno for its master.

He'd seen him only once: aquiline face, yellow eyes, skin a lacework of black runes. A conjurer.

This was no natural conflagration. Like the others, this one moved with ravenous purpose. What the Baltic Raiders hadn't destroyed, this witchfire demolished—even his company, save him and one other. What were Academy swordsmen against sorcery?

Movement ahead.

Hiro darted for the shore.

It was a sea wolf. Shrieking, it twisted on a broken leg as the flames devoured its fur.

He sheathed his greatsword into the beast's heart, kicked its corpse free into the bubbling water. Hissing followed, the angry spit of a hellcat, then nothing.

"Where are you?" he shouted into the light.

The fire swirled, parted sinuously as if by the sweep of an unseen hand. An exit? Or an invitation? Mother had always taught him to be polite.

Hiro moved through the flames, shivered as they closed behind him.

There.

Departing the pebbled beach were the langskips: long, shallow boats with slots for oars and a mast for one large sail. Gap-toothed skulls and the severed heads of their enemies were lashed to the gunwales. He recognized them—Pietro, Wulfgar, Allen, sweet Samara. Even the faces scorched by witchfire. He saw them all.

An enraged cry ripped from his throat.

The boats were all in the water now, rowing for their haven with languid strokes. Except one. A canoe, the private transport for the conjurer and his attendants. Though they treated them with reverence, the Baltic Raiders were just as suspicious of their sorcerers as the mainlanders.

The conjurer stood with a foot upon its prow, one hand outstretched to prevent the fire from encroaching. His runes were red now, embers trapped beneath his skin. He turned his face toward Hiro and smiled.

Hiro launched forward with a roar, greatsword slashing the smoky air with every stride.

The conjurer flicked the fingers of his other hand, and his attendants sprang from the canoe. Drawing dirks from their bearskin kilts, the six sloshed through the water onto the beach to meet him.

4

The big one reached him first. He put all his weight behind a downward stab at Hiro's chest. Amateur.

Hiro pivoted and swung, the arc of his greatsword cleaving the attendant's head from his shoulders as he stumbled past. The headless corpse took two more fumbling steps before collapsing into the shallows.

A spray of pebbles rained against his boots as the rest of them skidded to a stop. Their banshee cries died in their throats as they stared at their headless companion. His death seemed to confuse them, rattle them.

Hiro raised his greatsword; blood oozed down the fullers and dripped over the crossbar. The ground sizzled with every drop.

As one, the five attacked.

Hiro rolled forward as the dirks sliced above his head, driving his blade into the gut of the second. He spun on his knees, twisted his blade free, severed the hamstrings of the third. The third went down with a howl, stabbed at him with his dirk and sliced only air. Hiro caught the fourth and heaved him over his shoulder. The fifth he sliced across the chest before he returned to silence the third with a stab through his caterwauling mouth.

The fourth was back on his feet; pebbles dripped from his skin like shedding scales. He was quicker than the others, his face familiar. He darted forward, slicing Hiro's arm. Received a left cross that shattered his nose. Hissing, Hiro stepped back and pressed his hand against the wound. It was a shallow cut but stung like nettle.

Poison.

Hiro stormed forward, batted the dirk aside, and seized the fourth by the throat. Squeezed.

Behind him, the conjurer shouted.

Even as the fourth's eyes bulged and his shaved pate purpled, Hiro saw the resemblance. He swung around, dropped the conjurer's relative to the ground. With the hand of his weakening arm, he jerked the fourth's chin up and to the side, rested the edge of his greatsword against the gasping jugular.

"The antidote," Hiro demanded.

His lip twisted into a snarl, the conjurer snapped his outstretched hand into a fist.

The witchfire surrounding them snuffed out with a whoosh of heat. Behind them, the fire continued to feast upon the forsaken village, but it was no longer commanded by sorcery. It would burn itself out.

Hiro sucked in a ragged breath of blissfully cool air. His arm throbbed.

Bare feet crunching along the shore, the conjurer approached. His runes had faded to black. Two yellow eyes glared at Hiro, darted around his face. Noted the soot, the blood, the sweat. The smugness returned with his smile.

Hiro was sweating now, his weakened arm trembling.

The conjurer stopped a few paces away, crossed his arms over his bare chest. "You're not like the others," he said in flawless Layman, "but you're not strong enough to withstand nightshade poison."

Hiro cleared the tightness in his throat. "Give me the antidote."

"You'll be dead in another heartbeat. We can wait." The conjurer smoothed a hand over his bearskin pelt, flicked some ash off the edge.

Hiro heard the faintest *clink* of glass above the bubbling of the seawater. He staggered back a step.

"See? Even now you're fail—"

Hiro sliced the young man's throat and hurled his greatsword.

The blade sank deep into the conjurer's chest, knocked him flat. Eyes bulging, red spume bubbled at the corner of his mouth.

Hiro stumbled forward, wheezing. He pawed at the conjurer's kilt, ignored the feeble attempts to fend him off. He yanked the vial loose from its fine chain under the pelt and gulped the yellow liquid down before his throat closed.

Flopped on his back, he watched the smoke drift across the stars, heard the gurgling of the dying man beside him choking on his own blood. His heartbeat slowed. The stars turned black.

HIRO LURCHED UPRIGHT, hand clutched over his racing heart. His throat, paper dry, gasped for breath. Groaning, he rolled onto his side, met the gaze of angry yellow eyes. There was life still in them, venomous and vengeful as wasps.

Hiro tossed the vial aside and got to his feet. "Thank you." Mother had always taught him to be polite. He loomed over the dying man, gripped the hilt of his greatsword.

The conjurer's hands snatched the blade, and witchfire raced up the steel to engulf his hand. "*Ese, ese, esejen!*" Amber vapor spewed from the conjurer's mouth.

Screaming, Hiro tore off his glove, cradled the singed flesh against his chest. One last chuckle from the conjurer, watery and weak. Baring his teeth, Hiro yanked the greatsword free with his other hand. Then he dragged the body down to the village and fed it to the flames.

The fishing town was in ruins now, just like the others they'd been unable to save. His captain and his fellows were dead – ornaments – redheaded Alistair hidden in a cave with a broken arm and a concussion. It was just him and the souls of the thousands they'd failed.

Hiro returned to the water, plunged his blade into the steaming sea to clean it. A dark form bobbed nearby like an ominous cork; waves pushed it closer. The sea wolf.

He hauled it onto the beach, ignored the salt stinging his burned hand. Its belly was distended, swollen. Pregnant.

Hiro passed a hand over the thick fur. The fire had only singed it in places, hadn't yet melted skin. Drawing his dagger, he set to work skinning the wolf. He removed the mandible and kept the skull, scraped out the gray bits and sluiced it clean. Then he layered the pelt over his mail and settled the skull over his brow. The long fangs flanked his vision, kept him focused ahead.

He returned to the abandoned canoe, tossed out anything that would slow him down.

"Come," he told the spirit of the she-wolf, "lend me your strength, and I will set this right."

PART II

CHAPTER 2

THE MAN WAS ALONE IN THE WASHROOM WHEN THEY CAME FOR HIM. Sleeves rolled up to his shoulders and his arms elbow-deep in soapy water, he released the robe he'd been scrubbing with a long sigh. Three priests blocked the doorway, the steam immediately beading on their foreheads. Their eyes shone bright and hard as one hefted a poker; its end still glowed red from the fire.

"How did you find out?" he asked.

"Does it really matter now?" the one with the poker said.

He'd been at the temple for almost two years and had yet to learn any of their names. He'd been far too busy in the library.

"No, I suppose it doesn't. What do you plan to do with that?" He gestured to the poker.

The other two rushed him, grabbing his arms and pinning his back against the washtub. These notué priests were quick. Each straddled a leg to keep him from thrashing and locked his arms up at the joints. Just a pulse of pressure from either one of them would tear muscle from bone. He was no stranger to pain, but he fought to remain still. Primal instinct made him flinch; he tried to turn his head away.

"If I am who you think I am," he said, "then you know you're making a huge mistake."

"The Great Delphi forbids murder," the one with the poker said, "but your deeds cannot go unpunished."

CHAPTER 3

Daybreak was fast approaching when Amelia reached the crest of Mount Taru. The mountain mist muffled her footsteps, obscuring everything in shadow. It was the perfect spot to meditate, or purge her gift.

Throwing her satchel aside, she dropped to her knees and pressed her palms against the dewy summit. Silver fire jumped from her hands, scuttling over the rocks like grease dropped into a hot frying pan. Since the equinox it'd been harder to suppress, to keep hidden, and she found herself making excuses to sneak away and disperse it.

She wasn't supposed to have it. It was sorcery of the foulest kind. The Militum Dei hunted people like her. She'd been trying to get rid of it for years, retreating to this secluded spire to bleed her gift into the stone that kept no memory. It was *impure*, and she was Sanu, a virgin priestess devoted to the Blessed Lady.

When the first rays of the sun warmed her back, Amelia closed her fists with a groan. The fire snuffed out beneath her fingers. She had to hurry now. It was a special day: the Ciel Pass was open.

Amelia scrambled over to her discarded satchel and retrieved twin fans of painted silk. A quick flick to open them and she began the Dance of the Morning. The summit had been worn smooth by the years of her dancing; her sandals hardly rasped against the ground now. The silken fans grew heavy with moisture until they began to spray precious drops upon the rocks.

Her dance ended as the tide of dawn swept over the mountainside. Orange and pink azaleas, drooped with sleep, lifted their floral faces to the light and shone like tiny suns themselves. Amelia turned her back to the glare and guided the mist collected by her fans into the mouth of a jade flask.

Slinging the satchel over her shoulder, she raced to the eastern edge of the spire. Upon its craggy face clung the peach tree sacred to Lady Bosetsanu. Ripe fruit, white with a faint blush of pink, nestled in its purple leaves.

"Thank you for this gift," she murmured, plucking two peaches and pillowing them in the folds of her sari.

Before she left, Amelia touched the tips of her fingers to her lips and pressed the kiss against the ground at the base of the sacred tree. To the body buried deep within the earth.

The narrow trail meandered in a loose coil down the spire until it emptied onto a flat expanse where the temple of Bosetsanu flourished. Its pale gray stone gleamed with an inner radiance, an opalescence hardly brighter than starlight. Orchards flooded the air with the scent of peach blossoms, and the warm southern breeze hummed with the droning wings of honeybees.

Amelia scattered a pair of red-crowned cranes as she stepped over the threshold. Petals strewn across the ancient flagstones flew into brief and violent twirls of life as she hurried past. Outside the sanctuary, she hopped from one foot to the other as she shucked her sandals. The pungent smell of incense perfumed the air. Bowing her head, she walked between the columns of kneeling sisters to the altar.

Revered Onu Jocasta de Taru awaited her with a small smile and eyes that crinkled at the corners. Her white hair flowed like snow to the floor and was brushed to a fluffy fineness that rivaled the most delicate of cirrus clouds. Behind her, the black mica of the Blessed Lady's statue glittered. Her dragon curled under her feet, open maw filled with fresh flowers.

Amelia presented the peaches and scurried to her place beside the other young priestesses and unmarked novices.

The ancient sister lifted the fruits heavenward with her withered arms. "With this sacred gift, let us begin another day devoted to Lady Bosetsanu's love and truth."

When nothing else seemed forthcoming, the priestesses glanced about. This was a *special* day. A century had passed and the Ciel Pass was open. Surely that merited some sort of announcement.

But the Revered Onu simply fed one peach to the altar's white flame and sliced the second into paper-thin portions. Frowning, Amelia took the slice offered to her and ate without tasting it. After the moon peach had been consumed, there was a pregnant pause as the sisters waited. Now?

Amelia strained forward as the Revered Onu cleared her throat. No one dared breathe, lest the sound of her breath muffle the ancient's weakened voice.

"A century has passed, and Yueshu is required of us once again. As you all might have noticed, I'm getting on in years."

A soft chuckle rippled through the assembly; Jocasta was nearing her one hundred twenty-ninth birthday.

The Revered Onu smiled and raised a wrinkled hand for silence. "It is the duty of the Onu of the Sanu sect to perform this ritual, but such a journey would claim my life. From among you, I must select a sister to assume my authority and go in my stead, as Maitre. The Voice of Onu."

Whispers took wing like cicadas in summertime as the sisters guessed who it might be. Amelia leaned back on her heels and cast a glance at her friend, Yuki. The jet-haired girl pressed her hands together in mock prayer and silently mouthed, "Matilde." Stern Sister Matilde, whose dominion was the washroom, always complained that there were too many bubbles and too much laughter and not enough scrubbing when Amelia and Yuki shared the same laundry shift.

An elbow to the ribs choked off Amelia's chuckle and jerked her chin upright.

The sisters had all craned around, their eyes fixated on her like she was some rare menagerie exhibit.

"Amelia?" the Revered Onu said, clearly repeating herself. "Would you come up here, please?"

Amelia's bare feet rasped against the reed mats as she approached. Her gaze flicked to the sister standing behind Jocasta – to Aunt Saoirse – seeking understanding or some explanation, but the elder sister's eyes held no answers, only warning.

The Revered Onu carefully lifted a length of multicolored pearls from around her neck, plucked the white tassel from its end, and held it out in front of her. "Kneel, child, and receive the mark of your new station."

CHAPTER 4

"*Kneel*," the drill instructor barked.

Prince Hiro Ishida knelt in the mud, the spring rain soaking through his gi. He shivered with outrage, not cold. He sank his hands into the sludge of the training yard until he was on all fours. Then the beating began. Wooden swords thrashed across his back and shoulders. Sparks like fireflies flittered across his vision. His arms shook, but he did not go down.

The drill instructor finally called them off with a sharp word. He tapped his bokken against Hiro's thigh. "Get up. If you can."

Someone spat near his head. Trembling, his gaze remained on the patch of mire between his hands. Rain swirled the mud like cream poured into tea. He was rooted in this spot, fought to stay conscious. The blood roaring in his ears drowned out their retreating steps, masked Kale's light-footed approach from some hiding place.

The boy's hand fluttered against Hiro's hair. "Hiro? Are you okay?"

Hiro barked out a single laugh. "Not really, Kale."

"I'm gonna get help."

This time he heard the splashing of boots when Kale returned. Hiro cocked his head, eyed the new arrival: lanky, wearing a gi too large in the shoulders, flaming red hair that burst from his scalp like a thousand springs. Alistair Lochlan. His only friend.

"Why didn't you say anything?" Alistair thrust his books into Kale's hands, grabbed Hiro's arm. Hauled him to his feet. Once upright, Hiro retched. Nothing but a little bile surfaced; his breakfast had been digested long ago. The hard life of the Academy burned fuel efficiently. "Let's get you out of the rain."

They managed to get one of Hiro's muscled arms looped over Alistair's narrow shoulders, struggled across the yard to the covered porch. The training hall was dark; no one was around to see Hiro's weakness except Alistair and Kale. He collapsed on the floorboards, the wet of his thick black hair pooling into a damp halo around his head.

"Kale, get some towels," Alistair said.

The boy dumped the books into a pile and ran off, pounded a rhythm into Hiro's skull.

Hiro hissed as Alistair began pulling apart his gi.

"You're an idiot," Alistair said, yanking at the fabric. "You should've just gone down."

"Hn."

"Why didn't you come to me? I could've gone to Uncle—"

"And Domo Tanaka would've still ordered the same sentence, despite the pleas of his nephew. He must remain impartial. You know that."

"I know, but…" Alistair shook his head with a sigh, his red springs dampened to amber curls in the rain.

The pounding in Hiro's head returned. He cracked open an eye.

Kale ran up, arms overflowing with towels. "Here." The boy dumped his bundle onto the ground.

"Not in the puddles, Kale!"

"Sorry." He hastily scraped the towels aside with his foot.

Groaning, Hiro lifted an arm so Alistair could finish tugging off the gi. "Kale, think you can wring that out?"

"Absolutely, sir!"

"Now wait just a minute," Alistair said. "Hiro, you don't mean to still compete, do you?"

"Yes, I do. Now help me." He grabbed a towel, started drying his hair.

"But you were just beaten half to death."

"Then they'll see what a half-beaten man can accomplish." Hiro snatched another towel from the pile. "They need to pay for what they did."

"Didn't they the first time?"

"Not enough if they went squealing to Master Kozlovsky. Their humiliation must be absolute."

With a huff, Alistair helped Hiro back into his damp clothes. "Kale, get some ginger tea. Apparently I'm taking this fathead to the stables."

Hiro refused his friend's hand and limped across the training yard, each step an agonizing lance of pain up his spine. At the stables, he turned his head to one side and retched again. Dragging his sleeve across his mouth, he entered his mare's stall. Alistair hovered right behind him.

"Here's the tea." Kale's head popped into view over the stall door, sloshing half of it over the lip of the cup. He offered a sheepish smile in apology.

Hiro ignored the burning in his throat as he guzzled the scalding liquid. He just needed to get warm again.

"Help me with the armor, Kale." Alistair yanked at the lacings. "We need to protect this huge, *stubborn* head of his."

"This would go faster if you'd stop complaining." Hiro fitted the bit between the palomino's teeth. "That's a good girl." He led her out of the stall, finished saddling her in the aisle.

"Hiro, you can't," Alistair tried again. "Domo Tanaka banned you from competing after dishonoring Domo Favino's son. You know, the reason why you were beaten? I shouldn't even be holding this." He flung the mail shirt on the ground.

"The point of competition is to win," Hiro said. Grimacing, he dragged the mail off the ground and settled it over his gi, each fine link making a gentle *clink* as they rippled into place. "Honor has no meaning on the battlefield when it's your survival pitted against another's."

"But we're not *on* the battlefield."

"Irrelevant. Now hand me that helmet."

Alistair pivoted away as Hiro grabbed after it, kept it nestled in the crook of his elbow. "Even this helmet won't disguise you. You're too big."

"There are half a dozen other men of my size competing. Give it here." Hiro flicked Alistair's ear, snatched the helmet free. Smirking, he fitted it over his wet hair.

Alistair rubbed the sting from his ear. "But none have your brutality."

"I'll try to keep it in check this one time."

His friend snorted but handed him his bow.

"The sword, too," Hiro said.

"This is a yatsusame course, not a fight."

"It stays with me. You know that."

Alistair struggled to lift the heavy greatsword. "I still don't see why you can't just get a rabbit's foot like everyone else. And isn't bringing a lucky talisman with you cheating?"

"Tell that to everyone else with a rabbit's foot." Hiro settled the greatsword onto his back with ease. Its hilt was scaled like dragon's hide, the pommel a serene reptilian face whose fangs gripped a sapphire the size of a cherry. Forged in dragon's breath, not of Damascus steel as most thought, it'd been his mother's sword, and every Ishida general's before her. "Keep the boy out from underfoot, will you, Alistair?"

"Fine. But I get a share of your winnings."

"Hn. Thirty percent?"

"Make it forty. I'm sure I'm going to get an earful from Uncle after this."

Hiro ruffled Kale's hair, swung himself into the saddle. He fought a swell of nausea as he snapped his visor down. Putting his heel to the horse, he joined the string of competitors in the misery of the rain.

Twice a week a new competition was held at the Academy to

determine rank upon the leaderboard. Martial combat, mounted archery, cross-country races, the events always varied. Privileges were granted to those who scored the highest – private sleeping quarters, free time, increased rations – and Hiro Ishida had been very privileged until recently. *Dishonorable methods* was the term they'd thrown about at his hearing. His punishment had been dispensed this morning to ensure he was physically unable to compete. Fools.

A trumpet blast signaled the start of his run; his horse surged forward. This yatsusame course was on a forested trail with ten hidden targets. The archer never knew how quickly to draw and fire, yet each whistling arrow from his bow *thumped* into a target. A smug smile on his lips, Hiro urged his horse to the end of the course.

Four figures blurred by the rain loomed ahead, blocking his path.

Hiro jerked hard on the reins, drew his mare up short with a churning of hooves.

Faces with swollen eyes and broken noses glowered at him.

Hiro held his breath. If they caught him, he wasn't sure he'd survive another beating.

"*Ryushutsu!*" Luca Favino bellowed.

Hiro wheeled his horse, bolted for the trees.

CHAPTER 5

AMELIA'S SANDALS MADE HOLLOW *THUNKS* AGAINST THE WOODEN PLANKS of the boardwalk behind the Hall of Lilies. The walkway meandered through a garden of gnarled cherry blossom trees to the Revered Onu's private residence. Toro lanterns popped from the vining ground cover like crocuses from snow.

Dazed, she'd remained on her knees in the sanctuary long after her sisters had filed out to start their chores. Now, she caught up to the Revered Onu and Aunt Saoirse on the bridge spanning the koi pond. Alerted by their shadows, the rainbow fish surged to the surface, churning the water with their gaping mouths.

"Revered Onu, Aunt—"

The ancient sister gave her a sharp look.

"I-I mean, Sister Saoirse. Please, *wait.*" Amelia skidded to a halt and grabbed the railing to catch her breath. The pearl necklace of her new station caught around her knees; she yanked it free and flicked it aside. "Onu, why me?"

The Revered Onu looked puzzled. "Why not you, Amelia? Have you forgotten the verses about the Gate?"

"Of course not. *'The salt of my grief shall be masked by my Mother's water, and my Father's light upon its mirrored plane will guide you back to me. With the blood of Heaven, I will make a way for you.'*

"Then you must've forgotten the dance forms?"

Yueshu, the Blessing of the Gate, was a dance that was never taught in its entirety. It'd been broken into three segments centuries ago, each taught by a different instructor so no one person could perform it. Only the Onu knew its sequence.

"No, I remember. But Onu, wouldn't another priestess be better? Maybe Sister Isobel or Sister Suleika? Both are older and wiser in the faith."

"Age has nothing to do with faith, otherwise I might've picked one of them. You've only ever known Bosetsanu. You are the best choice, child. Besides, who other at this temple has shown more fascination at the pilgrims' stories than you? Or has read the Bethany Journals cover to cover a dozen times? I believe that in your heart, you long to see the outside world."

"But what about the library and the artifacts? Sister Saoirse hasn't finished training me—"

"Life is out *there*, Amelia. Not buried in one of your books. Can you give me one compelling reason why it shouldn't be you?"

Sorcery. Sorcery was a compelling reason.

The ancient raised her eyebrows, awaiting an answer.

If Amelia answered truthfully, she'd be expelled from the order. Maybe even persecuted. Hunted. So she did what no other Sanu could do. She lied.

"N-no," she said, wincing against the sudden pain that lanced through her chest. "But Onu, if I should fail..."

The Revered Onu nodded slowly. "The End Times. It will not come to that, Amelia. You will not fail. Nine hundred ninety-nine Sanu have completed this ritual. You are the thousandth. And one marked as Bosetsanu's Chosen. Some might call that auspicious."

Amelia touched her sternum where the V of her collar just barely concealed the golden tattoo. The confirmation ceremony required a novice stick her hand into the white fire that burned in the Lady's altar. It needed no earthly fuel but sustained itself on the devotion of the faithful. If deemed pure, a golden lily appeared on the back of the hand. But Amelia's tattoo had appeared on the center of her chest.

The Revered Onu squeezed Amelia's hand. "Trust in my decision. Sister Saoirse will help you prepare, and... say good-bye. You leave tomorrow at dawn."

It was only when Amelia was alone in her room that she realized the reality of her new situation. She was Maitre, the Voice of Onu. No one under the age of fifty had ever achieved that honor. When she left the mountain, she would have the most powerful influence in the world. She'd been selected for Yueshu, the Blessing of the Gate—the holiest of rituals that prevented the apocalypse and ensured an end to the drudgery of reincarnation. It was every Sanu's dream.

Amelia dropped to her knees and retched.

CHAPTER 6

WHEN IT WAS OVER, HIRO RETURNED HIS MARE TO HER STALL. HE limped across the training yard to the infirmary, clutching the arrow sprouting from his thigh. A lucky shot.

Cadets scattered out of his way. A hundred pairs of eyes trailed after him; whispers dogged his heels.

"Ishida!"

Hiro glanced at the drill instructor, kept his face a mask. If the scrappy Siberian saw weakness of any kind, he'd root it out more viciously than a terrier in a den of weasels.

"You should be in the infirmary," Master Kozlovsky said, tapping his wooden sword against his leg, "or I didn't do my job right."

"I'm headed that way now, sir."

"You're a cockroach, Ishida. No matter how many times you're stepped on, you keep popping back up."

"You trained me well, sir."

The drill instructor snorted, circled his bokken in the air. "On me." He smacked a cadet across her backside with the wooden sword for dawdling, ignored her squeal.

Hiro dragged his wounded leg up the steps, shouldered open the infirmary door.

Kale stood just inside, smiling. The novelty of the boy's sudden and providential appearances had worn off years ago. Hiro expected it now. "He's here now, Mistress Glenna," Kale called to the physician. "And only one arrow."

The fat Celt waddled over, her bottom lip pushed out in disapproval as she examined him. She felt his forehead with the back of her hand, gave his cheek a light pat. Stooping, she wiggled the shaft stuck in his thigh.

Hiro growled.

"Ack, boy," she said, cuffing his shoulder. "None of yer nonsense. Get to a bed. We'll patch ye up."

He refused the leather strap, gritted his teeth when she yanked the arrow free. A splash of alcohol, the repetitive prick of the suturing needle, and the wound was bandaged. An orderly helped him strip, put him into an ice bath for his back. The cold dragged him toward oblivion.

Mistress Glenna slapped at his cheek. "Ack, boy, stay awake. Drink this."

She put a mug to his lips: watery tomato juice with herbs drifting like flotsam over its surface. Hiro wrinkled his nose.

"All of it."

The physician tilted the cup until runnels of juice dripped off his chin. Hiro choked the concoction down, gripping the edge of the tub as his stomach churned.

Mistress Glenna grabbed Kale's arm and sat him on a stool. "Wee lad, stay here and make sure he doesna drown, eh?"

The physician gave him work to do as he kept a watchful eye on his master. There were herbs to grind and coils of thread to stuff into phials of alcohol for sterilized stitching. Finished, the boy wrested a guqin off a dusty shelf of forgotten things and began to play. Hiro's eyelids drooped.

"When they told me the great Hiro Ishida was in the infirmary, I didn't believe it," a husky voice said.

Hiro jerked around, snarled at the bolt of pain that lanced up his side.

A soft laughter filled his ears.

"Lakshmi," Hiro said. "I didn't see you in the yard this morning."

The voluptuous figure of Lakshmi Khan sauntered into view, hands on her hips.

"Not everyone has to attend morning drills." She shooed Kale off the stool, trailed her fingers in the ice water. The boy set the guqin aside and disappeared. "I was in the armory getting weapons ready for the blooding."

"*You're* leading the blooding?"

Lakshmi pouted. "And why shouldn't I? Top of my class, undefeated in the khukuri knife, I could go on. Why? Afraid you'll miss me?" She submerged her hand, caressed the length of his thigh. Hiro stiffened, shook his head warningly. Smirking, Lakshmi withdrew her touch.

"I'm just surprised," he said. "Your family could lose its candidacy for the Tybetan Seat if something happened to you."

Candidates were chosen from the Houses of the particular province that proved their proficiency in furthering their lineage. With only one child and no extended family, Domo Khan's chances were slim at being elected. Unless he had a powerful benefactor. Like Hiro's father.

"Hiro." Lakshmi pursed her full lips. "I am a *Khan*. Nothing will happen to me. At least I don't need to be worried about being dispatched to Biscay Bay. The Baltic Raiders have been silent since your blooding."

He glared at her.

"Still won't talk about it?" She stroked a manicured finger down his burned hand.

He plunged it beneath the ice.

"Not even after six years? You and Alistair were the only survivors. The Academy has never known that kind of defeat. That blooding file has been placed in the *restricted* section of the Academy annals."

Hiro scowled.

"Don't scowl at me," Lakshmi crossed her arms. They pushed her breasts forward, bulged out the V of her gi. Her chocolate eyes were dark, hungry. "You know what your scowl does to me."

She slipped her hand back into the water.

"Not now," he growled.

"Then when?" she whispered. "It's been too long, Hiro—"

"Lakshmi Khan," the Celt's voice trumpeted across the infirmary. "Ye've business here?"

"Yes, mistress." Lakshmi stood, flicked her fingers dry. "I've come with a list of supplies needed for the blooding. I was just checking on my friend."

"Well, ye've seen 'im." Mistress Glenna seized her arm, hauled her away.

Hiro watched under lowered lashes as Lakshmi's hips swayed after the physician. Sighing, he sank another foot into the ice bath.

"*There* you are," came another voice.

"Gods above, now what?" Hiro groaned.

Alistair tossed a spare gi onto the vacated stool. "If you think for one minute that you're excused from noontime lecture, you've got another thing coming."

"Alistair? How did you—"

Kale poked his head out from behind his friend, auburn curls framing his impish smile.

Alistair extended a hand, flapped his fingers. "Come on."

Hiro didn't budge. "I haven't been released yet."

"Can you stand?"

"Frankly, I don't want to try."

"Alistair Lochlan, ye leave my patient alone." Mistress Glenna bustled from the storeroom, Lakshmi on her heels.

"Hello, Master Alistair." Lakshmi clasped her hands behind her back, smiling warmly.

Alistair ducked his head, mumbled something inaudible. Shifted his books under one arm to the other. Hiro glared at Lakshmi. She was only standing that way to push her breasts out and fluster his friend. She knew he couldn't talk to women. At least none under the age of sixty.

Mistress Glenna flapped her fingers at him. "*Shoo.* My patient needs rest."

"Aren't you lecturing today, Alistair?" Hiro asked.

"Yes."

"Then I'm definitely not coming."

Alistair cuffed him on the side of the head. "Some friend *you* are."

"Leave him be." The physician nudged him aside. "Boy, ye've got more drinking to do."

Hiro grimaced at the mug of foul elixir. He set it aside, grabbed the gi. "I feel an overwhelming urge to be lectured at. Shall we?"

"I'll get you a towel."

"Is anyone here listening ta me?" the fat Celt asked the air. She snatched Lakshmi, yanked her around as he dressed.

Clothed, Hiro grabbed Kale and presented him in front of the physician. "Kale will help you with whatever you need, mistress. Compensation for my premature exodus."

"I will?"

Hiro bent until his mouth was near the boy's ear. "*That's* for getting Alistair."

The boy huffed, trailed after the physician as she rattled off a list of tasks.

When they reached the lecture hall, just a glare made the nearest cadets jump to close the gaps between them. Lakshmi sat beside him, tapped her thumbs together in her lap. She shifted along the bench until her leg brushed his.

Alistair shuffled some papers, pounded his hand against the podium.

Silence, a tide of snuffed-out whispers.

"Today's lecture in battle strategy is the last stand of the great General Bethsaida Ishida."

Hiro felt his stomach drop to his knees.

The memory of the day his mother had left, never to return, threatened to overwhelm him. He was fifteen again – just barely a man – standing in front of the gate to the rose garden. She came to him dressed in her gold chainmail, the Ishida Dragon helmet tucked under her left arm. Her black hair was gathered into a topknot banded with gold, the rest of it braided into one thick rope down her back. Unshed tears in her eyes.

His mother crushed him against her. Her armor bit into his flesh; he refused to let her go. She told him to be kind to his younger brother, kissed the top of his head. From her helmet, she withdrew a carving of an ugly Steppe horse, pressed it into his hands. Short legs, fuzz of mane; she was always whittling things.

"I love you," she whispered, turning away into the sunlight.

It had blinded him, forced him to shield his eyes until she had gone. Alone with his Steppe horse by the rose garden gate. She would never come back.

CHAPTER 7

AMELIA SCRAPED THE PEARLS OUT OF THE POOL OF BILE AND WIPED HER mouth with the back of her hand. She clutched her head with a groan. "Blessed Lady, give me strength."

She staggered to her feet and went to find something to clean up her mess. When she returned, an elderly sister stood by her futon, arms laden with supplies, her gaze fixed on the vomit on the floor. The sister's gray hair, streaked with brown, vined in puckish curls down to her knees. It'd been chocolate-brown in her youth, luscious and shiny, and as a child Amelia had called her 'Selkie.'

"Aunt Saoirse!" Amelia scurried around her and mopped the floor clean with a rag. When she stole a glance into the elderly sister's face, she found her green eyes soft and sympathetic. She plucked the ceremonial fans and the bottle of gold henna from the top of the pile before Saoirse deposited the heap onto her futon. Sticking out of the mound was not just one pouch of dried peaches, but two. Her favorite. Lastly, Saoirse produced a large jar of pickled eggs.

Amelia wrinkled her nose at the sight. She hated pickled eggs. "Thank you, Aunt Saoirse."

"You're welcome. Yuki asked that I make sure to give you the largest jar we had on hand since you like them so much."

"She is such a thoughtful friend," Amelia said through gritted teeth.

"Yes, she is." Saoirse cast a furtive glance over her shoulder at the closed door. Shadows passed in the hallway. "Is there anything else you need that I forgot, Maitre?"

Amelia winced. Her elevated position had already created a schism between her and the woman who'd raised her. After years of fighting to belong, she was being set apart. Again. Amelia swallowed past a hard lump in her throat.

The shadows in the hallway moved on. Sister Saoirse unexpectedly reached out, smoothing Amelia's hair back behind her ears and framing her cheeks with her aging hands. Leaning forward, she placed a gentle kiss on Amelia's forehead. She hadn't been permitted to show Amelia such affection in years.

Amelia clutched Saoirse's wrists. "It shouldn't be me. Aunt Saoirse, I'm afraid."

Saoirse's grip tightened on her cheeks. "There is nothing wrong with you, *ma petite*. We Atlanticans still remember the old days when the Most Holies walked this earth and freely bestowed their gifts. They might be silent now, and their gifts rare, but they are gifts all the same, regardless of what others might say. But have no illusions, Amelia," she said, "you must keep your gift hidden. The Revered Onu is sending you into the lion's den. This mountain range secludes us and protects us against outside influence. It's even created this micro-climate that keeps us in perpetual warmth. When you leave tomorrow, you'll be at the world's mercy. I tell you this not to frighten you, but to forewarn you. You *must* take precautions."

Amelia's heart pounded in her chest. "I've never left this mountain. How will I know the way? I know Lhasa's east of here, but the star charts can only guide so much. And... how will I be safe?"

The holy city of Lhasa was on the other side of the continent on a plateau abutting a seaside cliff. Before weathering had rendered the pilgrim's path impassable, the faithful had climbed the Chehara Cliff in order to pay their respects at the temple. The temple whose doors could only be opened by the gentle-hearted. Now, those wishing to visit the city were forced to prove their devotion by crossing the Himalayan Mountains first.

Amelia gulped.

"Just as the Most Holies is a partnership, so is Yueshu." Saoirse released her cheeks and adjusted the pearls around Amelia's neck. "A Delphian priest from Bastogne will accompany you. They are masters in notué and have been protecting the Sanu for centuries. They know the way. One will be waiting for you at the crossroad."

The elderly Sanu stepped back and rifled through the folds of her sari. She withdrew a thin book bound with a cover of woven reeds. Wedged in its spine was a little wand of red lacquered wood. With the wand, she flipped open the cover and tilted it for Amelia to see.

"The Bethany Journals?" Amelia asked in surprise. "It's so small."

Saoirse smiled. "I made a copy for the library. It's on rice paper, so you need to use the wand so you don't leave fingerprints. I know Sanu are not to give or receive gifts, but take it with you. Your favorite stories will keep you company on the road."

Amelia held the book tight against her chest.

"Now I must leave, *ma petite*, otherwise I fear I'll never let you go." The elder Sanu smeared the tears from her eyes and left, sliding the screen shut behind her.

Alone again. Amelia turned to her futon and started packing with numb fingers. Jasmine soap, packages of dried vegetables for soup, a traveling cloak of undyed flax, they all disappeared into her rucksack with room to spare. She dropped the pack by the door and fled.

It was too hot in there. The air had grown thin, and she gasped for breath. In the courtyard, her sisters exclaimed in alarm. They touched her brow and hair, tried to soothe her, to suffocate her. Someone brought a gourd to her lips, offered her a drink, tried to drown her. Silver sparks fizzled from her fingertips. She pushed them away, broke free of their pawing hands.

Her heart hammered in her chest as she made the climb for the second time that day. Amelia scrambled up the spire, falling in her haste and splitting her knee on a jagged chip of rock. Half-blinded by tears, she pushed onward to the summit and collapsed at the base of the sacred peach tree.

The exposed rock was hot, and her tears dried upon her cheeks. She shored up against the trunk and into its meager shade, tucking her legs to her chest and hiding her face on her knees. She inhaled deep, shuddering breaths.

It was no use. The panic had her.

If she refused to go, they would discover her secret. They would force her hand into the altar's white flame and she would sing the truth then. She would be abandoned again, a leaf on a hurricane wind. But if she went, she would fail. Sorcery tainted her, and the ritual required a pure vessel. She would *not* be the harbinger of the apocalypse.

It had to be someone else.

Leaning forward, she pressed her hands into the ground. It was over for her. She would never dance here again, never sneak sips of young wine from the cellars with Yuki, never smell the blossoms of moon peaches. Wailing, she released her gift into the rock.

The silver flame erupted into the sky, a pillar of swirling light. Amelia scuttled away from the blaze, clamping her hands to her chest. Instead of extinguishing, the fire engulfed her. Screaming, she shrank into a ball and squeezed her eyes shut, praying for it to stop.

She didn't burn.

Amelia peeked open an eye and stood.

The silver flame was cool, and the wind of its passage teased her hair into the air above her. The fire rippled like water, twisting around her like a playful hound. Laughing, she swept a hand through the flames. They vanished into the cloudless sky, and her hair fell about her once more. She pushed the disheveled mess out of her eyes and stopped, her hair halfway behind her shoulders.

Yuki stood at the trailhead, eyes white and her full lips frozen in mid-gasp. The bottle of wine slipped from her fingers and shattered against the rocks.

"*Yuki.*" Amelia chased her down the trail. "Please, *stop.*"

The jet-haired girl slipped and slid down the path, a cascade of loose scree showering off the cliff-side.

Amelia grabbed an exposed root to slow her descent and extended her hand to her friend. "It's not what you think."

Yuki smacked her hand away and dusted off her sari. "I don't know what I think, Amelia. I came up here because you were having one of your panic attacks, and…" She shook her head and turned back to the trail.

Amelia trailed after her, choking on the dust. She caught up to Yuki again and grabbed her arm. "What are you going to do?"

"I don't know," Yuki said, tugging free. "Sanu can't lie, and we don't keep secrets from our best friends. Why didn't you *tell* me?"

"Because of the way you're looking at me right now."

It was true that Sanu couldn't lie. In exchange for the golden tattoo, the white flame took away their ability to lie. It was impossible. Except for her. But if and when she did, a pain – hot as a branding iron – lanced from her tattoo down every nerve in her body.

Yuki was looking away, down the curve of the trail. She folded her arms across her chest and took a step back, but she did not flee. A swallowtail butterfly flitted past, tickling Amelia's arm and fluttering in Yuki's face before disappearing over the ledge. Yuki started forward, craning over the edge to catch another glimpse of Boset-sanu's messenger. Amelia felt her heart leap to her throat.

"I figure the Blessed Lady would've blasted you back a hundred feet at our confirmation ceremony if you hadn't been worthy," the jet-haired girl said after a while. "And she wouldn't have given you that." She pointed to the hidden tattoo on Amelia's chest. "Does Onu know?"

Amelia shook her head.

"I can forgive you if you haven't held back anything else."

She nodded quickly. "I haven't, Yuki, I swear."

"Good. Now come on." She took Amelia's hand and gave it a tug. "We need to tell Onu. She has to know. Rotten timing too. A pilgrim just arrived—"

"Wait."

"What is it?"

There it was again. A cry. Gryphons were said to have nested in this area, but no one had seen one for hundreds of years.

Amelia froze.

Screams came from below, their echoes dying on the rocks.

CHAPTER 8

"GET UP," HIRO HISSED TO LAKSHMI. STARTLED BY THE VENOM IN HIS voice, she fell out of her seat.

Hiro stalked out of the lecture hall without being excused. Outside, the sky roiled with dark clouds, threatened to unleash their fury upon the earth once more. He stormed to his room, nearly ripped the sliding door out of its track. Lakshmi forced herself in behind him, wedged the brazier stoker in the track.

He turned on her, wild. "I have no time for your games, Lakshmi. I want to be alone."

"What you want is to forget." She untied her gi, let the jacket slip from her shoulders. Hiro swallowed, turned his eyes away from the dusky flesh. She took his hand, molded it against her breast. He couldn't deny that it promised something he so desperately wanted. "Can't you see what you do to me?"

She slid her hands up his arms, along the strong column of his neck, threaded into his hair. She drew his face down to hers, pressed her mouth against his.

He kissed her hungrily, sought oblivion in her passion. Growling, she broke the kiss to pry apart his gi so she could rub her hands along the great slabs of muscle underneath. He took a fistful of her hair, wrenched her head back. Kissed her again. Her lips parted, let him have his way with her. She wrapped one arm around his neck, plunged the other beneath his waistband. Hiro moaned against her mouth when she found what she was looking for.

"You get nothing for free, Ishida," she reminded him. She took his hand, guided it down her trousers. *"There."* She arched against his fingers.

And their hands granted them each the release they searched so desperately for.

Later, alone in the dark of his room and staring at the ceiling, a knock rapped on the doorframe. Hiro tensed one breath, relaxed the next. He and Lakshmi were the epitome of discretion. They had to be if they didn't want to be beaten and sent from the Academy with naught but their skins.

He limped to the door.

Of the three figures in the gloom, only one took a step forward into the wan afternoon light. Impeccable posture, piercing eyes, full mouth set in a disapproving slant. Hiro recognized him immediately. He bowed as deeply as he could.

"Domo Tanaka."

The Academy Proctor's voice was as crisp as autumn leaves. "You will attend me in my office, Hiro Ishida. We have much to discuss."

A GREAT PAGODA sprouted from the mud like an oni demon, hulking, the tips of its curved roofs piercing the clouds like horns. They climbed the exposed stairway to the top floor. One of the six guards posted there slid open the door.

Domo Masaru Tanaka swept inside, shucked his coat. He went around his desk, lifted the lid of a porcelain teacup. Steam rose, tendrils of smoke from a miniature dragon. "Please, be seated." The Proctor gestured to a cushion on the floor.

"I'll stand, Domo."

Domo Tanaka sent him a sharp look.

"My leg, Domo," Hiro said hastily.

Domo Tanaka nodded, his topknot not once moving a hair out of position. The Academy Proctor wore his banded with gold, a right shared only with Lords and generals of the highest order. Upon graduation, a cadet wore copper, either banding his topknot or wearing ear cuffs. Rank was achieved through battle. Hiro had already seen combat – no, *massacre* – and had a silver ear cuff hidden in his room to prove it. Domo Tanaka had presented it to Hiro in secret; the two had never spoken of it again.

Hacking, the Academy Proctor picked up his teacup.

Hiro averted his gaze to the only frivolous item in the entire office: a stunning painting of a leaping carp hanging behind the domo's desk. Hiro knew it'd been painted by the domo's nephew. When his sister had run off to marry a flame-haired Celt, the Tanaka House had vowed to disown her forever. But when Alistair had been born, the Academy Proctor had become smitten with the redheaded child.

"When I spoke with Alistair," he said, clearing his throat, "he said you would, and I quote, 'show them what a half-beaten man can accomplish.' Apparently a great many things. Tell me, will we ever discover the bodies?"

The heavy rain had dampened everything; it had been easy to get lost in the forest. Or hide in it. He took them one at a time, disappeared into the dark undergrowth between each strike. He let the forest sounds gnaw at their nerves. The creak of a branch, the rustling of loosened scree, the scream of their suddenly misplaced companion. He'd left them dangling in the trees, strung up by their feet.

"If they've learned anything here, they ought to be able to free themselves," Hiro said with a shrug. "Eventually."

"I see. So you completed our most difficult yatsusame course without flaw, successfully evaded a force of superior numbers, found your way back to a secure location amidst miserable weather conditions without being seen or caught—"

Hiro felt the pride swelling his shoulders start to dissipate.

"—and yet"—Domo Tanaka slammed his palm against the desk —"you have learned *nothing*."

"'Learned nothing?'" Hiro hissed. "How can you say that?"

"You haven't learned teamwork. How many friends, even non-hostile acquaintances, have you made here besides Alistair and the boy? You haven't learned the worth of a man, or subtlety, or graciousness, or mercy—"

"Mercy is for the *weak*. It has no place upon the battlefield."

Domo Tanaka shook his head. "Nothing. Not even honor."

Hiro exploded. "My honor was stripped from me twenty years ago when my father banished me here. He stripped my home from me because I had the gall to challenge him. To speak for those he was sending to their deaths. And my reward was being sent to this Academy of *cowardly old men*."

The door snapped open. Four guards rushed in, katana glinting in the gray light.

Domo Tanaka stilled them with a gesture.

"Forgive us, Domo," said the first. "We heard raised voices."

"Thank you, Captain, but I don't need your services."

The four bowed, slid the door closed behind them.

The Proctor picked up his cup again. "You were sent here because it was Lord Ishida's fervent wish that you learn strategy, composure, and *respect* at this Academy."

Hiro gritted his teeth. "My father's strategy killed my mother."

"As his general, it was her duty to carry out the will of her lord."

"It was suicide!"

"Perhaps that's why you are here, Hiro, to be better. So you will not make the same mistake when you assume the mantle of leadership. Honestly, how are you supposed to lead without the respect of your men?"

"It is my duty to lead and their duty to follow. I do not need their respect or admiration or comradery. I need only their compliance."

"You fail to understand that to lead is to empathize, to serve is to sacrifice. You know only how to take, not receive. You would not even sit when I, your superior, offered it to you, knowing how painful it must be to stand."

Hiro said nothing. Outside the rain picked up, rushed down the slates and sluiced over the roof. Hiro could barely hear him above the roar.

"Do you know what they call you, when they whisper behind your back?"

He clenched his burned hand. "The Beast of Biscay."

"Though only you and I know how true that appellation actually is." The domo rubbed his chin. "Not too dissimilar from a title given to another man twenty-one years ago, don't you think?"

Hiro glared at the Academy Proctor. He was about to cross a line that would leave him in a bloody heap upon the floor and Hiro dangling from a noose in the training yard for murder.

The Proctor dropped his gaze, a subtle act of apology. Smothering another cough, he poured himself some more tea. "I'm resolved not to graduate you until you learn—"

"You won't graduate me because my father does not permit it."

The Lord of Jianshu had requested that Hiro stay put, and no one, not even the impartial Academy Proctor, refused the Lord of Jianshu anything. Not when it had been *his* army that had defeated the Tybetan Monster and had liberated the whole of Eurasia.

"—*but*, my hand is being forced." Domo Tanaka picked up a scroll from the corner of his desk. "Unfortunately, I don't have the time to correct the rather egregious lapses in your education. You've been summoned to Jianshu at your father's request. He expects you back no later than the summer solstice."

Home.

"W-what? Why now, after all this time?"

"The notué priests of Bastogne have been exterminated. Soon the entire continent will know. It was only by some miracle that one of our graduates was returning home that way; it might've gone unnoticed for weeks."

Of course he wouldn't let me return unless he needed something from me. But Toshiro. I'll get to see my brother again.

"I know my father is a religious man, but why would a bunch of slain priests—"

The Proctor raised a hand to silence Hiro's question, smothered a cough, gave him the scroll instead. "Your father did not explain himself. Here are your release papers and graduation certificate. A duplicate was made and sent out to Arashiyama this afternoon.

"Wear the silver cuff you were given for your service at Biscay Bay until your hair grows. You leave tomorrow morning, bringing the boy with you, of course. Master Pindar will have supplies ready for you in the pantry." He gestured to the door. "May Delphi the Protector guard your steps."

Stunned, Hiro bowed, limped to the door.

"Prince Ishida." The Proctor's voice was soft, urgent. Domo Tanaka came out from behind his desk and knelt. He pressed his forehead to the floor in the ancient gesture of deepest respect. "Thank you, for saving my nephew."

Hiro clenched his burned hand, nodded. "Always."

CHAPTER 9

AMELIA SLID TO A STOP AND DOVE INTO THE BRUSH. SHE SNATCHED Yuki off the trail and yanked her down beside her. With trembling hands, she parted the screen of jasmine.

Beyond the red torii gate, the sisters screamed and scattered. Their orange saris streamed behind them like flares as they sought refuge. Any refuge. By the dining hall, a red-crowned crane nudged its mutilated mate, ruffling its beak through the blood-stained feathers. Someone had knocked over the fire bowl of fragrant oil, and a line of yellow flames zipped across the courtyard to the library. Sister Mika screeched and swatted the fire that gnawed at the fringe of her sari. A dark form hit her from behind, pinned her squalling to the ground, and sank iridescent teeth into her neck.

Amelia clamped her hand over Yuki's mouth to smother her scream. They fell back into the jasmine, the star-like flowers smothering them with perfume.

The demon's head snapped up at the sound. It flashed to the torii gate.

Amelia tightened her grip on Yuki's mouth and stifled her own shriek. The demon had disappeared and reappeared within a heartbeat, first across the courtyard and then only feet away from their hiding place. Black, its form shimmered around the edges, like something seen through a haze. Twice the height as the tallest of them, it had long arms for climbing and claws that sprouted from cat-like paws. Powerful hind legs coiled beneath it, as thickly muscled as a greyhound's. It had no eyes but a big set of nostrils that snuffled the air, searching for them.

Her blood turned to ice. She'd read about them, heard stories about them, but she didn't believe in them. Demons never breached the Abyss. Yet here one stood, a myth made flesh.

Amelia blinked the sweat from her eyes and kept very still. Yuki shivered in her arms, her tears dribbling over Amelia's hand and making her skin itch. Her heart hammered hot in her chest, threatening to melt her from the inside out. The air, thick as honey, tried to strangle her. It was only Yuki's cold and clammy hands digging into her forearm that kept the panic at bay.

A bee droned by, bringing the scent of peach blossoms from the orchard.

The demon snuffled the jasmine, a great snort dislodging the bee from a flower. It plummeted to the ground and writhed on its back, legs furiously kicking to right itself.

Amelia ignored its plight, riveted by the large nostrils huffing about the blossoms.

Growling, the demon lifted a paw, gorged the ground, and flashed away.

She and Yuki jumped as fresh shrieks sounded by the orchards.

Amelia surged to her feet and pulled Yuki after her. Peering around the gate, she saw only the mayhem left in the demon's wake but no sign of the creature itself. She skirted around the Hall of Lilies, heading for the sanctuary.

On feast days, the golden hall would be festooned with hundreds of paper lanterns. Now the lily murals were splattered with blood, and the precious honey cakes meant for her farewell feast were scattered across the floor. Their sweet smell mingled with the stench of smoke and gore.

Distracted by muffled whimpers, she diverted from the sanctuary.

Amelia rounded the corner and threw a finger to her lips, silencing the startled cries of a cluster of unmarked novices.

"It passed us by," Nylah blubbered. "It saw us and left. Why—"

Amelia shook her head and beckoned to them. *Come.* Yuki grabbed the hands of the nearest girls and tugged them after her, heading for the sanctuary. She, like every Sanu, knew no demon could enter a structure that housed the white flame. Together the priestesses shepherded the novices toward the hallowed ground.

A mutilated sister sobbed as her frail arms struggled to pull her up the few stairs to the sanctuary. Amelia pushed Yuki forward, toward safety. "Ring the gong. Wake the guardian." She turned and crouched beside the struggling sister. "Onu."

The Revered Onu's cirrus-like hair was tacky with blood, and one leg twisted out at an odd angle behind her. "Maitre, you must flee," she urged, ignoring Amelia's attempt to help. "Leave me."

The gong clanged, and the dust between the flagstones shivered. Amelia glanced over her shoulder, half expecting to see a dragon erupt from the sanctuary. Nothing came. The gong continued to sound, frantic now.

Amelia seized the ancient's arm. "Onu, I don't know the sequence of the dance."

Jocasta's eyes widened in alarm. "It's—"

In the sanctuary, one of the novices screeched.

The demon had returned.

Lurching forward, Amelia wedged her hands under the sister's arms and heaved. The Revered Onu yelped as her broken leg smacked against each step.

Amelia managed to get her halfway into the sanctuary before the demon flashed onto the porch. She lost her grip and toppled backward.

The beams strained and snapped over its hulking shoulders, and slate shingles splintered on the ground. The demon extended one claw, pierced the Revered Onu through her broken leg, and peeled back its lips into a ghastly smile.

Howling, the Revered Onu's fingernails tore ribbons of lacquer from the floorboards as the demon dragged her across the porch. Amelia lunged for the sister's flailing hand. "Elwynn. Find El—"

Amelia's fingers grazed the ancient's withered flesh as lightly as a butterfly's kiss before the demon flung her into the torii gate. A wet thud, followed by another as her body dropped to the flagstones, leaving a smear of crimson behind.

The temple guardian never appeared.

Stunned, Amelia stared at the crumpled body for only a moment. She ran.

She sprinted for the jasmine on the west side of the sanctuary and disappeared into the blooms. Heedless of Yuki's cries, she didn't look back and she didn't stop. She just had to get away.

Amelia caught the trunk of a young imperial maple and swung hard to the south, racing for the dormitories. Farther away, the cacophony of terrified priestesses and demonic howls continued to rage. She finally risked a look behind her; there was nothing but the broken underbrush of her passage.

A jagged hole in the wall was all that remained of the dormitory door. Amelia picked her way through the debris, refusing to look at the bodies of her slain sisters. The demon hadn't just killed them, it had mutilated them. Dismembered limbs littered the hallway; pools of viscera congealed in the doorways; blood dripped from the ceiling. She shuddered as a fat drop splattered on the back of her hand. With a cry, she shook it off and snatched her rucksack from her room.

Amelia bolted from the carnage and vanished into the azaleas. Their pink and orange faces were so thick she nearly missed the path. It was a narrow thread of bare earth, hardly more than a game trail, which would peter out north of the temple road. She would be exposed then.

She yanked the rucksack over her shoulders and took a deep breath.

Trembling, she poked her head above the flowers.

The demon bellowed in triumph, and the screaming began anew.

Amelia clamped her hands over her ears and fled.

CHAPTER 10

THE SORCERER WRENCHED OPEN THE DOOR.

Behind him, the skein gleefully roared, flashing here and there and painting the temple scarlet with the blood of its priestesses. Demons loved mayhem, and this one had been eager to answer his summons.

He stalked into the library, pausing just inside to let his eyes adjust to the gloom. They still hurt from before, and the smoke from the overturned fire bowl irritated them. There was smoke in here too, not the sweet smell from fragrant oil, but the acrid bite from burning parchment.

Hurrying forward, his robes flapped about his knees as he checked down each row. An orange glow flickered behind a honeycombed shelf of scrolls. The faint crackling drowned out the cacophony of the massacre outside.

He rounded the corner, startling an elderly Sanu with a mass of gray-and-brown curls. She stood over a wastebasket, frantically tearing a scroll to bits and feeding the orange glow until it grew into a tall yellow flame. The scraps of paper singed at the edges, curling like dried leaves, the golden ink melting away and hissing in the heat.

At his appearance, the Sanu snatched a rosewood chest from the table beside her. She clutched it tightly between her hands and thrust it over the flame. It was a small thing, no larger than a girl's jewelry box, with a silver knotwork inlay where the keyhole would be.

The Raion Chest.

It was the reason why he was here.

"Put it down," he ordered. His swept his cloak aside and rested his hand on the pommel of his dragonbone knife.

The Sanu's green eyes flashed in defiance.

"You know fire cannot destroy it," he said.

"No ordinary fire, yes," the priestess agreed. "But this one has been fed with the scroll of the sacred texts. It'll burn anything. Even this." She lowered the box to the grasping flames.

"*No!*"

The Sanu paused. "Call off the attack."

"No." He couldn't even if he wanted to. The summoning could not be changed. Once bound with a task, a demon would complete it or die. And they were near impossible to kill.

"Then it must be done."

The priestess jumped as her sister was thrown into the window. Her shadow pressed against the linen screen, scrambling to get away, when the demon pounced. A terrified scream turned into a gurgling gasp as the demon slashed her throat, spraying the linen with red. Blood soaked into the fibers, spreading like spilled ink.

He took a quick step forward, raising his hands to stay her. "Stop, and I will end your life quickly. The skein will never touch you. Burn it, and you'll wish for death by its hand, for I will not be so merciful."

She hesitated, eyes riveted on the window.

He took another step forward, boot rasping against the stone. He was almost close enough to—

The Sanu flung the box into the fire.

She jumped back as he pounced, but the flame had already engulfed the box. It burned like seasoned timber, flaring white with incredible heat before reducing to ash. Even the silver inlay was disintegrating.

With a roar, he yanked his dragonbone knife clear of its sheath. He spun, hurling it into the back of the fleeing priestess.

The Sanu collapsed to the floor with a cry, pawing for the knife she couldn't reach. Keening, she crawled for the door and a quicker death.

He turned back to the wastebasket. The holy fire winked out with one final flash, its task complete. Nothing but a mound of black sand remained.

He gave a frustrated huff and stalked after the dying Sanu.

She'd gotten farther than he'd expected; the red smear of her passage ended at the library threshold. Outside, the stench of death greeted them. The demon had the last of the priestesses trapped in the sanctuary, deterred by the sacred white flame and unable to pursue. It didn't concern him; eventually they would have to venture beyond its protection if they wanted to eat, and then the demon would have them.

He crouched by her side and tugged the knife out of her back. Grabbing a fistful of graying curls, he yanked back her head. The priestess gasped, spraying the stones with bloody spittle.

He gave her head a little shake. "What have you done, witch?"

But she was laughing, a dry croaking noise that grated in his ears. "Fool," she said. "Only a Sanu could open it. And you've killed us."

"No! The notué priests have a key—"

"A decoy. Did you think this secret was protected by an ordinary lock?"

His blood curdled. Sanu could not lie; the golden lily on their hands prevented it. He would be *manabudh* – a Forsaken One – if he did not make this right.

Snarling, he slammed her croaking face into the stones. Grinding her head into the ground, he pushed himself upright. He went to the ash and collected it into a pouch, taking the time to capture every grain.

When he was done, the Sanu's bloody face was wan, her mouth slack, her green eyes dull. Dead.

He wiped his blade clean on her orange sari and left. As he trudged down the mountain path, he pulled a long-stemmed pipe from his pocket. He relit the pipe with a match and sucked hard on the smokeweed. Runes glittered across its bone-pale surface, glowing green with the summoning. Tiny things, they flickered like fireflies.

The skein flashed before him, deep chest heaving and long indigo tongue lolling to one side. Its shadowy hide was striped with blood and gore, its iridescent teeth stained pink.

A task could not be changed, but the time of its completion could be.

"When you find that last Sanu, bring her to me alive and unhurt," he instructed. "I want to speak with her before you kill her."

The demon nodded once and vanished.

He picked up his pace, determined to reach the crossroad before the demon returned with its prize. There was a priest there he needed to kill.

CHAPTER 11

THE DEMON'S ROAR ECHOED INTO THE NIGHT.

Amelia shucked her pack and wormed herself feet-first into the hole of a rotting pine log. She yanked her pack in after her, closing the gap. Various holes bored into the wood gave her a spotted view of the sky. The Great Bear dipped low, hugging the treeline. Something blackened the stars, and something snuffled and scrabbled along the bark.

Amelia froze.

A rodent's whiskered face popped into view, moonlight illuminating its ears like pearls. Its head cocked, shiny black eyes examining the unwanted guest encroaching on its den. Those shiny eyes bulged a heartbeat later, a piercing squeak trumpeting from its tiny mouth. Five black claws punctured the rotting wood; one dripped blood onto her cheek.

Amelia turned her face away and bit her lower lip to keep from screaming.

The log creaked as the demon shifted its weight, snuffling along the holes. One nostril filled the hole where the mouse's face had been, blasting her with sulfuric fumes with each exhale.

She couldn't hold her breath any longer.

The demon howled and tore away at the log.

Amelia shrieked as she was pelted with bits of rotting wood and pine straw. The demon reared back, a triumphant squeal gurgling from its throat, and lunged.

With a cry, she threw her hands up to cover her face.

The blast of silver fire knocked the demon aside. Amelia scrambled from the debris and crouched, both hands rippling with silver flame. The demon whined, clawing at its burned face. It bashed into trees, scrabbled against the ground, utterly senseless. It rooted its ruined nose against the pine straw one moment only to shriek the next. Then it raced off into the night, the splintering of pine following in its wake.

Shaking, Amelia turned to the wet on her hand. It was black and oily-thick, shining like crushed crystal in the starlight. Demon ichor. Frantic, she rubbed it off on the pine straw before it could burn her. Grabbing her rucksack, she turned in the opposite direction of the flailing demon and ran.

CHAPTER 12

ALISTAIR LEANED AGAINST THE DORMITORY WALL, PICKED HIS fingernails.

Hiro seized him by the throat. "You're an ass. The Battle of the Xinjiang Plains? *Really?*"

Alistair's books bounced against the floorboards as he squirmed, clawing at Hiro's fist. "That's a first edition *The Phoenix Tomb and Other Lost Wonders* and its pages are getting—"

Hiro ignored him, gave him a little shake.

"I'm a battle strategist," Alistair squeaked. "It's the most famous battle in the last century. If I didn't lecture on it, I wouldn't be doing my job!"

"You didn't have to pick *that* battle for today's lecture."

"It was meant to honor—"

Shadows behind his door. He gave Alistair a warning look, slid the door open a crack.

Kale was pouring tea into three cups amidst a low table laden with food. Actual food. Not the shapeless fuel the Academy fed its cadets.

A farewell feast.

Hiro released his gasping friend, helped pick up the strewn books. "He told you?"

"I *am* his favorite nephew." Alistair pushed past him. "Though I'm considering throwing all this to the pigs."

"*No*," the boy cried. He dropped the teapot, clamped the edges of the table in his small fists.

"No, you won't," Hiro said. "You don't eat this well either, *Master* Alistair."

"True, but I asked Kale to swipe some wine for us from the pantry. Perhaps I'll make him put it back." He picked up a dark bottle of purplish liquid. "What kind did you get, anyway?"

"It said mûremei on the shelf—"

The bottle slipped from his hand. "You took Uncle's special reserve blackberry brandy?"

Hiro caught the bottle midair, yanked the cork out with his teeth.

"Give me that." Alistair swiped the bottle. He took a long pull, followed by another. "Oh my, that's delicious."

Hiro plucked the brandy from his friend's hands, drank deeply.

"Rude," Alistair said. "But I suppose it *is* your party. Let's eat before it gets cold."

Roasted chicken in apricot glaze, grilled seafood over fat noodles in butter sauce, even Old Imperial egg custard tarts for dessert.

Kale dropped his chopsticks, done drawing knotwork designs in the apricot glaze, and dragged himself to bed.

Hiro draped a blanket over him, smiled as the distended belly swelled with each snore. It reminded him of the bullfrogs he used to catch in the summer as a boy.

"This is for you too." Alistair tossed him the winnings from the yatsusame course. "I donated my forty percent. You'll need it more than me."

"You didn't need to do this, you know. The feast, the money. It wasn't—"

"I'm your friend, Hiro."

"But why?" He couldn't shake what Domo Tanaka had said in his office. "I'm too angry, too *toxic*—" The brandy had flooded his system, made him almost delirious. His thoughts blurred, darted like fish in muddied waters. His pains lessened. He thought Alistair wasn't going to answer him, but his friend said,

"You saved me. Despite being the domo's nephew, my youth here was, well… you know how bad it was. I wasn't exactly Academy material. And then you found the boy in the garden. Why were you there again?"

The mûremei made it hard to remember. Hiro grasped at the murky fish for the right answer. "Manual labor for mouthing off to Kozlovsky."

"Ah, that's right. That temper. Well, you could've left Kale alone, or put him back into the river from whence he came, but you took him in, like you did me. Despite your crusty exterior, you have an affinity for misfits."

"I do not."

"And then there's…" Alistair looked at Hiro's burned hand. The pink flesh puckered like a morel mushroom.

Hiro lowered it onto his lap, out of sight.

"You haven't been the same," Alistair whispered. "Please, don't let that night consume you."

Hiro turned his head away. "It already has."

"I've moved on, and my dreams are no longer troubled. You should, too."

"You sound like your uncle."

"It must run in the family." Clutching his head, Alistair struggled to his feet. "Ugh, I have lectures to give tomorrow."

"Some day you should actually lead a strategy instead of teach about them."

"Maybe I will! Delphi knows you'll need me if you ever go to war, Hiro. You with that fat head of yours." Alistair giggled, then hiccupped. Collected his books. "Gods above, that brandy…"

Hiro helped him to the door, pulled him hard against him. "Thank you, Alistair, for everything."

The redhead gave him a slurred smile, patted his shoulder. "Delphi protect you. And the boy. Both."

Hiro rolled the bullfrog boy onto his side, lowered himself on the futon beside him. Dozed fitfully. The crackling briquettes in the brazier a lullaby; the flesh-memory of his beating a throbbing purgatory. And the cackling of a dead conjurer flitting in between.

HE WOKE BEFORE DAWN, packed his few belongings. Kale had even less than him: a spare gi, an oilskin jacket, a comb he never used.

In the gray light, he double-checked the room. His foot pressed on a loose floorboard by the window.

Kale sprang to his feet at the creak, eyes barely open.

"Easy," Hiro said. "I've already packed. Go get yourself a sword at the armory, then get the supplies from Master Pindar. I'll meet you at the stables."

The boy disappeared into the morning gloom like a puff of smoke. Hiro watched long after he had vanished. The boy was part child, part sage, and part something else entirely.

Hiro eased his foot off the loose board, knelt to pry it up. It lifted after a good tug, revealed a dusty cache beneath. Dipping his hand in, he felt the texture of a shaggy pelt against his palm. An old comrade.

Wrapped inside the pelt were a silver cuff, a tanto knife, and a small package bound in a ribbon of dark-green silk. He tugged on one end; the knot slithered apart. He thumbed through the letters. There were twelve in all, the last only read once, five years ago. It contents sprang fresh into his mind.

He tossed the letters onto the brazier. The three cypress trees stamped into the wax melted, trickled away. The letters flared once as the fire took them, brilliant and brief as the love they bore within their pages. He should've kept Toshiro's letters instead.

Slipping the tanto knife into his belt at the small of his back, he considered tossing the pelt onto the coals as well. It was just as full of dark memories. The embers glowed, waited to devour the dangling fur. Howling. A lacework of black runes turning red. *Boom. Boom. Boom-boom-boom.* Always the drums. Clutching his head, he stumbled away from the brazier.

Hiro stuffed the pelt into the bottom of his pack.

Kale caught up to him at the stables, two burlap sacks over his shoulder. An onigiri rice ball stuck out of his eager mouth. Pinned under his arm was a guqin.

Hiro plucked the instrument free with a shake of his head. "No sword, but you'll take a musical instrument with you?"

The boy shrugged as he swallowed a huge mouthful of food. "I couldn't find a sword I liked."

Hiro sighed. The boy never seemed to find a weapon that suited him. He was pickier than a bride at a flower market selecting her wedding bouquet. "Did you eat all of our breakfast or do I get any?"

Kale plopped a slightly mashed ball into Hiro's hand.

He ruffled the boy's mane of auburn hair, leaned the guqin against a trough.

"But—" Kale protested.

"It's too much weight. I'll get you one in Arashiyama."

"But how will you sleep?"

Hiro paused just inside the stables, glanced at the guqin. He could almost hear its haunting melody plucked from the silken strings, Kale crooning a lullaby. His burned hand tightened into a fist. "I'll manage."

He collected his mare, saddled her in the aisle. He'd bought his palomino warhorse with the spoils of Biscay Bay, trained her himself. She'd been a spirited filly, full of teeth and bucking hooves. A mane and tail of moonlight, golden hair, all covered in mud. Like her master, she had scars now and a burly body to carry them.

Hiro swung up into the saddle, hauled Kale up behind him. They passed under the portcullis, left the Academy and its pagodas and training yards behind. Headed north toward the Silk Road that would bring them to Jianshu.

Home. It'd been twenty years and the ache hadn't lessened. It was as sharp as the tanto knife, twisting with the memory of his slain mother.

He narrowed his eyes against the mist that had started. There would be plenty of time to plan his vengeance.

57

CHAPTER 13

AMELIA BREATHED A SIGH OF RELIEF AS SHE ENTERED THE GRASSLANDS. Boulders scattered the landscape: the bones of ancient mountains left to rot in the wind and rain.

Shortly after the azaleas had thinned, the path down Mount Taru had widened into steps. One thousand of them. At their end, the way leveled into a cobbled road overrun with moss. A lichen-speckled torii gate grew from the road, straddling an upright block of stone. Upon its top was the worn carving of a blooming lily. A marker of Bosetsanu. It hadn't protected them.

Black pines threw themselves into the sky like spears. Everywhere it was green and black and the burnt orange of pine straw. Suspicion clung to the Rothaar Mountains like dew to spiders' webs, and the sporadic creaking of its forests only reminded her that she was being hunted.

Amelia hadn't seen the demon since that first night. She'd traveled only during the day, hiding at night for almost a week until the Rothaar Mountains had finally deposited her into the grasslands.

Amelia shaded her eyes with a hand, squinting at the ring of vultures drifting in the sky. They were close enough that she would reach whatever had caught their attention in an hour or so. Unbidden, silver flames rippled over her fingers. She hadn't purged her power in days, convinced the demon could use it to track her, and now it surfaced whenever her emotions peaked.

"Fear is the hungry mouth that devours all you give it. Give nothing. Fear nothing." She repeated the mantra until the fire winked out.

Amelia followed the dirt road until it divided at a crossroad. A monolith erupted from the ground. Carved into its center was the symbol of the Most Holies: Delphi's open hand and Bosetsanu's blooming lily in its palm encircled by a ring of interlocking suns. She kissed her fingertips and transferred it to the carving before looking down the right fork.

The vultures were picking at a heap off the side of the road, half-hidden in the shade of a boulder. There were smaller, crow-like birds among them, cawing and flapping and generally being a nuisance. She crept forward, peering over the milling mounds of feathers, until one such bird pecked at a turquoise sash.

"Shoo," she cried, swatting at the lumbering birds.

Squawking, they surrendered their prize and flapped out of her way. The bolder, crow-like birds remained close, watching with beady red eyes and ready to resume their pecking whenever she moved away.

It was a young man. A staff lay limp in his long-fingered hand. Golden hair curled around a chiseled face, fluttered against chapped lips with every shallow breath. He wore the white robes and turquoise sash of a Delphian priest, though rust-colored spots speckled the wool. There were matching stains on the bandage across his eyes.

His face had been clawed; five scabby lines marred his otherwise pleasant features. Another bandage lay thick on his forearm. He'd probably thrown up his arm to protect his face. Unsuccessfully.

She crouched and withdrew her canteen. A thin trickle of water, no more than a crystalline thread, splashed into the trough of his lips. It sluiced into the golden down on his cheeks, disappearing under his collar. Delphian priests were required to be clean shaven; he'd been stranded just as long as her. He moaned softly.

She squeezed his shoulder. "Brother."

The priest roused with a cry, swinging with his staff.

Amelia dodged hastily, catching a glancing blow against her arm. *"Hey—"*

"Get away from me," the priest shouted. He scrambled to his feet, keeping one hand anchored to the rock as he swung the staff with the other. "Begone, demon!"

"My name's Amelia."

The priest faltered.

"And that demon will surely hear you if you don't stop shouting."

"Y-you believe me?" he said.

She caught his staff and pushed it aside. Taking a tentative step forward, she placed a hand on his shoulder. He jumped at her touch. *"Pax, brother." Peace.*

The priest collapsed against her, weeping.

Struggling, she lowered him to the ground and sat beside him. Amelia pressed the canteen into his trembling hands, urging him to drink. He spared none of it and mumbled an apology.

"They're all dead," he sobbed into his hands. "It butchered my brothers like cattle. Killed our cranes so we couldn't warn anyone. I managed to get away before it could finish its work." His fingers grazed against his bandage. "I can still see its face, that ghastly grin before—"

His shoulders shook.

Amelia slid her hand over his. Her sect discouraged touching anyone but a fellow sister, but he needed the comfort as much as she did. His long fingers intertwined with hers and squeezed.

She drew her legs up to her chest and rested her chin on her knees. "It came for my temple, too. Maybe not the same one, but a demon anyway."

"What of your sisters?"

Amelia looked away, squeezing her eyes shut. The grief was still too near, and the threat of the demon hadn't given her any respite to mourn. "They're gone. I am the last." She wrapped her arms around her legs, hugging herself.

She'd never see Yuki again. The demon had probably torn her to bits, just like the others. Tears soaked into her pink trousers, darkening them to red.

The priest placed a gentle hand on her shoulder. It was forbidden to touch a Sanu without permission, but she didn't reprimand him.

"I'm sorry. My brothers are dead, your sisters—" He jolted upright. "Gods above, what about Yueshu?"

She'd been heartsick over the same thing for days.

But no one could discover she didn't know how to perform the ritual, not even this priest. It would only incite a wildfire of panic.

"There is one Sanu left. Come on." She smeared the tears from her eyes and pulled him to his feet. "Let's go."

"Go where? Nowhere is safe with that *thing* running around."

"Lhasa. Lhasa is safe."

"It's on the other side of the continent—"

She gripped his shoulders and gave him a little shake. "The Sanctisum Seats must be *warned*. They need to prepare for the worst. And I need to go. Though..." She looked about the boulder-strewn grasslands, fighting a rising dread. "I do not know the way."

The priest squared his shoulders. "I do. If you'll be my guide, I will be your map." His fingers tightened on his staff. "Besides, there is nothing left for me here. Deal?"

He stuck out his hand in the Western way.

On one hand, she couldn't very well leave a wounded man to wander about in the wilderness. On the other hand, he was blind, and the journey promised to be an arduous one.

Behind them, the crow-like birds cawed, scratching at the rocks with their little talons. Amelia flicked her hand at them, silencing them. They hooted and milled around, pacing impatiently.

She had no choice. She needed his help.

Slowly, Amelia clasped the young priest's outstretched hand. "Agreed. I'm Amelia de Taru."

"Isen de Bastogne. Very pleased to meet you." He smiled a disarming smile, the strip of cloth crinkling at the corners of his eyes.

"We'll skirt south of the mountains until we hit the Silk Road. Then east to Nov Praga. But first, do you have any food?"

"Yes… How do you feel about pickled eggs?"

CHAPTER 14

THE SIGH THAT ESCAPED AMELIA'S LIPS WAS BORDERLINE LUSTFUL. SHE'D never seen so much water. The river was a lazy thing, broad and shallow, its water clear and peppered with schools of little fish. Its banks, free of reeds, were framed with flat pebbles. Dragonflies zoomed here and there, like little flashes of color zipping by. The spring sunlight dappled the slow current with a thousand tiny mirrors.

Isen cocked his head in a birdlike way, listening. "This must be the Rhine River."

"We're stopping."

"We're stopping?"

"Have you smelled yourself?" Hopping from one foot to the next, she shucked her sandals.

"That's rather rude." He sniffed under an arm and grimaced. "Though, you make an excellent point."

Amelia laughed and trotted down the shore a ways, just out of sight. She stripped to her underclothes and plunged into the brisk water.

She'd never felt so alive.

The water caressed her skin; bubbles tickled her feet as she kicked to the surface. She sucked in another lungful of air and dove to the bottom. Little crayfish disappeared into crevices; schools of minnows parted around her only to reform downstream, flashing their silver bellies. Her long hair swept around her like spun sugar, the water's current teasing it back and forth, tugging lightly at her scalp.

Amelia had never swum before. Mount Taru had only one spring, and its water was harvested in buckets to be heated for sponge baths. To be fully submersed, nearly weightless in another world, was intoxicating. For the first time since the attack, her heart beat with joy.Silver light exploded from her hands.

It condensed against her skin, glittering like crystal. The shimmering light lengthened into talons at her fingertips, and feather-like scales rippled up her bare arms as a triumphant growl rose from the back of her throat.

A mask of bubbles obscured her face as she screamed.

Amelia struggled for the surface, fighting the panic of her burning lungs. Breaching, she choked on air and clawed her way out of the water. She scuttled away from the shore and that *thing* in the water. Exhausted, she flopped onto her back and pressed a hand against her hammering heart.

Fear is the hungry mouth that devours all you give it. Give nothing. Fear nothing.

"Amelia?" Isen's voice was frantic.

"I'm alright," she said hoarsely. "I'm… coming."

Amelia pushed herself upright and plunged her hands into the river. The silver light raced away into the current, gleeful as an unleashed hound. The feather-scales never reappeared.

What was *that?*

She purged her gift until her chest felt hollow, empty. Weak, she gathered her things and stuffed them into her pack.

Her fingers grazed the strand of pearls.

Amelia rubbed a green one between thumb and forefinger. She'd hidden the pearls and the ceremonial fans in the bottom of her pack, and now the orange sari and its beaded fringe joined them. Anyone looking for a Sanu would recognize them immediately. She slung the pack over her shoulder.

Yuki had said a pilgrim had arrived at the temple, and shortly thereafter a demon had attacked. Amelia was not naïve enough to think the two events unrelated. She thought she heard it sometimes at night, snuffling, howling, but when she strained to listen, there were only crickets.

Isen had stripped to his black undershirt and sat in the shallows, one hand on his staff. It was rooted in the riverbed, anchoring him against the current. He trailed his hand along the water, tickling its surface. His robe and turquoise sash were in a tidy square on the shore.

Amelia dropped her pack next to the bundle and waded into the water.

Tentative, she sank into the shallows. She flexed her hands under the water, but no glittering talons appeared.

I must've imagined—

Isen's quiet voice cut through her thoughts. "I used to dive for aeris off the docks of Balasore, you know."

Amelia inched closer. In the weeks they'd traveled together, Isen had proven himself a wonderful storyteller. There was the sheep-stealing witch of Vienna, the kraken who thwarted all who dove for a mysterious amulet, how Suyin the Dragon had been tricked into eternal imprisonment. She sometimes entertained him with daring escapes from ice bears or horse racing with the Bédu from the Bethany Journal, but mostly she liked to listen to him weave fantas-tical tales.

"Sometimes sunken treasure if a ship foundered in a storm. But it was never enough. *I* wasn't enough. In that part of Tybet, a caste system still lingers. I was *harijan*, an untouchable." He scooped a stone from the riverbed and chucked it across the water. "I lived off the scraps from the fishermen before saving up enough to get out of there."

"And then you became a priest."

"Why not? I've always had a long fascination with the division of Heaven and Earth."

"Fascination isn't enough to become a priest, Isen. Especially a notué priest. You need faith."

"Oh, I don't have faith," he scoffed. "I *know*." He smiled in her general direction.

She returned the smile, though he couldn't see it, and snagged his shirt when he rose from the water. "What are you doing?"

"I don't swim. Not anymore." His fingers grazed against his bandage.

"I'm sorry, Isen, but you're not going another step until you've bathed. I can't stand it anymore."

"But—"

"Bath. Now." Amelia grabbed the soap and guided him into deeper water. She dunked his head back and started to scrub out his hair.

"This is humiliating."

"Don't sulk. And don't forget your armpits." She rinsed out his hair and sluiced water to remove the suds still clinging to the golden tufts on his jaw. "You tried to shave, didn't you?"

"*Tried?*" He ran a hand across his patchy chin. "Sweet mercy, I must look ridiculous."

Amelia took his knife and dragged it carefully along his cheek. He held still, his hands resting on her waist. She fought to ignore his touch, but the warmth of his hands seeped through her cotton camisole into her skin. It was all she could think about.

It was so… intimate.

"Amelia? You're shaking."

She was suddenly aware of how the water beading at the ends of his hair looked like drops of gold; how his underclothes clung tight to his body like a second skin, hinting at the ridges of taut muscle beneath. He startled her when he took her hand, slipping it off his chin.

"Thank you."

Her cheeks felt like they were on fire. "Y-you're welcome."

"Well, you did a finer job than me." He lifted his chin, running a hand along his throat.

Something gold winked at his collar. It was a chain, disappearing under his shirt. A pendant swelled under the wet cloth at his sternum.

"What's this?" Amelia traced the pendant with a fingertip.

Isen yanked her hand away.

For an instant, the world stopped. They stood there as if frozen together, knee-deep in the river, her hand against Isen's chest where he'd yanked it aside.

"It's—"

The world came back to her in a rush as the rhythmic beating of his heart under her hand sent tingles up her arm.

"It's private." His breath fluttered against her cheek.

"I-I'm sorry."

"It's nothing." He stepped away from her. "I think it's time to get dry now."

Flushing, Amelia stretched out on the shore, pillowing her hands behind her head and letting the sun warm her skin.

"So, uh, where do we go from here?" Anything to take her mind off her burning cheeks. Her heartbeat still hadn't slowed.

"East, still, until we hit Salzburg. After that, the city of Vienna where we'll turn south…"

His voice lulled her away. She drifted in the clouds, floating closer to the sun—

The fingers that gripped her hand dug in hard, like the pincers of a crab.

She blinked rapidly, trying to clear the sun spots from her vision. "Ow! Isen, what the-"

"Quiet. We're not alone."

RIDERS APPROACHED.

Isen snatched up his staff. Amelia yanked her cloak down over her underclothes and jumped to her feet. The riders were hard-looking men in worn clothing and dust-stained boots, dirks tucked into their belts.

"And what's this?" the first said with a leer. "A lovers' sun spot?"

"Good afternoon." Isen lifted a hand in greeting. Only Amelia could see the muscles tensing in his forearm.

"We've got ourselves a lecherous priest, Sam." The second rider rubbed his palm against the pommel of his dagger over and over again. Amelia found the action to be quite vulgar.

"Right you are, Jakub. And by the looks of her, I'd forsake my vows as well."

"You were never that picky to begin with, Sam."

The first one shrugged. "She must have other charms to lure a brother from his faith. Especially a blind one. Tell me, priest, how does she feel—"

"Excuse me?" Amelia bristled.

"We don't want any trouble," Isen said. "Please, be on your way."

"But we need to water our horses."

"There are plenty of other places."

"Nah, we like the look of this one."

The two dismounted. The dirks *snicked* from their sheaths, flashing cold and bright.

Isen shifted himself in front of Amelia, cocking his head in his birdlike way. With one hand, he slowly pushed her away from him.

"Isen—"

The two rushed him, and the two were put into the ground with a few strokes of Isen's staff.

He paused, white-knuckled, cocking his head again as he listened. "Are they down?"

Amelia was speechless, her hands covering her mouth. Blood pooled from one man's nose, and the other stared into the grass without blinking. She didn't think he was breathing—

"*Amelia.* Are. They. Down?"

"Y-yes."

"Get the horses."

Amelia stumbled into action, snatching up the reins and tugging the horses forward. She handed them off to Isen and gathered up their things.

"Mount up."

She clumsily pulled herself into a saddle as Isen swung fluidly into his. He turned his horse's head to the east and spurred it forward, Amelia's horse following in its wake. They rode with reckless abandon for too long, the sun dipping low in the sky and the jostling of the saddle making her thighs scream. Close to tears, she begged him to stop. Isen slowed his horse, and she fell out of the saddle, her legs buckling.

"What have you done? Those men—"

Isen dismounted and tapped his way to her. She shied away from his touch, but he grabbed her, cupping her wet cheeks in his gentle hands. "Would've killed me and raped you," he said. "They might've killed you too and looted our bodies before getting back on their horses and continuing down the road to talk of merry and pointless things."

"But you *killed* them."

"No, sweet girl. I merely beat them. And we took their horses so they cannot follow."

"'*Thou shalt not steal.*'"

"You're quite right." He turned their horses around and slapped them on the flanks. The two ambled off, heads low, back to their beastly masters. "There they go. We merely borrowed them for the afternoon."

"Why? Why would they do something like this?"

Isen sighed, pulling her against him. He stroked her back, resting his chin on the top of her head.

She hadn't been held since she'd been a child; it was oddly comforting. She leaned against him, the shock of the assault still washing over her like the waves of a relentless tide. She would've fallen again if he hadn't held her upright.

"You are no longer on your mountain top, sweet girl," he murmured. "The outside world is harsher than you realize."

Amelia shut her eyes, spilling the last of her tears onto her cheeks. "May Delphi the Protector guard our steps and the grace of the Blessed Lady be upon us always," she whispered. "I should pray for the souls of those men."

"Some are beyond saving, but it's good of you to try. Now let's get a fire going and banish these dark thoughts. Make sure you rub your legs tonight, or you won't be able to walk at all tomorrow."

"Isen, h-how did you know how to ride? How to fight those men?"

A smile flickered across his lips in the falling twilight. "I wasn't born a priest, sweet girl."

CHAPTER 15

Hiro shouldered open the door to the inn, threw back his hood. A fine mist of raindrops sprayed across the wooden floor. This was the only inn between Salzburg and Vienna for miles, and the dining room was packed. It took a few minutes of agitated waving for the innkeeper to notice his presence. Steel hair, sharp eyes, broad shoulders. Innkeeper hadn't been his first occupation.

"Good evening, sir." He set down a tray of cups. "If you want a hot meal, aye we have that, but the rooms're all filled up."

"I am the heir to Lord Ishida of the Jianshu Province, and I require a room." Hiro placed a doros on the counter.

The innkeeper paused a moment, placed his finger on the gold coin, slid it back toward its master. "My apologies, Prince, but the rooms're full. I'll not be turning out those've already paid."

Hiro placed another doros on the counter.

The innkeeper's face soured. "Attempt to bribe me again, and you'll find no supper here either." He hoisted his tray onto a thick shoulder, disappeared among the tables.

Hiro glared after him. None seemed to notice or care about the hulk of a man standing by the counter.

Kale appeared at his side, soaked and covered in straw. At least his mare had found some respite from the rain.

He clamped a hand onto the boy's shoulder and waded into the crowd. They found the only unoccupied table, sat. He'd have preferred a table off to the side, even in a corner, where he could survey the room for trouble. None were available, and the nearest corner was darkened by a man in a hooded cloak packing smokeweed into a long-stemmed pipe.

Kale turned down the wick of the oil lamp until it was only a blue wisp, slid it to the opposite end of the table.

Hiro signaled the innkeeper, who promptly ignored him.

"I'm hungry." Kale looked around for some unguarded morsel.

"We both are." Hiro tried to catch the innkeeper's attention. He was about to rise and force himself into the kitchens when a voice behind him said,

"Excuse me, but would you care for these? The staff forgot that I don't eat meat."

A woman in a flaxen cloak stood at his elbow. The cloth flowed to the floor; not even her feet poked out beneath the hem. She looked like a milkweed seed. The hand breaching the shapeless mass was sleeved in yellow silk almost to her fingertips and held a plate of fat sausages. Steam hissed from their plump casings; the juices inside sizzled.

Kale drooled.

Hiro stood and bowed. Mother had always taught him to be polite. "Thank—" His voice died in his throat. He'd never seen eyes like that, blue as the ocean deep.

The woman looked away, embarrassed.

"Thank you," Kale said. He wedged himself in front of Hiro, accepted the plate with a bright smile. Returning to his seat, he started devouring the sausages.

"Mistress," the innkeeper exclaimed, hurrying over, "this ruffian isn't disturbing you, is he?"

Hiro bristled.

"Not at all, Master Torben. Your server simply gave me meat by mistake. And they looked hungry."

"I can't apologize enough. I'll bring you pierogi myself. Or would you prefer tempura eggplant?"

Hiro cringed. Tempura eggplant outside the Jianshu Province promised to taste little better than a soggy sponge. Abomination.

"Pierogi, please. I don't care much for eggplant."

"And ale," Hiro added.

The innkeeper frowned, bustled away.

The woman gave him a parting smile and waded through the tables back to her companion in the corner. She plucked her cloak free of a drunk's hand, chastised him with a stern word. His companions rebuked him too, cuffing his head and flicking his ears. The scent of jasmine – faint, teasing – followed in her wake.

Master Torben dropped a mug of ale onto the table. Yellow foam sloshed over the rim, oozed across the worn wood. He held a plate of steaming pierogi fried with onions, all artfully arranged, in his other hand.

Hiro jerked his chin at the woman. "Who's she?"

"A healer. And too good for the likes of you, prince or not," the innkeeper sniffed. "She is *raffiné*."

"Hn." Hiro pointed at the mug. "You didn't spit in this, did you?"

"And dishonor Mistress Amelia?" The innkeeper huffed and stalked away.

Nevertheless, Hiro investigated the remains of the foam before thirst got the better of him. Setting the empty mug aside, he cocked a finger at the boy. Kale leaned in, a half-masticated sausage in his fist. "Any room in the barn?"

"No, sir. Even the horse has barely enough room to turn around."

Hiro grunted. "Then it's another night on the road."

"Aww."

"Shush." He gave the boy a silver mark. "Get a bottle of wine. One with the wax still intact. And a hot milk for yourself."

"Thanks, sir!"

The wine was barely tolerable. Hiro was draining his second cup when the music began. With a groan, he poured a third. These country folk enjoyed their dark ale, fat wenches, and the dastardly cheerful music that infested every tavern and inn along the Silk Road. People pushed the trestle tables aside to make room, started to dance. Kale clapped his hands and stomped his feet, a grin splitting his grease-covered lips. Hiro tossed him a napkin and hunched over his wine, tried to disappear in it.

Ale, brown and frothy, splashed against his neck and dribbled into his clothes.

Kale's face went white.

Hiro whipped around.

A beefy villager with half a dozen teeth missing smiled at him.

"Do you have any idea who I am?" Hiro demanded. "*Apologize.*"

"Ack, ain't but a bit o' beer," the man said, spraying Hiro's face with a fine mist of spittle. "Ooh! Wine! *In vino verititties*, right?"

Kale shook his head, pleading.

"Go away," Hiro growled.

"Celebrating, eh? What's tha occasion?"

He turned back to his wine. "I said, go away."

"*Pssh.* No one's tah celebrate alone." He slapped Hiro's shoulder with a grin.

"Hiro…" Kale warned.

Hiro brought his fist up into the villager's face, relieved him of yet another tooth.

The man toppled onto a table, scattering its patrons.

The fiddle player's bow skidded to a halt; the final note faded like a yowling cat. The one thing guaranteed to spoil an honest man's night after a hard day's work is to spill his drink. These men were no exception, and indignant and inebriated chaos ensued.

Hiro grabbed Kale's collar, yanked the wine bottle out of his hand before he could crack it over someone's head. Nothing was out of bounds: hair was torn free by the roots, bellies were punched, food was thrown, knees were knocked out, the legs of chairs were broken off to use as clubs.

Kale's pure voice cut through the din. "*Hey.* You leave her *alone.*"

Hiro looked up from dropping his elbow into the back of some man who'd tried to tackle him, saw the Delphian priest – *wait, isn't he blind?* – lashing out with his staff. The woman screamed as someone grabbed her wrist, tried to wrest her out of her hiding space. Thrashing, she kicked over the table's oil lamp.

Flames spewed across the table, zipped along the floor. The man released her wrist with a cry, smacked at the fire that gnawed at his leg.

The flames were not high, just tall enough to nip at her calves, but in his mind's eye they clawed to the ceiling. Scorched the rafters. Behind their twisting screen of heat and light, he saw not her, but the thousands of faces he could never forget.

Hiro barreled through the crowd, ripped off his greatcoat. Wild, he slapped at the flames, smothered the smaller ones with his boot. Kale joined him, stomping a fiendish jig.

Hiro grabbed the woman, wrenched her upright. "Are you hurt?"

"No, I—" She shied away suddenly.

Hiro pivoted, catching the blow. A bottle crashed against his shoulders, splattered him with glass and wine. The woman shrank back, shielding her face. He paused for a moment, brushed the glass from her hair. She hadn't been cut.

Hiro wrenched around, backhanded his attacker. Sent him sprawling into the tumultuous crowd. They turned on him as one, shouting curses at him for attacking Mistress Amelia.

He grabbed a man in mid-leap at the priest, slammed him into the ground. A clay mug sailed out of the crowd, shattered against the blind man's head.

He collapsed to the floor, groaning.

"*Isen,*" the woman cried, abandoning her corner. Kneeling by the priest, she cradled his head her hands.

Hiro snatched the staff from his limp hands, laid the nearest men flat out on their backs. Broken noses squirted blood; ribs cracked like splintering wood. Battle-lust throbbed in his veins. He'd missed this.

"*Stop!*"

The ferocity of the voice silenced the room. A shiver rippled down the length of his spine.

The woman stepped out in front of him, eyes ablaze.

"No—" He made a grab for her arm, missed.

"*Shame* on you," she cried. "Look what you've done. You've ruined Master Torben's business and vandalized his home. And over what? A few spilled beers? How *dare* you treat Master Torben with such disrespect?"

Whatever residual mutterings of discontent wafting through the crowd were snuffed out.

The man closest to her swiped his hat off his head. "Sorry, Mistress Amelia."

"I expect each and every one of you to help clean this up. *Immediately.*"

Like the crack of a whip, her order lashed the patrons into movement.

Hiro signaled Kale, turned to go. They had miles to go before they were even halfway home, and there was no lodging here for them tonight.

"Excuse me, sir," the woman called after him. "That means you, too."

Frowning, he glanced over his shoulder.

The woman's hands were on her hips. "This is your fault. You were the one who threw the first punch. You can start by helping me right this table."

The crowd stopped cleaning, stared at him balefully. All except the group that was hauling the drunk who'd attacked Mistress Amelia outside to be put up in the stocks. The young woman nearest them, a server, wrung out a dishcloth like she hated it. Her fingers dug into the cloth, twisted it mercilessly. Like she was imagining it was Hiro's throat.

Kale immediately started collecting strewn cutlery.

With a huff, Hiro clenched the edge of the trestle table, righted it with a mighty heave.

"Thank you," the woman said. "That's one."

Scowling, Hiro stalked about the dining room, righting tables and chairs. When he finished, he scanned the room for Kale. Not surprising, the boy was with the woman. She'd fed him after all, earning the boy's immediate loyalty.

She was feeling about the priest's head, searching for injury. Finding something, she stood on tiptoe to examine it. The cloak hiked up, revealed pink trousers underneath.

Hiro arched an eyebrow. Only one sect of women wore pink trousers, and they never hid their identity.

CHAPTER 16

KALE HELD THE BOWL OF WATER AS THE WOMAN CLEANED THE PRIEST'S head.

She rinsed the cloth, dabbed at the wound again. "It's shallow. It'll heal without stitching."

"It hurts," the priest said. "A lot."

"Well, there is some minor swelling. I'll get you something for that."

"It looks like your head's trying to lay an egg," the boy said.

The priest groaned. "Not helping."

Hiro approached the group, rested a hand on the boy's shoulder. "Kale, it's time we go."

"Not until I look at his knee," the woman said.

"You're hurt?"

"Nah…"

"Here, let's clear off this table and you can take a seat, little man." She swept the debris off to the side, snatched her hand back with a hiss.

"You're bleeding," Kale exclaimed. "I'll get you a bandage." The boy darted into the kitchen.

"Amelia?" the priest asked.

"It's just a scratch."

If she was who Hiro thought, touching her without permission was forbidden. Hiro snatched her hand.

She let out an indignant squeak but didn't pull away. Interesting.

A long splinter had buried itself in her left palm. Without preamble, he drew his dagger, wiggled the splinter loose with its tip. He bent his head, pressed his tongue against her palm, and sucked the splinter out. He spat off to one side and rubbed his thumb against her skin. He'd gotten all of it.

"T-thank you."

He shrugged, sheathed his dagger.

The boy returned with a roll of linen and bound up her hand.

She winked at him. "Thanks, little man. Now let's take a look at that knee."

Hiro snatched Kale under the armpits, hoisted him onto the table. He rolled up the boy's torn trouser leg, hissed at the mangled flesh. He cuffed Kale's head. "What I tell you about being careful?"

"Sorry, sir."

Hiro sluiced the wound clean, splashed some wine into it, and wrapped it up. He ruffled the boy's hair. "Alright. You're good to go."

The woman hovered over his shoulder. "You're not going to put a poultice on it?"

"What do I look like, a medicine woman?"

"Don't worry, Miss Amelia." The boy hopped off the table with a smile. "I'll be better in minutes."

Hiro clamped a hand onto the boy's shoulder. Squeezed warningly. "*Kale.* Let's go."

"But it's pouring outside—"

"There's no room here, and I doubt the innkeeper will let us stay here after tonight's entertainment."

"Then share our rooms."

Hiro turned to the woman, raised an eyebrow. "You're offering to share your bed?"

The priest stiffened, his fingers tightening on his staff.

"You would bunk with Isen, and the boy would stay with me," she clarified. He couldn't tell if she was being coy or naïve.

Kale looked up at him pleadingly.

Hiro considered the offer. Him: lean but muscular, a disarming smile, sunshine-golden hair. Her: ocean-blue eyes, mildly attractive, knee-length hair the color of caramel. Just like the sweets his mother used to give him when he'd been especially good. Neither one of them seemed the type to slit his throat in the night.

"I don't sleep on the floor," Hiro said.

Isen cocked his head to the side like a bird, a tight smile stretched upon his lips. "Nor do I."

"I'll let you two figure that out," the woman said. "I'm going to get some more blankets. Master Torben? Do you have a minute?"

Kale trailed after her like an excited puppy.

A staff blocked his path before Hiro could follow. "Walk out of our room before dawn this night, and you'll never walk again."

Hiro could've picked the blind man up and broken his back over his knee with the same amount of effort it would take to snap a twig in half, but he paused. The vehemence in the priest's voice demanded respect. "I will not," he promised. "And the boy will guard her with his life."

Isen snorted. Hiro smiled to himself, knowing what the boy was truly capable of.

"Then it's settled. What's your name?" Isen asked.

"Prince Hiro Ishida."

And he walked off to find his bed.

KNOWING GLANCES. Secretive smiles. Isen's hand flitting about looking for the salt.

Glancing from one conspirator to the other, Hiro dropped his spoon into his breakfast bowl. Slid the salt shaker into Isen's searching hand.

"Ah ha," the priest said.

"What is it?" Hiro demanded.

"Tell him," Kale said.

"We have a proposition for you." The woman slid her bowl to the side.

Kale hooked a finger over the lip, dragged it halfway across the table before Hiro slapped the back of his hand.

"Please continue."

"We propose you join us on the road," she said. "We're headed to Lhasa, but Kale tells me you're headed east, at least for a time, and—"

"Can you pay?"

She blinked. "Pardon me?"

"Can. You. Pay?"

She glanced at Isen before answering, "N-not exactly. We don't have any coin, but we all have our individual talents. Plus there's strength in numbers—"

Hiro sat back and laughed.

Isen drummed his fingers on the table. "You're being very rude."

"There are robbers out there," she said, "and... much worse."

"Then you should've sent for the Militum Dei. Protecting clergy is one of their duties." He leaned forward. "Isn't it, *Sanu?*"

The woman froze, eyes large. She looked away, sat back in her chair.

The priest cleared his throat. "Just what are you insinuating—"

"Then this is where we part ways. Kale, we're leaving."

"You're making a mistake," Isen called after him.

"No, I'm not," he cast over his shoulder on the way out.

In the stables, Kale ran his hand down the mare's burly leg. "We could help them, you know." He dug the muck out of the her hoof as Hiro brushed her down. "Protect them."

"I just want to go home, Kale. It's been twenty years—"

"Then what's a few more weeks?"

"*And* I have enough trouble keeping *you* safe. I don't need to compound that by adding an elite priestess and her blind brother to the list."

Hiro hauled the boy up behind him on the warhorse, left the inn and its unusual patrons behind.

At sundown they hit a thick swath of washed-out road. Hiro dismounted to lead his mare. He swung the tails of his greatcoat around his shoulders to keep the worst of the filth free of it, started to wade.

In the distance, the night creatures began to howl. His mare threw up her head with a snort. They had to clear this swath quickly.

Behind him, Kale hopped in the divots left by his boots.

"You're being especially quiet," Hiro said.

The boy said nothing, continued to hop from one divot to the other.

"Are you sulking?"

Kale stopped, crossed his arms over his chest.

"Look," Hiro said. "We're not a charity, and a larger group would just slow us down."

The boy frowned.

"And I have to report to my father without delay."

Kale's eyes narrowed.

"*Ugh.* Why do you *care* so much?"

A smile broke out on the boy's face. He took the mare's reins, led her back the way they'd come. Back to her. "She reminds me of someone."

The howling continued, closer now.

Kale jumped.

"It's just wolves." Hiro tapped his greatsword. "We'll be fine."

"No," the boy said. "It's something... else."

CHAPTER 17

THE SORCERER STOOD ON A HILL FAR AWAY, A ROOK PERCHED ON HIS shoulder.

The crow-like bird's gaze tracked the prince and the boy as they led the warhorse through the mire. He blinked twice and saw through its cabochon eyes. A red lens snapped over his vision, heightened it, sharpened it, until he saw them as clearly as if he was walking right beside them.

He couldn't hear them, but it was clear they were arguing about something. The boy was petulant, stomping in the divots left by the prince. The prince was frustrated, a resolute set to his jaw.

His gaze lingered over the prince. He'd grown from a chubby boy into a well-muscled beast of a man. He had his mother's impressive height and his father's authoritative air. A prince indeed.

The son of his master's most hated rival.

It wasn't his mission, but it was too good an opportunity to miss.

The rook cawed once when he broke their connection. Withdrawing the pipe from his pocket, he used the mouthpiece to cut a shallow line in his forearm. The last one had not yet healed; that demon hadn't returned. It was still hunting, its prey elusive.

It boggled him. Skeins did not see the way mortals did. They could see past every illusion, every concealment, and yet it'd been weeks since the attack on the Sanu temple and still nothing.

"Kill the Sanu," he'd instructed it. "You will know them by the golden lily tattoo on their hands."

Maybe it was defective.

He lit the pipe and sucked on the smokeweed. He hated its taste, preferring the cool tobacco smoke of his hookah back home. Tiny runes, sparkling like emeralds caught in sunlight, rippled down the length of the bone-white surface.

The skein that appeared before him now was leaner, smaller, more vicious than the one he'd summoned before. Before it could attack him, he bound it with its name.

"Jezebul."

The demon shrilled, thrashing its head in a blur as if harassed by a swarm of bees. Green runes flickered from its head to its flanks, completing the binding, and the skein reluctantly settled.

"Kill the prince," he commanded. He gave the demon a mental image of its quarry. "Then find out what's taking Azelbul so long. Begone."

With a sinister howl, the demon flashed away.

He shrugged his shoulders, and the rook took flight. Sucking in a deep breath, he flung his arms out to the sides. His body exploded into a flock of blackbirds, the avian cloud banking east and vanishing into the twilight.

CHAPTER 18

AMELIA SLUNG THE MUD OF OUT HER SANDAL WITH A GRUNT. THESE wretched spring roads threatened to twist her ankles with every step. She wiggled the sandal back onto her foot, took Isen's hand, and trudged for firmer ground.

The sky was a dreary gray and a drizzle had started, covering everything with a fine mist of diamond dust. Sighing, she clutched her cloak tighter around her and leaned into the wind. It wouldn't have bothered her nearly as much if it hadn't been for that disappointing conversation with the prince.

"You're brooding, aren't you?" Isen said.

"I thought you were blind."

"And I'm soon to be a cripple, given the state of this ground." Isen yanked his staff free with a squelch. "Does it look any better up ahead?"

"No. But we need to find a dry patch soon otherwise we're going to be sleeping in the mud."

"Delightful."

Amelia tugged on his hand, steering him away from a particularly washed-out section. "I just... I just thought he'd help us," she confessed. "The prince, I mean. He obviously knows how to handle himself, and he's—"

"Fat? I bet he's fat. He sounds fat."

Amelia laughed. *Safe*. That was the word she was going to say. A stranger, he had shielded her from a blow that would've knocked her unconscious. Brushing the glass from her hair, he'd been far gentler than she'd expected anyone of his size to be.

"No, he's not fat. But he's big. And his eyes... it's like they could strip flesh from bone."

"Thank Delphi the Protector they could not. 'Twould be improper for a Sanu to be running around the country with naught but her bones."

"I wish they could. We haven't seen the demon in weeks, but I can't shake that—"

"It's out there." His fingers tightened in hers. "I know."

In the distance, the night creatures began to howl.

Amelia froze.

Isen gave a defiant shake of his head. "That's not ominous at all."

"There's a group of trees up ahead. Come on. We'll shelter there."

They both knew a cluster of trees wouldn't deter a demon, but they hurried nonetheless. Silver sparks flickered at her fingertips. She thrust her hand under her cloak, balling it tight to her chest.

Not now, she begged. Her power was still a secret, and she took great care to seclude herself before purging it. Notué priests were more in tune with the mysteries of the four realms than other Delphian priests, but they still drew a hard line at sorcery.

"We're almost there," she said, panting.

"Do I hear hooves?"

She scanned the darkened hills. "A rider."

Amelia diverted into the slick grass, hoping to put as much distance as possible between them and the rider. Their experiences with other travelers on the road had left them wary.

To her dismay, the rider slowed.

Isen hefted his staff.

"Amelia!" The boy slid down from the palomino horse and ran over to them. "Please, you have to come with me."

"Kale? What's that on your face? Is that *blood*?"

"Please, it's Hiro—" He broke off, starting to cry.

Isen grabbed the boy by the shoulders and gave him a little shake. "*Kale*. What happened?"

"You wouldn't believe me if I told you. It was—"

Amelia gripped the boy's chin in her hand. In the failing light, she saw dark splotches on his neck. Black and oily, they glittered like crystal. "Demon ichor." She hastily wiped it off the boy's neck before it burned him.

"What about Hiro? Is he alive?" Isen pressed.

The boy sniffled, wiping his snotty nose on his sleeve. "I hope so."

"Everyone on the horse," she ordered.

"Amelia, *that* is a trained warhorse. It'll never let us near it."

"Yes, she will." Kale ran over to the mare and led her back to them. She was meek under his hands.

"Now listen here." Amelia took hold of the bridle, pointing a finger into the horse's face. "I want no nonsense out of you. You're going to take us to your master so we can help him, okay?"

"Amelia, it's a horse—"

"It never hurts to be polite," she snapped. She pulled herself into the saddle and helped Isen up after her.

"She can't take three," Kale said. "It's okay. I'll run."

"You'll never keep up," Isen exclaimed.

Determination darkened the boy's face. "You've never seen me run."

THE DYING prince was covered in ichor.

He was unconscious, sprawled in the middle of the road. All around him, the tarry remains of the slain demon bubbled and hissed upon the ground.

"That's not possible," Isen gasped.

Amelia tiptoed around the gelatinous ooze and crouched down by his head. His face was ashen, and blood trickled out of the corner of his mouth.

Panting, Kale appeared a moment later, falling to his knees on the other side of him. "He got cut here," he said, pointing to a spot on Hiro's abdomen, "but the demon bit him on the leg."

Amelia parted the torn fabric, exposing his flesh to the moonlight. Demon ichor bubbled out of a gash in his calf. Ugly black lines, just beneath the skin, crept up the prince's leg like a ragged spider web. *"Sweet mercy."*

She tore the fabric, chasing the vining lines until they ended at mid-thigh. Their progress was slow, but before her very eyes they slunk up toward his heart.

"They said you're a healer," Kale cried. "Please, *do* something."

She leaned forward and swept the hair away from the prince's face. Bending down, she lowered her ear to his mouth. A whisper caressed her cheek. Gooseflesh rippled across her skin as his cold breath sighed again. "He's alive, but I don't think—"

"Please."

The boy's plea cut her. He held his master's hand, squeezing it over and over, trying to chafe some warmth back into him.

Frozen, she watched his hands, remembering she had done the same thing years ago for the man she had called father.

"I'll do anything," he said. "Anything to save him. Please."

She had said that, too.

Amelia exhaled sharply and stood. Muttering, she brushed through the scrub on the side of the road.

"Amelia, what are you—"

"Sangnon," she said, still searching. "It's common everywhere – spreads over fields like a purplish-red carpet – but most people don't know of its healing properties. It might just buy him some time."

"What's it look like?"

"Like purple deadnettle. But it smells more like lemon balm."

"You mean god's-herb?" The boy fished around in a saddlebag and produced a pouch. "Hiro always has some, though I didn't know what it was for."

Amelia seized it and wiggled her fingers into the paper packet. The faint scent of lemons mingled with the tar of the decomposing demon. She stuffed the plant into her mouth and chewed. When it was a mushy paste, she spat it into her hand and smeared it into the wound.

Hiro moaned faintly.

"We need to get him on the horse."

Isen grabbed her arm. "Amelia, you can't do anything—"

She shook him off violently. "No. I'll never not do anything again. Vienna isn't too far. There's a temple there. They might have something to stop this."

"It's pointless, Amelia. Besides, that temple's been—"

"Enough! How do I find it?"

The priest sighed. "Follow this road. It leads directly to the city. The temple's on the west side."

"Thank you."

It took the three of them to get Hiro across the saddle. Isen stumbled back, sagging against his staff.

"Kale, will you stay with Isen? Sweet mercy, hold *still*."

Snorting, the mare sidestepped as Amelia hauled herself into the saddle.

The boy took the horse's bridle and pulled her head down. He whispered something in her ear, and the beast quieted with a huff.

"I'll come back for you," she promised.

"We'll follow," Isen said, grasping the boy's hand. "Delphi protect you, Amelia."

Wheeling the horse to the east, they galloped away, racing the vines that slithered ever onward to the prince's heart.

CHAPTER 19

Amelia kneaded her hands into the mare's neck, urging her forward. The beast's chest and flanks were lathered with sweat, but her stride never slackened. Across her withers, her master bounced in time with her hooves. Amelia put a hand on his back to steady him, feeling the coolness of his flesh through his clothing slink up her arm. She knew he was alive only from his occasional groan.

"Hold on, Hiro."

Howling sounded behind her.

Three dark shapes flashed across the moonlight-dappled hills. Behind them, the snowy peaks of the Alps gleamed silver. One raised its head, nosing the air, and yipped with glee. They loped after her, closing the distance between them with each flash. Their entries and exits into this world were like the soft *foom* of far-away mining blasts.

Their claws tore through the fields, dashing the wildflowers and sending the shredded petals high into the air. The floral rain caught the wind and brushed against her neck even here, thousands of yards ahead of them.

Faster, the caress urged.

She dug her heels into the horse's ribs.

No longer beads on the horizon, the lamplight illuminated the shape of the sleeping city. She could glean none of its details, except that it was cleaved by a river that carved the landscape like a silver sickle.

Snuffling.

The demons were close enough for her to hear their great nostrils scenting the air.

Amelia lashed the warhorse with the reins.

A demon sprang, slicing a paw through the mare's tail. White strands, pale as cream, fluttered away. The warhorse shrilled and surged forward.

Amelia hunched low over her neck, her whipping mane stinging her cheeks. The city was close now, close enough to see the looming shapes of buildings. Desperately, she looked for the one with a steeple or a torii gate.

The horse stumbled, thrown off balance as a demon rammed into her.

With a cry, Amelia dropped the reins and clutched onto the prince as the warhorse regained her footing. Pain, hot as a branding iron, seared across her thigh. Amelia pressed her hand there, withdrew a palm slick with red.

Lightning split the sky. The clouds that had been building all day finally released their deluge upon the earth. The horse started to slow, the wet ground sucking at her hooves.

Terrified, Amelia hunched low over the mare's neck and shut her eyes. All she could hear was the snorting of the horse and the snuffling of the demons and the roar of the rain. The noises jumbled together, surrounding her, suffocating her. She sucked in a ragged breath, desperate for air. It was hot, too hot. Silver fire threatened to consume her from the inside out.

No, not now, she pleaded. *Not in the open where everyone can see.*

The mare whinnied in fear, jerking sideways. Her eyes rattled open. The temple was just yards ahead. Its steeple had crumbled into a nub, the jasmine shrubs had wildly overgrown, but the pale stone still gleamed with an inner brilliance even in the rain. A beacon to any who sought it.

The horse raced right over the threshold, the demons swiping at her hooves. Exhausted, the poor beast floundered on the courtyard's slippery flagstones, pitching her riders to the ground. Hiro rolled to a stop, shoring up against a pillar. Whimpering, Amelia struggled to free her wounded leg out from under him.

The demons didn't flash now, their target finally pinned. Their claws clicked against the flagstones as they paced, lips peeled back and long indigo tongues lolling to the side. Their deep chests heaved, exhaling sulfuric fumes.

Her breathing wouldn't slow. The air was impossibly thin. Heat burned in her blood, bubbling to the surface.

As one, the demons lunged.

Silver fire bloomed from her skin, radiated out like a flower bud bursting to full blossom in a single instant.

The demons fell back, fumbling, trying to reverse direction, but the blast had them. Their bodies disintegrated in the light. Not even ash remained.

The blaze faded, and the rain, which had been blown heavenward from the blast, resumed its descending migration.

Gasping, Amelia yanked her leg loose and pushed apart Hiro's gi. The black vines had spread to his neck and arms, but his chest was still free. There was a mark there, something on his sternum that she couldn't make out, that the ichor could not pass. Even now she could see the vines twisting, worming, probing for access. His heart beat very faintly, just a tremor under his skin.

"That looks bad," a husky voice commented.

Amelia turned, raising her hand warningly.

A hunched crone, swathed head to foot in rags, sidled out from behind a pillar with a snort. "Don't make me laugh. You've got nothing left."

Amelia scrambled to her feet. Her wounded leg throbbed. "Please, will you help me?"

The crone turned, her rags trailing behind her like a tail, rasping along the flagstones like scales. "No."

CHAPTER 20

AMELIA HOBBLED AFTER THE CRONE, SLIPPING ON THE SLICK flagstones. "Tell me what you want. I'll—"

"If you have to ask, then you are blind. You have nothing I want. Begone."

"Why won't you help us?"

"Why should I? When you refused to help those who needed you the most, *Sanu Maitre.*"

Amelia blanched. "I-I am not—" She winced, the white hot pain of the lie searing through her veins.

"No, you aren't. Haven't been for a while. You've been too busy hiding who you are." The crone made a guttural snort of disgust and ambled into the sanctuary.

Weak light shone through the broken windows and made strange shadows on the floor. Many of the pews had rotted away, and the smell of decay lay heavy in the air. A few candles burned in haphazard niches, providing very little light and even less warmth. The gold sigil of the Most Holies, covered in thick cobwebs, still hung on the wall behind the altar, but the copper bowl where the white flame should be burning was eerily vacant.

"I'm being hunted," Amelia tried to explain.

"I'm not talking about your clothes. *This!*" The crone jabbed a claw-like finger into Amelia's chest. To the lily tattoo hidden there. But the finger pressed deeper, toward something beyond the golden mark. When she spoke again, the crone's voice was almost crooning. "That flame inside you."

Amelia rubbed the poke out of her chest. "It's unpredictable. I can't control it."

"You've never *tried*. No, you just bleed it off to do whatever it will. Did you think that kind of power goes unnoticed? Foolish whelp."

"How can you know this?" Amelia drew back as she remembered Isen's stories. "Are you really a witch?"

"*A witch?*" the crone shrieked. Her rags shook as the body beneath it trembled with outrage. "How quickly you humans forget."

The crone stormed away, weaving through the scattered debris of the decrepit temple until she got to the altar. She gazed at the sigil for a long time.

Amelia crept closer, tripping over the rotting pews and prayer cushions. The crone's shoulders had stopped shaking. Her gnarled hands, white as paper, clutched the lip of the empty fire bowl. Peering over the rim, Amelia saw the bones of some ruminant – picked clean – where the white flame should've burned.

"I made a mistake," Amelia said. "Is that what you want to hear? I ran because I was afraid. *Am* afraid."

The crone grabbed Amelia's chin and yanked it down to meet her gaze. Her face was not pale, but void of any color. Her eyes were as clear as ice, yet they burned with such intensity that Amelia flinched. Sharp white teeth snarled at her. "You'll never control it that way," the crone sneered. "You're a disgrace to our mother, to our sisters."

Amelia jerked free, her hands balling into fists. Silver flame crackled over her flesh. "You are no sister of mine," she snapped. "You faithless, condescending, merciless snake!"

"*Snake?*" the crone roared. Her voice shook the temple walls; dust rained from the rafters, coating everything in a fresh film of gray. She lunged forward, but Amelia didn't budge.

"My *sister* would help that man regardless of what she thought about me," Amelia said. "He doesn't deserve this."

"No one deserves that fate."

"And yet you won't help him! Bosetsanu's love and forgiveness is without reservation. She would never punish him for my transgressions. She—"

"Ha! Bosetsanu is not our mother."

"You live in her house and deny it?" Amelia spat. "You blaspheming—"

"I've heard enough," the crone cried, drawing herself up. When she wasn't hunched over, she stood a foot taller than Amelia.

Amelia staggered back a step, her weak leg unable to support her weight anymore.

"I would challenge you right now—" The crone could only hold her height for a heartbeat. She sank back down to her wizened stature, huffing in defeat. "But you are Mother's favorite."

Amelia felt a trickle of hope flutter in her chest. "As Sanu Maitre, and as Bosetsanu's

Chosen, I *order* you to help me."

The crone's gnarled hands cracked and popped as she clenched them into fists. Her body trembled violently, as if she strained against something. Amelia almost thought she saw tendrils of smoke wafting out from the crone's enraged nostrils. Whatever inner turmoil she faced, she lost.

"Bring him out of the rain, foolish whelp," she said with a sigh. "Because he'll die of fever if the demon ichor doesn't claim him first."

AMELIA RUMMAGED through the horse's saddlebags and fished out a length of rope. She looped it under Hiro's arms and tied the ends to the saddle horn. Taking a firm grip of the bridle, she guided the weary beast forward into the only shelter available: the sanctuary.

Blessed Lady, forgive me.

A little fire was burning in the nave now, suffusing the space with light and heat. Amelia winced; the holy place was more desolate than she had first imagined. She dragged Hiro as close to the fire as she dared and freed him from the rope.

The crone crouched beside the prince's shoulder, cocking her head first one way and then the other as she examined him. One claw-like finger traced the mark on his chest. The vines had crept closer, the nearest one only a finger's width away. "Hurry now," the crone said. "He's almost gone. Put your hands on his wound."

Amelia glanced at her hands. "But you said—"

"You renew quickly."

"But I can't call it on command!"

The crone threw up her hands. "You're a priestess, aren't you? Don't you meditate? It's the same thing. Calm your spirit, and your power will obey. Now go." The crone jabbed her with her claw-like fingers, urging her forward. "No more questions."

Amelia knelt and yanked the shredded fabric away from Hiro's leg. The gash was black now, the ichor completely saturating it. Shuddering, she clamped her hands around the wound. The ichor started to hiss.

"Deep inhale through your nose and exhale through your mouth," the crone said. "Draw the ichor out."

She did as instructed and felt nothing. There was no change in Hiro's pallor, no change in the vines clawing their way to claim his heart. She only felt the heat of her hands as her power coursed through his body.

Inhaling, she felt a thick substance coat the back of her throat. She coughed, glaring at the film that covered everything like the dust of moth wings. She was going to sneeze for weeks after this. Her cough turned into a hack, and a black blob ejected from her mouth. It hit the stone with a sizzle, bubbling like tar. Amelia yelped.

"What? Did you think it would just take a pretty twirl of your hand? Don't stop," the crone said. "You have it by the tail now. Drag it out!"

With each exhalation, Amelia expelled more ichor. Each glob hit the floor with a sizzle, bubbled once or twice before silver fire engulfed it and burned it away. The vines began to shrivel and slink back toward their root. Amelia fought a swell of nausea with every expulsion. The process was abhorrent but effective. She knew her task was complete when it was blood she spat out, not ichor.

She hobbled to the nearest window and vomited.

"If you're quite finished," the crone drawled, "your work is not yet done. Those wounds could still kill him."

"No, I can't use my... gift on those."

The crone gave her a bewildered look. "What do you think you just did?"

"I could claim that herbs from the temple healed him of the poison. But the wounds need to be stitched. No one knows about... me. Sorcery is—"

"You are not a sorceress. You were born with this. Conjurers have to learn and at great personal cost."

"I doubt the world makes much of a distinction between us." Amelia shook her head. "I can't risk it. The Militum Dei would hunt me down."

The crone gave the prince an appraising look. "He might be big, but he's not stupid. He'll figure out it wasn't just herbs and stitching that saved him."

"I have to try." Amelia peeled back the jacket to reveal the cut on his abdomen, and the crone hissed.

"Stitching won't save that one. You have no choice if you want him to live."

Amelia sucked in a shuddering breath. "Then show me."

She stripped him of everything not necessary to preserving his modesty and got to work. There were dozens of cuts that needed cleaning and three that needed stitching. The crone taught her how to heal, how to focus her power to do the most delicate of tasks. After years of suppression, the silver fire was eager to work.

Hours later, when his wounds were packed with poultices, she draped her bedroll over him. His skin was flush again, but his chest rose and fell with troubled breaths. His fingers twitched, plucking on a phantom fiddle's strings.

"He dreams." The crone dragged a nail across his forehead. "Fire and blood... and drums."

Amelia staggered against a pew, the words triggering her own memoires of carnage. "Crone, are there cranes here? I need to get a message to the Sanctisum Seats."

"They're gone. Dead or flown."

"Will more come? Demons, I mean." She could barely keep her eyes open. She wrestled another scrap from a rotting pew and almost toppled over.

"Lie down, whelp," the crone said, shuffling for the doorway. "I'll watch the gate tonight. But sleep lightly. If they come, you must wake, otherwise you won't see the dawn."

CHAPTER 21

THE SORCRER COLLAPSED AGAINST THE TABLE WITH A SHOUT, scattering the wine glasses and pitching a platter of food over the side. The fried fish split in two and mired in a puddle of white wine; it stared sullenly at him with one dull eye.

The rooks screeched and flapped down from their roost to peck at the unguarded morsels.

Sagging into a chair, he jerked his sleeve up to the elbow. The three cuts closest to his elbow knitted into thin black lines, just like the other one. Failure.

His olive-toned skin, supple and smooth, turned dry and wrinkled. It spread from his hands up his arms and over his shoulders. It crawled over his entire torso and down his back to his hips. Snarling, he pounded his fists on the table. His fragile skin hurt. He wouldn't have the strength to try again – not until he returned home – and he wasn't sure he wanted to. Four skeins had been defeated. It was unthinkable.

He packed his things at once.

A tentative knock on the door jerked him to a halt.

"Sir? It's Master Rajesh…"

Nosy *abn haram*. But he'd been forbidden from killing him; the hotel proprietor was important to the cause.

"… heard a noise, do you need any assist—"

"No," he barked. "Go away."

"… sure? I could get a maid…"

By the state of his skin, he'd need a dozen maids. "Send three."

"T-three?" There was a tremor in the man's voice, like he'd misheard. Or wanted to mishear.

"When I'm done, send someone to clean up. I'll be going. After."

"…okay…"

He waited until he heard the proprietor shuffle off before he resumed packing. He kicked the rooks aside and snatched up the pipe that had fallen into the apple strudel. With a flick of his wrist, he slung the whipped cream off its stem and put it in his pocket. His fingertips grazed against the velvet pouch full of black sand. At least none had scattered during his spasm.

Clapping his hands twice, he captured the rooks' attention. There were four of them, and four pairs of red cabochon eyes stared at him. "Go. Keep watch. One of you go to Bucharest and get our friend there to send out mercenaries. *Capture* only. I'll be along."

The rooks cawed and abandoned the remains of the fish. They flew out the window and into the night sky, blotting out the stars.

He picked up the last thing from the floor, a pair of fingerless gloves of golden silk. He tugged them over his aging hands and picked up the wine bottle. Pouring himself what remained in a glass, he sat down to wait for his cleaning service.

CHAPTER 22

THE MOON WAS LOW IN THE SKY WHEN AMELIA LEFT THE TEMPLE.

A popping ember had startled her awake. It had the same snappish demeanor as the crone, reminding her of something she had forgotten. The fire was nearly burned out, and there was no sign of the crone. She took the horse, leaving Hiro to sleep – dreaming less fitfully now – and went to collect their companions.

Her thighs were sore, but there wasn't any pain where the demon had cut her. Instead there was only a white scar, long and narrow, as imperceptible as a hair unless it hit the light just right.

Amelia found them in the ruined wildflower fields at daybreak. The boy, eyes half-lidded, leaned against the stumbling priest. Isen jerked his staff into both hands when she hailed them.

"It's okay," Kale said, tugging on Isen's sleeve. "Amelia, is Hiro…?"

"He'll be fine," she said, dismounting. "He's still sleeping—oof!" Amelia staggered back a step as the boy gave her a fierce hug. She gave his back a few awkward pats and gently pulled away. He didn't know she was Sanu and forbidden to touch.

No sooner had she pried herself loose than Isen crushed her in an embrace. His golden curls tickled her face, the pendant he wore hidden beneath his robes pinching her skin. He knew better than to touch her without permission, but she was just as relieved to see him.

Amelia passed a hand over his hair, guiding his forehead to press against hers in the ancient gesture of connection.

"I heard their howls," he mumbled, his voice thick. "I didn't know—"

"*Pax*," she murmured. "I'm alright."

"How did you...?"

"When we crossed the temple threshold, they vanished. There was a silver light... and..." She grunted in pain, the hand on his robes balling into a fist. The lily tattoo seared her flesh, white-hot with the lie.

"It's okay," Isen soothed, "you don't need to talk about it."

Amelia released him with a gasp, turning away to rub the spot on her sternum.

Isen fumbled into the saddle, and Kale sprang up behind him, looping his skinny arms around the priest's waist.

She took the reins and guided the warhorse back they way they had come.

They walked the crests and troughs of countless little hills speckled with white and yellow wildflowers under the springtime sun. The morning air was cool and full of birdsong, as if the world had been completely oblivious to the frantic chase that had happened only last night. The menfolk were fast asleep, and the weary warhorse trudged after her, nearly at the length of its reins. Amelia propped herself up on Isen's staff and focused on putting one foot in front of the other.

Vienna finally revealed itself beyond the next hill, and as they approached, Amelia could see the entire city buzzing. The people swarmed around the abandoned temple, bustling to and fro from the city proper.

A dark patch emanated from the holy ground; blight that turned all greenery to black and ash. Yet the people traversed the cursed earth without care. Some were even singing.

Their songs woke Isen and Kale, and the boy peered around the blind priest, eyes wide with wonder. Children his age were scurrying about, plucking things from the blight. The black earth faded to gray even as she watched, and green sprouts poked up from the ash to wave sprigs of tiny bell-shaped flowers.

Kale slipped from the horse and ran into the temple, his mane of auburn hair bouncing with every stride. His passage startled the workers, and a cry rose up when they saw her. Amelia shrank beside the warhorse, clutching her breast collar for support. The mare snorted and stamped at the crowd, eyes rolling.

Ignoring the horse, women with their hair swept back under kerchiefs and men with rolled-up sleeves swarmed her, praising and calling her "Maiglöckchen." Young girls and boys stuffed bouquets of the bell-shaped flowers into her hands until her arms overflowed.

"Sanu," they cried. "Thank you, Sanu!"

Amelia smoothed a hand down her flaxen cloak. "But how did you—"

"Only a Sanu could defeat the Witch of Vienna," the closest woman said, beaming.

"There goes our anonymity," Isen muttered.

"The Witch has plagued us for nigh on twenty-one years," the same woman said. "Stealing sheep, spreading blight, haunting the temple—"

"Legend said a Sanu would come and drive her out—"

"She'd bring the maiglöckchen back-"

A red-cheeked man with bright eyes pushed forward. "Last night the city watch said they saw a golden woman on a golden horse ride straight into the temple. *You*, my lady," he said, remembering a moment too late to remove his hat. "Then there was a blast of silver light, pure as lightning, that drove the witch away. We all saw it, didn't we?"

The crush of men and women cheered.

"Then the maiglöckchen began to grow again." An old woman pressed forward and added her own bouquet to the pile in Amelia's arms. "And we knew the Lady had come to help us."

"Come, Sanu," the red-cheeked man said, waving her forward. "We're restoring the temple in your honor. Everyone's come!"

The lily of the valley carpeted the once-cursed ground, perfuming the morning air with their waving bells. It was impossible not to trample them as the crowd followed her into the temple.

There were even more people within, furiously cleaning. The vines had all been torn from the mildew-speckled pillars; the rotting leaves and scraps of garbage had all been wrested from the courtyard's corners and burned away; women and men were scrubbing the flagstones free of grime. Even the sanctuary had been cleaned, the last of the rotting pews burned and the salvageable ones repaired. The golden sigil of the Most Holies gleamed once again.

The copper bowl in the altar remained silent. The sheep's bones had been cleared away and the bowl wiped clean to a brilliant gleam.

Amelia approached the altar and touched the cold stone with a hand. It should be warm, humming even, like the soft purr of a sleeping kitten. But with no sacred white flame, no temple guardian, the altar was cold, lifeless.

She felt the silence of the crowd like a crushing weight on her shoulders. They all watched her, breath held, as she placed her hand against the bowl. But she could not restore the flame. Only a temple guardian could do that, and this one had long since fled.

She still felt the need to try; the crowd expected it of her.

If you are there, return home. By the Lady and her Lord, please come back.

I never left.

The white flame blazed to life, flaring to the ceiling as the crowd gasped and shuffled back. The fire shrank to its normal height, snapping and writhing.

Amelia withdrew her hand, frowning. She wasn't one to think that fire could have a personality, but this one seemed ornery, like a tired old woman too set in her ways.

"Crone?" she whispered.

My name is Niobe. Your debt is paid; I have my home again.

"H-how?"

I told you before, we have the same mother. And now, I can finally rest.

The flame's voice started to fade.

"Wait." She hunched over the copper bowl, lowering her voice even more. "Crone – Niobe – have you ever heard of a man named Elwynn? The Revered Onu told me—"

No man. Her voice was slipping away.

If she'd been the crone, Amelia would've shaken her awake. "But-"

Pax vobis... sister.

She sighed, stepping away from the altar. *"Pax vobis." Peace to you.*

"Now that the Sanu has restored the flame," a rough voice growled, "I'd appreciate it if you'd give us a minute. We have much to discuss."

Amelia jumped. The crowd shrank from the hulking figure, creeping past her to place bundles of maiglöckchen on the altar before dispersing.

Her cheeks flamed. In the bustling activity, she had quite forgotten about the prince.

He sat on a stool by the window, mending the rents in his greatcoat in the mid-morning light. The muscles poking above the yards of bandage encircling his abdomen twitched with each stab of his needle. When the last of the townsfolk had cleared the sanctuary, he tossed his coat aside and stood.

"Hiro, I—"

He crossed the space between them in three great strides and flipped her onto the altar stone, hand clamped around her throat. Amelia shouted, but only a squeak passed through her teeth. She writhed on the stone, wiggling to get free, but the prince had her pinned.

"I should be dead," he shouted. *"What did you do to me?"*

CHAPTER 23

"I WAS DYING," HIRO SNARLED. "NO SANU COULD'VE PREVENTED IT. I know your kind. The strongest of you can cure a headache with a touch, but that's it. *What did you do to me?*"

The priestess clawed at his hand, ocean blue eyes rolling in her head as her lips turned a similar shade. He released her, yanked his dagger out of its sheath. She rolled onto her side; great hacking coughs shuddered through her body. He flattened her with a yank to the shoulder, laid the blade against her bruised skin.

"*Hiro.*" Kale's voice echoed from the doorway.

"Well?" Hiro gave the priestess a little shake.

She coughed again, sucked in a rattling breath. "The crone—"

"You let some *witch* touch me?"

"Leave. Her. *Alone.*" Kale yanked on his arm; Hiro shook him off. The boy jumped to his feet, rushed around to the other side of the altar. He threw his arms across the gasping priestess.

"Kale, you know how I feel about sorcery—"

"It was the only way—"

Hiro reared back, eyes ablaze. The blade lifted from the Sanu's throat. "You *let* her—"

"What wouldn't I do to save you?" The boy was crying now; great fat tears splattered on the Sanu's flaxen cloak. His face was red, strained.

The priestess clamped a hand to her throat, used the other to push herself away. Her ocean-blue eyes were bulging, fearful. The boy pushed her behind him, a little cat protecting its injured littermate.

Hiro looked past the boy's tears, noted the grim set of his jaw. The boy was crouched, ready to fight his master if he took another step. He'd seen that crouch before. Hiro sheathed the dagger, swallowed thickly. "Kale. She must answer—" His gaze flicked to the Sanu as she extended a hand in mute warning.

A staff cracked against his skull, shattered, and felled him and the splinters into a bloody heap before the altar.

SOMETHING WAS TUGGING at his hair.

The fingers were nimble, precise, small.

Kale.

The boy was wrapping his head with a bandage. The smell of lemons, not quite lemon balm, lingered in the air. There was something thick the boy was binding to his head. God's-herb poultice. He saw clippings of the purple-fuzzed leaves and its tiny purple flowers scattered on the stones beside him. It was fresh, not the dried stuff he kept in his saddlebags.

Someone had given it to him.

In front of the altar, the Sanu knelt at the feet of an old woman. The crone was covered head to foot in rags that trailed behind her like a tail. The priestess twirled a stalk of god's-herb between her fingers as the old woman spoke.

Hiro groaned, tried to sit up. "What happened?"

The boy gave a little cry of delight, urged him to stay still. "I need to finish this or else your head might fall off."

"I doubt it's that serious."

"It could be. It looks nasty." The boy cringed, continued to wind the bandage. "How far back can you remember? Do you remember this morning, when all the townsfolk were here? Did you know that Kogu – I mean, the Tybetan Monster – had marched through here and put all the temple's priests and priestesses to the sword? Said something about them being false prophets, that obedience to the Most Holies was demeaning and useless. He even torched their library. At least that's what Kurt's father's mother said. That's when the witch moved in—"

"Boy, enough of your chatter. My head hurts enough." Hiro got to his feet. He paused, let his vision stop swimming. "I remember all of it."

"But Amelia says you shouldn't move." The boy tugged on his sleeve. "You'll bust open your stitches and get blood everywhere. She's threatened to cauterize them, and you don't like fire…"

Hiro stalked straight for the priestess.

The blind priest blocked his path, hefted his broken staff. "I'll break this to kindling over your head if I have to."

"You'll never get another chance."

The boy yanked on his arm. "Hiro, don't—"

Hiro pointed to the old woman in rags. "Is that the witch talking with the Sanu?"

The old crone's head shot up; a pair of colorless eyes, like chips of crystal, glared at him. She hissed, bared a set of sharp white teeth. Witch indeed.

The priest cocked his head in a birdlike way, puzzled. "There is no other. Amelia is meditating. And you'd best be polite and keep your voice down. She's saved your life twice now."

"She's right *there*." Hiro stabbed a finger in the witch's direction.

"Don't bother pointing." The priest waved a hand in front of his bandaged eyes. "Blind, remember?"

The boy peered around them, shook his head. "Hiro, maybe you got hit harder than-"

When Hiro looked again, the crone was gone. Vanished. The Sanu rose, tossed the god's-herb onto the nearest brazier. Its lemony scent mingled with the smoldering incense.

Wild, Hiro whipped around. "Where'd she go?" He thrust out a hand to steady himself. His vision swam, his pulse throbbing in the back of his head. "Where is she?"

A hand grasped his, pulled him down into a pew. "Peace, Hiro," the Sanu said, her voice hoarse. "Your wounds. Kale, didn't you tell him?"

"I did, but—" Kale began.

"*You.*" Hiro ripped away from her. "What did you do to me? I was dying. That… that *thing* bit me and… my flesh turned to ice yet fire burned in my blood. Then silver light, like a hook, dragging it away."

The Sanu's ocean-blue eyes were cool, guarded. Waiting.

"*You.*"

"Me." The priestess nodded once. She winced, probed her bruised skin with gentle fingertips.

"You mentioned a crone."

"You see a white flame, I see an old woman."

His eyes narrowed. Sanu were known conduits to the divine realms; this one had restored a sacred flame. It was unprecedented. Unless it was something else.

Hiro seized her hand, the right one with the golden lily tattoo. The yellow silk of her sleeve crinkled under his fingers. Sanu were bound by that tattoo, utterly incapable of falsehood. "Tell me, did you use sorcery?"

The guarded look faded from her eyes. Replaced by hurt. Pain. "No."

Hiro released her hand, dropped to his knees. His throbbing head could no longer bear to keep him upright. Relief, powerful as a riptide, threatened to topple him. Black runes stoked to ember red floated in his mind's eye. The conjurer's chuckle echoed faintly in his ears. He clutched his head. *Gods above, if she'd said yes—*

There was a startled cry as he yanked his greatsword clear of its sheath. He set the point against the floor, gripped the hilt with both hands. The sapphire held in the dragon's teeth winked in the candle-light. "Sanu, you came to my aid for no other reason than compassion. My honor demands that I repay this debt. I will get you to Lhasa. On my life, I, Prince Hiro Ishida, do swear this oath."

Panic. Dismay. Emotions flickered over her face like a shadow puppet show. "I can't possibly accept—"

"It's already done." He rose to his feet. Red bloomed from the bandage on his calf, where that *thing* had bitten him.

The Sanu huffed, went to the nearest brazier and plucked up a coal with a pair of tongs. Without preamble, she yanked down the bandage on his leg, pressed the glowing coal against the wound. Flesh sizzled.

Hiro howled.

"*That* is for my throat."

CHAPTER 24

THE DANUBE RIVER CUT THROUGH VIENNA'S WARREN OF multicolored buildings, a fissure of blue against white and green. A dam nestled under its primary bridge, fueled the lampposts lining the main square and river ways. Even some of the wealthier neighborhoods had electricity. The Sanu openly gaped at the wonder of hydropower.

A cathedral dedicated to Delphi the Protector towered above the crush: glittering beige stone, colored windows, blue dome. Beyond it, a great white arc of a building that used to be a palace.

Hiro led them into the thick of it. Tension seized his shoulders as the throngs flocked to see the Maiglöckchen. Without permission, he hoisted her into the saddle.

"Hands!" the priestess shrieked. "It is *forbidden* to touch a Sanu-"

"Can't afford you getting lost."

"You can *ask* next time."

"I'll try to remember that."

"Maiglöckchen," a woman cried, waving her hand. "Sanu!"

Hiro glanced behind him. The Sanu was stained from travel, but her caramel hair streamed behind her like a banner. The breeze pushed her cloak behind her shoulders, revealed the pink and yellow silks beneath.

Wide-eyed, the Sanu twisted around in the saddle. He doubted she'd ever seen this many people in her entire life. Slowly, she waved back to the old woman, and the crowd erupted. They tossed flowers, hoisted children onto their shoulders, shouted pleas for healing and good fortune. The press tightened until Hiro had to shove his way forward.

"Do you know where you're going?" Isen called.

"I'm looking for a hotel. *Obviously*," Hiro shouted back against the din.

"Try the Green Pearl. It's on the southwest side of the plaza."

"I'm not interested in a hostel, priest."

"It's perfectly capable of catering to your more refined tastes," came a sour reply.

It was the old palace. It dominated half of the plaza, a great white building dotted with windows and statues and topped with three domes like cherries on a cake. The Green Pearls, more like it.

Inside was the same white stone, gray-veined, furnished with green and silver. It was as ornate as any Council Lodge: high ceilings, sweeping staircases, skillful architecture. Electric lamps shaped like scallop shells furnished every wall; he smacked the Sanu's hand away when she reached up to touch one.

The man behind a slab of marble countertop gave an excited cry. Hiro grabbed him by the shoulder, held him at arm's length before he could come any closer. Chocolate-colored skin and hair, a simpering smile, fancy clothes with gold thread. Sleeves that extended past his wrists, like the Sanu's.

"Something wrong with your hands?" Hiro asked sharply.

Isen stiffened beside him, clutched his staff hard enough to make the wood creak.

"I-I have an unsightly—" the man began.

"*Show me.*"

"Hiro," the Sanu scolded. "You're being extremely rude—"

"It's nothing, my lady." With a flick of his wrists, the elongated cuffs slithered down his forearms. Revealed terribly marred hands. The chocolate skin was the withered rind of a spoiled avocado. "A rather nasty grease fire," the man explained, shaking his cuffs back into place. "A small price to pay for the best Siamese fried fish."

"Satisfied?" the priestess hissed.

"Hn." Hiro released him.

"I am Master Rajesh Chandanmal, the owner of this humble establishment." He extended a hand to the priestess. "If I may?"

She nodded, cast Hiro a satisfied look. *This is what manners look like.*

The proprietor kissed the back of her hand with barely constrained delight. "May the blessings of the Lady be upon you. The city has been simply *buzzing* since last night. We are honored by your presence. I expect you need rooms, yes? I must apologize." Rajesh wrung his hands. "Our finest suite is undergoing some cleaning. Its previous guest was rather... untidy."

"It's no trouble. Thank you for accommodating us on such short notice."

"*Anything* for you, Maiglöckchen."

A young woman approached, eyebrows lifted expectantly. She had the same chocolate skin, dark hair as Lakshmi. A pang of lust shot through his stomach.

"No, Priya, I'll show our guests myself." Rajesh eyed Hiro, dismissed Priya with a flick of his hand. "This way, please."

They climbed one of the staircases, trailed down a long marble hall hung with paintings in gilded frames. Their steps echoed in the vaulted ceilings, joined the clatter of the hotel's other guests going about their business.

"... have everything you need," Rajesh continued chattily. "This establishment houses a butterfly garden, the local Hadi Center, and the only remaining Lipizzaner riding school in the entire continent! Attached is also a Dollhouse—"

"Dollhouse?"

Doll or Gent, the Whites were adepts in the arts of massage and conversation, whereas the Reds were erotic experts. Respectable and accredited, it was still just highly regulated prostitution. At least for the Reds.

Hiro was shocked the proprietor had even brought it up. "She is *Sanu*, you simpering *hundan*."

"Hiro!"

"I only meant in their capacity to massage away the wearies of the road."

"Thank you, but I'm not allowed to indulge."

"Not a problem! There are three gourmet restaurants and four gardens, two of which are reserved for the private use of our guests."

The Sanu shifted nervously. "A-and what would one-night's stay here cost?"

"My lady," Rajesh exclaimed. He stopped in front of a door at the end of the hall. Unlike the others of polished wood, this one was caved with prancing horses. He unlocked the door, gestured them inside the plush suite. "I could no sooner ask the Blessed Lady or her Mighty Lord for payment than you, Sanu."

Hiro's eyes bulged. Never had he, the heir to the esteemed Lord Ishida, been offered a free night's stay anywhere.

"Surely we can offer you something for your service-" the Sanu began.

He wanted to elbow her, keep her mouth shut.

"Stay an extra day. Bless my establishment. Anything more would be too much." Rajesh took her hand again, smothered it with a kiss. "Now I'll send my boy up to draw your bath – these old pipes can be finicky, you know – and my daughter Priya with some refreshments." He turned to Hiro, looked him over head to foot. Sniffed. "I expect her back *promptly*."

Hiro glared, fists tightening at his sides.

"If you're wanting any entertainment, like I said before, there *is* the Dollhouse."

"That depends," Hiro said. "Any Red Dolls there that look like your daughter?"

The Sanu took a quick step between them. "Thank you, Master Rajesh. You've been more than generous."

His features smoothed, and he flashed her a smile. "Please, Sanu, enjoy your stay. *Gentlemen.*" The man bobbed a smart bow, glared at Hiro, and hurried off to his other guests. Or gossip that the Maiglöckchen was at *his* establishment. *Hundan.*

"I can't wait for that bath," Hiro groaned.

"You'll have to wait a bit longer." The Sanu sauntered to the largest room, blocked the doorway.

"*Oh?*"

"Master Rajesh said he's sending his boy to draw water for *my* bath. Maybe if you decide to be polite for once, he'll do the same for you. Until this evening, then?"

She shut the door in his face, slid the bolt into place.

Hiro's hand twitched; he contemplated breaking down the door to give her a piece of his mind. Master Rajesh would certainly throw them out. And the boy was hungry. Kale hadn't had a decent meal or a bed to sleep in in weeks. He'd have to control his temper.

He pounded his fist against her door. "I thought Sanu were supposed to shun modern technology. That *includes* indoor plumbing."

"Not when it would insult someone's hospitality."

"I hope your bathwater's cold!"

"It won't be," came the singsong reply.

Hiro gritted his teeth, pushed past the snickering priest into the second room, and steeled himself for a wash with a pitcher of cold water and a cloth.

CHAPTER 25

Amelia sipped at a glass of wine and tried to keep from fidgeting.

News of her arrival at the Green Pearl had spread like wildfire, and visitors flocked to her like moths to flame. They came from the city, from the shepherding hills, from the Elbe forests where laumė were rumored to haunt. The crush forced them onto the plaza, where even more people pressed forward to see the Maiglöckchen.

They sat on the rim of a wide fountain outside the Green Pearl. Eight spouts, two on each face of the plinth, arced water in twisting rivulets into the pool. Upon the plinth reared a magnificent warhorse and its rider, both green with age.

Hiro sat next to her, presumably to supervise her safety yet seemed wholly occupied with cleaning his nails with the tip of his dagger. He wouldn't admit that he didn't have the strength to stand long; the strike from Isen's staff had been a powerful one. The proud prince had yanked the bandage off his head that morning, insisting he had healed enough.

The priest had retreated with Master Rajesh to the Hadi Center to entertain the destitute with his stories, and Kale had stolen off to the stables to play with the barn cats under the guise of tending to the horse. That'd been hours ago. Amelia took another long swallow and set the glass down with a trembling hand.

"You know," Hiro drawled, never looking up from his nails, "it'd be inappropriate for a Sanu to get drunk in public."

"I'm *not* drunk." She hiccupped and glared at him. "That was a coincidence."

"Uh-huh. Have some water."

"I'm just… nervous."

"Nervous? About what? I thought you priestesses were used to this kind of stuff. Praying over the sick and blessing babies and whatnot."

She leaned in close, lowering her voice to a whisper. "The only people I ever saw were my sisters and the rare pilgrim. This *ocean* of faces, it's… Look, I just wanted to get to Lhasa unnoticed. Less trouble, you know? Now I am this Maiglöckchen. They even call me Argenti, the Silver One. Everyone knows my face!"

He wagged his dagger at her. "*You* let that cat out of the bag."

"When I saved *you*."

"Stop worrying. No one'll try anything out in the open like this. And so far I've seen nothing—"

"Of course you haven't. You're too busy cleaning your nails and antagonizing the supplicants. Why do you have to look at their hands? And did you really have to punch that one in the face?"

Hiro glowered. "He'd just confessed to falling in love with the wife of another man. Of course I had to punch him in the face."

"He hadn't *done* anything yet. He was seeking help."

"He can think of it as warning of what's to come should he pursue her. Hn. I hope a laumė gets him."

Amelia huffed. "You're no help at all."

"No help, huh? *That* man—"—he jerked his chin at one by the lace shop—"—has done nothing but stare at you since you got here. Pretty soon I'm going to go over there and ask why. And *not* politely."

Predatory. That's the only word she could think to describe the man leaning just outside the door of the shop, arms crossed over his chest. A faded red scarf looped several times around his neck, blending in with his chestnut hair. He wore it in partial canerows, tied off with bits of colored sea glass. Even from across the plaza, she could see his sun-browned skin was stretched tight over lean muscle.

Amelia stood. *"Come, mariner,"* she called in Atlantican. *"What do you need? Your stares are making my friend uncomfortable."*

The man straightened, dropping his arms in surprise. Then he threw his head back with a laugh and returned to his slouch against the wall. *"Only uncomfortable? I'll have to do better."*

"Suit yourself. He won't be polite if he questions you."

He waved a hand in cavalier dismissal. *"Feh, he doesn't look the type for manners anyway, my lady. You might consider getting a more genteel replacement."*

"Like you?"

He put a hand over his heart and inclined his head. *"It would be an honor, Argenti."*

She grinned, until Hiro yanked her down beside him.

"What are you doing?" Hiro snapped.

"Hands!" Amelia smoothed her clothes and gave him an imperious look. "Now that he knows we're aware of him, he should be less trouble, right?"

He rolled his eyes. "Sanu, you don't—" He cut himself off as a child stumbled forward. His father's hand clutched a wad of the boy's jacket, keeping him close in front of him.

Amelia smiled at the father – who didn't return it – before she looked at the little boy.

"Left hand," Hiro said.

The little boy didn't return the smile, either. Amelia frowned. The boy's eyes were brown, seal-brown like Hiro's, wide and full of unshed tears.

"Are you hurt?" she asked gently. She extended her hand, beckoning him. He snatched it and strained forward, but the father's hand on his jacket prevented him from coming much closer.

"Left. Hand," Hiro said again.

"Are you alright?" she whispered to the boy. "Did your father… hurt you?"

Tears spilled over the boy's cheeks, but he never made a sound. He just kept his eyes glued to her face, pleading. Willing her to understand.

"Are you deaf? *Left hand.*" Hiro rose from his seat.

The boy started to shake, but he wasn't looking at the prince. "He's not my father."

Hiro shoved Amelia back, knocking her into the fountain.

She thrashed in the shallow water, trying to get her legs under her. Staggering upright, she smeared her hair from her face.

The plaza was in chaos. The people scattered, feet thundering against the bricks. Stone statues on their ledges of the old palace trembled, showering dust on the stampeding crowd.

Hiro was locked in battle with the boy's father. He had a crazed glint in his eye as he slashed at Hiro with a small sickle. The prince caught the sickle with his dagger, snatched the man's hand, and yanked the blades aside. He knocked the man into a heap with a head-butt that left him staggering. The prince lurched forward, pressing his boot into the man's wrist until he released the sickle.

The man spat the blood out of his mouth. *"Via—"*

The dagger silenced the cry with a swift cut.

Amelia crawled out of the fountain as Hiro wiped the dagger clean on the man's clothes.

"Wha... what—"

He yanked back the sleeve on the dead man's left hand. The faded tattoo of a rampant lion clawed at the air. Hiro turned his head to the side and spat.

"That's why I look at their hands."

THEY LEFT the city the same night.

Five others with the same mark had been slain, their bodies scattered across the plaza. A red scarf, faded from the sun, had fluttered among the carnage.

Hiro had forbidden conversation indefinitely, but when he told them to stay put in a thicket as he back-tracked to check if they were being followed, Amelia couldn't help herself.

"*Isen.*" She crawled over to him, tugging her cloak free as it caught on the brush. The priest sat with his back against a tree, Kale curled up beside him and fast asleep. Isen cocked his head at her voice.

"Amelia? Hiro told us—"

"I think we can risk it now, so long as we're quiet. We're miles away." She glanced from the city – nothing more than a cluster of children's building blocks – to the sky. The Archer's bow was behind the horizon. "Besides, he's been gone for at least an hour now."

"Well... just keep it down. He's the sort to slash-first-ask-questions-never, and I want to keep my tongue in my head."

She rolled her eyes. "Listen, when Hiro was looking at everybody's hands, I just thought he was being really rude, but—"

"He's just being extremely *cautious.* Kogusanji had his followers tattooed with a rampant lion on the back of the left hand. Right here, in the web between forefinger and thumb."

"How sacrilegious could he get?"

The rampant lion was a sigil reserved only for the Crown Prince of Heaven, the Lion Before the Storm.

Isen shrugged. "After the Great War, there was a time known as the Purge where his supporters were hunted down and executed."

"That's barbaric."

He shrugged again. "It's just like cutting off diseased limbs from a tree. The victors can't have the losers spreading their propaganda, can they? But some escaped."

"But why now? Why would a loyalist attack Hiro after all this time?"

"He's finally free of the Academy's walls. He's an *Ishida.* His family was instrumental in Kogusanji's defeat. I expect it's only natural for them to want to extract some sort of revenge. But... are you sure Hiro was his target?"

Amelia sat back on her heels. "You mean *me?*"

"Why not? Kogusanji was only ever truly afraid of the Sanu. *Someone* is summoning those demons."

"But Kogusanji's dead."

"Is he? The body was never found—"

Amelia silenced him with a hand on his arm.

Snuffling.

Fear seized her, turning her blood to ice. Inside, the silver fire flared.

Sweet mercy, will we never be free of them?

CHAPTER 26

"I TOLD YOU TO BE *QUIET*." HIRO PARTED THE BRUSH WITH AN ANGRY swipe. "I could hear you—"

The Sanu scuttled away with a cry. Her face pale as moonlight, she raised a hand to ward him off.

"Sanu—"

"It's the horse. It's the *snorting* horse." She dropped her hand with a relieved giggle. Borderline hysterical.

"Were we being followed?" Isen asked. He roused the boy with a little shake.

Hiro shook his head. "Not anymore."

"Hiro, '*all who draw the sword will die by the sword.*' Maybe you should try something el—"

"That's enough sermonizing for one night." He pulled the Sanu roughly out of the thicket.

"Hands! And I *don't* sermonize."

"Of course not. Kale, hurry up."

"I don't," she insisted.

"Uh-huh."

She shrieked when he picked her up and plopped her into the saddle.

"*Hands!*"

"Hush. Kale, up you go. There's a better spot to camp up here."

The trees of this grove grew so thick the mare had a hard time squeezing between their trunks. Not even the moonlight penetrated here. They dug deeper into the arboreal haven until at last they breached its heart, where the trees were old and spaced farther apart.

Kale scrounged around for deadwood, built a fire just large enough to heat the tea kettle. Hiro passed around the food he'd swiped from the Green Pearl: paneer momo for the Sanu and some sort of baked fish for the rest of them.

"It's like shoe leather." Kale ripped a hunk off with his teeth.

Isen gnawed at his piece, plucked the needle-like bones from his mouth between forefinger and thumb before flicking them into the fire.

Hiro just spat his off to the side.

"When I was in Sundsvall, I ate nothing but dried fish for weeks," the priest said. "*That* was shoe leather. This, well… it's just slightly over-cooked."

Hiro started. Sundsvall was the tip of the Scandinavian Archipelago, the birthplace of the Baltic Raiders. "What business did you have that far north?"

"Priests travel, you know. It's called missionary work."

"Do we have any more of those momos?" Kale dragged the sack between his legs, rooted around.

Hiro cuffed his head. "Those're for the Sanu."

"I don't mind sharing," the Sanu said.

"It's not your job to feed him."

"'*If you knew what I know about the powers of giving, you would not let a single meal pass without sharing it in some way.*'" She stood, gave the boy her last momo. "I'm done anyway."

"Don't go too far," he said.

"I know, I know."

Hiro grunted.

The priest began telling a story, something about a kraken

guarding a sunken treasure. Kale inched closer, capturing every word. They were all too wired for sleep but too tired to do much more than sit and talk.

Hiro listened with half an ear, ground out the nicks in his dagger left by the sickle. It'd been an opium sickle, the hilt goat's horn, a rarity outside the poppy fields of western Tybet. A poor choice for a weapon.

Unless you were trying to send a message—

The fire popped loudly.

The priest had moved onto another story, and the priestess wasn't back yet.

"Damn it." Hiro snatched up his bow.

She was nearby in a glade just large enough to dance in. Of course. Mother had always said the Sanu were more likely to dance their devotions than kneel. Above, the thinnest fingernail of a crescent moon cut the night sky. Her movements were languid, ethereal. They seemed to caress the moonlight, wove it into her dance until her skin shone silver. Mesmerizing.

"What is that?"

She yelped.

He waved in the gloom. "I'm not going to bite."

The Sanu plucked her sleeves down to her fingers, smoothed back a wisp of hair with a trembling hand. "Moon Song. We perform it on the eve of the new moon, a plea for it to return to the sky. It's said that in the Beginning when Heaven and Earth were one, the Most Holies lived upon the earth with their Creation. But the people began to drift away, choosing greed instead of love. And—"

He'd heard it before. "In order to reconcile us after our rebellion, the Crown Prince sacrificed himself to create the Gate of Heaven. Upon his rebirth, the Moon returned to the sky. Something like that?"

She pursed her lips. "It's a cycle of rebirth that his sacrifice can free us from."

Hiro was quiet a moment. "You know the new moon occurs because its rotation brings it between the Earth and the Sun, right?"

The Sanu shrugged. "Why can't it be both?"

"Uh-huh. I told you not to wander off."

She held her hands out, crossed at the wrist as if he were a jailer come to take her into custody. "I've had my moment of freedom." She sighed wistfully. "You can drag me back now."

"Hn." He rolled his eyes. "Don't tempt me."

CHAPTER 27

"ARE YOU GOING TO STOP AT *EVERY* MARKER?"

The Sanu lagged behind, stood with her hand pressed against the sigil on a stone pillar. Eyes closed, her lips moved in a soundless prayer.

"Yes, yes, may Delphi the Protector guard our steps and the grace of the Blessed Lady be upon us always, we *know*." Hiro clamped a hand around her wrist, dragged her forward to the others. Isen and Kale rode the horse, the priest's staff slung across his lap threatening to smack the unwary.

With an indignant cry, she wrested her arm free of him and smoothed her cloak with a flounce. "Hands! It is forbidden to touch a Sanu—"

"Without permission, I know. We *all* know. But if you keep slowing us down with all your prayers, I'm going to put you over my shoulder and *carry* you the rest of the way to Lhasa."

The priestess planted her hands on her hips. "Is there something *wrong* with taking a moment to give thanks for our blessings?"

Hiro yanked the broken staff from Isen's hands, herded the priestess forward. A shepherd's crook redirecting a wayward lamb. With a squeak, the Sanu lurched out of reach. "There's nothing wrong with a moment. But you take dozens of moments a day. And don't get me started on the *hours* you spend reading that book or meditating. Is the cosmos really that fascinating? And what have we been blessed with anyway, Sanu? The weather's been *goushi*, our grain stores are low because *somebody* doesn't eat meat, Isen's just getting over the flux, *you* can barely walk in those forsaken sandals—"

"I never knew Academy graduates were so *whiny*," the Sanu said. "I thought they were people of substance, fortitude, indomitable spirit. You've done nothing but complain or bark orders since Vienna. *'Endurance is one of the most difficult disciplines, but it is to the one who endures that final victory comes.'*"

"You've never had to train twelve hours a day for *years*, have someone beat you and break you down and mold you into something else, to give up everything – *everything* – for a failed cause. What do you know of endurance?"

The Sanu's eyes were chips of flint. "I'm enduring *you*, aren't I?"

Hiro's lip curled into a snarl.

"Yes, *yes*, the road can be difficult," Isen interrupted firmly. "When we get to Bucharest let's take a few days to *relax*."

"At this rate it'll take us a month."

"I wasn't aware we were in a rush," the priestess said sourly. "Arashiyama isn't going anywhere." The Sanu snatched the mare's breast collar to steady her stumbling gait. The warhorse pulled her forward as if she weighed nothing at all.

Hiro shoved the staff back into Isen's hands, reclaimed the reins from Kale. "I… I have responsibilities there." He clenched his jaw, felt the tanto knife dig into his lower back. *And vengeance.*

"I bet it's a woman," Isen announced.

"Well, there was one girl named Ellaria—"

"*Kale.*"

Isen clapped his hands. "I may be blind, but I can hear you're blushing. Tell me, Kale, is he as red as a beet?"

The boy giggled. "Redder."

Hiro *tsked* at him. The sound of a viper's hiss with the vehemence to match.

"How romantic," the priestess mused. "It turns out our brooding prince has a heart after all."

Hiro rounded on her. "Oh, yes. Nothing is more *romantic* than your fiancée sending you a letter telling you her love has been misplaced. That she's run off to marry another man."

The air stifled with its silence. No birdsong, no insect wings, even the jingling of his mare's harness had vanished.

"Hiro, I'm s—"

He turned around, yanked on the reins. "It's just as well. Mother never would've let such a treacherous woman marry into our family. She was *raffiné*."

"I thought your mother was a famous general," the priestess said, frowning. "How can she be *raffiné*?"

"She was both!"

"Her last stand at The Battle of the Xinjiang Plains is legendary," Isen said. "Happened, what? Twenty, twenty-one years ago?"

"Twenty," Hiro answered through tight lips. He knew what was coming next, tried not to listen. Isen had a flair for storytelling.

"She had the Tybetan Monster bottled up between the Hotun River and the Pamir Mountains." Isen chopped the air with his hands, created a wedge. "Harassed his war-host with just three hundred cavalry for *days*. Day attacks. Night attacks. She drove them to drown in the river, pinched them against the mountains with nowhere to go." He smacked his hands together. Kale giggled. "She was clever, swapping out their Imperial horses for the hardier and nimbler Steppe horse. On the fifth day, she was defeated by Kogusanji himself." Isen shook his head. "He thought the war won, but General Bethsaida had been just a diversion."

"A sacrifice." Hiro spat out the word.

"Lord Ishida had gathered the rest of his Guard and met him on the Plains. Slaughtered Kogusanji's war-host, though some managed to get away and go into hiding. And so, the defeat of the Tybetan Monster and the liberation of Eurasia. I'm told the Xinjiang Plains are more fertile now than ever."

Kale winced.

Hiro dragged Isen from the saddle. Rammed him against the mare's side.

"*Hey—*"

"Speak that way about my mother again, and I'll kill you."

"What? *I* wasn't the one who sent her to die."

"Stop it!" The Sanu wedged herself between them, tried to separate them with her elbows. Her ocean-blue eyes snapped with fire. "*Stop. We need to get ahead of this storm.*"

She jerked her chin to the west. Clouds, gray as an anvil with a shape to match, crawled across the sky. The storm's shadow darkened the valley below like a shade shuttering closed one slat at a time. The rain it carried promised to be cold.

Hiro released the priest with a shove.

The Sanu was taking another moment at another marker when the rain caught them. Droplets as fat as his thumbnail, heavy, bone-chilling.

"Come *on*, Sanu. The rest of us would like to get out of the rain. We don't have the same fortitude of spirit that makes us water-proof."

Hiro turned up the hood of his greatcoat, dug the oilskin jacket out of the saddlebags for Kale. Isen had already tugged the cowl of his woolen robes over his head, a blind turtle hiding in its shell. Hiro pressed on, let the Sanu fall behind. She only adhered to her own timetable anyway.

"H-Hiro," the Sanu called. "Might we s-stop for the d-day?"

"The storm isn't that bad." But the path was getting washed out. He stepped off to the side to avoid the stream churning down the dip in the road. "And if you hadn't wasted all that time talking to the air we'd be in the next town by now. You know, with *roofs*."

"I w-would greatly appreciate it if we c-could."

"Do you see any shelter?" He whipped around. "Gods above – why didn't you *say* anything?"

She was soaked. Shivering. The thin cloak hugged her every curve. "I d-did."

"You stupid girl," he hissed. "Get on the horse."

As she took another step, her eyes rolled back into her head.

"*No—*" Hiro caught her as she collapsed. He dug in hard with his right foot, halting their slide down the muddy road.

With his teeth, he yanked the glove off his burned hand. He pressed the puckered flesh against her forehead. Ice cold. His blistered fingers hovered, debating, then peeled the long strands of caramel hair away from her face. He replaced his glove, hoisted her into his arms.

"You stupid, stupid girl."

CHAPTER 28

AMELIA FELT A STRONG ARM SNAKE AROUND HER MIDDLE, PRESSING HER close against a broad chest. She was about to protest at the indecency of it all but found her mouth frozen shut. Numb, she wasn't even aware they were moving, except when Hiro was suddenly pulling her out of the saddle. He carried her into a darker patch of gloom, and she was no longer wet, just cold. She blinked once, twice, and then he was gone. When she blinked a third time, he had returned with the rest of their party.

"Take off your clothes."

Her head felt heavy, murky. Surely she hadn't heard him correctly. "Huh?"

"She'll do nothing of the sort, you animal," Isen snarled. "She is Sanu, the highest priestess of the Blessed Bosetsanu—"

"Sanu or not, she'll die of hypothermia. I can't get a fire going in this wet so the only course is to get the wet off her."

"Not a chance," Isen snapped. "The sheer notion of such impropriety and disrespect—"

"Because propriety is *so* good at keeping you warm—"

"It's not your job to protect her."

"Maybe it should be!"

"H-help," she whispered. She could no longer feel her legs.

"That's *it*. Move aside, priest."

Scuffling. Then silence.

THE SOFT SPLATTER of raindrops on stone coaxed her awake. The cavern was dark except for the meager light at the entrance. The four of them were huddled in a rudimentary cave, hardly more than a wide ledge jutting from the hillside. Vining tendrils shadowed the opening to the outside world; water beaded at their ends and dripped onto the mossy stones with a soft *pit-pat*.

She was buried beneath a heap of blankets that smelled faintly of horse, but she didn't care. She was dry and deliciously warm and—

The cave floor stirred.

Hiro sighed in his sleep, the rise of his bare chest brushing against her cheek. She lay nestled against his side, his muscled arm draped heavily over her shoulders, his naked thigh wedged between her own.

Amelia was wide awake in a heartbeat, instantly aware of every inch of him that pressed against every inch of her. "*Hiro Ishida!*" she screamed, thumping him in the chest. Her fist merely bounced aside.

His eyes flew open.

"How *dare* you." She thumped him again.

Unalarmed, he unwound himself and tossed the blankets aside. The pale light curved around his naked silhouette as he reached for his gi.

Speechless, her cheeks stained crimson, Amelia wrenched her gaze away.

There was an abrupt throb deep in her abdomen, hot and insistent. She pressed a hand against her belly and willed it to go away.

Gods above, what is happening to me?

Silver fire threatened to erupt from every pore. She crushed the surge with a snarl and chased after him.

"I *trusted* you. What kind of man takes advantage of a helpless—"

"The kind that keeps her alive," Hiro roared, rounding on her.

His voice was muffled by the thick fog that masked everything in an impenetrable veil of gray. Trees towered above them, dark as shadows behind the crystalline shroud. Even the Alps with their ever-present blanket of snow were invisible.

"Nothing happened. As you can see, you're still wearing your underclothes."

Amelia glanced down at the cotton camisole and drawers she wore beneath her uniform. She'd been so angry she hadn't even checked. The collar of the camisole barely covered the tattoo on her sternum. She clamped her hands together against the chill. "Then what were you doing naked in my bed?" she shrilled.

"Keeping you from dying from hypothermia, you stupid girl. You were so cold you blacked out. The only way to save you was skin-on-skin contact."

"Then why did you leave this on me?" She plucked at her hem. Triumph swelled her shoulders at finding a hole in his story.

"I was *trying* to preserve your modesty. Would you've preferred me to strip you utterly naked?" His seal-brown eyes narrowed. "Because I could do that. You'd just have to ask me nicely."

Amelia retreated a few steps. When he didn't come any closer, she lifted her chin. "In your dreams. And what are you looking at?"

Hiro gave her a wolfish smile. "It's wet out here, and your clothes are hardly better than gauze. What do you *think* I'm looking at?"

Horrified, Amelia clamped her arms over her chest. "You're a *beast*, Hiro Ishida."

She rushed back inside the cave, smacking the dripping tendrils out of her way. She tugged her cloak around her, shuddering at its damp cling. "Isen!" She would throttle him awake if she had to. "Why didn't you—"

The blind priest rested on his side, a gag in his mouth and his hands tied to his ankles behind his back.

"*Isen.*"

Amelia tugged the gag loose, but her numb fingers fumbled at the knots at his wrists.

"Let me," Kale offered. He untied the ropes with swift, precise movements.

"I slept well, considering." Isen smacked his lips. "Though my throat's rather dry. And Kale, I thought a smart boy like you would've *immediately* seen how wrong it was for you to tie me up."

The boy mumbled an apology.

"Hiro's word is not *law*, you know. Use your head—"

"*Enough.*" The menace in Hiro's voice filled the small cave. "Kale was acting on my orders. If he hadn't, you would've intervened."

"I would've protected her—"

"And she would've died. You're welcome, all of you. Now leave the boy alone."

"That's not much in the way of an apology," Isen snorted.

"It wasn't meant to be. I won't apologize for doing what had to be done, and that includes your bruised jaw, priest."

"He *struck* you?" Amelia cradled Isen's chin in her hands, probing for injury.

Flushing, he slid his long-fingered hands against hers and gently removed them from his face. "Thank you, sweet girl, but it's rather tender. I'll just be a little less handsome for a while." The priest tried to smile but gave up, wincing.

Amelia whipped around. "You *beast*—"

Hiro had her by the throat in a heartbeat. "Call me that again, and I will reconsider saving your life in the future."

The silver fire surged to her fingertips. She clenched her hands into fists, smothering it, and forced herself to relax. The fire diminished to a growling flame, pacing, circling, like a caged hound unable to protect its master. "Y-you vowed you would get me safely to Lhasa."

He released her with a sneer. "I made no such oath. I swore I would get you there. I did not say in what condition you would arrive."

Amelia scrambled away from him. She wormed into the warmth of her bedroll, drawing the edge up to her throat is if it would protect her.

Isen felt his way near her and sat very close. His hand curled tentatively around her knee. "He didn't touch, or do—"

"No, Isen. I'm still... I'm fine. Really."

"Good. Otherwise I'll kill him."

She gave a nervous chuckle. "You're a priest. Violence is not your way."

"It was, a long time ago." His hand tightened on her knee.

"Catch up on your sleep," Hiro said loudly. "We're not going anywhere until this fog lets up."

Sleep did not come. The fog dissipated when the rain started up again. Amelia huddled under the bedroll, waiting impatiently for her uniform to dry.

She read the tales of Yueyeux from the Bethany Journals, the general with the moon-pale eyes who'd presented Bethany with a lily, listened to Isen tell his stories – Kale particularly liked the one about the kraken guarding the lost amulet – and tried her best to ignore the rasping coming from the other side of the cave. The sound paused periodically so he could hack another wad of spit onto the whetstone. Amelia bit back a surge of bile.

Hiro had all of his weapons spread out on his greatcoat: the Damascus steel greatsword, the curved dagger, two blades he kept hidden in his sleeves, a dirk he secreted in his boot, a small knife in a black lacquered sheath. The man even had a hatchet.

He was wiping the filings off the knife when Old Imperial characters glinted on the steel.

Amelia leaned forward. "I've never seen that knife before. What's that writing on it?"

Hiro slid the knife into its lacquered sheath without so much as a look in her direction. He plucked a black arrow from his quiver and slid it down the whetstone. He'd sharpened two of them before Amelia leaned back with an irritated huff.

Rasp-rasp-hack-spit, rasp-rasp-hack-spit.

She clamped her hands over her ears and burrowed beneath the covers. She must've dozed off, for she awoke when something rooted around by her feet. Peering over the edge of her bedroll, she saw Hiro jerking. He was asleep, spasming, caught in one of his nightmares. Kale was dug into the prince's side like a tick, mouth open and drooling, until a violent lurch jolted him upright.

The boy pressed his small hand against his master's forehead. He stroked Hiro's hair like he would a frightened dog, crooning softly. She'd seen the boy minister to the prince before several times. Just a few caresses and the spasms abated, but this time his thrashing only grew more impatient, more frantic.

Amelia crawled over to them.

"This usually works." Kale's fingers trembled. "He won't wake, either. When he gets this bad I usually play a song on my guqin, but Hiro said it was too much weight to bring." The boy choked on a sob.

"My... father used to sing to me." Amelia shifted the prince's head onto her lap and combed her fingers through his hair. Without meaning to, she wove a thread of silver fire into her voice.

> *Sleep softly now, the night's at peace*
> *The wolf has fled, let crying cease*
> *Above the hearth, my sword is hung*
> *Never to slash, its battle won*
> *Sleep softly now, the stars watch on*
> *I'll love you, dear, 'til there are none*

The prince sighed, a great exhale, head lolling to one side. His body was limp, surrendered to a deep and dreamless sleep.

Wide-eyed, Kale peered over him. The boy pressed a finger into the prince's cheek, testing the depth of his slumber.

Amelia swatted his hand away.

She traced the silver cuff on his ear. "I thought Academy graduates wore copper. How did he get this?"

"Battle."

"Is that what he dreams about?"

"That, and witchfire."

"Witchfire?" She'd never heard the term before.

"A conjurer burned his hand. Destroyed whole villages Hiro'd been tasked to protect. He hates sorcery."

An icy touch trailed down her spine. "Is that why he reacted that way, back in Vienna?"

Kale nodded. "He'll kill a sorcerer on sight. No questions. And the marked. But I don't mind those."

"Kale," she said sharply, "*'thou shalt not murder.'*"

"Oh, it's not murder."

"Then what is it?"

"Retribution."

Amelia blinked. He'd said it so matter-of-factly. Oblivious to her alarm, the boy smothered a lion-sized yawn behind both hands.

"Help me with him?" she asked. "His head weighs a ton."

"Everything about him weighs a ton."

They propped Hiro's head on the saddle bags, and Amelia returned to her bed. She wiggled, searching for a more comfortable position on the uneven floor. She knew where one was – the very same she had woken up to that morning – and flushed at the thought.

A foot rammed her in the leg.

"Quit moving around," Hiro barked. "You'll wake everybody up."

Amelia threw back her bedroll with a glare.

Kale shook his head. His hazel eyes pleaded with her

With a huff, she gave one final wiggle and settled down. A rock dug into her side, but it hurt less than being kicked by an insufferable prince.

Minutes – hours – later, she was kicked again.

It was lighter this time, more like a nudge, but she was groggy with sleep and irritable.

She threw back her bedroll a second time. *"What?"*

Hiro's gaze was riveted on something outside.

Slowly, he drew his dagger.

CHAPTER 29

THE RASP OF THE BLADE CLEARING ITS SHEATH WOKE THE BOY.

Hiro lifted his arm; Kale slunk away, gave him room to move.

Hiro rolled into a crouch, parted the tendrils with his dagger and peered through the gap. Then he darted out of the cave.

When he returned a few minutes later, blood dripped down his left hand. "Time to go."

Kale grabbed their gear, shot past him outside.

"What happened?" the Sanu demanded. "Whose *blood* is that?"

"What's going on?" Isen yawned, groped for his broken staff.

"Let's move, priest. You too, Sanu." He stuffed the rest of her things into her pack, tugged her bedroll out from under her.

"Hiro, what the – hands!"

Taking her by the elbow, he hustled her out of the cave. The Sanu looked wildly about, spied a wide swath of flattened grass stained red. The trail disappeared under a nearby bush, where two pairs of boots peeked out.

Sputtering, she tried to turn around. He propelled her forward.

"Hiro, who—"

"Horse thieves." He glanced over his shoulder. "Isen, hurry *up*."

"But—"

"Up you get." Hiro tossed her into the saddle.

"It is *forbidden* to touch a Sanu—"

"Even after all that cuddling we just did?"

Gasps. A face gone purple with rage.

"We've got no time for your dawdling." He threw her pack and bedroll up after her.

She yanked the bedroll out of her face. "It's called the Dance of the Morning, and it's *not* dawdling."

"Uh-huh." He stuffed her foot into a stirrup.

"I don't interfere with your morning training sessions!"

"No, you do not," he agreed. "*Isen.* Come *on.* There could be more—"

"The sword is not always the answer," the Sanu pressed. "You could've just run them off. Honestly, one look at you and any attempt would've been snuffed out."

"What's *that* supposed to mean?"

"Only that you look like a man who knows how to use that greatsword you carry," she said hastily. "And what example are you setting for the boy? First you tell him to hog-tie Isen, and then it's pay no nevermind to the bodies you've stashed in the woods? Honestly, Hiro, did you have to kill them?"

"But—" Kale began.

"They were trying to steal my horse!" Hiro said. "Did you think I was going to sit down with them over a cup of tea and discuss their reasons why?"

"What if they were just desperate? A little charity could've alleviated the whole thing."

"So I pay them *not* to steal my horse? How does that make any sense?"

"'*One moment can change a day, one day can change a life, and one life can change the world.*'"

"You're assuming because you saw a little blood that I killed them. You might not know this, Sanu, but a man tends to resist when you're trying to knock him out. They're both fine. *Isen*, get out here."

"Then why hide the bodies?"

Hiro gestured to the boy. "Kale? Care to explain?"

"Hiding the bodies prevents your enemy from knowing your position. It'll also slow down any pursuit." The reply was quick, brief, military-efficient.

"Very good, Kale."

The boy beamed.

"Tell me again, Sanu, what kind of example I'm setting for him?"

"And," the boy added, "Hiro hid the bodies to keep the animals away until they woke up."

"O-oh." Her cheeks reddened like twin cherries.

"'Judge not lest ye be judged,' eh, Sanu?"

"That's enough, Hiro," Isen said, emerging from the cave.

"Did you get enough beauty sleep, priest? When I tell you to get out here, you'd better—"

"Did anyone bother to ask themselves *why* a couple of horse thieves – in the middle of the woods, mind you – decided to try to steal a trained warhorse?" The priest flapped the leaf litter from his robes. He remained at the cave's entrance, hefted his broken staff into both hands. His head cocked to the side in that birdlike way, listening. "Maybe they were trying to get away from something."

Hiro glanced around, saw nothing. "Okay, I'll bite. There might be the occasional wolf around here, even the rarer laumė, but nothing that would provoke two strangers to try to steal a horse. Except common greed. Now—"

"What about *that?*" The priest pointed with his staff.

The mare reared with a strangled whinny, dumped the priestess onto the ground.

The Sanu scrambled away from the flailing hooves, froze like a rabbit in the middle of the road.

A nightmarish hellbeast stood on the rise of the hill, chest taut. Its edges rippled like smoke or shadow, hazy and undefined. Great snorts of sulfuric fumes blasted the ground. Its claws pierced the road, sank in deep. A ruined nose snuffled the sky; an eyeless face locked onto them. Its lips peeled back with a triumphant squeal.

"It found me," the Sanu whispered.

⚜

THE SANU WHEEZED as she hit the ground. The hellbeast flashed, lifted a paw to strike her again.

Hiro rammed into its shoulder, knocked it into a heap of sprawling limbs. The hellbeast righted itself with a roar. From the side, a rock whizzed into its face. Followed by another. And another. Kale and Isen snatched up loose gravel from the road, pelted it mercilessly. The hellbeast shook it off, snarled with annoyance. Hiro cleared his greatsword of its sheath just as a stone zinged its ruined nose.

The hellbeast reared back with a scream. It flashed right in front of them, slashed with its claws. Isen yanked Kale out of way. They fell backward into the brush and tumbled down the slope. Shored up against a fallen log, Isen clutched his head as Kale struggled to his feet. The hellbeast gave a laughing hiss, choked off when Hiro rammed it again.

Off-balance, it couldn't defend itself from the downward slice of the greatsword. The blade bit into its back, cleaved just behind the shoulder. Black ichor, thick and oily, sizzled as it dripped onto the road.

The hellbeast screeched, flashed away.

It reappeared right in front of the priestess. Hiro ran for her, greatsword slicing the air with every stride. The Sanu sidled away, but the hellbeast pinned her to the ground with a massive paw. It snuffled at her hand, then her chest, snorted in frustration. The Sanu was paralyzed, eyes white with fear. She didn't move, didn't struggle. The hellbeast crushed her into the ground and she did nothing. It was fixated on her, oblivious to everything else.

Hiro punched its ruined snout. As it flung its head back with a screech, he lunged. Plunged his greatsword into the hellbeast's exposed neck. The blade sank deep into its gullet, squelching to a stop at its ribcage. Its spasming lungs threatened to suck the hilt from his grasp, swallow his greatsword whole. Hiro braced a hand on the hellbeast's slack jaw and yanked his sword free with a twist of his shoulders.

The Sanu scrambled out from under the corpse before the ichor could burn her.

Hiro grabbed her elbow, hauled her to her feet. "You stupid girl," he said, giving her a shake. He passed a hand over her hair, lifted her chin and checked for cuts. "Why didn't you get out of the way? Why didn't you move, or fight, or—"

He stopped when he realized she was panting. The short, fast gasps of a vole pinned beneath a fox's paw. Sweat glistened on her cold hands. She shook violently, the sky blue of her eyes a pale imitation of its ocean depths.

"Gods above, you're in shock." He shucked his greatcoat, swirled it around her shoulders. It swallowed her in shadow. "Stay here."

She nodded numbly.

Hiro trotted to the side of the road where it sloped down into a small glade. "Kale? Isen?"

"Coming," the priest answered with a groan.

Kale appeared first, a forest sprite with twigs poking out from his auburn mane, mud and leaves plastered to his face and clothes. Both hands were clamped onto a branch as he hauled Isen up behind him. The priest held the other end, using a free hand to grasp at brush and roots.

Hiro leaned forward, dragged him onto the road by his sodden robes.

"Well, I got a new staff," the priest said. "Amelia? *Amelia?*"

"I'm h-here." The priestess only trembled now, eyes half-lidded, arms hugged around herself.

"Is it... dead?" Kale asked.

Hiro nodded. The hellbeast was already decomposing into tar, bubbling and hissing.

"I didn't know Damascus steel could do that." The priest ran his fingers down the blade. "You can just barely feel the ridges of different steel—" He stopped, encountering demon ichor, and hastily wiped his hand on the wet leaves.

"It's not Damascus steel. It was forged in dragon's breath, after the Great Cataclysm." Hiro knelt, cleaned his greatsword off in a puddle. The ichor shimmered like crushed crystal in the rainwater. When he was done, he kept the naked sword in his fist and turned to the priestess. "'It found me?' Care to explain?"

The Sanu froze, eyes darting everywhere. "I... I told you there were things out there—"

"Not even the Militum Dei could've protected you from *that*," Hiro shouted. "Whatever that thing—"

"It's a demon."

"A demon? A *demon*? That's the thing that almost killed me. It's been after you this *entire* time?"

"Please." She'd started to cry. Her arms tightened around herself, the only things keeping her from shaking apart. "Please, I am the last."

"What?"

"It killed my sisters. *All* of them." Her voice broke with misery. Sorrow. "You don't understand—"

"You're talking about the apocalypse."

Her weeping paused, replaced by surprise.

"You think I'm an ignorant grunt who doesn't understand religion." Hiro wiped a hand over his face. "So you're the last Sanu. You're the only one standing in the way of the End Times."

She nodded once.

"Gods above." He turned away with a snort, sheathed his greatsword. He collected his mare, paused to press his forehead into her thick shoulder. He'd been an idiot to swear himself to her. He should've just ridden away, let honor be damned.

The priest seized his arm. "Hiro, you must—"

"I *must* do nothing," he snarled, shaking him off. He eyed the Sanu. After a long sigh, he extended his hand. "Except keep my vow. I'll get you to Lhasa, just as before."

"Thank you." She took his hand, let him help her into the saddle.

"But no more delays, Sanu, I mean it. Not with those *things* running around."

"I'm so glad you believe me."

144

"I *understand*, Sanu. There's a difference." Hiro shoved her pack and bedroll into her hands. "Don't think for a minute you'll get special treatment."

"From you?" She gave him a watery smile, returned his greatcoat. "I wouldn't dream of it."

CHAPTER 30

Hiro dreamt of fire and blood.

It wasn't the first time.

The Sanu was there. She danced beneath a full moon, each movement serene, ethereal in its beauty. Beckoning.

Fire ignited from his step, encircled the priestess with flames that reached the clouds.

Boom. Boom. Boom-boom-boom.

The bodies of the slain rose up between them. He cut them all down again, even the children, over and over with hands that no longer obeyed him. The priestess screamed in horror – of the flames, the death, *him* – until the moon descended and swallowed her away from the madness.

He groped after her, found nothing but smoke.

Hiro pushed the panic aside, opened his eyes. Camp sounds: a spoon scraping against the pot as it stirred porridge, the stamp of his mare shifting in her sleep, bare feet whispering in the grass. The Sanu was dancing to welcome the dawn. Alive.

Groaning, he let the adrenaline drain from his body.

A mane of auburn hair and a worried face popped into his field of vision. "Sir?"

"Hn." He ruffled the boy's hair.

"Late start to the morning?" Isen said, stirring the porridge. "You and Kale are usually beating on each other by now."

Hiro grunted, wiped the dregs of sleep from his eyes.

"What's it today? Knives? Bare knuckles? Harsh language?"

"Why are you always so chatty in the morning, priest?"

"It's better than grunting like a rooting pig. You should try expressing yourself in words."

"Uh-huh. Maybe if you talked less you wouldn't burn breakfast as much."

"I don't see *you* doing any of the cooking."

"How would you?"

The priest dropped the spoon, launched to his feet.

The Sanu stepped between them, stayed Isen with a hand to his chest.

"I'd appreciate if you'd wait until this afternoon to start antagonizing each other. It's been weeks; *stop* baiting each other." She pushed between them, gave the pot a stir. "And breakfast's burned."

"It *is*?" the boy cried.

Isen snarled, retreated to salvage the porridge.

With a shout, Kale barreled into Hiro.

He stumbled back a few steps, heaved the boy aside. "Kale, what are you—"

"Isen was making my *favorite*."

"Sounds like bare knuckles to me," the priest said.

The boy lashed a series of punches, so quick they stung like bees. This wasn't the tae-do taught at the Academy. Hiro barely got his feet rooted before Kale struck again. A kick buckled his knee, but Hiro caught Kale's ankle, punched his chest. The strike was open-palmed, but the boy went down hard.

"Kale?" Hiro said.

The boy sprang from the dirt, howling. His attack was too fast to see, a thunderstorm of lightning strikes.

"Almonds, cinnamon"—Kale sliced his leg, caught Hiro's feet. He crashed onto his back, the boy on top of him and smothering his windpipe with a knee— "and the last of the chocolate!"

The boy punched. The fist stopped, hovered above Hiro's eye. When he blinked, his eyelashes grazed the boy's knuckles. With deliberate slowness, the boy opened his fist and gave Hiro's cheek a smart little pat. Kale flashed a grin, jumped off before Hiro could throttle him.

"What was *that?*"

"Isen taught me notué while you slept this morning. For a priest from Bastogne, he's pretty bad at it."

"*Hey*," Isen said.

"You learned notué in an *hour?*" the Sanu exclaimed. "It takes years—"

The boy beamed. "I've always been a quick study."

"So what's it like being beaten into the dirt by a little boy?" Isen spooned out the rescued porridge. He gave the first bowl to Kale. With a gleeful whoop, the boy retreated to a log to devour his breakfast.

Hiro growled something inaudible.

Isen ladled out another bowl for the Sanu and the last for himself. "Well, Hiro, I'd offer you some breakfast but it *sounds* like you're choking on your pride."

The boy and the priest laughed; the Sanu offered her half-eaten porridge with a sympathetic smile.

Clenching his jaw, Hiro shoved his way past them. "We leave in five minutes," he barked.

HIRO GLANCED INTO THE SKY.

Three crow-like birds lazily soared on an updraft. They were dark blots against a vast blue expanse, circling. Occasionally he heard them caw to each other, a small sound to alert the others of its location.

Like scouts.

It'd been weeks since they'd left Vienna. They stayed off the main roads, traveling east to the Council Seat in Bucharest. No other travelers, no pursuit. Yet still he felt like they were being watched.

Hiro glared at them, squinted to make out any details. Nothing.

Swiftly, he unshouldered his bow and nocked an arrow, aimed it at the sky. The birds squawked and scattered, rejoined in a flutter of feathers when he didn't fire.

"Something the matter, O Brooding Leader?" the priest laughed.

Sorcery.

Hiro returned the black arrow to its quiver, kept his stride confident. Carefree. *They* were watching.

Kale's eyes narrowed. "What is it?"

"We need to hurry," he said. "It's taking too long by foot."

"In case you haven't noticed, there isn't a lot of civilization around." The priest's voice was sullen. "*You* keep us off the main roads."

The Sanu, who'd been ahead of them for once, paused at the crest of a small hill. She turned back, swept the caramel hair out of her face. The puckish wind plucked a few strands free, swirled them like ribbons of honey. They whispered against his face when he joined her, tickling. Teasing. She pointed past the vineyard sprawling across the low valley to the pier jutting out into the river.

"I have an idea."

CHAPTER 31

HIRO ADJUSTED HIS GRIP ON THE MARE'S BRIDLE. HE SPOKE SOFTLY, murmuring nonsense, until she calmed. She'd never been on a boat before, didn't like how the ground shifted under her hooves. They'd made a makeshift stall for her in the deckhouse; no one wanted a frightened warhorse thundering along the deck.

He found Isen where he'd left him, clinging to the side and vomiting. There was nothing in his stomach now, just bile. The nearest Atlantican offered him some rum; the priest guzzled like a man dying of thirst. Anything to dull the nausea.

Atlanticans.

The ship was full of them, swarthy with blue or green eyes, hair cropped short or braided in canerows. He'd been hesitant at first, but when the priestess had approached them in their native tongue, they'd leapt at the chance to help the Argenti. At no charge.

But it'd cost the rest of them a doros apiece. Despite being laden with wine barrels, the ship slipped over the water. Left their crow-like spies behind.

The Sanu and Kale stood at the bow, laughing with the captain. Thick braid of black hair, wiry, a golden ring pierced through one nostril. Mercedes Medianu ran her ship with the efficiency of an

Academy graduate. The *Espada* sliced through the Danube, carried them and its cargo – wine, weaponry, and a very special present for her cousin – toward the Great Black Sea.

Hiro cleared his throat.

The Sanu shrieked, grabbed the railing for support.

He rolled his eyes. "Should I wear a bell?"

"That'd be immensely helpful, thank you."

The captain chuckled. She held a young cat in her hands, rubbed its scruff between thumb and forefinger. The Atlanticans always had cats on their boats.

Calm again, the priestess turned back to the water, lifting her chin to the breeze. The tension melted from her shoulders. Until the captain murmured something in her ear.

The Sanu's cheeks ignited with embarrassment. He flicked his gaze to Mercedes. White teeth dragged against a plump lower lip, eyes crawled along the breadth of his shoulders. Her eyebrow cocked in invitation. She asked the Sanu her question again.

"Sanu. What?" Hiro said.

She coughed, spoke in a rush. "Captain Medianu would like to know if you'd like to join her in her cabin later."

Kale wrinkled his forehead. "I thought she said she wanted to see Hiro nak—"

The priestess clamped a hand over the boy's mouth.

"Hn. How... brazen. Perhaps another time."

The priestess relayed his words; the captain smiled broadly. She rattled off something fast, poured the orange cat into Kale's arms and sauntered away with another appreciative look.

"She says it will be many days before we reach Bucharest," the priestess said. "Many opportunities for..."

"Wrestling," Kale finished. "I don't get it."

"Maybe when you're older." Hiro ruffled the boy's hair. "Who knew I'd live to see the day when a Sanu became a procuress?"

The priestess gasped. Hiro laughed. He caught the gunwale when the ship pitched through some choppy waves, shot a hand out to steady Kale. The Sanu merely shifted her weight.

They'd only been on the water for a day, but the Sanu seemed to have come alive. A smile was never far from her face, her skin glowed, her ocean-blue eyes were brighter than twin sapphires.

"You seem remarkably at home on the water," he said.

"A trait I picked up from my... father."

Hiro lifted an eyebrow.

"The Atlantican who found me." Her attention was on the dark water cleaving beneath the prow. "He took me out of the surf and gave me a home... for a little while, anyway."

Kale slipped his hand into hers. She never chastised him.

"So you're an orphan, like me?"

Hiro caught the railing for support. The chop was far behind them, the water smooth and steady.

The Sanu swept the boy's wind-tousled mane out of his eyes. "We're hardly orphans, Kale. We've got Hiro and Isen. And the horse."

His heart started to beat again.

"And Arancio." The boy cuddled the young cat close to his face.

"Arancio?" Hiro scowled. "What have I told you before? *No pets.*"

"But the others were picking on him. And Mercedes said—"

"No pets. *Leave* it." Hiro plucked the cat from the boy's arms, set it down hard on the deck. He nudged it on its way with his boot. "*Shoo.*"

The beast fluffed its fur with a little hiss and entwined itself in Kale's legs.

"I was little once, and you didn't abandon me."

It felt like Hiro had been knifed through the heart.

No, he'd been hoeing weeds in the garden patch when he'd pulled the half-drowned boy out of the river. Adopted him, fed and clothed him. Protected him. Thrashed Luca Favino and his friends for taking a swing at the boy for defending a three-legged puppy they'd been tormenting. After the hearing, Hiro'd been put on his knees and beaten for disorderly conduct.

He stuck the crook of his finger under the boy's chin, forced him to look up. "To rescue a life is to take responsibility of it. That responsibility cannot be discarded simply because it becomes wearisome or too demanding or time-consuming. It is a promise that once given cannot be revoked. Do you understand me?"

"Yes, sir."

Hiro paused, searched the boy's face. He let go of his chin. "That cat has a job to do on this boat. We can't take it with us. But until we reach Bucharest, consider it yours. You will feed it, you will care for it, you will pick off every flea. Is that clear?"

Kale hugged him hard around the middle. He snatched the cat off the deck and slung it over his shoulder. Its purr was loud enough to drown out the water slapping against the hull.

"Now go check on the horse."

"Yes, sir." The boy snuggled the cat as he walked away. "You can be Beleza's new friend. She doesn't like sailing."

"And when you're done, see that one-eyed swordmaster. You need a blade, Kale." Hiro turned back to the Sanu, drummed his fingers against the railing. "Beleza?"

"It's what he named your mare. It means 'beauty' in Atlantican."

"You taught him Atlantican?"

It was a dead tongue, a bastardization of the ancient Romance languages. When the Great Cataclysm destroyed most of the Atlantic coast, its wayward people had blended together on the remaining isles. Atlanticans. Sea gypsies. Their language was hardly ever heard on the mainland, except in pockets near Roma and the Academy.

"I don't know how. He just... picked it up." She shook her head. "That boy is remarkable."

She didn't know the half of it. But he was a gift that needed to be protected, even from her.

"Thank you... for what you said about Kale not being an orphan."

"Of course. We're all in this toge—"

"But let me be clear about something." His eyes were chips of flint. "We are not some happy family. I have a debt to repay you, nothing more. When I get you and Isen to Lhasa, we're done."

The Sanu blinked, mouth agape. "Hiro, I—"

"And don't convince the boy otherwise, understand? I don't – I mean *he* – doesn't have time for it."

"You can't deny that we've all become at least *friendly* over the last few weeks. Is that so terrible? Why do you insist on being so detached?"

"Why are you so desperate for connection?"

The Sanu's face grew stormy, eyes snapping with silver lightning. "That's just what you do, isn't it? You push people away. I think that this"—she gestured to all of him—"is just a façade. That contempt you always wear? A smokescreen. You're *afraid*."

"Me, afraid?" he laughed bitterly. "Of what?"

"Having to rely on anyone other than yourself. Of letting your guard down just *once*."

He shoved a finger in her face. "Dependence is for the weak. Let me quote some scripture so you'll understand: '*You only lose what you cling to.*'"

She swatted his hand aside. "'*To live a life without love is no life at all.*'"

"That's your solution to everything, isn't it, Sanu?" He threw his hands into the air. "Love for everyone."

"It's what saved you from dying in a ditch."

He clenched his jaw, upper lip curled into a snarl.

"This might be difficult to hear, Hiro."

"What could it *possibly* be now?"

She leaned forward, had to go on tiptoe to get close to his ear. Her whisper teased his hair, rippled a shiver down to his toes. "You are loved."

Hiro ripped away from her. "Don't. *Don't.*"

He pushed away from the gunwale. Fled.

CHAPTER 32

"Stay close."

Captain Medianu had docked at the quayside in the middle of the night, when the customs agents were more likely to keep their mouths shut. Bucharest's streets were deserted except for the night market. Stalls by the riverside sported great tubs of ice packed with fish and oysters. Farther in were dozens of stalls cooking their own version of the regional favorite: sarmale. Cabbage rolls.

The crowd pressed and tightened around them. The traffic shifted so much like a school of fish that it was easy to get sucked away in an unseen current and lost from sight. The noise was typical of vendors hawking their goods, but there was a strain to their voices. A fear of being too brash, too noticeable. Suspicious glances were as common as the pigeons scurrying about.

Afraid of being jostled away, Amelia snagged the back of Hiro's shirt.

He glanced behind with a raised eyebrow before taking her hand and pulling her along. The leather of his gloves pinched her skin, but she didn't let go. Isen rode with Kale astride the warhorse, the boy keeping a lookout from his elevated perch.

At the city gate, it only took the flash of a jade identification card for the guards to wave them through. A contingent of the city watch was all too eager to escort a Jianshu prince and his entourage to the Council Lodge.

The Lodge was nestled in the affluent part of the city, a tall establishment of gleaming wood and myriad windows that towered above the neighboring buildings. A wrought iron gate encircled the Lodge and its gardens, the golden tips both beautiful and deadly. Guards in black-and-violet livery patrolled the fence with large black dogs straining against their leashes. The ones at the gate raised a cacophony of slavering snarls. Kale quieted them with a word.

Another brief inspection of the identification card opened the Lodge gates. A soft trumpet blast announced their arrival; moments later the double doors were wrenched open by none other than the steward himself. His hair was disheveled, his eyes bloodshot from being asleep just five minutes ago. Doubled over with his panting, the golden chain of his office almost dangled to his knees.

Hiro cleared his throat.

The steward raked his hands through his brown hair, bowed, and gestured them into the foyer. A crystal chandelier larger than a lady's ball gown floated above their heads, sparkling with electric light. It scattered bits of rainbow across the marble floor. The vast expanse of gray-veined stone was broken up by the Council crest: a shield of the five provincial sigils linked in an unbreakable circle.

The steward introduced himself as Domo István and led them up the sweeping staircase. Glass lamps festooned the walls, the shades blown to resemble unfurling tulips with crenulated tips. Amelia kept her hands to herself this time.

"... suite already prepared, Prince Ishida," the steward was saying. "One for you and your courtesan, and another for the rest—"

Amelia gasped. She knew her uniform was hidden by the cloak, but—

"*Courtesan?*" Hiro exploded. "Do I look like some depraved Siber prince to you? I am this woman's *escort*. Imagine her status now, to command the services of an Ishida prince."

The steward bowed hastily. "My sincerest apologies, my lady. I

meant no disrespect. I'll have another suite prepared. Sonja!" He practically screamed the woman's name.

A tall woman with white hair cut even with her jaw hurried down
the hall. She wore a uniform of black satin with a purple shield
embroidered over her heart. Matching purple slippers covering her
feet whispered against the carpet.

"Take my lady to the Tulip Suite." He turned to the prince. "It is
our *finest* available—"

"I want a guard at her door."

"Our best *fema* quad will be assigned in the morn—"

Hiro glared.

"—right away. Of course. Sonja, when you get my lady settled,
reassign Kala's quad."

"But they're in the middle—"

"*Immediately*," Domo István shrilled. He forced a smile and
smoothed back his hair. "Immediately, Sonja."

"Is that entirely necessary?" Amelia asked. "I mean, so long as I
have my own room, there's no reason for us to be separated."

"It's Council regulations. Unmarried women stay in their own
wing. The *fema* will look after you when I can't." Hiro started to put a
hand on her shoulder, but caught himself halfway. It fell back to his
side. "You'll be fine. We'll meet up after we've had some rest."

They stopped at a Y-intersection where an arched window rose
from floor to ceiling. The morning was already in the east, the sky a
dove gray with clouds streaked pink and lilac. The dark shapes of
birds flitted about, and one crow-like bird came to perch on the
branch nearest the window. It was close enough to see the white
feathers around its beak, the red cabochon eyes. A rook.

Amelia squinted, trying to remember why it looked so familiar—

"This way, my lady," Sonja interrupted. "You'll have plenty of time
to see the gardens when your *fema* arrive."

She took her eyes off the rook to notice the gardens for the first
time. Beautiful. Following Sonja down the hallway, she glanced over
her shoulder at the window. The bird was gone.

CHAPTER 33

Unable to sleep, Amelia wore the carpet bare as she paced in the lavish Tulip Suite. Her room in the Green Pearl – in an ancient Baroque palace – seemed dull compared to this extravagance. Twin settees boasted cushions fat as storm clouds; the carpet was so thick it swallowed her toes; the four-poster bed was so massive it required three steps of polished mahogany to mount it. A closet nearly as large at the suite itself boasted hundreds of spare outfits, shoes, even jewelry from the daintiest silver anklet to a gold torque studded with white pearls the size of tulip bulbs.

She jumped at the soft knock on her door. Outside in the hallway was Isen. Amelia grabbed his arm and hustled him down the corridor.

"Amelia, what's going on? Why did you ask for me? And why does it feel like we're going down the stairs?"

"Because we are. We're getting out of here."

"We are?"

"Just for a few hours. Now hurry, before the *fema* arrive."

"But Hiro told us to stay put."

"Do you always do as you're told? I'm not going to stay locked in my room like some prisoner. I need to *breathe*, Isen. I've already arranged a carriage for us. Are you with me or not?"

They stopped in front of the doors, freedom just a few feet beyond.

"This is a terrible idea. Hiro'll be furious. Let's go."

"Where to, my lady?" the driver asked. "There are the fighting pits, the gambling courts, the Rue d'Huit Tasses for all your drinking needs…"

She winced. "Perhaps something a little more refined?"

"There's the city park, and well, I'm not sure it's more *refined*, but there's always the Temple of the Lady or the Doll—"

"Where do we get breakfast?" Isen clutched his rumbling stomach.

"The park has some of the best street vendors."

"Park and breakfast first, Temple second." Amelia clutched the leather seat as the carriage lurched forward. "I'll feel better with a full stomach before we have to send those cranes."

ENDLESS GREENERY and old trees stretched on in either direction. Their carriage rolled to a stop on a boulevard of flowering pear trees. Delicate white petals, teased loose by the morning breeze, fluttered like snowflakes. Peeking above the tree line was a dome of pink marble crowned with an unfurling gold tulip.

"Florin, what's that dome over there?" Amelia asked the driver.

"That's the Jardin Seat, my lady. The palace is truly something. I'm sure you'd enjoy it."

"Is Lady Cosette in residence?"

"She normally is, but she keeps rather busy," the driver replied quickly. "She has, uh, so many responsibilities that it's almost impossible to see her without an appointment."

"Best leave her to it, then."

Amelia guided Isen onto the gravel path. Tulips were everywhere: purple, yellow, red-and-white striped, some pink and orange like the azaleas of Mount Taru. She balked as a pang of homesickness twisted in her gut.

We should've gone to the temple. I can't believe *I thought about my stomach first instead of sending a crane to the High Sister. And maybe someone there will know who this Elwynn is—*

"Amelia, sweet girl, you're squeezing my arm. If you're worried about Hiro—"

"No, no, it's not that."

"We can always go back."

"No. It's... nice."

"Amelia, you don't need to feel guilty about going for a walk in a park. We don't *need* Hiro's permission. And we could just leave, you know. We were getting along fine without them."

She shook her head. "He'd find us. You know he would. Besides, he'll get us to Lhasa and then he's gone. He's made that perfectly clear to me."

"I'm just worried about the meantime. Amelia, you are the *last*. Yueshu requires a pure vessel, both heart and body. You can't afford to get compromised, and Hiro is an irreverent *hundan*."

"Isen, language—"

"Well he *is*. You're just too polite to say it."

"He'd never do anything like that."

"No? He's already been naked with you."

Amelia gasped. *"Isen."*

"Through no fault of your own, of course! But what do we really know about him anyway? He's a banished prince. The Ishidas are a proud family. He must've done something terrible."

"I believe in second chances and so should you."

"I know, I know. Let's forget about him, okay? He's the whole reason we're playing hooky, anyway."

"Right." Amelia readjusted her hand and gave his arm a squeeze. "I could get used to a place like this."

"Especially one that smells like this. Are those donuts?"

Up ahead, a vendor was frying a batch of the irregularly shaped gogoși. Vanilla and orange and hot pastry perfumed the air.

Amelia swallowed against a suddenly moist throat. "We're getting some. Let's go."

The vendor was an older man with twinkling eyes and a bushy

mustache that curled up at its ends. His gnarled hands deftly scooped the donuts from the hot fat and smothered them in powdered sugar. As he offered them the paper sack, the twinkling vanished from his blue eyes.

"I don't hear the birds anymore," Isen said suddenly.

Amelia glanced over her shoulder.

A man leaned against a tree, examining the nails of one hand with feigned interest. The other shoved in his pocket was balled into a fist. A yellow shirt peeked out from his black jacket like a prisoner's face between cell bars. There was another man in the same uniform behind the vendor by the pond, supposedly watching the swans.

It was then she realized the park was empty. Its patrons were gone.

Amelia snatched the vendor's hand. "Who are they?"

"Canaris," the man hissed. He wrenched his hand free, and the sack of gogoși dropped onto the gravel. The vendor packed up his cart. "*Go.* I don't want any trouble."

She yanked Isen away, trying to keep her pace brisk but not rushed. Running would draw too much attention. "We're being followed. Come *on.*"

The silver fire paced restlessly, but it did not flare. She had too tight a hold on it, strangling it with her fear. Amelia gulped in a breath and hurried for where they'd left the carriage.

There were four of them now. They moved quickly, keeping pace with her. Amelia stepped off the path into the tulips, cutting across the gardens. Two followed while the others kept their distance, flanking. The one on their right snuck a hand into his jacket and withdrew a narrow cylinder.

The carriage was in sight now, and the two behind them were close enough she could hear them huffing to keep up.

She dug her fingers into Isen's arm. "*Run.*"

There was a startled shout from behind, then the pounding of feet on turf. The two that were flanking dropped all pretenses and sprinted. One scattered a pair of napping swans that angrily gave chase.

Pfft.

A wooden skewer with a tuft of feather zipped by her left ear.

"*Florin*," Amelia shouted above the honking. "Time to *go.*"

The carriage driver snapped the reins. Amelia released Isen's arm and threw open the door. Another skewer buried into the padded leather by her hand. The priest spun around, clobbering the closest one with his staff. She jumped into the moving carriage, spun, and yanked Isen in after her. She just managed to get the door shut and locked when the second canaris slapped his palm against it. There was a brief jiggling of the latch before the carriage pulled away.

Amelia peeked out the rear window; two were helping the one Isen had felled to his feet. The fourth caught her eye and raised a hand, saluting her with his blowgun. She sank low in her seat and smacked the side of the carriage.

"*Faster*, Florin."

AMELIA RACED down the deserted hallway and skidded to a halt a few doors away from her room.

Four women in red snapped to attention. Each was lean and well-muscled with a pair of stern eyes peering over the gauzy veil covering the lower half of her face. Long, thin rapiers dangled in silver scabbards at their hips.

Fema.

The brunette crossed her wiry arms over her chest with a disapproving scowl.

Amelia forced a nervous smile and gave them a little wave. "Um, hi. I'm Amelia. Thanks for coming?"

CHAPTER 34

HIRO POURED HIMSELF ANOTHER GLASS OF WINE, GLANCED OUT THE window. It was twilight, and the Sanu was late. He finished his glass, steeled himself to go search for her. She was always wandering off. Dancing. Meditating. No doubt Little Miss Sanctimonious had found some injustice that needed righting at the expense of their suppertime.

"Once, just *once*," he grumbled, "I wish she'd just—"

The double doors opened to the laughter of women. The *fema*, renowned for their stoicism and martial ferocity, were giggling like a pack of schoolgirls. The Sanu was in the middle of them, face flushed with mirth. Of course she'd make friends with them.

The *fema* sobered at the sight of him, bowed and closed the doors after her.

Hiro lurched to his feet.

The Sanu had abandoned her cloak and uniform for a long-sleeved dress of imperial jade green. It clung to her curves, flowed to her feet. She smelled of jasmine, delicate and faint. Her hair, dark with water, hung like a sheet of bronze to her thighs. Obscured the swell where her legs met her back—

Hiro hastily looked away, cleared his throat. "I thought you were trying to be inconspicuous."

"My uniform is still drying. *Oof.*"

Kale hugged her hard around the middle. "I'm so happy you're here. We can eat now!"

Isen tapped his way over to her, nudged Kale away. "Yes, and we don't have to listen to this little beast whine anymore. Shoo. Listen, I did a little digging into our *friends—*"

"How about we eat first and talk later?" Hiro snapped his fingers at the servers. "We've been kept waiting long enough, Sanu."

He tried to keep his eyes on his food, listened with only half an ear to the conversation – some nonsense about bath bubble sculptures – but they kept returning to the priestess. Imperial green was a Jianshu color, an *Ishida* color, and it looked stunning on her. It was... distracting.

"Do I have something in my teeth?" she whispered. Her spoon hovered above a quenelle of strawberry sorbet.

He blinked. Since when had they moved on to dessert? "No. Why?"

"You're staring at me."

He rolled his eyes with a snort. "I am not."

"Yes, you are."

"I am *not.*"

"Not what?" Isen wanted to know.

"Not interested in listening to your mindless chatter any longer." He pushed his uneaten sorbet aside. Kale eagerly plunged his spoon into the melting mound. "It's time we discussed business."

"Oh?"

"Primarily the acquisition of funds. We're low and won't make it to Jianshu without more than what we have."

"Don't Lodges also act as banks for Council Houses?"

Hiro's eyes narrowed. "*That* is a closely guarded fact. How did you know that?"

Isen shrugged.

"But doesn't that solve our problem?" the Sanu asked.

"It does not. That is my father's money, and I don't take charity."

"Then what do you propose?"

"You there"—Hiro hailed the nearest server—"tell me where to find the fighting pits."

"THIS IS NO PLACE FOR A SANU," Hiro growled. "It's not safe."

"This *city* isn't safe. And it's no place for a boy either, but I don't hear you telling Kale to stay behind," Amelia fired back. She bunched up her cloak and pulled herself into the carriage. "Or Isen, for that matter, and he's a *priest*."

"I'm only going because you're going," the priest said.

"You sure you don't want to stay?" Hiro pressed.

She crossed her arms over her chest and looked out the window. "Waiting on you now."

Kale giggled until Hiro thumped him in the leg. He called to the driver, and the carriage rumbled away.

"This is idiotic. You know that, right?" she snapped.

"Save your sermons, Sanu. You can't convince me otherwise."

"Until you enter that pit, that's *exactly* what I'll try to do."

Too soon the carriage stopped in a rough-looking part of the city, and the men got out. Before she could follow, Hiro blocked the door. He loomed over her, his seal brown eyes willing her to stay put. "Last chance."

"Will you move or must I shove my way out?"

He snorted but backed away. "As if you could."

"Amelia, sweet girl, you've got to be out of your mind," the priest hissed. "Get back in the carriage."

She ignored him and pressed through the crowd to catch up to Hiro. There was a crush of people eager to see two men pound each other into the sand. "Hiro, don't do this."

Deaf to her pleas, Hiro signed into the rosters under a pseudonym.

"Pit seven," the man said. "Three-to-one odds."

"No. I need a larger margin."

The man shrugged. "More risk."

"I'll take it."

"No you will *not*," Amelia declared, tugging on his arm. It was like trying to uproot a tree.

"Pit nine. Eight-to-one. Highest we got." He jerked his chin. "Over there. Fight's in three minutes."

"Place your bets here," someone called. "All pits, all bets! Coin only."

Hiro began shedding his gear as he pushed his way toward the pit. Kale trailed behind, collecting it all into the greatcoat.

The crowd smelled the oncoming challenge and began to cheer. People jostled into position, pressing toward the pit. The champion was already waiting for him, stripped to a leather codpiece and heavy, blade-studded cestus on each hand. He was taller than Hiro and heavier, his pale white skin and shock of yellow hair already speckled with the blood of his last opponent.

"Hiro, *please*," Amelia tried again. "Just take some money from the House accounts."

"That money belongs to my *father*." Hiro spat. "The same father that dismissed me from my House. I haven't depended on his *generosity* in decades. I won't start now."

He shrugged out of his gi jacket, and the crowd went wild. The torches bathed every swell of muscle with flickering yellow light. His scars rippled like stripes of molten brass as he moved.

Amelia looked away, a blush creeping up her neck.

The brute in the pit bellowed at the sight of him. This was going to be an actual contest, and he knew it. Already the masses were pushing her out of the way so they could see better. The stink of sweat and gore and urine was suffocating.

"*Ladies and gentlemen, welcome to the second match of the evening for Pit Nine.*"

Amelia elbowed her way to his side. Someone had tossed him a roll of leather and he was in the middle of wrapping his wrists.

"Give 'im a kiss for luck," someone shouted. "He'll need it!"

"Hiro, if anything should happen to you, where would that leave the rest of us? I – I mean *we* – depend on you—"

"And we *need* this."

"Please, let's just go. We'll get money another way. This city... it's not safe."

"There something you want to tell me?"

She chewed her lip as she groped for an answer. "Have you ever heard of the canaris?"

Hiro laughed. "They're a *myth*. A story told to frighten children." He waggled his fingers at her. "Don't step out of line, or the secret police will stun you with their blowguns and drag you off to the dungeons."

"Only the insane *dare challenge the champion of our deadliest pit!"*

"Fight already," someone else screamed.

"Hiro, you're not *listening—*"

Still chuckling, he stepped around her.

Then she did something she shouldn't have; she placed her hand on his cheek. His freshly shaved skin felt like velvet against her palm.

Hiro froze, eyes wide.

"Please. Don't go."

Isen shoved his way beside them. Empty, her hand fell back to her side. "Gods above, Hiro, listen to her," he implored. "You can get *killed* in there."

"Is he brave, or is he just stupid? Challenging our reigning champion today is Sjávar Ulfur!"

Hiro took a step away from her and rolled his shoulders. "I'll see you when it's done."

He dropped into the pit.

"If you don't bleed out first," Isen shouted.

The brute was already charging. Amelia craned over the edge as far as she dared and watched Hiro, weaponless, deflect the hulk of a man with a simultaneous strike to the leg and shoulder. The champion crashed onto his side, stunned for only a moment, then rolled onto his knees. Before he could launch forward, Hiro snatched his head between his two large hands. Blood sprayed across the sand at her feet as Hiro drove his knee into the man's nose. A feral gleam she'd never seen before shone in his seal-brown eyes.

"Why do I even bother?" she shouted at the air.

She smothered the tingling sensation in her fingertips, snatched Isen's arm, and waded out of the crowd. The people surged forward, eagerly taking their places and screaming encouragement at the two men beating each other senseless in the pit. "Stay with Kale."

The boy stood on the wooden stands, peering over the crowd's heads. He held his master's bundle under his arm with one hand and clenched the priest's hand with the other. "Wait, where you going?"

"To pray!"

"TAKE me to the Temple of the Lady," Amelia barked. She winced and unclenched her hands. "Please, Florin."

The driver glanced back at her. "You're sure? Maybe you'd prefer the Dollhouse? I'm sure there's a White Gent who'd—"

"I don't see how a Gent could help me. I'm sure, Florin. Now please, drive on."

"Yes, my lady."

By the time they reached the temple, Amelia was seething. It took all of her self-control to keep the silver fire contained. It strained to release like a hound after a hare.

"I'll wait for you here," Florin said.

Nodding curtly, she slammed the carriage door shut behind her. She marched up the temple stairs, bathed yellow in the light of a dozen fire bowls. The oil smelled sweet and floral, just like it was supposed to. At least *something* was right in this world. She passed under the colonnade and entered the sanctuary.

A whore greeted her.

"Welcome to the Temple of the Lady."

CHAPTER 35

AMELIA STAGGERED BACK A STEP. THE TEMPLE WAS OVERRUN WITH women dressed in yellow gauze that hid nothing and revealed everything. Prayer cushions were strewn in heaps upon the floor where clients reclined, their fingers tangled in the hair of the women buried between their legs.

Splashes of paint and strips of cloth adorned the statue of the Blessed Lady. Her cistern of blessed waters was defiled with wine, and one of her red-crowned cranes roasted on a nearby spit. The altar's white flame was gone, extinguished. Hundreds of candles flickered there instead.

There was music coming from somewhere, sinuous and subtle. And everywhere there were the sounds and smells and sights of primal ecstasy.

Amelia gaped at the orgy unfolding around her.

"We're delighted that you've come," the whore said, twirling a lock of her red hair. "We're all masters in the art of love here. What would you like?"

Amelia backhanded the whore to the ground. "What have you done?"

"W-what?" the whore asked, clutching her cheek.

"What have you done?"

She was attracting attention now. The people closest to her shrank away from the look on her face.

Amelia turned to the closest couple, snatched the whore by the hair, and yanked her off of the woman she was servicing. She threw her to the ground and did the same to the couple on her right.

The man gave an outraged cry at the interruption and surged to his feet. None of them even had the decency to do their deeds in private.

"This is a temple of the Lady Bosetsanu," Amelia shouted. "And you have *defiled* it."

"But Bosetsanu is the Lady of Love—"

"And you've made her temple a den of lust. Get out. *Get out!*"

"Who's gonna make us?" The man she'd interrupted just stood there, naked, hands on his hips and an angry crease in his forehead.

Silver fire burst from her fingertips and snaked up her arms. The flame swirled around her, cool to the touch, twisting her hair into a long rope above her head. Her eyes snapped with lightning. *"I am."*

Her voice was not her own. It chimed like a chorus of bells, deep and ancient. For a moment the silver flame flared into a serpentine shape with long fangs and sharper talons.

The man stumbled away with a curse and scrambled for his clothes. The whores scattered, knocking into other couples and kicking over wine glasses. The wine sluiced red over the white bricks.

Engulfed in silver fire, Amelia stalked to the altar stone. She swiped the candles aside and pressed her palm into the copper bowl. "Come, and avenge your home."

The sacred flame shot in a pillar of white light to the ceiling. It crawled over the dome and down the pillars, covering everything in rippling white fire.

Amelia spun on her heel, snatched up the offertory box – now collecting service fees – and threw down every fire bowl she could find.

The slick oil flowed over every surface and ignited everything it touched. The strips of silk that had once been Sanuset uniforms caught fire and dropped twisting from Bosetsanu's arms to the ground like a nest of vipers. The goose down pillows exploded with resounding pops; glass shattered in the heat. Flames spouted out the windows, clawing at the sky. Ugly black smoke charred the white stone and boiled into the night, blotting out the stars.

Screams of the frightened mixed with the wails of the burnt. The whores and their clients fled, but she was not finished.

Amelia threw out her arm, and a wall of silver light sprang up from the floor, blocking the doorway. The whores cowered away from her, backs pressed as close as they dared to the silver fire. Many tried to cover themselves with their hands; the redhead she'd backhanded only glared, the ribbons of her clothes hiding nothing.

"*Kneel,*" Amelia thundered.

Those that did not fall to their knees were yanked there by their colleagues.

"You do not deserve to live for the crimes you've committed against the Blessed Lady," she hissed. "Bosetsanu is a symbol of love, and you have twisted it beyond recognition."

"We give love—"

"You sell *lust,*" she roared. "Love is not something that can be *bought.* It is not carnal passion or desire. Love is selfless and encouraging. It inspires us to be better, to place others before ourselves and not serve our own *petty interests.*"

"You speak of love and compassion yet you burn down our home." The whore's red hair snapped in the air like the flags of flame that demolished the temple. Her honey-colored eyes glittered with hatred. "*It's a mercy you're not burning with it!*"

The whores, even the redhead, shrank away from her.

Amelia gulped in a breath and then another, trying to restore some of her calm. When her fingers stopped shaking, she broke open the offertory box and fished out the coins. "Each one of you will receive two doros: one for clothes, food, lodging, and one for starting your new life. If you are wise, you'll spend this money well. It will be hard work, but it'll be honest and honorable.

"I am Sanu Maitre Amelia de Taru, the Voice of Onu. I am headed to the Temple of Lhasa and the Sanctisum Seats. When I arrive, I will order the Militum Dei to return to Bucharest with the explicit command to put to the sword any one of you should you be found in this temple under false pretenses. Now take your money and go!"

Amelia placed two gold coins into each hand. Some wept, some glared at her, some were too stupefied to move. Clenching her hand into a fist, the barrier vanished. The silver flame undulating over her flesh snuffed out, her hair cascading about her shoulders once more.

She stalked into the cold evening air and left them to their fates without another thought.

AMELIA RAN WITH WILD ABANDON. Behind her, the night sky blazed with the fires of the temple. She had to get away from that disaster, that disgrace to her Blessed Lady.

A great sob tore through her chest, forcing her to stop. She vomited into the grass, purging her dinner and her grief along with it. Amelia spat the filth from her mouth and continued to walk until she reached the park. Collapsing among the tulips, she drew her knees up to her chest and wept.

Her whole body ached with misery. She was cold and alone, but nothing could harm her the way the scene at the temple had. No matter how hard she suppressed those memories, they resurfaced like ghosts. All of those screams. The smoke. The flames scorching the Lady's serene statue. She'd gone to the temple for peace and had received agony instead.

"What have I done?"

Pfft.

She grunted and pulled a dart from her neck. The wooden skewer had been dipped in something iridescent green, now smeared with the red of her blood. Amelia slumped over in the grass, the dart rolling out of her palm.

CHAPTER 36

THE SOFT DRIP OF WATER AGAINST STONE TEASED HER AWAKE. SHE blinked; blurred lines focused into iron bars. To the left, a torch flickered in the damp. The shadows scurried across the wall like rats.

Amelia jumped to her feet and staggered against the bars. Groaning, she rubbed the cramp out of her right thigh.

"I thought you'd never wake up." The voice was soft, lightly accented with Sarabi.

She lurched away from the bars, back into the shadows of her cell.

On the opposite side of the iron rungs, a man in a hooded robe leaned against a table. Gold fingerless gloves peeked out from the cuffs. A shiny beard, slicked to a point with pomade, poked out from the hood.

"Who... who are you?"

The man rolled up his sleeve to the elbow, bared his olive-skinned forearm and its five black scars. "It was only supposed to take one. One summoning. One skein. It had no difficulty killing your sisters, yet you thwarted it. Killed it, even. Tell me, Sanu, what makes you so special?"

Her breath froze in her lungs. Thunder roared in her ears as her heart threatened to hammer straight out of her chest.

The sorcerer.

"I-I'm not Sanu." She fought to stay still as the tattoo hidden on her chest seared white hot with the lie.

He cocked his head to the side as he rolled down his sleeve. "Your kind cannot lie. Jasper! Come in here. You're sure this is the right one?"

A canaris stepped into the torchlight. He was tall, lean, with hair as dark as his eyes. He was the one who'd saluted her with his blowgun. "Yes, my lord. She's the one from the park."

"Send in the whore."

A woman with fiery red hair and hateful honey eyes entered and trailed her hand along the bars. Amelia watched her as she would a snake, paralyzed to come any closer but too terrified to blink.

"*And by fire I shall refine Man into his greatest self.*' I guess yours wasn't strong enough, *biaozi.*"

Amelia swallowed, anger stirring in the pit of her stomach.

The whore flicked her red hairs over her shoulder and sauntered to the sorcerer's side. "She calls herself Amelia de Taru, Sanu Maitre. She summoned a silver dragon and burned the temple down."

"You're sure."

"Absolutely." The whore trailed her hand down the sorcerer's arm. "Now about my reward—"

The sorcerer chuckled and stood, lifting the whore's hand to his lips. "There'll be time for that soon. Besides, I'm not done with your services just yet. Now go and wait upstairs."

"Satisfied?" It was another woman's voice, high and grating.

Amelia inched along the far wall of her cell until the speaker came into sight. Rather, her stomach came into sight. Whoever she was, she was a voluminous mound of fat smothered in dusky rose satin.

The sorcerer shrugged. "Enough."

"See, I told you it'd be easy. My canaris never fail." Her voice was so shrill it was like a needle driving into Amelia's skull.

"Yes. It was – what's that phrase you Westerners use? – A piece of pie?"

"*Cake.* It's 'a piece of cake.'"

"Piece of cake, piece of pie. You Westerners love your desserts."

The voluminous mound of fat jiggled with laughter. "True. And I expect to be well taken care of, *sadiq*. My province is to be left *untouched*, understand?"

"Yes, yes. It's all been agreed."

"Then I'll see you upstairs for some refreshment when you're done?"

He nodded. "I won't be long."

Amelia shivered.

The sorcerer went around to the back of the table. His body had obscured a copper bowl, not unlike the ones that housed the sacred white flame. He dug around in his pocket and produced a velvet pouch. Very carefully, he poured the contents into the bowl. A mound of black sand glittered like crushed mica in the torchlight. "So... clearly we have some conflicting ideas as to your identity." He came to the bars. "Give me your hand."

Amelia shrank away from him.

"Give me your hand."

The voice compelled her to move, peeling her away from the wall. The silver fire writhed in outrage at the command. It urged her to resist, to fight, but the power of the voice dragged one foot in front of the other.

Panic seized her limbs as she watched the bars come involuntarily closer. The sorcerer impatiently thrust his hand through the rungs and pulled her the rest of the way. He rubbed his thumb against the bare skin on the back of her right hand.

"No tattoo, yet the witnesses swear you are Sanu. Are you just a novice?" He laughed softly. "Even a novice would be put to death for such a claim. Brazen."

She tried to yank her hand away. "I'm not—"

"We'll see."

He flipped her hand over and dragged a knife across her palm. An opium sickle. Amelia yelped, but the sorcerer held her fast, coating the blade in her blood before he let her go. "Let's see who the liar is." He returned to the copper bowl and held the sickle aloft, point down. "It's said that only a Sanu can open this box. Imagine my chagrin when that old librarian enlightened me of that pertinent piece of information."

"Saoirse," she murmured.

He hadn't heard her. "It's a good thing that skein failed. I had to collect every grain in the hope that this would work. Do you even *know* how long that took? Almost the same amount of time as for the demon to slaughter your sisters."

Beads of her blood dropped like rubies into the black sand. It hissed on contact and started to smoke. A silver glow emanated from the bowl, and the sound of scales on stone whispered into the air. Amelia pressed forward on tiptoe to peer over the rim.

The black sand shifted, writhed over itself as each grain jostled for a particular position. The rough form of a rectangular box began to take shape.

"But you have no…" The sorcerer looked up from the bowl, but his hood still shadowed most of his face. "What *are* you?"

Amelia flung herself away from the bars, back to the safety of the shadows.

The sorcerer laughed. *"Pathetic."*

He left the bowl to shimmer on the table and closed the door behind him. There was a scrape of a key in the lock and then footfalls ascending a flight of stairs.

Amelia sank to the floor and drew her knees up to her chest. Shivering, she wrapped her arms around her legs. Saoirse had given her life to protect the secret of that relic. Now Amelia's blood threatened to undo her sacrifice, and all because she'd been too stubborn to stay in the safety of the Lodge.

She sought the silver flame, but it was dormant, unresponsive. She had strangled it with her fear, and it was too weak to rise. Reduced to an ember, it pulsed like a weak heartbeat.

Amelia buried her head into her knees and wept.

CHAPTER 37

HIRO RAMMED THE STEWARD'S HEAD INTO THE WALL.

"The *key*."

"I d-don't have it—"

"Then I will flay the flesh off your finger and chisel one out of your bone."

"*Please*. I don't have it! This is the *private* dungeon. Only Lady Cosette has the key—"

"*Fine*." He tested the door with his foot, felt the lock give just a little. He grabbed the steward and hurled both of them into the door.

The steward screamed as the door ripped from its hinges. Howling, he collapsed onto the floor, cradled his ruined shoulder.

Hiro side-stepped around the whimpering man, paused a moment to stare at the copper bowl of writhing black sand.

Sorcery. He rushed to the cell and the figure huddled within. "Gods above – *Sanu*."

She had her legs drawn up to her chest, her shoulders shaking. He jimmied the lock with the tip of his dagger, yanked the door open. There was blood on her hand, dried, but no wound. He dropped to his knees, parted her hair from her face with a tentative hand.

"Sanu, I'm here." He said it gently, like to a wounded animal.

She lifted her eyes slowly. They were dull. Numb.

"Sanu, we have to go." Hiro hauled her to her feet. Gave her a little shake. "Sanu. *Sanu.*"

She wasn't listening. Her gaze was distant, unseeing; her hands pale, trembling. She felt so cold. He cupped her cheek with his hand; she didn't even protest.

"Sanu, I can't carry you and haul that piece of *goushi* around. You need to snap out of it. *Sanu.*"

No response.

Frustrated, he bent his head and pressed his mouth against hers. She was as soft as satin. His grip tightened instinctively, melded her against him. He'd meant only to distract her, to shock her, but when her lips parted in surprise, his tongue delved to caress hers. Sweet, the faint taste of strawberry sorbet—

The punch hit like a lightning strike.

Hiro staggered away, rubbing his jaw.

The Sanu's eyes snapped with silver fire. "It is *forbidden* to touch—"

"There she is."

The priestess shook her head as if to clear it. "W-what are you doing here?"

"Rescuing you, of course. You're always wandering off." He drew his greatsword. "We need to go. I've kicked a hornets' nest getting in here."

His third fight in the pits had been interrupted with the news of the burning temple. The blind priest had blubbered something about the Sanu going off to pray, and that was the last he'd heard before sprinting to the conflagration.

Flames clawed out of every window, every door. Red wine from the broken cistern sluiced across the floor, dripped down the stairs. Evaporated in an acrid sizzle. For a moment, the seamless bricks turned into a pebbled seashore, the wine washing over them into blood. The cries and stench of the mangled and dying filled the air; an echo from the past.

Then he'd seen the canaris, wide-eyed and mesmerized by the destruction. It'd taken only a few well-placed cuts for the spy to sing like a canary and tell him where the Sanu had been taken. The Jardin Seat, formerly the People's Palace, was a fortress. The canaris took him to a secret entrance – still full of spies, but less populated than the front door – and Hiro had set to maiming.

"Please, don't kill me," the last canaris gasped, sidling along the floor.

Hiro glanced behind him at the carnage in the corridor. The spy's brethren lay strewn in various states of bloody incapacitation, but all would live. He snatched the nearest blowgun off the floor, extracted the dart.

He rammed the iridescent tip into the spy's neck. "She wouldn't want me to."

That's when the palace steward had arrived, furious at the commotion he'd heard from the secret passages behind the walls. Perfumed, ears pierced with ruby studs, silver tunic and dusky rose trousers. The man had shrieked at the bloodshed, tucked one foot up like a crane away from the gore.

Hiro yanked the steward to his feet by his dislocated arm, smothered the man's scream with a gloved hand. "Let's *go*, priestess."

But the Sanu was by the table, eyes glued to the bowl of shifting sand. Without warning, she plunged her hand into the bowl, screamed as fire raced up her arm.

"Sanu!"

The priestess gritted her teeth and kept her hand submerged. Her face contorted with agony as the fire grew hotter.

"*Amelia!*" Hiro tackled her. They hit the ground hard, and he shucked off his greatcoat, ready to smother the flames.

Dazed, the Sanu raised a hand to smother her cough. Her flesh was untouched. Even the yellow sleeve of her tunic wasn't singed.

"Sanu, what—"

"*That* is the Raion Chest."

"I'm going to pretend to know what you're talking about."

She scrambled to her feet, smeared the tears from her eyes. "It holds the true name of the Crown Prince of Heaven. The power to *summon* him, Hiro. Unfathomable power."

"Can we destroy it?"

"No. I mean, I just tried, but…"

Hiro stared at the writhing sand. "What happens when that stops?"

Her blubbering stopped as her eyes widened. "He'll use me to open it."

"Then we'd best not be here when that happens. Come on."

"*Wait.*"

Hiro jerked on the steward's collar. The man ceased his sniveling, started to shake as a new fear took hold of him.

The Sanu approached with all the presence and fury of a hurricane. "Take us to Lady Cosette. *Now.*"

"No, Sanu. We don't have the strength—"

Her ocean blue-eyes were cold. Determined. "I have *you*, don't I?"

"I'm flattered, but I'm not stupid." He shook his head. "This is tactically dangerous. Suicidal."

She closed the distance between them in two quick steps, poked him in the chest. "That temple was a *whorehouse*, Hiro. I can't let that go. You're either coming with me, or I'll see you back at the Lodge."

The disrespect to such a holy place made his skin crawl. Hiro turned a disgusted glare to the steward. "You heard the priestess."

The steward made little noises in his throat, protesting. Hiro jabbed him in the spine with his greatsword and made him comply.

They went up a flight of stairs and through a maze of corridors before ascending another staircase. At each junction they were beset by palace guards, called to action by the terrified steward. Hiro merely kept his grip on the man's collar, dispatched his combatants with cold efficiency.

He never heard a peep of protest from the Sanu. Then again, he hadn't killed anyone, either. They went down another hall, just as garishly decorated as the last half dozen, before the steward skidded to a halt in front of wide double doors.

Carved with an unfurling tulip flanked by wheat sheaves and gilded in gold, the doors were guarded by four burly men. Each was Hiro's size, maybe even larger. Lady Cosette's personal guard.

Having done his duty, the palace steward attempted to flee. Hiro kicked his knee out of joint, let the man collapse on the tiled floor with a cry.

"We are not expected, if you were going to ask," the Sanu informed them coldly.

The captain flicked his eyes from the priestess to Hiro to the writhing palace steward and back again. The bodyguards shifted away from each other, allowing room for combat. Their leather armor and metal gauntlets creaked as they adjusted their grips on their spears.

"*Attack them, you idiots,*" the steward screamed.

The captain rolled his thick neck, limbered up for a fight.

The priestess took a stomping step forward. "How can you not recognize me?"

The bodyguards eyed her warily.

"Have you all been led so astray?" she demanded. "Do these colors mean *nothing* to you? You are the personal guards of the Jardin Seat! An official who's tasked with maintaining respect for all. How could you let a temple of Bosetsanu become a whorehouse? How could you just do nothing?"

She kept clenching her hands, as if smothering something. Or grasping at self-control. Hiro risked a glance into her face. Stormy. A tempest of righteous rage.

Three of the four averted their eyes, shifted on their feet.

"It's not what you think," one of them whispered.

"*Quiet,* Sandstone," their captain barked.

Hiro lashed out, not with his sword as the captain had expected, but with his bow. The wood caught around the captain's throat, wrenched him to his knees. Hiro pressed his foot into the captain's back, pulled hard on the ends of the bow. The captain's fingers scrabbled at the wood as his face turned purple. With a choking gasp, he collapsed to the floor. Unconscious.

The others had not rushed to help him.

Hiro untangled his bow, rolled the body toward the whimpering steward. "Okay." He took a deep breath, surveyed the remainders. "Who's next?"

"My lady." The one named Sandstone dropped to one knee. "We had no choice."

"I doubt that."

"If we did not obey," he whispered, "she would kill them."

"Kill whom?"

"Our families," another guard answered. "She has a hostage from each of us."

"And where are these hostages?"

As one, the three guards glared at the steward.

"He'd know," the third said darkly. "He *visits* my niece."

Gulping, the steward shied away. Bumped into Hiro's immovable frame. "S-she keeps they key around her neck," he blurted.

"How could this have happened?" Hiro asked. He shoved the steward away from him. "Surely someone could have sent an eagle to another Council Seat for intervention."

Sandstone shook his head. "Lady Cosette's reach is very long. The canaris… it's how she stays in power. She's got leverage on everyone who could make a difference."

"Not anymore," the Sanu snarled.

She threw open the gilded doors.

CHAPTER 38

"*KYRIL*," A FEMALE VOICE SHRILLED. "I *TOLD* YOU WE WERE NOT TO BE disturbed."

Lady Cosette Bavaria was a whale of a woman.

She had piggy little black eyes sunk into a doughy face with red lips as fat as leeches. Her blond hair was long and curly and very pretty, but did little to enhance her looks as it cascaded down her rolls of flesh. She was swathed in dusky rose satin, and her dainty feet with their pink painted toes were perched upon a footstool. A fire roared in a hearth beside her, illuminating her half of the room but keeping the rest of them in shadow. Hiro had hauled the steward Kyril in after him, keeping one gloved hand firmly clamped over the man's mouth.

On one side of her settee was a table laden with delicacies – crispy duck in orange sauce and thinly sliced Iberian ham – and on the other side in front of the hearth was a thick Pirsan rug. The whore with the fiery red hair was shackled to a ring in the floor, naked, her face crushed into the rug.

The sorcerer had his back to them, his robe hanging from his elbows and exposing a large swath of olive skin. It was desert dry, cracked and flaking like a forgotten riverbed. He'd mounted the whore like a dog, fingers digging into the flesh at her hips. Grunting, he pounded away at her as Lady Cosette watched.

"Do her harder," she whispered, sucking the syrup off a slice of poached pear.

The sorcerer barked a laugh and redoubled his efforts. The whore whimpered.

Amelia choked.

The redhead's honey eyes found her, the hatred replaced by misery. A spark of hope flickered in their golden depths, and she gurgled an unintelligible plea. Her jaw was broken.

The sorcerer flung his head back with a shout. As his body shuddered in ecstasy, the cracks on his back and arms began to soften. They fused, and the skin became supple and soft. The flakes drifted away like pollen.

The whore's pink skin turned the greenish-gray of withered grass. Her red hair became white, dull, no more than a tangle of dead brambles. The sorcerer disengaged himself and shrugged his robe back into place. With just a flick of his fingers, the shriveled remains of the whore crashed to the rug in a shower of dust.

"The trick is to pull out before they desiccate. Nothing worse than a raspy husk wrapped around your—"

Hiro swept into the firelight, his black greatcoat whipping out behind him like a thundercloud. Lady Cosette screamed, and the sorcerer spun into a crouch.

The rippling steel of the greatsword bit into the sorcerer's shoulder just as he exploded into a flock of blackbirds. Cawing, flapping madly, the dark flurry crashed through the nearest window and into the night. A blackbird lay pinned to the carpet under the greatsword, oozing ichor. With a frustrated cry, Hiro hurled the bird into the fire. It flared green with a loud hiss.

Panting with rage, he spun, raising his greatsword at the Lady of Jardin.

Amelia flung up her hand, shaking her head. *No*, she mouthed.

"Darius!" Lady Cosette had pitched herself upright with flabby arms that wobbled under the strain. "*Darius!*"

"He can't hear you," Amelia said. "There is no one out there. And no one is coming."

A ripple of fear passed over Lady Cosette's face. It was quickly replaced by disdain. "My canaris will find you. But this time their darts won't be dipped in a sedative. You're a walking corpse, girl. A *walking—*"

The prince backhanded her into silence. "I doubt that. None of them have working fingers right now. Who was that?"

"The sorcerer?" She craned around to look at him, but the rolls of fat kept her neck locked forward. "I'm not foolish enough to know his name."

Hiro laid the ichor-dripping tip of his greatsword against her flesh. She squealed as her skin started to sizzle. "You'll have to do better than that."

"He wanted the Sanu! That's all. In exchange, Jardin would be left out of the coming war."

"War?"

Lady Cosette sneered. "*Via Leao.*"

"I could almost forgive my kidnapping if you hadn't defaced the Temple of the Lady," Amelia said.

Lady Cosette pushed the greatsword away with a sausage-like finger and dabbed at the blood dribbling from the split on her lip. "I've done no such thing—"

"You've allowed a holy place to be defiled. And judging by the scene I just saw, it's no wonder why. You are a sad, depraved woman."

"How *dare* you judge me? I am the ruler of this province. I—"

"You do not *rule* here. You govern. But not anymore." Amelia kicked the footstool out from under the Lady's painted toes. "It's a Seat's duty to keep the sanctity of its holy places so that others might find refuge in them. It is *respect*, Lady Cosette. Hiro, your dagger, please."

"*Hiro?*" The woman truly looked at him for the first time, her piggy black eyes bulging from her head. "*Hiro Ishida?* You have her stop this right now or I'll tell your father—"

Hiro handed Amelia his dagger as calmly as if she'd asked to use it to slice a piece of bread.

As she approached, Lady Cosette started to scream.

Amelia took a fistful of the lady's hair and sliced the dagger through it. She was rough in her punishment, grabbing and yanking and cutting and oblivious to Lady Cosette's shrieks and wails and thrashing until all of that beautiful blond hair lay in heaps on the ground. Only patchy clumps like haystacks remained.

Overwhelmed, Lady Cosette slumped into a faint.

Amelia returned the dagger. "Thank you."

Hiro wiped the last whisps of hair away. "I thought she'd never shut up."

"One of the guards mentioned a key. It should be around her neck."

"And?"

"And you're the one wearing gloves."

Upper lip twisted in revulsion, Hiro peered around the Lady's vast bosom until he found a chain half-hidden in a valley of fat. He gave it a jerk, and a key freed itself from between her breasts with a pop like an uncorked bottle.

Still grimacing, he marched over to the mewling steward. He rammed two gloved fingers into the terrified man's mouth.

"Hiro, what are you doing?"

Hiro lowered the key and its chain into the steward's mouth and clamped his hand over his lips. The steward thrashed uselessly; Hiro had one knee rammed into his chest to keep him pinned to the floor. He finally swallowed, or choked, and the prince released him.

"Give our regards to her Ladyship when she wakes, you piece of *goushi*." He clapped the man on the shoulder. "If you're still alive, that is."

Grabbing her arm, Hiro hustled her from the room. "Gentlemen," he told the guards, "the key is in the steward's stomach. Happy hunting."

Three grim smiles darkened their faces as the guards filed into the room.

They were halfway down the hall when they heard the steward start to scream.

"I HAVE TO STOP." Amelia braced her hands on her knees, gasping. "I can't run anymore."

"Then find whatever inner strength you priestesses preach about and *keep going*."

She shook off the hand clamped around her arm.

"Sanu, we need to get back to the Lodge. We needed to leave this city hours ago."

She straightened indignantly. "And we would have if you'd just listened to me. I told you it wasn't safe here."

"I wasn't the one who wandered off and set a temple on *fire*."

"*You* abandoned us first. You risked not only your life, but all of ours, when you went to the fighting pits. It's *pride*, Hiro."

"Uh-huh. Well, I'd love to stand here in the middle of the street and point fingers with you, but in case you've forgotten, we've just assaulted the Jardin Seat. Whatever forces are still loyal to her are out hunting for us right now and you want to compare sins." He raked a hand through his hair. "Ridiculous. Now move or so help me I will *drag* you the rest of the way."

Pfft.

A dart buried itself into the thick column of his neck.

Hiro threw the skewer aside and drew his greatsword. He circled around once, blade poised at shoulder height and ready to stab.

Amelia crouched, hunching her shoulders to protect her neck, and peered around in the gloom. "Hiro—"

"Stay behind me."

She flattened her back against his, moving with him as he circled. "I don't see—"

Pfft.

The prince grunted. He tugged the dart from his flesh with sluggish fingers. His legs wobbled. The sword clattered against the street as he pitched forward.

"*Hiro—*" Amelia grabbed his coat and wrenched him upright. She only succeeded in collapsing under him. His limp frame trapped her against the ground, head lolling in the crook between her shoulder and neck. His seal-brown eyes glazed up at her. "You. Big. *Ox.*" She strained to wiggle out from under him.

Three shadows stepped from the gloom, the one in front tossing the blowgun carelessly aside. The miserly lamplight glinted on the sea glass woven into the man's canerows. A red scarf, a new one not yet faded from the sun, looped several times over a sinewy chest. She'd recognize those sharp eyes and sharper cheekbones anywhere.

"Drag *a woman?*" he said in Atlantican. "*See? I told you he was rude.*" He pressed a hand against his heart and bowed. "*His genteel replacement at your service, my lady.*"

CHAPTER 39

A FLOCK OF BLACKBIRDS PELTED INTO THE TULIPS. PETALS PUFFED INTO the wind like feathers.

The sorcerer stumbled out of the flower bed, clutching the wound at his shoulder. The rippling steel of the greatsword had bitten in deep. Forged in dragon's breath, the blade had left an intolerable sting. A chunk of flesh was missing, and bright red blood seeped between his fingers.

Acrid smoke from the burning temple mixed with something sweeter in the night breeze. Oranges and sugar.

It was almost dawn now, and the lampposts of the park were starting to dim. Down the gravel path he spied a cart. Hunched over it was a lone figure, a match blooming yellow in his hands. The fire rippled across the charcoal, and the scent of frying oil lay heavy in the air.

He staggered down the path, his steps clumsy from the blood loss.

The gogoși vendor looked up in surprise as he knocked into the cart. He was an older man with twinkling eyes and a bushy mustache that curled up at its ends. "You're a bit early, sir," the vendor apologized. "I just put the oil on. The gogoși won't be ready for at least another quarter hour. There's a café just up the way here if you want a coffee... Sir?"

The vendor threw up his hands as he lunged for him. A hand slapped a slotted spoon, splashing hot oil into his face. Snarling, he grabbed the old vendor by the collar and pressed his lips against his. Repulsed by the mustache that prickled his face, he kept his lips firm against the vendor's as the man's life drained into his.

Finished, he pushed the desiccated husk away from him. It disintegrated into dust before it'd even reached the ground. The wound in his shoulder had stopped bleeding, but a gaping wedge remained in his flesh. The sting of the dragon's breath sword hadn't lessened. He needed more.

Footsteps crunched along the gravel to his left. "Papa! Have you started frying yet? Andrei and I brought you the nutmeg—" The young woman dropped a paper sack as she jerked out a hand to steady him. Both of them were young, fresh-faced, full of life.

"Where'd Papa go?"

"Are you alright, sir?" Andrei asked. "Do you need help?"

"Why, yes. Yes, I do."

CHAPTER 40

AMELIA CHEWED ON HER THUMBNAIL AS SHE PACED IN FRONT OF THE AFT window. The water was as black as the night, the reflecting stars churning into foam in the ship's wake. The flame of the oil lamp wavered as the ship banked to starboard. A ribbon of oily smoke threaded into the air. It seemed to expand, to smother everything in darkness. Except the light of the flame. It had clawed free of the lamp, devoured the desk and its maps, and now turned its hungry gaze toward her. Voices not her own screamed in her ears. Amelia clawed at the window, desperate for a way out.

The door banged open. In sauntered the Atlantican, a jug in one hand and two glasses pinched between the fingers of his other. She flattened herself against the window, panting. He cocked an eyebrow in question. She cast a worried look at the oil lamp; its flame was no larger than her thumb, perfectly contained behind soot-streaked glass.

The Atlantican jerked his chin to the seat behind the desk.

Amelia sat, wringing her hands in her lap. Cold sweat clammed in her armpits and dribbled between her breasts. Her tattoo itched like a nettle sting.

Oblivious to her discomfort, the Atlantican set a glass in front of her and poured a brown liquid up to the rim. The spice stung her nose.

She leaned forward and took the glass with a trembling hand. Half the rum disappeared with a sputter. *"W-where are my friends?"*

He sat close on the edge of the desk and took a large swallow from his glass. Amelia looked away. Salt water and rum rolled off him like a tide. Leather pants hugged his hips, and a ruby drop earring winked from his left ear. A necklace of amber beads studded with silver charms clicked against his brown chest. The man seemed incapable of keeping his shirt closed. *"They're fine. Already that priest is in a stupor. Green-bellied, that one."*

"And the boy?"

"You mean the little lion?" He rubbed his jaw and smiled, flashing sharp white teeth. *"He's in the hold protecting your gear, but he's really just playing with the other cats."*

"What of the warhorse? The palomino one."

"That golden terror? Yes, her too. The boy refused to be parted from her."

"And... Hiro?"

"Sleeping off a double dose of ever-sleep. Potent stuff." He paused, sharp eyes never leaving her face.

"How did you manage to get into the Lodge anyway?" she asked irritably. *"It's a fortress."*

"My cousin is a Doll there. Red, the little minx. Argenti, you've nothing to worry about."

She jumped upright. *"'Nothing to worry about?' You drugged my friend and* kidnapped *us."*

"Rescued, Argenti. Rescued." He motioned for her to sit back down.

She looked him in the eye. They were pale green, like the sea glass in his hair. *"Why would you rescue us? You don't even know me."*

He smiled down at her. Boldly. He had that predatory look she'd seen before.

The silver fire stirred. It flared once, not in defense, but with a tranquil sigh. As if it recognized a friend. Amelia pressed her hand against her chest, rubbing the tattoo with a puzzled frown.

"Don't know you? We met in Vienna. Don't break my heart and say you don't remember."

"A brief conversation can hardly merit a rescue." She finished off her rum in another large swallow, winced, and put the glass on the desk. Already it was dulling the panic. The avenging fire was fading into a haze. The terrified cries of the people it had punished sounded no more than a buzz in her ears.

The Atlantican chuckled and refilled her glass.

"So?" she prompted.

"You speak the language of the sea, yet you are not one of us. I believe you are an eridani."

Amelia retrieved her rum with a scoff. She took a swallow and started to laugh at the ridiculous idea. He fixed her with a serious look. *"Y-you think I'm a daughter of water?"*

The Atlantican shrugged and took another sip. *"I've never met someone with eyes as blue as yours. Surely you must have siren's blood."*

She shook her head.

He leaned forward, eyes intent. "You were an orphan. Discovered by the surf?"

Amelia shifted uncomfortably. *"What do you know of it?"*

The Atlantican nodded, as if she had just proven his point. *"Eridani."*

"Eridani are a myth."

He winked at her. *"I'm Atlantican, a sea gypsy. We believe all myths, especially those about our beloved sea. Anyway, my cousin Mercedes told me she had ferried the Argenti to the city, and when the temple burned, I searched for you. In a dangerous city and away from the water."* He clicked his tongue disapprovingly. *"Risky, Eridani."*

Amelia rolled her eyes. *"Then it'll shock you to know I've never seen the sea until now."*

"So sad." He whispered it, his pale green eyes capturing hers. They were soft, caressing.

She cleared her throat. *"I'm Sanu and an eridani, not an undine. So you can stop trying to... beguile me."*

He laughed, a great guffaw that teased a smile from her. *"Don't blame me for checking."*

"Are you a merchant like Mercedes?"

He stood with a smirk and refilled both their glasses. *"After a fashion. Where are my manners? I am Captain Aurelio Serrano of the* Siren's Call."

"Amelia de Taru, Sanu Maitre, Maiglöckchen, Argenti, and eridani, apparently."

Aurelio's eyes twinkled. *"I feel the need to clarify, my lady. The* raider *Aurelio Serrano."*

The smile vanished from her face.

"Sweet mercy," she breathed. *"You're a* pirate."

She bolted away from the desk.

"Aw, come now. We were getting along so well." Aurelio remained seated on its edge, sipping his rum. *"You've nothing to fear from me or my crew, Eridani."*

"I shouldn't be... here."

"With us sea gypsies? An eridani is more at home with us than anywhere else." He picked up her glass and gave it a little wiggle.

Instead, she took the chair and dragged it a modest distance away from the immodestly dressed pirate. Then she returned for her rum. She clinked her glass against his, took another large swallow, and sat. Anything to dull the guilt.

"So, um, aren't raiders the same as pirates?" she asked.

"Not at all. Pirate *implies a certain lust for bloodshed that* raider *does not. Think of a raider as someone who merely liberates and redistributes surplus goods. Of course, if the crew fights, I don't deter my men from defending themselves."*

"Semantics aside, you should not pirate or raid or liberate."

"And why not? A man has to eat."

Aurelio twirled his glass in circles with small movements from his thumb and middle finger. A ring resembling a mermaid curling around an emerald crowned his index finger. The detail was... explicit. She found the wavering lamplight glinting on the mermaid's voluptuous curves rather distracting.

"*Because. It's. Wrong.*" She spoke slowly, cutting through the carefree haze.

"*It's wrong for harbormasters to line their own pockets with the profits others have died to make. If I did not liberate as freely as I do, the villages along the Medi coast would shrivel up and bake in the sun like bleached bones.*"

"*They're not all like that.*"

"*They're everywhere, from Nice to Istanbul. Vashti is riddled with them. Those bastardos prey upon the weak and rape—*" He cut himself off with an angry huff. The sea gypsy toyed with the ruby dangling from his ear. "*Except for them, I only raid from those who can afford it and return it to those that need it.*"

She hiccupped. "*How very noble of you.*"

"*I follow the Tenets like any gods-fearing man.*"

"'Thou shalt not steal.'"

"*Liberate. And I redistribute it—*"

"*You mean sell it back.*"

He waved her words aside with a flick of a hand as he took another swallow. "*At a fraction of the cost. I should be paid for the hard work I do. A man has to eat.*"

Aurelio offered her more rum, but she kept her glass close and shook her head. Any more and she'd be singing shanties with him in a minute.

"*So why were you outside the lace shop in Vienna?*" she asked. "*That seems pretty far away from the sea.*"

"*I knew you remembered.*" He grinned and rifled around in his desk drawer. He withdrew a thin cigar and lit it from the oil lamp. After a puff, he offered it to her. "*Cigarillo?*"

She shook her head, wrinkling her nose.

Aurelio was careful to blow the smoke away from her. "*Elizabetta's getting married soon,*" he explained. "*She was there for a fitting. Blasted woman was determined to have Viennese lace. It's the least I could do after... Anyway, Mercedes transported the dress for me when it was done."*

"*Aw, the pirate with a heart of gold.*" She slurred her words this time, a sloppy grin on her face.

"Raider." He wagged the bejeweled finger at her. "*And don't be saying such things, Eridani. Imagine if word got out that the Great Aurelio Serrano was shopping for lace for his sister's bride clothes? I would have to resort to* pirating *just to get my reputation back.*"

She nodded as seriously as she could. "*Well, I can assure you that would* never *happen.*"

"*Oh?*" He cocked an eyebrow.

"*You are not so great. I've never heard of you before today.*"

The raider grinned, green eyes laughing.

Amelia giggled and looked down into her cup. Empty. With an indignant sound, she held it out for more.

"*Where are my manners?*" Aurelio wedged his cigarillo between his lips and jumped off the desk. He uncorked the bottle with a flourish and steadied her glass with his hand. His fingers lingered against hers even after the rum trickled over the sides.

"Not *an undine.*" She wiped the smile from her face so he'd take her seriously, but it just snapped back like a rubber band.

He grinned again. "*Sorry. It's always good to double-check.*"

"*Feh, even if I was I wouldn't fall for you.*"

"*No?*" His voice had turned soft, his mouth hinting at a seductive smile. Those pale green eyes tried to persuade her differently. They were very convincing.

"*You're an incorrigible flirt, Aurelio,*" she said matter-of-factly. "*You'd break my heart.*"

"Never, *Eridani.*"

Amelia sloshed half the rum down her clothes as a bellow echoed outside the door. She staggered to her feet as Aurelio sighed, grounding out the end of his cigarillo on the bottom of his boot. There was another shout, this one closer, and the rattle of a body being thrown into a wall.

"*I must ask your forgiveness for drugging your bodyguard. He seemed the type to put up a fight.*"

The door burst open.

Amelia steeled herself for the inevitable brawl and downed the rest of her rum. "*Ask him yourself.*"

CHAPTER 41

Hiro leaned against the doorframe for a heartbeat, his brain still addled from the sedative. He pushed himself into the room, dagger drawn.

The pirate glanced at the blade. "No blood," he said in halting Layman. "My thanks."

"Get away from her."

The Sanu came around the desk. Red-faced, bleary eyes, reeking of blackstrap rum. Even drunk, she merely shifted her weight as the ship rocked.

Hiro stumbled into the wall, caught himself on the bookshelf. He shoved himself away, spread his legs wide for balance.

"Hiro, I'm... fine." Her voice was slow, halting. "Put it... away."

"We've been abducted by pirates—"

"'Raiders.'" The priestess and the pirate shared a grin.

"Semantics! We've been kidnapped—"

"*Rescued.*" She staggered to the bed, sat.

"—and here I find you laughing and drinking like a... like a—"

"Like those whores?" She met his gaze for the first time. Her-ocean blue eyes, dull with drink, still burned with a smoldering fire. The Sanu finished the rum in her hand, held her glass out to the pirate.

She rattled off something in Atlantican, and the pirate put her glass on the desk.

He sidled around Hiro, hands opened at his sides. No threat. The pirate closed the door on his way out.

The Sanu pulled her legs up to her chest, wrapped her arms around them. Like she did every time she needed to comfort herself.

Hiro sheathed his dagger, dropped down on the bed beside her. He knew he shouldn't touch her. Slowly, he shrugged out of his greatcoat and draped it around her. Consoled her with its warmth.

Her fingers curled around the lapels, clutched it closer. Her voice was a whisper. "I'm a monster, Hiro. What I did tonight—"

"You did what was necessary. Righteous anger is not the same as wrath, Sanu."

"I could've *killed* them. What kind of Sanu could do that?"

"But you didn't. Some walked away with a few burns… I'm told you even gave the whores money?"

The Sanu had had every right by every law to slaughter those whores on the spot. They hadn't deserved her mercy or her generosity.

"I can still see their faces. They were *terrified*."

"It'll get better, Sanu," he lied softly. "Just give it time. And if you're a monster, well, then there's no hope for me."

The priestess looked up from her knees, glanced at his burned hand. The unspoken question lay heavy in the silence between them.

She'll never look at me the same way again. He rubbed the puckered flesh. "Six years ago I was stationed at Biscay Bay. Gods above, I can't do this sober."

He went to the desk, uncorked the bottle. The rum disappeared in a few gulps. He slammed the bottle down with a *thunk*, passed a hand over his face. Hiro sat back down, swallowed. Steeled himself.

"Baltic Raiders were pillaging along the coast, disrupting trade. One chieftain was Red Ellick, and his clan specialized in destruction. It was not enough to steal and rape and murder; they had a conjurer set fire to everything. Whole villages were lost. They were… unbeatable."

He paused, shoved the echoes of their screams from his mind.

"I killed their conjurer, but it wasn't enough. Baltic clans never stop even if only one is left breathing. They would get another sorcerer. So that night, I disguised myself in the pelt of a sea wolf and took a canoe to Red Ellick's camp. He was like any other chieftain, bringing his entire clan with him on a raid, the women and children too. They were not expecting an attack so close to home.

"I destroyed his clan. I burned the camp to the ground, left nothing but ash behind. I had to send a message. Their butchering would be revisited tenfold. That morning there was no raid. Nor was there a raid in Biscay Bay the following day, or the day after that, or ever again. The Baltic Raiders fled back to their home islands whispering about the death that came in the guise of a sea wolf. At the Academy, I became known as the Beast of Biscay."

He'd never spoken of that day to anyone except Domo Tanaka. The two Academy survivors had been sworn to secrecy. Even Kale knew none of the details of his blooding. He remembered – vividly – the deaths of each one of Red Ellick's clansmen. Even the innocent faces of the babes as their mothers came at him with knives. He cut them all down like rabid dogs. Merciless. Convinced himself he was avenging the hundreds that had already perished, saving countless others from a similar fate.

He'd left none alive.

Hiro forced a humorless laugh. "Like I said, Sanu, there's no hope for me. Not after what I've done. But your hands are clean, and your nightmares will go away. I'm sure of it." He cleared his throat. "I… know you must think differently about me now, but…"

You can't send me away. Whatever honor I have left has been pledged to you.

He waited an eternity for a response. Any response. The Sanu was always quick to voice whatever was on her mind, but now she was eerily silent.

Hiro shifted in his seat, impatient. Anxious.

She shifted away from him. Even in her drunken haze, she knew to be repulsed.

Then her hand crept out from under his greatcoat. Her fingers curled around his.

Speechless, he stared at her hand.

How can you even touch me?

Holding his breath, he risked a glance at her face.

"Anyone can see you are a haunted man, Hiro. But, I believe in second chances," she whispered. "There is hope enough for both of us." She gave his fingers a gentle squeeze, withdrew her hand back to the warmth of his greatcoat. "Is there any rum left?"

His heart roared in his ears. "N-no."

"I could use... a little more."

I could use a barrelful.

He pushed her shoulder. Barely. The Sanu toppled onto her side with a muted groan. He got her legs onto the bed with a gruff toss. "Sleep it off, Sanu. We have more to talk about."

"'Bout what?" Her words were muffled by the pillow.

"About how you can stick your hand into a bowl of witchfire without getting burned."

She rolled onto her back with a sleepy smile. "I'm Sanu."

"Hn. And that makes you fireproof now, does it?"

"Eridani don't burn."

"Uh-huh. Show me your tattoo, and I'll forget all of this."

He'd never seen it before. The long sleeves of her tunic had always covered the backs of her hands.

A small giggle. "That would be... indecent exposure."

He rolled his eyes. There was no talking to her like this.

With a gentle tug, he rolled her onto her side so she wouldn't choke if she vomited. Her head lolled against her arm, her lips smooshed against the greatcoat. Her hair lay in disarray around her head, a thousand strands of caramel.

He took her right hand, pinched the cuff between thumb and forefinger. Briefly, he contemplated waking to discover someone gawking at the puckered flesh on his own hand.

She sighed, a little huff of contentment. Security. Even after what he'd confessed. Her fingertips curled slightly in his palm.

She'd never given him reason to doubt her. He smoothed the sleeve back into place with his thumb, nestled her hand under her chin.

The Sanu stirred. "Daughter of…water."

"What was that?"

But she was already asleep, drooling into his greatcoat.

CHAPTER 42

"*LAND.*" ISEN SAGGED TO HIS KNEES, DUG HIS HANDS INTO THE SANDY beach. He prostrated himself with a blissful sigh.

Hiro rolled his eyes. "You'd think the priest would have a little more self-respect."

The Sanu smiled, twirled her hair into rope and coiled it around her arm to keep the wind from whipping it into everyone's face.

"My tribulations are *over*," Isen cried, rolling onto his back. "*Never again. You hear me? Never again.* My best regards, Captain Serrano, but *good riddance.*"

"The feeling's mutual," Hiro said. "You were drinking all of their rum."

The priest pointed to himself. "Pot." Then he pointed in Hiro's general direction. "Kettle."

The Atlantican shook his head, held the rowboat steady as the Sanu got out. Hiro offered her his hand, but she just handed him her pack instead. She'd been militant about maintaining her personal space.

What'd you expect? You told her you killed women and children, even if it was for the greater good. That's still... murder. She's a priestess, you idiot. She doesn't see a gray area for acts like that.

The priestess hiked up her cloak, sloshed through the shadows. Taking her pack, she nudged Isen playfully in the side with her foot.

"Scamp." Isen flailed a hand, missed.

Hiro nudged him in the leg, not so playfully. "Sober up. You're wasting time."

"I don't criticize when *you* self-medicate." The priest brushed himself off. "That rum saved my life. I would've wasted away to nothing—"

"And spared us all this racket. C'mon. Get on the horse."

"I'll walk, thank you." He flounced his robes, flicked out his sash. "I've ridden enough."

He started up the dune in the opposite direction.

"Over here, Isen," Hiro said.

The priest changed direction without a word.

Kale giggled, followed after him.

Hiro glanced over his shoulder. "Finish your good-byes, Sanu."

The pirate pried a ring off his finger, pressed it into her palm. Wrapped her fingers closed around it. They spoke in foreign whispers, his voice intent, hers acquiescent. Then he pressed his lips to the hand that enclosed his ring.

Hiro cleared his throat warningly.

"Ciao, Eridani." The pirate gave him a mocking salute. "Prince."

Hiro rolled his eyes, helped Serrano push the rowboat back into the surf. "Farewell, *pirate*."

The priestess was already halfway up the dune, the palomino warhorse dragging her along. The mare's step was high as she tossed her head. White mane thrashing in the sea breeze. He didn't know who was more content to be rid of the boat, his horse or the priest.

Over the rise was a small town. Just a few families that maintained the fresh water supply. Ships traded goods to have their barrels refilled from the precious well. Beyond the little town stretched a barren wasteland. A T-intersection on the eastern outskirts provided three choices. North to Balkanabat, east to Mashhad, and southeast across the wasteland to Zahedan. A carriage waited for them.

Serrano's ship had had messenger eagles, large ospreys with yellow eyes. They'd sent messages ahead to this very hamlet, and to the mayor of the nearest town that an Ishida prince was in need of a carriage. Isen had even used one for a personal message with a surly, "I have *friends*, you know."

It was an armed escort: two men clung to the footman post at the carriage's rear, a woman with a deadly-looking crossbow sat beside the driver. Hiro secured their packs on top beside the barrels of water.

"Where to, my prince?" the driver asked.

"We'll take the Wasteland Fork."

"We'll take the *what?*" Isen's head popped out of the carriage window. "Are you insane?"

"It's the fastest route—"

"To your *father*, maybe."

"To *Lhasa*," Hiro growled.

"We're supposed to arrive in one piece. Not *pieces*."

"Why do you think I requested an armed escort?"

"Hiro," the Sanu said, "if it's as dangerous as Isen says—"

"He's overreacting, as *usual*. We take the Wasteland Fork, and you're in Lhasa in a matter of weeks and I'm home at the end of the month. *When I'm supposed to be.* We take any other route and we'll add unnecessary weeks to our trip. And what for? To assuage the doubts of a cowardly priest?"

"That unfounded remark aside, I still don't see why we can't just cut east and take the Shogun Pass into Jianshu and then head south-"

"*No.*" Nothing could make him go to the Xinjiang Plains.

Isen snorted in disgust, pulled his head back through the window.

Hiro clapped his hands. "Alright, everybody *in*. We've wasted enough time."

The Sanu waited for Kale to scramble into the seat next to Isen before blocking the carriage door with her arm. "Isen is not a coward." Her mouth was set in a thin line, her brow furrowed over her eyes. "He is the most honorable one among us. I'd appreciate if you didn't foist your own shortcomings on him. And I think you should ride your horse. You know how she gets when she hasn't been ridden in a while. Besides, there's no room in here for both you *and* your ego."

She stepped into the carriage, latched the door behind her. The priestess even went so far as to close the shutters. She thumped her fist against the wall with a stout, "Drive on!"

Hiro's left eye twitched as the carriage rumbled down the southeast road. Hissing, he swung up into the mare's saddle and followed in its dusty wake.

THE WASTELAND FORK WAS A ROUGH, less-traveled road that cut through the heart of the Pirsan Province. An endless expanse of bleached rock and scrub beaten down by the wind. There were no signs of life, no insects, not even the wayward lizard.

Hiro hunched over in the saddle, drew up the hood of his greatcoat to shade his eyes. No doubt Little Miss Sanctimonious wore a smirk at her perceived victory.

He was used to the sun and sand.

Half Pirsan on her mother's side, Ellaria often went to visit her mother's family in Herat. Hiro'd gone a few times, learned in their fields how to ride bareback like the Bédu, the last to formally petition for their blessing.

He returned to Jianshu feeling like a king. Ellaria Matsu sat opposite him in the dark green of her House, her chestnut hair done up in the geisha style with golden hairpins. Shy. Happy. Like him.

The carriage rolled down the streets of Arashiyama as its citizens waved bamboo branches in celebration of their engagement. Cherry blossom trees filled the air with pink petals. Under their floral branches, his mother gifted him the tanto knife, inscribed with *Protect Always* in her own hand. Six months later, his mother was dead and he was banished to the Academy. Eleven years passed, and Ellaria ran off with another man.

A caw wrenched him from his thoughts.

Wild, he scanned the brush and the barren rocks beyond. The dust kicked up by the carriage's passage obscured almost everything in a beige haze. He rode off the road, upwind of the dust cloud.

There.

A blot of black and white among the scrub. A magpie.

Hiro huffed a sigh, put his heel to his warhorse. Every birdcall, whether a gull over the water or the gabbering of a magpie, reminded him that he'd killed only one blackbird. The sorcerer was still alive.

Still hunting the priestess.

CHAPTER 43

On the fourth night in the wasteland, they were attacked.

Hiro was under the carriage keeping watch, plunged his greatsword up into the bandit's gut. The scream as his entrails gushed in bloody coils onto the dirt woke the rest of the camp.

He rolled out from under the carriage, sprang to his feet. Another half dozen men scurried about in the dark. Jackals, harrying their heels. Hiro thumped his fist against the door. *"Kale. The horses."*

The boy darted out of the carriage like a shadow.

Someone lit a firebrand to the ground; the scrub erupted into a blaze of red and yellow.

Hiro retreated from the sudden bloom of light, shielded his face from the heat. His burned hand twitched in phantom pain.

The carriage horses screamed; hooves trampled the sky. The driver fumbled at the harness of the horse nearest him, got kicked in the chest for his trouble. Beside him, the woman with the crossbow loosed a bolt into the smoke. It churned from the arrow's passage, swirled into the spectral faces of the dead. He hadn't protected them. They screamed in fury, lunged with silver claws.

Hiro blinked numbly, caught the glint of a knife slicing through the gloom. He pivoted. The edge caught his shoulder, bit deep enough to sting. Hiro caught the hand, rammed his greatsword into the bandit's chest. Pushed hard against the bone. He braced a foot against the body and wrenched the steel free.

He shook his head to clear it, and the smoke became faceless once again. He still heard their cries, their pleas, their—

A shriek by the carriage.

A man had the Sanu by the hair, dragging her away. The priest was still in the carriage, whacking around with his staff as he searched for a way out. He stumbled free; Hiro shoved him aside and ran after the priestess.

She had her hands clamped over her scalp, tried to keep the man from pulling her hair out from its roots.

Hiro lunged. His greatsword sliced through hand and hair with a *snick*.

Long strands glinted like threads of honey as they fluttered away in the wind.

The Sanu stumbled forward, suddenly free.

With a wet thud, the severed hand fell to the ground. Hiro stabbed the man through the throat, smothering his mutilated cry.

But the cry turned into a scream.

It was the Sanu, her hands cradling her shorn hair. When once it had brushed against her knees, its ragged edges now swayed by her waist.

"Did I cut you?"

She just kept screaming, her eyes white and wide.

It was attracting attention now. Hiro snatched her hand – she tried to rip away from him – and hauled her over to Isen. The priest gently pushed her behind him, tilted his head in that birdlike way of his. Hiro scrambled on top of the carriage to salvage their gear.

Isen swung his staff, split open a man's head like a melon. Another rushed him, but the blind priest just listened. Ignored the sounds of the encroaching inferno, the creaking of Hiro jostling the luggage, the cries as men were stabbed. Found the harsh breath of the man running at him and put him into the ground with the other.

It had to be the uncanny hearing. No one had intuition like that. No one but Kale—

The carriage shifted under his feet as a wheel collapsed with a shower of sparks.

Hiro yanked his bow and quiver free – paused to skewer a fleeing bandit through the back – and threw down the rest of their packs before the smoke forced him away.

"Get upwind of it," he shouted.

They searched for a hole in the raging fire, somewhere where the scrub was thin. Hiro ripped off his greatcoat and slapped at the ground, created a gap in the flames for just for a moment. He shoved Isen through, then the Sanu, and followed last. He had no idea where Kale was, and the last time he'd seen their escort, they were slumped in odd heaps upon the ground. Dead.

They did not stop until they were on top of a slope and able to see the path of the spreading fire. It illuminated the night with a fearsome glow, churned smoke into the cloudless sky. At the center of the blaze, their carriage and all of its supplies burned even brighter. There were a few loud *pops* followed by long hisses as the barrels of water exploded from the heat.

Hiro whistled shrilly, paused to listen. He whistled again, louder, and his warhorse thundered up the rise. Her nostrils flared as her great chest heaved, dark gold with sweat. "Good girl." He rubbed her neck before tightening her girth and gathering the reins. In one fluid motion he swung himself into the saddle.

"Where are you going?" Isen demanded.

"Stay upwind of the fire," he said. "I will return."

"What about Kale?" the Sanu sputtered.

Hiro swallowed a hard lump in his throat. "The boy's smart. He would've gotten clear. Call to him, and he will find you."

Isen shook his head violently. "Hiro, *no*—"

But he turned his horse to the north and put his heels to her.

HIRO FOUND them at first light, a small camp of no more than ten. Some were burned from last night, and one had a small, black tattoo of a rampant lion on his left hand. He had died last and very slowly, blubbering *"Via Leao"* like a prayer as his blood gushed out of a dozen cuts.

He left as quickly as he'd come, squinted his eyes against the grit kicked up by the wind. The smoke was still trickling into the air from the smoldering scrub, the fire not yet extinguished. The swath of the conflagration stretched from one horizon to the other.

The Sanu and the others were nowhere in sight.

Hiro slowed his mare to a halt on top of the nearest rise. Her sides heaved with exhaustion and heat, her tacky lips fumbled around the bit.

Nothing.

Shading his eyes with a hand, he scanned in all directions. Heat rose from the rocks in sinuous waves, and the lonesome cry of a desert hawk echoed uninterrupted for miles. Hiro tightened his grip on the reins, urged his horse east.

They would've headed east. Northeast possibly, farther into the wasteland but away from the fire. Its desolation was still too hot to approach. The thicker roots hidden by the parched ground were glowing coals, and collectively they baked the rocks like one great oven.

He crested another slope and another. Panic threatened him with an icy caress down the back of his neck.

The sun reached its zenith, lowered to the western horizon, and still no sight of them. Twilight lingered out here in the wasteland, a smear of color speckled with the brightest stars. The last sliver of orange sun winked behind him, reflected on a flash of color to his left.

It was the Sanu's orange sari fluttering in the wind, a flare against the darkening sky. She had her arm outstretched like a flag pole, and the breeze pulled the yards of fabric high into the air. Kale was with them, led a carriage horse by its severed reins.

Hiro spurred his mare forward with a shout.

He threw himself out of the saddle and gathered the boy into his arms. "You are so brave."

Kale hugged him tight around the neck.

When he set the boy down, he saw tears in his hazel eyes. He found his own eyes damp. Blinked quickly. "None of that." He tousled the boy's auburn mane. "It's alright now."

He ventured a glance at the others.

Isen's mouth was set in a pursed line; the Sanu busily rewrapped the sari around her waist. The ragged ends of her hair swirled about her face, too short now to be twisted and coiled around her arm.

He raked a hand through his hair. "I'm glad you're all okay. What you did with the sari was brilliant, Sanu."

"Yeah! It's how I found them," Kale said. "Can't hear anything over that wind, you know?"

"It was Isen's idea." She hoisted her pack onto her shoulders, still looking at anywhere but him.

"Well *someone* had to make sure this group stayed together."

"I know you're upset, but I had to go after them—"

"And what if they come back?" Isen said. "If you've gone and stirred up a hornets' nest and they come back, we don't have any means of outrunning them!"

"There aren't any *to* come back," Hiro said flatly.

The priest swallowed. "Oh."

"Their camp had little, but I reclaimed our money and whatever we could use." He gestured to the packs burdening his warhorse. "Some food and water. Some wine."

"I think we all could use a drink," Isen said.

"Sparingly, and only the wine. The water is for the horses. They'll determine whether we live or die."

He watered the horses much less than they would've liked as Isen passed the wineskin around. Kale went straight for the food; there was only dried meat, possibly wild hare, and the Sanu passed with a tight smile.

"I'll wait," she said. "Surely we're not too far from the other side."

It's what they all hoped. It took a week to cross the wastelands, and yesterday had been their fourth day. The fire had driven them drastically off course; there was no way to tell how far yet they had to go.

Without the trail, any direction would be a death sentence. There was no food or water to be had, at least none they could spend time searching for. And without the carriage, they were all at risk of exposure.

"Everyone rest," Hiro said. "Just for a few hours. We travel at night from now on and sleep during the day. We'll head southeast for the border."

Kale hobbled the horses and retreated to the patchy shade of a clump of wormwood. The boy was asleep, mouth open and snoring lightly, in a heartbeat.

Hiro stretched out in his own patch of miserly shade as the Sanu took the first watch.

Eerily silent, she sat with her knees drawn up to her chest and watched the stretch of smoldering wasteland. She toyed a lock of shortened hair between her fingers, her ocean-blue eyes distant.

When he woke a few hours later, she was curled into a ball on her side, away from him. The boy was nestled against her back like a kitten. Isen was keeping watch, face into the wind to ferret out any threats by smell and sound.

"How long has she been asleep?" Hiro draped his greatcoat over the Sanu and the boy. It was big enough to cover them both.

"Just a little while."

There was a heavy silence.

"You can't do that again," the priest said.

"Do what?"

"Run off. Even if it's to pursue a threat. You lead and protect this group. If you go, we have nothing. Kale is a boy, and Amelia… Amelia shouldn't have to know how cruel this world can be. Well, how much crueler, anyway. And I can only do so much."

"You seemed proficient with that staff."

"I wasn't born a priest," he replied. "But not having my sight severely reduces what I can contribute to this group. So, are we agreed? No more running off?"

"Someday you'll have to tell me about the time you weren't a priest."

A thin smile stretched across Isen's face. "Perhaps one day I will."

CHAPTER 44

THE SANU WAS DYING.

In the three days since the attack, the Sanu had had nothing but a few mouthfuls of wine a day to sustain her. She'd refused to eat her meager portions of dried meat, and her body was shutting down.

Hiro was desperate to find the forest he knew was on the opposite side of the wasteland. As of yet, there were no trees in sight. He fought to stay cognizant. The wine made his head buzz. He needed water – they all did – but the horses needed it more. They were the means by which they would finally be free of this hellish waste.

The Sanu's head rolled back, knocked into his shoulder.

"That's *it.*" He yanked his horse to a halt. He pulled the priestess out of the saddle and into the scrub, pillowed her head with his great-coat. "Sanu. *Sanu.*" He gave her cheek a light smack.

Her ocean-blue eyes snapped open for a moment before rolling back into her head.

"Get me some food and water," he barked to no one in particular.

Someone stuffed a piece of jerky into his hand.

He slapped the Sanu awake again, held the meat under her nose. "You're going to eat this."

She gathered enough strength to lift her hand and push the jerky aside. "No meat," she rasped.

"*Damn* it, Sanu," Hiro shouted. "If you don't eat this, you'll *die*."

Kale dropped to his knees beside her head, started to cry. He stroked her hair as no tears fell from his red eyes. He was too dehydrated, just like the rest of them. The Sanu's hair had lost its lustrous shine, her face was pinched, her lips blanched and cracked. No longer soft as satin pillows.

"Amelia, you *must* eat," Isen said. "Who else will bless the Gate?"

The Sanu's eyes fluttered but did not open.

"Bring me a bowl," Hiro snapped. He tore the jerky into bits, added some precious water, and ground it into a thin paste.

Isen knelt in the scrub, grasped the priestess's shoulders. He gave her a shake. "If you don't eat, you cannot perform Yueshu. The cycle will be broken and the Gate will crumble. The *apocalypse*, Amelia. All mortals on this side of Heaven will be condemned."

The Sanu's eyes flew opened, panicked.

"Could you do that to someone like Kale?"

She barely shook her head.

"Then eat this," Hiro said. "*All* of it." He put the lip of the bowl to her mouth, forced her to drink.

The Sanu gagged, but he clamped his hand over her mouth until it subsided. She choked down the rest, and Hiro got her back on the horse.

They rode hard until dawn. When they stopped to rest, he forced another bowl of paste down her throat before letting her sleep. They'd been using the yards of her orange sari to construct a tent, pitched with Isen's staff and some rope from the saddlebags. The gold from the beaded fringe cast a sallow glow upon her face.

Hiro watched over her the entire time, frantic. If she died, he wouldn't know what to do with himself. This foolishness had gone on far longer than it should have. He should've made her eat much sooner than this.

Running his hands through his hair, he paced like a caged beast. He checked her pulse again. When the sun was high in the sky, he finally succumbed to a fitful sleep. The others took the watches, but there was nothing in the wasteland except them.

At sundown they mounted the horses and continued east. Hiro was convinced they'd traveled far enough south to make the decision to head due east a sound one. Isen and Kale had enough sense to keep their mouths shut even if they didn't agree with him. It had been *his* decision to take the Wasteland Fork, a route that only worked with a heavily supplied carriage or a caravan. Right now they had neither.

He wanted to reach Jianshu as quickly as possible, and his haste had brought them this disaster. The Sanu was dying because of *him*. Isen and Kale were starving because of *him*. They were desperate for water. He'd have to slaughter the carriage horse—

His mare stumbled, pitched her riders forward. Hiro grabbed the saddle horn in one fist and gripped the limp Sanu with the other. He dismounted, checked the mare's hooves. She seemed fine – dehydrated, exhausted, blood trickling from one nostril – the new norm. He searched around for what had caused her to stumble.

A black mass, not more than a few feet tall, leaned to one side out of the cracked earth behind them. The weak moonlight provided little help in identifying it, so he put a hand down and felt around. It rasped against his fingers.

He gasped, touched some more. Let out a weak whoop.

"What is it?" Isen asked. His voice was hoarse with thirst.

"It's a sapling."

"You're sure?"

"Here." Hiro yanked the tree free, thrust it into his face.

The priest's hands roamed over the branches. "Praise the gods."

Hiro swung up into the saddle, encircled the priestess with his arm. She was so skinny. "Hold on, Sanu," he pleaded softly.

They entered the forest at dawn, just as the sky opened up with a deluge. For the first time in over a decade, Hiro praised the Most Holies for their deliverance.

CHAPTER 45

AMELIA RECLINED ON A MOUND OF PILLOWS, SHADED FROM THE SUN BY A carved screen. Sunlight dappled in a pattern across her legs. She was secluded in one corner of the outer garden, present enough to hear the trickling fountain and smell the occasional perfume of the jasmine flowers, but removed enough to have some privacy as she recovered.

The last few days were a haze of disjointed memories: breaking free of the Pirsan Waste, the cotton and tobacco fields outside Janpur, the bazaar with its pungent spices and loud noises, finding refuge in this villa. Their host was currently out of town but would be returning any day. Beside her on a low table were an empty cup and a clay pitcher of goat's milk. She strained forward, her fingertips rattling the pitcher against the mosaic tabletop.

A shadow passed on the other side of the screen and came into view. Hiro crouched beside the table and filled the cup. He lifted it to her lips.

"I can manage," she said icily.

"You can *manage* to dribble it all down your clothes."

She turned her head away. "I'm not hungry."

Hiro leaned back on his heels, taking the cup with him. "We can both hear your stomach growling. Do you want some of that flatbread instead? The nâni?"

"I *want* you to go away."

The prince set the cup on the table with a clatter. Milk sluiced over the sides and pooled in the cracks between the tiles. "Damn it, Sanu, I couldn't let you die. I *had* to."

Her eyes flashed. "Do you know what you've done? I am *Sanu*. My body is supposed to be a pure vessel for Yueshu. I'm the last, remember? And you fed me *meat!*"

"Nowhere in the sacred texts does it say a Sanu cannot eat meat," he fired back. "That is a tradition, nothing more. But it does say '*do not call unclean what I have made clean.*' If it makes you feel any better, you protested as much as you were able. I had to force it down your throat."

Amelia grabbed a handful of her shorn hair and shook it at him. "*This* was my last show of faith! And you've *kissed* me. I'm supposed to be chaste and now you've gone and stirred up… *feelings.* How much more can you take away from me?"

She was crying now. She wanted to rage, wanted to hurl herself against him and throw her fists into his chest. But she was still too weak to get up other than to relieve herself.

His mouth had burned an imprint on her lips that would not be scrubbed away. The kiss lingered in the background of her mind, always present but never fully focused, like a fly buzzing about her head. That it affected her so made her angrier than the actual kiss.

Amelia took a deep breath and squeezed the tears from her eyes. Roiling inside her was the silver flame, eager for retribution. If she lost control, he'd know. He'd kill her. How she ever thought he could deserve a second chance—

"You were supposed to protect me." The words were a whisper. Hot, and full of pain. "Get. Out."

He didn't move, and she couldn't make him. His face was an impassive slate, his seal-brown eyes glittering with something unsaid.

"You heard her." The voice was as cold as frostbite. Isen stood behind him, staff clenched in one fist. He held a platter in his other hand, the knuckles white with tension. The priest bent, slid the platter onto the table, and straightened into a menacing stance. "Get out," he repeated.

The prince left without another word. Only when his shadow had passed beyond her screen did she look at the priest.

Isen knelt down on a pillow, fingertips fluttering over the platter. "Mango, dates, boiled eggs, and cheese curds. Everything an emaciated priestess needs. Some of that seeded flatbread too." His fingers found some and tore off a hunk. "It's time you started eating something more than milk and honey."

"Thank you." She picked at the fruit and curds with marginal interest. "When does your friend return?"

"Tonight. He sent an eagle this morning while you were sleeping. But I'll leave you to eat." He stood, rolling his shoulders. "I'm going to have a word with our prince."

"No fighting."

"If I had eyes, I'd roll them." He shook his head instead. "With you... I get protective. But I promise. Enjoy your meal, sweet girl."

No sooner did he leave than Kale's mane of auburn curls peek around the screen.

Amelia swallowed a mouthful of mango and looked at the boy warily. He had appeared too conveniently. "If you're here to plead your master's case—"

"Yes." The boy sat down directly in front of her. "And no."

She knew he was serious when he didn't even so much as glance at the food.

"Kale," she sighed, "I'm not in the mood—"

"Then just listen. You have panic attacks. And they're starting to affect the group."

She opened her mouth to protest.

"It's true. You know it is. When you freeze up, someone else has to intervene. And it's usually Hiro. First with the demon, then with the wildfire in the wastelands. I know he told you about his blooding. He doesn't know I know about it. Do you have any idea what it takes for him to overcome his own fear to help you?"

Amelia shut her mouth and shook her head.

"He hides it. He can't ever be seen as weak. In those moments, he only focuses on one thing: *survival*."

"But the means to that end matter, Kale. What's the point of surviving if you've destroyed yourself – and others – in the process?"

"I didn't say it was right. I just wanted you to understand. He doesn't mean to hurt you. Or... us." The boy's eyes dropped to his hands. They had bunched the hem of his gi into fistfuls of wrinkles. He smoothed them out briskly. When he looked up again, his hazel eyes were intent. "What are you afraid of, anyway? I've seen you. You... hesitate. As if you *could* do something but are afraid to."

"I-I don't know what you're talking about." Amelia winced as her tattoo flared with pain. "I'm Sanu. What could I possibly do in that kind of situation?"

"You could not freeze up."

Amelia's eyes narrowed. She'd never been angry with the boy before, but there was always a first time. "You think I do it on purpose?"

"I think you're holding something back. And it's time to set it free." The boy stood and held out his hand.

Amelia groaned as Kale helped her to her feet.

"It's called taiji. Brother Leiji – the Academy's priest – taught me. It's a type of meditation. It allows your inner energy – your taijitu – to balance. He says it's like having two koi fish in a pond. When they're on their own, just swimming about, the pool is choppy with all these random currents. But when the fish come together and circle, the pond smooths out and makes one harmonizing current. This whirlpool protects the fish, renews the water, and creates focus."

"You should teach it to Hiro," she grumbled.

"Hiro doesn't have panic attacks."

The boy led her out from behind the screen into the sunlight. Amelia squinted and turned away, seeking the refuge of the shade.

"Nuh-uh." Kale grabbed her hand and sat her down in the sun. "Just keep your eyes closed. I'll guide you through it."

Amelia folded her legs under her in the lotus position, clasping her hands loosely in her lap. "I *have* meditated before, you know."

"For spiritual connection, not for inner balance. Instead of pushing your thoughts outward, look inward. For now, just feel the sun on your face and listen to the fountain. When these fade away, you know you're there."

She opened one eye. "You sound unusually wi—"

"No peeking."

Amelia shut her eye and focused on the heat of the sun. It was almost too hot; she could feel sweat starting to itch in her hairline. She turned her focus to the fountain instead, enjoying the gurgling sound of its water. It reminded her of her swim in the Rhine, fully submerged for the first time. That feeling of weightlessness, the cool embrace of the water. Joy. It had felt like coming home.

Inside, the flame burst into a blaze of silver light. Heat flooded through every vein, down to her fingers and out every strand of her hair. There was no stopping it now. Whatever dam had kept it contained ruptured, and the flame lengthened into a serpentine form with a roar. The sound reberverated in her bones, chiming like a chorus of bells, deep and ancient. No longer smothered, no longer choked into an ember, it wiggled like a cat enjoying its first sunbath after a long winter.

"Amelia."

The silver dragon burned even brighter at the sound of his voice. It stretched wings of silver light and tossed its head, flicking the long whiskers of its muzzle to swirl about its spiraling horns. Strength poured into her limbs.

When she opened her eyes, the boy was looking at her strangely.

"What?"

"You're glowing."

She looked down at her hands, panicked.

"Not there. *There.*" Kale pointed to her chest.

Amelia clamped a hand over her tattoo and rushed behind her screen.

The boy followed on her heels, hazel eyes bright with wonder.

"How are you walking without hobbling right now? And what's with that gl—"

She smooshed a hand against his mouth. *"Shh."*

He nodded earnestly, mouth still pressed against her palm.

She took her hand away and gently pulled her collar down. The lily tattoo blazed like a small sun on her chest. The light slowly dimmed until only the golden mark remained.

"Bosetsanu's Chosen," he whispered. "Has it ever done that before?"

"No. What did you do to me?"

"I *told* you taijitu would balance your inner energy. Only trauma will close the pathway now. And then it's almost impossible to—"

Amelia let out an exasperated sigh. "Well I can't very well have it glowing at random."

"It's already stopped." Kale reached forward and tentatively placed a fingertip on her tattoo. His touch was warm, and the silver dragon strained toward him. Her tattoo began to glow again.

Amelia pulled away, smoothing her tunic back into place. The glow snuffed out, and she gave the boy a wary look. "Who are you?"

Kale cocked his head to the side like a cat examining something of enormous curiosity. "I was going to ask you the same thing."

CHAPTER 46

THE BOY SPRANG TO HIS FEET AS A COMMOTION SOUNDED BY THE garden gate.

"… in the garden like some common *beggar*," a man was shouting. He threw his bow and quiver into the arms of a startled servant. Green-fletched arrows clattered to the ground. "He should've been admitted into the inner villa *at once*. Where is Faruk? Get that gazelle to the kitchen immediately. And let Camila know I've returned."

Amelia peeked around the screen.

Their host was middle-aged and olive-skinned with a close-cropped head of hair and a pointed beard, not unlike almost every Pirsan man she'd seen thus far. A scar over his left eye marred his otherwise handsome face. An emerald-green sash encircled his trim waist, and the broad shoulders beneath the white Bédu robe bulged with tension.

After he finished berating the steward Faruk, he rushed over to Isen and yanked him into a familiar embrace. He planted a brief kiss on Isen's cheek and took a half-step back, still holding onto the priest's hand. "*Takrim* Isen. Please, let me welcome you to my home properly."

"Thank you, Tareq, but I have others with me. Amelia? Kale? I don't know where H-"

"My lady." Tareq bowed low as she emerged from behind the screen. Kale held onto her hand. Hard. "You must forgive my staff for your inhospitable treatment. They might be familiar with every *zaeim* in the province, but the Sanctisum clergy are a bit foreign to them. After all, your kind only leaves your mountaintop once every hundred years."

Tareq's smiled a smile as full of charm as it was of white teeth and held out his hand. Amelia kept her arms at her sides. The hand in the fingerless gloves of golden cloth waited patiently.

"Your gloves..." she said.

"Every *zaeim* wears them. A symbol of our status. That we don't perform manual labor. Domo Tareq Imal Sharif, Mayor of Janpur, and your host for as long as you'd like."

Amelia glanced at Isen. He leaned against his staff, perfectly at ease. Swallowing, she put her hand into Tareq's. His thumb curled over her fingers as he lifted her hand to his lips.

The silver dragon bristled, snarling. She yanked her hand away as silver fire sparked from her fingertips. Amelia thrust her hand behind her back, squeezing it into a fist. *Not now.*

The mayor blinked kohl-rimmed eyes, startled.

"Amelia de Taru, Sanu Maitre. I-I'm so sorry. Sanu aren't normally so... familiar. You surprised me."

"My apologies. We Pirsans can seem too forward to foreigners."

She nodded, rubbing her hand where he had kissed it.

He turned to the boy. "And who's this young man? A gaze like a lion."

Isen approached and slid his arm around the boy's shoulders. "This is Kale. He's—"

"... said *get off me.*"

They turned to the garden gate to see Hiro shrug off the offending touch. Men in red Bédu robes with golden sashes herded him forward, one of them covering a bruised eye with a hand. Every one of the Pirsan men had his weapon bared.

"What's this?" Tareq asked in Sarabi.

"We found him in the stables, zaeim."

"Then cut off his hands and balls like you would any other horse thief—"

"No!" she cried.

The Mayor of Janpur raised his eyebrows in surprise. "My lady?"

"I am a guest," Hiro slapped the sword aside of someone who got too close. "A friend. *Sadiq*, get it?"

"Please," Amelia said. "He's with us."

"Your bodyguard, then? Doesn't look Militum Dei to me." Tareq jerked his chin with a *tsk*. The men in the red Bédu robes backed off a few paces but didn't sheath their weapons. "Not a very good one. I didn't want to say anything, but your hair... isn't it supposed to be much longer than that?"

"Yes," she said. "I was *attacked*."

Hiro snorted. "That's a rather extreme—"

"And this strong fellow here did not protect you?"

Amelia looked Hiro in the eye for the first time in days. "Evidently not."

Hiro's gaze hardened.

"Well," Tareq scoffed, "what's the use of hiring a guard if he doesn't do his job?"

"I haven't the faintest idea."

"I must apologize for my earlier haste. We Pirsans treasure our Sarabi horses. Rest assured anyone that would try to harm you while you're under my roof will suffer a greater misfortune," the mayor of Janpur assured. "My guards are completely competent and attentive. You see them in those red robes? Only the most elite of my guards are fit to wear that color." He turned to Hiro with a sniff. "You, guard, feel free to train with them. Maybe you'll learn how better to protect your mistress. What's your name again?"

Isen winced. "This is Prince Hiro Ishida."

"Ishida." The name rolled off Tareq's tongue like something sour. He didn't bow. "So, not a guard after all."

Hiro's lip curled into a snarl.

"You are all welcome here," the mayor said, addressing the group.

"Please, let's retire to the terrace. I'll have dinner prepared straight-away."

"Thank you," Amelia said.

"Think nothing of it. Now *takrim*, come here and tell me of all your adventures since I saw you last. Politeness demands I wait for you to tell me, but since we are such good friends, surely you'll forgive me as I ask about your eyes. What *happened?*"

The mayor swept them under the archway into the inner villa, leaving Hiro to follow as if he was only a servant instead of a prince.

HIRO LEFT the priestess and the rest of them to chatter in Sarabi – he'd been ostracized enough and had no ear for the language – and found a secluded fountain in this inner sanctuary to defile by washing himself in it. He needed to repay the kindness of his host, after all. Shucking his gi, he splashed water onto his chest and arms. Screened the foliage from the corners of his eyes.

Movement.

Behind the acacia tree.

Hiro snatched up his jacket. Slung it over his shoulder and continued his walk in that direction.

His stalker stepped out of the shadows, blocked his path. Pirsan, red Bédu robe, piercing eyes. No older than twenty.

"You're in my way," Hiro said.

The young man started jabbering in Sarabi, but Hiro shook his head, not understanding. The Pirsan pointed a finger, directed Hiro back the way he had come.

"I want to go *this* way."

The young man shook his head vehemently, crossed his arms over his chest.

Why would a garden trail be off-limits? Hiro took a step forward. "Move aside, or—"

The Pirsan punched him.

It was not a lucky shot; it was a well-placed strike from someone who knew what he was doing.

Hiro spat the blood from his mouth.

He backed out of the brush, forced his opponent to follow him into the open. The Pirsan ran at him, feinted a head strike only to drop down and jab his fist into Hiro's gut. He blocked the swing to his head with his forearm, stumbled back with a wheezing cough. The Pirsan rammed his knee into his face, and blood squirted over his lips.

The Pirsan laughed, threw his last punch at Hiro's jaw.

Hiro whipped the jacket off his shoulder, caught the punch in the fabric. He twisted the sleeves around the Pirsan's arm and pivoted. The Pirsan's fist crushed against his own windpipe. Hiro kept his jacket taut, waited for the struggling to cease. The young man flailed, thrashed, but Hiro was stronger, heavier.

The Pirsan slumped against him. Hiro waited another heartbeat more, then untangled his jacket and dressed. He returned to the fountain and cleaned the blood from his face. His nose wasn't broken. Worth it.

He pressed forward into the forbidden garden. Brightly colored birds flittered in the branches, quick lizards scuttled underfoot. Heavily shaded by date palms, the humid air made him sweat again. He pushed farther in, past the bromeliads, and the perfume of jasmine almost floored him.

That scent was irrevocably tied to the Sanu. He thought of her hair, its jagged edges, the proud lift of her head, her eyes. They were the same ocean blue, no longer warm as the summer waves, but cool as the winter deep. Obliviously happy and preachy he could deal with, sullen he could not. Not from her.

He slapped aside a frond, tore it free of its trunk without meaning to. Just when he was good and lost, the pale yellow of the perimeter wall peeked through the foliage. He traipsed through the undergrowth, pressed his hand against the wall. A narrow trail ran along its length where the gardeners had kept the ground clear for easier maintenance. Keeping his hand on the wall, he followed its curve toward the terrace.

A square of beige stone popped into sight just ahead. The distinction was slight, but in the otherwise flawless yellow stone, it stuck out like a pimple. The growth around the tile was just as lush, yet a path, no wider than a game trail, snaked away from the tile and into the garden.

Hiro pressed his palm against the beige square.

A faint *whoosh* of air.

The section of the wall containing the tile slid back a few feet, left just barely enough room for him to squeeze through. The wall slid back into place behind him. He was in a narrow corridor of the same yellow stone. High walls, no ceiling, a wood-and-iron door at the far end. There was a keyhole but no key; Hiro drew one of his smaller knives from his sleeve and forced his way in.

The room was the shape of a circle with bookshelves built into the entire length of its curving wall, halved by a hanging map of Eurasia. It was as large as the one in the Academy chartroom, finely detailed down to the smallest stream. Sunlight fought through the latticework windows, cut through the gloom in great crosshatches of creamy yellow.

One beam glittered on the cover of a book forgotten on the table. It was edged in silver with a clasp to keep its aged pages from bursting loose. Carefully, Hiro thumbed the latch free, flipped to the first page. He read only a few lines before he slammed it shut. It was only then he realized that the table was carved with a house crest that had been banished from every heraldic annal. One paw raised and its mouth grinning, the spotted hyena laughed silently at him.

Hiro shoved the journal into the folds of his gi.

When he was back in the garden and following the half-hidden trail, he loosened his dagger in its scabbard. He would need to draw it very soon.

CHAPTER 47

TAREQ'S HOME WAS A WEALTH OF DIVERSION. HIS ENTOURAGE BUSIED themselves on the lower terrace, racing the Saluki hounds with a rabbit lure or sitting in a ring and taking turns touching the tail of a cobra. The women of his household, their hair covered under colorful scarves, sat off to the side on a mound of cushions and strummed on lute-like instruments called ouds. Four green parrots perched in a row on the stand near Tareq's chair, bobbing in time to the music.

The servers brought platter after platter of delicious things to eat, catering to Isen first as one would do for an honored guest. All of them, including the mayor of Janpur, referred to him as *takrim* – honored one – despite him being the youngest man present.

She hadn't seen Hiro since he'd left over an hour ago, and frankly she didn't care. Her focus was on food. Whatever that taijitu lesson with Kale had unlocked, it was ravenous. She busied herself with a whole khachapuri, a boat made of bread filled with melty cheese crowned with an egg and a dollop of deep yellow butter. That was before Tareq introduced her to these little jellied fruit candies covered in powdered sugar. He smiled at her delight and called for more.

Beside her, Kale ate slowly, never once taking his eyes off his food.

"Frankly, my lady," Tareq commented, "I'm rather impressed with your knowledge of languages. Isen never got a handle on Latan, and his Sarabi needs some work. Doesn't it, *takrim*? But you, my lady, you speak Sarabi almost as well as one born to it."

"Thank you. The Sanu have high standards of education."

He nodded and smiled as if they shared a secret. "The better to create missionaries, I think."

She laughed. "So much of a culture can be gleaned from a language. Since the Great Cataclysm, all of these peoples have been forced to mesh and intermix, creating new languages, new cultures. It's absolutely fascinating."

He picked up a piece of fruit and sank his teeth into the ripe flesh. "So are you."

She noticed he was particularly careful to pick up everything with just his fingertips, lest he sully his golden gloves.

"Don't tease her," Isen said. "She has no defense against your charm, Tareq."

"I am Sanu. That is defense enough."

"But you are also a woman." Tareq leaned forward to pluck a kebab from a platter.

"A woman who knows her own mind."

"A formidable foe." The mayor's eyes twinkled. "But isn't that a contradiction? I've never known a woman to know her own mind because she changes it more frequently than the wind changes its direction."

Shocked, Amelia lobbed a date at him. The parrots screeched, flapping their wings.

"*Quiet*," Tareq snapped.

Amelia covered her mouth with her hands, eyes wide. "Domo, I'm so sorry—"

"What an elegant response." He brushed the offending fruit off his lap with a flick of his fingers. "Truly cultured and elegant. You, my lady, are a credit to your upbringing."

"Thank you." She held his somber gaze for only a moment before they both burst into a fit of laughter.

"Oh, Isen," Tareq said, grabbing his friend's hand. "Must you all go tomorrow? You have brought this delightful woman to my door and now you tease me saying she has to leave. Isen, it simply isn't *fair*."

"We would be honored to stay, but Hiro has us on a tight schedule. Where is he, anyway?"

"I'm sure the man is off sulking somewhere because I mistook him as a guard. I can't *honestly* be expected to know a prince from a pauper if he chooses to dress in such shabby clothing."

Kale stopped eating. The boiled egg in his fist popped, oozing yellow yolk over his fingers.

"It has its uses." Amelia said it for the boy, not for Hiro.

"My apologies for any offense. I know you must feel indebted to the man for keeping you safe on the road so far." He glanced at her ragged locks. "More or less. You *must* permit my barber to straighten your hair."

"That would be greatly appreciated, Domo, thank you."

"*Tareq*," he corrected her. "And you must permit me to send with you a squad of my personal guards to protect you on your journey. Lhasa is not too far, and I have plenty of staff that a half dozen will not be missed."

"Thank you, but I don't—"

"Think about it. I would see you properly tended to." He lifted the plate of jellied confections. "Try the mango one next. It's not a traditional flavor, but I'm sure you'll love it."

Amelia fumbled the piece of powdery lokum when the blast of a ram's horn punctuated the women's music. A wailing cry followed the blast, and all activity within the villa ceased. Tareq's entourage filed out of the villa, and the women discarded their instruments and left by a different door. One remained, an older woman swathed in midnight blue, an oud in her hands.

"It's sunset," Tareq said, smiling. "Time for devotions. They've gone to the *salla*, the place of prayer. Perhaps you saw the one when you arrived? It's a red dome with a single long spire?"

She shook her head. "I was unconscious for most of that time."

Tareq nodded. "Of course. Forgive me for dredging up such unpleasant memories."

Isen stood. "Do you need to go, or should we...?"

"Sit, *takrim*. I don't go to the *sallas*. My devotions are here."

As if on cue, a woman appeared. She was about forty, curvy with charcoal-colored skin scantily clad in lilac gauze. Gold henna dotted and swirled on her arms and legs, and a heavy gold torque encircled her throat. Tiny bells jingled at her ankles and wrists.

"Ah, Camila." The warmth in his voice sent a shiver down Amelia's spine. It was so intimate that she flushed, embarrassed she'd overheard him.

The woman bowed. On the lower terrace, the older woman with the oud began to play. Camila danced, her thick black hair swirling like the coming night. Her dance was sinuous and unrefined, tugging at a primal instinct long since forgotten. Amelia stared at the woman, unable to look away. Something red, a garnet the size of a walnut, flashed between her breasts.

"Nothing is more divine than a beautiful woman dancing," Tareq murmured. "It's ethereal. No amount of prayer could lift me up as watching her. *Takrim* Isen, if only you had eyes to see."

"I see enough."

The oud's melody trailed off into the night, and the woman's bells became silent.

Tareq extended his hand. The dancer placed her hand in his, her dark face impassive as he kissed her knuckles. Something glinted in her eyes. "Ah, that was wonderful, Camila. Thank you."

The woman bowed and retreated back to wherever she had come from. Amelia heard the bang of a distant door being closed.

She started, the hushed atmosphere suddenly gone. "Your... wife?"

"Camila is my companion. I snatched her up from the slave market when she was only twelve. Beautiful then, stunning now. I'll make her my wife when I finally settle."

"*Slave* market?"

The mayor slouched in his seat, content. "They're abolished now, my lady. When Camila came of age, I released her from my household, but she stayed to dance for me. Wonderful woman. She lulls me into such a calm that not even the apocalypse could disturb."

"I'd like to try." Hiro took the stairs from the lower terrace three at a time.

The mayor squinted, looking for something behind the prince. "Where is Pudi?"

"Your *spy* is taking a nap."

Tareq cleared his throat and shifted in his seat. "Pudi is *khadim*, a servant. He was sent after you to assist you with whatever you needed."

"*Itoko*," Hiro spat. Amelia's eyes widened at the profanity. "Your *servant* attacked me. What sort of man allows his servants to attack his guests?"

"Hiro," Isen said sharply. "This man is our host."

"This *man*," he spat, "is not who he says he is. He is Tareq Imal *Nadir*, loyal supporter of Kogusanji. Sharif is his mother's maiden name."

Tareq remained seated, but his knife was suddenly in his hands. Its ivory hilt was studded with jewels the size of mustard seeds, winking as Tareq twirled the point against his fingertip.

Amelia glanced at Isen; his mouth was set in a grim line, the knuckles on his hands gripping the edge of the table were stark white.

"Technically I am Tareq Imal Nadir the Second," the mayor clarified. "The Nadir you speak of was my father."

"*Your* prowess upon the battlefield is well recorded. Your passion for torturing your adversaries was so renowned that even Kogusanji mentioned it here in his personal journal." Hiro threw the book onto the table, scattering the dishes. "You were his prodigy!"

The green parrots flapped from their perch, screaming.

"Where did you find that?" Tareq hissed.

"You know where. I saw that map too, the one where your father and the Tybetan Monster planned their attacks."

"And they would have succeeded, had it not been for that troublesome bitch you call your *mother*."

Hiro drew his dagger.

Tareq jumped to his feet.

"*Tareq.*" Isen's voice was gravely quiet. "You will put that knife down. *Immediately.*"

The mayor of Janpur slowly set his knife on the table.

"Hiro, you will refrain from attacking our host," Isen ordered. "We cannot hold him responsible for the crimes he committed under coercion from his father."

"He was with Kogusanji for *years.* That journal states—"

"*That* journal contains the ravings of a lunatic." Isen waved his concern aside. "We all know the Tybetan Monster was charismatic, deceptive, powerful. There was not a man who could stand before him and not be persuaded to join his cause. Tareq was a *boy* who was no less than brainwashed."

"Who are *you* to defend him?"

"He showed me a better path," Tareq fired back.

"What does *that* mean?"

"It's not really any of your business, is it?" Isen cocked his head in that birdlike way of his. "Let it suffice to say that the Council punished him severely, and now he uses his mother's name to move on with his life.

"Tareq has improved education, not just in Janpur, but all across Pirsa; he's even the one who created the Hadi Centers to provide for the war orphans. He works to unite the Bédu tribes and end the blood-feuds. To judge the man he is by the boy he was would be a grave mistake."

"Kogusanji molded him into the man he is today, and he just hides behind his mother's name," Hiro snarled. "That room back there in the garden is nothing less than a *shrine* dedicated to the Tybetan Monster. He cannot be trusted."

"*Enough,*" Isen roared. "He has answered for his crimes, and to accuse him again of the same is an affront to the Council's ruling, which, by the way, was presided over by *your* father." The furious priest turned to the mayor. "And *you,* Tareq, will apologize for that rude remark about Hiro's mother. General Bethsaida bravely did her duty and deserves your respect."

The mayor bowed his head. "Yes, *takrim*. Prince Ishida, I apologize for calling your mother a troublesome bitch."

Amelia was not entirely sure she believed him, and clearly Hiro did not.

"This is absurd—"

"You know where the door is," Tareq said.

"We're leaving," Hiro told them.

Isen slapped his hands on the table. "I'm staying."

Hiro turned to her, his hand outstretched. "Sanu."

Amelia looked at his gloved hand and then into his seal-brown eyes. He wasn't asking permission. It was an order, not a request. She rose from her chair and moved around to the opposite side of the table. She held onto the back of Isen's chair, anchoring herself for the inevitable confrontation. "I'm staying."

"What?"

"Isen's right. And I'm not leaving without him."

"What do you even *need* him for?"

"Yueshu is a partnership, Hiro. I'm staying with Isen."

"Sanu, I cannot stay here—"

"Then go."

He blinked, the anger in his face replaced by shock.

"You heard Tareq, you know where the door is." She gestured to the archway. "Sanctisum teaches us to forgive. Without it we cannot hope to break the cycle of rebirth. Tareq is clearly on a better path and is using his life for good instead of evil. He should be praised for his perseverance, not dragged through the mud of his past."

"Sanu, this man is a *snake*. Now is not the time to be spouting that religious nonsense—"

Isen snorted.

"'Nonsense?'" Amelia hissed. "*That* is the doctrine that guides my life. If you think these beliefs are nonsense then clearly you cannot think much of the person who holds them. Thank you for clarifying your position on the matter. I had no idea I was such an *idiot*. Please, let me trouble you with my idiocy no longer. Tareq has offered us a guard detail to get us to Lhasa. I thank you for your assistance in getting us this far, but I believe it's time for us to part ways."

"Sanu, he tortured people."

"Was he any different than you were at Biscay Bay?"

He staggered back a step as if struck, then his eyes sharpened to spear points. "I never *tortured* anyone."

She looked away. "I'm staying."

"Amelia, *no*." Kale grabbed her hand. "You can't. Please."

She combed her fingers through his auburn mane. "Thank you for everything, Kale. You truly are a remarkable boy. But you need to go with Hiro. I will see you again."

The boy fought against his tears. "You promise?"

"Absolutely."

Kale pressed his fist against his chest. It was the spot on his sternum that mirrored her tattoo. "Be safe." He released her hand and went to the prince's side.

"You're making a mistake," Hiro pressed.

"May Delphi the Protector guard—"

But he turned and walked out before she could finish her blessing.

CHAPTER 48

She didn't know how long she stood there, her eyes riveted on the archway.

"Amelia, sweet girl," Isen said calmly, "you're going to shake me right out of my chair." He slid one of his long-fingered hands over hers and gently peeled it free. He felt around for a chair and guided her into it.

Amelia sat heavily, the impact jarring the unshed tears from her eyes.

"You're trembling, sweet girl."

She wrapped her arms around her chest, trying to hold herself together so she wouldn't shake apart.

"*Khadim*, bring my lady a large *shrub aleasl*."

There was a rasping of sandals upon stone as the mayor's wishes were swiftly carried out.

Tareq got up from the table when the tea service arrived and busily prepared the beverage. He peeled strips from an orange and dropped them into silver cups. Then he poured the steaming liquid from a great height, as far as he could lift his arm, letting a thin rope of molten gold snake into the glasses. Cinnamon and cardamom perfumed the air. He gave each a swirl with a silver spoon before replacing the cups on the tray.

"That was very brave thing you did," Isen murmured to her. "Thank you for defending my friend."

"I believe in second chances," she said. *Even thirds or fourths. But not whatever number Hiro's on.*

The mayor offered her the tray. "Here, my lady, drink this. Be careful; it's quite warm."

"'Honey drink?'" Amelia questioned, not sure in her translation.

The mayor nodded. "A command of Tilk Alnidal. *'Taste not ye the fermentation of wheat or grape.'* However, fermented honey is completely acceptable. You'll love it."

She took a cautious sip of the golden liquid and felt its warmth slide down her throat all the way to her toes. "That is... delicious."

Tareq grinned. "*Shrub aleasl* makes everything better. It'll erase all memory of that horrid scene."

Amelia took a larger swallow.

The mayor chuckled as he removed his golden gloves. A rampant lion marked his left hand. The insult to the Crown Prince of Heaven made her blood boil. Noting her stare, Tareq massaged the tattoo like it hurt. "One of my many youthful mistakes. Apparently."

Amelia tore her gaze away and took another sip of the honey liquor. "Well," she forced herself to say, "you're making amends now."

"We've seen the Hadi Centers in all the major cities. Well done, Tareq." Isen saluted him with his glass.

"Thank you, *takrim*. I was just finishing some administrative work at the one in Masjed when you arrived."

"And what of the recruitment centers?"

"It's arduous work convincing the Bédu tribes to work together. Old rivalries and such. But the centers are rallying all those who wish for unification. They've put their differences aside to create an alliance to help hold the Pirsan tribes together. Over two thousand new recruits in the last week."

"That's incredible."

"But Shiraz is proving difficult. It's led by some prince named Malik. You've always been very persuasive. Maybe when you're done with your other obligations, you would be an ambassador for me?"

"Tareq, I would be honored."

"Isen," Amelia sputtered. "You'd leave the order?"

"Well, getting the tribes – who already adhere to the same religion – to unite is difficult enough without an infidel trying to get it done."

"So you'd have to convert?"

"Not exactly, but I can't very well go around wearing this either." He ran his hand along his turquoise sash.

"And the tribes would have greater respect for you as a man if you had a wife," Tareq added.

"Is that what you want, Isen?" Amelia asked.

The priest blushed deeply. "Maybe. I've grown to appreciate female companionship."

Amelia choked. The liquor burned in her nostrils. She hastily wiped her face with a napkin.

Tareq refilled their glasses, a sly look in his eye. "I do believe if my lady wasn't Sanu, Isen would be getting down on one knee right now."

The priest's hands pressed into the table so hard it made the tendons in his forearms pop. He sat rigid, his mouth set in a thin line.

Tareq looked from one to the other. "What?"

"That is enough, Tareq."

"*In vino veritas*," he replied in slurred Latan. "The spirits release the mind and set the tongue free. It's clear you fancy her."

"*That is enough, Tareq*," the priest repeated in Sarabi.

"Ack, Isen—"

"*You will remember your place, khadim.*"

Tareq shot out of his seat, knelt before Isen, and bent until his forehead touched the ground.

"Isen, this man is our host and you called him—"

"*Takrim* Isen saved me. Saved my soul, my lady," the mayor said quickly, voice muffled by the ground. "I am what he says."

Isen drummed his fingers against the table. "You will apologize to Amelia for embarrassing her, and then I'll forget about this."

"Yes, *takrim*." The mayor did was he was told and then sat back in his chair, his eyes lowered.

Amelia did her best to ignore the tension and sipped at her spiced honey liquor. It was thick and sweet and gave her the most delightful feeling in her stomach and a pleasant fuzziness to her thoughts. They churned around what Tareq had said. "If I wasn't Sanu, I might accept."

Isen's head snapped in her direction. "Amelia—"

"It's true." The liquor was making her tongue loose, and she had to make an effort to speak clearly. "You're kind and thoughtful and inspiring." She hiccupped. "And you're very handsome, even with that cloth over your eyes."

"It does lend a rather debonair element to your overall appearance, *takrim*."

Isen wet his lips and swallowed. The expression on his face was unreadable.

"Sorry, Isen. I've embarrassed you, haven't I?"

"Sweet girl, I think you're drunk."

"Rubbish."

"How many glasses have you had?"

"I…" Amelia looked down at her empty cup. "I can't remember."

Isen chuckled. "Then you've had enough."

"Nuh-uh."

"Cultured and eloquent." Tareq nodded sagely. "Truly, my lady, you make a persuasive argument."

"Where are the dates so I can throw another one at you?"

"*Khadim*," he bellowed to no one in particular, "my lady requires dates!"

"Must I be the adult here?" Isen demanded. "And send you all to bed?"

"Pish, it's too early. The moon is not even overhead yet. We have plenty of time to dance still."

"I'm not dancing." Isen crossed his arms over his chest. He unfolded them and quickly drained the rest of his cup before folding them once again.

"My lady?" Tareq extended his hand. The fingers wobbled slightly.

Amelia hiccupped. "I don't know any Sarabi dances."

"We'll start with *basit*; it's the one that children learn. It's just kicking your feet. Come, come." He gestured for her to stand. "It's a piece of pie."

"*Cake*," Isen corrected. "It's 'a piece of *cake*.' Honestly, Tareq, who taught you Layman?"

"Piece of cake, piece of pie. You Westerners love your desserts."

Amelia lurched to her feet, spilling her glass. *Shrub aleasl* soaked into the white tablecloth. She'd heard that phrase only once before. In the dungeons of Bucharest.

She stumbled back a step, knocking over her chair. The green parrots screeched, flapping madly until Tareq snapped his fingers. They settled reluctantly, feathers ruffled and looking malcontent. They glared at her with red eyes.

"My lady?" the mayor said.

"S-sorry, I stood too quickly." She clamped her jaw to keep her teeth from chattering. "I think I've had t-too much to drink? I should probably go to bed. Isen, you're practically asleep at the table. I'll help to your room."

The priest swayed on his feet, both hands on his staff. "It's not bedtime yet."

"Must I be the adult here?"

Isen giggled. "Very funny, Amelia."

She shook her head impatiently and grabbed his arm.

"My lady, perhaps I could help you with—"

"*No.* I mean, no thank you. We're fine. We're not used to, uh, celebrating like this. See you in the morning?"

The domo looked at a loss for words. "O-of course."

Amelia risked a glance over her shoulder once they'd stumbled halfway down the colonnade. Tareq was nowhere in sight. She pushed Isen roughly into an alcove.

He turned, snaking an arm around her waist and threading a hand into her hair. Lips parted, he bent his head toward hers. "Amelia, I know what we said, but you're Sanu and you really shouldn't be taking advantage of me like this—"

She slapped him.

"Ugh! Why—"

Amelia snatched him by the collar. "*Listen* to me." She swayed against him, fighting the haze of the honey liquor. His hand left her hair and cupped her cheek, his thumb brushing against her mouth. His touch was electric. She flushed with heat. She'd never been so close to him before, and the way his fingers caressed her so tenderly—

"Amelia, I lov—"

She pushed away from him. "We… need to go."

"I agree. An alcove is no place—"

"*No.* I mean the villa. Right. Now."

"But—"

"Isen, *please*. Trust me."

The priest released her with a sigh, hands trailing down her arms and leaving fire in their wake. "Okay."

Amelia took his hand and yanked him after her. She retrieved their things from their rooms and snuck to the archway to the outer villa. The compound was eerily silent, nothing but the snapping of torches in the hot evening breeze.

After a furtive glance in all directions, she crept under the archway. The outer villa and its fountain were deserted. The water bubbled quietly, as if it knew not to make a sound. Amelia stumbled to the gate, her legs too rubbery to run. The gate rattled in her hands, locked.

Panicked, she whipped around, searching for another way out.

Guards in red Bédu robes emerged from the garden like shadows.

A dozen spear points leveled in their direction.

Amelia grabbed Isen's hand and pulled him close.

The spears parted for a figure in white, his booted footfalls echoing in the silent garden.

Isen cocked his head to the side. "Tareq?"

The sorcerer crossed his arms over his chest and shook his head with a disapproving click of his teeth. Four red-eyed rooks hissed from his shoulders.

"What kind of host would I be to let my guests leave in the middle of the night?"

CHAPTER 49

AMELIA HUDDLED IN THE CORNER, HANDS CLAMPED OVER HER EARS TO drown out Isen's screams. He'd been yanked from their cell – minutes? hours? – ago. Each crack of the whip was echoed by an agonizing cry. Sweat trickled into her eyes, but she was too afraid to wipe it away.

Two guards in red Bédu robes returned, dragging the priest between them. One opened the cell door, and together they heaved him into the dirt. Only when they had gone did Amelia inch from her corner and place a shaking hand on his shoulder. Blood seeped into his robes from the latticework of a dozen lashes. Isen curled into her thigh, tears darkening her pink trousers red.

She jumped when Tareq trailed his hand across the iron bars. "This is so familiar."

"Tareq," Isen moaned. "Why—"

"This has nothing to do with you, dear friend. I just needed to make sure our Sanu here would cooperate."

"With what? What could you possibly want with her?"

"I have a dilemma." Tareq opened the door and crouched in front of them. He plucked a rosewood chest from his emerald sash. The silver of its knotwork inlay glinted in the torchlight. The Raion. "*This* has no keyhole. And only a Sanu can open it."

"I don't know how-"

"Don't *lie* to me," Tareq shouted. "You have no idea what I've sacrificed to get this, to get this far. I'll not be denied by some *woman*." He slapped her so hard it left her ears ringing.

Amelia sidled away, cradling her stinging cheek. "I don't know how," she shouted back. "Do you think I want to see my friend tortured? I'd open it if I could!"

"No, you wouldn't," the sorcerer sneered. "Not if you knew what this truly was. Give me your hand." He snatched her right hand, pressed her palm against the silver inlay, but the box remained closed. He tried again with her other hand to no avail. "*Fine.* Isen, you're coming with me again."

"*No.*" The priest clung to her, too weak to do more than pluck at her sari.

"Leave him alone!"

Tareq slapped her again, and this time she did not get up.

Isen clawed at her leg, even removed her sandal, before the guards hauled him away. His sniveling pleas turned to ear-piercing screams as the whip lashed him again.

The sorcerer placed the Raion on the ground at her feet. "When I return, I expect you to have figured it out. Isen doesn't have much time."

He left, wrenching the door shut behind him.

Amelia dragged herself back into her corner, hiding her face against the warm stone and trying to drown out Isen's cries. After a particularly shrill shriek, she dared a look at the chest. The torchlight gleamed on its rosy surface.

Aunt Saoirse had never told her how to open it. They'd never gotten that far in her training. But after Tareq had pressed her hands against the inlay, it wasn't too hard to guess how. He didn't know her tattoo was on her chest.

She didn't dare open it. The power contained in that relic was unfathomable. It was worth Isen's life. It was worth hers.

The priest's sobs hung heavy in the air.

Amelia pressed a hand over her heart, willing its racing pulse to slow. It didn't listen. She couldn't *think* when she was this afraid. She couldn't *focus*—

She scrubbed her face with her hands. They came away wet with sweat from the sultry heat. The torchlight sparkled across her palms, like sunlight dappling a stream.

"Water," she murmured. "Remember the water."

The Rhine had enveloped her like the embrace of an old friend, dazzling her with a hidden world. She'd felt free under its surface. Its caressing waters had plucked every worry away, carrying them far downstream.

Exhaling slowly, Amelia relaxed.

Unleashed, the silver dragon trumpeted in triumph. It flared its wings and stretched, its scaly hide ruffling then smoothing flat like fur. A roar sent fire flooding into every nerve.

Amelia surged to her feet. She stuffed the rosewood chest into the folds of her silks and hurried to the cell door. She was just about to press a glowing hand against the lock when the jingling of bells startled her.

She retreated into the shadows, snuffing out the fire. Her heart beat wildly, but she wasn't afraid. The silver dragon reared its head at the challenge.

A hand as dark as charcoal kept the door steady as the lock glowed red. The tumblers fell into place, and the door swung open with a grating creak. A familiar face peered inside.

"Sanu?"

"*Camila?*"

The dark woman yanked her out of the cell and stuffed her into the bromeliads on the other side of the path. Camila pulled the cell door closed before joining her in the foliage. This close, Amelia could see it wasn't henna that adorned her skin, but tattoos embedded with gold dust. They swirled over her skin like flames or the wings of firebirds. The garnet around her neck glowed as if it housed a tiny ember. As Amelia watched, the light flickered out.

"Phoenix Tear quartz. Burns through anything."

"Camila, what are—"

The dark woman pressed a heavy key into Amelia's hand. "This unlocks the stable gate. I've already put your things there."

Amelia stuffed the key into her pocket. "Come with us."

Camila shook her head, her black eyes glittering like onyx in the firelight. She fingered the torque around her neck. It gleamed brightly even in these shadows. "No, cousin. I cannot raise a hand against him. Go, Sanu. Set us both free."

Amelia nodded.

The dark woman pressed a firm kiss onto Amelia's forehead and rushed off into the garden.

Amelia stood, the silver dragon flexing beneath her skin. It was time to find her friend.

ISEN SMEARED the blood from his bottom lip with the back of his hand and spat off to the side. "I thought we were *friends*, Tareq."

The sorcerer shrugged, twirling his ivory knife in his hands. "Your Sanu is proving most uncooperative, *takrim*."

"And you sound out of breath. Too many summonings will do that. You're working harder, not smarter."

"It was an opportunity I couldn't pass up—"

"Have you lost your *goushi* mind?"

Amelia peered through the palm fronds. Tareq and Isen were on opposite sides of the dinner table, as if they were engaged in a friendly chat instead of an interrogation. Four men in red Bédu robes loitered nearby. One of them had a whip, its barbed tails scratching wetly against the stone as he tapped the coils against his thigh. Blood. Isen's blood.

Silver fire engulfed her, snapping with soundless flames. They were cool to the touch, slipping over her skin like water. Rage burned through her veins.

Amelia stalked into the torchlight, and the silver dragon roared.

"*Shaytan!*" a guard shouted. *Demon!*

Isen lurched across the table, snatching the ivory knife from Tareq's surprised hands and slashing wildly at the sorcerer.

Amelia stomped her foot. A silver line ripped through the garden, shredding trees and flowers like confetti. Without slowing, it raced up the terrace and blasted the dinner table into splinters. Isen hit the ground hard, sliding on his side in front of the guardsmen.

There was no sign of Tareq.

Two grabbed Isen's arms, but a silver arc knocked them back before they could drag him away. Amelia flicked her hand again, and a second arc flattened the four guardsmen against the far wall. They slumped in stunned heaps upon the bricks, blood trickling from the corners of their mouths as little yellow flames guttered out on their clothes.

The silver fire vanished, and Amelia sprinted through the ruined garden. Scrambling over the rubble, she dropped by Isen's side and cradled his head in her hands. Nicks peppered his forehead and a few shallow cuts grazed his neck.

He groaned as she slung his arm over her neck. "A-Amelia?"

"It's okay, Isen. Lean on me."

"*Sanu!*"

Amelia snatched up the discarded whip and lashed its barbed tails. Silver fire rippled down the braided leather and flung a round of roiling light into the sorcerer's chest.

Tareq crossed his arms in front of his face, dissipating the blast. His feet slid across the bricks, but he remained upright, his sleeves scorched and smoking. He lowered his arms, amber eyes wide with surprise. "What *are*—"

She snapped the whip again, and the bricks shattered under his feet. Fire erupted from below in a geyser of light. Tareq exploded into a flock of blackbirds, scattering like shadows. But the fire had them. The birds splattered into blots of oily ichor against the wall. The yellow stone shuddered, a dozen cracks spider-webbing across its flawless surface. Groaning, the wall crumbled into a heap of rubble, spraying them with sand.

Amelia shielded her face with a hand, her heart pounding. When the yellow dust had cleared, she saw no trace of the sorcerer.

Readjusting her grip on Isen, she hurried to the stables. One last silver arc snuffed out the remaining pocket of resistance. Amelia wrested their packs from behind a palm, unlocked the gate, and rushed back to the priest. She picked the closest horse and hoisted Isen in front of the saddle. He cried out in pain as she draped their packs over his shoulders and slumped against her, too weak to protest anymore.

A furtive glance over her shoulder revealed a quiet garden. No one pursued them. In the archway beyond, the glow of an unchecked fire emanated from the inner villa. Amelia wheeled the horse to the gate and put her heels to its flanks. She wasn't sure if the sorcerer was dead or just incapacitated, and she wasn't going to stay and find out.

CHAPTER 50

Black blobs of oily tar oozed across the rubble. They sought each other out, dribbling over stone and trailing across the grass. A blackbird, its head wrenched at an odd angle, hobbled out of the bubbling pool, followed by another. The birds clambered over themselves out of the tar, squawking and flapping and screeching.

Groaning, the sorcerer crawled out of the wreckage. He clutched his throbbing head and staggered upright.

His elite guards were sprawled across the bricks, unconscious or dead. The terrace was ruined, blasted apart down to the scorched dirt. A fire chewed away at the garden, destroying generations of meticulous landscaping.

He wiped the blood from his mouth with the back of his hand. Such destruction. He knew she'd been different ever since her blood had reconstructed the chest, but this—

"No wonder the skeins failed."

The sorcerer withdrew the pipe from his pocket. Instead of cutting another shallow line, he rammed the mouthpiece into the meat of his forearm. He buckled to his knees with a cry as the runes on the pipe flared orange. Smoke poured from the bowl, ballooning into a shadowy mass as dense and dark as a storm cloud.

"Malason."

The smoke shifted, and two glowing coals for eyes bored into him. *You will need more than my name to bind me, human.* It made no sound, but the voice rattled in his bones.

The sorcerer jabbed the pipe deeper into his arm, providing more blood for the summoning.

Rolling thunder deafened him as the erebus purred with the flood of extra energy. *You know the price of failure,* the demon warned. *I am not some petty skein.*

"I know. Your prey carries something precious. I would see it returned, unharmed."

No promises.

"You are *bound* to obey."

For now.

The erebus laughed, a cacophony of clashing cymbals, and slithered into the shadows.

CHAPTER 51

THEY CAME FOR HIM.

Four men, each one with the rampant lion tattooed on his left hand. Kale was hunched over the campfire, drawing a knotwork design in its ashes with a stick, when the first sprinted out of the morning mist. With a startled cry, the boy rolled away from the downswing of the saber, his stick flinging hot ash into the Pirsan's eyes. Hiro sent the man howling into the dirt with a straight arm, snatched his head between his hands and snapped. Two more went after Kale; the fourth ran up from behind him. Hiro feinted to the right, swung his leg out and hit the fourth man across the backs of his knees. The Pirsan stumbled, catching himself against a tree. Dodged as the greatsword buried itself into the bark where his head had just been. Quick. A tuff of brown hair stuck in the sap.

There was a giggle off to the side; the boy was toying with his attackers. A smack across the backside with his stick, a feint so one man would collide into the other. A cat playing with a pair of mice.

Kale giggled and evaded until someone swore so profusely in Sarabi that the boy stopped, his face a thundercloud. *"That* was not nice." He broke his stick over the offending man's head.

The man dropped, and the boy prowled toward the second.

"You should've brought more men," Hiro sneered.

With a shout, the fourth slashed with his sabers. Hiro danced away from the twin blades, wary. The Pirsan swept his sabers in a whirl of steel, and a cold wind buffeted Hiro's face.

He sank his greatsword into the ground, thrust his hands out to his sides as if in surrender. The knives he kept hidden in his sleeves slipped into his hands. The Pirsan sprang as Hiro flicked his wrists. One knife sank into the man's thigh, the other into his shoulder. The sabers dropped for an instant in mute surprise; Hiro yanked his greatsword from the dirt in a wide arc. Cleaved flesh from gut to neck.

He squinted as blood sprayed across his face. A wayward spout jettisoned into the air like some macabre fountain. Hiro flicked a piece of gore off the rippling steel, let the man finish dying in the dirt.

"Kale?"

"Here, sir." The boy ran up, wiped the sweat from his eyes.

"Ready the horse. We're leaving."

Hiro dragged all the bodies into a row – after slicing the throats of the men Kale had left unconscious – and looted them. He took their weapons and threw them a far as he could in separate directions. He took their food, water, money, anything else he could use. The Pirsans were dressed in plain Bédu robes – no crest of allegiance anywhere – but the tattoos on their left hands didn't make it hard to guess. Finished, he turned the warhorse around, spurred her back along the road they'd traveled yesterday.

When they'd left the villa, he and Kale had fled the city in a hurry. It was already dark, and trading cities were breeding grounds for thieves. They got past the city walls and galloped down the eastern road; Hiro wanted to put as much distance between him and the Sanu as possible. While he was tense with fury, Kale pressed his head into Hiro's back and cried the whole time. "You're *abandoning* her."

"She *sent* me away."

"You gave her your word you would—"

"Well she did a pretty good job of releasing me from my vow when she chose to side with that traitorous piece of *goushi.*"

His small fists rained weakly against Hiro's back. "That is *not* how vows work and you know it. You have to do what you promised."

Kale had not spoken to him since that night. He did as he was told: set up camp, brushed down the horse, sparred as ordered, gathered firewood. The easy comradery they'd built had had vanished.

They'd crossed the Indus River yesterday morning. Hiro braved the churning current with his warhorse as Kale scampered across the rickety footbridge. Had he been any other man, and his horse not the stalwart beast she was, they both would have drowned. Twice. Traveling the twenty miles downriver to the ferry was out of the question; he wanted to get away and forget her as soon as possible.

Forget her sermonizing, her wandering off, her prayers at the markers, shrieking "hands" at every hour of the day, the warmth of her ocean-blue eyes. The way her caramel hair lifted in the wind like spun sugar. The coldness in her eyes after he'd cut that hair. The nights she'd wept softly in her bedroll when she thought no one would hear.

You were supposed to protect me.

Hiro rammed his heels into the warhorse's ribs.

The mare's hooves thundered on the packed dirt of the road, matched the drumming of his heart. Not soon enough, the bridge came into view. The churning white river beneath it threw spume into the air, covered everything in a slick sheen. The alpine cedars grew almost horizontal out of the rocky slopes; the ground was treacherous with loose scree and wet needles. Rocks jutted from the surface of the river, and rapids whipped the water into foam and spray.

When they were close, he dropped from the saddle. Without being told, Kale took to the high ground to scout. The forest was thick, the needle-strewn ground muffling his footfalls. After the attack this morning, it made sense that a second contingent would be posted at the crossing to finish the job if they others didn't return.

Six Pirsans in plain Bédu robes with sabers milled about on their sleek Sarabi horses. They were on the eastern side of the river, their desert horses light enough to cross the footbridge.

Hiro shrugged off his bow, selected an arrow from his quiver. He drew the fletching to his lips and loosed.

The Pirsans shouted as their companion fell from his saddle. Hiro already had another arrow nocked, his next target selected, when the Pirsans wheeled their horses around to face the bridge.

A dappled gray horse thundered up the road. Its long tail streamed like moonlight behind its sweat-streaked flanks. Just out of reach from the roiling shadow with glowing orange eyes. Two tendrils snaked out from the smoky mantle, condensed into talons each as long as a sword. They spread wide, like an eagle's feet just before striking, and snapped shut over air.

The gray had jerked sharply uphill, dumping a rider in its panic to evade the demon.

A priest, his white robes stained with old blood, staggered to his feet. He struggled under the weight of the two packs slung haphazardly over his shoulders. Head cocked to the side, he tapped toward the bridge with his staff. His other hand clutched a rosewood box tightly to his chest.

"Isen!" Hiro shouted.

The roar of the river snatched his voice and carried it downstream. The Pirsans dismounted, the *shiing* of their unsheathed sabers unheard by the churning water.

Hiro surged forward, skittered down the needle-strewn side of the slope to a game trail below. He had to get clear of these damn trees. He scrabbled at a tree root to slow his descent, coming into view of the guards. One abandoned the group, bolted for the bridge. His sprinting steps forced the priest to abandon his staff and cling to the rope railing.

Hiro slid free of the trees, loosed arrows into the four remaining Pirsans in quick succession. They buried into their chests so deep the fletching seemed to grow from their flesh like nightmarish flowers.

"*Isen,*" he shouted again.

The priest's head snapped up, cocked to the sound of the Pirsan racing along the planks. The bridge rippled like a wave caught in a maelstrom. Isen clung to the ropes, vomited over the side.

Hiro skidded to a stop, nocked another arrow into his bow. He drew back and pitched the arrow high before releasing. The shaft whistled in the air, arced, and sank like a diving falcon into the Pirsan's neck. He toppled sideways, pitched over the rope railing, and disappeared into the spume below.

The bridge no longer swaying, the priest hurried across the wooden planks. The rosewood box remained clenched to his chest like a treasured keepsake.

The cypress trees on the other side of the river exploded. The dappled gray horse emerged from the spray of red kindling, another rider hunched low into its white mane. It shied away from another splintering tree, trumpeted as the roiling shadow surged behind it. It raced for the bridge just strides away. The demon reared back, flared its smoky mantle like the hood of a cobra, and struck.

Caramel hair caught the sunlight like a thousand threads of honey as the rider wrenched around. She threw up a hand as the demon engulfed her.

Silver light erupted from the saddle. The horse brayed in terror, hit the bridge at a gallop.

Isen was thrown against the ropes, the rosewood chest fumbling from his grasp. It tumbled through the air as the priest groped after it, disappeared into the white froth of the river. *"NO!"*

Behind him, the demon shrieked, its shadow fragmenting like a broken mirror. Threads of silver spread like a spider's web across its billowing mantle, shredded its existence into a thousand wisps of smoke. The blast threw the rider from the horse and into the churning waters below.

"AMELIA!" Hiro screamed.

CHAPTER 52

The priestess plummeted into the rapids. Her head breached the surface once before the coursing river sucked her back under.

Hiro dropped his bow and bolted. He shucked everything as he ran, his greatsword, his dagger, his belt, his quiver, anything that would drag him down.

The slopes were steep but began to level out as the river widened. His feet drummed a frantic rhythm along the treacherous ground. The damp earth shifted underfoot, but he didn't slow. Downriver, a waterfall churned the air for fifty feet over a bed of jagged rock. She'd never survive. Hiro sprang onto a fallen tree, ran down its trunk and dove into the water.

Cold hit him like a hammer striking an anvil, threatened to suck the air out of his lungs. He surfaced and kicked, worked with the swells and eddies of the river. The Sanu was not far ahead, unconscious. She just bobbed like a cork, bounced limply between the rocks. She'd drown before he got to her.

Hiro fumbled against a rock, got his feet braced against its slimy surface. A mighty kick and he sliced through the water, catching her flaccid hand. Yanking hard, he pulled her head above the water. "*Sanu*," he shouted.

Her eyes cracked open into slits.

A small drop jerked them apart. When Hiro snatched her back from the greedy current, her eyes were wide. Panicked. The river grew faster, dragged them onward toward the falls. Hiro scrambled for purchase against rocks, fallen logs, whatever he could get his hands on.

She spat out a mouthful of water. *"Hiro."*

The river was disappearing into a haze of white foam.

Ahead, a tree daringly grew straight out from the slope before curving up into the sunlight. Its branches barely skimmed the water, but the trunk seemed thick enough to support their weight. If they could reach it.

"Let go," he told her. "Trust me, let *go.*"

With a strangled cry, the Sanu released him.

Hiro swam forward as fast as he could and launched out of the water. He hit the trunk with his chest, and the coarse bark bit into his palms. The water pulled at his legs, hard, but his desperation made him stronger. He hauled himself free of the river and twisted onto his stomach. *"Reach for me."*

The Sanu flung herself at him, grazed his hand. Missed.

Hiro did not.

He lurched down, muscles screaming, and grabbed her sleeve. Before it could tear, his other hand grabbed the only thing it could find: her hair. He jerked on both. The Sanu's head erupted from the water with a screech. He let go of her sleeve and snatched her wrist. Released her hair and caught her other flailing hand. Wrenched her out of the river.

The tree started to groan, started to sag.

"Move."

The priestess scuttled forward on hands and knees, Hiro right behind her. The tree was coming loose at its base, the roots unable to grip the wet soil and support the weight of two sopping-wet humans scrambling along its trunk.

Groaning, the roots pried loose of the bank. The Sanu yelped as the trunk dropped, its branches caught in the water. The river plucked the tree free of the shore, splintered it against the rocks and threw its remains over the falls, Hiro and the Sanu along with it.

SOMETHING CAUGHT him around the waist.

At first he thought it was a rock or the battered tree trunk, but the force dragged him against the current. The water was an impenetrable curtain of bubbles, blinding white. Suffocating.

He was pulled free of the water, deposited roughly on the riverbank. Hiro rolled to a stop, lurched to his side to expel the water from his lungs. The coughing burned, and his whole body trembled with the effort. He squeezed the tears from his eyes. Searched blearily for his savior.

The Sanu crawled away from him. A silver shimmer, fine as frost, hovered above her skin. The crystalline shell had its own shape, serpentine with opalescent pearl horns and two long whiskers, superimposed upon the priestess beneath it.

"Hiro!" The boy's voice sounded from the ridge above, but he didn't hear him.

Exhausted, the Sanu slumped to the ground. The serpentine form rippled, dissipated into flecks of silver that fluttered away on the wind. The priestess remained, head pillowed on her hands.

There was something different about them.

"*Hiro.*" Kale dumped his bundle and slammed into him.

Hiro yanked him aside, behind him, eyes glued on the panting priestess.

The boy forgot the rough treatment when he spied the Sanu. "Amelia!"

Hiro caught Kale's collar as he rushed forward, hauled him out of the way. He bent and retrieved his greatsword from the bundle Kale had brought. It was his greatcoat, filled with everything he'd discarded in his pursuit of the Sanu. Of this monster.

"Hiro, *no.*"

"Get out of my way, Kale."

Moaning, the Sanu stirred.

Hiro knocked Kale aside, sprawled him into the pine straw. He hefted his sword to shoulder height and advanced.

"What..." The priestess gasped, eyes white. She scrambled away from the sword raised above her head. "Hiro, what are you—"

"*What are you?*"

"I... I'm Sanu—"

"*Itoko.*" He adjusted his grip on his sword. "Sanus can't lie, and you've fooled me all this time. Who are you to command spirits?"

"Sanus are bridges—"

"You are no Sanu. Your hands are bare! Where is your tattoo? You are *yaoguai* or some other nefarious being—"

"*Stop it.*" Seething, Kale lurched between them, Hiro's dagger in his fist. He slashed at him, large arcs that forced Hiro back a step. "If you can't see that she is *good*, then you truly are lost!"

"*Get away from her.*"

"*No.*"

"She has you under a spell, boy!"

The Sanu rose to her feet, slipped a hand over Kale's shoulder.

Hiro lurched forward. "Don't you touch him—"

But she guided the boy away from her. Her ocean-blue eyes, so familiar and yet so foreign, pleaded with him. Her fingers curled around the V of her tunic and pulled the fabric down.

"You can't seduce me, you foul—" His words died in his throat. A golden lily tattoo glinted on her sternum. The tip of his sword wavered. "A trick—"

"You know it can't be." Her voice was soft, firm. "Give me your hand."

"Not a chance."

"*Trust* me, Hiro, as you once did."

Hiro hesitated. Then he put his left hand into his mouth, pulled his glove off with his teeth. He spat it off to the side, leveled his blade with her stomach. Cautiously, he approached until the tip of his greatsword indented her sari and his fingers hovered a hair's breath away from her tattoo.

The priestess trembled, but her eyes stared resolutely into his.

"You try anything," he warned, "and I'll run you through."

She gave him a tiny nod.

Hiro pressed his fingers against her skin. The golden tattoo was slightly raised, embossed like the designs of an illuminated manuscript. Yet it was still part of her skin, smooth, supple. He traced it all, determined to find a flaw and found none.

Bosetsanu's Chosen.

Her virgin flesh trembled under his touch. Sweat swelled in the dip of her collarbone, trickled down the tattoo and disappeared into the shadowy valley between her breasts. He should not be touching—

Hiro yanked his hand away, withdrew his sword.

The Sanu buckled to the ground with a sob, clenched her legs to her chest.

"Gods above…"

The priestess trembled violently, the muscles in her arms taut as she held herself from shaking apart. Even the pine straw shivered around her.

Kale collapsed beside her, flung his arms around her.

Hiro watched her like he would a snake, still unsure if it was harmless or concealed venom behind its beautiful scales. His burned hand twitched; Kale was too close. "Kale."

The boy lifted his head from her hair, blinked away his tears.

"Go get some firewood."

The boy didn't move.

"*Kale.*" Hiro stuck his greatsword into the soft earth. He moved away from it, crouched down. "Can't you see she's cold?"

The boy glanced at the shaking priestess, chewed his bottom lip. "I'll be right back."

Kale wiped his nose on the back of his sleeve, handed Hiro his dagger. He took it gently, passed a hand over the boy's auburn mane. Sniffling, the boy nodded and went about his task.

Hiro never took his eyes off the trembling priestess. Not once had she moved, and the crystalline dragon had never reappeared. When Kale got the fire going, Hiro sent him to collect the priest. The boy gripped the priestess's shoulder once, then scrambled up the slope. The weather was warmer now, summer just weeks away, but the Indus River had had an icy grip.

Hiro inched as close to the fire – and the priestess – as he dared."Sanu, I… I'm sorry—"

She lifted her face from her knees, ocean-blue eyes blurred with tears. "How could I ever believe you?"

He opened his mouth, but no words came out. There was nothing he could say.

"Do you have any idea what it's like to live in perpetual fear that the man sleeping across the campfire at night might one day murder you in your bed?"

He raked a hand through his hair. "Sanu, I… My life is black and white, okay? And here you come into it just *frolicking* in the gray. Spirits and sorcery… How am I supposed to rationalize that?"

"It's *not* sorcery," she said angrily. "I was *born* this way. I can't help it. And I've had to hide it for *years* because of people like you! From people who don't try or want to understand. How am I any different than Kale?"

Hiro froze. "*What?*"

"Spend any amount of time with him and you'll know he's… special. How can you condone him and condemn me? I've done nothing but save your life, when you've only threatened mine. What are you even *doing* here?"

"I-I came back for you."

The Sanu sniffled. "Why?"

"I should have never left. When Tareq sent men to kill us, I knew you were in danger. And… I'd made you a promise."

"I told you before, I release you. Now that you know what I am – sweet mercy, I don't even know what that is – how could we possibly rely on each other like that?"

Hiro stood, plucked his greatsword from the ground. "The boy."

"What about Kale?"

"He reminded me of the nature of a promise. It must be fulfilled." He stomped out the fire, collected his things. "I won't pretend I'm fine with all this. I can't do that. But I can swear to you that I'll keep my promise. I will get you to Lhasa, and... I will keep your secret."

The Sanu wobbled to her feet. At one time Hiro would've put out a hand to steady her, but now it remained at his side. If she noticed, she didn't say anything. "Will I have to sleep with one eye open?"

He shook his head. "No."

Something in the set of her mouth said she didn't quite believe him.

He wasn't sure he believed himself.

CHAPTER 53

THE SORCERER GASPED FOR AIR.

His skin shriveled and flaked away into dust. His legs buckled, unable to support his weight. A cloud of greenish-gray skin puffed into the air as he collapsed. Muffled popping, the sound of his bones snapping under the strain, roared in his ears like mining explosions.

His throat was so dry it tore as he screamed. Blood, thick and syrupy, choked off his cry as it oozed down his throat.

The rooks, their lidless cabochon eyes glinting like garnets, screeched and flapped around his head.

The rasp of bare feet against stone was no less than a woodcutter's saw grating against his ears. The jingling of tiny bells reverberated like clashing cymbals. He screamed to make it stop but only gurgled on more blood.

A figure crouched by his head, and a face as dark as charcoal peered over him. The luster of the heavy torque around her neck was fading.

"Camila," he rasped. He stretched a withering hand toward her. "Help me—"

"You've gone too far this time, *shaytan*." She smoothed her fingers over his peeling brow and rammed them against his nose. "Breathe deep the scent of your mortality."

The stench of his own decay was overwhelming. He twisted his head away. "You have to help me."

Camila threw her head back and laughed. "The change is already too far gone."

He lurched forward to strangle her, but his arms just flailed in the air between them. She smacked them aside as if she would a pair of gnats. They fell back to his sides, fractured and useless.

She started to hum, a little tune from her home village where they'd met, as she rooted through the pockets of his robes. There'd been a time, long ago, when she'd torn his clothes from his body with impassioned fingers.

"Ah, here we are." Camila held up her hand, twirling the stem between her fingers. She looked down at him with fiery eyes. "I'll be taking my pipe back now, *shaytan*."

He shouted obscenities at her, but his mouth didn't move. His lips just chapped and flaked away. His vision darkened as her hips sauntered out of sight, the pipe tapping against her thigh.

CHAPTER 54

Isen was silent for a long moment. "Well, that would explain a lot of things."

The fire popped, sent a fizzle of cinders into the night air. The Sanu sat on the other side of the fire from Hiro, just a few feet away, but it might as well have been a chasm separating them.

Isen leaned forward, refilled his cup from the kettle.

"That's it?" Hiro asked. "You have *nothing* else to say?"

The priest sipped, shrugged. "Amelia has a gift. She's also Boset-sanu's Chosen. I've always known she was special. Though, I don't know why it took you this long to tell me, Amelia."

The Sanu winced. "Sorry."

"And I'm sorry about the Raion Chest. It just..." Isen clenched his jaw, the knuckles on his staff turning white. His shoulders shook.

After they had climbed out of the ravine, they'd found Isen on his knees by the bridge, tearing out his hair. He had screamed at the river, beaten his fists against the needle-strewn banks, had even threatened to kill the Sarabi horse for making him drop it. Hiro had wrenched the knife out of his hand, pinned him to the ground until the priest had come to his senses.

"It's for the best." The Sanu placed a hand on his arm, squeezed.

"That was a priceless artifact, Amelia. Utterly irreplaceable. A relic—"

"Tareq doesn't have it. That's the most important thing."

"I still can't believe—"

"That he was the sorcerer?" Hiro scoffed. "I told you he wasn't to be trusted."

"He's still out there." The Sanu drew her knees up to her chest, stared into the fire.

Isen's voice was hard. "I don't know about that. Conjuring a shadow-demon like the one you described must take incredible energy. Sacrifice. He was already weak when we left him. He might not have survived its defeat."

"You sound disappointed, priest."

"He was my friend," Isen snarled. "Or had been, for a long time. Then he tortured me and apparently has been trying to kill Amelia for some time now. Of course I'd have mixed feelings about him!"

"Good riddance."

The Sanu glanced up at the venom in his voice. Apprehension flickered across her ocean-blue eyes.

Hiro huffed a sigh, stirred the fire with a stick. The wood was wetter than he'd like, hissing and smoking and threatening to gutter out.

The priestess snapped her fingers. Hiro fell back as the fire flared silver. It returned to a healthy yellow a blink later, gnawed at the dry wood with renewed vigor. "*Don't,*" he whispered.

The Sanu lowered her gaze, hugged her legs a little closer to her chest.

Kale stretched his fingers toward the warmth. "That feels nice now."

Hiro glared murderously at him.

"Well it *does.*"

"It's just a tool like anything else." Isen picked up his cup again. "And it's reheated my tea perfectly. Thank you."

"For a priest, you're remarkably cool about all this."

"And you're the only one making a fuss. The Sanctisum clergy are well aware of demons and spirits and everything in between. Even if they haven't been sighted in centuries and the rest of you heathens have turned them into the stuff of legend. Why would this be so far-fetched?"

"Because... because—"

"Because it doesn't fit *your* norm of daily life?" The priest barked a laugh. "You don't get to pick and choose what kind of supernatural mysteries you believe in. They just *exist*."

Hiro kept his eyes resolutely away from Kale. The boy was different, special, something he'd come to accept years ago. Especially after he'd stopped aging.

So why him and not the Sanu, too?

Isen snorted. "You need to get out more, Hiro. Sanus are *bridges*. Being in the company of one is bound to show you some interesting things. Given your slash-first-ask-questions-never outlook on life, do we need to be worried?"

Kale cast him a questioning glance.

Hiro's eye twitched. "*No*. I made her a promise I intend to keep."

"She is the *last* Sanu, Hiro. Get that through your head, no matter whatever else you think about her. She is the only thing standing between us and the apocalypse. Surely you're not stupid enough to satisfy your own vendetta and sacrifice the rest of us."

"I *told* you—"

"Excellent." He set his cup down, rubbed his hands together. "Now that I know she'll wake up tomorrow morning *alive* and I won't be expelled from the Delphian order for murder, I think I'll turn in."

The Sanu caught his sleeve. "Isen, your wounds—"

"Already tended to, sweet girl. Thank you. Good-night all."

Hiro remained on his side of the fire, needlessly poked it some more. He was exhausted, battered from his battle with the river. Too wired for sleep, he turned his back on the fire. Despite Isen's confidence that they had nothing else to fear from Tareq, Hiro peered into the night.

Nothing.

No rooks, no shadow demons, no sorcerers.

He didn't wake Kale for the second watch, nor Isen for the third. A few hours before dawn, a whimper drew his attention from the gloom.

Shaking, the Sanu was curled on her side in her bedroll. Hands clasped under her chin, they shook until they rattled her teeth. Their chattering roused the boy; Kale kicked off his blanket and scurried to her side. He knelt by her head, his small hand smoothing back her hair. Above the crackling fire, Hiro heard his voice croon a soft melody.

> *Sleep softly now, the night's at peace*
> *The wolf has fled, let crying cease*
> *Above the hearth, my sword is hung*
> *Never to slash, its battle won*
> *Sleep softly now, the stars watch on*
> *I'll love you, dear, 'til there are none*

The creases in her forehead smoothed, her hands unclenched. Kale continued to comb his fingers through her hair until she relaxed completely.

"Where did you hear that?" It wasn't the one Hiro had sung to him as a child.

Kale dusted off his knees. "It's the one she sings to you, when the nightmares – when you can't sleep."

"She... sings to me?"

"You've been able to sleep through the night for weeks now. Didn't you know that?"

Hiro poked at the fire. "I-I hadn't noticed."

Kale came around to his side of the fire, sat down. He looked at the graying sky on the horizon, wiped the crust out of his eyes. "You let us sleep."

"Yeah, well, you all had a pretty big day yesterday."

"So did you. Unless you get thrown over a waterfall every day that I don't know about."

"Every morning before breakfast."

Kale laughed, a sweet sound he hadn't heard in a while.

Hiro smiled, yanked the boy under his arm and ruffled his hair.

Kale popped his head free, shoved him away with a grin. "Thanks, Hiro, I mean for Amelia-"

Hiro sobered quickly. "I'm not doing this for her. I'm doing it for you."

The boy's hazel eyes gleamed gold in the firelight. "I know."

CHAPTER 55

Hiro jerked hard on the reins. "Well... *goushi.*"

Isen gripped his sleeve. "What is it? Why've we stopped?"

Hiro shook him off. The priest rode behind him on the warhorse, had this habit of grabbing onto Hiro's arm instead of his belt to steady himself. The mare snorted, tossed her head. Tired of the bit jerking around in her mouth.

"Is that..." The Sanu's voice trailed away in the wind. "Is that an *army?*"

The Sanu reined the Sarabi stallion beside them, not too close to the temperamental mare. Kale clutched the stallion's mane, craned over its dappled gray neck to peer over the ridge.

The trees hid them well enough, but Hiro didn't want to linger. An army this size would have scouts everywhere.

They were like ants, or bees, thick and clustered. Crestless black flags flapped in the breeze. There was no order to their camp, yet they moved easily. It was quiet too. Not even the cry of an eagle pierced the silence of the valley. There should've been idle chatter, the clang of weapons or cookware, the pounding of feet running drills. Nothing. Only the braying of the thousands of mules they had corralled in some crude paddock.

"I-Is there another way through?" the priestess asked.

As far as the eye could see, the Himalaya Mountains marred the sky. The saw-toothed spine of a wild boar frosted white. Even on this ridge, he had to crane his head back to see their cloud-obscured peaks.

Hiro pointed to the cleft northeast of the army. "They're camped directly in front of the Qiang Pass. There is no other way. We'll... we'll have to go around. North. They'll be watching the Bhutan Steppes."

Isen started. "But that would take us to the Shogun Pass. You said you never wanted to—"

"I know what I said. And we're not taking the Shogun Pass."

"Then—"

"Quiet. We need to slip past unnoticed, so *shut your mouth*, priest. If this was the Tybetan Guard, they'd be flying the banner of the new governing House. But they're not. They've choked off Pathankot and the Beas."

One of the largest trading cities in the continent, Pathankot sprawled across the valley where the Pirsan, Tybetan, and Jianshu Provinces collided. Textiles, tea, porcelain from Jianshu. Spices, timber, opium from Tybet. Silver, livestock, limestone from Pirsa. All traded along the Beas River. To control this city was to control commerce in the East.

"This is... something else." *Loyalists.* The rumor of their resurgence had been the reason he'd been called home, hadn't it? He just hadn't thought there was much truth to it. Hiro clicked his tongue at his mare. "Come on. We need to hurry."

They're on Jianshu's doorstep.

HE TOOK them deep into the mountains. Black rock, untouched snow, crevasses of pale blue that cleaved deep into the earth. His burly warhorse lowered her head and trudged through the snow, the smaller Sarabi stallion in her wake. Behind them, their tracks stretched in a zigzag that mirrored the terrain before the wind wiped them away.

It'd been three days since Pathankot; three days of climbing and sweating in blinding snow; three nights of being packed together like sardines in dens they'd hollowed out of the ice so they wouldn't freeze. Slowly, the twin peaks they sought crept ever closer.

"Are we there yet?" the priest shouted above the wind.

Hiro ground to a halt. That was the fourth time today. He wrenched around to throttle the priest, and the Sanu collided right into him. She bounced back like a rubber ball, sprawled in the snow. A turtle on its back. Grimacing, he snatched her flailing arm and plucked her out of the depression.

He let her go immediately, turned back into the wind without throttling the priest. The Sanu no longer resembled a milkweed thistle. Her flaxen cloak ballooned around her, swollen from the extra layers she wore underneath. A red felt hat, bartered last minute from a village on the slopes, crowned her head like the proverbial cherry. She looked more like a *capezzoli di venere*, a confection native to Roma and the Academy and renowned for its suggestive appearance.

Hiro shoved the thought from his mind, focused on putting one boot in front of the other. "At least you get to ride the horse," he shouted back at the priest.

Moonrise transformed the snow into the purest silver. The warhorse's pace had slowed to a fatigued crawl. Kale, fat as a tick under his spare gi and oilskin jacket, hunched low over the saddle. He tapped her flanks with Isen's staff, but the horse refused to quicken.

"Hiro," the Sanu wheezed. "Why haven't we stopped? This is madness—"

"Because we're here."

Hiro took hold of the mare's bridle at the bit, pulled her forward into the shelter of a fissure in the rocks. The warhorse stumbled out of the wind with a great huff of relief. They wound through the narrow ravine, disappeared under a ledge of snow and ice only to emerge under the moon once more. It was silent; nothing but the occasional crunch of compacting snow beneath their feet, the occasional snort of discomfort from the horses.

The ravine widened into a tunnel that swallowed them whole. Stairs hewn out of the bedrock rose in a gentle incline. A crack in the cavern ceiling allowed weak blades of moonlight to cut through the gloom below. They passed in and out of shadow for eighty-eight steps before the ground leveled out.

A monolith loomed over the exit, glittered under a layer of frost. Moonlight glinted on its jagged teeth and bulbous eyes. Fins like moth's wings hugged its oval, fish-like body. The Sanu shrank from the hideous creature, jostling the mare. The warhorse stamped irritably.

Beyond the statue, across a vast courtyard nestled between the cliffs, a pagoda sprang from the mountainside. Sweeping roof tips, multiple tiers, majestic balconies, it protruded from the cliff like a prolific underbite. Snow piled on the railings, on the slopes of the roofs.

He smothered a jolt of panic. His memory of this place was one of life: men practicing with spears, women weaving yak wool into cloth, children playing with arctic dogs.

It was deserted.

"Hello?" His voice echoed between the cliffs, rattled icicles free to shatter against the courtyard.

"Gods above," Isen hissed. "This is the Pirsan Wasteland all over again. Only we'll freeze to death instead of—"

A light, small and yellow as a pea, popped into life in one of the windows. Another followed, and another, then dozens. They speckled the silent pagoda like fireflies.

"Ye of little faith—" Hiro began.

A spear whistled past his ear.

CHAPTER 56

"EVERYBODY, GET DOWN ON YOUR KNEES. PUT YOUR HANDS ON YOUR legs, palms out."

Amelia winced as the cold stone bit into her knees. The silver dragon huffed a sigh, numbing the pain. It was weaker now, wings tucked tight against its sides and shivering. It needed rest. *She* needed rest.

Hiro made a show of unsheathing his greatsword and resting it on the ground. "I'll handle this, Sanu. We don't need your... help."

Amelia bit back a retort. Her *help* had kept them warm at night, had kept their horses from becoming lame, had strengthened them when their meager rations could not. It was why the silver dragon could only numb the pain in her knees instead of flood her body with heat.

The oncoming stampede of men fanned out in an arc around them, rows deep, the pounding of their booted feet rumbling between the cliffs like thunder. Covered head to toe in gray, they blocked off further entry into the courtyard like a rock slide. Spears and khukuri knives bristled in the moonlight. Black eyes glittered behind thick scarves of yak wool. More than one set was riveted on her.

"How's it going?" Isen whispered.

"Sounds like Hiro's doing a fabulous job butchering the language," Amelia said. "He's doing this thing with his hands that seems... vulgar."

"So we have a fifty-fifty chance of being skewered with spears or invited to dinner."

"I'd say sixty-forty," Kale whispered. "And I'm hungry."

"And I'm f-freezing." Isen stuck his hands into his armpits.

The desert horse shivered behind them, side-stepped to cozy up to the burly mare. The warhorse stamped a foot but didn't have the energy to bite him. She just stood with her head lowered, eyes half-lidded. Her breath crystallized into ice on her velvet muzzle.

Amelia scowled. "This has gone on long enough. If he doesn't—"

"... son of Bethsaida Ishida."

A man approached from the back, parting the others with the butt of his spear. A red bindi marked the brown skin between his eyes. He appraised Hiro with stoic black eyes.

"Ishida?"

Hiro threw up his hands. "Gods above, *yes*. Like I've been saying, I am *Prince* Hiro Ishida, son of *Bethsaida Ishida*—"

"Shirt. Off."

"*What? It's freezing* out—"

The man with the red bindi jerked his chin.

The two men beside him surged forward. One yanked Hiro's head back by his hair and laid the curved edge of a khukuri knife against his throat.

"*No!*" Amelia yelled.

Hiro flung up his hand to stay her.

Trembling, Amelia remained where she was. She bunched her hands into fists at her sides; silver flame raced to her fingertips, ready to ignite.

The second man tugged open Hiro's clothes, baring his chest to the icy air. The man with the red bindi smoothed his thumb against the mark over Hiro's heart. Satisfied, he clicked his tongue at his men, and they released the prince.

Hiro yanked his clothes back into place with a scowl.

The man with the red bindi jerked his chin toward the pagoda. "Come."

Hiro was brusquely stripped of his weapons, and Isen had barely enough time to retrieve his staff before the horses were led away. Despite the lights they'd seen earlier, the passageways were deserted. The lantern's weak yellow glow did little to penetrate the gloom. Behind them, three of the leader's men followed, barring any retreat with their spears.

Amelia gripped her cloak tightly at the throat and hurried to keep up.

A blast of mountain wind flattened her against the wall as they exited into an open-air room. A half-moon balcony dangled over a hundred feet of air, high enough to afford a view over the twin peaks hiding pagoda and down into the valley below. Dominating the opposite wall was a swirling symbol carved deep into the rock. Tassels of dyed yak wool were nailed on either side of the carving, fluttering in the cold mountain air.

Oblivious to the chill, Amelia stopped and stared. She'd never seen it before, but the symbol curled in a familiar pattern, as if from a dream. She took a hesitant step forward, raising her hand to touch—

"*Sanu.*"

Hiro's voice goaded her forward. She hurried after them. After another flight of stairs, the man stopped at a wooden door. He knocked and waited to enter until he heard a muffled reply.

An old woman with a white bindi between her eyes watched them with an unreadable stare as they filed into the room. Gold hoops glinted in her ears and nose. Gnarled, nut-brown hands protruded from the shaggy white pelt enveloping her body. On the floor in front of her sat a young woman, her eyes lowered demurely to the carpet's dizzying pattern of red and black stripes. Candles dribbled wax into every available crevice, their light almost blinding after the darkness of the passageways.

In the corner, an old man in a variegated kaftan plucked at a guqin. His eyes were cloudy, unseeing, but his withered fingers effortlessly teased a gentle melody from the strings. The music melded with the snapping candle flames, filling the room with an eerie sense of reverence.

Amelia jumped when the door behind her snapped close.

The young woman, her forehead marked with a red bindi, gestured to the cushions on the opposite side of a low table. It was littered with cutlery, a copper cylinder with a long serpentine spout, and a large steamer basket. Apparently their sudden arrival had interrupted their supper. They sat, and the young woman loosely tied a white scarf around each of their necks. All but Hiro's.

"My name is Aarti, and I speak for the Old Mother. You are her honored guests," the young woman said in Old Imperial. She lifted a copper cylinder from the table and poured a thick and oily substance into each of their cups. All but Hiro's. *"It's po cha. It will restore you."*

Amelia brought her cup to her nose and sniffed. It smelled faintly of tea and strongly of butter. She took a small swallow. It was hot, silky with fat, and laced with salt. Isen let out a small moan as the heat from the cup seeped into his fingers. Kale guzzled his.

Hiro elbowed him in the ribs. The boy yanked the cup from his lips with an embarrassed smile. *"It's, uh, very good. Thank you."*

The old woman had never taken her eyes off the Ishida prince. And his gaze had never wavered from hers.

Amelia set her half-drunk *po cha* on the table.

"Is it not good?" Aarti asked. *"Please, you must drink. You are weak—"*

"I just... I just can't have any more when my friend isn't offered any."

The young woman's eyebrows lifted in surprise. *"Friend?"*

Hiro flinched.

The Old Mother clicked her tongue. Aarti hastened to fill another cup. She slid it across the table to Hiro instead of putting it into his hands as she had done the rest of him. He took it after a long pause and drained it in one draught.

Amelia leaned forward. *"Thank you for your hospitality, Old Mother. My name is—"*

Aarti shook her head, cutting her off. Her eyes were kind, but warning.

Amelia sat back on her cushion, glanced over Kale's head. "Hiro," she whispered, "I think you're expected to—"

"I've not been given leave to speak," he hissed through tight lips.

The old woman leaned forward and clamped the young woman's shoulder with a clawed hand. Aarti's dark eyes became chips of flint.

"We struck your name from the histories, guardian," the Old Mother said. *"Why have you come back?"*

CHAPTER 57

"I had no choice, Old Mother. In the leaving, or in the returning."

The Old Mother clicked her tongue. *"For our love of Bethsaida, we did not kill you. Now, why have you come back?"*

"I need Dongxue Shandian."

The old woman hissed between her teeth. *"That path is closed to you, guardian."*

"Sanu," Hiro said, his attention still riveted on the Old Mother, "show them who you are."

"I thought you didn't need my help."

"Sanu."

"Amelia, sweet girl," Isen whispered, "I don't think now is the *best* time to—"

"I know, I know."

She shed her cloak and untied the straps that kept Hiro's spare gi lashed to her body. Wiggling free of the mass of black wool, she straightened her uniform. The gold beads of her sari's fringe clacked against each other softly, yet loud enough to startle the guqin master. His spidery fingers skipped a beat. Hesitantly, Amelia pulled the V of her tunic down to reveal the tattoo on her chest.

The seams in the old woman's forehead doubled as her eyebrows lifted. Aarti broke into a delighted smile and clapped her hands together. The Old Mother's clawed hand reasserted command. The young woman's shoulders slumped, her face becoming a stoic mask once more.

"This is Sanu Maitre Amelia de Taru," Hiro said. *"I'm bound to bring her to Lhasa. The Qiang Pass was blocked. I had no other choice than to come here."*

The Old Mother laughed, her raspy voice whistling like a reed in the wind. *"You're a fool, guardian. You're as blind as that priest."*

Isen frowned and shifted on his cushion.

Hiro pursed his lips. *"Will you help me?"*

"No."

Amelia lurched forward on her cushion. *"Please, Old Mother. I... I am the last of my kind. I must get to Lhasa."*

"Do you know what this man has done?"

"I know enough. I trust him to help me."

"He treats you with contempt, yet you vouch for him?"

Hiro looked at the floor.

"I..." Amelia faltered at the pang in her chest. Everything had changed since the Indus River. *"I know. But he made me a promise—"*

"He made us a promise, too."

"No, I didn't," Hiro snarled. *"I—"*

The Old Mother silenced him with a jerk of her chin.

Amelia cast him a worried look. "Hiro... what did you do?"

"It's what I *didn't* do." He stared at the carpet like he was trying to burn a hole into it with his eyes.

"We're waiting," Isen prompted.

Hiro pulled aside the folds of his gi. A russet birthmark hovered on the taut skin over his heart, shaped like a coiled dragon ready to strike.

"Every Ishida has this mark. And every firstborn comes here when they turn sixteen. *Every. One.* It's a pact we've had with Mirka people since Rukio Ishida's time. Back when Jianshu was founded."

"What for?"

"They never say. You find out when you go. And I... I didn't come."

"Why not?" Isen asked. "If it's *that* important, why would you—"

Hiro glared at him. "I was sent to the Academy shortly before. My father—"

"The Himalayas divide Jianshu from the rest of the world. You could've stopped—"

"I was distraught. I'd just lost my home, my mother—"

"*It's always someone else's fault, isn't it?*" the Old Mother said. "*Your father, your mother, her.*" She pointed to Amelia. "*In the five hundred years your family has been coming here, did you think you're the only one who's ever known war? Or loss? Still they came to honor the pact.*"

"*I came here as a child. And I'm here now,*" he grumbled.

"*It was too early then, and it's too late now. The chain has been broken. Yet...destiny seems to have given us another chance.*" The Old Mother nodded to Amelia. "*We will help her.*" She released Aarti and clicked her tongue.

The young woman sprang to her feet, clasping her hands in front of her. "*Old Mother wishes you all to stay tonight.*" Her voice had regained its cheerful cadence. "*You will be taken to Matha Gupha tomorrow after you have rested.*"

Aarti lifted the lid of the steamer basket and distributed the rest of the dumplings among them. She served Hiro last, sliding the bowl across the table toward him like she'd done the *po cha*.

Amelia nudged the purse-like dumplings around in their orange sauce with her chopsticks.

The young woman smiled. "*They're paneer momo, Sanu. Vegetarian.*"

"Mine's beef," Kale said through a mouthful of food. "*So good.*"

Aarti tittered at his enthusiasm.

"It's probably yak," Isen told him. "These mountain folk survive almost solely on the products of yak: milk, cheese, meat, wool for their clothing, and manure for their fires."

"Gross." Kale wrinkled his nose.

Hiro ate his without comment.

"*Old Mother.*" The boy set his empty bowl on the table and bowed. "*Thank you for the food. May I give you a gift in return?*"

The ancient woman nodded.

Kale scuttled over to the guqin master. He sat beside him, his young fingers plucking a harmony to the old man's melody. The Old Mother's eyes fluttered closed, the straw billets of her pallet creaking as she swayed to the music. Aarti leaned against the old woman's pallet, face softening in contentment.

The Old Mother whispered something, her voice low and raspy.

"What was that?" Amelia asked.

"Old Mother says 'the boy knows.'"

"Brother Leiji taught him at the Academy," Hiro murmured, not looking at her. "After just one lesson, well… you know he's a quick study."

Amelia blinked. It was the most he'd said to her in a week. "He plays beautifully."

"It was his favorite instrument."

Kale glanced up with a smile. "Hiro promised me he'd get me one once we get to Arashiyama."

"Focus on your music, boy."

The song ended, the last strains disappearing into the sputtering of the candles. Aarti stood and gestured to the door. *"Yueshan comes. You must rest, Sanu. Old Mother sleeps."*

The ancient woman was hunched under the shaggy white pelt, snoring lightly.

"Wait." Amelia lingered by the sleeping woman. *"I have questions—"*

"Tomorrow, Sanu. Old Mother sleeps."

IN THE MORNING, the Old Mother was dead. Silent tears darkening her nut-brown skin, Aarti took the shaggy white pelt from the ancient woman and settled it on her shoulders. Then she donned a heavy gray jacket and thick leather boots and took them into the snow.

Breathless, Amelia fought to keep up with Aarti's brisk stride. The young Mirka woman shuffled ahead on her snowshoes as relentless as the mountain wind that wiped away her tracks. Kale hopped in the divots left by her feet, leading Isen by his staff. At the rear, Hiro had his head lowered against the gusting snowfall as he pulled the two horses after him.

They'd left the pagoda as the Mirka people were burning the Old Mother. Aarti shielded her eyes so the sight of the mourning people would not taint her reign with bad luck. Only after the winding cleft in the rocks had emptied them into this snow-covered valley did she lower her hands.

The valley was actually a mountain lake, frozen to its depths and blanketed in white. Stretching in every direction, the Himalayas choked the sky, blotting out the sun so only their jagged tips sparkled in the light.

Aarti finally slowed and came to a halt in front of a dark blot of stone. An arcing ledge kept the rock below it free of snow. Dark as obsidian, it was so smooth they could see their reflections in it. Dangling from the underside of the ledge was a heavy metal bell.

Aarti perched up on tiptoe and gave the worn tassel a shake. The bell resounded low, shattering the glass-like wall behind it. Across the valley, ice shifted, cascading in a thunderous roar down the mountainside.

Amelia shrank away from the avalanche, but the Mirka woman just regarded it as a common annoyance.

"It won't reach us here." She gestured to the cave entrance. "Matha Gupha. Safe journey, Sanu Amelia. It truly was a pleasure to meet you. I'm sorry it was under less joyous circumstances." Aarti regarded Hiro with cool eyes like it was somehow his fault. "Guardian."

He nodded once. "Old Mother." He stepped around her and herded them inside the cave.

"Wait!" Amelia slogged back a few steps and grabbed Aarti's arm. "I meant to ask the Old Mother last night... I have to know—"

The young woman nodded solemnly. "I am Old Mother now. Her wisdom flows through me. I will answer what I can."

"What is that symbol carved into the wall? The one that overlooks the valley?"

Aarti bent in the snow and drew the symbol.

Amelia traced a finger over the design, straining to understand. Its meaning was a butterfly flittering above her head that she couldn't catch.

"Om. You've seen it before."

Frustrated, Amelia shook her head. "No."

"Not with your eyes, Sanu. With your feet."

"My feet?"

"I'm sorry. That's the only answer I have." Aarti smeared the fresh tears from her eyes before they could harden into ice. "I must go now. At moonrise, I must make my farewells to the previous Old Mother. Go, Sanu. Matha Gupha does not wait."

CHAPTER 58

THE FOUR OF THEM STOOD AT THE EDGE OF THE CAVE, THE LIGHT OF THE failing sun illuminating the tunnel with streaks of white and blue. The walls were waves of ice frozen in mid-crest, indigo at the bottom and cyan at the top with myriad swirls of aqua, turquoise, and teal in between.

Teeth chattering, Amelia took a step forward.

"Sanu, *stop*," Hiro hissed, pointing to the ceiling.

Icicles, some as thick around as her waist, dangled from above. Needle-like points pierced the air just feet above their heads.

"Quiet. Everyone." He tied a cloth around each horse's eyes and led them down the slope into the cavern. The clopping of their hooves reverberated off the walls and tremored in the dangling ice. The sound of tinkling crystal intensified into a chandelier caught in a hurricane.

The Sarabi stallion panicked, trumpeting a terrified neigh.

Daggers of ice dropped free of the ceiling, shattering into glassy shards upon the cavern floor.

The horses bolted, dragging Hiro between them. Amelia grabbed Kale's hand and ran between the splintering stalactites. Isen stumbled behind them, hauled along by his staff. Kale yelped as the priest slipped and fell, yanking him down with him. Amelia pulled Kale to his feet and shoved him forward.

An icicle shattered between them, the blast throwing Isen onto his backside and her back toward the entrance. The silver dragon tensed, and crystalline claws shadowed over her fingers. They gouged deep into the ice, grating her to a halt. She scrambled onto her feet and raced for the flailing priest. Amelia dove into him, grabbing his robes. She hid her face into his chest as the ice exploded around them. They slid across the slippery floor, shoring up against the far wall.

Moaning, Isen clutched his head as Amelia scrambled off of him.

Bulbous eyes and needle-like fangs bored down at her. Shrieking, she scuttled away from the gaping maw.

"What? What is it?"

The stone statue snarled silently at her, the same fish-like creature with fins like moth wings she'd seen before.

The cave groaned.

She wrenched away from the frightening sentry, shielding her head from a spray of tiny icicles.

A massive shelf broke free of the ceiling, the frozen teeth dropping down like a portcullis. The ground shuddered as the ice splintered, jostling her off her feet. Shaking the blur from her eyes, she caught a glimpse of auburn hair just as the final cascade of icicles smashed into the floor. She flung out her hand.

"*KALE!*" Choking on the crystalline dust, Hiro sprinted to the rubble. He tore chunks of ice from the heap and tossed them aside like a madman. "*Kale.* Can you hear me?"

Amelia staggered to her feet and limped to the frozen mound. Balancing on one leg, she yanked aside whatever she could. Tears froze upon her cheeks as the ice bit through her gloves.

Hiro pried loose a chunk the size of a hay bale and flung it behind him. The rubble shifted and toppled over itself like sand spilling down a dune, skittering across the icy floor.

Huddled into a ball was the boy. Ice chips glittered in his hair and across the backs of his hands. His cheek was cut; the blood had already slowed to an ooze from the cold.

Encasing him was a shimmering shell. Its silver light rippled in an unseen current, weakening. It fizzled out with a crackle, and the ice it had prevented from crushing the boy sagged like a wave upon the shore.

Kale peeked out from under his hands, took a wary look around, and scrambled to his feet.

Hiro plucked the boy from the ice and collapsed on the ground, Kale's arms tight around his neck. The prince's shoulders shook with a silent sob.

Amelia cried out in relief, sagging against the rubble. She scrubbed the tears from her eyes and sucked in a deep, shuddering breath. She grunted as the boy hugged her hard around the middle.

He lifted a delighted face from her flaxen cloak, hazel eyes sparkling. "Thanks, Amelia." He pulled away, wiping his nose on his sleeve. "I'm gonna get Beleza and Amai. They could use a hug, too."

The boy raced off into the indigo shadows, calling for the wayward horses.

Amelia stole a glance into Hiro's face. His seal-brown eyes were red, his jaw clenched so hard she could hear his teeth grinding.

His hand shot out as if to yank her into an embrace, but halfway between them it fell listlessly to his side. He looked at the icy ground as his fingers curled into a fist. "Thank you, Sanu." He raked a hand through his hair. "We, uh, we should get out of—"

"Right. It's just I—"

"What?"

"I can't put any weight on my right leg."

"Oh. It looks sprained." He turned and slunk across the ice. Then he snatched Isen's staff, returned, and presented it to her. "Here. Take your time."

"Thank... you." She shimmied to the far side, trembling with exertion. It took all of her remaining strength to haul herself into Amai's saddle.

Hiro's hand on her foot made her jump. Biting her lower lip, she fought to remain still as he removed her boot and sock. The fingers of his burned hand gently probed her ankle. "Gods above, it's the size of a potato. It'll need to be iced."

"You might have some difficulty finding some."

He barked a laugh. He sorted through the chunks until he found one he wanted. He dropped it into her sock and wound it around her ankle. Pulling the scarf from around his neck, he wrapped it around her foot. Amelia sighed at the sudden bloom of heat.

"Can... can you heal yourself?"

She blinked. He never asked about her gift. "I don't have the energy right now. After Kale, I—"

"Forget it. The ice will give you a head start." He took the stallion's reins and whumped him in the shoulder. The horse ignored the abuse and worried Hiro's pocket with his lips, searching for a carrot. "You idiot," the prince muttered.

"Isen, how's your head?" she asked.

"I'll live." He was sprawled over the mare's neck, his hands tangled into her mane. "Hiro, would it be safe to say we can expect more of the same? Because if you say 'yes' we're turning straight around and trying our chances sneaking around that army."

"There shouldn't be any more of this particular hazard."

"*This* hazard?"

"It's three days to the other side. We must be quick and silent. There are more than just icicles in Dongxue Shandian."

"Then shouldn't we be getting a move on?" Isen squeezed the mare's ribs with his heels. The warhorse snorted, ignoring him.

"We need to wait until nightfall. There can't be any light in here. It won't be long."

"What are we supposed to do until then? It's *freezing* in here."

"Cuddle?"

WHEN THE SUN SET, Dongxue Shandian came alive.

The cave was black as the Abyss; not even a whisper of twilight penetrated the frigid darkness. Hiro waved a hand in front of his face, unseeing.

One by one, beads of light popped into existence. In the tunnel beyond the statue of the fish-creature, the cave ceiling burst into a riot of light. Little stars – pale green, azure, white – twinkled from the icicles. Dangling threads, fine as silver filament, rippled with pulses of light. Lightning along a thread.

The priestess gasped in wonder. "What is this place?"

"*Matha Gupha*, Moth Cave. I know it as Dongxue Shandian, the Cave of Lights."

"More like the Cave of *Ice*." Isen briskly rubbed his arms.

Kale approached a low-dangling thread. "Can I touch one?"

Hiro snatched his hand. "*No.* That light you see rippling down them has enough power to throw you fifty feet and stop your heart."

Kale stuffed his hands into his armpits.

"What are these things?" The Sanu peered into the ceiling.

Dark-gray shapes loomed above them, clustered like bees on a prized flower.

"Ice worms," Hiro replied, "although they look more like the angler fish of the deep. For every bead of light you see, you don't see a foot-long and voraciously hungry creature with needle-like teeth. Those threads are actually their tongues."

"*Ugh.*" Isen gagged. "What do they eat? There's nothing here."

"Moon moths. The ice worms stun the moths, then reel up their tongues. The moths' migration path takes them through this pass, and that's how the Mirka first discovered it centuries ago. They travel the pass to their breeding grounds on the western side of the mountains each full moon, then return to the eastern side to live. That means a great amount of moths on a frequent basis. The Mirka ring the bell on the eve of the full moon to make sure the moths can get through. They feed on them, too."

Kale stuck out his tongue.

Hiro ruffled the boy's hair. "Let's go, and don't touch the threads."

The ice worms only populated the meandering path the moths traveled, settled so thickly the light of their tongues and lures was almost blinding. The ice gave way to the hard bedrock of the mountain heart, and the freezing chill abated. True stalagmites and stalactites erupted along the path, left over from when water had coursed here centuries ago. Some were spindly things striped with ochre, yellow, orange, and russet; others were creamy white blobs all piled haphazardly upon each other.

The way condensed to narrow tunnels and expanded into great caverns whose tops shone to rival a hundred crystal chandeliers. It was in one of these great caverns that Kale found a bone the size of his leg. Hiro put a halt on their gawking, hurried them to the narrower passages beyond.

The natives had spoken of Meh-teh, great hairy white beasts with massive fangs, ice-blue eyes, claws as long as daggers that roamed in these mountains. They might not be much more than folklore, but battling an ice-demon twice his height was most definitely not on his list of things to do.

Night and day were relative terms in the depths of the mountain; the light of the ice worms never wavered. Their 'days' consisted of traveling as far as they could before exhaustion forced them to rest again.

Hiro woke with a start one of these times, blinked in the gloom. The ice worms overhead were dark, their brethren to either side shining only faintly. He rolled into a crouch, unsheathed his greatsword. The ice worms feared only one thing in these caves: the one beast strong enough to withstand the jolt of their electric tongues.

Behind him, a silver glow teased at the corner of his eye. The Sanu had her leg drawn up to her chest, massaged her ankle with silver hands. The glow was faint, unobtrusive, but the ice worms abhorred competition. Her fingers stopped working when she caught him watching at her. The light vanished from her hands. "I-I'm sorry. I know you don't like seeing—"

"No. I don't mind… anymore."

The Sanu was fully healed when they reached the other side. The lights flickered and went out as midmorning sunshine streamed from the jagged exit. Even through her blind, his mare sensed the open sky and strained forward. He could barely keep ahold of her as he yanked the cloth from her eyes. The warhorse whinnied, thundered down the slope into the wildflowers. The stallion chased after her. Kale was not far behind, his hands in the air and whooping.

Hiro shaded his eyes against the sun. Before him stretched the rolling green pastureland of Jianshu's Xinjiang Plains, lush under an expanse of blue sky streaked with white.

His home.

His mother's grave.

CHAPTER 59

THE BONES OF THE DEAD LAY HIDDEN HERE.

Hiro crouched, passing a hand over the long grass. White bone – the tips of a horse's ribcage – poked out from the ground like a straining hand. Clawing for the sunlight. Desperate to run beneath the sky.

He swung up into the saddle, barked to the others to do the same.

"Ack, Hiro," the priest yelped, "you're pulling my arm out of its socket!"

Before the priest was even settled behind him, he put his heels to the mare's sides.

The lush pastureland of Xinjiang passed by in a blur of green. Each day it took to cross only compounded his anger. His rage. This was where his father had sent his mother to die. This was where he'd first met Ellaria – the love of his life – who'd traded that love to another man.

It'd been a chance encounter at the Wind Runner Festival, the national horse race that declared the arrival of spring in Jianshu. The Ishida House broke free of the Jade Palace to preside over the auspicious event, and it was the Matsus' horse who won. A twelve-year-old Hiro approaching the chestnut mare to present the rider with a cherry blossom branch gilded in gold, the crowd gasping as the jockey removed her mask, revealing fifteen-year-old Ellaria Matsu underneath. He'd been smitten ever since.

His eyes watered, tears lashed free by the wind. He bent low over his mare's neck, let the wind stream harmlessly over his back. Just as she'd taught him.

THE JADE PALACE of Arashiyama was nestled in a valley surrounded by ridges thick with bamboo and imperial maple trees that burned crimson in autumn. Its gold trim shone like fire in the sunlight, its malachite walls finer and grander than any majestic tree. A sea of rhododendron, plump with clusters of purple and pink flowers, carpeted the valley in a floral embrace. A city with red lacquered roofs sprawled in a half-circle on the southwest side of the palace; a river threaded its way through the rhododendrons on its northeast side.

The bamboo forest around them sighed in the wind. A thousand little leaves showered down, teased him with gentle touches as if they were welcoming their prince home. A tiny gasp from his right. The Sanu, face full of wonder and delight, had her hands stretched out to the fluttering leaves.

"That's the *palace*?" Kale's eyes bulged from his head. "You grew up there?"

"I grew up at the Academy."

"It's stunning," the Sanu said.

"Yes, quite lovely." Isen stuck his head out from behind Hiro's shoulder. "I can see what the fuss is about."

Kale giggled.

"Come," Hiro said. "If we're quick, we can get through the city before nightfall."

After the Great Cataclysm, the city had returned to its more natural roots, forsaking electricity and other technology other than to facilitate indoor plumbing and illuminate the Council Lodge. Even the palace shunned excessive use, preferring the old ways of fire.

They passed through the city without delay. Its people were friendly but respectful; no one wanted to bother a hulk of a man and his ragtag group of road-strained travelers. He should've been greeted with fanfare, but these people didn't know him. He'd been gone too long.

They passed under the red torii gate separating the palace grounds from the city, followed a winding path through the rhododendrons. Fat bumblebees zoomed about the blooms, hairy legs heavy with yellow pollen.

An imperial green door, bearing the Ishida crest in silver and gold, appeared out of the flowers. A serpentine head growled down at them, golden teeth bared in a warning snarl.

The Dragon Gate.

Unguarded, only an Ishida could enter through its fortified door.

Hiro pulled the glove off his burned hand, pressed it against the pomelo-sized pearl the dragon held in its claws. He turned it in a complicated pattern of twists, the final one emitting a hiss of air from the dragon's nostrils as the door opened.

Fire erupted from the dragon's horns, pierced the sky with scarlet flares. An answering flare erupted from the Jade Palace, announcing his arrival.

Within minutes, the rhododendrons shook with the pounding feet of the Home Guard. Hiro tightened the reins as his mare side-stepped under him, eyes rolling. Shaking violently, the bushes ejected only one man from their blossoms. Plump cheeks, twinkling eyes, bushy salt-and-pepper hair with a matching moustache. He looked more walrus than man, even chuffed like one when he was in a reprimanding mood.

Hiro blinked in surprise, dismounted. "Domo... Ignatius?"

"Prince Hiro!" The palace steward hurried forward, red-faced and puffing from exertion, threw his meaty arms around Hiro's waist.

Hiro felt his back pop. "Gods above, you've gotten fat."

The steward laughed, slapped his ample belly. "You're looking at the Jianshu drinking champion four years running."

"Maybe you should give up the title."

"Now that you're back, maybe I will."

Hiro placed a hand on the steward's sloping shoulder. Slid it up to the side of his jowly cheek. Miserable gray eyes found his.

"I've missed you, boy. Seeing you is like seeing her all over again."

Hiro leaned his forehead against the steward's sweaty one. The domo's chubby fingers clung to his arms. "I've missed you too, Ignatius." He pulled away, smoothed the wrinkles from the steward's rumpled tunic.

The domo wiped his eyes with gentle dabs of his embroidered cuffs.

"I've come to make things right." Hiro tapped the hilt of the tanto knife in his belt.

Frowning, the steward peered at the knife. His bushy eyebrows shot skyward as realization struck him. His meaty hand grabbed the hilt, but Hiro locked Ignatius's hand against him in a powerful grip. "*No*, my prince," the domo hissed. "Absolutely not. Your mother—"

"Is exactly why I'm doing this."

"No. *No*, Hiro. Not until we've talked. Please. Promise me this."

Hiro thawed. "It must be soon, steward. And where is Toshiro? I haven't seen my little brother—"

But Ignatius plastered a smile onto his face and turned to Hiro's companions. "Where are my manners?" He bowed dramatically. "I am Domo Ignatius, steward of the Jade Palace. I'll get your names in a moment, gentlemen. Who, my prince, is this *divine* ray of sunshine?"

Hiro glanced at the Sanu. Travel-strained, hair disheveled, bags of weariness under her eyes. Yet she glowed, her ocean-blue eyes alight with mirth.

"That is *Sanu Maitre* Amelia de Taru, you old lecher."

"Don't listen to him." The steward kissed the back of the priestess's hand. "He's just jealous of our *instant* connection."

She tried her best to smother a smile. "Indeed."

Hiro rolled his eyes. "This is my ward, Kale, and this is Isen... Isen, I don't know your last name."

"We've been traveling together for *months*—"

"I never thought to ask."

"Unbelievable." The priest pursed his lips, flicked his turquoise sash. "Sanctisum clergy give up all familial ties when inducted into the order, so it doesn't matter anyway. But seriously, haven't you ever wondered why Amelia calls herself 'de Taru?'"

"No."

"Well… that awkward exchange aside, I'm delighted to meet you all. But we mustn't keep Lord Ishida waiting." The domo clapped his hands briskly. "Up we go." The steward spun on his heel, squared his shoulders for the hike up the hill.

"Domo, get on the horse."

"And disgrace your homecoming, paltry event that it is? Not a chance. Now we'll go over proper protocol when meeting Lord Ishida." The steward paused three steps into the climb, hands on his knees and puffing into the dirt. "Do not approach unless he invites you. Do not speak unless spoken to." The domo paused to hack into the bushes. He mopped the runnels of sweat from his face with a handkerchief, stuffed it up one of his embroidered sleeves for later.

The Sanu dismounted. "Domo Ignatius, please—"

The steward forced a smile, shook his head. As Hiro nudged his mare into the lead, Ignatius snatched the warhorse's breast collar for support. The mare grunted at the added weight, dug her hooves deeper into the path. "Do not… make direct eye contact. When you bow… keep your eyes fixed on the ground… until… until…" He paused to wheeze and swab off his brow. "Gods above, are we *there* yet?"

Hiro smothered a chuckle. "Almost. You're doing *great*, Domo."

"Shut up, Prince. Back for ten minutes and already insolent. Didn't they teach you manners at the Academy?"

"It didn't take."

"Clearly. Now where was I? Ah, yes. Don't raise your voice. Address him as 'my lord' or as 'Lord Ishida.'" He fanned himself with a hand the size of a snowshoe. "There, I think I've covered enough to keep the Home Guard from cutting you to pieces."

The Sanu looked sick.

"That's it?" Isen snorted. "That doesn't sound so bad."

"Wait until I get started on dinner etiquette."

"Later, Ignatius. We're here."

They passed under a gold torii onto a vast terrace. Fat urns painted with the Ishida dragon flanked the entrance, boasted Mother's favorite yellow-and-orange roses. Flames in the fire bowls danced into the twilight sky, twisted like ribbons of light. The malachite palace rose in the background, regal and unyielding as the man in front of them.

Hiro dismounted, a hand sliding to the hilt of the tanto in his belt. "Father."

CHAPTER 60

"PRINCE HIRO. YOU'RE LATE."

The summer heat that had warmed the air vanished, leaving an icy stillness in its stead.

Dressed in gold and imperial green, the Lord of Jianshu had the bearing of a king. The cuff that banded his silver-streaked hair into a topknot was no less than a crown. An orange-and-blue mandala hung from proud shoulders, a blaze of color against the gold of his tunic. Shorter than his son by at least a foot, Lord Akio Ishida had no trouble looking down his nose at him.

Hiro lowered himself to one knee, bowing his head. Kale did the same, pulling Isen down beside him. Amelia remained standing and kept her gaze averted politely; she was Sanu and bowed to no one.

"I have returned upon your request, my lord," the prince said. "I trust you received my commendations from Domo Tanaka and the messenger eagles I had sent to alert you of my progress?"

"Yes..." Lord Ishida said in Old Imperial, "... *and your blooding file.*"

Something flickered in Hiro's eyes, but his face remained impassive like stone.

"You did not say you would be bringing others with you."

"*I had not planned on bringing them this far,*" Hiro replied. "*I meant to drop them off in Lhasa but for the army—*"

"*Later. The boy there, is he your bastard? And that woman, is she his whore mother? Why does she not bow before me? Have you forgotten the teachings of your mother?*"

Hiro's hand clamped at something on his belt as the boy launched to his feet, seething.

"*Amelia is* not *a whore,*" Kale snarled. "*And I am not his bastard, but he may as well be my father. And he's a better one than you are, if you should think such dishonorable things about him.*"

The Lord of Jianshu blinked.

"*Kale.*" Hiro yanked the boy back down beside him.

"*You must be devoted to the prince to come so immediately to his defense.*" Lord Ishida's eyes narrowed. "*So, boy, if you are not his bastard, what are you to him?*"

"*My name's Kale, and I'm his ward. He found me abandoned by a river and raised me.*"

The lord cocked an eyebrow and gave Hiro an appraising look. "*Did he now?*"

"*You need to apologize to Amelia,*" the boy said.

The corners of Lord Ishida's mouth quirked up, patronizing. He looked beyond his son to her, his forehead creasing as his gaze dropped down to the pink trousers peeking out from under her cloak. She loosened the ties, and the flax cascaded into a pile around her feet.

"*Sanu.*" He dropped to his knees, pressing his forehead against the floor. His attendants and guards scrambled over themselves to mimic him.

Amelia stalked around Hiro, stopping in front of the Lord of Jianshu when she was sure he could see her sandals peering up at him.

Lord Ishida sat back on his heels, but kept his head bowed. "My lady, forgive a man his folly. May Delphi the Protector guard your steps and the grace of the Blessed Lady be upon you always."

"I am Amelia de Taru, Sanu Maitre," she said. "And you are forgiven. I pray you will remember humility in the future when dealing with strangers and familiars alike."

"As you say, my lady," the lord said, lifting his gaze. "I am blessed to have you..." His voice trailed off in alarm. She was staring at him, captivated by his ice blue eyes. A crescent scar marked his right brow, blinding his right eye.

"Y-Yueyeux?"

Lord Ishida went white. *"How do you know that name?"*

HIS HAND FLEW to a gold band on his finger. Behind him, his guards loosened their swords. Lord Ishida waved them off with an impatient gesture.

"The Bethany Journals." Amelia withdrew the thin book with its worn wand from her pack. "This is just a copy of the originals, but they're the writings of Bethany Cavill. She was a Sanuset missionary before her Release. She wrote about a general she called Yueyeux – Moon Eyes – because of a knife wound he'd received in a skirmish with the Samoyedic Horde. *You.*"

"Did you know her?" His voice cracked with hope. His good eye blurred, and he passed a trembling hand over his brow. "Of course not. Forgive me. You are too young."

She shook her head. "But I grew up reading her journals. She's the one who inspired my desire to see the world. It's partly the reason why I was chosen for Yueshu." She paused. "She... She must've loved you very much to accept the lily."

Lord Ishida rose to his feet, a picture of dignity though his shoulders trembled.

"Bethany?" Hiro's grip faltered on his belt. "Mother's name was Bethsaida."

"Your mother changed it after her Release. It's not uncommon among Released clergy." He turned back to Amelia, hands cupped in supplication. "Would you consider loaning me your copy for the duration of your stay? I would like to read my wife's words."

"O-Of course. I know how much it means to you, but..."

He smiled at her. It was genuine this time. "It is precious to you, too. I understand." He caressed the woven binding with his fingertips, biting his lower lip.

Behind her, the domo softly cleared his throat.

Flushing, Amelia took a step back and glanced at the prince. He was still down on one knee, jaw clenched. "I'm sorry, Hiro. Please forgive me for interrupting."

He nodded fractionally.

"There is nothing to forgive." Lord Ishida clasped the book to his chest. "You will all accompany me to supper, with you, my lady, as my honored guest. Domo Ignatius—"

"My lord."

"—see that they are washed and given clean clothes. We'll dine in one hour. And summon the rest of the Ishida family to the dining suite."

The portly palace steward bowed low. "At once, my lord."

They waited for the Lord of Jianshu and his retinue to leave before Domo Ignatius hustled them inside like a mother hen.

The Jade Palace was grander than any Council Lodge. Its magnificence came from its simplicity, the natural beauty of the malachite stone, and the fresh-cut chrysanthemums. Verdant columns veined with gold supported a vaulted ceiling; raw silk tapestries depicting colorful dragons of all sorts hung upon the walls; crackling flames from the fire bowls flickered light and shadow in an eternal duel across the polished green stone.

"... will take care of your horses and luggage. My lady – please try to keep up, we only have an hour now – you'll be in the Lotus Suite. My prince, you'll be in the Cherry Suite. Brother Isen—"

"The *Cherry* Suite?" Hiro said.

The steward shrugged sympathetically. "I'm sorry, but—"

"What's the fuss about?" Isen asked. "It sounds delightful."

Hiro stormed past the priest into the palace. "It's in the guest wing, Isen. I'm a *guest* in my own home."

CHAPTER 61

HIRO CLUTCHED THE EDGE OF THE TABLE WITH WHITE-KNUCKLED FISTS. It was the only thing keeping his hand away from the tanto knife. "What new hell is this?"

"Even after twenty years I'd expect you to recognize your own brother," Toshiro said.

It was like looking in a mirror: obsidian hair, brown eyes, muscular build. Even the way his upper lip curled in disdain was the same.

"I mean *her*," Hiro growled.

She was still as beautiful as he remembered: gleaming chestnut hair, honey eyes, voluptuous curves. Her kimono was too tight, left little to the imagination as supple pink mounds burst over her neckline. She still knew how to turn his mind into pudding. The *biaozi*.

Toshiro gulped down his sake and gestured drunkenly to the woman seated beside him. "Allow me to introduce you. Princess Ellaria Matsu Ishida. My wife."

"Well... that would explain why you stopped writing me letters, little brother."

Toshiro sloshed more sake into his cup, tapped the empty bottle on the table. Ellaria's handmaiden sprang from her spot against the wall with a murmured apology. Light-brown skin, hazel eyes, the same gracefulness of a gazelle. She set another bottle of sake by his hand.

"You didn't dilute this one, did you, Viane?"

A rosy tint to her cheeks. "No, my prince."

Tapping chopsticks gnawed at Hiro's attention. Irritably, he flicked his gaze to the Sanu. She was pushing pieces of tempura eggplant around her plate, not eating. He snapped his fingers at the nearest server, shoved the offending plate into his hands. "She doesn't like eggplant. Bring mushroom xiaolong bao instead."

"Hiro, please, you don't need to—"

"You're a guest, and you'll have what you like."

The table was quiet until the servers returned with the suggested appetizer. She picked up a bun with her chopsticks, hovered a soup spoon underneath. "*Itadakimasu*," she said in Old Imperial. *Let us eat.*

Lord Ishida smiled.

Toshiro shot back another swallow of rice liquor. "So…we missed you at the wedding."

Hiro choked on his plum wine. Isen thumped him hard on the back. Hiro shrugged him off, set his cup down so hard it shattered. A server lunged forward, cleaned up the glass, and poured him another drink.

He almost jumped when the Sanu pressed her napkin into his hand.

"You're bleeding," she whispered. She shook her head once, her eyes kind. *It's not worth it.*

Hiro forced himself to relax. "I was otherwise detained." He held up his burned hand, a memento of his service at Biscay Bay.

"It's rude to miss the wedding of your only brother."

"It's also rude to wed and bed my fiancée, but you don't see me getting all huffy about it."

Toshiro glared at his older brother, was met with an unflinching stare.

"Where are your children?" Hiro asked. "Surely you must've had many fat, happy babies by now."

Princess Ellaria shifted in her seat. "We have not been blessed—"

"*Be silent,*" Toshiro hissed in Old Imperial.

Ellaria set her chopsticks down with a little rattle, finished the last of her plum wine. When she looked up from her plate, her honey eyes were wet.

Hiro averted his gaze, pushed the curried boar around his plate. He knew it should be spicy and tender, but it tasted like ash in his mouth.

"I see you've forgotten the teachings of our mother while you were away." Toshiro jerked his chin in the boy's direction. "I can't believe you had the gall to bring your bastard to dinner."

Hiro bristled.

Kale looked up from stuffing food into his mouth, stopped chewing. "*Bastard?*"

"He didn't mean it," Isen whispered.

"Kale is Hiro's ward, Prince Toshiro," the priestess said. "And before you voice any assumptions about me, I am Sanu. My uniform is being laundered, thanks to the graciousness of our host. Though we all were formally introduced, I can understand how you'd forget about us when you're so clearly distracted by the return of your brother. Truly, you must be *overwhelmed* by his many accomplishments."

Hiro glanced at the Sanu. She was being polite – as always – but the set of her shoulders revealed just how tense she was. If she'd been a cat, her tail would've been lashing.

"You look lovely in imperial green, Sanu," Princess Ellaria said quickly.

Far more modest than Ellaria's, the kimono's collar still drooped between her shoulder blades. With her hair twisted into a coil over one shoulder, the kimono revealed much more of her back than he'd ever seen. A caramel strand had slipped loose from her twist, swung tantalizingly over the expanse of smooth skin.

"Thank you, Princess."

"Do you not eat meat, Sanu?"

"*Don't be ridiculous,*" Toshiro admonished his wife. "*She is Sanu; all life is sacred to them, remember? They won't even kill the mosquito that bites them."*

Hiro remembered the priestess killing many a mosquito and other insects that had harassed her, though she always tried to shoo them away first.

The Sanu's eye twitched at his tone. "And what have you been up to in Hiro's absence, Prince Toshiro?"

"I command the Jianshu Guard. The most fearsome army on the entire continent."

"I wasn't aware you had any military training."

Toshiro's upper lip curled into a snarl over the rim of his sake cup. "I'm an Ishida."

"So it's your birthright."

"Well, when *someone* abandons his responsibilities—"

Chopsticks slipped from Hiro's fingers, clattered against his plate. *"Abandons?"*

"—it's up to *others* to uphold the family name."

The Sanu thrust her rice bowl into Hiro's startled hands. "Would you get me a little more, please?" She bared her teeth into a bright smile. "I assume Princess Ellaria must find many a diversion while you are on deployment."

"Oh, yes. I attend many concerts—"

"She was speaking to me, not you," Toshiro hissed again. *"You will be mindful of your place—"*

"Disrespect your wife in front of me again, and I will dismiss you from this table," the Sanu interrupted icily. *"As your father's honored guest, it is my right."*

Toshiro swallowed his mouthful of sake with great difficulty. "Father, my Guard duties require me to be up early. May my wife and I have your permission to be dismissed?"

Lord Ishida dabbed his lips with a napkin. "No. You'll miss dessert."

Hiro watched with grim satisfaction as his younger brother squirmed in his seat.

"I'll have lychees," Ellaria said. She nibbled on the succulent fruit, slowly dragged the pits from her pouty lips.

Hiro ignored her, smothered the memory of them sharing the same fruit one sultry summer day. It'd been the first time he'd kissed her. He plunged his spoon into the dessert without thinking, reeled as a burst of summertime fruit flooded his mouth. Strawberry sorbet. He glanced at the Sanu.

"Is it too cold, Sanu?" Ellaria asked. "You look... in pain."

The priestess's cheeks were flushed crimson. "No, no. It's... fine."

For a heartbeat, the murderous thoughts vanished. Lust took their place. Clamping a shaking hand on the table, he shoved the sorbet aside. "I prefer egg tarts. Would you like the rest of mine, Sanu?"

She hunched over her bowl, shook her head vigorously.

"I'll take it," Kale volunteered.

"Don't eat too many of those tarts, Hiro," Toshiro sneered. "You'll get fat again."

"Hiro was *fat?*" Isen sputtered.

"Not as fat as you were, Toshi-Tum."

"*Don't* call me that."

Lord Ishida dropped his spoon onto the saucer with a loud ring. His eyes were chips of flint, his mouth set in a disapproving line. He rose from his seat, extended his arm to the Sanu. "If you please, my lady, I will escort you from this... humiliation."

Hiro bowed his head, glared at Toshiro from under lowered lids.

"*Princes* Hiro and Toshiro, you will wait for my summons tomorrow. Brother Isen, Kale, good-evening."

Once the Sanu and their father had exited the room, Toshiro bolted upright. Decorum dictated he wait until his elder brother left before him. Hiro took the time to straighten his place setting, then rose with deliberate slowness. Toshiro fidgeted.

"Kale, I'll see you for training tomorrow at dawn on the eastern terrace. Bring your staff. Isen, do you need someone to help you back to your suite?"

"What do you think Kale's going to do?" Isen said.

The boy looked up from Hiro's bowl of sorbet. "I am?"

Isen cuffed the boy's head. "I gave you the rest of my dessert! It's the least you can do."

Hiro turned back to his brother and his wife. His hand slid to his tanto knife, fingers stroked the hilt.

She wouldn't want you to.

He snapped a short bow and left.

OUT ON THE NORTHERN BALCONY, Hiro raked his hands through his hair. The night had not gone at all as he had envisioned. Being welcomed back with open arms was so far beyond his father's personality it was laughable, but being so thoroughly dismissed in favor of the Sanu was something he did not expect either. And Toshiro—

His fingers slipped to the tanto knife.

Gods above, he's *the one she left me for? He was the only family I had left—*

He raked his hands through his hair again, nearly yanking it out by the roots.

A scrape of leather against stone. He peered into the gloom for the boy. He'd know that footstep anywhere. But Kale remained in the shadows, discreet.

"Hiro?"

Ellaria stepped into the moonlight. Throwing her arms around his neck, she kissed him hard on the lips.

CHAPTER 62

HER TONGUE WAS HALF-WAY DOWN HIS THROAT BEFORE HE REMEMBERED himself and pushed her away. She tasted of lychees, cloyingly sweet.

"Ellaria—" Hiro gasped for air.

"Oh, Hiro," she moaned, hands tugging at his clothes. "I've missed you so much—" She pulled his head down to kiss him again.

"Princess Ellaria." He forced her away from him.

She laughed. "You needn't be so formal with me, Hiro."

He cocked an eyebrow, straightened his clothes. "Don't I?"

The smile faded from her face. "Hiro, you must understand—"

"That you were engaged to me but married my brother?" Hiro shouted. "My. *Brother.* Did those letters you wrote to me mean *nothing?*"

"Hiro, please! You were sent off in dishonor. My parents insisted upon a good match and refused to let me marry you, regardless of what I felt."

"Since when have you ever followed the advice of your family? You wanted to be just like your rebellious brother—"

"I'm not a *child* anymore, Hiro." Ellaria shook the anger from her features, slid her hand up his arm to his shoulder. "Surely you must have known how I felt about you. How I... *still* feel about you."

He grabbed her hand, wrenched it back at the wrist. She gasped, the pink mounds that burst from her kimono heaving with every breath. "Then why didn't you fight for me, for us?" he snarled. "I waited for you, preserved my honor for you, all of those years I was in the Academy. I never ceased to think of you."

It was true. He'd only succumbed to Lakshmi's incessant advances after the last letter. His fingers dug into her wrist.

"Hiro, please—"

"You are my brother's wife. You are nothing to me now other than a sister-in-law." He released her with a little shove.

"Is there someone else?" she demanded. "What of that, that *woman*, you brought to dinner?"

"What? No! Of course not."

"Is it because she's *pure*? Untouched by a man?"

Untouched? Unbidden, the image of them entangled together to prevent hypothermia sprang to mind. They had touched plenty. His cheeks burned at the memory.

"Any woman can be deflowered—"

"She is Sanu, and I'll not tolerate that tone about her. She's my... friend."

"*Friend?* Oh come on, Hiro," Ellaria laughed. "You were never the religious type. What could some priestess—"

"*Leave her out of this.*" The venom in his voice startled even him.

"So there *is* something between you."

"I am honor-bound to her. And why would you care?"

Ellaria's face twisted in rage. "You were sworn to me first."

"You are sworn to another now by your own hand."

"Your *father* made me do it."

Hiro snorted. "My father is not so cruel as to destroy the dreams of a son by marrying off his fiancée to his brother."

"You know nothing, Hiro."

They faced off in the moonlight, seething.

Abruptly, Ellaria smoothed her features as if pulling a mask down over her face. She tugged on her kimono to straighten it, drew his eyes to the fabric that clung to her breasts. He wet his lips involuntarily.

"Can't you see I belong with you?" She leaned into him, pressed each luscious curve against him. Her arms encircled his waist as she gazed into his eyes. Their honey depths threatened to drown him. Gods above, she felt amazing—

"Don't you want me?" she purred. Her mouth was so close he could taste the lychees on her breath. It mingled with the strawberry on his tongue, soured.

He pushed away from her. "It doesn't matter what I want. You belong to another."

"I belong to no one," she snarled.

"Yes, you do. And so long as you're married I cannot and *will not* look at you in that way."

She paused, wetting her lips. "What if I wasn't married anymore?"

"Don't be ridiculous. Your parents – my *father* – would never allow a divorce."

Ellaria would not be dissuaded. She crossed her arms over her ample chest. "What if they knew my heart still belonged to another?"

"My father would tell you a heart is not required to birth Ishida heirs. Face it, Ellaria, you were never meant for me."

"But you still love me, I can see it in your eyes," she cried. "Don't you know it's *your* name I call out when your brother comes to my bed?"

Disgusted, he turned away from her.

She tried again, rubbing against him like a cat in heat.

"Go away, Ellaria." He didn't know how much more of this he could take. His fingers slipped to the tanto knife. He'd wanted to plunge this into her gut for so long, but now—

"There is an ancient law, *intus familia*," she whispered, her hands trailing below his waist, "wherein a brother could have relations with his brother's wife—"

"That law is meant for the protection of widows, not wives with healthy husbands. And that law is ancient for a *reason*." He pushed her away more forcefully than he meant to. She fell to the ground, pouty lips parted in surprise.

Manners demanded he apologize and offer to assist to her feet. Mother had always taught him to be polite.

He remained rigid, ignored the teachings of his mother. "You will never again mention *intus familia* to me," he warned. "You will never proposition me again. And you will address me with the formality due to my station. Good-night, Princess Ellaria. Give my best to your husband."

He turned, left her there upon the cold stone floor as she burst into tears.

CHAPTER 63

"This is not the Lotus Suite." Amelia paused in front of azure doors carved with a dragon holding a waterlily in its claws. She snatched her hand from Lord Ishida's arm. The silver dragon reared its head, feathery scales bristling on its neck.

"No, it is not," Lord Ishida agreed. "Domo, if you would."

The walrus bustled forward and swung the doors open for them.

A bright shaft of moonlight pierced through the oculus and turned the rainwater of the recessed pool to cream. Paintings of the Most Holies covered every inch of the curved walls. There was Lady Boset-sanu in an orange gown creating the first lilies, Delphi the Protector and his phoenix defeating the Crocodile King, the Crown Prince of Heaven shining like a sun in the midst of a massive thunderstorm, his sword of white fire held above his head in both hands.

It was a chapel.

"I wanted to show you this," Lord Ishida said, gesturing her inside.

They removed their shoes, and Amelia took a tentative step, not sure where to place her foot. The floor was a mosaic of underwater creatures from jellyfish to turtles to sailfish. There was even a kraken in onyx tiles on the other side of the pool. Above, the tiles extended across the domed ceiling in depictions of various sea birds.

"It is the Ishidas' private chapel, but you are welcome to use it whenever you'd like during your stay. However long that may be."

"Shorter than I'd like, I'm afraid."

The Lord of Jianshu sighed. "I hope tonight's dinner—"

"Oh, no. It's just I'm impatient to be in Lhasa. I've had far too many adventures getting even this far. Not all of them good."

Lord Ishida frowned. "I'd very much like to hear about those. Not tonight, of course. I've heard some disturbing reports since I've summoned my son home."

They stopped in front of an oil painting suspended over a rendition of waterlilies.

"Is this your family?" she asked.

"Yes. As you can see, I had black hair back then."

"Hiro looks so much like Bethany. Lady Bethsaida, I mean."

"Painfully so."

Amelia stole a glance at him. Lord Ishida's eyes were soft, yet his teeth ground together. His fingertip traced the curve of his wife's face. He snatched his hand back when boots pounded into the sanctuary.

"Lord Ishida, an eagle has just arrived," the messenger panted. "Sealed in red."

"Would you like me to go?" Amelia asked.

He turned to her, bowing low. "Please stay as long as you'd like. I must attend to this. Domo Ignatius, if you'd remain with the Sanu?"

"Of course, my lord. And Master Cheng has your tonic ready."

Lord Ishida plucked the letter from the panting messenger and broke the seal on his way out. His retinue swarmed around him, breaking off as he gave them instructions. Domo Ignatius closed the door after them and picked up a candle snuffer. He hummed a tune to himself as he went about the room, extinguishing the little flames.

Amelia sat by the edge of the recessed pool, legs drawn up to her chest as she watched the pink candles floating carefree in the water. Soon they were all that remained.

"Tell me, Domo, are all family dinners with the Ishidas that... intense?"

The steward chuckled. "My lord prefers to let matters resolve themselves between those involved and step in only to prevent unfor-givable offense or action. His subjects know that if he has to settle their affairs they will not like the outcome."

"Why? Is he not just?"

"Brutally so, as in the punishment is more than you'd normally receive as a consequence for being a public nuance and wasting his time. He has an entire province to govern, not sit in judgement over the bickering of petty men. Or princes. He has other things on his mind." Domo Ignatius paused by the oil painting, flicking away a mote of dust clinging to the late Lady's gown.

"He still grieves for her, doesn't he? Even after twenty years?"

"We all do, my lady. Lord Ishida was always a stern man, but Lady Bethsaida brought life to this place. It… hasn't been the same."

"You miss her, too."

The domo forced a smile. "Of course."

"She wrote about you, you know. In the Bethany Journals."

"S-She did?"

"You were the one who found her when she was lost in the bamboo groves. You were hunting blood pheasant."

The domo groaned. "For Lord Ishida. He couldn't stand venison one more minute. We'd been in the north fighting the Samoyedic Horde for months already. Fool woman got lost during a blizzard and stumbled into a war zone."

Amelia smiled softly. "You cooked her the pheasant and lied to Lord Ishida that you hadn't found any."

"And I got sent back out the next night for my generosity." He laughed. "I'd do it the same all over again."

She trailed her fingers in the pool. "I wish I could've known her. She was so fearless."

"Hiro was much like her, before he left." The domo dragged a settee beside her and lowered his girth with a huff. The cushions wheezed in protest. "Fearless, compassionate, marveled at everything the world had to offer."

"*Hiro?*"

"Surely you've seen snatches of it. Just look at how he treats the boy."

Amelia sighed. "If only he'd put his anger aside and show the rest of us just a speck of such kindness."

"Sooner rather than later, I hope."

"What do you mean?"

Domo Ignatius shook his head and held a hand out to her. He helped her rise, but when he tried to take his hand away, Amelia held it even tighter.

"What do you mean, Domo?"

He looked at her sternly. Or tried to since his eyes were wet with tears. "I say this to you in confidence, Sanu. Lord Ishida is dying."

CHAPTER 64

Isen sat on a stone bench, head cocked to one side as he listened to Hiro and Kale spar. Mild grunts and the *thwack* of staffs filled the air of the otherwise quiet morning. Their jackets had been discarded long ago, and sweat dribbled between their shoulder blades.

Over a dozen servants milled about, watching the returned prince as they swept the terrace and watered the rose bushes. Amelia straightened her clean tunic with a sharp tug, relieved again that no one would mistake her as anything else but a devout priestess.

"Good-morning," Isen said as she joined him on the bench. "I trust you had a far more pleasant evening *after* dinner?"

She chuckled. "Yes. I can't believe how tense that was."

"It's a shame we don't get to pick our families," he sighed. "We must simply live with the one we have and try to surround ourselves with better friends."

"Like you."

He found her hand and held it. "You're such a sweet girl, Amelia."

"Isen, you call me 'girl,' but I'm not that much older than you."

"And yet I have a maturity you will never reach," he lamented, holding his nose high into the air.

She pinched him on the arm, and he laughed.

He leaned his shoulder against hers. "Now that we're in one of the most heavily guarded places on Earth, do you think we could slip away sometime? I've rather had my fill of Ishidas."

Amelia thought it over, chewing her lip. "It'd probably be best not to wander..."

"Yeah, but we haven't seen any rooks, no demons, *nothing* since the Indus River. I think we'll be alright. Besides, if there's trouble you can do that glowy thing you do."

"*Shh.* Not so loud. And what's this 'glowy thing?'"

"It's what Kale calls it. 'Magic' sounds too far-fetched, and we all know you're not a sorceress, so... glowy thing."

"We're *not* calling it that and – ack, *what?*" Amelia pried her hand free, shaking the feeling back into it.

"Trouble."

Toshiro sauntered onto the terrace, flanked by his attendants. He wore an open sparring gi, the cleft in his chest sporting the Ishida birthmark. Otherwise his skin was unmarred. Toshiro shrugged out of his jacket and rested a hand on the hilt of his katana.

"Good-morning, little brother," Hiro greeted, waving Kale off. "Slept in, did we? I thought you said your duties began early, and here it is an hour past dawn."

"It's a much shorter walk to the terrace from the guest wing than it is from the family suites."

"Bet that hangover didn't help you move any faster, either." Hiro motioned for Kale to resume his attack.

"My wife says you propositioned her last night," Toshiro continued loudly. "Something about how you can't move on, that you're still in love with her."

Hiro's face darkened. "Don't be ridiculous. She's your wife."

"I know what she is! And you'll do well to keep your eyes off her."

"That's hard to do when she dresses so provocatively. Tell me, does she dress that way for you or for someone else?"

With a roar, Toshiro drew his katana and swung at his brother. Kale dove out of the way. Hiro blocked and used his greater weight to shove Toshiro back a few steps.

Amelia grabbed Isen's hand.

"She chose *me*," Toshiro bellowed. "She left you for *me*."

This was not a training exercise; it was a fight between two men who wanted to hurt each other. The anger in Hiro's face was building to a volcanic level. Toshiro was about to get a thrashing he might not walk away from.

"You *stole* her," Hiro roared. "You twisted her into a pernicious *biaozi* to be just. Like. *You.*"

"That *biaozi* is my *wife*," Toshiro snarled, stabbing for Hiro's gut and missing. "You're just jealous her legs spread for me now instead of you. You can't stand the thought that I rut like a stag between those creamy thighs—"

Hiro's face had gone purple with rage. "Then why did she come on to me last night? You're delusional, Toshi-Tum. If you were taking care of business, she wouldn't be seeking it elsewhere."

Toshiro let out a strangled cry and attacked his brother with renewed fervor.

"I. Don't. Want. Her." Hiro insisted as he blocked his brother's strikes. "Leave *off*, Toshiro." He slammed his staff against his younger brother's shoulder, shattering his collarbone.

Toshiro crumbled to the ground with a howl. Amelia bolted from her seat and raced to the fallen prince's side. She tried to help him up but he lunged at her, screaming. Hiro knocked her out of the way and cracked his fist into Toshiro's jaw. His younger brother slumped against the ground, unmoving. Hiro drew his fist back to his cheek, readying another strike.

"*Stop it!*" Amelia shouted, pushing Hiro away. She would've had more success getting a glacier to move. She jabbed him in his chest with her finger, nearly breaking it. "You're *better* than this, Hiro Ishida!"

Hiro retreated, panting. He turned his glare upon his brother's retinue, who stood frozen by the stairs. "What are you waiting for?" he bellowed at them. "Your prince requires your assistance. *Immediately.*"

As the attendants surged forward, Amelia grabbed Kale's jacket and shoved it into his hands. She clamped a hand onto his shoulder and steered him away. "You're coming with me, Kale. Isen, let's go."

"Amelia, you're shaking."

The boy looked nervously over his shoulder. "I haven't been dismissed yet..."

"Sanu, where are you going? *Sanu.*"

She ignored the prince, tightening her grip on Kale's shoulder. "Hiro promised you a guqin, didn't he? We're going to get you one."

"So we're going to play hooky again?" Isen asked, perking up.

"Absolutely," she growled. "I've had enough of the Ishidas for one day."

THE MARKETPLACE WAS a bustling hive of activity. The storefronts were nothing more than a conglomerate of open-air stalls held together by little lanterns strung on silver wire. People jostled good-naturedly in the narrow streets, and the occasional Guardsman put enough fear into would-be pickpockets to keep them honest.

They shouldered past ramen stalls and dim sum carts, lingered by the calligraphy supplies, tailors and the candle-makers, until Kale let go of her hand and ran to the guqin-maker. He ducked under the noren curtains, winking out of sight.

Instruments in various stages of curing hung on the walls next to strings of twisted silk. The craftsman greeted them with a smile but continued working on the guqin between his knees, sanding the edges to butter smoothness. The instruments for sale were on display in front of him, from the simple to the ornate with mother-of-pearl inlay.

Amelia gave a low whistle. "I had no idea making one of these was so complicated."

"It's a complete instrument." Kale sat and hefted the simplest one onto his lap. His fingers teased a haunting melody from the silken strings.

Isen smoothed his hand down another's cords. "It's said that the

Crown Prince was so devastated when Heaven and Earth divided that he made the guqin as an attempt to reunite the two halves."

Kale gestured for her to join him. His left hand strummed while his right hand pointed. "See, this top board is round like the Heavens, and the bottom board is flat like Earth. This narrow end here is known as the dragon's gums, and the broader end with the pegs is called the phoenix's tongue. You know, because the dragon and the phoenix are the dual protectors of the four realms." His fingertip glided over the raised bed where the silk strings were gathered. "And this is yueshan, the bridge. A connection between the two realms."

Amelia started, remembering the Old Mother's words. *The boy knows.*

Yueshan. She'd thought it was just a mistranslation, but—

"Boy, you know more about the instrument than my apprentice," the craftsman said. He blew the shavings aside and smoothed his hand down the soundboard. "Have you a master? Perhaps you're in the wrong business. You should work here."

"Prince Hiro would never allow it," Isen scoffed.

Kale stopped playing. "You don't know that."

"I don't? Your master's a brawling hothead. Why do you think we're here?"

Ignoring him, the boy put the instrument on the counter. "I'd like to purchase this one, please."

"You're sure, Kale?" Amelia asked. "There are others that are prettier."

He smiled. "A guqin's beauty is its music. This one sounded perfect."

The craftsman wrapped the instrument in silk and tied the bundle snug with a satin cord. "I'll send the bill to the palace, young master. Thank you for the song."

Amelia ruffled the boy's mane of auburn curls.

"You do play rather well, Kale," the priest said. "Maybe Hiro would reconsider." His fingers snagged on a string, and the silk broke with a yowling twang.

The master raised an incredulous gaze, snatched the guqin and threw it into the fire behind him. "Bad luck. Forgive me, Brother, but please go."

"I didn't mean any offense—"

"Just *go.*"

Despite the master's pleas, Amelia was rooted to spot. She couldn't tear her gaze from the burning instrument, its silken strings snapping, the lacquer peeling with the heat. "But—"

Kale snagged her arm, pulling her away. "Just leave it. Bad luck, Amelia. Who knows what it's summoned?"

CHAPTER 65

THE PILE OF DUST BEGAN TO SWIRL. SLOW AT FIRST, AN UNSEEN HAND whipped the flakes into a seething coil. The whirlpool churned against the terrace, sucking everything within reach into its sandy maw.

The rooks screamed.

They dug their little claws into the bricks, raked their pinions into tattered shreds as they fought against the pull. One by one, the wind dragged them into the vortex. The last disappeared with a strangled caw, and the dust turned black.

A figure stepped from the writhing sand, swathed in shadow. The gauze-like fabric twisted and fluttered like flames in an unseen breeze. Only gleaming green eyes in a strip of ashen flesh could be seen behind the shemagh that smothered its head and face. They flicked to the bow hanging above the garden door. This vessel's hands itched to grip the familiar wood; it was as good a weapon as any.

His hand convulsed, and a rook exploded from his palm. The bird clawed its way out of his flesh, but his fingers snapped shut around its beak and head before any more of the bird could wrestle free. His hand tightened, crushing, smothering the death caws until a green flash winked once behind the seams in his fingers. When they uncurled, a barbed arrowhead rested in his palm.

Tiny hooks fringed the double-tiered broadhead, primed to punch through and embed in flesh. A scrollwork of miniscule runes decorated the bone-white surface, flaring green with his touch. He summoned the remaining rooks one by one, transforming their skulls until four identical arrowheads clinked in his hands like oracle bones. They disappeared into his shadowy robes, the green light dimming into dormancy.

The *manabudh* snatched the bow from its pegs, slung the quiver over his shoulder, and went to find the master.

CHAPTER 66

Hiro paused in front of the azure doors, his hand hovering above the dragon's snout. It'd been twenty years since he'd entered this chapel, or any other for that matter.

He pushed the doors open, half hoped they'd be locked and forbid him entry. Stumbling into the chapel, he shaded his eyes against the glare of the evening sun. He left his boots off to the side, padded forward on stockinged feet. He found himself tracing the tiled tentacle of a rose-colored octopus the same way he had as a child. Diverting from the cephalopod, he knelt by the recessed pool.

Mother had schooled Toshiro and him here, not just in religion, but in every subject imaginable. Once she'd even let them put captured frog's eggs in the pool to watch how they'd grow. The frogs had infested the palace like a plague, their chirping heard for months.

His hand slipped to the tanto knife. The frogs were long gone now, and so was she. Sent off to die on a suicide mission by his father. That tyrant had taken everything from him. His home, his family, his fiancée. The tanto slipped free of its lacquered sheath with a *snick*. The Lord of Jianshu had just welcomed a wolf into the henhouse.

"For you, Mother."

✦

A MUFFLED WHOOSH, quiet footfalls of slippered feet, the hem of a golden tunic rippling into his peripheral vision.

"Hiro. I... didn't know you were here."

He rolled to his feet, slid the tanto up his sleeve. "Father." *Hundan.* "Would you like me to go?"

"No, stay if you'd like. I just come here to see your mother before dinner."

Don't you talk about her! "Oh?" He followed his father to the family portrait.

Lord Ishida touched his wife's face with a gentle fingertip.

Don't act like you miss her, ryushutsu. The tanto slipped into Hiro's his palm until just the tip protruded past his fingers.

"Your mother would've been very disappointed in you for injuring your brother, you know."

And I'm very disappointed you murdered my mother. "He started it." He hadn't meant to hurt Toshiro, but his younger brother still knew how to goad him to violence.

Lord Ishida *tsked*, shook his head. "I did not summon you home so you two could fight over a woman. Especially *that* one."

The tanto dropped a little lower, his fingers curled around the slick hilt. *She's not the woman I want your blood for.* "Then why did you? Over a bunch of slain priests?"

His father's eye twitched. "Show some respect. Those men used to be your mother's brothers. If not for that, for the lives they lost."

Hiro barked a laugh. "Since when have you shown any respect for the life of your fellow man? Or woman? Or *wife?*"

Lord Ishida glowered. *"My wife?"*

"Yes, surely you must remember the woman you pitted against Kogusanji's war-host, knowing she stood no chance. My *mother?*"

The tanto was free now. Half-hidden behind his back, he gripped the blade firmly between thumb and forefinger like a razor. Just one swift cut across the jugular—

"*Oh.* Lord Ishida, Hiro, forgive me for interrupting."

Dammit, Sanu!

The priestess lingered in the doorway, a small sack in her hands. Domo Ignatius stood beside her, a fizzing glass of tonic in one hand. "I-I wanted to... I can come back later."

Good. Go far away—

"No, Sanu. Please stay," Lord Ishida said, beckoning her. "I've done my devotions."

"Thank you."

"Your tonic, my lord." Domo Ignatius bustled forth, handed him the glass with a sharp bow, and wedged his girth between them. "Let's see how that cut is healing, Prince Hiro." He seized Hiro's hand, squeezed his fingers until the bones started to pop. His gray eyes flashed warningly, but Hiro just gritted his teeth and held onto the knife.

"If it's okay, Lord Ishida, I'd like to add this to the pool." The Sanu fished around in her sack, withdrew a carved candle.

Lord Ishida sucked in his breath, took the candle with trembling fingers. Orange, black-spotted, a cluster of pale stamen. The candle was carved to resemble a tiger lily. "Just like the one I gave Bethsaida." He lit it from the nearest candelabra, knelt to float it among the others in the pool. "I searched the garden for over a week to find it."

The Sanu smiled softly. "I'm sure she appreciated your dedication. Oh, and we got Kale a guqin. He's been practicing all afternoon. I think he wants to put on a concert for you at dinner."

Hiro faltered. Ignatius took advantage of the lapse in his grip, got ahold of the hilt. "Sanu, you didn't need to—"

"Don't worry; I sent the bill to the palace. And... I got this for you, Hiro. I was going to give it to you later, but you're here now." Her fingers cupped around a purple lotus flower. "The petals are used to heal lacerations. You just layer them on and that's it."

That was the hand holding the tanto knife.

"I was just... looking at that wound... myself," Domo Ignatius said through gritted teeth.

They strained against each other, Hiro trying to conceal the knife and the steward trying to relieve him of it, all the while pretending nothing was happening.

"It's... fine," Hiro growled.

"Oh no, my prince...it looks... really bad."

The Sanu looked at him expectantly. "So... may I see your hand?" Her ocean-blue eyes were earnest, compassionate. She'd already forgiven him for the horrible way he'd acted this morning.

Hiro sighed, relinquished the blade. Ignatius snatched it away, made a show of presenting Hiro's wounded palm while he stuffed the tanto into the back of his sash.

"That looks really inflamed," she said. "Does it hurt?"

He shook his head fractionally.

The Sanu layered the purple petals onto his hand, curled his fingers over them to keep them in place.

"That was very kind of you, my lady," Lord Ishida said. "His mother used to do the same thing when he was a boy. The summers were always full of scraped knees."

His fist trembled in her hands. He dropped his hand, bruised the petals to a pulp.

"Well, that's all the time I have now," the Sanu said, dropping the remaining flower into the sack. "Domo Ignatius, would you give this to Prince Toshiro, please? If the petals are steeped into a tea, they can help reduced the swelling in his shoulder."

The steward accepted the sack with a small bow. "Certainly. I'll let him know it was from you."

"Why don't you just give them to him yourself?" Hiro asked.

"Princess Ellaria has invited me to a private dinner in her suite this evening. And I mustn't be late." She hopped from one foot to the other as she put on her sandals, gave them a little wave in farewell.

Beside him, Lord Ishida sighed softly. On his face was something Hiro hadn't seen in decades. Affection.

Just a heartbeat later, the emotion was gone.

"Domo, we'll take our supper in the war room now," Lord Ishida announced. "Summon Toshiro, if you would."

"Certainly, my lord."

"Come along, Hiro."

Before Hiro could follow, Ignatius snatched his arm. He held up the tanto knife, his gray eyes bright with anger. "I know what this is, boy. And I'm going to keep it until we've talked. None of this foolishness, now, do you hear me?"

Hiro scowled. "You know I'll find another way."

The steward cuffed his head like a child. "Mind me, boy. I'll not see you go down this path. Your mother wouldn't want this. Don't you remember the words she inscribed onto this blade?"

"But she's not here anymore, is she?"

CHAPTER 67

THE PRINCES CROWDED AROUND THE CHART TABLE. BAMBOO STEAMER baskets of dim sum delicacies nestled together at one end like a cluster of penny buns. A map of Eurasia dominated the rest of the table, its worn parchment yellowed with age.

Hiro poured three flutes of plum wine, handed one to his brother.

Toshiro glared murderously at him, one eye swollen shut and his lip split and leaking. Refused to accept the glass.

Shrugging, Hiro set it down on the table next to his hand. He took a long swallow from his own glass, selected a shrimp dumpling with his chopsticks.

"Hiro," Lord Ishida said, "I recalled you from the Academy because I believe Kogusanji is creating another army."

Hiro choked on his dumpling. *"What?* Isn't he dead?"

"We... never actually found his body."

"Worst secret *ever.*" Toshiro picked up the plum wine, drained it in one gulp.

"Regardless, either he has risen again or he has a successor. The loyalists are calling it *Via Leao* – the Way of the Lion – and more and more have been found bearing Kogusanji's sacrilegious mark."

"I've heard the term. But what's this have to do with the slaughtered priests of Bastogne? Domo Tanaka said *that* was the reason why you summoned me home."

"It's the manner of their deaths that concerns me. The priests were hung by their hands, abdomens slit, entrails burned beneath them. It's how Kogusanji dealt with those who had greatly offended him."

Toshiro poured some more wine. "So it could be a loyalist or just a psycho with a penchant for murdering clergy."

"Don't be flippant, Toshiro."

"But aren't those priests known for their mastery of notué? Who could've possibly attacked them and live? Kogusanji was just a man."

Demons.

Lord Ishida shrugged. "It could've been an inside job. Or both. It doesn't matter—"

"It *does* matter." Hiro set his flute down with a rattle. "There was a sorcerer who conjured demons to kill the Sanu. Just one of those things wiped out her entire temple. It could've attacked the notué priests as well."

"Surely you must be joking—"

Lord Ishida silenced Toshiro with a slice of his hand. "She'd told me she'd had many unpleasant adventures. But clearly you all survived. How?"

"Steel forged in dragon's breath seems to kill them just fine."

"And the sorcerer?"

"His name was – or is – Tareq Imal Nadir, the mayor of Janpur."

"How am I just hearing about this now? There should've been reports coming in from Jardin and Pirsa. I heard about a temple in Bucharest being set on fire, but—"

"Yeah... the Sanu did that."

"*What?*"

"It'd become a prostitution den. The Sanu drove out the whores and burned it down."

"Damn," Toshiro murmured.

"Did Lady Cosette know of this?" Lord Ishida demanded.

"Of course. She's the one who kidnapped her and gave her over to the sorcerer."

"*What?*"

Hiro sighed. "Briefly, he wanted her to open some artifact or other to summon the gods and bring about the apocalypse. You know, zealotry at its best. Anyway, we sort of toppled Lady Cosette's regime. I think the sorcerer's dead now since we haven't been attacked since crossing the Indus River."

Toshiro and Lord Ishida gaped at him.

Hiro picked up another dumpling. "It's been a busy few months."

"That would explain why the reports I was getting were not from the usual sources..." The Lord of Jianshu launched to his feet. "The Council will know of this. I'll have that *biaozi* stripped of her Seat and hung in the public square. Fraternizing with sorcerers—"

He started to cough, pressed a cloth to his mouth. After a ragged breath, he went to the sideboard and hastily mixed a drink. The herbs floating about in the bubbling water smelled strongly of ginger and licorice.

Lord Ishida sat back down. "More of that later. Yesterday when you arrived, you mentioned an army."

"They're here." Hiro tapped the Qiang Pass on the map. "No crests, just black banners. They're choking off Pathanok."

"Well, that army has started to move southeast. Deeper into Tybet, toward the Bhutan Steppes and Lhasa."

"How do you know that?"

"I sent out eagles that very night to our outposts along the border. They've been sending back reports ever since. That army is definitely moving on the holy city."

"It'll take weeks – months – to get an army of that size through the Himalayas, regardless of what path they choose."

"Plenty of time to attack them from behind."

"But—"

"Tomorrow I will publicly return you into the family fold, and then you will lead the Jianshu Guard against this threat."

Hiro swallowed.

"But the Jianshu Guard is under *my* command," Toshiro protested.

"*You are not fit to lead,*" Lord Ishida barked. "That broken collarbone is just a timely excuse to relieve you of your post. Instead, *you* will command the Home Guard and attempt to keep our capital city safe. Praise Delphi that Arashiyama is nowhere near the mountains. So even if you oversleep as you're so fond of doing, we'll still have plenty of time to muster the soldiers before the enemy is knocking at the palace door."

Lord Ishida ripped the Imperial dragon crest from Toshiro's shoulder. Bottom lip trembling, his younger brother stood rigid as their father picked the fabric out from the pin.

Lord Ishida turned back to his firstborn. "The Pirsan Guard has already been roused and is marching toward Jaipur as we speak. Apparently someone has been intercepting their messenger eagles. I've sent word to my beneficiary Domo Nameer Khan, but you know what Tybet is like. Nothing but a bunch of squabbling city-states. He'll get them in line if he wants my continued support.

"But the Jardin Guard cannot mobilize because of the riots in all of the major cities. Though I'm sure in light of recent news it's more of Lady Cosette's making than Kogusanji's. The Siber Guard is still assembling, but will march from the north. They will be at our northern border within two weeks. Hopefully we can crush this threat before it does what it was formed to do, whatever that is."

"I need a small contingent of Guardsmen to help me escort the Sanu to Lhasa first," Hiro said. "A squad should suffice."

"We need every man we can get," Toshiro complained. "Sending an entire squad to escort a priestess is *ridiculous*—"

"*Quiet.* To help *you*?" Lord Ishida clarified. "Perhaps you do not understand, Prince Hiro, but you are to take command effective immediately. I'll give you a squad, even a platoon, if you so wish, to escort the Sanu Maitre, but *you* will not be going."

"Father, I gave her my word—"

"I didn't recall you from the Academy for you to abandon your people in their time of need! Do you want history to look back on this time and blame the Ishida House for the destruction of the world through inaction? I'll not be second best, not again, not by you or your mo—" He cut himself off abruptly, swallowed before continuing more calmly. "You have two choices, Hiro. Escort the priestess by *yourself* and be forever stricken from this House, or return to the fold and lead the Jianshu Guard against the threat to your *family* and *province*. Do that, and the priestess will be escorted to Lhasa with an armed company."

"A company?" Toshiro sputtered. "First it's a squad, then a platoon, now a *company*? Why not send an entire regiment? What will remain of the Home Guard afterward?"

"*Silence.* She is the last Sanu, isn't she? A regiment might not even be enough. Whatever wars we wage on this earth are nothing compared to the one she battles for our souls."

"Then let me *go*," Hiro said.

"It's arrogance to believe that you, a single man, can smuggle her across the country and successfully evade such a force."

"I agree. It *would* be arrogance if I actually hadn't done it already."

He made a cutting motion with his hand. "*Enough*, Hiro. You are needed here to provide stability to the province. That is what *your* presence does. And that will inspire hope and courage in our troops to face the threat at our doorstep! What do you choose?"

"There's only one choice and you know it," Hiro snarled. "I'll be no better than an oath breaker. Is that the kind of man you want for your son?"

"*Well?*"

Hiro hated this moment more than when he'd found out Ellaria had married his brother. He hated his father for putting him in this position. He glared into his father's blue eyes with a fury that could melt flesh from bone. But his father was made of ice, through and through. He would never yield. There would be no coming back from this.

With a defeated sigh, Hiro bowed his head in submission.

"It's done then." Lord Ishida nodded briskly. "The regiment will be outfitted as soon as you pick them out, General. When it is done, the Pirsan Guard is expecting you to join them at Kanpur."

"I understand, my lord." Hiro couldn't bear to call this man 'father' any more.

Lord Ishida came around the table, placed his hands on his general's muscled shoulders. "The first army of Kogusanji's nearly destroyed this world. I need the Beast to defeat the Monster."

Hiro gritted his teeth. "I relive that day in my nightmares," he hissed. "And you want me to do that *again?*"

"I want you to do what is necessary."

Even if it cost him the rest of his soul.

"It... shall be done as you say."

"Very good. You two are dismissed."

Hiro bowed to his lord, gripped the empty sheath of the tanto knife hidden in his belt.

He's killed us both, Mother. But I will have vengeance.

CHAPTER 68

AMELIA WAS USHERED INTO PRINCESS ELLARIA'S PRIVATE APARTMENTS BY one of the princess's handmaidens. She squinted against the harsh electric light, the garish colors of the wallpaper and furniture blinding her. Princess Ellaria rose from the table when her guest arrived, coming to Amelia's side and grasping her hands like they were old friends.

"I'm so pleased you accepted my invitation to dine with me, my lady," the princess said. "I've been so long without cultured female companionship in this dreary palace."

"Dreary? The palace is stunning."

"Well, you probably don't know any better, my lady. You *do* live on a mountaintop." Ellaria laughed, her voice like the tinkling of water on crystal. "I suppose if Lady Bethsaida was still alive, this place would be different. Anyway, please come with me. I have a seat already prepared for you."

The princess led her to the lacquered table by the window and gestured her to sit.

Amelia sat on a plump cushion, folding her hands in her lap. The evening sun shone directly into her face.

The princess sat off to one side, smiling.

Amelia lifted a hand to shade her eyes. "Princess Ellaria, if I may—"

"Would you like some wine?" the princess interrupted. "It's made with the local ume plums. I've visited the fermentation houses myself a few times; it's *quite* fascinating."

"I would prefer tea—"

"What are you all gawking at?" the princess snapped at her hand-maidens. "Bring out the wine!" She turned her attention back to Amelia, smiling again. "So, you must have plenty of stories to tell after traveling so far away from home."

"I could say the same for you, my lady," Amelia said, trying to lean out of the direct path of the sun. It was hopeless. "You must miss your home."

Princess Ellaria sighed wistfully. "I do. It's strange though, I didn't expect to miss the cedar swamps as much as I do. They can be quite beautiful and depressing at the same time, do you know what I mean?"

Mount Taru came to mind, isolated yet enrobed in azalea flowers. "Yes—"

"Of course you don't. How could you? Mount Taru is the closest thing to Heaven on Earth, I'm told."

"It's one of the most beautiful places I've ever seen, though I might be a little biased. But this place… This place holds a beauty I don't think I'll ever fathom. I'd be tempted to stay—"

"But you have to move on again so quickly, don't you?" Ellaria interrupted, nodding as if in sympathy. "Besides, you've taken up so much of Hiro's time already, haven't you, poor dear?"

Amelia pursed her lips. She was not a 'poor dear,' and Hiro owed her a life-debt, a vow of his very own choosing no less. She bristled at the insinuation that she was a grindstone around his neck.

"Of course not deliberately, of course not," Ellaria plowed on, still nodding. "But, yes you have, all the same. So you're headed straight to Lhasa?"

Amelia nodded, smoothing her ruffled feathers. Perhaps Ellaria was just being chatty and borderline impolite because she was nervous. "I've been tasked to perform Yueshu," she answered. *Lady Bosetsanu help me. I still don't know the sequence of the dance—*

"Quite the archaic ritual, yes? I mean, is there any *real* use to it anymore? *Where is that wine?*"

Amelia bristled again. "There is *every* reason to perform the ritual. It maintains the natural order, ensures a path to paradise, prevents the *apocalypse—*"

"Ah, *finally.*"

Viane, the pretty handmaiden from last night, rushed forward with a bottle of wine and two small glasses etched with flowers. A handful of ume plums swam drunkenly at the bottom of the bottle as she poured the wine.

Amelia's upper lip twitched at the blatant disregard of etiquette as Ellaria took the first glass instead of offering it to her guest. Shocked, a small gasp escaped from the handmaiden.

Ellaria gave the young woman a scathing look, plucked the bottle off the tray, and set it on the lacquered table with a loud *thump*. She flicked her manicured fingers impatiently, and Viane scurried away.

When Ellaria turned her attention back to Amelia, it was like a mask had shuttered into place over her face. No longer distorted by anger, her features were as smooth as cream. Her eyes, though, remained sharp. It didn't make any sense. She was a picture of perfection with her voluptuous curves, gleaming chestnut hair, and flawless makeup. Her pink kimono was embroidered with gingko leaves in silver thread; matching silver-and-opal hair ornaments studded her coiffure; jewelry adorned her fingers and neck. Yet her honey-colored eyes were as hard and cold as amber.

Amelia finished her wine and set the glass down on the table. Instead of offering to refill it, Ellaria just drummed her manicured nails against her glass, eyes glittering.

Okay... Amelia poured herself another and was about to set the bottle down when the princess wiggled her empty glass in front of her nose. Amelia ground her teeth and topped it off. She wondered what Lord Ishida would think if he knew the Sanu Maitre was catering to a mere princess.

The uncomfortable silence was broken when another handmaiden appeared with a tray of hot towels. Princess Ellaria made a show of removing her rings, each one clattering against the silver tray. Amelia was done washing her hands before Ellaria had even picked up her towel.

Amelia refilled her wineglass – again – and forced herself to make small compliments about the decorations around the room that Ellaria interrupted her to embellish on. That vase was not just *any* vase, but a Ziyi; the Matsu Cedars tapestry was woven with silver thread mined from Pirsa; the caged bird was an extremely rare Kamuy owl and thought to bring good luck and protection; the silk screen was not painted by just *anyone*, but by Henry Shang himself.

Amelia let out a sigh of relief when dinner arrived.

Covered dishes littered the lacquered table, not one of them she could eat. Frog legs in white wine and shallots, grilled cod with black bean sauce, suckling baby rabbits in tarragon cream, crispy pheasant in orange glaze, curried noodles with prawns.

She couldn't even eat anything that had been cooked with meat, but the curried noodles beckoned her. The beady little eyes of the prawns glared back at her. Glancing around the table one last time, she searched for the bowl of rice traditionally served with every Old Imperial meal. It was missing.

"May I ask for some tea?" Her head was starting to hurt from all the wine.

"It'll come out later." The princess plucked a prawn from the noodles with her chopsticks. "Otherwise it'll dilute the taste of the meal. Well, help yourself, Sanu."

The princess ripped a baby rabbit in half and sucked the cream off of the meat.

Amelia nearly retched.

She watched, dismayed, as the princess pulled the meat off the frog legs, crunched on crispy pheasant skin, and pried the cheeks out of the cod. There was such a cacophony of crunching and snapping and ripping that if she closed her eyes it was not hard to pretend she was having supper with a troll.

Despite her headache, Amelia poured herself another glass of plum wine. She was desperate to drown out the sounds of the princess munching on all those carcasses. Hiro had once disgusted her with his generous consumption of animal flesh, but one afternoon spent teaching Kale how to make a snare had changed her mind.

"This snare will break the neck instantly," Hiro had explained, touching it with a stick. The noose snapped closed, and the snare thrashed in an arc. "Why is this important?"

"It's so the rabbit doesn't suffer." Kale carefully reset the trap.

"Exactly. The rabbit is giving its life so that *you* can keep yours. That demands respect. Understand?"

The boy nodded. "And that's why we use the pelts and throw the offal to the other animals to eat. Nothing goes to waste."

"Exactly. Good boy."

Across from her, Ellaria ate what she deemed the most succulent parts, leaving good food discarded.

Amelia rotated the stem of her wine glass with little pushes of her fingertips, starting to think she might have enjoyed supper better with the brooding Ishidas.

"Is my banquet not to your liking, Sanu?" Princess Ellaria flicked her gaze from Amelia's face to her empty plate and back again. "I feel almost embarrassed to eat while you just sit there eating nothing."

"I have a sensitive stomach," she replied, refusing to take the bait.

"That's unfortunate," Ellaria said, shaking her head.

The princess *knew* she didn't eat meat. It was a trap, and she decided to do some baiting of her own.

"I know being away from your family must be difficult. I'm sure starting your own family would assuage some of that homesickness. I'm quite good at preparing herbal remedies. Perhaps I can make you an infusion to, um, promote..."

The princess laughed. "Oh, my dear. There's nothing wrong with *me*. It's all to do with Toshiro."

"How can you know that? If neither of you have strayed from wedlock, it's impossible to tell who the deficient one is."

"Indeed." The princess's eyes narrowed. "I'm just confident it's him because I come from a very bountiful line."

"Bountiful or not, there is the issue of your age difference. You are *much* older than Toshiro, aren't you? And to my knowledge the Ishida family tree has had no issues bearing fruit, no matter their age."

"A master in fertility, are we?" the princess tittered, though the mirth stopped at her brittle smile. "That hardly seems *appropriate* for a Sanu priestess."

Amelia's eye twitched.

The princess snapped her fingers until a handmaiden appeared. "Viane, clear this away and bring out the tea," the princess ordered. "I know there's a lot left, but I was the *only* one eating."

"Would my princess's guest prefer—"

Ellaria just waved her hand. "Throw it to the pigs or something."

"Give it to the poor instead," Amelia protested. "I'm sure they're hungrier than the pigs."

"Oh, my dear! That's so thoughtful of you, but no doubt they'd retch from all the richness and spread their diseases *everywhere*. No, I think it's best that it's given to the pigs, for the sake and health of us all."

"But—"

"Viane. The tea. *Now!*"

Amelia shut her mouth, clenching her hands under the table. The silver dragon bristled, and fire flickered over her fingertips. She snuffed it out. *You're an idiot, Hiro. What did you see in her besides... Well, her looks are rather distracting.*

This woman was a snake. A passive-aggressive, manipulative, condescending, patronizing, jealous—

That was it.

Her rude treatment was due to jealousy.

But why would the princess be jealous of me?

Viane set the tea service in front of them with two pots of tea. One was a graceful porcelain swan embellished with gold filigree... and the other was a fat little pot shaped like a koi.

What? Was she not good enough to drink from the princess's own teapot? Was her own pot made from moss scraped off the nearest stone instead of the jasmine tea that grew on the southern slopes? Maybe it was filled with tea after all. Maybe they'd burnt the tea leaves before steeping it. Or maybe they'd used tea leaves but had steeped it in moss water.

She was going to drink it, whatever it was. She was not going to give that nasty woman any satisfaction.

"What a delightful little fish," Amelia exclaimed. She even meant it. "I assume this pot is for me?"

Disgruntled, the princess shifted in her seat. "Um, yes. My own dietary issues require a specific type of tea. I'm sure you'll indulge me."

Amelia forced a smiled. It was small. "Of course."

Her tea was actually wonderful. Delicate jasmine tea, perfectly steeped in plain, clean water, piping hot. She guzzled it. Anything to fill her empty belly and stave off her throbbing headache.

Ellaria put three sugar cubes into her teacup before swirling it with a golden spoon. She rapped the spoon against the cup's rim three *tinks* more than Amelia thought necessary before nesting it on the saucer.

"The tea was brought out not a moment too soon, wasn't it?" Ellaria whispered, as if sharing a secret. "You'll have plenty of time to sober up before you leave tonight."

Amelia choked on her tea. She was *not* drunk, and she was *not* trying to sober up. It was time to end this insulting behavior.

"I believe we were discussing the impropriety of your interest in fertility?" the princess quipped.

"People have all sorts of problems, fertility being one among many." She tried hard to keep her voice conversational. "You'd be amazed what secrets and problems people confess to us: theft, lust, *cheating*. I wonder if your marriage to Hiro had gone through, if you would've had children by now. Some say the firstborns are the more virile of the siblings."

"Unfortunately, I'll never know," the princess replied icily. "I couldn't marry a man in disgrace. It would've shamed me, not to mention my family. But Toshiro tries, Gods above. He tries so much I can hardly *walk* the day after." She laughed, but her eyes were like flint. "Oh, I can't imagine what it's like to be a Sanu priestess, to be a virgin *forever*, to never know the touch of a man."

Unbidden, the memory of her and Hiro entangled together to prevent hypothermia sprang to mind. They had touched plenty. She was tempted to see what kind of look would be on Ellaria's face when she told her she knew exactly what it felt like to have Hiro's naked thigh wedged between her own.

"—it's almost like you're incomplete without it," the princess was saying, "like you're not a full woman."

"I wouldn't know." Amelia poured herself some more tea so she wouldn't reach across to slap the patronizing smile off the princess's face.

"I suppose you never will. But you have a higher calling. Someone's got to do it, right?"

"Indeed. One of my favorite duties of my *higher* calling is joining people in matrimony. I've performed one wedding already. Perhaps I'll have the pleasure to reside over Hiro's when he finally takes a wife. We've been through *so much* together that I'm sure he'd let me do the honor. That should be a marvelous affair, him being the heir to the Jianshu Seat and all."

Hatred burned in the princess's eyes.

"I'm sure that'll be soon," Amelia continued chattily, "now that he's returned home. Remind me, how long have you and Toshiro been happily married?"

The princess cleared her throat. "It'll be five years this winter."

"Oh, I bet that must've been a beautiful ceremony. Mmm, white snow and red winterberry bouquets—"

"Winterberries are for commoners," she sniffed. "I had lion's head dahlias from the greenhouse."

"Equally gorgeous, I'm sure."

The princess scoffed. "Hardly. They have a beauty second to none. If you'll excuse me for a moment, I've drunk too much tea." The princess rose from her cushion, still as pretty as a picture, and left Amelia to herself.

Amelia wanted to bolt, but decorum demanded she stay until she had bidden her hostess a proper farewell.

To the Abyss with etiquette.

She hefted her teapot, but only a few drops came from the koi's mouth. It was empty. Of course it was.

She set it back down with a rattle. Casting a furtive glance about, Amelia poured herself a cup from the princess's teapot. It was as black as molasses and smelled horrible.

Black like your soul. She gave a quick shake of her head. *You're better than that, Amelia.*

She took a cautious sip before gagging. She added three – no, four – sugar cubes to the cup and drank it down. The tea was terrible, but her stomach was happy for the sugar, so she forced another cup down before Ellaria returned.

"Sanu, it's getting late and I'm sure your duties require you to rise before dawn," the princess said.

First she was insulted, and now she was being kicked out? Amelia glanced out the window; it was barely even twilight. A sliver of sun still shone from the western horizon.

"Shall I show you to the door?" Ellaria prompted.

"I'm sure I can find my own way out, princess."

"That would not be very polite of me." But she made no move to usher Amelia to the door.

"Believe me, princess, your manners have no equal."

"It was a *pleasure*, Sanu."

Liar.

"We must do it again sometime," the princess said.

"I wouldn't want to inconvenience you."

Viane flashed to the door and opened it for her.

Ameliea gave the young woman a smile. *At least her staff knows how to properly treat a guest.* "And by the way," Amelia paused, looking over her shoulder, "that vase is *not* a Ziyi. Its design is indigo, and everybody knows Ziyi worked exclusively with cyan. I hope you didn't pay too much for it. Good-evening."

Even in the hallway, the sound of a vase shattering against a wall echoed. Amelia smiled grimly and went on her way. She would rather get lost in this enormous palace than spend another minute with that horrible woman. And she did. Eventually she fumbled her way to the terrace and breathed a sigh of relief as the night air blasted against her sweaty skin. She knew how to find the Lotus Suite from here.

"Lost?" a voice asked from behind her.

She spun, catching sight of a hulking figure leaning against one of the pillars.

"Oh, Hiro," she cried, running over to him. "I've just had the most wretched—"

His hand shot out, clamped onto her wrist, and pulled her in tight against him. His breath reeked of liquor.

"Hiro," she exclaimed. *"Hands—"*

"I'm not Hiro."

CHAPTER 69

"You know," the voice slurred, "I've never had another woman in my arms in almost five years—"

Amelia realized there was an arm in a sling pressing against her chest. She lurched away.

"—but maybe I'd find more love if I did."

Toshiro took a stumbling step toward her into the firelight. In his free hand he held a fat bottle of shochu liquor. He took another swig, staggering. His handsome face was marred by his bleary eyes and swollen lips.

"Forgive me." Amelia retreated another step. "I didn't realize it was you."

"Yep. It's me. Just me," he confirmed, swinging the bottle for emphasis. "Not the golden boy, Hiro Ishida. Just the second-born. Just the nobody."

"But you're the commander of the Jianshu Guard."

"Not anymore," he shouted at her. "Noooooo! Hiro is now. Now I'm just the head of the Home Guard. Feh."

"I'm sure that's still an honorable position."

"A monkey could do it. I guess that's me, isn't it? The Ishida monkey. Want me to dance next, Father?" he shouted to the stars. "Bang my cymbals? Oh wait, *I only have one arm.*"

"I think you should give me that bottle now."

"Get your own bottle." He took another swill.

"Toshiro," she said quietly, "why are you doing this?"

"Because he takes *everything.* He takes my Guard, he takes Father's attention, he takes Ellaria—" The prince stumbled against a fire bowl.

Shrieking, Amelia smacked on his injured arm, smothering the flames.

The prince howled, shoved her away from him. *"Damn woman—"*

She slapped him across the face. Hard. "Remember who you're talking to, *Prince.*" She snatched the bottle from his hand and gave him a small push.

He easily collapsed, cradling his head in his good hand. A soft sound, watery and choked, emanated from his hunched shoulders.

Wary, Amelia knelt, touching him lightly on the shoulder. He was crying.

"She doesn't love me," he blubbered. "She's always loved *him*. He wasn't even in the same province, and he still had her heart." He groped for the bottle, but she gently pushed his hand away. "Mother was gone, Father was... And Hiro left. Didn't he *care?* Didn't he know I *needed* him? I was so lost..." He wiped his nose on his sleeve. "Now I just trudge through this muck day in and day out, never pleasing her, never pleasing Father, and now *he's* back, and I'm nothing again."

"There's... there's nothing I can say that can make this any better, Toshiro. But I can promise you that things will work out. You're not *nothing*, Toshiro." Amelia wrapped her arms around him.

He buried his head into her shoulder, clutching onto her sari with his good hand. The silver dragon stretched out its neck and blew a sigh into his hair. His shaking subsided, and he became calm once again. His brown eyes cleared, and he looked at her as if for the first time.

The prince scuttled away, lurching to his feet. "Forgive me, my lady. I'm so embarrassed. I should've never been so close—"

"I hugged *you*, Prince Toshiro."

He flushed red, raking a hand through his hair. Like his brother. "Still, I'm so sorry—"

"You should be."

They turned as the crisp voice cut through the night air.

"F-Father."

Lord Ishida stalked into the light, his ice-blue eyes glittering. "Disgracing yourself in front of the Sanu. Deplorable. *Go.*"

Toshiro bobbed a hasty bow and scurried away.

Amelia eyed him, mouth pursed in a disapproving moue. "That was unnecessary, Lord Ishida."

"He should have more shame—"

"I think he's been shamed enough."

Lord Ishida cocked an eyebrow.

"Your family is rotting from the inside out, Lord Ishida. But so long as nobody sees, then it's all fine, isn't it?" She shoved the shochu bottle into his startled hands. "The Ishida dragon is a symbol of strength and humility. And all I've seen since coming here is one of you trying to assert dominance over the other. Where is the humility? There is no dragon among you, just a bunch of snakes."

Lord Ishida threw the bottle aside. It shattered into clay shards, the liquor evaporating into the summer night air. "You overstep, Sanu."

"Sanu *Maitre*. The Voice of Onu. Higher even than the Sanctisum Seats. If I don't chastise you, who will?"

His upper lip curled into a sneer.

"What would Bethsaida have to say about you? About her sons? The woman I read about in the Bethany Journals would be *appalled.*"

His hands tightened into fists. "Don't say her name—"

"You've taken her legacy and thrown it to the wind! Kind, understanding, forgiving. Your sons have none of her traits because you didn't enforce them after you sent her away—"

"*She* left *me*!" Lord Ishida bellowed.

Amelia stumbled back a step.

"She just took her cavalry and her armor and she *left*. When I finally found out what had happened, it was too late to do anything to stop it. And you know who told me? *Hiro*. She'd stopped to see *him*. Not her husband, but her *son*."

He hefted the mandala pendant. With a snick, the pendant separated into two pieces.

"This used to be hers. I found it on my pillow... after. Maybe she thought I'd try to stop her. Maybe I might have ordered her to go. I think either choice would've been too much for us to bear the truth of it."

He put the two halves back together, smoothed it flat against his golden tunic.

"She left me to be both father and mother to our sons. She left me with no time to grieve and mourn. She left me with a shattered heart. She left me with all these things, but made the time to see Hiro."

Amelia sputtered. "You have to tell them the truth—"

"And have them hate their mother? Even her memory? *No*. Not ever. It's easier for them to hate me."

"Lord Ishida, your wife is *dead*. You'd have your sons hate their only living parent for the sake of her memory? It's only ripping your family apart."

"And risk their wrath with what little time I—" He cut himself off, shaking his head. "No... it's better this way."

Scowling, Amelia pressed her finger into his chest. His ice-blue eyes blazed at the impertinence, but she was Sanu, and bowed to no one. "Get your house in order, Lord Ishida, or you'll be lord of nothing."

CHAPTER 70

HIRO STOOD ON A WOODEN PLATFORM ON THE SOUTHERN SIDE OF THE palace overlooking the training yard. The sun was still hidden behind the eastern ridge; only the small streak of gray fringing the summits revealed that dawn was on its way. Below him in rigid formation stood thirty colonels – a mixture of men and women – all with topknots banded in imperial green ribbon.

"Prince Toshiro has been relieved of his command." His voice boomed across the yard. "I will be your general until death takes me or Lord Ishida releases me. While I was at the Academy, I spoke very highly of the Jianshu Guard. Let's see if you were worthy of my praise."

Hiro descended from the platform. Stalking through the ranks, he scrutinized the officers. Each of them had tens of thousands of fighters under his or her command. If the colonel was not fit, then the troops were not fit. He stopped in front of a man who had let his waistline get the better of him.

"You," he said. "Get out."

The colonel blinked in surprise.

"Did I stutter?" Hiro loomed over him, nose a hair's breadth from the colonel's. "Get. *Out.*"

Shaking, the colonel bowed, took three steps back, and waddled away.

Hiro proceeded down the rows, dismissed another colonel for poor hygiene, and yet another for being overweight.

"General, sir, if I may?" An officer leaned out of formation with a little wave of his hand. Wavy brown hair, bright-green eyes, a face that would cause a woman of any age to swoon. "Colonel Branson, at your service. We're used to doing things a certain way under Prince Toshiro—"

Hiro's eyes blazed. "Get. *Out.*"

"But, *sir,* I was just trying to be helpful—"

"Get out or I'll order your former comrades to tie your feet to the nearest horse and drag you out." Hiro turned to the nearest colonel, a man with a scar marring his left cheek and neck. "You, this man is *goushi* fouling my training yard. Take care of it, would you?"

The colonel snapped a nod, yanked his bokken from his belt and rammed it across the backs of Branson's knees. He dropped to the dirt with a howl.

"Sir," the scarred colonel said, "I don't see any horses. Permission to drag him out by his ear instead?"

"Granted."

Branson squealed as the colonel twisted his ear, dragged him to his feet. Sniveling, he was thrown out of the yard.

"You've all grown complacent under my brother's command," Hiro snapped. "You are lazy, you are undisciplined, you are a disgrace to Jianshu and its Guard.

"Those of you who survive my training will retain your posts. Those who do not will be dismissed like the others. You are free to rejoin the Guard as infantrymen and work your way through the ranks, if you have the ambition to do so." He cracked his knuckles; the crackle echoed across the yard like thunder. "Shall we begin?"

The sun was well over the eastern ridge when Hiro called for a halt. Panting, he wiped the sweat from his eyes. The ranks had thinned by nearly a third; most of those remaining had collapsed in the dirt, retching. Those that remained upright received a silver hair ribbon.

"Those of you with silver ribbons will be my brigadiers," he announced. "From your regiments you will choose those worthy of being your colonels. You will also present me with candidates for the colonels I've dismissed. Those of you unable to stand will retain your posts. I am relieved to see that my praise of the Jianshu Guard was not misplaced. Get some water. Not you."

Hiro intercepted the scarred colonel. Blond hair, brown eyes, that ugly scar destroying otherwise pleasant features, he'd remained standing by sheer force of will. He'd drawn Hiro's attention early in the training: neither the fastest nor the strongest, his ferocity to succeed had eclipsed everything else. The colonel wrenched himself upright as Hiro approached, nearly pitched himself backward.

"Sir."

"How'd you get that scar?" he asked.

"A Bering raider, sir." He grinned, flashed sharp white teeth. "He got worse, though."

Hiro returned the wolfish smile. "Very good. Your name?"

"Harrison Jin, sir."

"I have a special assignment for you, Brigadier Harrison. You will attend me this afternoon."

"Sir."

"You can get your water now."

"Thank you, sir."

Hiro trudged up the stairs to the platform. He halted on the last step, eyed the man by the railing overlooking the yard.

"Toshiro."

His younger brother turned, arm lashed against his body as his collarbone healed. There was something different about him. Something earnest.

He's sober.

Hiro went to the bucket, splashed some water on his face and neck. "What are you doing here? This isn't your command any—"

"I know. I know that." Toshiro raked a hand through his hair, looked back at the decimated ranks of his former officers. "I've shirked my responsibility to our Guard to its detriment, Hiro. With your permission, I'd like to oversee the training of the colonels you've dismissed. Give them a second chance. It's my fault they were not up to standard, and I would be doing them a disservice if I did not try to make amends."

Hiro blinked. "Toshiro... that's surprisingly...unselfish."

His younger brother barked a laugh. "*Hundan.*"

"Despite that disrespectful comment to both your older brother and commanding officer, your request is granted. *Hundan.*"

The ladle dropped into the water bucket with a splash as a ripple of startled cries sounded through the training yard.

"What the—" Hiro gripped the railing, craned over the side facing the barracks.

A handmaiden sprinted into the yard, her kimono yanked above her knees. Long brown legs churned the dirt.

"*Viane?*" Toshiro sputtered.

"Prince Hiro," she hailed, waving her arms. "Come quickly, the Sanu—"

"You are dismissed," Hiro barked to the officers.

He trotted down the stairs, grabbed the handmaiden's elbow, and wrenched her around. He escorted her from the yard at a brisk march. A general was always in control of the situation, no matter how dire. However, when they were inside and the door behind them shut, Hiro released the handmaiden and began to run.

CHAPTER 71

AMELIA AWOKE TO BLOOD.

Her sheets were soaked in it.

Screaming, she wiggled out of the bed, pawing at her groin. Her thighs were slick and bright red, her nightclothes fused to her skin.

Someone was banging on her door, but she was too frantic to answer it. She raised her bloody hands to her face and started to cry.

"My lady?" a handmaiden called, rattling the doorknob. "Sanu Amelia? You there, go get the domo!"

With trembling hands, Amelia tore a sheet into strips and started to bind her abdomen and groin. Tears splattered onto her fingertips, making them even more slippery.

"Blessed Lady, help me," she prayed between sobs, deaf to the pounding on her door. "Lord Delphi, *please...* dear gods, why won't it *stop?*"

Inside, the silver dragon writhed in agony, twisting and coiling over itself like a beheaded snake.

The door burst from its hinges.

Hiro staggered into the room, naked greatsword in hand. Covered in dirt, he looked like he'd just run off a battlefield.

Just for a moment, her heart fluttered in relief.

"*Sanu*," he exclaimed.

The world came crashing back, and she lifted her shaking hands, blood dripping from her fingertips.

"It won't s-stop. I can't heal m-myself—"

Hiro sheathed his sword and took both of her bloody hands in one of his. He reeked of sweat, but she didn't care. Without permission, he placed his other hand against her tear-soaked cheek. His seal-brown eyes bored into hers.

Domo Ignatius arrived, skidding to a stop. He clamped a hand on Hiro's shoulder to peer around him. His eyes widened. "Sweet mercy. What happened?"

"You're going to be alright, Sanu." Hiro swept her into his arms and marched out of the room.

"It won't stop, it won't—"

"Shh. We're going to fix this."

"Seal that door," the domo barked at the staff. "No one goes in there. And not a word about this to anyone or else I'll cut your tongues from your heads, do you understand me?"

The servants nodded hurriedly.

The *click-clop* of Hiro's boots echoed as he carried her down the hallway. She clutched her belly with one hand, clung to his gi with the other. Droplets of blood trailed behind them. Two women followed at a distance, hastily cleaning the floor.

"Ignatius, we need to get her to the hospital."

"No," she rasped. "Take me to the chapel. If I'm going to die, I'm going to be looking upon my Lady and Lord."

"You're not going to die," Hiro said gruffly, but he changed direction anyway. "Ignatius, bring the physician."

She moaned, clutching her belly. The silver dragon panted, its scales glowing brighter with each exhale. Whatever it was doing, it was sucking what little energy she had left.

"We're nearly there," he whispered. "Just hold on."

Amelia just wanted the pain to go away. She shut her eyes against her bloody hands and prayed as Hiro carried her down the hall. He kicked open the chapel door and sat down by the edge of the recessed pool, cradling her in his lap.

"There's s-so much blood," she moaned.

"I've seen worse."

She forced a laugh, but it quickly turned to sobs.

He placed one of his large hands, stained red, on her abdomen and applied pressure. "Does this help?"

She nodded.

"Okay." He wet his lips. "We can do this. The physician's almost here. Think happy thoughts like, I don't know, sunbeams and rainbows and kittens and stuff."

Amelia giggled feebly, nearing the edge of hysteria. It took so much effort just to keep her eyes open. "You're not really good at this."

"In my defense, it works on Kale. He loves kittens. And I've never had to comfort a woman like this before. *Hey.*" He jostled her with his shoulder. "You need to stay awake, Sanu. Stay—"

"Tired..." Her head rolled into his shoulder.

"Don't you die on me, Sanu. Don't make me come after you."

Amelia grunted as he jostled her again. Why couldn't he just let her sleep?

Something wet hit her cheek. She cracked open an eye and squinted. "Are you... crying?"

"*No.*" He shook his head. "It's just dirt from – Gods above, take your *time*, Master Cheng."

The physician skidded to their side and moved Hiro's hand away from her abdomen. An elderly man with a long braid of gray hair draped over his shoulder, his hands were still nimble and strong. The muscles in his forearms bulged as he rolled back his sleeves. He peeled away the bandages and her drawers and peered down at her. Hiro averted his eyes, and Amelia bit her lower lip, mortified. Fighting back another wave of tears, she turned her head into Hiro's shoulder and did her best to ignore the physician's gentle touch. Hiro squeezed her reassuringly.

Master Cheng muttered something and frantically tore up some leaves. Sangnon. She stiffened as the physician applied a bandage soaked in the herb to her groin. She wanted to die. She wanted to sleep. A small whimper escaped her.

Hiro cupped her cheek with his palm. "Look at me. Look only at me."

Her eyes wandered all over his face, taking in every detail and forgetting them instantly. Only his seal-brown eyes remained constant. They were clear, focused, willing her to lose herself in them.

"That direct application will help stop the bleeding," the physician said. "My lady, I'm going to give you a coagulant, and I need you to drink it all as fast as you can. We'll give it a little time to work, and then we're going to put you in the pool and clean you off."

"I'll summon some women," Domo Ignatius said.

Hiro wiped the sweat-dampened hair from her face and helped her force the drink down. He spoke to her of many things: the western shores of Eurasia where the striped porpoises liked to play, the cherry blossom festival in the springtime where it rained pink petals for weeks, Dragon Day where they celebrated First Lord Rukio Ishida's birthday with fireworks and spicy fried foods, his mother reading the *Tale of the Mouse and the Lion* to him before bed.

The silver dragon thrived under the sound of his rough voice, each word like a bellows stoking a forge. She turned away, the glow of its scales unbearably bright. The beast flung out its neck, and silver fire poured out of the dragon's mouth. Thick as lava, the fire incinerated the poison and cauterized her wounds. Hiro's grip tightened, his brown eyes wet with worry.

"Amelia? Master Cheng, *get over here.*"

Too weak to protest, she lay limp in Hiro's arms as the physician examined her again.

"It should've taken longer." The physician shook his head, bewildered. "Much longer than this, but... I do believe the bleeding's stopped. Let's get her cleaned up."

Hiro lowered her into the pool, and the army of women swarmed to help her. They came armed with towels and spare clothes and bandages and brushes and soaps and all manner of things.

The physician gestured to the door. "If you'd like to wait outside…"

"Out of the question." Hiro dragged the settee away from the wall to a spot in front of the door. He sat, his back to the pool, as unmoving as a gargoyle sentry. "I'll tell you when they're done."

The women scooped the floating candles out of the pool and set her down to soak. Blood, like spilled ink, wafted away from her abdomen and stained the water red. The women peeled off her clothes and bandages, and Amelia sat huddled with her legs drawn up to her chest as they drained and refilled the pool. She kept her eyes on Hiro's broad back the entire time, fearful he would turn around. He never did.

Clean, the women toweled her off and helped her dress in the spare clothes. She was too weak to do it herself. Inside, the silver dragon lay in a heap, its chest heaving with short breaths. They helped her to the settee and started sanitizing the pool.

Someone had given Hiro a clean shirt and a washcloth, but he still reeked of the training yard. Without a word, he encircled her shoulders with his arm and pulled her close. Shivering, she leaned in against him.

"And don't give me that 'hands' tirade," he warned her. "Not after what we've just been through."

She nodded, her head rubbing against his shoulder.

"You gave me a fright, Sanu," he murmured, his breath teasing her hair. "You need to stop doing that."

"I'm s-sorry."

"Damn right you are." He smiled.

Amelia stared at him, stunned how that smile brightened his face, even when studded with flecks of dirt and filth. His seal-brown eyes crinkled at the corners, shining with warmth. Her heart beat painfully against her ribs.

Clutching her chest, she coughed against a suddenly dry throat.

The smile faded from his lips. "Are you alright? How is... you know..."

The silver dragon was calmer now, eyes half-lidded and legs curled up under it. Threads of smoke drifted from its nostrils.

"I'm good... I think. And thank you." She leaned away from him, pulled her legs up to her chest. It was cold without his arm around her. "I didn't expect you to... you know..." *You couldn't bring yourself to touch me since the Indus River.* Her cheeks flushed. *Not that I've missed it or anything—*

He raked a hand through his hair. "Yeah, well... what are friends for?"

"We're... friends?"

His seal-brown eyes became guarded, his tone defensive. "Aren't we?"

"Yes...? I mean, if we weren't before, we kinda have to be after *that.*" She jerked her chin to the pool.

The physician approached, clearing his throat. "Sorry to interrupt, Prince Hiro, my lady. So did the, ah, vigorous cleansing restart the flow?"

She shook her head, unable to look at him.

He clapped his hands. "*Excellent.* Then I believe we're out of harm's way. You are a *remarkably* fast healer. But I want you to drink another cup of that infusion to be on the safe side. I'll come by to check on you this evening."

"Thank you."

"Any time, my lady," he said gently.

"Master Cheng, what happened to her?" Hiro demanded. "Was she poisoned?"

The physician wrung his hands. "My lady...was it time for your monthly cycle?"

Flushing, Amelia shook her head.

"Considering you've no other symptoms, I'd think you must've ingested a strong abortive."

Amelia dropped her feet to the floor. "An *abortive*? I think I'd know if I ingested something like that!"

"Well, many are dissolved in liquid to mask the flavor. Maybe you had what you thought was soured wine or bad tea?"

Amelia swallowed and looked at Hiro. His seal-brown eyes searched her face, questioning.

"Hiro, we need to speak with your father."

CHAPTER 72

"Prince Hiro, stop pacing and sit down at once," Lord Ishida said. "You are *not* a caged tiger."

Hiro sat with a huff. Amelia knew he was still agitated when his left heel continued to bounce on the carpet.

"Have another mushroom bun, my lady," Domo Ignatius said, offering the plate. "Master Cheng said you need to eat."

She nibbled on one half-heartedly; she just wanted to sleep. It felt like she'd spent the whole day running, and it wasn't even noon yet. The jiggling couch cushions weren't helping, either. She put her hand on Kale's knee, silently begging him to stop swinging his legs. The boy was so furious he didn't even beg for food.

"Sorry," he mumbled.

"So… Master Cheng thinks it's an abortive," Isen summarized. "Where on earth would you have ingested something like that, Amelia?"

"As you know, I had dinner with Princess Ellaria last night. When the tea service was brought out, there were two teapots. She said she had dietary issues and needed a special tea."

Toshiro snorted. "That woman can eat anything. I've never heard her discuss dietary 'issues' before."

"You probably wouldn't. It's an embarrassing topic." Amelia shrugged. "I didn't think anything of it at the time. Anyway, I was really hungry—"

"Wait." Hiro held up a hand. "You said you were having dinner with her-"

"I wasn't offered anything I *could* eat. Nothing vegetarian."

Toshiro's face contorted with anger. "She knows you're Sanu; that was made clear your first night here. I think I need to have a discussion with my wife about proper decorum. I apologize for your mistreatment, my lady."

"Enough interruptions," Lord Ishida ordered irritably. "Please continue, Sanu."

"I was hungry and had finished all of my tea, so I had two cups of hers. It was foul. I had to load it with sugar just to get it down. This morning I started to... hemorrhage."

Kale snatched a bao bun from the plate and started tearing away large, angry mouthfuls.

"You're talking about child's bane," Lord Ishida said. "It's usually masked in liquid."

"That's what I suspected was in Princess Ellaria's tea."

"Now wait just a minute." Toshiro pushed himself away from the wall. "Are you saying my wife was drinking an abortive? On *purpose?*"

"I believe your marriage to Ellaria is *haichi*, a business alliance? And... you've yet to produce an heir in the five years you've been married."

"Sweet mercy," Lord Ishida hissed. "She's trying for *absolvere negotium.*"

"What?" Toshiro asked.

"If an heir is not produced from *haichi* within the probationary period, the marriage may be dissolved with half of the marital assets being awarded to each party, regardless if they entered the marriage with equal assets. The tramp is trying to swindle you out of your inheritance!"

"Why would she do that?" Isen asked. "Being married to a Jianshu

Prince is far more lucrative than not being married to one. It's in her best interest to remain with the prince."

Toshiro swallowed. "But I'm not the prince she wants. Now that Hiro has returned, he's reclaimed his birthright as primary heir, along with all its assets. She'll get close to nothing now."

Lord Ishida slammed his fists on the armrests. "She knows I need her father's business. She plans to divorce you and sink her claws into Hiro, the clever *biaozi*."

Domo Ignatius raised a tentative finger. "But Lord Ishida, if we can prove she's been taking child's bane, *absolvere negotium* is void. And—"

"The offended party is granted *all* of the offender's assets," Lord Ishida finished with a cold smile.

Toshiro slumped into a seat, cradling his head in his good hand.

"Toshiro, I'm so sorry," Amelia said.

He shook his head. "I don't want to believe it."

"Believe it," Lord Ishida said. "You knew she was a treacherous woman—"

"Then why did you force me to marry her?" Toshiro bellowed. "Did you want me to suffer the rest of my life for a mistake I made as a boy? Do you hate me that much, Father?"

"That was the consequence for betraying your brother," his father shouted back.

Hiro launched out of his seat. *"What's going on here?"*

Lord Ishida glanced at Amelia, shifting uncomfortably in his seat.

"Anyone?" Hiro pressed.

"I dissolved your engagement to Ellaria when I found her and Toshiro *fornicating*. I forced them to marry so this scandal wouldn't tarnish the Ishida name. Toshiro needed to be punished for bedding your fiancée."

"You did what?" Hiro thundered, turning to his brother.

"We weren't fornicating—"

Lord Ishida sniffed and looked away. "I know what I saw, what we *all* saw. She threw herself at you, and you took advantage of it. Heaven knows what else you two may have been up to—"

"We just kissed," Toshiro insisted.

Lord Ishida fixed his son with a scathing look.

"A-and yes, I touched her, but—"

"She was my fiancée," Hiro shouted. "I *loved* her."

"You were sent away," Toshiro shouted back. "We were both distraught after you left. She was left alone in the palace, and so was I, now that Mother... And Father was *never* around. We started to spend time together. It was mostly to talk about you, Hiro. We became friends. And then one day I found her crying. She had a letter from you. I sat down to comfort her, that's *all*.

"Then... she leaned over and kissed me. I knew she had to be imagining you, Hiro, but you know how she was. She was so kind and friendly and loving and when she kissed me, I lost my head! I was *fifteen*. Then Father and Domo Matsu stumbled across us, but Hiro, I swear, *nothing happened*."

"*That* time," Lord Ishida huffed.

"That was the *only* time," Toshiro insisted furiously. "But apparently this one instance of youthful folly is enough to damn me for the rest of my life!"

Emotions danced over Hiro's features like a shadow puppet show. "You should've told me your marriage was *haichi*, Toshiro. Why did you goad me then, at dinner and again on the terrace? I could've..." He looked down at his clenched fists.

"*Because I wanted you to put me out of my misery,*" his younger brother screamed.

"Y-you wanted me to... *kill* you?"

"Just one cut, and it'd all be over. I'd be free of this hell. Free of a loveless marriage, free of Father's disapproval, free of never living up to your shadow."

The muscles in Hiro's jaw popped. He rounded on his father. "And you forced him to marry her? Toshiro was a *boy*."

"I taught him better—"

"You never taught him," Hiro raged. "Ignatius and I taught him. You were too busy fighting a war to spend any time with your sons. Even Mother – your *general* – took time to write to us, to teach us from afar. She was closer to us on the front lines than you were down

365

the hall! And then when you sent me away, who was left to guide him?"

"You will *not* speak to me in such a manner." Lord Ishida surged to his feet. "I am—"

"You are *nothing!*" Hiro spun around and snatched something from the steward's belt. He shoved the steward off his feet and turned back to his father.

"Hiro, *no*—" Ignatius rolled on his back like a beetle, flailing to right himself.

The short blade of the tanto gleamed in his fist.

"You've hurt this family enough," Hiro seethed. "First with Mother, then pitting one brother against the other just for a business alliance. You are not fit to govern this House."

He lunged.

Lord Ishida stumbled backward, falling over his chair.

Domo Ignatius toppled the prince, pinning Hiro beneath his girth. The knife hovered inches from Lord Ishida's blind eye. The steward's meaty fist clamped around Hiro's wrist, fighting for control.

"You're a *monster,*" Hiro shrilled. "A *murderer*—"

Lord Ishida convulsed, spewing black blood over his son's face.

CHAPTER 73

"*Akio,*" Ignatius cried. "Don't move, don't—"

Lord Ishida frantically unbuttoned his gold tunic, fighting to breathe. The Ishida birthmark shone stark white against his heaving chest.

Amelia staggered off the couch.

"Amelia, *no,*" Isen protested. He held Kale in his arms, the boy squirming to get free. "Don't go any closer."

She touched Lord Ishida's shoulder, and a silver thread seeped into his skin. It was all she had left. It wasn't enough.

Back wrenching, he expelled another volley of black blood. He inched away from the vomit, breath coming in shuddering gasps, and slumped against the overturned chair.

Amelia turned to Hiro and placed her hand on the one that held the knife.

"My lady—" Ignatius warned. He still struggled with the prince's wrist.

"Don't," Hiro gasped. "Don't take this away from me, Sanu."

She slipped her hand to the blade itself, grasping it firmly between thumb and forefinger.

Hiro shook violently. "Don't, Sanu. This anger is all I have. He killed my mother."

"No, he didn't. Give me the knife, Hiro."

The wrath in his seal-brown eyes faltered. "He... he needs to pay—"

"He already is." She'd felt the sickness in him when the silver fire had penetrated his skin. "It was Bethsaida's decision to face Kogusanji. She went to stall him so her family could live. *All* of you."

Tears dribbled down his cheeks, but he continued to thrash. "*No. He sent her and drove me away.*"

"I exiled you because every time I looked into your face I saw her staring back at me," Lord Ishida whispered.

"Hiro." Her voice was soft. "What is written on this knife?"

Shaking, he squeezed his eyes shut. "*Protect Always.*"

The blade slipped from his hand.

Amelia sagged back, the tanto in her palm.

Isen let the boy down and hurried to her side. His long-fingered hands scooped under her arms and dragged her back to the couch. "You foolish girl. Are you alright?" He passed a hand over her face and down her arm to the knife in her lap. He plucked it from her feeble grasp and tossed it under the couch, out of reach.

Groaning, the steward eased his bulk off the prince. Hiro rolled onto his side, gasping. "That's what I was *trying* to tell you." Ignatius cuffed his head and went to his Lord. "Lord Ishida, let me help you."

The Lord of Jianshu kept his eyes on his son as the steward helped him into his seat.

"Prince Toshiro, go to your father while I make a tonic. *Now,*" the steward ordered.

Toshiro jumped into action.

"He doesn't need... protection." Hiro scraped himself off the floor, panting.

"Oh?" Lord Ishida pressed a cloth to his mouth with a trembling hand.

"I could never accept your word, but I can accept hers."

Lord Ishida balled the cloth in an angry fist. Toshiro put a restraining hand on his father's shoulder as he lurched half out of his seat. "I should have you arrested and thrown in prison, not to mention *hanged*—"

"No, you won't," Hiro sneered. "You imprison me, and we'll look weak. We can be a squabbling pack of wild dogs on the inside, so long as we present a united front. You need me to fight your war. Isn't that why you summoned me home? Here I am, the Beast you always wanted. You just never thought I'd turn my claws on you."

"That is *enough*. Get out of my sight."

"Gladly." Hiro bowed mockingly and swept out of the room.

Kale ran after him.

"You're just going to let him *go*?" Isen gasped. "He almost committed patricide and regicide and probably a host of other 'cides, and you're just going to *let him walk?*"

Lord Ishida took small sips of his tonic. "He is my son. He will do what is right."

Isen snorted. "This assassination attempt aside."

Lord Ishida glanced at Amelia. "It's my fault for not telling them the truth. He was just trying to avenge his mother."

Toshiro backed away from his side, disgusted. "You forgive him instantly for trying to murder you, but for my *mild* indiscretion, you saddle me with a wife who's made my life a living hell for the last five years? I wanted my own brother to kill me. You're unbelievable."

The prince stormed out of the room.

"I need to rest," Amelia whispered.

"I'll take you back to your room." Isen slipped an arm around her waist and helped her to her feet. "Good-*day*, Lord Ishida."

"*Wait.*" Lord Ishida's good eye burned. "How did you do that, my lady? The fits are usually more... violent than that. You healed—"

"Assuaged. Temporarily. I'm Sanu, Lord Ishida. Surely your wife told you about us."

"O-of course. Thank you, my lady."

She glanced over her shoulder as they left; Lord Ishida was tracing the scar over his ruined eye with shaking fingers, his mouth set in a firm line.

Amelia leaned heavily against Isen as he helped her down the hall, tapping his staff with his other hand. His fingers dug into her side as the muscles in his arm strained under her weight. Her legs fumbled along awkwardly beside his, as unsteady as a newborn foal's.

"You'd think in a palace *this* size, they'd have palanquins," Isen growled. "Especially for a guest injured under their very own roof."

"I'm sorry, Isen," she said. "I'm—"

"It's not your fault, sweet girl. Here." He propped her against a pillar. "I'm going to find someone to help. I'd carry you, but I'm sure I'd walk into a wall, and then where would we be? Don't wander off."

"Isen." She caught his sleeve as he turned to go. "We're leaving. Tomorrow."

"Is that wise? You're so weak—"

"We're going. You, me, and Amai, if that's what it takes. We'll take our chances. I'm afraid if we stay any longer, we'll be ripped apart just like them."

CHAPTER 74

HIRO STOOD OUTSIDE THE GREAT HALL, LISTENED TO THE CHATTER behind the double doors with only half an ear. He plucked at his cuffs, straightened the haori jacket over his silk shirt. His fingernail caught on something, flaked away. A spot of red on the inside of his left wrist: the Sanu's blood. Amelia's blood. He wet his thumb and rubbed it away.

There had been so much of it. He'd seen severed limbs and cleaved muscles on the battlefield, but never blood like that. And the look of terror on her face; it'd nearly killed him.

His hand went to the nape of his neck, searched for the greatsword that should be there. Of course Lord Ishida's guards had deprived him of it. It was for the best. He'd sheath it into Ellaria's belly given half a chance. It was just a tomb there anyway.

Rolling his shoulders, he shrugged off all the years he'd spent pining for that treacherous woman. She wasn't worthy of his loyalty and devotion like—

Kale's footsteps padded down the corridor. The boy was dressed in black and imperial green, his wild hair brushed out and tidy. Ish. Forehead creased in worry.

"How is she?" Hiro asked. He'd seen neither hide nor hair of Kale all afternoon.

"Isen told her stories, and she slept a lot," the boy answered. "I got her soup and hot tea. She said she was cold."

"Good boy." He smoothed his hand over Kale's mane of auburn curls.

The boy looked up at him, bottom lip quivering. His hazel eyes were wet with unshed tears.

"What is it, Kale?"

"Are you... okay? I know you were angry with your father, but earlier... that was *wrath*."

"It's... complicated. You wouldn't understand."

"I understand more than you think."

Hiro eyed him. Of course he did. He knelt, a heavy hand resting on his ward's shoulder. "I spent the last two decades under the assumption that Lord Ishida had sent my mother to die. That he had exiled me for defending her. Now I find out that she went under her own volition... that she sacrificed herself to buy Lord Ishida time to defend Arashiyama. To defend *us*. And that he perpetuated a lie so we wouldn't blame Mother. That's nothing I can forgive and forget in just a few hours."

He smoothed a hand over his hair, careful not to muss the topknot. "I've spent more of my life hating that man than loving him. I don't know how to turn it off. At least not right now. And after that foolish stunt in Lord Ishida's chambers—"

Kale wrinkled his nose. "Why do you call him that?"

"What?"

"'Lord Ishida.' He's your *father*."

Hiro sighed, straightened. "He hasn't been my father for some time."

"It doesn't sound like he has much time left being your not-father."

Hiro sighed. "Yes. But I can't let his imminent death just wipe the slate clean. This isn't a fairytale, Kale. We don't always get our happy ending."

The boy nodded, chewed his bottom lip.

"There's more, isn't there? What aren't you saying, Kale?"

"Amelia and Isen are leaving tomorrow," he bawled.

"*What?*"

"She won't stay here another minute. She's determined to go."

"As much as I... I can't *force* her to stay, Kale. She has a job to do. The Jianshu Guard will see that she gets there safely."

"But how do you know if you're not the one doing it?" The boy smeared the tears from his eyes. "You promised—"

"You know why. That was the price. Kale, I've wanted this more than anything: to come home."

"This is not *home*. Home is your family, and look at your father, your brother—"

"This is the only way I can protect her and have my banishment lifted."

"It's not the same."

"I know. Do... do you want to go with her?"

He was afraid of the response. The boy treasured the priestess. But Kale kept him grounded, made him want to be better. Better than the Beast. He never realized how much he cared for – no, *loved* – the boy until this very moment. This moment when he was going to let him go.

Kale threw his arms around Hiro's middle, cried into his silk shirt. "*Yes...* and no. You need me more."

Hiro crushed the boy against him, felt his own eyes burn as his heart swelled. "I do. But she's not gone yet. We've got one more night with her, so let's make it the best, shall we?"

"Yes, sir."

"Good boy. Now dry your eyes; she mustn't see you sad."

The reverberating thunder of a gong announced his entrance.

The hall was an ocean of green malachite, the people packed more tightly than mackerel in a fisherman's net. All the prominent Houses, the headmen of the various guilds, the brigadier generals he'd promoted that morning, the chief members of the palace staff. A Council scribe sat in attendance to the left of the Seat dais, his swan feather quill poised above a sheaf of paper.

The assembly gawked as Hiro strode down the center aisle, faces frozen in awe or appreciation. Many had difficulty reconciling the chubby, laughing boy they'd known with the muscled, stern-faced man he was. The Ishida Dragon embroidered on the back of his haori jacket snarled and snapped at them as he passed. A little push to Kale's nape, and the boy ran off to join Isen in the crowd.

Hiro marched up to the dais, snapped a smart bow at Lord Ishida. Gold tunic, imperial green trousers, the mandala pendant a duel of orange-and-blue on his chest. Clean. No traces of blood. The hands on his knees were balled into fists. The Sanu sat in a chair on the opposite side of the scribe, too weak to stand. Her cheeks had a faint tinge of pink, no longer ashen.

His eye caught something garish. Ellaria in a Western gown with a V-neckline that plunged almost to her navel. Vermillion velvet against creamy skin. His burned hand twitched, ached to hold the greatsword. Toshiro stood beside her, the arm not bound by a sling taut with tension.

Lord Ishida pushed off his seat, straightening carefully. Others might think it was a deliberate show of authority; Hiro knew it was because he was weak.

"Prince Hiro Cavill Ishida, you were sent away as an impulsive boy and have returned as an Academy-forged man of honor."

Hiro's eye twitched. *Trying to shame me won't work.*

Lord Ishida padded down the stairs of the dais, a gold dragon dangling from a thick chain in his hands. He was so tall that Lord Ishida would be forced to go on tiptoe to slip it over his head.

That'll teach the old man some humility.

The Sanu glared at him, ocean-blue eyes cold as the winter wind. Lip twitching, Hiro bowed. Lord Ishida slipped the necklace over his head. It was heavier than he thought. Jade and pearls as fat as marbles studded the chain even to the clasp. It was a magnificent collar for a Beast.

"Let it be known throughout Eurasia that my son has been restored to his rightful place, the Heir of Jianshu."

The Council scribe scribbled away as the applause rumbled like an earthquake.

He followed his lord up the dais, took his place at the Seat's right side. He rested a hand on the back of the magnificent chair, and the crowd erupted into another round of cheers.

Lord Ishida raised a hand. "And now for the other matter. Prince Toshiro, Princess Ellaria, come forth."

They shifted from the crowd, presented themselves with a bow. The tops of Ellaria's breasts could be seen perfectly from this angle. Add some rouge and a jaded look to her eye and she'd actually look like the whore she was.

Hiro met his brother's gaze, gave him an encouraging nod. Neither one of them knew what to expect. It was never a good thing to be presented to Lord Ishida unless there was a medal waiting for you. His younger brother needed all the bolstering he could get.

Lord Ishida cleared his throat. "Princess Ellaria, did you or did you not murder your own children for the last five years?"

CHAPTER 75

SILENCE.

Even the flames in the fire bowls devoured their wood quietly.

"My lord?" Ellaria stammered.

"You are accused of sabotaging your *haichi* to Prince Toshiro through the regular consumption of the abortive child's bane," Lord Ishida said. "Furthermore, you are accused of adultery by propositioning Prince Hiro under the guise of *intus familia.*"

"My lord, I'm *horrified* that you'd accuse me – the heir of the Matsu House and your daughter-in-law – of such things. And to do so without my family present—"

"They're over there." Lord Ishida pointed a finger to the far corner of the room. "I had the Guard fetch them this morning. What do you have to say for yourself?"

"I've always been a faithful wife to my husband," she shrilled. "I will *not* tolerate such slander. And to suggest that I would forsake my wedding vows—"

"I *suggest* nothing. Prince Hiro is never without his shadow, his ward, Kale. The boy witnessed you trying to seduce the prince the very night he returned."

"You'll take the word of his ward over mine? His testimony is biased at best," Ellaria spat.

"I'll also take the word of my son over you. He's been honorable in exile, whereas you've done nothing but lie," Lord Ishida sneered. "What do you have to say about the abortive?"

"I deny it, of course. Search my rooms, you'll not find it *anywhere.*"

"We did, and you're right. We found no such thing in your suite. We did, however, find a considerable amount of child's bane in the rooms of your handmaiden, Viane. I believe she accompanied you from the Matsu estate when you came to live here?"

The handmaiden wilted under Ellaria's glower and shifted away from her mistress. The princess smoothed her features, raised a haughty eyebrow. "My handmaiden possessing such an offensive herb doesn't reflect any guilt upon me."

"Except you drank an infusion of it at your private dinner last evening with the Sanu Maitre. The Maitre drank from *your* teapot out of hunger and thirst as a direct result of *your* egregious lapse in etiquette. It was so potent that she almost hemorrhaged to death this morning. The imperial physician has confirmed that drinking such a large dose is only done by women who intake it regularly, having grown immune to its effects over time.

"You, madam, were taking abortives to prevent producing an heir in hopes of invoking *absolvere negotium* to gain half of Prince Toshiro's assets. As the former primary heir, you stood to gain half the province."

Ellaria started to deny it, but Lord Ishida cut her off.

"I have no less than two dozen witnesses to corroborate the Sanu Maitre's story. Plus I have the full confession from your handmaiden, Viane. It turns out she very much did *not* want to be executed for treason against the Jianshu Seat."

"Why you little—"

Toshiro snatched his wife's wrist out of the air before she could slap her handmaiden. Shifted between them with a glare.

Ellaria grabbed his good arm. "Please, Toshiro, you have to believe me—"

"You have killed my sons and daughters." His voice was as dead and lifeless as the spirits of his children. "*Your* sons. *Your* daughters. I'm sorry I wasn't enough for you, but there can be no forgiveness for what you've done." Toshiro shook her off, turned his back on her.

A gasp rippled through the assembly until it was a crashing wave upon the shore. In the corner, the crowd closest to the Matsu family shifted away. Afraid to be guilty by proximity.

The Sanu eased out of her chair and went to the scribe's desk. She signed three pages, limped back to her seat. An exhausted sigh passed her lips.

"Ellaria Matsu, the Sanu Maitre bears witness to your divorce from Prince Toshiro. You are forthwith stripped of your title," Lord Ishida declared. "According to the laws of *haichi*, all of your family assets now belong to the offended party, the Ishida House."

She screeched in outrage, the sentiment shared by her family in the corner. Lord Ishida sliced the air with his hand.

"You and the members of the Matsu House will leave this city at once. You are henceforth evicted from your family home, and should you take any possessions with you, you will be charged with theft and punished in accordance with the law. Now get out!"

Toshiro kept his back to her, heedless of her pawing hands.

Ellaria spun to Hiro, fell to her knees, and threw out her hands to him. "Hiro, *please*. I did all of this for *you*. I've only ever loved *you*, Hiro. I only wanted to bear *your* children. Please, you must understand. If you ever loved me at all, you'll help me now. *Please*, Hiro."

He walked down the dais steps, took each step with deliberate slowness.

She scrambled toward him, the plunging neckline of her gown threatening to expose her in a most unseemly way.

"I could've forgiven you if you'd only loved him. But you tortured him instead with the memory of me." He avoided her touch, went to his brother. He put his arm around Toshiro's slumped shoulders. His younger brother leaned into him. "Brigadier Harrison, you were so helpful this morning in the yard. It seems like your assistance is needed again. Clearly this woman needs help leaving the palace."

The scarred brigadier advanced, withdrew a bokken from his belt.

Ellaria screamed, dragged herself off her knees. Harrison merely followed her, the bokken out to his side, tip whispering against the malachite floor.

Hiro squeezed his brother's shoulders. He was certain Toshiro would think of her for some time, but the moment she was out of sight, she was out of Hiro's mind forever.

CHAPTER 76

HE WAS EXPECTED TO MINGLE, ENJOY THE PARTY, REVEL IN HIS RETURN to the fold. But he couldn't get the Sanu out of his mind. Her scowl, in particular.

Someone had dragged out a settee for her on the terrace. She leaned against one armrest, picked at some food from the little plate beside her. A shawl of robin's egg blue, thinner than gauze, attempted to keep the cooler night air at bay. Little cranes of silver thread danced along its edges.

Hiro dropped onto the adjacent cushion, set a flute of sparkling cherry wine next to the half-eaten egg tart.

"Ellaria's exit was *overly* dramatic, don't you think?" she asked flatly.

Hiro sighed. "Not dramatic enough, I'd say. I wished she'd put up more of a fight. It would've made her humiliation that much greater."

The Sanu played with the beaded fringe of her sari. "That's a bit callous."

"She'd shamed Toshiro and my House for years. Turnabout is fair play."

"Hmph."

She didn't touch the glass. She didn't look at him either.

"So… how're you doing?"

"Master Cheng says I'll be fine."

"Good."

Another awkward silence.

"So… aren't you going to congratulate me?" he asked.

"Congratulations."

"But…?"

She rounded on him. "I'm having a difficult time reconciling the man who held me this morning with the one before me. You tried to kill your *father*. How am I supposed to overlook that?"

"I was justified—"

"Based on a *lie*."

"A lie perpetuated by *him*. How was I supposed to know?"

"I can't believe – You've been planning this the whole time, haven't you?"

He gritted his teeth. Behind them, music and clinking glassware drifted out onto the terrace. Oblivious to the building thunderstorm.

"His death would've been on *my* hands, too. Did you ever think about that?" she demanded. "*I* was the one who saved you in Vienna. *I* took responsibility for your life."

"My actions are my own. I drew the knife."

"But I am the one who enabled you to do it. Sweet mercy, I am the *last* Sanu. The only person who can perform Yueshu. Can you imagine the consequences of my heart being impure? Of being tainted by the blood of your father?"

"Sanu, you're overreacting—"

She flung herself off the settee. "Am I?"

"It's just some superstitious ritual—"

"How can you say that to me? After all we've been through, after all we've seen? You're *lying*—"

Hiro lurched to his feet. "There's an army wreaking havoc out there in the name of a dead tyrant, and you want to go gallivanting around the province so you can dance in the moonlight! Can't you see how ludicrous that is? Can't you see how dangerous it is? *Stay.* Here, where it's safe. With… me."

She snorted. "*You*. You who plot to kill your own family members. That's *safe?*"

"I'm sworn to protect you."

"You're *sworn* to get me to Lhasa. After that, we're done. Weren't those your exact words?"

"You know it's more than that. That *we* are more than that."

"And what are 'we' now? *Friends?* Friends don't encourage each other to shirk their responsibilities." She threw her hands into the air. "Sweet mercy, was that your plan all along? Prey upon my trust, bring me here, then sabotage me with your boyish affections?"

"'Boyish affections?'" His eyes narrowed.

"Only an immature *boy* would ask me to abandon everything I've worked for. Now I'll not hear another word. We're leaving tomorrow."

"Yes." He picked up her untouched wine, gulped it down. "You have a long ride ahead of you."

Her forehead creased. Confusion. "The way you said that sounds like you're not coming."

"That's because I'm not."

She crossed her arms over her chest.

"What? I figured you'd be pleased that you don't have a scheming murderer accompanying you. I thought you believed in second chances. Weren't *those* your exact words?"

The priestess glowered. "This outrageous proposition aside, you promised me you'd get me to Lhasa."

"A regiment of the Jianshu Guard will get you there."

"That's not the same, and you know it."

"Won't my 'boyish affections' get in the way? And why does it matter? You'll be in Lhasa, whether by my hand or the Guard's."

She shook her head, eyes glinting. "I wish I could weasel out of my vows as easily as you do yours."

"Listen," Hiro snarled. "It was either that or be exiled from my House *forever*."

"'*Health is the greatest gift, contentment is the greatest wealth, and* faithfulness *the best relationship.*' How can you achieve any of this with the people who demand you break your vows?"

"Tell me, what would've you done in my place?"

"I would've kept my promise!"

Hiro shook his head. "That's easy for you to say. You have no family."

She staggered back as if he'd slapped her. The shawl fluttered from her shoulders, limp as a broken bird.

"Amelia, I didn't mean—" Hiro reached for her.

She batted his hand aside, stepped out of his reach. Her face twisted in rage. "Better to have no family than to be a slave to one," she hissed.

CHAPTER 77

Gauzy wisps of mist still clung to the bamboo trees, covered the rhododendrons in diamond dust. The sun peeked over the imperial maples just as the carriage winked out of the sight into the folds of the forest. The hooves of three hundred imperial horses galloped after it. It was warm for a summer morning, but he shivered nonetheless.

They were on the southern balcony, which offered an unhindered view of the forest and the city. If they stared long enough, there was a chance they would see the carriage again before it passed through the hills. After that, it would be forever out of their sight.

Moments passed; they did not see the carriage again.

Hiro stuffed the blue shawl into the folds of his gi, over his heart. His finger snagged against the point of the Ishida crest pin. Blood, red as the imperial maples, dribbled down his finger.

Kale withdrew his white-knuckled hands from the railing, let them fall listless to his sides. Hiro gently slid his arm around the boy's slumped shoulders.

"She didn't say good-bye."

PART III

CHAPTER 78

THE UPSWING OF THE BATTLEAX RIPPED THE HELMET FROM HIRO'S HEAD. He pivoted, slashed down with his greatsword. His assailant collapsed, his left arm cleaved from his body. Hiro stabbed him through the chest, kicked the body free of his blade and moved forward. His personal guard swirled around him as he pushed farther down the battlefield. A hurricane of steel and fury.

A wound on his right arm where he'd caught the glancing blow of a spear trickled blood down his sleeve, made his glove tacky. There was another nick in his left knee where someone had thought to hamstring him. No time to bind them.

Only one battalion of the Shadow Army, one thousand souls, had been sent to deter them. One battalion of the Shadow Army was put to the sword by his Guard. His fighters were ferocious, merciless. Devoted to their task.

Hiro thrust his greatsword into the dirt, shrugged his bow off his shoulder. The fletching tickled his lips as he nocked a black arrow. Bellowing horses, screaming men and women, the bitter clang of metal striking metal. The bugle calls coming from the hill to direct their Guardsmen. He was deaf to everything but the stretch of his bow, the twang of its string. The brief pocket of silence as the arrow found a fatal mark. He emptied his quiver: twenty-four pockets of sweet silence peppered the cacophony of battle.

An enemy arrow answered him.

Hiro twisted out of the way; green fletching kissed his cheek as the arrow whizzed past. It lodged into a Guardsman behind him, knocked him flat into the dirt with a howl. Hiro scrambled to his feet, searching for the bowman.

Up until now, the Shadow Army had only engaged them with swords. Arrows required more skill than the enemy had yet demonstrated. They were just grunts hacking away with their swords with no regard for personal safety. Like drones.

"Boss, look." The Tanin gestured with his sledgehammer.

On the closest rise, the bowman nocked another arrow.

Hiro plucked the nearest shaft free of its corpse, arched his bow high to make the distance. The arrow whistled through the sky—

—and was shot down by the bowman. Instead of nocking another arrow, the bowman turned and disappeared down the other side of the hill.

Hiro watched the vacant spot where the bowman had been for only a moment before snatching up his greatsword. A double blast from his horn reassembled his Guard.

A sea of warriors in black-and-imperial-green livery swarmed around him, created a wedge. Driving forward, they cut down everything in their path. The Shadow Army made no sound even as they fell beneath the sword or spear. The brief pockets of silence he'd created with his arrows were just the breaths of his Guardsmen between one enemy and the next. Their enemy was clad head to toe in black, a black cloth masking the lower half of the face. Their eyes, rimmed with kohl like the pharaohs of the ancient world, were blank and soulless. They made coordinated attacks with seemingly no external communication. Like bees.

He plunged his dagger through the last's soulless eye as the unmistakable *whaaa* of the water buffalo horn signaled the march. Someone found his helmet, pressed it into his hands. A whistle brought his warhorse thundering from wherever he'd leapt out of the saddle.

They filed back to camp, salvaging arrows and carrying their dead. The Shadow soldiers had come like ghosts, carrying nothing of importance, and were left to rot under the sun.

As they returned to camp, the chant rippled through the tents. Hiro had fought with nearly every single Guardsman at least once, and his ferocity had quickly become a legend. Each time they returned from a skirmish, they chanted his name.

"Dragon! Dragon! Dragon!"

No longer was he the Beast. His title now was one of strength and honor, not savagery. If only he was actually worthy of it. He was a traitor, and every man he cut down was a fleeting moment of relief where he didn't have to think about what he had done.

Hiro raised his good arm, waved once to acknowledge their praise. The camp exploded into a frenzy of cheers as it always did. And as it always did, it only warmed him for a little while.

His mare trudged up the hill to the command tent. On the crest overlooking the battlefield was a thick Pirsan rug. A chair, a footstool, a small table with a bugle and a forgotten cup of mint tea. All this makeshift sitting room needed was an umbrella to keep the Jaipur sun away. Beyond the rug, a brass spyglass on its spindly tripod stared into the grass beside the warhorn. Over six feet long, the warhorn must've come from the grandfather of all water buffalo.

Hiro dismounted, left a trail of blood down his warhorse's neck. He winced, pressed a hand to his arm. It must've been deeper than he thought.

"Hiro!" Kale shot out of the orange tent, threw his arms around Hiro's waist.

He ruffled the boy's mane of auburn curls.

He'd tried to leave the boy back at the Jade Palace, had even believed he had succeeded, only to find him following the Jianshu Guard a day later. From that day on, Kale squired for him. Took care of his armor, cleaned his weapons, fed and groomed the horse.

He pressed her reins into Kale's hands.

The boy clicked his tongue. "What'd you do to Beleza? She's got blood on her."

"It's mine." He shrugged off the boy's concerned look. "Just a scratch. Clean her up. She fought well today."

"Is that a piece of *skull* sticking out of her shoe?"

"Probably."

Hiro pushed aside the tent flap with another wince.

With a delighted smile, the Pirsan general struggled to rise from his chair. He succeeded as he always did, left hand clamped over the golden knob of his cane. Stocky, thick-shouldered, skin like leather from years by the seaside. The leopard pelt of his rank draped over weathered armor. "Another victory," Vasilios Constantinos crowed. "Come, come. We must toast our success." He poured two cups of wine, presented Hiro with the larger cup.

Hiro drank the dark red liquid down in one swallow, nodded his thanks to the general.

Vasilios refilled it for him, slid the plate of cold goat kebabs and pita forward.

"That's our third skirmish this week." Hiro tore into the food. "No more than a battalion, just like always. You'd think they'd get tired of losing and just send the main force."

"Perhaps this is their goal, to tire us out or to lull us into false confidence." Vasilios tugged at his beard. "We cannot be sure, and thus cannot move on their position."

"We don't even know where their position *is*," Hiro grumbled. "Our scouts never return. Poor *hundan*."

"I pray Delphi the Protector has taken mercy upon their souls." The Pirsan general bowed his head for only a moment. Then it was back to business. Battle never waited. He moved some pieces on a map of the area. "How many did we lose today?"

"Not more than twenty dead, and they're already being burned. Another fifty or so are wounded."

"Yourself included it seems."

Hiro glanced at the blood soaked bandage on his arm. It'd probably need stitches.

At last Vasilios sat, absently rubbed at the scar on his leg. "I've set the usual watch rotations, and Master Fong tells me the food stores are in good supply."

Lord Diren had called the famous general out of retirement, ripped him away from his black-haired wife and home by the sea. Unfit for battle, Vasilios used his spyglass and his uncanny knack for strategy to relay commands via bugle and warhorn. Hiro, the general on the ground, made sure those commands were carried out.

He looked away from the scar and its emaciated leg, picked up another kebab. "I want our best men who weren't in the battle rotation today to go hunting. Our livestock won't last. Ashar'll have to make kebabs out of something other than goat."

Ashar, the Bédu brigadier and the Pirsan second-in-command, loved only three things: cooking, fighting, and horses. He kept his recipe for herbed goat kebabs hidden in a special compartment in his horse's saddle and had his Sarabi mare sleep inside his tent every night.

Vasilios snorted. "*You* can tell him that news."

"We don't know how much longer these guerrilla tactics are going to continue. Better to start supplementing our meat with the local game. The best way to beat an army is to starve them out."

Vasilios nodded. "I'll see that it's done. You go and see to your arm. And sleep. The third battalion is already on alert should an attack come. Ashar will lead them while you rest."

"Vasilios... they have an archer now."

"After all this time? We've been fighting them for months now and they've never used archers."

"*Archer*. Singular."

"An annoyance—"

"He picked me out on the battlefield. *Me*. I had no defining marks. I wasn't even wearing my helmet."

Frowning, Vasilios drummed his fingers on the table.

"We need to send more scouts."

The general sighed. "You mean send them to their deaths."

"I'll do it myself if that's what it takes."

"*You?* A general? Go out scouting?"

Hiro slapped the table. "We need to know where that army is. They've moved from Pathankot and have disappeared into the wind. An army that size cannot simply vanish. It's impossible. They *must* be somewhere."

Vasilios sighed again. "We'll speak of this tomorrow. Go sleep." He swiped the wine from Hiro's hand and finished it himself as he shooed Hiro from the tent.

Their camp sprawled like a honeycomb across northern Jaipur. Rings – instead of rows – of tents made little clusters of communities. The Pirsan and Jianshu Guards mostly segregated themselves, but those who'd spent their lives growing up closer to the melting pot of Pathankot preferred to mingle.

A familiar camp song coaxed Hiro to divert to one such cluster. Matching red ribbons marked the tents of the Si Tanin. Selected from the elite, the Four Little Dragons comprised Hiro's personal guard. Takāto: joyous, enormously fat, wielder of the Foehammer. Calliope: tall, stoic, muscles larger than most men's. Liked to remind herself of her home near Mersin by carving sea creatures into the shaft of her spear. Azelie: petite, lithe, a master knife-thrower and poker prodigy. Shin: mute, brooding. He used a katana with more precision than a surgeon.

Shin hunched over a grill, turned a spatchcock chicken with a pair of tongs. Takāto sat on the other side of the fire, boisterously singing as he simmered the sauce. Muscles bulging, Calliope stirred a large pot of cooling rice with a wooden paddle. Azelie had a blade in each hand, minced garlic and ginger in a blur. Swept it into the sauce with an invisible flick of her knife. When they weren't fighting, the Si Tanin made the best teriyaki chicken onigiri in the entire continent. It was a taste of home Hiro always made time for.

"Hey, boss." Takāto paused in his singing to give him a nod. "Got some leftover ones from yesterday, if you're hungry."

"I'll wait."

Takāto tapped his spoon on the rim of the saucepan. "Shin, *today*, man. Boss's hungry."

Shin flicked the fat man a scathing stare before turning the chicken again with deliberate slowness.

"You should get yourself to the medic, boss." Calliope jerked her chin at Hiro's arm. "That's not closing."

"I know, I know."

"Shin'll have some onigiri ready for you when you get back. *Right*, Shin?"

The mute swordsman pursed his lips. Met Hiro's gaze and nodded.

"I want some crispy skin in mine." Azelie trailed her fingers up Shin's arm, smoothed his black hair behind his ear.

"No fair flirting with the chef," Takāto complained. "C'mere, Shin. I'll massage your shoulders."

Shin hefted a cleaver.

"Maybe not."

Screams cut through the fog of camp noise, silenced their good-natured bickering. Hiro snatched one of Shin's cooking rags, tied it over his wound.

Calliope stopped stirring. "Boss, you want me...?"

"No. Feed Kale whenever he shows up. It just sounds like amateur hour at the medic station. I'll be right back."

CHAPTER 79

HIRO PUSHED THROUGH THE THRONG TO THE MEDIC STATION. A PIRSAN man – no, a boy – thrashed on the table. His brethren fought to keep him still as the physician yanked on an arrow.

The boy had taken the arrow meant for him. Hiro pressed a hand against the Pirsan's sweat-soaked forehead. His screams lessened to mewling cries as he looked up at the famous Dragon. Tried to be brave.

"Pull it *out*, master," Hiro commanded. "Why torture the boy?"

"G-General." The physician fumbled some vague resemblance to a bow. "The arrowhead, sir. It's barbed or—"

Hiro pushed him aside, clamped a hand onto the boy's chest and ripped the shaft free.

The Pirsan bit through the leather belt and into his lip. Hiro rolled him onto his side so he wouldn't choke on his own blood. Ignoring the boy's screams, he wiped the gore from the arrowhead.

It was indeed barbed. Tiny hooks rippled along the double-tiered broadhead like the saw-toothed edge of an elm leaf. There were carvings on it too, miniscule and impossible to see in the failing light if it wasn't for the green glow emanating from within.

Hiro snapped off the arrowhead and threw it into the fire. The flames snarled, flared green.

Sorcery.

Behind him, the boy's gurgled cries turned more desperate as he fought for air.

"Dammit," the physician said, "keep him on his *side—*"

The boy was convulsing now.

Hiro drew his greatsword just as the boy knocked his brethren aside. He jumped upright on the table, eyes shining green with sorcery. His nut-brown skin had paled to curdled milk, and teeth – inhumanly long – bared in a snarl.

"*Shaytan,*" the physician breathed.

The boy pounced, dug his teeth into the physician's neck. The Guardsmen scattered back with surprised shouts, drawing their swords. The boy killed twenty of them before their blades were even clear of their sheaths. Snapped necks, torn throats, hearts plucked from their ribcages. He moved like a shadow, an immaterial puff of smoke one moment and solid the next.

The Si Tanin stampeded into the fray. A strangled cry escaped Calliope's lips.

Hissing, the boy crouched and flicked his hands. Nails lengthened into four-inch points from his fingertips.

"*Boy,*" Hiro thundered.

The possessed Pirsan whipped its gleaming gaze around. Those green eyes, glowing like lanterns, threatened to freeze him where he stood. Hiro raised his greatsword as the boy appeared in front of him. Cold hands enclosed his neck, an impossibly wide smile revealed twin rows of needle-like teeth.

The glowing eyes rolled up into his head as Hiro slid his greatsword into the boy's chest. The rippling steel parted the flesh like a hot knife through butter, burned out the infection. The Pirsan's skin returned to its former shade of brown, paler now in death.

Hiro caught the boy as he slumped to the ground. "What was his name?" he bellowed.

"Haluk, boss." Calliope sank to her knees, leaned her forehead against her spear shaft. "He's my cousin's son."

Takāto set aside his sledgehammer, started closing the eyes of the dead.

Shin made piles of their gear and valuables, bundled them in the dead's clothes to be sent to their families.

"Get a pyre ready," Azelie barked.

Dark hair, crooked nose, brown eyes lightened with golden flecks. Shaking, Hiro held the boy until the funeral pyre was complete. He laid Haluk on top in the place of honor himself, handed the torch to Calliope. Tears slipped down her stony cheeks as she thrust the brand into the kindling.

"Boss... you want a beer?"

I don't want anyone else to die for me. "No, Takāto. Just feed Kale."

It was late when he made it to his tent. Larger than most, an inner division cordoned off his sleeping area from the rest of the interior. The small glow of an oil lamp from within cast shadows on the canvas. So Kale had been by. That meant there was fresh water, enough to clean out the wound on his arm. It still stung.

He pushed through the hanging folds of the entryway and drew his dagger.

A figure dressed in black armor and a purple, waist-length cape was helping himself to the bottle of wine at the table.

"You've got the wrong tent," Hiro growled.

"What's this? Tell me the Dragon doesn't waste his time with a *diary*." The figure hefted the booklet carelessly, and the lacquered wand slipped loose from the binding. "Huh. Who's Bethany?"

Lord Ishida had given it to him before he'd left for the front. *She left this here, by mistake I think. Take it, Hiro. These were your mother's words. Perhaps they'll comfort you as they've comforted me.*

The binding of woven reeds creaked under his gauntlets as the figure examined it.

"*Put it down,*" Hiro ordered. "Like I said, stranger, you've got the wrong tent."

The figure turned, pulled back his hood. Raven-black hair spilled out of the hood, cascaded in soft curls just below the shoulder line. Part of it was gathered into a topknot banded in copper. A smile lit up a dusky face.

"No, I don't think I do," Lakshmi purred.

Hiro sheathed his dagger as Lakshmi pulled off her gauntlets. "How did you—"

She put a finger to his lips, covered them with her mouth. Her tongue tangled against his as she slid a hand into his hair. His mind went blank. "Let's talk later," she panted. Her fingers were already frantically at work at her armor.

Hiro had his armor shucked before she did, peeled hers off like a crustacean's shell. She pressed against him, clawing and nipping and moaning. He pushed them into his sleeping partition, pinned her beneath him on the cot. The light made him pause; he fumbled with the lamp wick. If it shone too brightly, it'd cast their shadows for anyone to see.

"No," Lakshmi whined, "I want to see you."

"Feel me instead."

He gripped the edge of the cot and thrust against her hard. Her breath caught with a little hitch. Hissing, he yanked his fingers away from the hot glass of the oil lamp. Lakshmi swirled her tongue around his fingers, sucked them into her mouth. Her dark eyes full of promise. Hiro pulled his fingers free and kissed her again. She wrapped her thighs around his hips as she raked her fingers down his back. He slid a hand up her shirt, stroked the firm flesh beneath. She bucked under him.

"Hiro," she gasped as he kissed her neck, "I want more than what we did at the Academy. We're no longer bound by its rules. Hiro, please—"

He paused, lips hovering above her skin. Her chest heaved under him, each breath teasing him with a brush of two hard nubs.

Even now, he couldn't forget *her.*

"No," he growled. He moved his mouth to a spot low on her neck and sucked hard.

Lakshmi let out a pleasured moan before she shoved her hand down the front of his trousers and brought him to oblivion.

It was good to forget. Even for a little while.

Later, Hiro tossed her a washcloth. He peeled off the rest of his clothes, finally looked at the wound on his arm. The nick by his knee had already scabbed over.

"So... why are you here?" He kept one eye on Lakshmi's toned body as she washed herself. Gods above, she was beautiful.

"I've been assigned here, stupid." She threw the washcloth at him, hit him on the side of the head. "And not just me – Alistair too."

"Alistair's here?"

"I daresay you're more excited to see that bookworm than me."

Hiro rolled his eyes. "Don't be jealous."

Still pouting, Lakshmi shimmied into her trousers. "Anyway, he's not here yet. I've come ahead of him with my blooding company. After we fought off some pirate bastards in Mersin, we received a messenger eagle detailing the situation. The Academy promoted me to brigadier and instructed me to take the company east to join with the Guards."

"Congratulations. Toss me that jacket, would you?"

A crumpled wad of blue gauze tumbled out of its sleeve; Lakshmi snatched it up. "*Now* I'm jealous. What's this?"

He made a swipe for it, but she wrenched her hand away. "It's nothing, Lakshmi. Give it back."

"*Nothing?*" She grabbed his chin in her hand. Her nails dug into his cheeks. "I'm the *only* one, right?"

He shook her off, plucked the blue cloth free and stuffed it into his pocket. "As much as 'one' can be."

"Good. Now sit down so I can stitch your arm."

Hiro clenched his jaw as Lakshmi cleaned out his wound. Her naked breasts brushed against his arm, a needed distraction from her rough ministrations. She lacked the tender touch that *she*—

Lakshmi splashed wine into the wound. Hiro hissed.

"Stay still." She stitched it up, grabbed a roll of bandaging.

"You're not going to put a poultice on it?"

She would've mixed something up to prevent swelling and infection.

"Do I look like a medicine woman to you?" When she was done, she gave him a slap on the shoulder. "Done. Now get dressed. I need food. Perhaps after dinner we could have some more fun?"

"We'll have to be careful. I *mean* it, Lakshmi. Fraternization is severely discouraged in camp."

Undeterred, she stood on tiptoe and nibbled on his ear. "Then we'll just do it on the battlefield."

Hiro pulled back, not in the mood.

"Hiro, I just made you scream my name into your pillow. How're you brooding already?"

The battlefield. No matter how much blood he spilt to keep *her* safe, nothing would ever wash his conscience clean.

CHAPTER 80

THE HOLY CITY OF LHASA GREW FROM THE PLATEAU TO TOUCH THE SKY.
Domed buildings of white stone rose from lush gardens. Everywhere
there were brightly colored birds and streets of smooth, paved stone
and tinkling water fountains. A low wall of the same white stone
encircled the city, protecting it from an encroaching banyan forest to
the north and from the steep Chehara Cliff in the south.

The waves of the Bengal Sea crashed upon its face, spraying ocean
mist thousands of feet into the air and coating everything in a thin
salty crust. The bend of the Brahma Rush snaked through a few
rounded hills to the east before disappearing on its sinuous course
between Tybet and Jianshu to the shores of Nan Phet and its teal
waters.

It was hard to imagine that twenty years ago this province had
nearly been destroyed by the fury of the Monster Kogusanji.

The man had risen to power in the west and had swept across
Eurasia like a plague. His victories were decisive and quick, and he
moved across the land as if upon the wind. When his war-host
reached Tybet, he lingered, intent on annihilating the province. While
a third of his army laid siege to the capital, the rest burned through

the poppy fields of western Tybet and flooded through the mountain pass into Jianshu. The continent had never seen such wrathful destruction. Yet Lhasa, though it had no standing army of its own, thwarted him for thirty-three days before General Bethsaida Ishida came to challenge him in the Shogun Pass. Kogusanji had met her upon the Xinjiang Plains, and though she fell to his sword, she had defeated him in the end.

"I've longed to enter this city for years. Too many years." Isen absently rubbed the pendant he kept hidden beneath his robes. "Tell me, Amelia, is it as beautiful as they say?"

Amelia stepped away from the doors and leaned back. The pale stone had the same luminescent quality as any other temple that housed the white flame, but this one glittered like an opal. Lilies, lanterns, and lions decorated the columns and along the base of the vast dome. Covered in gold leaf, the dome shone like a second sun.

Amelia shaded her eyes. "More, Isen. It's more beautiful than I could possibly describe."

Behind the dome, a great white obelisk speared the sky, its cap covered in the same gold leaf. The Militum Dei called that obelisk home, its warrior monks ready at a moment's notice to carry out the whim of the Sanctisum Seats. Sometimes it was to defend a temple, or safeguard the way of pilgrims, or hunt down those accused of sorcery.

Amelia shifted uncomfortably and approached the doors. There was no going back now.

The polished red wood depicted a meadow of lilies with swallow-tail butterflies flitting about on an unseen breeze. Rampant lions, mirror images of each other, pawed the air between them as an oil lamp in each corner spilled stars into the sky.

Amelia knocked on the doors and heard its echo roll like tympani drums within.

The doors cracked open just enough to emit a Sanuset priestess's head. "Welcome to the Temple of Lhasa, home of the Sanctisum Seats," the young woman drawled. "I am Sister Penelope de Lhasa, how many I serve…"

Her voice trailed off as she actually looked at them. She jerked open the door just enough to reveal her lemony yellow sari. Instead of bowing, she thrust out her hand. The invitation was clear and demanding.

Cautiously, Amelia slipped her hand into the young woman's grasp. "I'm Sanu—"

"Amelia." The Sanuset priestess's fingers closed around hers.

"How did you-"

"Thank the gods you're here."

The young woman yanked her into the temple.

"HEY!" Isen snagged her sleeve and stumbled to keep up.

Sister Penelope hustled them into the rotunda before Amelia could wrench her hand free of the Sanuset's grip.

"I am Sanu *Maitre*, the Voice of Onu, and I will *not* be dragged in such an undignified manner—"

Amelia choked back the rest of her tirade. A much larger version of the chapel in the Jade Palace, sunlight poured from the oculus at the apex of the dome and glittered on the rainwater caught in the recessed pool. The dome arched so high it surely supported the sky itself.

Beneath its vast expanse was a sea of clergy. Delphian priests in white-and-turquoise and Sanuset priestesses in lemony yellow cowered like frightened sheep between the two great statues.

Well over thirty feet tall, the statues loomed out of the shadows into the sunlight.

Lady Bosetsanu, head slightly bowed and a soft smile on her lips, offered a blooming lily in her cupped hands. Strands of pearls hung from her neck and arms, and flowers sprouted beneath her bare feet.

Lord Delphi, strong and assuring, raised a lantern in one hand while the other beckoned. A great shield emblazoned with a bursting star rested against his legs.

They were perfect.

Encircling them all were Militum Dei, dressed in black with the red sun of their order emblazoned on their chests, naked swords digging into the marble floor.

Amelia shrank back into the shadows, heart hammering in her chest. There were so many. One of them was bound to guess—

"Please, Sanu, there is no *time*," Sister Penelope pressed. "You must come, quickly. The High Sister is waiting for you."

They kept to the shadows on the outside edge of the rotunda, well away from the Militum Dei. As they circled, she caught a glimpse between the monks' shoulders of a Sanuset priestess holding a copper bowl of the sacred white flame. With a hesitant wince, a Delphian priest stuck his hand into the flame. Unharmed, he withdrew his hand, and a Militum Dei monk smeared a stripe of red paint across it and sent him on his way.

"What are they doing?" Amelia whispered.

Sister Penelope shook her head, gesturing for silence.

They skirted the thousands of clergy and warrior monks without being seen. Every eye was fixed on the white flame, every person wondering when it would flare gold with righteous anger. It wasn't until they'd gone halfway that a monk turned his head into his elbow to smother a sneeze and saw them. He left the ranks with a stern frown etched into his face.

Amelia backed away, the silver dragon snarling like a cornered cat.

"Sister Penelope, you know the rules," the monk said. "All newcomers must get in line."

"But this is the Sanu Maitre—"

"I don't see a tattoo."

The Sanuset priestess blanched. Her brown eyes wavered from Amelia's uniform to her unmarked hands. "But, Amelia... you said..."

The warrior monk hefted his sword.

Amelia hushed the silver dragon and pulled down her collar with trembling hands.

The monk was so close the golden lily reflected in his dark eyes.

They widened, the lily expanding across their brown depths. The Militum Dei dropped onto one knee, pressing his forehead against the crossbar of his naked sword. "My lady, please forgive me."

She smoothed her clothes back into place. Her hands remained clustered by her sternum as she fought to slow her pulse. Inside, the silver dragon paced, snorting blasts of smoke from its nostrils.

"Captain Julian, I really must take Sanu Amelia to see the High Sister."

"Of course. Go ahead, Sister." The monk stood, tugging the sword point free of the marble. "But you, priest, go join the others."

Isen bristled. "Excuse me?"

The Militum Dei placed a heavy hand on the priest's shoulder. The calloused fingers dug into his robes. "You must be tested. The Seats' orders. The line starts after Brother Michael."

Isen's staff creaked as his hands tightened into fists. The soldier's fingers dug into his cowl. "I did not travel the length of this continent to be denied—"

"You will be tested or you will be imprisoned and *then* tested. Is that clear, priest? Do not make me ask you again."

Amelia put her hand on Isen's shoulder. "*Pax*, Isen. Do as he says."

He turned a bewildered face in her general direction. "But—"

"I'll find out what's going on. I'll come back for you as soon as I can." She turned to the soldier, frost in her eyes. "Get this over with quickly, please. I expect him to accompany me when I return. Is *that* clear?"

He nodded hurriedly, and Isen shoved his hand off his shoulder. With an agitated flounce of his robes, Isen tapped his way to the milling crowd of clergy. The soldier resumed his post, filling the gap in the chain of Militum Dei that encircled the priests and priestesses like the constricting coil of a python.

Amelia turned back to Sister Penelope, tightening her hands into fists to keep them from trembling. "I'm not going another step until you tell me what's going on in there. Why do they need *testing*?"

The Sanuset wrung her hands, glancing from the scene in the

rotunda to the candlelit hallway behind them. There was a light at its end, a moon gate leading to an expanse of green. The Garden of the Gate.

Sister Penelope took a step closer, far closer to a Sanu than she had any right to be. "There is a traitor in our midst," she whispered.

CHAPTER 81

"She'll meet you inside, Sanu." Sister Penelope gestured to the moon gate. "I must get back to the door now."

As the sister's footsteps retreated in a hasty staccato, Amelia turned to the archway of luminescent stone. Shielding her eyes from the green light, she stepped into the garden.

Every species of flowering plant and tree battled for space in this secluded oasis. Jacarandas overshadowed the gravel paths, littering the crushed stone with purple flowers. A thicket of heliconias sprang from the left and yellow azaleas to the right. Farther in there were foxglove and columbine, fuchsia crepe myrtle, and white magnolia.

Butterflies floated on the breeze scented with sea rose and honeysuckle; peafowl perched in the branches as red-crowned cranes disappeared between stalks of bamboo.

The sound of water was faint, and the sinuous path often curved away before twisting back in its direction. All around her, strong vines of climbing roses fused against the garden's walls bloomed orange in the summer heat. When at last the greenery parted, she found the source of the water.

A trough hollowed into the rim of a stone disk caught the water that bubbled up from somewhere beneath it. As if made of obsidian, the disk was so smooth it reflected the garden around it in a perfect mirror image. And breaching skyward from its stony depths was an arch. It towered into the air, dwarfing the tallest tree in the garden and encircling the sky before plunging back into the earth below.

The Gate of Heaven.

AMELIA CIRCLED THE GATE, trailing her hand along the rim of the trough. There were no markings of any kind, no clues as to the sequence of the dance. The black diamond merely dazzled in the light without so much as a hint to its secrets. It seemed cold, unwelcoming, and frankly... underwhelming. With a troubled sigh, she placed her hands on her hips.

"Expecting to see a glimpse of Heaven from the other side?"

Amelia jumped. She stuck her head out from behind the arch and found an ancient Sanuset priestess seated on a bench by the honeysuckle. "H-how did you get in here?"

The old woman smiled, her eyes crinkling at the corners. "This is my home, Sanu. I know all of its secrets. From the catacombs to the walls." She shaded her mouth with a hand and lowered her voice to a whisper. "It's not a divine presence that keeps these gardens lush. The tops of the walls are hollowed out into aqueducts that then feed an irrigation system below the soil."

Amelia could only blink in bewilderment.

Twig-like fingers braced on her knees, the Sanuset rocked forward onto her feet. "I am High Sister Rosara de Lhasa, sibyl of the white flame. Welcome, Sanu Amelia."

"How... how do you know my name? Sister Penelope—"

"Bless that child. I hear she let you in without even confirming you're *actually* a Sanu. And Bosetsanu's Chosen to boot. We have Captain Julian's allergies to thank for that. Poor man. You don't mind if I sit, do you? When you get to be as old as I am, all you want to do is sit."

Amelia blinked again. "N-no, of course not. Please, go ahead."

"Thank the gods." Rosara rocked back onto the bench with a cacophony of popping joints. She patted the vacant spot next to her. "Come sit, Sanu. That way I don't have to crane my neck to look up at you."

Amelia sat on the edge of the bench, hands tucked into her lap.

With a groan, the sister bent down and retrieved a bottle of purple liquid from under the bench. "Care for a drink? It's mûremei brandy. Fantastic stuff."

"Um... could I just have some water from the Gate?"

The High Sister scooted closer. "I hate to tell you, but the spring that feeds the Gate is actually the Pool of Heavenly Tears." She jerked her thumb over her left shoulder. "It's back that way, behind the heliconias. Beautiful water. Absolutely horrid taste. Won't kill you, but why suffer? Have some mûremei instead."

Amelia hesitated.

Rosara cocked an eyebrow. "Not what you were expecting of the Sanuset Seat?"

"Not exactly."

The old Sanuset shrugged. "It shocked the others at first, too. Me, a hard-drinking, man-chasing, meat-eating thief. Yet still the white flame chose me to be its sibyl. Life's just strange sometimes." She wiggled the bottle encouragingly.

When a cup wasn't offered, Amelia swigged from the bottle.

Grinning, the High Sister wiped it clean with her hand and took a large swallow. "It's one of the few delights I have left," she mused, nesting the cork back into place. "Now, are you hungry?"

"No, thank you. Sister, I really think—"

"Do you need to rest?"

Amelia shook her head impatiently. "*No. I'm fine.*"

"What about a bath?"

"*Sister Rosara.* I think we should concern ourselves with the *bigger* issue than whether I'm hungry and tired."

The High Sister slouched, blowing a raspberry between her lips. "You youth are all in a hurry."

"There is a *traitor*—"

She waved her hand in dismissal. "I know; the white flame told me. I'm the one who initiated the testing procedure. Abba Daniel is overseeing it personally. Perhaps you saw him? Mid-fifties, eyes blue as a summer's day, square jaw, *ravishingly* handsome?"

"I didn't notice. Sister, you don't seem overly concerned—"

"What's the point of being worried? There's nothing we can do at this point that isn't being done already. My, Jocasta never told me how high-strung you were."

Amelia looked away. "You have no idea what I've been through."

A hand of twig-like fingers slipped over hers. Amelia glared at the impropriety and found the old Sanuset's eyes glistening. "Oh, but I do, child. I know about the temple, the demon, about your sisters. That you are the last."

Amelia snatched her hand away. "How could you know? You weren't *there*."

"I am the sibyl of the white flame. When you restored its sisters to their temples, they showed me your memories. How did you *do* that, by the way? It's said only the Lady herself could restore a lost guardian."

"I-I just asked them to return."

"*Well*," the old woman huffed, throwing up her hands. "If I'd known it was that easy, I would've ordered the local chapter to do that *years* ago."

"How did it...?"

"Show me your memories? Sanu are bridges. The temple guardians, the flames, are a network to this mother flame in Lhasa. It speaks to me mostly in images – which is how I knew your face – and it felt the horror of that event as if it was its own."

Bitter, Amelia snorted. "Then it must've told you I don't know the sequence of the dance. That I might be the last Sanu, but I can't perform Yueshu?"

The High Sister blanched. "No... it did not. It seems I have something to be worried about after all."

CHAPTER 82

"Whether you know the sequence of the dance or not is *irrelevant* if you're not pure. Let's tackle one obstacle at a time. Sweet mercy, there are so many. Thank the gods you arrived early. Keep *up*, Amelia."

The High Sister could move quickly when she wanted to. Her lemony yellow silks streamed out behind her like a banner as she hurried out of the garden.

Feet crunching on the stone, Amelia jogged to keep up.

They returned to the inner sanctum, taking a right at the intersection. A door halfway down the corridor opened up into the sanctuary. Windowless, the room was lit from a copper bowl submerged into the floor. Bright as a star, the sacred flame danced fifteen feet into the air and threw white light into every corner of the room. Thousands of prayer cushions littered the gray stone like little drops of color flicked from a paintbrush.

Kneeling in front of the copper bowl was another Sanuset priestess, her iron gray hair piled into a tight bun on the top of her head. She stared into the flames without seeing, her pinched lips moving in a soundless prayer.

Rosara threaded through the cushions, the relentless *pad-pad* of her shuffling feet the only noise echoing in the sanctuary. The white flame, for all its dancing, was silent.

"That is Sister Ophelia, my prodigy and the sibylline," the High Sister whispered. "She will witness your testimony. Do not touch her; she is in the trance."

The sibylline's eyes glowed white, as if molten quicksilver writhed in her sockets.

"The traitor is here." Ophelia's voice resounded like a bell. "I can almost—" She blinked, the glow dissipating from her eyes. They were like Rosara's, gray as a dove's wing. The stern façade melted from her face, and she slumped back on her heels.

Amelia stared. Ophelia was younger than she first thought.

"I'm sorry, High Sister," Ophelia said. "I couldn't get a good look. The traitor is… hidden."

Rosara patted the younger woman's shoulder. "You'll find them. But now, you must witness. The Sanu Maitre has come."

The sibylline's face brightened. "Amelia. It's so good to finally meet you in person. We lost sight of you after Bucharest, but then something happened by the Indus River—"

Rosara cleared throat.

Amelia fidgeted. Clearly these women had been watching her through the flames.

Ophelia blushed, taking another ten years off her face. "I'm sorry. That must sound… creepy."

"I'm starting to get used to the unusual. Like… what's happening to your face."

The sibylline rubbed the fading wrinkles on her cheeks. They didn't disappear completely, but she no longer looked much older than forty. "The toll of being a sibyl. The longer you stare into the flames, the more it takes from you."

Amelia glanced at Rosara.

"No, I'm actually quite old," the High Sister said, flicking her long white braid over her shoulder. "But enough of these niceties. Normally I'd offer you days of rest and refreshment, Sanu, but we can't waste any more time with that traitor running around. It can't be

411

a coincidence. They must know somehow that the ritual cannot be completed."

Ophelia started. "Wait, what do you mean Yueshu—"

"But I've told no one," Amelia said. "Not even Isen, the notué priest who's been with me since the beginning."

"If only it'd showed me a *face*." Rosara balled her hands into fists. "Instead, I get Delphi's lantern and the bloody bones of a snake-like creature and the word 'traitor' burned so hotly into my eyes I almost went blind." She shook her head angrily. "It doesn't matter now. We'll find them. Anyway, once we start this interview, it cannot be stopped for any reason. Do you understand?"

Amelia bit her lower lip, nodding.

"Ophelia, prepare yourself."

The sibylline nodded and held out her hands to the flames, her eyes disappearing behind the white glow.

Rosara coiled her hair into a twist and pinned it against her scalp. "There could be an earthquake happening under our very feet and *still* you must go on. Are we clear?"

"Yes. But why?"

The High Sister stacked a few cushions on top of one another to make a seat. She wiped a wisp of white hair from her face with a sigh. "Because if you leave before the interview is complete, the flame will assume you're impure. And kill you."

Amelia hesitated at the rim of the copper bowl, the white flame rippling in an unseen current. The silver dragon flared its wings in challenge.

Fear is the hungry mouth that devours all you give it. Give nothing. Fear nothing.

She sucked in her breath and stepped into the fire.

CHAPTER 83

AMELIA STOOD IN THE CENTER OF SACRED WHITE FLAME, HAIR SWIRLING into a twist above her head. The flames engulfed her, ruffling her clothes and tickling between her toes. She felt weightless as if submerged in water, yet she could breathe. Everything was in shades of white or silver, and the crackling of the heatless fire was a dull roar in her ears.

"We will begin with your name." The sibyl's voice cut through the noise, demanding to be heard over the flames.

"The man who found me named me Amelia Brigantia."

Silver images danced across the swirling screen of flames, memories extracted from long ago. The feel of his strong hands plucking her from the surf, the way his eyes crinkled at the corners when he sang her his lullaby, his warmth as he sheltered her under his cloak during a snow storm in the Ciel Pass, gasping for one final breath as Sister Saoirse dabbed the sweat from his brow. The sisters' candlelight vigil as they buried him at the base of the sacred white peach tree.

Amelia smeared the tears from her cheeks and slapped the flames. The images shredded like tissue paper, swirling away in the updraft.

Do not be sad, child. It is as it should've been.

"So it was my fate to be an orphan and his to die?" she spat. "What divine purpose could that provide?"

"Sanu… who are you talking to?"

Amelia whirled around. The voice had been like a bell, deep and resonating. Her bones still tremored with its voice. No matter how hard she searched, she could see nothing but the white flames. Not even a shadow of the High Sister on the opposite side. "I… just forget it."

"Alright… Sanu Maitre, I will now ask you a series of questions. They will determine to what extent, if at all, you've strayed. We will begin with Wrath. Have you ever acted with a vengeful heart?"

Images of the whores in Bucharest appeared in the swirling flames. The orgy she had witnessed returned in explicit detail. Bodies writhed in front of the Lady's statue as their voices peaked in ecstasy.

She looked away, her nails digging into her palms. "No."

The white flames grew warm.

"That was righteous anger."

She clutched her head, swooning from the heat. "I-I spared them. I gave them a new opportunity—"

The heat intensified until it robbed her of breath.

Inside, the silver dragon roared. Snarling, the white flame blasted her with heat until the dragon tucked its tail and hid its face under a wing.

The Temple of the Lady was burning. The fire spared nothing, devouring everything like some starving hellbeast finally set loose. Smoke choked the night air, smothering the screams of the whores and its patrons. Their terror grasped at her like a hundred pawing hands, dragging her away from hope and suffocating her with despair. Their fingers pinched and clawed and tore—

I wanted to kill them," she shouted. "They deserved to *burn* for desecrating that temple. And I didn't… I *couldn't—*"

Wrath in our mistress's name is still wrath, child.

"Anyone else would've—"

You are not anyone *else. You are Chosen.*

Pictures of Tareq's ruined villa consumed the flames. Isen, lines of red blooming across his robes from the whip, blood dripping from his mouth. The anger was still fresh in her mind; she could taste its acidic bite in the back of her throat. She'd cut down his torturers like winter wheat with an arc of silver fire.

Do not let your rage drive you to kill.

"I didn't kill them. And they were *torturing* Isen because of *me*."

Rooks – the remains of the sorcerer – splattered against a crumbled wall loomed before her.

"He killed my sisters—"

Revenge is not for you.

An image of a dead tree flashed in the flames. In a blink it was gone, so fast she wasn't sure she'd even seen it at all. She strained forward, gritting her teeth against the insufferable heat. That wasn't her memory.

"Who *are* you?" she asked.

The heat disappeared.

Gasping for breath, Amelia wiped the sweat out of her eyes. It dripped off her hands and dribbled down her arms and pooled in her groin. She was soaked. Panting, she sat down before her trembling legs could buckle under her. "H-High Sister? How many more questions?"

"Six."

"SANU ARE FORBIDDEN ATTACHMENT. They are never to know anything more than chaste companionship. Have you loved, Sanu?"

Amelia was on her hands and knees, gasping for breath. She no longer had the strength to lift up her head, let alone stand. The silver dragon had curled into a tight ball, castigated into submission by the white flame.

She'd been interrogated about pride and envy, greed and gluttony. The white flame had plucked her memories from where she had shamefully hidden them, exposing them across its rippling surface. The myriad quotes she'd thrown into Hiro's face, abusing her title for personal gain, deluding herself that every time she bent a sect's rule she was doing it because she had no other choice. She'd eaten meat, slept in the arms of a man, gotten drunk to the point it had endangered her life.

The white flame stripped it all away and flung it back into her face.

Yet it could not tap into her memories without revealing some of its own.

The dead tree, parched earth cracked like shattered pottery, an orange moon glowering from the night sky. And anguish, hot as a branding iron, that rippled through every image.

"Sanu... have you ever loved?"

She gritted her teeth. "Of course I have."

The man she had called father. Saoirse. Yuki. Jocasta. And Kale. Wonderful Kale with his sunny smile and infectious giggle. Isen. Golden-haired and handsome. Encouraging. Compassionate.

The flames swirled with a picture of them standing in the Rhine River with her hand on his chest after he'd yanked away from his pendant; wedged together in the alcove of Tareq's palace. His hand in her hair, his lips hovering above hers as he was about to tell her something he shouldn't. Her lowered inhibitions had encouraged him to both their detriment.

"We were... I didn't mean... He's my *friend*. My brother."

Hiro appeared in the flames like a beacon. There were too many memories of him: brushing the glass from her hair in the tavern, tangling together for warmth in the cave, his mouth against hers in the Bucharest dungeon, yanking her out of the Indus River, the countless times he'd touched her without permission.

All of it had meant nothing until the day she had been poisoned. He'd pushed aside his prejudice, his fear, to cradle her in his arms as she'd bled. His words echoed in her ears. *Don't you die on me, Sanu. Don't make me come after you.*

Amelia squeezed the tears from her eyes. The white flames wicked them away before they could even drip off her cheeks. "He's killed children."

And nightmares haunt him. Yet he strives to redeem himself by protecting everyone else, even you, someone he fears.

"He tried to kill his father. He doesn't matter to me any—"

Your duty is to this world.

"You think I don't know that?" she bellowed.

Your relationships say otherwise. Distance yourself, for your heart's sake. There will come a time when you will have to give them up. You must be a true *bridge between realms, and attachments only tie you down to one side. The Gate cannot work without a bridge.*

"Yueshan."

The sacred fire flickered in acknowledgement.

"Then tell me," she said, lifting her gaze, "what good is a bridge if the Gate is broken?"

CHAPTER 84

THE WHITE FIRE SPAT HER OUT.

Amelia flung the cushion off her face and lurched to her feet.

Jaw hanging, Rosara's gray eyes bulged out of her head.

Ophelia was frozen on the ground, hands poised above the rim of the copper bowl. "What did you just—"

The High Sister reached for her. "Sanu, don't move. You've been in there for—"

But Amelia wasn't listening. She bolted out of the sanctuary, out of the temple, out of the city. Amai's hooves churned the earth as she drove him north toward the banyan forest. The once cloudless morning had darkened into a smothering swath of afternoon storm clouds. Lightning tore across the sky in crackles of purple and white.

Her mind was as scrambled as her morning eggs. Memories that weren't hers flashed silver across her vision. Her head throbbed as the images fought to overlap with whatever she was seeing. They were seeking something, driving her forward.

At the edge of the banyan forest, she spilled out of the saddle, clutching her head with a cry. The silver dragon snarled, flaring its wings wide. They glittered like crushed crystal, enveloping her mind and sealing out the fragments that sought to tear it apart.

The pain receded like an ebbing tide, and her vision cleared. Everything seemed sharper than before, more vibrant and alive. Blues were deeper, greens were brighter. She could even see dust motes glittering like flecks of gold in the sunlight. And there, like a ribbon of silver weaving through the trees, was the path of a memory. A spectral butterfly hovered above the path, flashing lilac wings.

Bosetsanu's messenger.

Amelia abandoned Amai and plunged into the forest.

The banyans were a tangled net so dense the sky was just a faint patchwork of blue. Their roots were slithering nests of wooden snakes; their hundred arms grasped greedily at the sky. She was a thread casting through the eye of a thousand needles as she wedged between tree trunks and scrambled over roots.

It was dark under the canopy, but the silver path of the memory shimmered with unwavering light. Myna birds with their yellow masks flitted about, chirping to each other as she passed. They scattered for their havens as the sky opened, flooding the forest with water. Amelia climbed into the arms of a tree and waited it out, hugging her legs to her chest. The lilac butterfly rested on her shoulder, wings flapping and sprinkling her with silvery dust. The air, once humid and stifling, became heavier and colder. She shivered as brown water sluiced over the roots, clawing even more soil away.

When it had lessened into a trickle, Amelia resumed her scrambling. She kept to the tree roots, avoiding the puddles trapped between them and the mud that threatened to twist her ankles. The ground rose more steeply now, and the banyans started to thin.

The silver path pulsed urgently.

She followed its sinuous trail to a cliff erupting from the forest floor. The butterfly spiraled up into the sky. Without hesitating, she began to climb.

The mesa rose just above the tree line, nestled deep in the heart of the banyan forest. Behind her, the golden domes of Lhasa rounded above the city wall like eggs in a nest. The Bengal Sea sparkled like sapphire, and the twist of the Brahma Rush in the west was a fat brown snake. All around her the forest rippled dark green across the land, from the Bhutan Steppes in the west to the Himalayas in the east.

The shimmering path pulsed again, demanding her attention. It cut across the mesa in a straight line to a dead tree. Even from this distance she could see it clearly: fat at its base and slender at the top with great arms of branches. They were bare of leaves, clawing at the sky like skeletal fingers.

Her sandals crunched on the dry rock as she crossed the mesa. A honeycomb lacework covered its surface, creating irregular wells that should've been filled with water from the storm.

Maybe it's porous?

She crouched and swept a hand over the white surface. Powder flung into the air, coating her tongue. Amelia spat. *It tastes like salt.*

She wiped her hand across her mouth and continued to the tree. Its bark had sloughed off long ago, leaving a bleak white trunk like an ancient bone of some bygone era.

It was a Bodhi tree. Its bark would've been gray like the sibyl's eyes, its leaves thin like those of bamboo but red as the setting sun. It was said each leaf teased loose by the wind was a prayer sent to Heaven.

The salt of my grief shall be masked by my Mother's water, and my Father's light will guide you back to me. With the blood of Heaven, I will make a way for you.

Amelia pressed her hand against its trunk.

The white flame's memory threatened to overwhelm her. With an anguished cry, she slumped to the ground, but her hand remained fused to the Bodhi tree. Pictures flashed across her mind like zipping dragonflies.

A river in the east. A bright light that blasted like a pillar of fire into Heaven. The cracking of the mesa's once mirror-like surface. The leaves of the dead Bodhi tree disintegrating into red powder.

With each ragged gasp, the memories faded.

So it's true. The Gate is broken. And I don't know how to perform Yueshu. We really are lost.

Inside, the silver dragon hummed. It was like a cat purring, trying to console her. She smeared the tears from her eyes and got to her feet.

But it wouldn't have shown me this if there wasn't a way to fix it. There has to be a way. Whatever happened on that river... that's got to be it.

She brushed herself off and marched back the way she had come. Night had fallen by the time she emerged from the banyan forest. Amai was nowhere to be found, so she started the trek across the farmland alone.

"It'll be fine," she told herself for the tenth time. "There's plenty of time. It's..."

Frowning, she looked more closely at the stars. The Whale wasn't supposed to rise for another four hours. The Hunting Dogs had already set, and the moon hovered above the southern horizon.

Amelia blanched. *"I've been in the flames for two weeks?"*

CHAPTER 85

A HUSH SETTLED OVER THE CROWD AS AMELIA STAGGERED OVER THE temple threshold. Sister Penelope backed away from her, covering her mouth with both hands. Then like a rabbit, she ran across the rotunda.

"*Amelia.*" Isen shoved his way through the crowd. He grabbed her arm, the tension in his face melting away. "Don't you scare me like that! They found Amai just wandering. Are you alright? Sweet mercy, you're soaking wet."

"Isen—"

"They found the traitor, by the way. Some brother named Michael. The Militum Dei dragged him—"

"Isen, I've *got* to talk to you—"

"*Not here.*" The High Sister's voice sliced through the air. "Sanu Maitre, you will accompany me at once."

Amelia gave Isen's arm a squeeze and pried herself loose. The ancient Sanuset clamped a hand around Amelia's wrist and hauled her off. "I *knew* there was something off about that Gate in the garden. The flames, they showed me—"

"Not another word," Rosara hissed. "Sister Penelope, send Sister Ophelia to my room at once."

"You don't need to drag me, Rosara. I *can* walk."

The High Sister refused to let her go. "The temple has been in an uproar, Amelia. Everyone saw you run out of here like a *tengu* out of the Abyss and now you've returned soaked and covered in filth. What possessed you—"

"I wasn't... myself."

Rosara rolled her eyes. "I could've told you that. For weeks Ophelia and I have listened to you talking to the flames. Actually *talking*. Except you didn't sound like you. Your voice... it *chimed* like bells."

When they arrived at a door carved with lilies and butterflies, Rosara withdrew a key from her pocket and opened it. Cozy with carpets and a crackling hearth, the High Sister's quarters were downright garish compared to the barren cell Amelia slept in. Above the mantle hung a tapestry map of Eurasia, embellished with Meh-teh peering out between the Himalayas and mysterious half-woman half-fish creatures popping out of the waves in the oceans.

Rosara shuffled to one of the stuffed chairs by the fireplace and sank into it with a groan.

Amelia collapsed into another, the adrenaline that had flooded her system now spent. "I was in the flames for two weeks. Sweet mercy, how is that possible?"

"The interview takes as long as it takes. The sacred flames delve deep. And how did you *talk* to it? I've been its sibyl for the last five decades and it's never once *spoken*."

There was a brief knock on the door, and Sister Ophelia rushed into the room.

"Lock it behind you, Ophelia."

The sibylline obeyed and hastily joined them at the hearth. She gripped the armrest of Amelia's chair, staring wildly into her eyes.

"Why would you think the Gate is broken?" Ophelia asked. "I can see its arch—"

"That *farce* in the gardens is not the Gate."

"Rosara... w-what is she talking about?"

The High Sister flicked her dove-gray eyes from Amelia to the sibylline, considering. At last she sighed, shaking her head. "You suspected even before the white flames told you. How many generations of clergy have come through this temple and haven't seen the truth? Tell me, what gave it away?"

"There was no life in it."

Ophelia slumped into the last chair. "If it's not in the garden, then where is it?"

"You'll find out when I'm on my deathbed, and not a moment sooner," Rosara said firmly.

"So why the deception?" Amelia asked.

"Tell me, Amelia, if you had the biggest, the most precious, the most wondrous jewel in the world, would you put it on display? Would you put it where just anyone could see it? Could touch it? Could *steal* it?"

Amelia shook her head.

"Certainly not," Rosara agreed. "You would put in its place a decoy. The Gate of Heaven is the most powerful force on this earth. What would a person do with that power, if they could access it?"

"But they can't."

"No, but *you* can, and every other Revered Onu or Maitre that's been trained. Who's to say you won't use the power for personal gain?"

Amelia lurched to her feet. "How *dare* you—"

Rosara held up her hands in surrender. "I am not saying *you* specifically, Amelia, of course not. You've proven your heart already."

She returned to her chair with a huff.

The High Sister's voice had gone quiet. "So now you know."

"But if it's broken," Ophelia ventured, "how can Yueshu be performed successfully?"

"I'm... not sure."

"When was it damaged?" Amelia asked.

"Twenty years ago." Rosara scrubbed her face with her twig-like hands. "There was a flash of light in the middle of the day, and then that was it. I've been trying to discover how to fix it ever since."

Unbidden, a pillar of fire erupting into the clouds flickered across

Amelia's vision. She shook her head, clearing her eyes of the spectral memory. Uncurling her fingers from the fists they'd made, she took a purging breath. "So you're telling me that in twenty years you haven't found a solution? How can we *possibly* fix it in time? Yueshan is in four weeks!" Feeling the need to throttle something, she grabbed the poker and stabbed at the fire. "Why didn't you send a crane to Mount Taru? Surely the Revered Onu could've helped."

"She could not make the trip, and her protégé had not yet finished her training. I would've sent others to do this years ago, but I couldn't trust just *anyone* with this secret. Except for Abba Daniel – and now Ophelia, thanks to you – I was the only one who knew the temple Gate was a decoy. I couldn't share the secret of its location, nor the fact that it was broken, with anyone but the Sanu sent here. I've been waiting for *you*, Amelia, for the last twenty years."

"And what a disappointment I've turned out to be." Amelia hid her face in her hands, biting her lip to keep from crying. "Onu Jocasta died before she could tell me the dance sequence. I'm *useless*."

"Heaven be merciful," Ophelia whispered.

"Fear not." Rosara leaned forward and patted her on the knee. "The last twenty years were not in vain. I've discovered someone who can help."

Amelia peeked over her fingertips. "Who?"

"A druid."

"High Sister, *no*. She'll never make it—"

"Of course she will. She has no other choice." Rosara leaned back in her chair. "Make no mistake, Amelia, this journey will be more treacherous than the one that brought you to us. But it's our only hope."

"Does this druid have a name?"

"Yes. Elwynn."

CHAPTER 86

LAKSHMI ENTERED THE COMMAND TENT, ELATED. GORE WAS SMEARED across her gauntlets, the scimitar in her fist scarlet with dried blood. She sauntered into the tent, snatching the nearest cup and draining it.

Hiro dropped into a chair, set his dragon helmet beside it. He rubbed a sore spot in his shoulder, rolling his arm to work out the strain.

The Bowman had been there again, his arrow missing its intended mark and possessing a Jianshu soldier. Eyes glowing green, she killed a dozen of her comrades before lunging at Hiro. Takāto barreled into her with a cry, knocked her off her feet, and crushed her head in with the Foehammer. Eye dangling from a socket, she sprang from the ground and sank her needle-like teeth into his forearm. Calliope had pinned her down with her spear before Shin had taken off her head off with his katana.

"Can you hear them outside?" Lakshmi crowed. *"Dragon! Tiger!* As if these very beasts have come alive in us. Isn't it absolutely thrilling?"

"Let us toast our success." General Vasilios handed him a cup of wine. "Is your man okay?"

Takāto was in the infirmary getting his arm sewn back together from the bite wound that had left his flesh in ragged strips. He'd been so pale—

"I don't know." Hiro set his cup aside, untouched. "Vasilios, this has to stop. That Bowman is targeting me. Imagine the destruction *I* would be capable if I was turned into one of those... *henge*."

"I'm surprised you've let these little skirmishes go unanswered." Lakshmi helped herself to a goat kebab. "Why haven't we struck at the heart of this Shadow Army yet? Each Guard has five divisions. We have plenty of fighters."

"We move in any direction, and they attack. When we defeat them and press forward, they're gone. We can't *find* them, *Brigadier* Khan."

"Then send some scouts."

"They don't come back."

Lakshmi stopped chewing. "Deserters?"

The Pirsan general pursed his lips, plucked the plate of kebabs out of her hands. "You dishonor the dead."

Hiro put a restraining hand on Vasilios's shoulder. "Lakshmi, I want to take some of your Academy troops and scout tomorrow."

"A general? *Scouting*? Whoever heard of such a thing?" She turned to Vasilios. "You'd allow this?"

"I allow him nothing," the Pirsan griped. "Hiro does as he pleases; you know this."

Hiro shrugged. "I do what is necessary."

"Then I'm coming with you."

"No," they both said.

"You and Ashar will need to lead the army as General Vasilios directs."

"They're my troops, and I go where they go," Lakshmi fired back. "You, Hiro, can stay here as you should."

"*General Ishida*," Vasilios corrected her.

"I'm the only one who's scouted them and lived." That was stretching the truth; discovering the army outside Pathankot had been an accident. "And I need to see what we're up against with my own eyes. What kind of man stays silent when he's being slashed apart?

What general sends entire battalions of his troops to needlessly die? And who is that Bowman?"

Vasilios stroked his beard. "We need to move camp. We've stayed in one place too long already."

"I'll take the scouts at the fourth watch, while it's still dark," Hiro said, standing.

"*We'll* take the scouts at that time," Lakshmi clarified.

There was no arguing with a Khan. Like her father, Domo Nameer Khan, she never took 'no' for an answer. They shared the same ruthlessness, the same ambitious drive.

"Fine." Hiro collected his gear. "Send groups of four to the east, south, and west. I'm going north."

"North?" Vasilios asked. "The Shadow Army is south of us."

"A blackbird was there today. It watched the battle and flew north. I want to know why." He touched his forehead. "Peace to you, General."

Vasilios mimicked the gesture. "Peace to you, General."

Hiro swept the tent flap aside, Lakshmi at his heels. "You should select your scouts. And go pack."

"Later. First come to my tent, *General* Ishida."

He caught her hand before she could touch him. Yanking her into the shadows between two tents, he crushed her wrist in his hand.

"Hiro, you know I like things a little rough, but this—"

"*Discretion*, Lakshmi," he hissed. "*Use* it. I might be a general and you a brigadier, but we are still soldiers in the same army. There are expectations."

"Hiro, you *know* how battle enflames me—"

He released her. "Go. I'll... see you later."

Her dusky face parted into a brilliant smile. Trailing her hand down his chest, she slunk off in the opposite direction.

With an exasperated huff, he went to the see the Si Tanin.

There was no singing, no delicious aroma of roasting chicken and bubbling teriyaki sauce. Only the rasping of whetstones.

Shin dragged his katana against the damp block, wiped the edge clean with a cloth and tested it against his thumb. Panting, Azelie hurled her knives into a wooden target. They bristled from the center like a steel thistle. Calliope sat by the fire, rewrapping the grips on her spear. The firelight curled into the carvings of the sea creatures along its shaft, illuminating them like sorcerer's runes. The Foehammer rested against a stump of wood, masterless.

"Boss." Azelie noticed him first. Her last throw went wild, the blade piecing the target a full inch lower than the rest clustered in the center.

"Takāto?"

"He's sewn up, but he's got a fever now." Biting her lip, she turned her head away.

Shin stopped sharpening his katana, placed a hand on her shoulder.

"Azelie... what aren't you telling me?"

"Black streaks," Calliope answered. The muscles in her arms bulged like grapefruits as she jerked on the leather straps. "Looks like blood poisoning but the physician says it isn't. He's treating it with god's-herb now, but..."

Demon ichor.

Hiro clenched his burned fist. "I'm scouting tomorrow. I'm going to find that piece of *goushi* Bowman and—"

"Boss, *no.*"

"Azelie, I want you with General Vasilios."

"Boss, don't be ridiculous. We're going with—"

"Kale will be with him."

Azelie shut her mouth, nodded. The Si Tanin knew nothing happened to the boy on their watch.

Hiro drew his greatsword, swiped a whetstone, and rasped it down one side. He caught the filings on a cloth and carefully bundled it up. Hiro pressed the wad in Calliope's hand. "Calliope, give this to the physician. Have him make an infusion and drip that into Takāto's wound. Steel forged in dragon's breath seems to dispel some sorcery, maybe it'll help. And stay with him. You're the only one strong enough to... subdue him if..."

She shook her head violently. "Don't say it, boss. Please."

"Shin. You're with me. You're the only one better than me with a bow. If we can get close enough, I want that Bowman put into the ground."

Shin sheathed his katana with a grim nod.

"Good. I'll check on Takāto before I go. When Kale comes for dinner, keep him here. I don't want him to know until it's time."

"Got it, boss."

Hiro nodded, disappeared to his own tent.

Scowling, he shucked his armor as Lakshmi shrugged out of her padded jacket. She flung it carelessly on Kale's guqin, teased a yowl from the strings. He hadn't even unbuckled his belt before her teeth were on his neck. He let his mind go blank, forgot about Takāto, ignored the Bowman, and let Lakshmi shatter his worries into oblivion.

CHAPTER 87

THE BLACKBIRD DROPPED TO THE GROUND IN A BLOB OF ICHOR, THE arrow lodged in its eye sizzling in the tar.

Shin nocked another arrow, drew the fletching back to his lips. He eyed the bird with baleful black eyes.

"Don't waste your arrow." Hiro plunged the tip of his greatsword into the bubbling mass, just to be sure.

"What *is* that?" Lakshmi's gaze was riveted on the disintegrating ichor.

"Sorcery. Come on, we're exposed on this ridge."

Hiro whistled, and the ranging scouts converged in the little valley where they'd left their horses.They continued north until just before daybreak, kept to the lowlands and scrub to mask their movements. The insects continued to chirp, the night birds their intermittent warbling. They had this habit of becoming deathly still when the Shadow Army was nearby, and the air was a cacophony of sound.

Maybe I was wrong. Maybe that blackbird was just following us. Maybe—

Dagmara whistled. She was already on her belly, clinging to the ground like a spider. Hiro dismounted, slunk up beside her, and parted the scrub with a silent hand.

The Shadow Army stretched for miles. They covered the earth like ants, dense and swarming with no glimpse of the ground beneath their feet. No fires, no camp sounds, just a swath of black stretching to the Himalayas.

Hiro felt his stomach drop to his boots. The only reason he didn't vomit on the spot was that he'd left four companies – twelve thousand souls – scattered in the Qiang Pass as a preventative measure. They were a cork in a bottle of shaken champagne. Ready to be blown apart. "I hate being right."

"How...?" Lakshmi's voice died in her throat.

"Look at their marching pattern. We drove them south, thinking to corner them against the sea, and all they did was cleave in half and swing wide around us. Back to the pass." The scrub splintered in his fist. "I should never have left home."

"But we've killed thousands—"

"A diversion. Just large enough to think we had them by the tail." He swallowed. "Gods above, there's got to be over a million of them."

Farther down the ridge, Shin threw a rock at him. He pointed to the sky.

Three blackbirds flapped overhead. They flew in a jerky jumble of feathers into the valley below, disappearing into the southernmost clot of soldiers. A whisper of green light welcomed them.

The Bowman.

Shin slid an arrow from his quiver, but he'd have to break cover in order to fire.

"It's too far," Hiro hissed, waving him off.

Shin nodded, kept the arrow nocked but flattened himself against the ground.

"Sir," Dagmara said, "what *is* that?"

Hiro strained forward as specks of green light popped into existence like hellish fireflies. Radiating from the Bowman, the light rippled through the ranks until hundreds were possessed by his power. *Henge.* They broke apart from the main host, formed a flanking line of glittering green light.

"Those things'll kill half our soldiers before we even reach their war-host." Lakshmi seized his arm. "We can't win this. Not even if the Siber Guard and their savage dogs came from the Borealis Pass tomorrow."

Hiro fought the rising bile in his throat. "We'll just have to change tactics. Beheading them seems to work just fine. Now—"

He was suddenly aware of how quiet it was. No birds chirped, no lizards rustled among the brush. The song of the insects had guttered out. Hiro spun, drawing his dagger.

The blade was only halfway clear of its scabbard when it blocked the downward swing of a sword. The drone's kohl-lined eyes had that empty look he'd seen a thousand times. Hiro grunted, cleared the dagger the rest of the way. He kicked the black-clad man in the gut, sent him sprawling.

Dagmara whistled a shrill alert, was answered by Jorge's scream. Lakshmi rolled to her feet and sliced Hiro's assailant across the chest with her scimitar before running to their horses. Hiro scrambled down the hill after her, sliding in the scree. Shin was already in the saddle, fired two arrows over their heads at the drones that appeared over the crest. More were coming.

Hiro swung up into the saddle. "We need to send that eagle—"

"Jorge had the bird."

"Damn it." He rammed his heels into his mare's flanks.

They'd been taken completely by surprise. He hadn't heard a cough, a curse, or a stumble to alert them of their presence. Their attackers had been ghosts. Even when Lakshmi had sliced that man's chest open, he hadn't made a sound.

Hiro pushed them hard, sometimes slowing but never stopping. The Shadow Army didn't use horses, but there was always a first time.

It was around midnight on the second day after their escape that Lakshmi ordered a halt. "We *have* to sleep. Even if it's only for a few hours. The horses need to stop, Hiro."

"*Fine*. Just for a few hours."

They didn't even bother to set up a camp. They just loosened the girths on their horses, slept wherever they dropped.

He was too wired to sleep. He had to alert Vasilios. Toshiro and the

Home Guard needed to know, if they didn't already. His troops in the Qiang Pass needed to know, if they hadn't been slaughtered already.

Lakshmi grabbed his arm. Her chocolate eyes were bright with fear. "Hiro, we'll be slaughtered."

"You *don't* know that."

"You saw how they snuck up on us," she hissed. "*Us.* Academy graduates! That's impossible."

"Nothing's impossible."

But Lakshmi was right; it shouldn't have happened. They were better than this.

"Don't be a *fool*." Her grip tightened painfully. The metal scales of her gauntlets creaked. "They'll kill us all. We have no defense against their stealth, their *henge*, they're too numerous to count—"

"What are you saying?" He pulled away from her. "We can't just up and leave."

"Can't we?" she asked softly.

Hiro blinked. "*What?*"

"Come south with me," she pleaded. "We would find refuge in my family's estate in Kolkata. No one would know. The scouts never return, remember?"

"And what of *them*?" He pointed to Shin, Dagmara.

Lakshmi touched the hilt of her scimitar with a shrug.

Hiro backhanded her across the face. Blood sprayed from her broken lip. "*Have you lost your mind?* I should cut your throat right now. Sedition, murder, cowardice, take your pick!"

Lakshmi gazed back into his fiery eyes with steel in hers. She spat the blood out of her mouth, lunged to her feet, and poked him in the chest. "You *know* I'm right."

"I *know* I'm within my rights as your general to hang you by the nearest tree and let the dogs have you," he snarled. "But I won't... out of respect for your previous service. I will not abandon my soldiers. Not for anything or *anyone*."

CHAPTER 88

Hiro threw himself from his horse. The *whaa* of the war-horn had announced their arrival a few minutes ago, and the camp had erupted into ragged cheers. He ignored them all, hurried to the orange command tent. Kale threw the flaps aside, Azelie hot on his heels.

Hiro knelt, let the boy fling his arms around his neck. He flattened the boy's mane of auburn curls and looked over his head at Azelie. "Takāto?" he mouthed.

She winced. "Alive. Calliope hasn't left his side, not even to sleep."

Hiro unwound himself from the boy. "I need to speak with Vasilios now, Kale. The hor – Beleza – needs you."

"You're staying now, right? You're not going out again?"

"We'll see."

"Boss... what about Shin?" Azelie twirled one of her knives against her fingertip, tried her best to look nonchalant.

Hiro rolled his eyes. "He's *fine*, Azelie. Go on."

"Thanks, boss!" The deadly knife-thrower practically skipped away.

Hiro plunged into the orange tent.

"Ishida," Vasilios exclaimed. "Praise the gods you've returned—"

Hiro grabbed the pitcher of water and drank from its mouth.

435

They'd run out of stores yesterday. He guzzled until there was nothing left.

"H-Hiro?"

"We need to send every messenger eagle we have." He snatched a plate of cold kebabs, tore into them.

The Pirsan general slid the bowls of pita and olive oil within reach. "So you don't have to crawl over the table."

Hiro glared at him, stuffed a wad of pita into his mouth.

"What did you see?"

"What of the other scouts?" Hiro asked instead. "Have they returned?"

"Not yet, but the Fifth just drove off another battalion hours before you arrived. It might've delayed them some. I must say, Harrison makes quicker work of the enemy than you do. And where is Brigadier Khan?"

"Who cares," he muttered into his food.

Vasilios snatched the kebab out of his hand. "*What did you see?*"

"Millions. They cover the earth like a plague." Hiro snatched a bottle of wine, poured two glasses. He took the second cup and drained it. "And they've flanked us. This southern pursuit has been a diversion. They're pouring into Jianshu and northern Tybet as we speak."

The Pirsan general paled, shook himself. "Then... we pursue. We'll send eagles to the Siber Guard, tell them to breach the Borealis Pass and meet them on the Xinjiang Plains. We'll pinch them—"

"There's more. A company of *henge* protect their flank."

"Heaven be merciful." Vasilios sank into a chair. "What can we do?"

"*Nothing.*" Lakshmi stormed into the tent, grabbed the general's wine cup and guzzled it. "It'll be a slaughter."

Hiro ignored her. "We *might* have a chance. I left four companies in the Qiang Pass. And I left Toshiro with the Home Guard on alert halfway across the province in Gasi."

"Why did you not tell me this?" Vasilios blustered.

"Because I don't trust people I've just met. And then... it seemed irrelevant."

"We'll need to send the eagles tonight to your brother."

"No, to Domo Nameer Khan. Any birds they see in the Qiang Pass they'll just shoot down. Send them to Nameer in Kolkata to redirect to the Jade Palace. It'll be safer for the birds to travel over the Bhutan Steppes."

"And you said you were never good at strategy."

Alistair ducked into the tent, a horsehair helmet under his arm instead of books. His red hair had lengthened into a fiery halo around his head. He'd even put on ten or twenty pounds of muscle; it no longer looked like a breeze would topple him over.

"*Alistair.*" Hiro crushed his friend against him.

Alistair dropped his helmet, hugged him back hard.

"Gods above, it's great to see you," Hiro said. "When did you get here?"

"A day or two after you left." Alistair whumped him in the shoulder. "You should never have left, *General*. You should've left it to—"

"The expendables," Lakshmi said. "I tried telling him, Alistair—"

"That's *General Lochlan* to you, Brigadier Khan," Alistair snapped. "And I was *going* to say 'the professionals.' And how are my Academy troops doing?"

Lakshmi pursed her lips. "They're living up to the Academy's reputation, sir."

"Very good. You are dismissed."

"But, sir—"

"That is *all*, brigadier."

After a moment, she bowed her head and left.

Hiro just stared at him. "Alistair, you just spoke to a woman. Without vomiting."

"I think I'm going to be sick." The redheaded scholar rushed to the nearest basin and heaved.

Smirking, General Vasilios rolled his eyes and refilled their wine glasses. Poured a large one for the Academy general.

Alistair wiped his mouth with the back of his hand and slumped into a seat. "I don't care if she's the daughter of the forerunner for the Tybetan Seat, she is rather impertinent."

"I'm still impressed."

His friend grinned. "I read a few self-help books after you left."

"Of course you did."

Alistair quickly grew serious. "Hiro, I've never seen anything like this. Not even... at our blooding. This enemy – I've looked into their eyes, Hiro. It's like they have no souls."

"I've always thought of them as puppets, but..." Hiro raked a hand through his hair. "Gods above, what if you're right?"

"Hiro," Vasilios said, "I don't think he means *literally*—"

"Don't be obtuse, Vasilios. The Bowman, the *henge*, it all makes *sense.*"

The Pirsan general pursed his lips. "That insult aside, I think you're run ragged, Hiro. Alistair and I will take care of the eagles. Why don't you go bathe and sleep? We'll have dinner when you're more... level-headed."

"And when you don't stink like an ox," Alistair added.

"*Fine.* I'll be back in an hour. After I've checked on Takāto."

"Your man is stable, Hiro. That infusion has stalled the poison. Hovering over him won't make any difference. Go *sleep.*"

When he ducked out of the tent, Lakshmi was waiting for him. He swept past her without so much as a glance.

"*Hiro.*" She grabbed his arm. "You haven't spoken to me—"

He shook her off. "I have *nothing* to say to you. You should keep your distance, *brigadier.* When we meet again, it'll be as comrades on the battlefield, and that is *all.*"

He stormed through the camp, acknowledged the hails of his troops with a curt wave of his hand. They chanted *Dragon! Dragon!* with his passing, but it only made his stomach churn. His province was about to be destroyed; what Dragon couldn't protect its home?

"Sir." One of his brigadiers ran up to him, saluted. "Pleasure to have you back, sir."

"Harrison. Heard your brigade fought well today." He stopped by a trough, pushed a horse's muzzle out of the way and splashed some of the water on his face.

The brigadier's nod was brisk. "They don't call me the Reaper for nothing, sir. Gotta make up for the time I lost in Lhasa. And sir, you have… guests. Zhang found them while on patrol in the east."

"They've been searched?"

"Of course, sir. Not a weapon among them."

"The fools. Fine, send for them. I'll be in my tent."

"Yes, sir."

Hiro ducked into his tent, turned up the wick and flooded the space with light. It was the only thing keeping him awake enough to bathe. Flinging his soiled clothes into the corner, he scrubbed himself raw with a washcloth. The water turned reddish-brown after the first rinse. A towel was still on his head as he struggled into a fresh pair of trousers when the curtains of his sleeping partition parted.

Lakshmi appeared wearing her purple cape, and *only* her cape. She released the ties, let it pool in a puddle of cloth at her feet. "Please, Hiro," she begged. "Forgive me."

Before he could react, she dropped to her knees and peeled down the waistband of his trousers. He felt her lips on his flesh. Thought he was going to explode.

With a shuddering breath, his hand threaded into her silken hair.

But she was dead to him. She'd been willing to kill her own troops for her own self-preservation. And Shin, one of *his* Tanin.

"I told you to leave me *alone*." He yanked her head off of him with a vicious jerk. Wrenching her upright, he shoved her cape into her hands and chased her from his sleeping partition. *"Get out."*

Hiro stumbled to a halt at the sight of his guest seated on the camp stool.

"Forgive me." Cheeks aflame, the Sanu turned her head away. "Harrison didn't tell me you were… entertaining."

CHAPTER 89

"I thought prostitutes weren't permitted in the camp," the Sanu said. "You're playing with fire, Prince Ishida."

"I am Brigadier Lakshmi Khan, daughter of Domo Nameer and Doma Latika Khan, Academy graduate," Lakshmi snarled. "Not some filthy *whore.*"

"You couldn't expect me to come to that conclusion given your nakedness." The priestess risked a glance up from the carpet. "It's not like you have an insignia of your rank branded on that vast expanse of skin I just witnessed."

Hiro choked back a chuckle.

"How *dare* you—"

He snatched Lakshmi's arm, wrenched her back a step. The Sanu remained on the camp stool, a picture of refined composure. Her ocean blue-eyes were distant, cool. Disapproving. "It's not like that," Hiro blurted. "No rules have been broken. We… we just use our hands—"

"*That* didn't look like her hand."

Hiro flushed. Belatedly, he remembered he'd turned up the wick. She would've seen everything. He'd thought of *her* every day, and now here she was, and their reunion was turning into a disaster.

"She's nothing to me, Sanu, I swear."

Lakshmi struggled out of his grip. *"Nothing?"*

"So you were just using her?" Her eyebrows had lifted doubtfully. "That makes it better?"

"No, we used each other—"

"So you were both tools. I see."

"We don't need to explain ourselves to some self-righteous Sanu," Lakshmi snapped. "Hiro—"

"There is no 'we,' you pernicious *biaozi*," Hiro thundered. "Now get *out.*"

Lakshmi clutched her cape tight around her and fled.

There was a tense moment where the priestess played with the beaded fringe of her sari and Hiro's mind reeled from this bizarre exchange. He just stood there, panting with frustration, his hands clenched into fists at his sides.

The Sanu glanced at him. "Maybe... you should go put on a shirt."

He ducked behind the curtain, ran his hands through his hair. Considered ripping some of it out. What was she *doing* here? Why was she not safely sequestered in Lhasa? How much had she seen?

She's seen enough, you idiot.

Hiro tugged on his gi jacket, smoothed his rumpled hair. He yanked socks onto his feet and shoved them into his boots. They still needed polishing. Gods above, why was he thinking of polishing his boots? Fate or Heaven or whatever had deposited Amelia back into his life, and—

Hiro stumbled out from behind the curtain, still struggling with a boot. "Are you hungry? Thirsty?"

"Water'll be fine, please."

She took the cup without looking at him. Was she embarrassed at what she had seen, or was she judging him? His thoughts buzzed about his head like a swarm of bees.

The Sanu cleared her throat, stared into her cup. "So... I see Brigadier Harrison's made it back safely to the Guard."

He'd sent Harrison to lead the Sanu's armed escort to the holy city. He'd wanted no one but the most ruthless fighters protecting her.

"Yeah… he leads the fifth brigade."

An awkward silence where only the sputtering of the oil lamp filled the air between them.

"Some might think his frankness a bit off-putting, but I rather like him," she said/

"I do too…?"

"And the company's returned too, of course. It's not like they stayed in Lhasa. That'd be silly…"

Another pause.

"Your cuff is different."

"Oh… yeah." He ran his fingertip along the golden band. "It's a – Sanu, what are you *doing* here?"

She fidgeted in her seat. "It's not like I planned a field trip to your camp. Your scouts picked us up as we were crossing the Bhutan Steppes on our way to the Brahma."

He scrubbed his face with his hands. "I mean why aren't you in Lhasa? Yueshu is less than four weeks away—"

"Oh, so you *care* now?"

"Don't do this, Sanu. I care about *you*," he growled. "*Why are you here?*"

"I… I've been tasked to go to Akuma Cove."

Hiro blanched. "Sanu, *no one* comes back from there."

"You can't talk me out of this, Prince Ishida." She shook her head resolutely. Sadly. "I *must* go."

Prince Ishida. So that's it then, we're nothing but formal acquaintances now?

He swallowed past a hard lump in his throat. "Then I'll go with you. We can't afford to spare even a squad. But one man can go."

Startled, she finally looked up from the floor. Those familiar ocean-blue depths bored into him, squeezed at his heart.

She shook her head vehemently. "I can't ask you to do that. You're needed here-"

"Amelia." He came out of his seat, knelt on the carpet in front of her. Without asking permission, he took the cup from her hands and squeezed her fingers. "I made a huge mistake back in Arashiyama. I should've gone with you. The things I've seen… Please, don't deny me the opportunity to make it up to you."

The priestess wetted her lips, slowly withdrew her fingers from his grasp. He knew it was forbidden to touch her, but as she withdrew her hands, he couldn't help but interpret it as a refusal to forgive him. "What of your men here?"

"They'll be fine. Alistair and Vasilios have enough brains for battle strategy to share among ten men. And there are enough brigadiers to carry out their commands."

"I hear they call you the Dragon. That you have *friends* now."

"Yes… the Si Tanin."

"However did you manage that?"

It was an innocent question, but it still stung. Swallowing his pride, he went to the table and retrieved the journal. "I took a page out your book, Sanu. I care for them."

"The Bethany Journals?" She sprang from her seat. A smile brightened her face for the first time. "I thought—"

"Lord Ishida gave them to me… after you left. They've been entertaining and educational. But they belong to you." He secured the wand in its spine, offered it to her. "Here."

"No." She kept her hands at her sides. "I know them by heart, and you seem to need them more than me."

He set the book on the table, trailed his finger across its woven cover. "Thank you."

"But seriously, you should stay here. I've heard whispers around the camp… You are too important to leave."

"Your mission is of the utmost priority. I'm going."

She crossed her arms over her chest, nudged a spot of carpet with her foot. "So there's nothing I can say—"

"Nothing."

A heavy sigh. "So be it."

He nodded. "We'll leave tomorrow. Give me the rest of this night to settle things here and gather supplies. You're more than welcome to sleep here. I can go somewhere else."

"Should I be worried about any more unexpected guests?"

Hiro flushed. "No. Not at all. I'll send for some food—"

Kale sprinted into the tent. The *whoosh* of night air harried the oil lamp, scattered jagged shadows across the canvas. His hazel eyes flashed with joy at the sight of the Sanu, but he didn't greet her.

A scream drifted on the wind behind him.

"Takāto," the boy panted.

CHAPTER 90

BLOOD DRIPPED DOWN CALLIOPE'S SPLIT LIP, SPLATTERED ONTO Takāto's snarling face. Her hands clamped his meaty shoulders flat against the table as his legs thrashed. Hiro grabbed a flailing foot, pinned it down. When the other kicked his way, he caught it in the crook of his arm. It took the last of his strength to keep Takāto from wriggling free.

"Hey, boss."

"I thought he was stable." Hiro grunted as he got kicked in the ribs.

Calliope leaned over, flipped open the writhing man's gi. Black lines streaked across pale skin. "How stable can he be with *that* in his body?"

"Just put him out of his misery already," the physician shrilled. "Before he kills us all."

"Shin. Remove that man."

The swordsman grabbed the physician's collar, hauled him out of the tent. Then he held open the flap, gestured with his naked katana for the rest to follow.

"That means *move it*, people," Azelie barked.

The staff hustled their patients through the gap at a quick march.

445

Kale pushed through the throng, clutched the edge of the table. "Vasilios says to—"

"I know what he'd say," Hiro barked. "Get out of here, Kale. You'll get hurt."

"You didn't find the Bowman, did you?" Calliope asked. "No remedy?" She pinned Takāto's thrashing head between her bulging forearms. His teeth had lengthened into points, his face white as lily petals, the greenish cast to his dark eyes growing stronger with every heartbeat.

"No remedy that doesn't involve a sword."

Calliope looked him straight in the eye. "We won't be able to restrain him much longer."

"What are you saying, Calliope?" Azelie demanded. "That we just give up?"

"Of course not."

A breath of air rolled through the tent as the flap opened again.

"Shin, don't let anyone—"

"My lady, you shouldn't be—"

The Sanu approached the table, dodged a thrashing arm. Calliope grabbed his wrists, braced her elbows into Takāto's shoulders. Her breasts wedged against his head. If he'd been cognizant, no doubt he'd be grinning ear to ear.

"Sanu..." Hiro began.

"Hold him as still as you can. He isn't going to like this." She unwound the bandage on his arm. Her thumb smeared away the poultice. "Are there... metal shavings in here? It looks like Damascus – Hiro, are these filings from your sword?"

He nodded briskly, struggled to keep Takāto's fat legs pinned under his arms.

"That was... brilliant."

"Don't sound so surprised, Sanu."

"Whatever you're going to do, do it fast, my lady," Calliope said through gritted teeth.

The Sanu gripped Takāto's wound with both hands, inhaled deeply. Her shoulders rose as her chest expanded like a bellows.

Takāto snarled, snapped his sharp teeth at her. She fixed him with a cold blue stare, continued to breathe.

Suddenly she turned her head to the side, spat out a glob of black tar. The ichor sizzled as it hit the ground, hissed as silver fire ignited across its oily surface. It disintegrated into ash, leaving a scorched spot on the grass.

Azelie rushed out of the tent, retching. Shin hovered nearby, hand clamped on his sword hilt. Calliope paled, raised her horrified gaze from the scorched grass to meet his. Hiro smothered the nausea that churned his stomach, forced himself to witness.

The Sanu expelled the demon ichor with each breath. Slowly, the black lines vining across Takāto's skin shriveled. Shrank. He didn't fight so much now. The greenish glow had vanished from his eyes. His teeth still seemed longer than usual, but he no longer snarled.

"You can let go now," she said.

Calliope straightened slowly, kept her hands planted on Takāto's shoulders.

The Sanu slid her hands down Takāto's arm, the flesh knitting together before their very eyes. She staggered back a step, grabbed a cloth and wiped her tongue. "He'll be fine now." She leaned against the table, panting. "But it might take him a little while to wake—"

The fat man's eyes popped open. He craned his head around. "Calliope, I had the most wondrous dream that your breasts were right in my face. Gods above, they felt per—"

The warrior woman smacked him across the mouth.

"*Ugh.* I said it was a *dream*, Calliope."

"*That* was for talking about my breasts." She wedged her hands under his shoulders, helped him sit up.

Hiro released his legs. "It's nice to have you back, Takāto. Now say 'thank you' to the Sanu. She saved your life."

Takāto heaved his girth off the table. "I heard your voice, my lady. Beautiful, like silver bells. You called me back from..." He shuddered, pressed his fist into his palm and bowed. "Thank you, my lady."

The Sanu smiled weakly.

Takāto leaned forward. "And might I say you are no less *radiant* in person-"

Hiro rolled his eyes. "She's *Sanu*, Takāto."

The fat man shrugged, gazed at Calliope. "I guess I'll just have to satisfy myself with our tender moment."

"Azelie?" Calliope called. "When you're done vomiting, I need one of your knives. Takāto has a problem with his tongue."

Hiro grabbed a stool before the Sanu could collapse. He guided her into it, ignored the happy reunion happening behind him as Azelie leapt into Takāto's arms. Lowering himself into the grass, he knelt at her feet.

She wouldn't look at him. Her shoulders shook from exertion, her fingers trembled in her lap.

He snatched a blanket from the nearest cot and draped it over her shoulders. "Sanu—"

"Please, don't say anything." Her voice was hoarse, irritated from all the hacking.

"I had no idea that's what you did for me."

She risked a glance at him. Her ocean-blue eyes were wet. Afraid.

Taking her hand, he pressed her knuckles against his forehead in the ancient gesture of respect. The trembling in her fingers vanished.

Something bumped his shoulder. The Si Tanin had joined him on the ground, heads bowed with their fists pressed into their palms.

The solemnness of the moment was shattered as Kale burst into the tent. He dragged a Delphian priest behind him. "Look who I found!"

Isen tripped over a wayward bedpan, banged his shin against a cot.

Sighing, Hiro stood. The Sanu's fingers slipped from his hand.

"Hiro? Is that you? I swear I recognize that mouth-breathing—"

"Hello, Isen."

"*Ah.* Fantastic. Back together again."

"I'm... thrilled." Hiro headed for the exit.

The Si Tanin swarmed around him.

"Boss, where are you going?"

"Yeah, stay and celebrate. I've just become not-possessed anymore. They're gonna sing songs about me, boss. I'll be famous!"

He looked over their heads at the Sanu. They followed his gaze. Disheveled caramel hair, her silks stained from travel, a smear of Takāto's blood across her cheek. His heart thumped painfully in his chest. "She is the last Sanu, and I am bound to her. Where she goes, I must follow."

Shin gripped his arm, shook his head warningly.

"Shin's right, boss," Azelie said. "You can't *leave*. That's desertion."

"No, it won't be."

Takāto crossed his arms over his chest. "Then we're coming with you."

"You're going to Lhasa." Hiro glanced at the priestess again. "Something's wrong there. Infiltrate, but do not engage. I'll return that way. Go tonight, while I am still your commanding officer."

"You'll always be our commanding officer," Calliope said. But she gave a sharp whistle, and the Si Tanin filed out of the tent behind her.

Kale appeared at his elbow. "Where are they going?"

Hiro raked a hand through his hair, tangled it in his topknot. He pulled the ribbon free, let his hair fall to his shoulders. "Kale, pack your things. We're leaving in the morning. I just... need to figure out how to tell Vasilios and Alistair."

The boy cringed. "Then you'd better bring your sword."

CHAPTER 91

Hiro kept one foot on the dock, looped his other leg over the gunwale, and offered his hand to the priestess. It was a modest catboat, black with *Xunsu* written in curling gold script along the stern.

Ignoring him, the Sanu hopped into the boat as nimbly as if she'd grown up on the sea instead of on a mountain.

Scowling, he helped the priest instead. Kale was already up the mast, clung to the ropes like a monkey.

Hiro led his warhorse last, put her in the makeshift stall of the recessed deckhouse beside the calmer Sarabi stallion. He kept her blindfolded; the last thing he needed was a panicky twelve-hundred-pound beast smashing through the gunwales.

"Kale, the sail."

The boy loosened the halyard. The orange sail snapped out like a fin, trembled in the wind until Hiro tightened the mainsheet. The *Xunsu* zipped away from the dock, sliced swiftly across the Brahma Rush. He hadn't sailed since his youth in the Academy, but after riding out a storm that had lasted three days, it was a skillset he was unlikely to forget.

Isen stumbled to the nearest gunwale and retched. The Sanu was at the bow, arms crossed over her chest to keep her sari from flying into her face. If the wind held, they'd reach the Irrawa River in the morning. Follow its course southwest into the wild heartland and shark-infested shores of Siam. To Akuma Cove.

She still hadn't said why they were going. In fact, she hadn't said much to him at all. The Sanu kept her distance, rarely looked in his direction, found every way to avoid him.

The tiller creaked in his fist, threatened to snap.

He'd apologized, hadn't he? He'd forsaken his troops, devastated his friends, angered his comrades.

Alistair had almost ripped his hair out. "We've just discovered that the Shadow Army is over twenty times our number, marching on Jianshu – your *homeland*, Hiro – and you're going to up and leave to follow a priestess on some fool's errand?"

"What Alistair is trying to say is, 'Have you lost your damn mind?'" Vasilios clarified.

"I can't expect you to understand, but I must go. This is a... holy mission."

"Are you invoking *dimittere*? Release for religious reasons?"

Hiro nodded. "I am."

Alistair threw up his hands.

"I'll note it in the log, but this is serious, Hiro," the Pirsan general said. "If the inquiry proves you used *dimittere* to cover your desertion, the penalty is death."

"I'm not deserting. Have I ever broken my word to you? Have I ever acted dishonorably?"

Both men shook their heads.

"Then trust me in this."

"But you *can't*—"

"One man does not tip the scales of battle, Alistair."

"How can you say that?" Vasilios demanded. "*You* are not a man. *You* are a Dragon. How will the troops react when their Dragon has left them on the eve of the largest battle they will ever fight? With a company of *henge* no less. How could *I* possibly..."

Hiro glanced at the ugly scar marring the general's leg. "Brigadier Harrison will lead in my stead."

"The Reaper?" Vasilios lifted an eyebrow. "Not Brigadier Khan?"

"But Hiro, no one returns from Akuma Cove," Alistair said.

"Just like no one returns from scouting our enemy?"

"Lord Ishida will not be pleased," Vasilios said. "He will know of this."

"I understand. Do as you must."

The day they'd arrived in port, a messenger eagle was waiting for him with the dockmaster. It was the largest message the bird could carry. A diatribe from Lord Ishida. Hiro scanned it, crumpled it, threw it into the water. Let some big-mouthed bottom-dweller feast on his words; Hiro had no time for them.

All that, and he was met with nothing but cool indifference.

"*Sanu*," he barked. "Come over here."

She looked over her shoulder with a scowl.

"What? Am I supposed to be the only one who steers the boat?" he asked. "I'll need to sleep eventually."

The Sanu pushed herself away from the bow, took her time checking on the nauseated priest. She gave him a wad of licorice root and eventually joined Hiro at the stern.

"Take the tiller," he said.

She waited for him to get well out of the way before she wrapped her arm around the tiller shaft.

"It's connected directly to the rudder. Even the slightest push or pull will adjust the boat's direction drastically."

The *Xunsu* lurched starboard, heaved port. Hiro yanked on the mainsheet to steady himself. Isen vomited loudly over the side.

"*Goushi*. Not so *much*, Sanu. You're giving the other captains heart attacks."

The nearby ships had fled, shouting curses on the wind.

When the *Xunsu* held a steady course, he put the mainsheet into her hands. "This is the line that controls the boom and the position of the sail. When the sail catches the wind just right, it's easy to get a couple of knots out of her."

"'Her?'" The Sanu struggled to keep the mainsheet taut.

"Boats are referred to as feminine."

"How chauvinistic."

"Boats are like women," Hiro said with a sneer. "When they're cantankerous, we call them *biaozi* too."

Scowling, the Sanu loosened her grip on the mainsheet. The pulley squealed as the wind caught the sail, swept the boom across the deck like a wrecking ball.

Hiro dropped and rolled out of the way. Felt the *whoosh* of the boom's passing ruffle his hair.

The priestess tightened her grip on the mainsheet, reeled it back in to catch the wind once more. "*Oh!* So *that's* what happens." She tired a bowline into the mainsheet, looped it over the nearest cleat. "She's all yours, Ishida."

He scrambled to the tiller. "Since when do you know how to tie knots?"

"Kale," she said over her shoulder. "He's smarter than most ten-year-olds, you know."

The boy scrambled down the pegs of the mast as she climbed the cargo rope onto the deckhouse. Folded her legs under her like he'd seen her do only a hundred times. There'd be no use trying to engage her now that she was meditating.

"Is Amelia going to steer again? That was fun."

"*Never. Again,*" Isen groaned.

Hiro crooked his finger, beckoned the boy closer. "What's wrong with the Sanu?"

"You mean why is she treating you so coldly and the rest of us like normal?"

"Yeah. That."

The boy shrugged. "No idea."

DAYBREAK, and they were the only poor souls steering toward the mouth of the Irrawa. The Forbidden River. The chop disappeared from the water, became smooth as glass. Narrow, the

trees strained over the water for the sunlight. Birds flitted overhead but didn't sing. The Sanu stopped trailing her hand in the water.

They furled the sail, and Hiro kept the *Xunsu* to the middle of the channel. Yellow cliffs erupted from the sapphire water on either side. Vines slithered down the rock, a green net against the pale stone. The smell of jasmine was heavy in the air, lulled them into a stupor.

"We're here," he murmured.

CHAPTER 92

SOMETHING BUMPED THE BOAT.

Hiro blinked, rubbed the sweat out of his eyes. Maybe he'd just imagined it. Maybe they'd passed over a submerged limb—

Off the starboard side, something pale flashed just below the surface before disappearing into the deep.

The boat rocked as they were struck from below.

The priestess climbed down from the deckhouse and went to soothe the horses.

"Kale," Hiro called, "anything ahead?"

From his perch on the mast, the boy shaded his eyes. "There's nothing. I don't see—"

They were hit from the port side, hard. The wood creaked with the strain as water sloshed over the gunwale.

"Gods above," Isen wailed. "Make it *stop*."

"Kale, get down here. Sanu, take the tiller." Hiro unsheathed his greatsword.

A jarring blow knocked the priestess off her feet. The water churned into white froth as they were struck from all sides. The boat jumped like grease dropped into a hot pan. The Sanu slid across the deck, slammed into the stern. Shrieking, Kale plummeted into the water.

Hiro sprinted up the deck as the horses screamed. Kale flailed off the starboard side, scrambling against the slick hull.

Lurching over the gunwale, Hiro grabbed the boy's collar. With a twist of his shoulders, he heaved Kale out of the water and plunged his sword into the gaping maw of the bull shark chasing after him. The shark ripped away from the blade, nearly jerking it out of his grasp.

"Unfurl the sail!"

Sharks swarmed around the boat, ramming it with their noses and thrashing at their competition.

Isen vomited.

Hiro pried the priest away from the edge, threw him against the deckhouse. Isen clung to the cargo net like a half-drowned rat.

The Sanu wrapped the mainsheet around her arm, braced herself against the tiller. She leaned back against the pull of the sail, crying out as the rope burned through her sleeve into her skin.

The boat pitched to port from another strike, threw him into the side. He caught himself before he could hurl overboard and slashed an opportunistic shark across its toothy jaws. The water bloomed red.

Kale shouted that he had the sail free. Too terrified to move, the boy clung to the mast like a barnacle. Behind them, dorsal fins of even larger sharks sliced through the surface waters, intent on joining the assault.

"They're *eating* the railing," the Sanu shouted.

A shark gnawed on the gunwale where Isen had been, thrashing between bites to rip the wood loose. Hiro chopped down with his greatsword. The severed head hit the deck with a wet *thunk*, its jaws still snapping.

"Rocks ahead," Kale shrilled from the mast. "Port side!"

The Sanu threw her weight into the tiller. The boat grazed the rocks, showered the water with black flakes of paint.

"Tree, starboard side!"

The boom hit Hiro across the chest. He crashed against the deck, the greatsword jarred from his hand. It skittered across the reddened planks for the hole in the gunwale.

The priestess abandoned the tiller and dove after it. A shark launched at her, shattering the weakened wood. With a scream, she rolled away, brought the sword up with her. It cut into the underside of the beast's jaw, catching in the bone.

The sharks below tore into their deceased companion, yanking it back into the water. Dragged the sword and the priestess with it. Hiro scrabbled across the deck. He reached around her, grabbed the crossbar with both hands, and gave the blade a mighty yank. The shark's jawbone snapped.

The Sanu slammed into him. The body of the dead shark slithered off the deck, leaving a trail of red in its wake. Panting, she released the greatsword and sagged against his chest. Sweaty, splattered with blood, a ribbon of flesh dangling from her shoulder. Their eyes met for only a heartbeat.

She pushed away from him, staggered back to the tiller. "Kale?"

"All clear ahead." The boy pointed to the water behind them. "It looks like they're retreating."

Hiro rolled to his side and dared a look over the edge. The water boiled as the sharks tore into their dead. Clots of pink froth floated by. "Kale, furl the sail."

He tossed the severed head overboard, drew up bucket after bucket of water to rinse everything down. Including himself. He held out a bucket for the Sanu. She didn't take it. "We can't leave a trail for them to follow."

"I... need help." She turned over her hands. She'd held onto his greatsword so hard its hilt had left its scaly pattern carved into her palms.

"Gods above, Sanu—"

She looked away. "I-I'm too tired to heal myself right now."

He poured the water over her head as carefully as he could. Scrubbed her scalp with his burned hand, combed her hair out with his fingers. He picked the gore from her silks, sluiced her until the water ran clear.

Shaking, she never once looked at him. "T-thank you."

"Take a break, Sanu." He gently took the tiller from her. "See to the horses?"

She nodded numbly. Stumbling off to the deckhouse, she paused to check on Isen. It was just a glance, just enough to verify he was alive. In the makeshift stable, a puff of tawny stalks shot into the air as she collapsed on the hay.

Kale peeled himself away from the mast. "I'll wake her up for the first watch."

"No. Let her sleep."

"But you're exhausted, too."

"I'm good for a while." He ruffled the boy's mane. "You need a haircut."

Kale pushed his hand away, skipped out of reach. "Nuh-uh."

"Hn. Just keep a lookout in case I doze off."

He slapped his cheeks, shook his head. Focused the scraps of his attention on steering.

The Forbidden River had them firmly within its grasp. They would be in Akuma Cove soon, if they survived.

CHAPTER 93

THE IRRAWA SNAKED AROUND THE HEAD OF AN ANCIENT STATUE THAT had crumbled from its body centuries ago. It rose lopsided out of the river, the water lapping against full lips. Its serene face was pitted with lichen, and jasmine vines clung to the snail-shell curls of hair. A cluster of swallowtail butterflies took flight from its nose. Amelia stared as *Xunsu* glided by, wondering whom it was the ancients had honored by carving such a colossal figure. They passed under its shadow and back into the dappled sunlight.

Kale stood at the bow, eyes riveted on the water. He no longer spoke but thrust his arm out to signal when he saw something they should avoid. He no longer climbed the mast either, preferring the safety of the deck.

The heart of Siam was quiet, as if a spell kept all of its creatures silent. She'd never been in a place so still; it felt like they were trespassing. Perhaps that's why they all spoke in whispers.

She pressed a cup of ginger tea into Isen's hands. It was the only thing he could keep down.

"Are we there yet?"

She ran her fingers through his golden hair. "Soon."

"Gods above, everything hurts. Except that. You can keep doing that." He leaned into her touch. "Whose bright idea was it to take a boat?"

"Yours, actually."

"Why do we have to find this druid anyway? I came with you, no questions asked, but now I need to know. For my stomach's sake."

Amelia wetted her lips. She wanted to tell him, but Rosara had sworn her to secrecy. "The High Sister asked me to."

"That's not cryptic at all."

She shrugged. He must've heard the rustle of her silks because he frowned.

"I can't help but think there's more you're not saying. You've been distant with me, and you've been nothing but a... well, a *biaozi* to Hiro."

"No I haven't! And so what if I'm... *reserved* around him? He takes far too many liberties—"

"I'm just saying your friends are here for you. Me, especially. Don't keep us in the dark."

She stood, wiping her hands on her sari. "I've got to go... Drink your tea, Isen. You're losing too much weight."

He smiled weakly. "How else do you think I keep these chiseled looks?"

Chuckling, she went to the stern to relieve the prince. Just the sight of him made her tense. The white flame's bell-like voice chimed in her ears. *Distance yourself, for your heart's sake. There will come a time when you will have to give them up.*

He flicked his seal-brown eyes in her direction but didn't release the tiller. "I'm fine, Sanu. Besides... your hands."

"Are healed now. Come on, Ishida. You've been at it since last night."

"Just sit down and stay out of the way." He wasn't looking at her. His attention was on the left bank.

"So you can collapse from exhaustion and crash us into the rocks? No, thank you."

"Sanu, I said—"

An arrow whistled from the left bank and buried itself in his shoulder. With a shout, Hiro clamped a hand around the shaft before a second and third nailed him in the torso. He stumbled back, pitching over the side.

"*Hiro!*"

ARROWS SLICED OVERHEAD. Amelia dropped to the deck. The splash where Hiro had gone over was already disappearing. He hadn't surfaced.

She grabbed the closest docking rope and tied a hasty bowline. "The sail, Kale!"

Amelia dived over the edge.

The water swallowed her. It was so dark that the dappled sunlight barely penetrated below the surface. Hiro disappeared into the indigo depths as his clothes and weapons pulled him down. The trail of bubbles escaping his mouth was the only sign of his panic.

Inside, the silver dragon surged into her lungs and limbs. Scales rippled down her arms, fluttering into place like tiny feathers. She swam deeper, faster, and a silver lens slid into place over her eyes. She could see him clearly now, as well as the shape that was racing toward him from the deep.

Amelia reached him first. She managed to slow his sinking just enough to get the bowline over his head and under the opposite arm. Suddenly the line grew taut, yanking him toward the surface. She had just enough time to grab onto his arm before she was left to drown.

An eerie swish of the water swirled just below her feet. Through the haze of a thousand little bubbles, a webbed hand strained after her ankle. With an effervescent shriek, Amelia tightened herself into a ball. A crescent tail fin flashed iridescent amber before disappearing to the gloom.

Gasping, she breached the surface. Its orange sail full to bursting, the *Xunsu* zipped along the channel, dragging them out of the water. Kale released the ropes, and the fin-like sail shuddered as it lost the wind. The boat slowed into a leisurely glide.

Isen reeled in the line, the tendons in his arm rippling like wire under his skin. Kale kept the tiller steady with his foot and leaned over the stern. It took all three of them to haul Hiro's limp body onto the deck.

Amelia crawled out of the water. "I think... I think I saw a mermaid."

"Don't be ridiculous. They haven't been seen for centuries."

She grabbed Isen's hand, tugged him down beside her. "Everybody stay low. We might not have seen the last of those arrows."

He cocked his head to the side in his birdlike way. "What's wrong with him? I don't hear him mouth-breathing."

Kale helped her roll him onto his back. Two arrows were missing, wrenched free by the water. She had to brace her foot against his ribs to yank the last one out of his shoulder. She threw the arrow aside and squeezed hard on the leather armor over his chest. No water bubbled out of his mouth. His face had gone white; his eyes bulged like those of a dead fish. Amelia hovered her ear above his lips.

Isen knelt, feeling around for the discarded arrow. His long fingers wrapped around the shaft and brought it to his nose. After a sniff, he gave the barb a cautious lick and spat. He turned, throwing the arrow overboard. "My tongue's tingling. Must be a paralytic."

"He's got a pulse." Amelia tried to wedge her finger between his lips, but his jaw was clamped shut. "I can't get his mouth open."

"The paralytic probably closed off his airway. Prevented him from drowning."

"Well it's preventing him from *breathing* now. Quick, help me get his armor off."

They fumbled with the lacings. Apparently the soak in the water had made the knots cinch even tighter. With a mild curse, Isen pulled a knife from his sash. Jewels the size of mustard seeds glittered in the ivory hilt. It was Tareq's blade.

He guided the knife under the stays and cut through them with little *snicks*. The armor peeled apart liked the cracked shell of a crab. Isen tossed it aside as Amelia yanked open Hiro's jacket. There was something dark and wet matted over his heart.

"Gods above, please don't let it be—" She withdrew a wad of blue silk. The arrows hadn't punctured his lungs. She sagged in relief.

"Amelia," Kale whimpered, "he's turning blue."

She grabbed the prince's cheeks and pressed her mouth against his. Her breath pooled against his teeth.

Her lips tingled with silver sparks. She breathed again, and the fire ignited. It pushed into his throat, burning through the paralysis. His mouth softened against hers. Once more, and the silver fire raced into his lungs and kindled his weakened pulse.

He gasped against her mouth, his lips no longer cold. Their warmth sent tingles racing down—

Amelia yanked her head back.

His seal-brown eyes cleared, the corner of his mouth quirking up into a little half-smile. "I liked our first kiss better. I was conscious for that one."

She scrambled away from him, glaring, and wiped her mouth with the back of her hand.

The knife slipped out of Isen's hand. "You two have *kissed?*"

"It was *nothing.*"

Hiro tried to sit up and managed to twitch his fingers instead. "Why can't I move?"

"You got *shot.* Here, here, and here." Kale peeled back the gi at Hiro's shoulder. "Looks like Amelia got this one healed already. Apparently they had this goo on them that made you go all stiff and stuff."

Isen waved his hands. "Wait just a minute here. You two. *Kissing?*"

"It was back in Bucharest, Isen. When I was having a panic attack in the dungeon. He… snapped me out of it."

"*With a kiss?*"

"Just forget it."

"Still can't move here." Hiro strained to lift his head up. It fell back to the deck with a wet thud. "And why am I soaked?"

"You fell into the water," Kale said. "Amelia dived in and saved you."

Hiro frowned. "I didn't know you cared."

463

"Of course I *care*," she snapped.

"She said she saw a mermaid, but Isen thinks she's delirious."

"Of course she's delirious if she's *kissing* people. Amelia, you are Sanu—"

"*I know what I am*," she shouted. She lurched to her feet. "And *you*, Ishida, can just lay there until that paralysis wears off."

"But who'll steer if he's—"

Amelia grabbed the priest by his collar and shoved him against the tiller. "You can push, and you can pull. Kale will be your eyes. *Right*, Kale?"

The boy nodded quickly.

"And where are *you* going?" Isen asked her.

"To gargle with boiling water!"

CHAPTER 94

AMELIA SANK INTO THE STRAW. UNCURLING HER FINGERS, THE WAD OF silk fell into her lap. It'd been the blue of a robin's egg at one time, darkened now from countless days of sweat. She rubbed her thumb against one of the embroidered cranes. Lord Ishida had given it to her, but she'd lost it on the balcony after her fight with Hiro.

He's kept it all this time?

Distance yourself, for your heart's sake, echoed the sacred flame. *There will come a time when you will have to give them up.*

Rosara had told her the same thing.

"All is not lost, but it *will* be if you continue to burden yourself with earthly attachments. I heard what the sacred flame said when that prince appeared in the fires. Trust me, I know too well the dangers of a handsome face—"

"Forget Hiro." Her nails gouged into the padded armrests as she lurched forward. "You said the druid's name was *Elwynn?*"

"Yes."

"Onu's last words told me to find him. But what does he have to do with the broken Gate?"

"When the Gate broke, a flash of light occurred by the Hotun River. The eye-witness accounts vary, but most agree seeing a glowing object floating in the middle of the river shortly thereafter. Although one report swears it was a child. As you know, the Hotun River intersects the Brahma Rush, but an offshoot of the Hotun is Xiaohotun, which feeds into the Volga Vast. And the Vast crosses the entire length of Eurasia."

"And what do geography and rivers have to do with anything?"

"I propose that whatever fell into the water is the key to repairing the Gate."

Amelia threw up her hands. "Who's to say it's not caught at the bottom of a river or lost at sea? We'll never find it—"

"What do you think I've been doing all these years? Twiddling my thumbs? I've sent cranes and eagles asking for any strange reports along the waterways – no matter how outlandish – and nothing. But three years ago, peculiar things were being reported in Balasore."

The city sounded vaguely familiar. "But Balasore isn't by any major river."

The High Sister lifted a finger. "Ah, but the currents of the Medi Sea draw whatever comes from the Forbidden River up along the coast. And whatever happened in Balasore was a singular event – something about a great kraken attacking the city – but from where did it originate? Akuma Cove."

Amelia snorted. This was just one of Isen's stories. "You think that because some giant octopus attacks a city it must be related?"

Rosara crossed her arms over her chest. "Have you ever heard of such a thing?"

"Only in the sacred texts-"

"*Exactly*. Nothing but the Most Holies or their influence could have roused the beast. Hence—"

"You think it's connected to the Gate."

"It's said the kraken reclaimed what was stolen and returned to the deep. Such a beast only makes its home in Akuma Cove."

"You know the word *akuma* means 'demon' in Old Imperial, right?" Amelia asked flatly. "You want me to go to *Demon* Cove? After what I've already been through?"

"What better place on earth to protect something from Heaven?" Rosara countered. "No one goes there."

"So what's this got to do with Elwynn? I need to find *him*, too."

"The druid makes his home there."

Amelia sagged in her seat with a sigh. "Of course he does. So I'm to go to Akuma Cove, find the druid, and ask a monster from the ancient world to give me whatever it's protecting. Well... I'd best be polite."

"And be back before the harvest moon so you can fix the Gate and perform Yueshu," Ophelia said. "That's in four weeks."

Rosara glared at the sibylline. "*Not. Helping.*" She turned her dove-gray eyes back to Amelia. "If anyone can help you – us – it'll be him. I know you've come a long way, but I'm asking you to go a little farther. You were Chosen for a reason, Amelia."

She hid her face in her hands. "This is overwhelming."

"Take the blind priest with you. He's tenacious and has been your bosom companion up until now. He can go a little farther, too."

Amelia bit her lip, hating the words she was going to say. "Isen is my brother, but do you *really* think a blind man will help me the most?"

"At the very least, he will encourage you. Bolster your strength when you have none. He's better than this Prince Hiro. You're too emotional about him. That man is dangerous to you in more ways than one, Amelia."

THERE WAS a knock on the deckhouse wall.

Amelia stuffed the blue silk into her pocket. "Yes?"

"Hey, Amelia..." Kale's head popped around the corner. "Um... could you come back out? Isen's tired and Hiro can only sorta sit up."

"Yeah, sorry. How long have I...?"

"All night."

"*What?*"

He ran a hand through his mane of hair. The gestured echoed of his master. "Yeah... and could you give Hiro a boost or something?"

She scowled. "No. He can suffer the inconvenience of being paralyzed a little while longer after *that* comment about us… you know…"

"Are you upset because he said it, or because you liked it?"

"*Excuse* me?"

"You get all blushy—"

"No, I don't." She pressed her hands to her hot cheeks. "I do *not*." Her tattoo seared white-hot like a branding iron against her skin.

"Okay." The boy shrugged. "Well, I just thought you'd want to see this."

The rising sun exploded into the sky. Clouds hovering above the horizon were aflame with pink and orange as the morning chased away the indigo of night.

The Forbidden River widened into a crescent-shaped cove fringed with white sand. The jungle prowled at its edges, trying to reclaim the beach with mangroves. A flock of white birds with thin, curved beaks the same dark pink as their spindly legs scurried about in the gentle surf. A few crabs scuttled about upon the shore, and one lazy, speckled shark flicked its tail to get out of their way.

An island rose from the sea just outside of the cove. A pinnacle of black rock erupted from its north-facing side as if a giant long since buried had finally freed himself of his restraint, plunging his fist skyward in triumph.

The *Xunsu* glided over the turquoise waters on an easy wind. It was quiet here, too, as if the sea was afraid to slap against the hull. The gentle groan as the boat ground to a halt echoed down the beach like thunder.

Amelia let out a breath she didn't know she held. "We're here."

CHAPTER 95

IT DIDN'T TAKE LONG TO DISCOVER THE ISLAND WAS DESERTED.

There were no insects, or birds, or snakes, or burrowing creatures or beasts of any kind. Gulls soared above the pinnacle but never touched down on the island to rest. No fish swam nearby; even the speckled sharks avoided its shores.

It was a small speck of an isle. After a pulse of silver fire had burned through the rest of Hiro's paralysis – which left him doubled over and wheezing for a few long, satisfactory minutes – they'd scouted the beach on the horses. A few hours later, they were back at the boat again. They'd found a freshwater stream, its source hidden behind a screen of fuchsia hibiscus, and a jungle so impenetrable they had to hack away at it with Hiro's greatsword.

Isen sat in the shade by the spring, weaving hats out of palm fronds. The tropical heat had already burned his nose and bleached his hair. His robes and sash were in a bundle beside him, his black underclothes plastered against his skin. On the beach, Kale wore one of Isen's hats as he collected coconuts. The haphazard pyramid of the green orbs grew as they boy darted around like a deranged squirrel.

Amelia sank to the ground, wiping the sweat from her eyes. With the fingers of her left hand, she peeled her right hand off of the hatchet. Her palm came away sticky with fluid. Blisters had formed and popped under the incessant chopping. She glared at the forest as a healing silver glow spread across her palm.

Hiro hacked without any evidence of slowing. His gi was wrapped around his head and neck to keep the worst of the sun away while Isen finished making him a hat. It was hypnotizing, watching his muscles ripple under that taut skin, the scars flashing like molten bronze, the sweat beading and spilling in little streams down his back to disappear beneath his waistband.

"Thirsty?"

Amelia jumped.

Kale stood at her elbow, offering a coconut.

"Um…"

Hiro abandoned his chopping. "I'll take one."

A runnel of water dribbled from the corner of his mouth, down the column of his neck, and coiled around the dragon-shaped birthmark on his chest. There it melted into the sweat trickling down six taut ridges into the trough of his hip—

Kale nudged her. "Coconut?"

"I-I'm fine." She snatched up the hatchet.

Hiro blocked her path, hands braced on his hips. She looked up at the sky, pretending to see something captivating. "Have one anyway, Sanu. Otherwise you'll faint, and I'll have to carry your unconscious body back to the boat. And then you'll wake up and yell at me for touching you without permission."

Glaring at him the entire time, she sucked the water out of a coconut.

He watched like a disciplining schoolteacher. "Eat it, too."

"I'm not a child, Ishida."

"*Do it.*"

She scooped out the jelly-like meat with her fingers. Finished, she chucked the coconut at him.

He caught it with one large hand. "Nice try. Now follow me. We've cleared enough to start climbing."

Amelia rushed past him. Kale dropped the coconut he'd been chopping and raced after her.

"Uh-uh, Kale. Stay here," Hiro said. "I want those canteens filled by the time we get back."

"Aww."

"I guess I'll wait here," Isen called after them.

The climb was easy.

The black rock undulated from the forest floor like crashing waves suddenly frozen and covered in pitch. Other mounds bubbled up like cotton balls covered in tar, and the leveler areas resembled elephant skin. The rock was coarse, flaky, and entirely speckled with mica. Amelia shielded her eyes against the glittering and climbed with one hand.

The rolls and mounds created a natural series of switchbacks to a summit worn flat by the wind. They were above the canopy now, the whole island stretching around them in panoramic display. Amelia forwent the view and ran the rest of the way to the pinnacle.

It erupted from the summit, towering into the sky. She inspected every side except for the eastern face that plummeted a sheer hundred feet into white sand below. No doors, no openings, no crevices of any kind.

Hiro peered over her shoulder. "Hn. Take a look at that."

She shifted away from him. "Do you have to stand so close, Ishida?"

"Just look."

At the base of the precipice, the sand cut a wedge through the dense forest to a lagoon. Teal water enveloped by pillowy mounds of white sand stared back at them like a giant eye.

"It's an atoll," she said.

"No, *that*. I didn't think they were indigenous to Siam."

A yellow swallowtail floated just below them. It caught the breeze and fluttered up into her face. Amelia closed her eyes against its gentle floundering, opened them again to see the butterfly circling down between the gap in the trees. Just above the sand, it pulled out of its descent and flapped away. "They're not. We have to get down there."

Hiro grabbed her arm. "Not today. We're exhausted. And we're going to need a rope to get down this."

"Can't we just cut through to the lagoon?"

"Sure, if you want to spend an entire day or two doing only that. Be my guest. I didn't think we had that kind of time."

Amelia gave the cliff another glance. "Maybe there's a way—"

He gave her a little tug. "Come on. Let's go back. Get a swim and cool off. We'll come back at first light."

She wrenched free of him, more violently than she meant to.

His eyes blazed. "What is *with* you?"

"I don't want to waste what little time I have going for a *swim*. I *want* to go down there and find this druid—"

"I'm not talking about that. I'm talking about *this*." He gestured to the air between them. "You and me. You can't look me in the eye, you barely speak to me, you don't even call me by my name."

She crossed her arms over her chest. "What do you want me to say?"

"I want you to forgive me."

"*Forgive* you?"

"I'm sorry, Sanu, alright? For everything. For my father, for abandoning you"—he raked his hands through his hair—"*gods above*, for kissing you. I'm risking everything to be here. To help you. How much more of this abuse do I have to take?"

She smeared the sweat off her forehead, flicking it aside with an angry swipe of her hand. "I don't have time for this."

He stepped in front of her. "*Make* time."

"You don't get to order me around, Ishida! I'm not your soldier, I'm not your friend. I'm just a Sanu trying to prevent the end of the world. Your *feelings* are the last thing I'm worried about. I didn't *ask* for your help. You're here because you insisted on coming. I didn't force you."

He snorted, shaking his head. The glint off his golden cuff was piercing. "You can't even show a little gratitude? You, a *priestess*?"

"Gratitude for what? Keeping the promise you should've kept months ago?"

"I just wanted to go *home*, Sanu. My father exploited that desire, and I let him. I'd been ripped away from everything I knew for so long that when the opportunity came, I didn't care what I said or who I hurt to get it." He paused, gritting his teeth. "But a home is nothing without a family. And I believed my only family were the ones who'd betrayed me... or I thought they had. Whatever, it doesn't matter anymore. I'd been making another one without realizing it. And... I ruined it. I'm *sorry*, Sanu."

She scrubbed her face with her hands. Anything to mask the brimming tears. "Whatever camaraderie we had is gone. I can't go through – You're just a hired sword, Ishida."

He nodded numbly and stepped out of her way.

She rushed past him and bolted down the rocks. When she was back by the trailhead, she paused, straining to hear his footsteps. There was nothing but the gurgling of the stream and the rustling of the wind.

Isen cocked his head, listening. "Amelia, did something happen?"

Kale looked up from drilling a hole into a coconut. "Where's Hiro?"

"He's... coming."

The boy stood, dropping the knife. "You look like you've been crying."

"I'm just sunburned."

She winced as the white-hot heat of the lie seared into her heart.

CHAPTER 96

AMELIA CLUNG TO THE ROPE UNTIL HER FINGERS ACHED. SHE DIDN'T think about the air she dangled over or the ground that waited below. She kept her eyes riveted on the pinnacle that grew taller with every heartbeat. And the man beside it, his face strained with concentration as he lowered her inch by trembling inch.

Sand as fine as flour wiggled up through her toes. It melded against her buttocks, then her back, then her head. With a shuddering breath, Amelia wormed out of the bowline and gave the rope a few hard tugs. "I'm down," she shouted.

The rope slithered back up the cliff.

Amelia retreated to the shade of the pinnacle as she waited. It was another cloudless day of relentless tropical sun, and the light was bright off the lagoon. The sand gleamed like molten silver; the trees glared green. She pulled the rim of her palm hat farther down over her eyes.

A soft grunt, and Hiro joined her on the sand. He was red-faced, completely soaked with sweat. His arms trembled as he untied the makeshift harness.

Amelia yanked one of the canteens out of her pack and handed it to him.

He took it without a word. They hadn't been on speaking terms since yesterday. "Kale," he called. "Your turn. Just like I showed you."

"Why are you shouting?"

They spun around as the boy jogged up from the north side of the pinnacle.

"How did you—"

"I took the stairs."

Hiro's eyes bulged. "There were *stairs?*"

"I was chasing this butterfly and just found them. But you were already over the side so there was no point in telling you."

"Hn." Hiro shook his head and passed the boy the canteen. "Everybody drink. Then let's spread out and—"

Amelia was already walking away. She went to the north face of the pinnacle and gaped at the neatly hewn stairs curving up to the summit. With a disbelieving snort, she inspected the stairs and the surrounding rock. No doors, no cleverly hidden passageways, simply coarse black rock that glittered with flecks of mica. With a sigh, she faced the jungle. A wall of tangled greenery, thick and inhospitable, stared right back. "Kale," she called. "Any luck?"

"No," came the boy's disheartened reply. He prowled the east side of the lagoon, moving south.

Hiro didn't offer any findings, and she didn't ask.

Amelia shook the sweat out of her eyes and took a sip from her canteen. That lagoon was looking more tantalizing the more time she spent under the sun. Abandoning the jungle, she trudged across the hot sand to the water. Halting at the coral-encrusted edge, she peered into its depths.

Blue water, darker than sapphire, plunged below like a chasm to another world. It consumed her vision, lured her with a promise of cool respite from the heat. Like an anchor, it dragged her gaze into the deep. A call, sweet and undulating like the peal of a chime, beckoned her. A flash of iridescent amber winked fathoms below.

Something clamped onto her shoulder. She fought against it. It was trying to take her away. The call pulled at her, insistent. A screen of bubbles tickled her nose, and a weight crushed against her chest.

The silver dragon trumpeted in alarm. But the deep promised relief, if only she could reach it. She strained a hand—

The water trembled. As if a great underwater beast sighed in its sleep, a frothing white bubble like an enormous mushroom roiled toward the surface.

Amelia sputtered as Hiro dragged her out of the water. Like a cat scruffing a kitten, he pulled her over the coral and dropped her into the sand. With frantic hands, Kale smeared the hair away from her face and rolled her onto her side. She clawed at her chest, her lungs like lead and prickling like hornet sting. A large hand slapped her back, hard, and she hacked up the seawater.

"What were you *doing*?"

She didn't get a chance to reply.

Water erupted from the lagoon. Like the wave that had destroyed the coasts during the Great Cataclysm, a wall of frothing water climbed toward the sky. Seawater pelted the sand like hail, tore through the palms and mangroves with the fury of a hurricane.

The ground convulsed with every strike. Craters of displaced sand overflowed with water returning to the deep. When its receding roar finally faded, she cracked open an eye.

Kale had fastened onto her tighter than a tick. Head buried into her ribs, the boy shook hard enough to shiver out of his own skin. She had one arm wrapped around him and the hand of the other tangled in Hiro's gi. He'd thrown himself over them, digging into the sand with his hands and knees. His face was still twisted in anticipatory pain. Above him, a crystalline shell of silver light rippled as the seawater washed over it.

"We're okay." She drew in a shuddering breath, said it again with more confidence. "We're okay."

Kale peeked out from under her arm. Hiro craned his head around, eyes widening at the shell that encased them.

Amelia relaxed, sinking back into the sand. The shield dissolved, sprinkling them with salty mist.

With gentle fingers, Hiro peeled her hand off his jacket and pushed onto his feet.

"Sorry," she mumbled. Then she sat upright in alarm. "Sweet mercy, *Isen*. We have to see if he's okay!"

Hiro pulled off his boots and rolled his trousers up to the knee. With a hypercritical glance in her direction, he set across the changed landscape. Divots like sinkholes trailed in his wake. Back bowed with exhaustion, he followed the sinuous path of a trench back to the pinnacle.

Kale darted along the crest of the same dune, sprinkling the water with sand kicked up by his feet.

Shucking her sandals, Amelia was just about to trudge after them when a shadow flickered across the sand. It was the butterfly. Perfectly unharmed, it fluttered across her sunburned arm and flitted after the prince. She chased after it.

Steep trenches of coursing seawater cut through the beach. Once in gentle swells, the sand crested into great dunes. Pockets of water made temporary tide pools that dwindled even as they watched. Debris scattered the previously pristine sand: leaves and fronds, branches and coconut husks.

The lagoon's eruption had even reached the pinnacle. Water cascaded from its peak in a narrow waterfall, mingling with the broad sheet cascading from the precipice's summit. It pulverized the beach at the pinnacle's root, flinging sand and spray for hundreds of yards. The butterfly approached the waterfall, circled a few times, and drifted away on the breeze.

"H– Ishida." Amelia clutched his arm. "Look over there."

She pointed to the spot where the sand met the rock. The assault of seawater had revealed more stairs curving around the base of the pinnacle. A steady red glow shone from a triangular gap at their end.

They shared a look before dropping their shoes and racing across the dunes.

"Wait for me!" Kale cried.

Hiro was the first to the gap and slid to a halt a few tentative feet away. He unsheathed his greatsword and probed the entrance with its tip. When no lurking beast emerged, he stabbed his blade into the sand and started to dig.

Amelia dropped to her knees beside him, sweeping the sand aside with her forearms. The hole widened, the red glow growing stronger and staining the sand scarlet. A tunnel slowly took shape. Its walls were impossibly smooth, shining like polished silver. The tunnel cut into the pinnacle only a few yards before disappearing in a curve. The red glow burned even brighter there.

Hiro leaned forward, running his hand along the wall. "Dragon fire. Only dragon fire could melt rock like this."

"Maybe the druid has a pet?" Kale whispered. He gulped as both Amelia and Hiro glared at him.

Hiro sheathed his sword, drew his dagger, and slid down the shifting sand into the tunnel. The pale grains skittered across the smooth stone like glass broken on tile. As soon as his bare feet touched the floor, a rumble trembled through the passageway. A voice, far away and muffled, answered it.

Hiro glanced back at her, tension tightening his bare shoulders. "Someone's home."

CHAPTER 97

HIRO HUNCHED, SIDLED ALONG THE TUNNEL LIKE A CRAB UNTIL HE CAME to the turn.

The glow washed everything in red. The walls were crimson, his skin a dark russet. He squinted against the glare and ignored the sweat dribbling off his nose.

Behind him, the skittering of sand and the padding of bare feet. The priestess's hand touched his back. So staying on the beach until he knew it was safe was out of the question.

The tunnel sloped deeper into the pinnacle, the air becoming humid, stagnant. Tinged with sulfur. Like the breath of the Abyss.

Hiro kept his hand against the wall, slid forward with little shuffles. The red light had grown so intense he couldn't see his outstretched hand. He stopped, shut his eyes and listened instead. Every hair on his body stood on end, quivered like the Sanu's hand pressed against his back.

There was a hum, low and droning, or it could've been the roar of his blood in his ears. Every instinct told him to run. Just turn around and bolt.

He glanced over his shoulder.

The Sanu was a palm tree in a hurricane. Shaking violently but

479

resolutely holding her ground. Kale clung to her arm, looked like a frightened kitten ready to hide under her sari.

He extended a hand. She slipped hers into his without hesitation, entwined her fingers. Forced a little nod.

Holding his breath, he walked into the enveloping light.

His vision cleared. The red glow was behind him. He pulled on the Sanu's hand, and they emerged one by one as if through a veil. Unseen in the crimson murk one moment and suddenly beside him the next. Nearby, stairs cut a series of switchbacks to the floor of an empty magma chamber.

But it was far from abandoned.

A bed of bamboo and canvas, a slab table with benches hewn from palm trees, lamps made from coconut shells. There were books stored in shelves cut right into the rock; a pot bubbling over a hearth; a saltwater distiller that dripped into a cistern at a steady dribble.

And on the far end, molten rock shifted behind a slit in the wall. No more than a foot wide, the fissure crackled across the wall like a demonic smile.

"Hello?" the priestess called.

"*Sanu.*" Hiro jerked on her hand. "We need to be careful. We don't want to startle—"

"Too late," Kale said, pointing.

Hiro pushed them behind him.

At the bottom of the stairs, the druid peered up at them through thick lenses. White hair adorned with silver beads, orange eyes, hand equally familiar with books and weapons. Hand. Singular. The sleeve of his homespun shirt knotted at the left shoulder.

The druid closed the book he was holding with a snap. Tossed it onto the slab table. "So how did you find me?"

Hiro gestured back the way they'd just come. "The tunnel."

"Yes, yes. But *how*? That entrance was blocked."

"The water shifted the sand—"

"Water? From the lagoon?" The druid clicked his tongue behind his teeth. "Erupted again, did it? Must be Wednesday."

"It's Saturday," Kale said.

Hiro shushed him.

"What?" The druid gave them an irritated look. His orange eyes, impossibly huge, seemed to rattle around behind the spectacles. "Are you just going to *lurk* there, or are you going to come down?"

Hiro kept his dagger bared, slunk down the winding steps. Strung the Sanu and Kale behind him. "Are you Elwynn?"

"Nope, don't know him."

The Sanu poked her head out from behind him. "Please, we're looking for a druid—"

The old man's face broke into a delighted grin. "*Amelia!* Dearie, I haven't seen you since you were a whelp. Sweet mercy, you look so much like your mother. Your eyes, anyway. I'm Elwynn."

Hiro frowned. "But you just said—"

The druid winked at him. "Never know who'll come asking, eh?"

The Sanu hurried forward. "You knew my mother? What about my father? Master Elwynn—"

"*Uncle* Elwynn to you, dearie." He beamed a smile. "What a nice fledgling you've grown into. You have a beautiful daughter."

"What?" She looked down at her hands; one clutched Kale's, the other entwined in Hiro's. She flew away from them both, wiped her palms against her thighs.

Kale frowned. "I'm a *boy*."

"Of course *you* are."

Hiro chuckled. "Told you you needed a haircut."

The druid was suddenly right in front of him, two fingers pressed under Hiro's chin. He hadn't heard him move.

Hiro jerked away from the touch, but the fingers kept him rigid. He couldn't even ram his dagger into the man's gut. Trembling, he could only balance on tiptoe as the druid dug his fingers like talons under his chin.

Those owlish eyes bored into his, gleaned details with every flick. "Look at you, guardian. Found your ward after all, didn't you?"

Hiro gasped as the druid released him. Weak, he staggered back a step.

481

The Sanu stepped between them before he could raise his dagger. She shook her head, ocean-blue eyes glinting.

Hiro coughed, rubbed the sore spot under his chin. "What do you mean 'found?' He's been—"

"*He?*" The druid wrinkled his nose. "Don't be obtuse."

"How about you make *sense?*"

"*Four.*" Elwynn shouted at the ceiling. "You said there were *four.*"

Hiro shared a dubious look with the boy.

"Sir?" Kale asked. "What are you...?"

"Look." The Sanu pointed to a scrap of yellow circling about. "The butterfly."

"So there *are* four. You, boy, go fetch him. Follow the krachiao flowers. Or return via that horrible path you all hacked through my jungle. Honestly, dearie, why didn't you just send a pulse through the ground? It would've shown you the path and my whereabouts instantly. I haven't been hiding from *you.*"

The Sanu cringed under Hiro's glare. "Uh... I didn't know I could do that."

The druid shrugged. "I suppose not. You *are* just a fledgling. And you, guardian, are you any good with that knife, or do you just pretend to know what you're doing?"

Hiro drew himself up to his full height and glowered down at the druid.

"Thought so. You can finish skinning the shark. Know how hard it is to do that with just one hand? Feel free to help yourself to the palm wine."

"Now wait just a minute—"

"And put your shirt back on. Honestly, there's a lady present. Have you no respect?"

Hiro blinked in bewilderment.

"*Today*, guardian. Dinner won't cook itself. Quick march now, boy."

Kale shrugged, raced up the stairs and back into the tunnel.

The druid put the Sanu's hand into the crook of his arm as if they were the oldest of friends.

"You said you knew my mother—"

"But that's not why you're here. Or it shouldn't be. I didn't expect to see you for another decade, dearie. Or was it a decade ago?" He shrugged. "What are you doing here?"

"The Revered Onu told me to find you."

"Why would Jocasta do that? She's not stupid. She wouldn't tell—"

"She's dead."

The druid paled.

"We were attacked. By demons."

"Demons? There are no *demons* in—" He whipped his head around, scrutinized the molten rock sliding behind the crack in the wall. "That can't be... has Yueshan happened yet?"

"No." She shook her head. "That's why I'm here."

Elwynn clicked his tongue against his teeth. "Ah. The Gate's broken now, isn't it?"

CHAPTER 98

"Pour me some of that palm wine, guardian. The world's about to end in a few weeks."

The cup slipped out of Hiro's fingers. "Gods above, Sanu. *That's* why we're here?"

"Please don't say anything." Amelia tugged on the druid's arm. "Is there somewhere where we can talk? *Privately?*"

"Oh, so he didn't know?"

She shook her head.

"Well... sorry." Elwynn paused to swipe the bottle from Hiro's slack hand. He took a couple of large glugs and smacked his lips with a sigh. "And what did I say? The only one being seduced today by that washboard you call your stomach is your own ego. Shirt. *On.*"

The druid hustled her to an archway hidden under the stairs. Those large eyes had no trouble seeing in the gloom. He guided her through a little passageway into an even larger cavern. It was cooler here, away from the molten rock, and their footsteps echoed in the dark.

"Would you do the honors, dearie? Just a flare will do. The jellies don't like competition."

She snapped her fingers, and a spurt of silver fire leapt into the air.

Immediately the cavern came alive with turquoise light. Blubbery mounds, rippling with bioluminescence, throbbed against the ceiling. The smallest had a diameter larger than the span of her arms outstretched.

Amelia cowered in the tunnel.

Elwynn chuckled. "Don't be frightened. They're harmless in their egg stage. Unless they fall on you. Then squash."

"What are they?"

"Ship-killers. Baby kraken."

"So the stories are real."

"More often than you'd think."

Amelia ventured back into the nursery. The wavering light of the eggs glinted on something slick smeared across the cavern floor. "It's metal."

"Treasure, actually."

There were heaps of coins, bejeweled chests with hidden delights, a fist-sized emerald haphazardly stuck in a crystal chalice, and strands upon strands of pearls. There were silver plates and copper armbands and rings studded with every jewel imaginable. Ornate suits of armor from different cultures and centuries framed a path with racks of spears, halberds, swords, pikes, axes, and other such weapons right behind. As they walked deeper into the splendor, she discovered a twist in the cavern, revealing additional mountains of treasure farther back, stacked all the way to the ceiling.

Baffled, she let out a low whistle. "What are you, a dragon?"

"Oh no, dearie," Elwynn chuckled. "The last dragon slumbers deep in the mountains, far away from here. How do you think krakens are trained to go after ships? Even as they incubate, these eggs are learning to hoard all manner of glittery things."

The cavern floor dropped away into a pool. The mounds of coins and stray jewels banked right against the lip of the mirror-like surface. A hundred feet across, it reminded her too much of the baleful eye of the lagoon. Amelia kept her distance this time, searching the black depths warily. The tang of salt lay heavy in the air.

Fearless, the druid walked right up to the edge. He puttered around the glittering shore, heedless of the coins his feet teased loose. They cascaded into the water, sending a shiver of ripples across the opaque surface. He made a full rotation, sighing in disappointment when he returned to her side far away from the pool.

"Nothing new. Lazy beast. I was expecting her back any day now. Or was it a week ago?" The druid scratched his chin with pointed nails. "Travels all over the world, you know. Finds all manner of things lost and forgotten."

"Like the broken piece of the Gate?"

The druid stopped scratching, fingers still curled in his scruff. "If I possessed something that powerful, there would be fireworks erupting from the top of the pinnacle. Something like that cannot stay hidden in this world. Might as well be walking and talking and attracting all manner of attention."

Amelia pointed to the water. "*That* is not our world. In the lagoon, I heard a voice—"

"*You went into the water?* No wonder it erupted. Damn fish-women been trying to flush me out for years, but you..." He put two fingers under her chin. His orange eyes gleamed. "Much bigger prize."

She wiggled away from his touch. "You really shouldn't—"

"Right. *Sanu*. Brilliant."

Amelia made a cutting motion with her hand. "Both Onu and the High Sister wouldn't have sent me if they weren't convinced you can *help* me. I need you to *focus*, Elwynn."

"Difficult, now." His eyes grew hazy behind the thick glass as he rubbed the empty sleeve at his left shoulder. "Damn crocodile."

She turned away so he wouldn't see her frustration. Inside, the silver dragon paced, snorting tendrils of smoke.

His hand perched on her shoulder like a bird, the nails pricking her sari like little talons. "Amelia... I'm not what I once was. Am. I'm sorry. But I can still help."

"How?" She tried to keep the sob out of her voice. This had been nothing but a fool's errand.

"I keep journals when time isn't... when I'm lucid. Come. We'll look. Then you can tell Jocasta I kept my promise."

"Elwynn... Jocasta's dead. Remember?"

Clenching his teeth, the druid pounded his forehead with his fist. "We are *then*, you stupid old hoot. *Then is now.*"

Amelia grabbed his hand and firmly pulled it away from his face. "Elwynn."

The druid's eyes cleared. "*Amelia*, dearie, it's so good to see you. Come to take a look at the books, did you? Or was it the prince that needed them? Either way, I don't keep them in the treasure room. Too moist. Quick march now!"

Amelia clenched her trembling fingers into fists as the druid disappeared behind a mountain of treasure. She waited until his footsteps receded into the tunnel before she sank to her knees. With a frustrated cry, she slammed her fists into the ground. Coins sprang away in a glittering spray as silver fire exploded from her skin. The blast rolled through the cavern in a thunderous wave, crashing against the walls and spraying the ceiling with silver light.

The turquoise glow of the eggs darkened to azure. The light pulsed in a frantic display as the baby kraken panicked. The cavern floor began to tremble; strands of pearls and precious gems shivered loose from the mounds of treasure. Once smooth as glass, the surface of the pool bubbled like a boiling soup pot.

She lurched to her feet as a groan emanated from the deep. Staggering through the hills, racing through the path framed by armor and weapons, she ducked inside the tunnel just as a tentacle erupted from the water.

CHAPTER 99

"*ELWYNN.*" AMELIA STUMBLED INTO THE MOLTEN LIGHT OF THE MAGMA chamber. "I think I just did something really bad – Elwynn?"

The druid had his hand wrapped around Isen's throat.

Hiro was just clearing his greatsword from its sheath as Kale scooted out of the way, a long handled spoon in his fist.

"What's going on in here?" she demanded.

The priest wedged a foot between them and kicked the druid away. Gasping for breath, Isen felt around for his staff and snatched it up. With a screech, the druid plucked the skinning knife from the shark carcass.

Kale ran to her side. "I just brought Isen back from the beach, and—"

Elwynn slashed at the priest, shaving wood from Isen's staff with every strike. The priest toppled over a barrel, feet flung toward the ceiling as coconuts rolled around the floor like bocce balls. Isen shoved the barrel away and scrambled upright. He caught a glancing slice of the skinning knife across his cheek before his staff pushed it away.

The druid dropped the knife and snatched the swinging staff. He yanked down as he pivoted on his right foot, his left leg arcing through the air. His heel caught Isen on the side of the neck, dropping the priest like a stone. Elwynn had Isen's arms pinned beneath knee and foot with his nails digging into the priest's throat when the tip of the greatsword kissed the back of his neck.

"Don't. Move," Hiro warned.

"I can't breathe," Isen rasped.

The druid clamped even harder. "That's the point."

Silver fire snapped along her fists. "Elwynn, let him go. *Immediately.*"

"Can't."

"Why not?"

"He's a fraud."

"*What?*" Hiro barked.

Isen writhed as his face turned purple. "He's insane—"

"Time like a scrambled egg," the druid hissed, "but not insane."

"Let him *go.* Isen's my friend—"

"*Friend,* you say?" The druid cocked his head like an owl examining the mouse pinned beneath its talons. He bent low over the suffocating priest and fixed him in one orange eye. "Shifty Noh mask. I don't know what you are now, but you certainly weren't born a priest."

Isen clawed at the hand. "How can anyone be *born* a—"

Elwynn let him go abruptly, springing to his feet. "Why is the ground shaking?"

"I was trying to tell you—"

"Conchita! I'm coming, my darling decapus." He paused at the archway under the stairs. "You, boy, why'd you stop stirring the soup? Back to it. Quick march!"

Amelia helped Isen onto the bench and healed the cut on his cheek with just a touch.

"'Follow me,' the boy said. 'There'll be dinner,' he said. Wonderful, but I'd very much prefer mine without the side of *crazy,*" Isen shouted after the druid.

"Elwynn's just a little eccentric."

"Let me put it another way. Bats in the belfry. *Lots.*" Isen rubbed his throat with a grimace. "I think we should go. Just call the whole thing off. What are we even *doing* here?"

"We're here because I don't know how to perform Yueshan, okay?" Amelia shouted.

"But—"

"I know the forms, but not the sequence. The Revered Onu sent me here to learn it, but that man's brain is a jumbled mess and we only have one more day here before we have to start the trip home or else we'll never make it in time, and I just need everyone to be supportive right now. Is that *too* much to ask?"

No one would look at her, except Hiro. A scowl hooded his seal-brown eyes. Isen nursed a cup of palm wine; Kale stared into the stew as he frantically stirred. Amelia smoothed her sari with an irritated flick. "Now if you'll excuse me, I'm—"

"A *word*, Sanu?"

Hiro herded her to the bookshelves on the opposite side of the chamber, out of earshot of the others. "Why didn't you tell me the Gate was broken?"

"What good would that have done?"

He raked a hand through his hair. "I don't know. Maybe I could've gotten us here faster, looked harder for the druid—"

"Ishida, it's not like you've had the missing piece all this time."

"A missing *piece*? Gods above, I thought you just needed an incantation or something. And what's this now about not even knowing the ritual? Yueshu is at the next full moon, and the *entire* world—"

Amelia gritted her teeth. "You think I don't know that's at stake?"

"We've got to find an alternative. The ramblings of this senile old man aren't enough-"

"Old? Who are you calling *old*?"

The druid stood directly behind them.

Amelia yelped and staggered into a bookcase; Elwynn caught Hiro's elbow as he spun around and pushed it harmlessly away from his face.

"Sorry," the prince mumbled. "Reflex."

"And what are we all doing over here?" The druid's orange eyes were hazy again behind the thick spectacles. His clothes were somewhat rumpled, as if hastily smoothed down over something, and very, very wet.

"You mentioned a book…?" she said.

"Oh, yes. That one. The one with the green spine. Is dinner ready yet?"

Amelia and Hiro glanced at each other.

Elwynn tapped the prince on the shoulder. "Why don't you find out? Off you go."

Hiro reluctantly stalked off, casting a glare over his shoulder.

Amelia felt a twinge of guilt as the druid dripped on the floor. The heat of the molten crack dried it away in seconds. "I'm sorry about the… decapus. Conchita?"

He flapped his fingers. "Oh, that was *ages* ago. Concha's already forgotten about it. And she even brought me a gift. I mean *you*. She brought *you* a gift. I think." The druid stuck his hand under his shirt and withdrew a rosewood chest no larger than a girl's jewelry box. "Lazy beast said she'd had it for quite some time. Just hadn't deposited it yet."

"That's the Raion Chest."

"Huh. Thought it looked vaguely familiar."

Amelia plucked the chest from his hands and shoved it into a gap on the bookshelf between *Practical Demonkeeping* and *Planetary Alignments and Their Inherent Risks*.

"Dearie," Elwynn said patiently, "*books* go there, not relics—"

"Shh!" She peered around corner, but the rest of the menfolk were busy getting the table set for supper. "We have to hide it. A sorcerer hunted this chest. Who knows who else—"

"Not a sorcerer, dearie. A *manabudh*. He waits for you if his master fails."

"That's not possible. I… incapacitated him."

"Remade. Take the Chehara Cliff. He doesn't watch that one."

"Elwynn, the pilgrim's path has been closed for centuries."

The druid tapped the side of his nose. "Only to those who don't know the way. *Those that wear the golden crown light the path through Heaven's Wall.* East side, remember that. Now get going."

She let out a huff. "I can't go yet. We need to *hide* this, Elwynn. No one can know it's been found."

The druid frowned. "That boy out there might as well be your son, that guardian your mate, and you say that *priest* is your friend. Why would you keep something like this from them?"

Amelia barked a laugh. "Are you kidding me? That prince is so *insufferable*, only a woman both blind and deaf could possibly tolerate him."

"Interesting how that's the *only* thing you took issue with." The druid's eyes had cleared, and they narrowed into thin slits. "You've been keeping a lot of secrets, Sanu."

"Only a few. The Sanu sect protects the Raion Chest. As I am the only one left, I am making the executive decision to keep it secret and have that leviathan hold it in trust for me. I'll just go in there and ask—"

"You'll have to keep it. Concha isn't on speaking terms with you right now."

"But you said she'd already forgotten!"

The druid snorted. "As if. You frightened her entire clutch not ten minutes ago, and expect a beast that lives for thousands of years to just forgive you in the length of time it takes for her to snap her tentacles? *Feh.*"

"*Fine.* I'll just read this, then."

"Good… Wait. Why are you reading my diary? Have you *no* shred of decency?"

Amelia let out a frustrated sigh as the druid plucked the book from her hand. "Elwynn, your mood swings are giving me whiplash. Is there something here I'm supposed to read or not?"

He rifled around in the honeycomb lattice of scrolls and selected one. Brittle at its edges, a cord of purple silk kept the yellow parchment snugly furled. "*This* one."

Amelia rolled her eyes as she untied the cord.

Something slipped from the scroll, a red gemstone that clattered against the floor.

"Ah-ha! So *that's* where I put that." The druid scooped it up and pressed it into her hand.

Its insides glowed faintly as if it housed a tiny ember. It flared when she rubbed it with her thumb, the stone cracking as the ember inside bloomed into a conflagration.

"Phoenix Tear quartz," she breathed.

"There are only two left in the world. This one belonged to your father."

"M-my father?"

Elwynn nodded, pointing at the scroll.

Painted in the Old Imperial style was a rendering of the Most Holies. Lady Bosetsanu and her Lord Delphi were depicted more or less like the statues in the Temple of Lhasa, but the Crown Prince of Heaven was definitely not.

Normally drawn as a sun shining between his parents, this was a young man with a mane of curls that threatened to obscure his impish eyes. He was the only one of them to wear armor: a breastplate etched with a knot of storm clouds expelled from a roaring lion's mouth. His mouth quirked up in a mischievous smile, the young prince rested his hands one over the other upon the hilt of a blade that crackled with angelfire.

Elwynn's finger hovered over the phoenix on Lord Delphi's shoulder.

"My father is a *bird*?"

"Not just any bird. A *firebird*."

Amelia rolled her eyes. "Uh-huh. And what is this? I've never seen—"

"It's how they looked in the old days. History forgets and bends the truth. Isn't that why the Crown Prince is depicted as just a sun nowadays? Not in his true form, with his armor and sword as the Lion Before the Storm?"

"I thought he gave those up when he created the Gate."

"How can you give up something that is just as much a part of you as your own flesh?"

"But the Gate is just a salt mesa—"

"Hmph. To *your* eyes."

Shaking her head, she traced the Crown Prince's familiar grin with a fingertip.

"Amelia, Elwynn sir," Kale called. "Suppertime."

"*Finally.*" The druid plucked the Raion Chest from the bookshelf and shoved it into her hands. "Time to hide this."

Amelia stuffed the chest and the quartz into her pocket as the druid scurried over to the pot.

He wafted the steam into his nose and ruffled the boy's hair. "Quick march, dearie. Before it gets cold."

She abandoned the scroll and sat at the freshly scrubbed table. "But I don't eat meat."

"Nonsense. You *love* seafood." The druid pounded his head with his fist. "*Later.* Right. Pigeon peas and rice for you, then? Care for some salt?"

He sprinkled some over her bowl with a flourish, flicking the grains that still clung to his fingers at Isen as if he were some bad luck spirit. The priest ignored the assault, nursing a cup of palm wine.

Hiro drained his own cup with a roll of his eyes. "I've been meaning to ask, druid. What is *that?*" With his spoon, he pointed to the molten rock that slid behind the slit in the wall. "And how is it not cooking us alive?"

"You know the demon of fire and earth that nearly destroyed the world during the Great Cataclysm?"

"You mean the volcanic eruptions?" Isen clarified skeptically. "The ones triggered by the ocean-miners digging too deep for oil?"

The druid shrugged. "To-*may*-to, to-*mah*-to. Either way, they don't just disappear."

CHAPTER 100

"DRINK UP, GENTLEMEN. PALM WINE IS BEST ENJOYED WHEN YOUNG. No, none for *you*, dearie. I need you alert."

Hiro lurched to his feet, catching the edge of the table for support. "Are you saying you have a *demon* trapped in that pinnacle?"

"Where *else* would you keep one?"

"I'm too sober to have this discussion." Isen lifted his cup with a heavy sigh. "Fill it up."

The druid readily obliged.

Hiro eyed the slit that crackled across the far wall. The *shiing* of his greatsword leaving its scabbard echoed like a wind chime in the cavern. He pointed it at the offending fissure... if it was three feet lower than it actually was.

"Oh, *relax*. It's shielded. So touchy for a guardian." Elwynn refilled Hiro's glass. "Sit down and drink that. Now, who wants to feed my darling decapus?"

Isen spewed his wine across the table. A breathless whistle of a laugh escaped him. *"Decapus."* Pushing his wrists together, he waggled his fingers in an inebriated imitation of a multi-appendaged sea creature. "Oogly oogly oogly."

Hiro snickered.

Kale glanced from prince to priest, spoon hovering halfway to his mouth.

"Ugh, we just had this table *cleaned*. Boy, you up to it? Take one of these coconut lamps but leave it just inside the tunnel. Then dump that shark carcass into the pool. Concha will do the rest."

"Don't get too close. Or else." Hiro slapped his hand against Isen's face and mimed sucking it off like a tentacle.

The priest giggled.

"Off you go, boy." The druid dumped the carcass into Kale's arms. "Conchita can get quite snappy if her dinner's delayed."

"Don't you mean *crabby?*"

Amelia's gentle poke sent Isen toppling out of his chair. "Elwynn, what did you—"

Hiro leaned over the table, losing his balance and sprawling among the cutlery. "*Goushi.* What are you doing down there?"

"Just leave them." Elwynn gestured for her to join him. "Young palm wine is quite strong. I warned them to go easy on it, otherwise it's stuffed colons and unpleasant dreams, but they're not very good listeners."

"You told them to drink up!"

"Did I?" Elwynn scratched his chin. "Whoops."

"No, don't go." Hiro flailed after her hand. His attempt to inconspicuously point at the fissure failed. "There's a demon. In. The. Wall."

"It's just *lava*, Hiro," Isen groaned from the floor. "Gods above, not everything is witchfire and brimstone."

"Witchfire? *Where?*"

Elwynn plucked the greatsword from his hands before he could impale any of them. He set it on the table and pushed the prince back into his seat. Hiro fell with a grunt. "Amelia and I are going to reseal its prison right now. Stop having a fit."

Hiro dug around in his pocket and dropped a whetstone on the table. His fingers scrambled after it. "Demons. *Henge.* I've got to get ready."

"Said no man in a Dollhouse ever."

496

The priest and the prince laughed, and the druid tugged her closer to the fissure.

Amelia shivered. The heat was forge-like this close to the crack in the wall. Molten rock slid thick and sluggish like syrup on a winter morning. Elwynn curled his hand around hers and pressed her fingertip against the rock under the slit. He dragged it in a series of swirls that ended with a crowning dot.

The rock turned red with the passage of her finger, like coals stoked from their slumber. The more she repeated the design, the more the rock flared to life. When it glowed golden, the druid took his hand away. "Just keep tracing in the way I showed you."

"How many times do I need to do this?"

"Twenty-nine. One for each star he took from Heaven. It'll turn blue when you're done."

"I know this symbol." She pressed forward eagerly, drawing faster.

"It's an om. The universal seal."

"I've seen it before. In the Himalayas, there was this prayer wall—"

"Not just there."

"The Old Mother said I'd seen it with my *feet*, but that doesn't make any sense."

"Of course it does. Yueshan is a *dance*, isn't it? Better that than the blood sacrifice it was created with if you ask me. I mean, you *could* do that if you needed to, but—"

The om shone as blue as starlight. Amelia shaded her eyes and backed away until she was even with the druid. "I know it's a dance. But I don't know the *sequence*. Without that, I'm just flailing around."

The om winked white and vanished.

"What do you think I just taught you?"

"You mean...?" With a cry, Amelia threw her arms around the druid's neck. "Thank the gods. I knew you weren't crazy. I knew you'd help me."

"Why does everyone keep saying I'm crazy?"

Laughing, she turned to the table. "Isen, H– Ishida, I told you Elwynn would..."

The men were slumped over the table: Isen's face buried in his sleeve and his overturned glass dripping wine onto the floor, Hiro's head lolled to one side with the whetstone and greatsword loose in limp hands.

"I didn't think they'd fall asleep so fast."

"They're not asleep. They're drugged."

Silver fire snapped from her fingertips. "Why would you—"

"It's forbidden to use such a sacred symbol for just *anything*. If you don't draw it right, it's just a bunch of squiggles. Draw it – or *dance* it – in its proper sequence, and its power is unfathomable. How else do you think this demon of the ancient world has been contained for the last millennium? Why else is it used in Yueshan? It prevents the apocalypse by resealing the Gate."

"I didn't know…" She glanced at the wall with the demonic smile, a phantom om shimmering white below its lip.

"So don't be doodling it mindlessly. Like that boy who keeps drawing that knotwork design in the dregs of his soup."

"I won't. But Elwynn, the Gate is still broken—"

The druid jumped, hazy eyes rolling like oranges behind his spectacles. "It is? Well that's not good. Not good at all."

Amelia sighed. She'd lost him again.

"I'm going to consult Concha. Maybe she's picked up something that can help."

She didn't have the heart to argue with him. "Thanks, Elwynn. I appreciate you checking."

"Not at all! Fate of the worlds, you know? Go ahead and use the bed; don't wait up for me. This could take a while. My Conchita is a lazy beast."

Amelia sank on the bed, forcing a smile onto her face. The druid waved encouragingly from the archway and disappeared into the tunnel. Groaning, she flopped face-first into the pillow. Inside, the silver dragon keened with sympathy.

"Amelia, are you awake?"

She cracked open one eye.

A mane of auburn hair framed hazel eyes bursting with excitement. "Amelia, he's got a *kraken*," Kale said excitedly. "Concha is a *kraken*."

"And were you polite? I hear they can suck your face clean off."

"Concha says she prefers whale to human." The boy crawled on top of the mattress next to her. The chopped palm fronds crinkled under his weight. "Hey, why are Hiro and Isen asleep like that?"

"Oh, that. Elwynn drugged them." Yawning, she closed her eye and wiggled into a more comfortable position on the bed.

Kale lowered his voice to a whisper. "Amelia, I know you like him, but I think he's a little crazy."

"Says the boy who talks to krakens."

RUMBLING.

Low, faraway or underground, it was enough to break through the fog.

Hiro forced his eyes into slits. Blurred by sleep, the druid stood before the crack of molten rock. Once no wider than a foot, it had expanded until it consumed half the width of the wall.

Impervious to the heat, Elwynn stuck out his hand. "It's time. Give it back."

Deep within the molten heart of the pinnacle, something answered.

"Yes, she will," he said.

The rock rumbled again.

"You'll do as I say," the druid commanded irritably. "Now give it back."

Red light flared. The druid stepped forward, stuck his arm up the shoulder into the gap. Whatever he withdrew burned white like lightning.

"*What?*" Hiro whispered.

There was no way the druid could've heard him, but the man's head snapped around to face him. The molten rock rumbled once more before the gap closed into the narrow slit. Hiro blinked in disbelief. When he opened his eyes again, the druid stood directly in front of him. Hiro jerked back, nearly fell out of his chair. His hand tightened on his sword, but the druid's fingers dug into his wrist like claws. Owlish eyes gleamed.

"You need to let the girl go," the druid said.

"What...?" His mind was as thick as a springtime fog.

"The girl. When it is time, *let her go.*"

Hiro clutched his spinning head. "I don't... Wait, what was—"

"You can't be a keeper of demons without a few side effects," the druid whispered. Pressed his thumb into Hiro's forehead.

His vision went dark.

CHAPTER 101

THERE WAS NO SIGN OF THE DRUID.

"We can't wait," Hiro said quietly. "Did you… get everything you need?"

The others were watching.

Amelia put on a brave face. "Of course. I just wanted to ask him more about my parents." The sear of a branding iron pierced her chest; she didn't even wince. She was too heartsick to feel the wrath of the lie.

Kale showed them the hidden path of the krachiao flowers to the beach, but she hardly admired their beauty. They were out of time, and the Gate was still broken.

Sacks of rice and pigeon peas leaned drunkenly in the sand. Barrels of fresh water and nets of coconuts nestled beside them, and the druid was loading them one-handed into the *Xunsu*. On one of the barrels was a tea service, a thread of steam twisting from the pot's spout.

"Gods above, please say that's the remedy," Isen moaned.

The druid heaved a sack into the boat. "Apparently *someone* had too much palm wine last night. I warned you of its side effects."

"*Elwynn.*" Amelia ran the rest of the way to him. "I thought—"

"I may be scatterbrained – *oof* – but I'm not bereft of manners." He encircled her tightly with his one arm. "Of course I'd say good-bye to my favorite niece."

"But the Gate—"

"What about it, dearie?"

The druid's eyes were hazy again, unfocused. Her hopes scattered on the sea breeze.

Hiro glared over the rim of his cup. "I had dreams of you, druid."

"I'm not surprised. I was quite handsome in my youth." Elwynn shrugged. "I like to think I'm well-seasoned now."

Hiro scoffed and drained the cup. "What's in this?"

"It tastes terrible." Isen clutched his stomach. "You sure it's a remedy?"

"It cures hangovers, settles the stomach, and promotes a healthy colon. I also use it to clean out the latrine."

"I think I'm going to be sick."

Hiro gave him a slight shove off to the side. "Then do it before we get on board."

"Quick march now. The tide's already leaving. Go north up the Medi to Vashti. It's the closest fresh-water source."

They loaded the rest of the supplies and stabled the horses. All five of them leaned against the prow of the *Xunsu* and shoved her back into to the sea.

As they scrambled aboard, the druid waved from the shore. "I almost forgot," he called. He rifled under his shirt. "Something for each of you." The druid tossed little bundles at them.

One hit Isen in the head before dropping to the deck with a jingle.

Kale shredded the fabric from his gift. "Look what I got!" He waved a blue opal the size of a chicken egg above his head.

"You gave him a rock?" Hiro shouted from the stern. "He *needed* a sword."

"You think I'd throw a *sword* at a *child*?"

"What you'd get, Hiro?" Kale asked.

"It's… personal." He stuffed the little wad into his pocket.

Isen leaned over the gunwale. "You give everybody else something meaningful and all I get is a sack of doros?"

The druid shrugged. "Too late now. *Pax vobis.*"

Amelia turned away from the others and pried the cloth apart with two fingers. Paper crinkled against her fingertips, wrapped around something warm and metallic.

What the—

She pulled the paper free and thrust it into the sunlight. Curling script flowed across the parchment: *I've kept this hidden for the last twenty years. And now you must do the same. Until it is time to dance.*

Amelia didn't even get to look at it. She stuffed it into her sari, along with the note, and sprinted to the bow. The druid was just an ant on a little hill. She cupped her hands around her mouth. "Thank you, Elwynn!"

His voice came back faint, just a thin thread of sound. "For... what?"

CHAPTER 102

VASHTI SPRAWLED ALONG THE CURVE OF THE BAY LIKE A SUNNING CRAB. Red and yellow roofs were speckles, the curving headlands its pincers. From their tips spouted twin watchtowers strung with a net of metal links, governing passage in and out of the port.

The *Xunsu* slipped under the shadows of the watchtowers, slid through the crowded water between junks and sloops and merchant galleons. She glided into an open spot on the pier, and no sooner had Hiro knotted a docking line around a piling did a hand thrust itself under his nose. Demanding payment.

Thin, drooping mustache, squinty eyes, a skulking rat of a man. Bold enough to charge them a gold piece to dock their boat.

"*One doros?*" Hiro exploded. "Are you out of your mind? Half a silver mark would still be extortion for a boat this size."

"No mooring permit. One doros."

Hiro slapped the fishing hand out of his face. "I want to see the harbormaster. Right *now.*"

Scowling, the rat-man skulked down the dock, barked at people in his way. They scurried out of their path like cockroaches. "Filthy *harijan*. Out of the *way.*" He kicked at a small pack of children too starved to move quick enough. Caught the little girl in the leg, dumped her onto the ground. The rat-man grabbed her eldest brother by the ear as he snatched up a harpoon. "Just try it, Kamal." Gave the boy's ear a twist and continued to the harbormaster's headquarters.

Thugs smoking thin cigarillos or tormenting the young women selling fruit with crude gestures loitered just outside. Sparse, stove in the corner, a neat stack of wood beside it. An old man scribbling a different number for the same line item in two different ledgers. He didn't even look up when Hiro marched across the room and shouldered open the office door.

Greeted with the harbormaster's naked backside ramming away between the legs of a whore seated on his desk.

She didn't even shriek. Her eyes widened in surprise only for a moment before they became dull again. Dead. Far-away. On his desk, a frame rattled in time with the man's frantic thrusting. Pinned to the navy felt with silver tacks were scraps of lace and cloth and even a ruby drop earring. Had the withered flesh of its previous owner still attached.

Hiro's lip curled in disgust.

The harbormaster groaned in release, disengaged himself. Pulled up his trousers as the whore tugged down her skirts. Sighing, he sauntered to the sideboard and poured himself a glass of wine. Selected a mangosteen from the fruit bowl. After a leisurely sip, he remembered to fish an aeris out of his pocket for the whore.

He still hadn't even glanced in Hiro's direction.

The whore gawked at the copper penny in her hand.

"Take a bath and brush your teeth before you come back tonight, Songla. You smell disgusting."

"But if I spend the money on a bath, how will I eat?"

"How will you earn money if you don't come back tonight?" He sliced into the mangosteen's purple rind, scooped out a segment of white fruit with his finger. He ate only a few bites before tossing it into the wastebasket. "If you don't please me, Songla, you'll please no one. I'll make it so no one will touch you, and you'll have to beg for your scraps. Do you want to beg, Songla?"

The whore stared at the half-eaten fruit. Flies already buzzed along its ripe flesh. She swallowed. "No."

"No *what?*"

"No, sir."

"Then I'll see you at ten. And bring that new girl from the Center. I've a need to add to my collection. Now get out."

The whore pocketed the penny and shuffled out the door.

"Women." The harbormaster finally looked at Hiro. Appraised him with shrewd eyes. "I'm Rufus Avital. What can I do for you?"

Die. For starters.

Forty-something, fit, utterly devoid of human decency. Superstitious too; a blade of blue sea glass dangled from his neck.

His eye twitched. "I am *Prince* Hiro Ishida. Your assistant is trying to charge me a gold doros to dock. It's extortion."

"Prince Ishida, is it? I've heard of you." Rufus didn't bother to get up, didn't bow, just sipped his wine. "Two dignitaries in as many days, what do you know? Patel, come in here."

The rat-faced man appeared, swiped off his cap.

"Why are you charging this *prince* a gold doros to dock here?"

The rat-faced man sneered at Hiro. "No mooring permit."

"Ah-ha!" The harbormaster slapped his hands on the desk. "No mooring permit. You'll pay Patel one doros."

"*Excuse* me?"

"Question the fee again and it'll be two doros." Rufus smiled. Bared his teeth like a dog warning another away from his bone. He crossed his arms over his sinewy chest. "A prince can afford such a paltry sum. And don't even bother trying to dock at the mayor's residence. Those moorings have been full for weeks. Have a pleasant stay in Vashti."

Hiro snorted and stormed out of the headquarters. Slammed the door behind him. The thugs straightened; the closest one flicked his stub of a cigarillo into the water. There were more of them, scattered everywhere along the piers.

An army.

Hiro hurried back to the *Xunsu.*

CHAPTER 103

Cursing under his breath the entire time, Hiro fished out a gold doros and slapped it into the rat-man's outstretched palm.

"An extra doros and we'll have the boys watch it while you folk are about your business." An oily smile of rotten teeth flashed up at him.

"Not a chance."

Striding down the pier, Hiro forced himself to look straight ahead. A backward glance showed weakness. He kept an eye on the reflective surfaces nearby – bits of sea glass, still water – and found two following him.

He diverted to the urchins the rat-man had threatened earlier. "You, boy. Three aeris for you if you go to *Xunsu* and watch it."

The boy hopped to his feet, puffed out his chest. Stick-like, each rib accounted for, eyes bright with defiance. A brown chip of sea glass around his neck. Three aeris was more than the boy could possibly steal in a week. "If I go, my crew comes with me."

Three younger boys and one tiny girl stood up from the salt-worn dock. The girl stopped prizing barnacles off the pilings, brushed the grime from her dress. Smeared it. They were probably his siblings, tossed out of their house or abandoned. No doubt their parents couldn't afford to feed so many mouths.

"If anything is stolen or broken, you'll have me to answer to," Hiro warned.

"If we choose to steal or break anything, good luck finding us."

He leaned down from the saddle, beckoned with a gloved finger. A flicker of hesitation. The boy took a brave step forward. "Do you know the harbormaster's assistant? The rat-man with that awful mustache?"

The boy nodded. "Patel Sim."

"I have no doubt Patel Sim will send some men to 'inspect' my ship. There will be a silver mark in it for you and your family if you do all you can to discourage him from boarding. Throw rocks, whatever you wish. What's mine is mine, and he can't have it."

A wolfish smile. "I'd like that very much, sir."

He dropped three aeris into the boy's grubby palms.

"What's this for? We haven't even protected your boat yet."

"Take that now and buy food. Nothing else. *Food.* Feed your family. I need you all strong to protect my boat. You'll get the rest when you've done your job."

"Thank you, sir!"

Hiro returned to the *Xunsu*, ignored the thugs trailing him. He saddled his mare, and the warhorse bolted down the gangplank with a wild neigh. Snorting, she wheeled and stamped at anyone who got too close. Accidentally bumped the two thugs off the dock with her hind hooves.

"Kale, stay here and watch the boat. I've sent you some help."

The urchins trotted up on spindly legs, mouths stuffed with half-chewed dumplings. The girl gasped at the sight of the Sanu on her dappled gray stallion. The dumpling slipped out of her hand, hit the deck with a wet *plop*. The brother nearest her scooped it up, brushed off the debris and stuffed it into his mouth.

"Kale, I want them and their clothes washed before we get back," she instructed. "And if they're still hungry, you feed them as much as they want. Make some tea for them too."

"They're here to protect the boat," Hiro growled. "Not to have a tea party."

"Best wait on that bath," Isen said. "The filthier they are, the better they'll be at protecting the boat."

"What? How?"

"They're *harijan*. Untouchables. Have them throw mud-covered rocks. Anyone interested in the boat will think they're throwing their own filth and leave it alone."

Hiro frowned. "Sounds like you have some experience—"

"Can we get going?" Isen snapped. "The sooner we can leave this place, the better."

They bypassed the floating market with its dried chilies, striped melons, and fly-harassed skewers of grilled octopus. Hiro wanted fresh, *clean* water and grain preferably free of weevils.

The poor lined the rubbish-strewn streets under the eaves, thrust begging bowls at anyone who passed. Some were too old or too tired or too sick, just sat with the bowl cradled in their laps. The young ones busied themselves stealing.

Stray cats and dogs – too thin, with patchy coats – competed with the monkeys and other animal vermin that overran the streets. Everywhere the noise of vendors shouting at the little thieves, drunks sluicing the streets with barley beer and palm wine, the moans and laughter drifting from the whorehouses, the screeching of sea birds trying to pluck some unguarded morsel. The people left the birds alone, lest they call the ocean winds into an avenging gale.

The Sanu's shoulders slumped. If she wasn't crying yet, she was sure to be biting her lower lip to keep the tears away. Hiro hurried them into the eastern market, hand on his dagger.

Swept streets and whitewashed walls, yet still strung with silver wire and sea glass. Blue and green here, not the brown and white prevalent in the west side. Tidy stalls of well-made goods and unspoiled food.

They were only in the marketplace for a matter of minutes before a squad of guards marched up to them. There were six of them: silver breastplates, talwar sabers at their hips, pointy caps of gold swathed in sheer white cloth. Spears with golden tassels near their points.

"Are you Prince Ishida?"

Despite the social divide, news traveled fast.

"And you are?" His warhorse side-stepped under him, eyes rolling.

"His Honor Mayor Kapoor requests your presence immediately." The guards lowered their spears, encircled them in a ring of glinting steel. "Right now."

THE SECOND FLOOR of the mayor's palace provided a panoramic view of the bay. From this height, the water looked blue, not brown. The Sanu was plastered against the window, watching the ships bob like buoys in the water. Frangipani coming from the gardens mingled with the tang of the sea air. Isen lifted his nose, breathed deeply.

Rooted before the view of the rotting city, Hiro clamped his arms over his chest. "So where's this mayor who'd threaten a prince?"

As if summoned, Mayor Ashley Kapoor appeared. Painfully white, blond, barrel-chested. Hair curled into spools of ringlets, a Western waistcoat of purple damask over an aqua shirt with ruffled collar and sleeves. He even had a gold ring studded with green sea glass on one pinky finger.

Hiro was looking at a patsy.

CHAPTER 104

"I'M *DELIGHTED* YOU ACCEPTED MY INVITATION TO JOIN ME FOR LUNCH." The mayor blinded them with a smile, went about shaking their hands in the Western way. "Mayor Ashley Kapoor, *delighted* to meet you all."

Hiro snatched his hand back. *"Invitation?"*

"Two visiting dignitaries in a week. How *wonderful*." He kissed the priestess's fingertips. "Please, my lady, have some of the passionfruit juice. This tropical heat is just *beastly* for us pale ones."

"Thank you, Mayor, but—"

"Ashley. Call me Ashley, my lady. Come, come. Everybody sit. Lunch will be served any minute. My chef is preparing his specialty: tandoori fish."

"You honor us with such... extravagance." The priest gritted his teeth in a tight smile.

"I doubt you priests are treated to such delicacies on a regular basis. Just mind that you don't eat the head or the tail."

"Why? Do you reserve those for the poor?"

Mayor Kapoor tittered. "Of course not. They get tossed into the water. If you eat the head and tail, it won't grow back, and then no more tandoori fish. There might be a temple devoted to Delphi overlooking the bay, but the old superstitions still hold sway here."

"Yeah... I could smell the hundred *harijan* getting over here."

"We're working on that problem. The Hadi Center is already over-flowing—"

"Hadi Center?" The Sanu paled.

Hiro's fingers itched for his dagger. The damn guards had it.

"It means 'serene' in Sarabi. Rufus Atival – the harbormaster – has been *instrumental* in getting it up and running. It gets the *harijan* off the streets and sets them up with honorable work. Many – especially the women – were being transferred regularly to the headquarters in Janpur up until recently. I guess the need for them dried up. No new openings for a month now."

The Sanu visibly relaxed.

"Here's a lassi for you, Brother. So we've been getting on as best we can here. Rufus has taken it on as his personal charity, and let me tell you, our city has just *flourished* now that they're being taken care of. Prince Ishida, you look like you might be able to stomach something a little stronger. How about a whisky?"

He poured some of the brown liquid into a glass, pressed it into Hiro's hand.

Hiro slammed the drink on the table and grabbed the mayor by his frilly collar. "You threaten me *and* a Sanu priestess at knife point. I don't want *whisky*. I want *answers*."

A faint report sounded across the bay, and the entire palace shivered. The glass rattled in their panes. The priestess seized the windowsill for support as the mayor's nervous smile evaporated.

"It's begun," the mayor sighed. "Right on time."

Hiro released him with a shove, gaped at the black sails anchored on the opposite side of the sea net.

The priestess squinted. "Does that flag have a mer—"

"Are those *cannon* blasts?" Isen clamped onto the edge of the table with both hands.

Hiro joined the Sanu at the window. "But we saw no other sails on the horizon."

"They're sea gypsies. Atlanticans." The mayor tugged down his waistcoat. "They're sneaky. They've probably got the sea blockaded by now."

"But the watchtowers, they've got cannons—"

Mayor Kapoor shook his head. "Just listen. Those ships have bigger guns. They'll be able to harass us all they want and our cannons won't even touch them. Though I'm not sure why they even bother. With the sea net up, they can't possibly get into the port."

The Sanu pushed away from the window as the palace shivered again. "But I have to be in Lhasa in ten days!"

"I'm sorry, my lady, but those pirates will be out there until winter. It's why I requested your presence, Prince Ishida. You have to help us!"

"Help? How?"

"You're an *Academy* man. Surely you must know how to thwart a fleet of pirates."

Hiro forced a laugh. "You want me – a *single* man – to persuade the pirates to desist? Impossible."

"What about you, my lady?" The mayor turned to the priestess. "We haven't had a Sanu visit our city in over a century. If you blessed the bay, it would certainly dispel the pirate scourge."

"I'd be happy to, but I don't think it works that—"

Hiro snorted. "It'll take more than a prayer to help this city get back on its feet. It's half-dead already. That *hundan* harbormaster is draining the lifeblood right out of your people, and here you sit on your frilly ass complaining about pirates. There are people *dying* in the streets."

The mayor slammed his glass of whisky on the table. "Rufus Atival is an honorable man. I wouldn't have made it two weeks without his guidance. And I've walked this city—"

"You've walked the *west* side?"

"N-not recently. Atival comes to the palace at the end of every week to review the books. With my schedule so busy and him already making the trip, there's really been no need."

"Then you're either blind or in the harbormaster's pocket. Is that why you can afford all this food while your people suffer? Does he bribe you with whores from the Hadi Center as well, or does he just keep them all for himself?"

"How *dare* you," Mayor Kapoor hissed. "I invite you into my home to share a meal and plead for your help and I am repaid with lies and slander and baseless accusations. Look, the filth spewed from your mouth has even curdled the mango lassi!"

Hiro swiped the offending drink aside; it shattered onto the floor like an egg, oozed its yellow liquid into the tiles.

"*Ishida*," the Sanu snapped. "You disrespect our host."

"How can you just sit there and indulge this idiot? Even Isen's been only one heartbeat away from strangling him. How are you so calm? What's wrong with *you*?"

"'*Cast not pearls before swine*.'" She said it in Old Imperial. Returned to Layman as she smoothed her features. "You should excuse yourself. The rest of us would like to enjoy our meal in peace. That is, Mayor Kapoor, if you'd still permit us? I'd be fascinated to learn what I can do to help you with your pirate problem."

"Certainly, my lady. And call me Ashley. It's always refreshing to be in polite and *civilized* company." He snapped his fingers at the doorway. "Gentlemen, if you would show the prince out?"

Four of the guards that had accosted them in the marketplace surrounded him.

Hiro shot the priestess a foul look, allowed himself to be led away.

The guards released him in the marketplace, returned his weapons and horse. An icy calm settled over him. He'd buy their supplies, then drag that priestess out by her hair if he had to.

The vendors cast nervous glances over the water. The cannon fire was louder out here, not too loud that he couldn't tune it out. The cannonballs mostly just buried themselves in the headlands or battered the watchtowers. The towers only trembled under the assault.

Hiro stole under the eaves of a nearby stall, hid from the sun as the vendors packed up his goods. He sliced into a mango and watched the young woman in the next stall carefully sort sea glass as her father hawked charms and jewelry.

"Patience will always be rewarded," a familiar voice said behind him.

The mango slipped from his hands.

Pfft. Then the prick of a dart.

Hiro whipped around, yanked the skewer from his neck. The ever-sleep already blurred the woman before him. She no longer wore her signature black armor, but the purple cape still fluttered at mid-thigh.

"Take him."

CHAPTER 105

"*Where is he?*"

The harbormaster shooed the dead-eyed whore off his lap. Another woman, this one young, sat in the far corner, hugging her knees to her chest and sobbing into her dress. It looked new, made from sky blue cloth and patterned with white albatrosses, but it was torn now in more than one spot. Rufus Atival was everything Hiro had said he was.

"Who?" He raked her over with his eyes. "My lady?"

Amelia forced her arms to stay at her sides instead of clamping them over her chest. Her fingernails bit into her palms, smothering the silver dragon. It raged against her control with every soft sob that shook the girl's shoulders. The dead-eyed whore rearranged her skirts and went over to the young one, drawing her up to her feet.

"I'm looking for Prince Hiro Ishida," Amelia said.

"And why would I know the whereabouts of a prince?" He lazily pulled his trousers up over his hips.

"Don't be coy," she snapped. "You have this city under your thumb. Someone must've told you where he's being held. *Now answer me.*"

"Aww, you're not going to ask nicely?" He poured two glasses of palm wine. "And where do you think you're going, Songla?"

The whore froze in the doorway. The younger woman cowered against her.

"I'm not done with her yet. Bring her back."

Tight-lipped, the whore dragged the young one back into the office. The harbormaster took her chin in his hand and wrenched her face up to look at him. He tore a scrap from her bird-patterned dress, slipped his hand under her skirt, and rammed it up hard between her legs. Shrieking, she tried to twist away, but the harbormaster held her tight. When he withdrew the scrap of cloth, the white birds had been dyed red.

The silver dragon bellowed.

Amelia clamped down on the fire that raced through her veins like jerking the reins of a disobedient horse. *We can't burn him alive until we find out where Hiro is.*

Grumbling, the dragon settled.

Without looking at them, the harbormaster flapped his fingers. "You can go now."

The whore grabbed the sobbing young woman and hurried out of the office.

Rufus Atival rifled through a dish on his desk and selected a silver pin. With unexpected care, he tacked the cloth stained with the woman's ruined maidenhead to an open spot on a frame of navy blue felt. In the row above it, a ruby drop earring with a piece of withered flesh still attached winked in the lamplight.

"You're disgusting," Amelia spat.

"If you're going to continue to insult me, I might not tell you where the prince is being held." He handed her a glass of palm wine. "Now why don't we talk like civilized individuals? Business is just business, after all."

Amelia dashed it into his face.

The harbormaster glared through the amber liquid dripping from his eyebrows. "I've restrained myself for this long because you're a lady, but now I'm beginning to think you need a firmer hand."

"*Try it.*" Silver lightning snapped in her eyes. "Now where is he?"

"Why should I tell you? He was a *hundan*, and you're not much better."

"I... can pay you," she ground out.

"Yeah? How much?"

"Five doros." The druid's gift to Isen.

The harbormaster didn't even blink. "For five doros you can have me, my lady. I swear I'm worth it."

"I doubt it."

"At any rate, my integrity is not for sale." He dropped into his chair, crossing one boot over the other on the edge of his desk.

"Then what about this?" She drew a blue opal the size of a chicken egg from her sari. Kale had begged her to take it. Anything to buy Hiro's freedom.

Rufus Atival sprang to his feet. "Is that the Lost Eye of Suyin?"

Amelia snatched her hand away before he could touch it. "What if it is?" She'd claim it was a crystallized tear from the Blessed Lady herself and bear the pain of the lie if it meant getting Hiro back.

"I've heard stories..." he trailed off. "That jewel is *priceless*."

"Not to me."

"The prince, yes, I know. Give me the opal, and I'll tell you."

She drew the gem to her chest. It felt warm and heavy in her hand, and she was not going to part with it until she had what she wanted. "Tell me first," she demanded.

With an exasperated sigh, the harbormaster rapped his knuckles on the desk.

Two men appeared in the doorway, each as big as an ox. They looked down at her with lecherous eyes.

"Give me the opal, and you can leave here unmolested. That should be a price you're willing to pay, *Sanu*."

She could roast them alive in their skins like sweet potatoes. Instead, she placed the opal on the desk.

Rufus snatched it up. He jerked his chin at the guards, dismissing them. He rubbed his thumb over the gem's flawless surface. "It was nice doing business with you, my lady."

Amelia snorted and spun on her heel.

"I suggest you forget about your friend and leave tonight," he called after her with a laugh. "Leave while you still can, my lady! Besides, tomorrow I might wonder what other treasures you keep hidden in your clothes."

CHAPTER 106

"How long does this ever-sleep last? He's been out for hours."

"He got a double dose, but it should be anytime now."

A foot nudged Hiro in the leg.

He cracked open an eye, squinted against the lamplight.

The stone floor was clammy under him. He lifted his head, let his vision focus. A room larger than the floorplan of most Vashti houses, shuttered bay windows, a rug of dueling sea serpents. Someone sat in an armchair – the big, overstuffed kind – and someone in purple prowled by the table scattered with bowls of fruit and torn loaves of bread. A half-eaten carcass of a roasted duck. A third in black and yellow crouched before him, peeled his eyelids apart.

Hiro snatched him by the throat. He didn't need his eyes to squeeze the life out of him.

The man scrambled for something in his jacket.

"No, don't dose him again." The one in purple rushed forward, put a knife against Hiro's neck. "Let him go, Hiro." The cold blade stung his feverish flesh.

Hiro released him, felt the blade lift. Shackles clinked at his wrists as he pushed himself onto his knees. The stone bit into his bare skin.

Naked. He tugged on one shackle, followed the chain to the ring in the wall behind him. Restrained like a beast. He yanked harder.

"I wouldn't bother if I were you. I change the pins when they get worn. Apparently some girl had it in her mind to stab me in the thigh with one once."

"*Atival*," he growled.

"Don't blame me. *I* didn't chain you there." He jerked his thumb to the left. "*She* did."

The woman in purple shrugged, twirled the khukuri knife in her hands.

"Let me go, Lakshmi," Hiro said. "*Now.*"

"And have you slaughter us? I don't think so." She sat at the table, crossed one leg over the other. Picked up a piece of yellow jackfruit and nibbled on it. "You're still drugged, and you almost killed Jasper. You won't be leaving that wall any time soon."

Hiro recognized the black-and-yellow clothes of the canaris. "Aren't you a little far away from home?"

Lady Cosette's spy only glared and rubbed his throat.

"Jasper's on loan," Lakshmi said. "We stumbled into each other at the Indus. Him headed east, me headed west."

"And why aren't you with the troops?"

"I could ask you the same question," she snarled. "You abandoned us weeks ago to face the threat of the Shadow Army *alone* on some 'holy mission,' as you call it. *Dimittere*, Hiro, really? *Itoko.*"

"You didn't answer the question."

"You don't think I was stupid enough to stick around and get slaughtered, did you? I'm a *Khan*, Hiro. Heir to this province, just as soon as they elect my father. If I die in battle, who'll inherit the province then?"

"Someone far more worthy," he spat. "Someone who'd go to battle in defense of its people."

"You don't get to lecture me about *honor*, Hiro. You abandoned your own fighters. Your precious Si Tanin."

"I left to save their souls."

She laughed. "Yueshu? *Please* tell me you don't believe in that garbage. Does that Sanu have you that tightly wrapped around her little finger?"

Hiro glowered at her.

"So she does." She threw the jackfruit aside. "You're a *fool*, Hiro."

"And why's that?"

"Because you chose a woman who could never choose you back. You chose her instead of *me*. You ran off with her instead of *me*!"

Hiro caught her hand before it could strike him, wrenched her wrist back. Her shriek turned into a gurgling cry as he clamped his fist around her throat. They never learned.

Lakshmi scratched, kicked, even punched him in the ribs. He'd release her when he had squeezed every last breath out of her traitorous lungs.

"You are guilty of desertion," he seethed, "and I am more than happy to carry out the sentence you so rightly deserve."

Something walloped him across the shoulders. He rolled away from the threat, taking Lakshmi with him. Rufus Atival struggled under the weight of the greatsword, heaved it over his head for another strike. The canaris darted forward, stabbed Hiro in the hand with another dart.

Fire raced up Hiro's arm. He scuttled back with a cry, his hand already swelling. Lakshmi scrambled away from him, latched onto the edge of the table and gasped for breath. Hiro sucked the poison out of his swollen flesh, spat it off to the side. The sting only intensified.

"What you'd give him?" Lakshmi asked.

The canaris drew a little vial of purple liquid from his jacket. "Nightmare fuel. It's mostly scorpion sting. With a little hallucinogenic."

Coughing, Lakshmi poured herself some wine and choked it down. "I want him alive, Jasper."

"But Lady Cosette—"

"She'll get her pound of flesh, but Hiro is *mine*."

The canaris shook his head stubbornly. "She wanted *both* of them."

"Since when is a Khan someone else's little *biaozi?*" Hiro shook, but he had the pain under control. Barely. Phantom flames danced like halos around their heads.

Lakshmi narrowed her eyes. "I'm no errand boy, Hiro. Lady Cosette and I have a mutually beneficial arrangement."

"Doesn't sound like it."

"She'll understand." She smoothed his hair away from his face. "I'm choosing *life*, Hiro, and I want you to choose it with me."

He lurched away from her touch. "The Academy will hunt you down. Your father cannot protect you now. You're a deserter. You've nowhere to go."

"Kolkata's not far. A lord or lady can deter the Academy from hunting down fugitives in their own provinces."

"But not prevent. They'll have you one way or another. You've besmirched their name, and they'll have *their* pound of flesh."

Her lip twitched. "My father will secure me a pardon."

Ghosts joined the phantom flames. Faces of the children he'd cut down like winter wheat.

"He'll never be Lord of Tybet," Hiro rasped. "When I get out, they'll know. They'll *all* know that Khans breed cowards. My father will withdraw his support, and the people will choose another."

"It doesn't have to be this way, Hiro. *Join me.* The Tiger and the Dragon united would be a force none could challenge."

He shook his head. "How did I not see this in you before? At the Academy?"

"You were only concerned with what I could do for you. You wanted release, and I granted it. Well, it's my turn now. I will have what I'm owed."

"You don't want *life*, Lakshmi, you want *power*. And those who crave it will never have it because they can't handle it. You're a kitten trying to prove she's got claws, and they're nothing but little stubs."

He was laughing now, laughing away the sting and the ghosts.

Lakshmi's beautiful face contorted into a demonic mask. "Jasper, make him more compliant. *Please.*"

The canaris dipped a dart into the purple liquid, slid it into his blowgun. Raised it to his lips.

"You'll fail, Lakshmi. It'll never—"

Pfft.

CHAPTER 107

"WHAT DO YOU MEAN 'THERE'S NOTHING YOU CAN DO?'" AMELIA slammed her hands down on the mahogany desk. The swan-feather quills jumped in their holder.

Flinching, Mayor Ashley Kapoor lurched forward to steady the ink bottle.

"Hiro – a *prince* of Jianshu – is being held against his will in the harbormaster's own house, and there's nothing you, the *mayor*, can do about it? Don't you outrank him or something?"

"My lady, it's not as simple as that. And why would Rufus kidnap him?"

He hadn't.

Kamal and his brothers had disappeared into the city while she'd been at the harbormaster's, and the *harijan* network had seen a Tybetan woman in a purple cape and her men dragging Hiro out of the eastern market. They'd sold his horse to some domo north of the city and had taken the prince to the fortress on the western ridge: Atival's home.

"A woman kidnapped him and brought him to the harbormaster's house. Though he's not directly involved, he's at least an accessory."

Sighing, the mayor tied his dressing gown and shuffled over to the sideboard. He poured himself a whisky, but she plucked it from his fingers before he'd even taken a sip. He sighed again, this time with a frown. "So you've been informed by some street urchin who told another one who told you. It's not uncommon to hear those in impoverished positions speak unkindly against those in better circumstances."

"Then go in and accuse his guest—"

"'Accuse his guest?'" The mayor swept past her with a sniff. "I would *never* be so rude. Besides, Rufus would've vouched for his guest, and he is a wonderful man. You must've been misinformed."

Cast not pearls before swine.

Amelia let out a short sigh. "I apologize for disturbing you, Mayor Kapoor. If Hiro does happen to turn up, would you tell him I've continued on to Lhasa? I can't afford any more delays."

"Y-you'll still bless the bay, right? Those pirates—"

She kept her voice as pleasant as she could. "Of course. Noon tomorrow, as the tide comes in."

The mayor clapped his hands. "*Wonderful.* I'm so thankful we can part as *friends* after this night's disagreement. I'll make the announcement first thing in the morning. The *entire* city will be out on the docks to witness it."

Nodding numbly, Amelia saw herself out.

She was no closer to freeing Hiro. She was not some battle-hardened warrior who could simply demand obedience. She had no name that would demand compliance through fear. And she couldn't just engulf everyone in flames. She was a Sanu priestess, devoted to spreading the love of the Most Holies. And she couldn't use her title for personal gain. Amelia just had her wits and her faith in the goodness of mankind, and so far they had gotten her nowhere.

Back at the pier, Kamal hailed her with a shout. His younger brothers scurried from their hiding places and presented themselves like little soldiers on the dock. Their younger sister, Sati, woke up from sleeping in a coil of rope and joined her brothers.

Kale ran to meet her.

"I lost the opal," Amelia whispered. "I'm so sorry, Kale."

The boy hugged her hard around the middle. "At least you tried."

Isen gripped the edge of the gunwale and leaned over the side. "Well?"

"The mayor won't help us."

"*Goushi.*" The priest scrubbed his face with his hands. "That's it then. We have to go."

"What?"

"The pirates have stopped their barrage for the night. I spoke with one of the merchants here. There's a gap between the sea net and the western watchtower big enough for the *Xunsu* to squeeze through. We can leave tonight."

"We're not leaving Hiro behind," Kale snarled.

"While you two spent the rest of the day searching for him, *I* went to the aviary," Isen said. "I've sent messages to Lord Ishida and to every local domo and doma beseeching their help. Someone *will* come, and we don't need to wait for them. He's not required for Yueshu, but *you* are, Amelia. We're just wasting time—"

"Isen, I'm not going without him."

"*Amelia.* Be reasonable! If you can't be, then I will. I'll sail this boat myself if I have to!"

"Good luck with that," Kale snorted.

"We've exhausted all of our resources. There's no one left who can help us. Or even wants to. Besides, he's probably already maiming whoever kidnapped him and will be back before we can even shove off. Amelia? Where are you going?"

Her sandals *thunked* against the salt-worn planks as she marched back up the pier. Her hand was in her pocket, her fingers curling around a silver-and-emerald ring. One that depicted a voluputious mermaid."I told you, I'm not leaving. Not yet. There's still one more thing I can try."

CHAPTER 108

Scorpions under his skin.

Hiro clawed at them. They bit him, stung him, laced his blood with fire.

Specters haunted him. Red Ellick and his clansman, their surprised faces as his sword took them one by one in the night. Thirsty steel.

The cries of their women gnawed at his ears. Mingled with the chuckle of the conjurer as he choked on his own blood. *Boom. Boom. Boom-boom-boom.* Hiro scratched at his head, ripped the memories free and flung them in red splashes against the far wall.

"...needs water."

"He'll get... later."

Purple. Black-and-yellow. An iris and a bumblebee.

"...heat'll kill him."

"Not yet... need *compliance*... won't get the Sanu."

Run, Amelia.

Was that steam rising from the floor?

His tongue felt thick, his mouth like paper. The throbbing in his head matched the cannon fire. There was so much light. Heat. He lifted a hand, strained against the chain that weighed him down.

Hiro panted, pawed at his throat. It threatened to collapse like an abandoned mine shaft at any moment.

Clang.

It sounded like the cannon fire, but it was close. Much too close.

A shutter closed.

He crawled into the shade.

"Thirsty? Of course you are."

A dribble of water, thinner than a gossamer thread, splattered against his lips. He strained after it.

"More?"

He groaned in response.

"Then stand."

He opened one eye. Glared.

She was naked. The dress of purple gauze pooled around her feet. At one time he would've drooled at the sight of her naked body, but now his eyes were fixated on the glass she held in one hand. "Stand, or you'll get nothing."

Hiro scraped himself off the floor. Swayed as his vision blurred. She didn't steady him. He wetted his chapped lips with a fuzzy tongue.

Lakshmi dribbled a thin stream across her bare chest. "Quickly now, or it'll evaporate."

It was humiliating. But he was so thirsty and already the precious water was dripping off the nub of one erect—

Lakshmi gasped as he captured her dripping nipple in his mouth. He sucked hard, frantic for the water. She bucked against him. He wrapped his arms around her, afraid this sole source of water would be plucked away from him.

Her flesh was firm under his tongue, smooth. Supple. When no more water came, he released her breast and ran his tongue along the moist line across her chest where the water had been. She threaded her free hand into his hair, curled against him. He found her other breast, licked that one dry as well. Her breathing had turned fast and shallow.

"More?" she panted.

Hiro looked up from her breast as she sucked the rest of the water into her mouth. Ignoring the pain in his chapped lips, he crushed his mouth against hers. The cup clattered against the floor as she wrapped her arms around his neck. She rubbed her naked body against his sweaty one, her hands roaming along the muscles of his back as her leg hiked up around his hip.

He sucked down the last of the water with a gasp.

"I want *us*, Hiro. The Tiger and the Dragon." Her hand slipped between his thighs, stroked methodically. "United. Our heirs will forge an empire—"

He bit her. Hard.

Lakshmi screeched, shoved him away.

Hiro spat the blood from his mouth.

She extracted a dart from her dress, sliced him across the chest.

Fire erupted from the shallow scratch as her eyes darkened into black, soulless orbs. Her face turned to ash, cracked with black veins.

He scuttled away from her.

"No one is coming for you. *I* am your only lifeline. You will be *mine*, Hiro Ishida."

"... NEVER SEEN... SURVIVE THIS MUCH."

"He bit..."

"... lose your temper... he dies."

He flinched away from the conjurer's touch. Yellow eyes swam in front of him. Ringed in black. Embers burned red beneath his skin. Called witchfire.

"Go... away." He forced the words out through chattering teeth. Not cold. Terrified.

"... incredible...this birthmark—"

"… burning up…"

Water chilled him. Threatened to drown him. It boiled into steam off his skin. He gasped for air. The river had him. Sucked him back under. No silver dragon heaved him onto the banks.

Run, Amelia.

CHAPTER 109

ONE WHITE-KNUCKLED FINGER TAPPED AN IMPATIENT RHYTHM AGAINST the wood of the staff. Isen lifted his face into the wind, nosing the sea air. "They're close. I can smell the mayor's perfume."

Amelia shifted from one foot to the other, crunching the shell walkway. "Isen, I know you don't agree with me—"

"It is that obvious? You're risking the fate of the world for *one* man. I can't even *begin* to explain how ludicrous it is."

She was quiet, squinting into the sun and watching the lavender pleasure barge approach the little dock by the western watchtower. Mayor Ashley Kapoor waved at her from under a tasseled umbrella. Behind them, the report of cannon fire resounded like mining blasts as the watchtowers exchanged volleys with the pirates. The ground shivered, and dust filled the air like pollen.

"I can't let him go," Amelia said.

"He'd agree with me, you know."

"I'd do the same for you, Isen."

He huffed a sigh. "I know. And I'd still berate you for it. The long game is what matters, Amelia. The bigger picture. If I had my sight, I would've taken a page out of Hiro's book and dragged you off by your hair." The drumming of his finger accelerated. "And where's Kale, anyway? I figured he'd want to be here for this."

"He has another task."

"Tell me you haven't been waiting long in the sun, my lady," the mayor said, landing lightly on the dock in his polished leather boots. "You'll get freckles."

Her ears were already sunburned, and sweat had created a swamp under her sari. She forced a smile. "Shall we?"

"I hope you two ate a good breakfast. It's three hundred stairs to the top." He clapped the priest on the shoulder and gestured to the watchtower.

It was blissfully cool inside the yellow walls. Amelia trailed her hand against the well-worn railing as she climbed the spiraling stair. Silver fire seeped into the stone, trickling like spilled ink into the foundations buried deep within the headland. A blueprint appeared in her mind's eye. She saw the cannon ports and the men hastily reloading their guns, the gear mechanism that adjusted the height of the sea net, the pyre at the top with its revolving golden disk that reflected the light out to sea.

A glance out an arrow-loop window revealed they were only halfway up. The pirate ships bobbed like angry black corks, spitting yellow and orange sparks with each cannonball. Acrid gray smoke swirled into the air, dispelling the sea birds that normally floated on the wind. Far away, crushed together on the beach and piers, the whole city had turned out to see the Sanu thwart the pirate scourge.

At the top, Mayor Kapoor leaned against the wall as if he would melt right into the stone. Blowing like an ox, he snapped his fingers at the nearest watchman. "Gods above, do I need to *ask* for water?"

A cup was hastily pressed into his hand as another watchman frantically fanned him with the log book.

The mayor slumped into a chair and loosened his collar. "Oh, that's heavenly. Thank you. I'm *famished*. Is there anything to eat around here?"

"Mayor, it's already noon," Amelia said. "I really must—"

He straightened in the chair. "Of course, my lady. Everything's been prepared as you've requested. That's driftwood from the beach, the oil's been scented with sea rose extract, and there's one of the watchtower's fans you can use. Is there anything else—"

"Light it. Now."

She went to the balcony, snapping the fan open with a flick of her wrist. The red silk burst like a poppy flower in her hand. The sweet scent of sea rose perfumed the salty air as the driftwood caught. Far away, the wondrous gasps from the crowd crashed like a wave upon the sand as the fire crackled with purple flames.

Amelia lifted the fan and began to dance.

CHAPTER 110

Hɪʀᴏ ɴᴏ ʟᴏɴɢᴇʀ ʜᴀᴅ ᴛʜᴇ ᴇɴᴇʀɢʏ ᴛᴏ ᴍᴏᴠᴇ. Jᴜꜱᴛ ʟᴇᴛ ʜɪꜱ ʙᴀᴄᴋ ꜱɪᴢᴢʟᴇ in the heat. Flakes of skin fluttered in time with his breath; tickled his lips when he inhaled, tore at them when he exhaled.

His hand hurt. The puckered flesh ballooned from the stab of the nightmare fuel. The line on his chest was as fat as a sausage. They pulsed with heartbeats of their own, incubating dozens of little scorpions. He'd popped the sore on his hand once, long ago. Released a plague of the tiny devils that swarmed up his arm, pinching and stinging as they went. But it might've been pus.

The door opened, shut like a peal of thunder.

Hiro scrambled to his feet. Went to the edge of his chain until his arms strained out behind him. Just as he'd been taught.

Lakshmi sauntered into view, her sheer dress fluttering like purple mist. She wore lipstick now, plum-colored to mask her bruised lip.

"Very good, Hiro. Would you like some water?"

"Yes, mistress." His voice came out thick, strained, as if it had to slog through a mouthful of syrup to get past his teeth.

Smiling, she poured water into a cup. Only half-full. He knew better than to protest. Non-compliance was met with another dose of nightmare fuel. More witchfire. More ghosts of the slain. Unblinking, yellow eyes that burned into him like the sun. He shuddered.

She came out of the shadows into the sunlight. Something glittered on her neck. Jade and pearls. Her fingers grazed against the fine chain. "I found it among your clothes. I think it looks rather good on me."

Lakshmi piled her hair on her head and lifted her chin. The necklace dipped low, the center pearl nesting between her breasts that strained against the purple gauze.

It'd been the druid's gift. Something he *wanted*. A necklace of white pearls and imperial jade set in gold. Delicate, elegant. Worthy of an Ishida Princess. Of an Ishida Lady.

It didn't belong on her neck.

He leaned forward, thought about ripping the chains out of the wall. Strangling her. She was soiling a gift meant for another.

Lakshmi combed her fingers through his sweat-soaked hair. Her nails felt good on his itchy scalp. "Open up."

He did as he was told, drank. Held still as her hand caressed whatever flesh it wanted to. Didn't flinch when she squeezed.

"Mmm... I like this obedience. I think I'll feed you today."

She went to the table. Her hand hovered over the half-eaten duck, congealing in orange sauce; the loaves of bread, laced with greenish mold; the fruit bowl. Rolled him an orange.

He seized it, clutched it to his chest.

Laughing softly, she left him alone. When the key scraped in its lock, Hiro tore into the food like an animal. Peel and fruit, his teeth gnashed it all just enough to turn it into a manageable pulp he could swallow without choking.

He was no longer the Dragon but the Beast, and this woman was turning him into a pet.

When it was gone, the pain returned. Acidic juice penetrated every break in his skin. Mouth burned as if he'd just rinsed it with vinegar.

Sliding to the floor, he curled away from the sun. Stuck his fingers in his mouth to suck off the remaining sweetness. Blood fouled his mouth. The sweat on his cheek hissed as he lowered his head on the hot stones.

Waited to die.

CHAPTER 111

AMELIA DANCED THE GIFT OF WATER, HER FAN TELLING THE STORY OF the first rain from Heaven. The red silk pierced the sky and swept low in an arc, mimicking the rains. It called rainclouds, birthed springs, rolled waves onto the shore.

And one by one, the pirates left.

The cannon fire petered out. The mayor fluttered about like a butterfly, whispering excitedly to anyone who'd listen. She drowned him out. She needed to concentrate.

The dance was one of the first ones Auntie Saoirse had taught her as a child. Simple and beautiful, it required less than a tenth of her attention to perform. The rest was devoted to severing the chain of the sea net. With each footfall, silver fire raced down into the belly of the watchtower and assaulted just one of the metal links. Its diameter was thicker than the length of her hand, but the silver fire had it glowing red now.

The dance ended with the fan thrust high into the air. Molten metal dripped onto the bedrock as the link flared white. Buckling, the chain tore apart. She whipped around and gave the mayor a sharp nod.

He urged the watchmen into action with frantic hand-flapping.

They signaled a barge anchored in the middle of the bay, and fire-works exploded into the sky in clouds of purple and green sparks.

Every eye was hypnotized by the rare sight. Every noise was drowned out by the deafening explosions, even the sound of the chain disappearing into the water.

"Oh, my lady, I can't thank you enough—"

An awed quiet settled over the crowd as one colossal firework appeared in the sky. It'd come from the south, arcing between the watchtowers and plummeting toward the barge.

The fireball detonated on impact.

A flurry of fireworks spiraled into the air and skipped across the water, exploding in a melee of light like a nest of enraged fireflies.

"Sails!" One of the watchmen leaned over the seaward railing. "Black and—"

They had the southern wind, their prows slicing effortlessly through the water. Three of them entered the bay, the center lobbing fireballs from twin trebuchets on its foredeck, the flanking ships bombarding the watchtowers with close-range cannon fire.

Amelia stumbled away from the balcony as the watchtower trembled under the assault.

"How're they getting through? The sea net"—Mayor Kapoor leaned over the edge—"where is the bloody thing?"

The lead ship broke away from the pack, the mermaid figurehead parting the waves as easily as a marlin. Its trebuchets hadn't ceased their fiery assault. The balls of flaming pitch targeted everything: the merchant galleons, the fishing junks, even the lavender pleasure barge.

Mayor Kapoor tore at his golden curls. "But your blessing – they were supposed to be gone!"

"Not gone. Just hidden."

Ashley turned to her as if he'd seen a ghost, the color leaching out of his sunburned face. He seized her by the shoulders and shook her. "*What have you done?*"

CHAPTER 112

Isen lunged forward and placed a chastising blow across the mayor's back with his staff. Yelping, the mayor released her.

Amelia rubbed her arms where his fingers and their fine rings had dug into her flesh. "You wouldn't help me, so I had to find someone who would."

"They'll destroy the *city*," Mayor Kapoor shouted. "Our ships, our goods… we'll be *destitute*."

"Now you know how the *harijan* feel," Isen spat.

"They've been instructed only to disable the cannons here at the watchtowers and to destroy the masts of your ships so you cannot sail. See for yourself." Amelia gestured to the balcony. "But if I don't signal them soon, they will attack the city. Starting with the *eastern* half."

With an angry huff, the mayor clutched the railing and leaned over the side. Black smoke billowed from the base of their watchtower. Across the bay, the eastern watchtower sagged as chunks of its yellow wall splashed into the sea.

There was a fleet of pirate warships now. Eight in the bay and four beyond the headlands, preventing escape and deterring the entry of any ship that unluckily chose this time to return to port. Like thunder at sea level, the concussive blasts of their attacks reverberated through the air and trembled the water. The masts of the trading ships, each as thick as five men linked together, shattered into splinters under the barrage of the incessant cannons.

The beach was a roiling mass of confusion. Panicked, the people trampled each other and everything around them, destroying their own city. Fires flared into life from overturned charcoal grills; glass shattered as the opportunistic began to loot; screams of protest at countless injustices.

Amelia cringed at the carnage. Even Delphi the Protector raged against those that threatened his family. Even Blessed Bosetsanu disciplined out of love when necessary. The Crown Prince of Heaven wore armor and wielded a sword. She'd taken no lives and had kept damage to the bay to a minimum. It could survive. It could thrive.

'No discipline seems pleasant at the time...' She swept her hair back from her face with trembling fingers. *In time they'll forgive me. Maybe I'll even forgive myself.*

Out of the mayhem, a flash of gold streaked up the gravel road to their watchtower. A boy straddled the golden flash, the white tail streaming behind it like a triumphant banner.

Her heart lifted—

"*My city,*" the mayor screamed. He rounded on her, angry tears streaming from his eyes.

—and sank into her toes.

"They are *dying* down there." The wind whipped his golden curls into his face like a hundred angry snakes. "By your own hand—"

"By *your* hand," Amelia snapped. "I came to you for help, and you turned me away because you *chose* to be ignorant. You *chose* to be blind. It's time you *woke up*, Mayor Kapoor."

"*No.* I—" His mouth worked but no words came out. He looked out at the burning ships, the muscle in his jaw bobbing as he ground his teeth. "Please, you are *Sanu*, help them—"

"It'd mean more to them if you did." She took a small step closer, laying her hand on his arm. "You have a good heart, Ashley. You've just been misguided."

"I can't bear to see it burn." He smeared the tears from his eyes. "I was just Mayor Hrithik's assistant. I owe that man everything. He had such vision for this place... and then he was murdered in the street. I was just trying to pick up where he left off."

Amelia raised her hand high above her head, and a heartbeat later the cannons and trebuchets were silent. Only the groaning of the ships and the dissipating shouts of the crowd remained. "Come with me."

He fell into step behind her. Inside, the three watchmen huddled together on the floor as far away from Isen as they could possibly get. He leaned against his staff, picking the grit out from under his fingernails.

"Let's go, Isen."

He pushed off his staff and rolled his shoulders. "I suppose you gentlemen are free to go now. Thank you for your cooperation."

The watchmen tripped over themselves to get away from him.

Isen started down the stairs, his staff clanging against each step.

The mayor trotted after him, only going a few steps before he paused to look back at her. "The pirates, the attack on the city... all of this for one man?"

She nodded. "It's Hiro."

CHAPTER 113

THE CANNON BLASTS GNAWED AWAY AT HIS SANITY, INTERFERED WITH the dehydration tempo already throbbing in his head. The concussive shocks showered him with dust, coated his burnt skin with a gritty film that his sweat turned into paste.

Some time ago, he began to empathize with the half-eaten duck still garnishing the table. Crispy skin: check. Vacant expression: check. Dry, stringy flesh from days of sitting in the sun: double check. Slathered in sauce: did sweat count?

Sweat-basted duck? He much rather have plum sauce—

Get a grip, you idiot.

The door erupted from its hinges.

Panic ripped through every nerve. He couldn't rise to his feet. Couldn't show he was obedient. There'd be no water, only nightmares.

"We've got to get you out of here." Lakshmi flew to the windows. "The city is under attack."

The shutters banged closed. It was like a knife being rammed into his ears.

A blanket hit him in the back, roughly smoothed out to cover him.

Hiro gritted his teeth. Even silk would've felt like the coarsest wool, and whatever this cloth was felt like barbed wire.

Lakshmi fussed at the locks of his shackles, wrenched them away from his wrists. Wafer-thin strips of chapped skin tore loose like fleshy ribbons as she threw the shackles away. "On your feet, Ishida!"

When he didn't move, she put her lips to his ear and screamed the order again. He barely had the energy to wince.

She grabbed his wrist, made a disgusted sound as her fingers curled around his oozing flesh. It was a battle – he didn't help, either – but the Academy made strong graduates. Lakshmi fought, inch by agonizing inch, screaming part of the way, and hauled him upright.

There was a commotion down the hall. Something shattered. The canaris and two others ran into the room.

"Get over here and help me with him," Lakshmi snapped.

The two men draped his arms over their shoulders and started to half-carry, half-drag him across the room.

"Just leave him," the canaris panted. "They're already—"

"*Let. Him. Go.*"

THE VOICE WAS SO cold it sucked the heat right out of the room.

Hiro peered through one eye.

His vision swam, but he recognized a figure dressed in pink, yellow, and orange silks. Since when were there three Sanu priestesses in Vashti? And why did they all sound like Amelia?

Lakshmi screeched something unintelligible, and the men dropped him into a heap on the floor. The canaris backed toward the window, calmly loading his blowgun. The men ripped their swords free and charged the doorway.

A swarthy man with hair in partial canerows surged from the hallway, a curved saber in each fist. Nut-brown skin, aquiline face, eyes the pale green of sea foam. There was a brief clash of metal against metal. Grunts, boots stomping against stone and rug, squelches.

The pirate dragged the bodies out of the way so the priestess wouldn't have to step around them. He returned to her side like an obedient hound, pressed her knuckles against his sweaty forehead before gesturing to the room.

But it wasn't safe yet.

Hiro warned them with a guttural gurgle.

Lakshmi inched toward the knife by the half-eaten duck.

"Don't you dare," the Sanu's voice lashed again.

The pirate rattled off something fast in Atlantican. By his expression, he seemed to be asking for the honor to kill Lakshmi.

"No, Aurelio." The Sanu's eyes flicked from Lakshmi to the canaris lurking by the window. *"You."*

"Get in there," another voice shouted.

The priestess stepped aside as Harbormaster Rufus Atival was shoved unceremoniously into the room. His dark face was covered in blood from his broken nose, matted in the coarse mesh of his beard. Rufus collided into the table, knocked over the fruit bowl and scattered the cutlery.

Lakshmi snatched the knife.

Pfft.

Aurelio Serrano snatched the dart from the air like a frog's tongue after a fly. It hovered inches from the Sanu's eye. Just as fast, he flicked the dart into the canaris's neck. The spy collapsed with a shriek, clawing at his skin.

Lakshmi jabbed the knife under Hiro's neck.

The priestess sucked in her breath. Hissed. The pirate lurched forward, but she flung up a hand to restrain him.

Oblivious to the tense scene already enfolding in the room, Mayor Ashley Kapoor shoved his way in between them. Fine droplets of red stained the frills of his shirt sleeve; his knuckles dripped blood onto the floor. When Rufus righted himself, the mayor punched him in the nose again. A sickening crunch as the cartilage broke into smaller pieces. Howling, the harbormaster clutched his face and stumbled back. Caught the leg of a chair and sprawled out onto the stone floor.

"I thought we were *friends*. I *trusted* you," the mayor bellowed. He kicked the harbormaster with every word. "You. Treacherous. Conniving. Evil. *Snake*."

"That's enough," the priestess informed him sharply.

"How long have you abused this city? That Hadi Center was supposed to be a *relief* station, not your own personal prostitution den," he hollered. "*And* you got blood on my favorite waistcoat, you *hundan*. It's *ruined* now."

Mayor Kapoor plucked an embroidered handkerchief from his waistcoat pocket. He dabbed the sweat off his face and rubbed the blood off his knuckles. With a sniff, he pocketed the fouled cloth and smoothed back his golden curls. He pointed at Lakshmi. "You, woman, are no longer welcome in my city. I'd have you arrested and thrown in prison to rot for the offense you've done me and my guests, but others have claim to you."

Lakshmi didn't move. The room was getting very crowded, but she still had a knife pressed into Hiro's throat. If they came at her, she would go down fighting. She might even succeed in getting away.

The mayor poured himself a glass of wine from the nearest bottle, resigning himself to one of the overstuffed chairs by the door. The harbormaster cowered against the table, away from the mayor's feet.

Ashley pulled his waistcoat out by the hem to examine it once again before mewling in despair. "Ruined. *Completely ruined.*"

"Who has claim to me?" Lakshmi demanded. "Certainly not that *biaozi*."

The Sanu's ocean-blue eyes narrowed. She kept her mouth shut and stepped aside.

"I do," Lakshmi's father answered.

CHAPTER 114

THICK HAIR CROPPED INTO SHORT CURLS, BLAZING EYES, A BUILD AS lean and fit as any one of his bodyguards. A purple cape gathered at one shoulder revealed black chainmail. His Tigers followed in his wake, the kohl stripe across their eyes glinting in the sunlight. Embellished cuffs on their hands bristled with four-inch blades like tigers' paws.

Domo Nameer Khan drummed his fingers against the hilt of his talwar sword.

The threat was obvious, but the knife did not lift from Hiro's neck.

"You alive down there, Prince Ishida?" he asked.

Hiro glared at the man as best as he could.

The domo snorted. "Like father, like son."

"Father, what are you doing here?" Lakshmi demanded.

"I could ask you the same question," he bellowed.

His daughter stumbled back a step, yanking on Hiro's hair.

"Imagine my surprise when I receive not one, but *two* letters telling me my daughter – my *heir* – kidnapped the son of my benefactor."

"Father, I—"

"Not only is he a prince, but this man is your commanding officer!"

"Not anymore." She shook her head smugly. "He claimed *dimittere*."

"So I've been informed by General Vasilios. The same general who wrote to me concerning your *desertion*."

Lakshmi's dusky face paled. "H-he was going to lead us into a slaughter. The Shadow Army's too big. We would've been worm fodder—"

"*What were you thinking?*"

"She wanted an empire," Hiro whispered. His voice grated against his burning throat.

"Shut *up*." She wrenched his hair, jerked his chin up.

The knife bit into his skin. Blood, thick as syrup, oozed down his neck. Congealed on his chest.

"What was that?" Domo Khan snapped.

"She wanted an empire," he rasped. "For our children."

Mayor Kapoor snorted. "The Tybetan Monster wanted an empire too and look what happened to him. And he even had an army."

The domo's dark eyes hardened. "I doubt you were consenting."

Hiro could barely shake his head.

"So not only is my daughter a kidnapper and a coward, she's a rapist as well!" The domo threw up his hands. "The Great Delphi smite me for spawning such a pathetic excuse for a human. Tell me, what was your plan? To wait here until the fighting was over and then suddenly appear at my doorstep with a kidnapped prince in tow? Do you think I would've welcomed you then?"

Lakshmi was shaking now. "With Hiro in our custody, the Council will have to back your succession to the Tybetan Seat. I did this for you, Father. For *us*."

"You stupid, ignorant child," her father snarled. "What would stop Lord Ishida from sending the Jianshu Guard to destroy Kolkata just to get his heir back?"

"We could kill him—"

"No." The protest was strained, barely audible. The canaris fought against the scorpion sting, swatted at the hallucinations flittering before his eyes. "Lady Cosette wants—"

Domo Khan ignored him. "A fine plan. That'll just give them even more of an excuse to slaughter us in our beds. Nothing like the murder of a golden prince to rouse the Houses to war."

"Fine, then we move him around until your Seat is secure."

"Just more opportunities to have him rescued. Honestly, did they teach you nothing about strategy at the Academy? Now take that knife away from his throat, or so help me—"

"Or what? You *need* me."

"Do I?" The domo crossed his arms over his chest. "Explain that to me."

"A lord or lady cannot succeed to a provincial Seat without an heir," she gloated. "I am the key to your ambitions."

"The world has already seen that your mother and I have no issue producing heirs. We'll just make another one."

The knife on Hiro's throat started to quiver. "M-Mother is old!" she protested.

"I'd like to hear you say that to her face. If she cannot bear any more children, then I'll take a concubine with her consent. Any offspring of that union would be seen as legitimate."

"But, Father, I am your *daughter*—"

"*Not anymore,*" he roared. "In fact, it was Lord Ishida's demand that I disown you in return for his continued support. I disown you, and the Seat is as good as mine."

"B-but you wouldn't. I am your flesh and blood!"

The domo regarded her coldly. "It's already done. Before I set sail this morning, I decreed it to the courts and sent messenger eagles to every Council Seat. You are no daughter of mine."

He snapped his fingers.

A blade sprouted from her right shoulder. Lakshmi howled, ripped away from him. Blood slung from her knife in a syrupy arc as the Tigers pounced.

In the confusion, Rufus launched himself at the door. Mayor Kapoor sprang from his seat, sloshing wine down the front of his clothes. "God's above, not *again*—"

The harbormaster shoved him aside and wheezed when Serrano

rammed a saber pommel into his stomach. The pirate elbowed him to the ground, pressed the point into the base of his skull.

Lakshmi gutted one of the Tigers. Heaved his body aside as she engaged the other five. Gore dangled from the man's open abdomen, draped the canaris with stinking coils. Shrieking something about snakes, the spy scrambled away from the corpse. A Tiger yanked him away before he could hurl out the window, put him to sleep in a choke-hold.

Crimson sprayed the floor as Lakshmi slashed low into a Tiger's inner thigh. She pivoted to cut at another's face when Hiro grabbed her ankle. It took the last of his strength just to tighten his fingers.

It was enough.

She glanced down in surprise, and the Tigers swarmed her. Her head snapped back as an elbow arced into her jaw. Someone ground her face into the rug as another clawed the knife from her grasp. Bound, gagged, she sat in the ruined shreds of her dress and glowered at her father.

"Take her to the brig," the domo ordered. "And bring Cosette's lapdog. Lord Ishida'll want to talk to *that* one."

CHAPTER 115

Lakshmi thrashed, kicking at anyone who came near.

The Tiger just absorbed the blow and tangled a clawed fist into her hair. Jabbing a dagger into her spleen, he marched her out the door.

Domo Nameer Khan stepped aside, ignoring her muffled obscenities with cool indifference. He turned to Amelia, pressing her knuckles against his forehead in the ancient gesture of respect. "My lady, you've earned the gratitude of my House. Should you need anything, just ask, and—"

"We need to get to Dhaka as soon as possible," she blurted.

His eyebrows lifted in surprise.

"Please."

"I'll have the ship prepared at once. We'll sail at your leisure." He bowed again and faced the mayor. "Should you need anything to help rebuild your city, let me know. The destruction looks substantial. Kolkata is a port city as well; we'll have much of what you might need."

Mayor Ashley Kapoor stood, smoothing his ruined waistcoat. "I greatly appreciate your offer to assist us, Domo Khan. I'll send an eagle after the assessment."

"Very good." He paused in the doorway. "And you, Prince Ishida.

Heal up. The army needs you when you're done with the Sanu. The fighting's gotten much worse. I'll take the liberty of telling your father you're alive."

Hiro just kept a hand pressed against the wound on his neck and grunted. He glanced at her. She looked away from the question in his seal brown eyes. "*Kale,*" she barked. "*Isen.*"

The boy appeared in the doorway. With a cry, he dropped the sack he'd been carrying and skidded to Hiro's side. The priest followed more slowly, tapping around the bodies with his staff.

Kale eased a pillow under Hiro's head as Isen fumbled around the table for a pitcher. After a sniff, he poured the water into a cup and dribbled it into Hiro's mouth. Kale peeled back the blanket with a hiss. Hiro's charred flesh was a bubbling swath of blisters, like eggs floating in tomato soup.

The silver dragon bellowed. Amelia clenched her hands into fists, wincing as her nails drew blood from her palms.

"Gods above," Mayor Kapoor breathed. "Please, excuse me." He turned his head aside and vomited. When he was finished, he sucked in a shuddering breath and dabbed his mouth with the handkerchief. "I'll order my palanquin delivered so you can get him to *The Wave Cutter* as painlessly as possible."

"Thank you." She tore her gaze from the ruined skin.

"Is there anything else I can do?"

"Yes." She fished two identical black books from the sack Kale had dropped. "These are Atival's ledgers. I had Kale liberate them during the... ceremony. They're the true account of what's been happening here."

The mayor wedged the books under his arm, glowering at the harbormaster. "They'll be an *informative* read, I'm sure. Now if you'll have your pirate friend remove that sword, I'll see to it that he's imprisoned and..."

The pirate didn't move.

"Come, come, man. I *assure* you he'll be in the dungeon with the most rats."

"Ashley, I'm afraid it is not that simple." Amelia bent and pulled the last item out of the muslin sack. Gagging, the mayor pressed the back of his hand against his mouth and turned his head away. She held out a frame of souvenirs tacked to navy felt with little silver pins.

The cavalier expression on Serrano's face hardened into wrath as he recognized one of the trophies. Its twin dangled in his ear.

He jabbed a question mark into the harbormaster's back. Atival yowled.

She nodded.

The raider plucked the ruby drop earring from the frame and waved it in front of Atival's face. "My *sister*. You *mine* now."

"Wait." Amelia rooted around in Atival's shirt and retrieved the blue opal. "Ciao, Aurelio."

Sword firmly pressed into Rufus's spine, Aurelio leaned over and kissed her briefly on the cheek. His green eyes twinkled. "Ciao, Eridani."

"W-where is he taking him?" Mayor Kapoor ducked his head out the doorway. "Um, *excuse* me. That's *my* prisoner?"

"Atival just needs to answer for his crimes against the Serrano family first. I'm sure Aurelio will return... whatever's left of him."

The mayor shuddered. "I don't even want to *think* about what they're going to do him."

"And you should expect the attacks on your port to stop now."

"Oh?" His eyes widened. "*Oh*. Well, *that's* a relief. Speaking of, I'd better go address the city. I-I need to apologize to them. This is as much my fault as it is Rufus's. I don't approve of your methods, my lady, but... thank you. If you'll excuse me, I'm going to go burn this disgusting display." The mayor held the trophy frame between thumb and forefinger as far away from his body as possible and followed after the sea gypsy.

Steeling herself, Amelia turned back to the group huddled on the floor. "H-how is he?"

"Alive." Isen dribbled more water into the prince's mouth. "*Barely*."

"They *tortured* him." Kale stroked his master's hair with shaking fingers. "He's got all these cuts full of pus—"

She didn't want to hear anymore. "Get him up."

"Amelia, he's too weak."

With an irritated shake of her head, she stormed over to them. She flung off the blanket and pressed her fingers against Hiro's cheek. Silver fire, unrefined and unfocused, surged into his skin. Gasping, his seal-brown eyes flared wide. "I did not go through all this trouble so you could die, Ishida. Now *get up.*"

Amelia looked away as he scraped himself off the floor. Spying the linen tablecloth, she yanked it free of the spoiling food and swept it around his shoulders. He shuddered at its touch. "Kale, Isen, get him out of here."

When they were gone, Amelia sagged to the rug. Sea serpents of green and amber silk dueled in the tempestuous waves. Red blotted out one of the serpent's tails. At the edge of the fringe was a pair of shackles, still sticky with peeled skin.

They'd chained him to the wall like an animal.

The silver dragon threw back its head, the scales on its chest brightening as molten fire bubbled up from the deep.

She let it out.

The silver fire sloughed off her skin like water off a seal's back. Cool to her touch, it incinerated everything. The rug and its sea serpents turned to ash; the discarded food on the table boiled away in acrid smoke; the furniture collapsed into smoldering embers. As the shackles dripped into pools of white metal, she stalked out of the room. She brought the conflagration with her, burning the harbormaster's house until it collapsed into the sea.

CHAPTER 116

THE WAVE CUTTER LIVED UP TO ITS NAME.

Its sharp keel and tiger figurehead sliced through the seas, and a strong wind kept the galleon's sails full to bursting. The purple canvas puffed out like voluminous storm clouds, propelling their ship forward at a relentless pace. They were actually gaining time.

Isen had abandoned the pitching of the main deck with a bottle of rum in his hand for the rocking of a corded hammock in the crew's quarters. She hadn't seen him since. Amelia clutched the taffrail of the quarterdeck, the blast of salty air doing little to lift her mood.

Hiro refused to see her.

When they'd loaded him on board that afternoon, he'd whispered only a few words to Domo Khan before beings whisked away into a private cabin. When Amelia made to follow, the domo blocked her path. "He wishes to be alone."

Only Kale and Master Abdullah were allowed in the cabin. There were even guards posted to ensure Hiro's wishes were met.

With Isen in a drunken slumber below decks and Hiro refusing her help, there was little for her to do. The crew of *The Wave Cutter* viewed her as something of a celebrity and refused to let her help in any way. Who else had the gall to persuade a pirate horde to hold a city for ransom for the sake of one man and actually *succeed?* They did everything for her, stumbling over themselves to fulfill her slightest whim. It was flattering and a little annoying.

Amelia watched the sailors scurry about their tasks; no one slacked off. There were ropes to coil, ropes to loosen, ropes to tighten, decks to swab, wood to polish, sails to mend, cannons to clean, grappling hooks to sharpen. Though they might not partake in piracy, they were definitely prepared for it.

At sunset, the door opened.

Amelia stumbled down the stairs. "How is he?"

"Sleeping," Kale said with a yawn. "He was able to pee earlier. The physician says that's good. Anyway, Domo Khan asked me to find you. Where's Isen, anyway?"

"Passed out below. At least he's not throwing up. Kale, I'm sorry I didn't ask straight away, but how are *you* doing?"

The boy gave her a tired smile. "We have Hiro back. So I'm good."

The guards moved away from the aftcastle door to let them pass. The hallway was poorly lit by the oil lamps at either end, and the air was stuffy with incense. The fragrant smoke streamed out from under the door of the cabin to the left.

Hiro.

She strained toward him. The guards on either side of the door stiffened warningly. Kale tugged on her hand, shaking his head. Light spilled into the hallway as the door on the right opened.

"*This* way, my lady," Domo Khan said, gesturing her inside.

The light of the setting sun bathed everything in an orange glow. The bed and its trunk were shoved up against the support wall beside the bookcase, and a cot with a thick pallet nestled against the sloping side of the hull. The chains that secured the books in their shelves twinkled like strands of gold.

Free of its charts and ledgers, the captain's table was crowded with food and drink. For two. Her stomach growled.

Kale released her hand. "I've got to get back now. Save some for me?"

"Kale, would you tell him I—"

"He doesn't want to see you." The boy's voice was kind, but it stung like bramble thorns.

She swallowed hard. "I know, but... just ask? Please?"

The boy nodded.

Domo Khan closed the door after him and gestured to the table. "You must be famished, my lady."

Amelia sat. "Yes, but I don't think you asked to see me just because it's dinnertime."

A thin smile stretched across his dusky lips. There was a lot of Lakshmi in his face, from his chocolate brown eyes to the sharp nose. He spooned some vegetable curry into a bowl for her. "Captain Salman and I have been questioning the prisoners."

"Prisoners? Last night Lakshmi was your daughter."

The domo shrugged. "I'm thankful the Academy gets its hands on her instead of my wife. Lakshmi might just live. Stripped of everything, of course, but she'll have her life. The Khans do not tolerate anyone besmirching the family name."

"You missed a drop of blood on your earlobe." She pointed. "Just there."

He wiped it away with the same concern as if it were a spot of gravy. "This compound has been supremely effective." He placed a vial of purplish liquid on the desk between them. "Turns out they'll tell you anything you want to know just to make the hallucinations stop. So... why does the former Lady of Jardin want your head on a spike?"

Amelia stopped swirling her spoon in her curry. "Hiro and I sort of deposed her?"

Domo Khan arched an eyebrow. "Remind me never to get on your bad side."

"I'm Sanu. I don't have a 'bad' side."

"But you have a vengeful side." He leaned across the table, eyes bright. "I've heard that Sanu are bridges, but I've never heard of your kind summoning silver—"

She pushed her food away. "I am not one of your prisoners to interrogate, Domo Khan."

"Of course not." He lifted his hands in submission. "I'm sending a company north to help the Councilary Army. With a woman as powerful as Cosette Bavaria sending her minions after you, allow them to escort you—"

"No." She forced a smile. "Thank you, but no. Speed is essential right now. Which is why Hiro must stay with you. He's too weak."

Domo Khan nodded. "I understand. He'll resist, you know."

"I know." Her words were soft. "But... it's for the best. For every-one." She stood suddenly. "Please excuse me."

He leaned across the table and picked up her bowl of uneaten curry. "I've had one of the officer's cabins prepared for you, my lady. I can show you, if you'd like."

When they were in the hallway, Amelia couldn't help herself. The guards shifted in front of the door. None of them were foolish enough to touch their weapons, but the warning was clear.

"What are your orders? Specifically?" she asked.

They eyed each other. "Not to let anyone enter but Domo Khan, Master Abdullah, and the boy."

"I just want to *look*."

They glanced over her head to their lord in the hallway. "My lady—"

"I am Amelia de Taru, Sanu Maitre. Lords and ladies *bow* before me. You think a *prince* can deny me entry anywhere? I am being respectful of your orders. I will not enter. I'll stay out here, I just want to see how my friend is."

The nearest guard wetted his lips, and shifted aside.

"Thank you." She wedged between them and tried the latch. The door opened just a crack.

Hiro was lying stark naked on his stomach on a wide bed, thick bandages encasing his wrists. Skin sloughed off his ruined back in ragged patches. Large sticks of incense smoldered on every available surface, the fragrant haze hanging in coils about the room.

The Sarabi physician painted a foul-smelling unguent along Hiro's tender skin as Kale sat near his master's head. His fingers plucked the silken strings of a guqin, playing a familiar melody. Amelia teased loose a thread of silver fire and wove it into the boy's voice.

Sleep softly now, the night's at peace
The wolf has fled, let crying cease—

Hiro's head snapped up. "*No.* Anything but her lullaby."

The silver thread snapped, dissipating into the night air.

"It's the only thing that gets you to sleep nowadays." The boy scowled. "She wouldn't stop to get you back, you know."

Hiro just turned his head away.

After a pregnant pause, Kale strummed the same song. But he didn't sing.

Biting her lower lip, she pulled the door shut until it clicked and turned away.

CHAPTER 117

ALONE IN THE CRAMPED SPACE OF THE OFFICER'S CABIN, AMELIA flopped onto the cot with a groan. All she wanted to do was put this day behind her but something jutting into her stomach was preventing it.

She rolled onto her side, stuck her hand into her sari, and found the offending object.

The druid's secret.

Ever since they'd left Akuma Cove, she'd never had a moment to herself. And their days had been so full of abductions and extortion that she'd almost forgotten about it.

Amelia scrambled to the end of her cot and thrust the object into the meager lamplight.

It was a hilt shaped like a lion's head: round-cut rubies for its eyes and a golden mane that flowed away from its face to form the grip. Its open maw formed a soundless roar. With a fingertip, she traced the gentle swells of its mane, felt the sharpness of its teeth, the smoothness of its ruby eyes.

Objects of power were said to hum with it, and this golden hilt purred.

But she'd been to the true Gate. There was no blade missing a hilt, nor a place to insert the hilt to act as a key. What was she supposed to do? Throw it at the Bodhi tree and hope something happened?

Shaking her head, she stuffed it back in her sari, her finger snagging on a wad of cloth. The length of blue silk slid through her fingers.

Hiro.

Every time she meant to give it back to him, something else got in the way. Like his capture. She'd wasted precious hours trying to rescue him instead of abandoning him to do her duty. Her duty that maintained the balance between Heaven and Earth. She had risked it all to get him back. With a huff, she balled up the cloth and stuffed it into her pocket.

Yueshan could fail because she couldn't give him up.

That night, she was plagued with dreams of fire. A silver dragon soared over the earth, incinerating everything with great belches of liquid flame. Stars plunged into the sea and mountains tore apart until the molten lifeblood of the earth bubbled free. But Hiro was safe, hand clasped in hers. Then his skin felt clammy, wet, as if he was sweating. When she looked, his flesh dissolved into mist. He slipped away from her, his bones plummeting into the fiery bowels of the torn earth. The roiling sky pulsed with thunder—

The incessant pounding on the door tore her from the nightmare. She kicked the sheets free of her legs and stumbled to the door.

Kale squinted with bloodshot eyes, his mane of auburn curls mussed with sleep. "You woke Hiro."

"I-I'm sorry."

The boy touched her cheek. "You've been crying." Kale pushed past her and crawled onto her cot. He fluffed the pillow, rolled onto his side, and started to snore.

Amelia got in next to him, drawing the blanket up to their necks. His presence was comforting, like a dog coming to lie at her feet because it knew she was frightened. In the dark, she smeared the tears away from her eyes. When they arrived in Dhaka, she knew what she had to do.

CHAPTER 118

"ARE YOU SURE YOU DON'T WANT AN ESCORT?"

Amelia shook her head and handed Isen her pack. "We'll be faster with just two. But thank you, Domo. For the hotel and… for everything else."

Domo Khan waved her gratitude aside. "It's nothing. You two spared my family great shame. Should you need anything in the future, just ask. If I am able, it shall be yours."

He gave her a leg up into the saddle. Isen encircled her waist with weak arms and leaned against her shoulder.

"Don't you dare throw up on me," she said.

"Trying," he groaned.

"*Pax vobis*, Domo." She wheeled Amai to the portside gangway.

"And just *where* do you think you're going?"

Amelia twisted around in the saddle.

Hiro emerged from the aftcastle, adjusting the fit of his black leather gloves. Instead of strapped across his back, his greatsword now hung from his left hip. He winced as the sea breeze flattened the silk shirt against his skin.

"Domo Khan—" she began.

"I told him if he could walk out of that room unassisted, I wouldn't detain him. And, well..." The domo shrugged.

She let out a frustrated sigh and tried to keep the annoyance off her face. Amai trotted down the pier, the warhorse and its master right on his heels.

Dhaka had a thriving night life. Tiny lanterns winked in the jacaranda trees, flickering shadows on the murals of sleek sailfish. There were tea houses that served the city's famous seven-color-teas and food carts that shaved portions off towers of mutton shawarma.

The horses' hooves clopped against the network of boardwalks spider-webbing across the tributary. They threaded through the stalls and up the nearest hill to the White Lotus Hotel. A rock garden speckled with junipers and lotus ponds encircled the establishment, and a wall of neatly stacked stones secured the little haven from the boisterous city.

From her window, Amelia clutched her flaxen cloak tighter around her shoulders as she watched the people enjoying the night market. Autumn was coming, and these last few days of summer had little heat to them.

A *thump* next door rattled the shutters. Loud voices followed soon after. The walls were thick enough to muffle most conversation, but not if the people were shouting.

Rolling her eyes, she shouldered open the door into the adjoining suite.

They were on opposite sides of a table, Hiro standing and Isen half out of his seat. Kale sat at the far end, trying to look small as he hunched over a plate of kebabs.

"They can hear you back in Vashti," Amelia hissed as she shut the door behind her. "What's going on in here?"

Isen pointed to the air somewhere beyond Hiro's right shoulder. "This *idiot* wants to take us up to Lhasa by way of the Bengal Sea instead of just continuing over land."

"If you thought the jungles of the druid's island were impassable, then you've *clearly* never been to eastern Tybet." Hiro started to cross his arms over his chest and stopped halfway, grimacing. "The sea's faster."

"Are you protesting because it'd mean more time on a ship?" Amelia asked.

"*No*," Isen scoffed. "I just don't see why we can't use our horses. Why do we have to risk autumn storms and drowning—"

"We don't know where the enemy is," Hiro argued. "They could've moved since the last time we were here, and we can't wait around for a report. The Bengal Sea—"

"Would take us to an impassable cliff a thousand feet tall. *Brilliant* plan."

Hiro ground his teeth. "We'll make port at Nagarze and continue via horse."

"And risk getting caught in a snow-storm from the Himalayas?"

"Hiro's right. We can go up the Bengal Sea," Amelia said. "I know of a shortcut. Trust me Isen, we'll be fine."

"*Fine?*" Isen snorted. "Amelia, I'm so *sick* of you defending him. We wouldn't be in this mess if you'd just left him behind in Vashti, and now we're risking *everything* on some ridiculous plan because he's got you wrapped around his little finger! Some pure vessel *you* are."

Silver flame crackled over her fists. She glared at Isen, wishing for once he had his sight so he could see the fury in her eyes.

"Get. Out," Hiro ordered.

Isen swallowed. "Amelia, I—"

She looked away from him.

"I said *get out*," Hiro snarled.

The blind priest snatched up his staff. Muffled curses trailed after him as he tapped his way down the stairs.

"Kale."

The boy dropped his skewer and chased after the priest.

This is the knife's edge.

Amelia smeared away the tears from her eyes. She'd already made her decision. "Hiro, I need to talk to you."

⚜

"I HAVE nothing to say to you." Hiro poured a glass of wine with a shaking hand. He drowned in its crimson depths so he wouldn't have to look at her.

"No?" She planted her hands on her hips. "I find that difficult to believe. I think I'm entitled to a 'thank you' or something for rescuing you."

"Thank you."

The Sanu crossed the room and slapped him across the face. Meant to startle, to capture his attention. "I don't believe you! Hiro, why are you *acting* like this?"

He glared into his wine. "So it's Hiro now, not Ishida?"

"How I address you is irrelevant—"

"*Itoko.*"

She scrubbed her face with her hands. "Rosara thought I was too attached to you, so she insisted I put some distance between us, okay? Referring to you in such a way helped me... compartmentalize. Between my duty and—"

"I get it." He finished his wine, poured another glass. "We done here?"

"No, we're not 'done here.' Why won't you *look* at me? I held a city *hostage* for you. Wasted time I didn't have to get you back. And then when I try to help you, you refuse to see me. You chose to suffer when I could've healed you." She slammed her hands on the table. "*Look at me.*"

"*I can't!*" He lurched to his feet, flung the bottle aside. Glass shattered; wine dribbled down the wall like spilled ink. He seized the Sanu by the arms and gave her a shake. "I can't look at you because I'm *ashamed.* I gave up in there, when Lakshmi had me dying of thirst and roasting away in the sun. And that drug... *I gave up.* Don't you understand? She *broke* me.

"I can't look at you because I don't deserve your pity. I'd vowed to protect you – a vow I'd already broken once – and I did it all over again. Don't you see I have no honor? I... I'm not worth saving."

Hiro released her with a slight push, slumped against the edge of the table. His head throbbed, his eyes burned. A watery sob choked in his throat.

The Sanu's hand was cool as she cupped his cheek, wiping the tears away with her thumb. He closed his eyes. She lifted his chin, pressed her forehead against his in the ancient gesture of connection.

Hiro slid his hand to the nape of her neck, wrapped the fingers of his burned hand in her caramel hair. Gentle heat bloomed where their foreheads touched. It seeped into his skin, lingered on his burns and cuts. Healed them. Relief flooded his limbs like a warm tide.

"Yes, you are," she whispered. "You *survived*, Hiro. You've nothing to be ashamed about. I know you. You would've broken free of her in time. I just couldn't wait that long."

"You shouldn't have waited at all. Yueshu's in three days. You should've left me behind."

She stiffened. "*Not a chance.* I was not going to leave you there."

"So that's why you unleashed a pirate horde?"

"Aggressive negotiations were in order. I thought you would've liked that."

Hiro snorted. She pulled away, his hand slipping from her hair. His fingers tightened on a caramel lock. "I never apologized for cutting your hair. Such beautiful hair." He released the silken length, cleared his throat. "I was insensitive and brutish and arrogant..."

"You can keep going." Her ocean-blue eyes twinkled.

He smirked, shook his head. "No, no. I think that was all of it."

Her smile was brief, faded into determination. Regret. She withdrew a lump of cloth from her pocket. Robin's egg blue, edged with silver cranes. Dropped it into his hands.

She found it? "I thought I'd lost this..." He stuffed the cloth into his shirt, over his heart.

"I kept meaning to give it back to you before this, but now..."

His eyes narrowed. "Now?"

She pursed her lips. "I'm going to Lhasa alone. After what Isen said, I doubt he wants to come with me. And you have an army to lead—"

"Sanu, that's the most *absurd—*"

She tossed her head irritably. "Why do you insist on calling me Sanu? My name is Amelia."

He swallowed. "I… I call you Sanu for the same reason you called me Ishida."

Her eyes widened. Bright as the ocean on a summer's day. Then she shrank away from him, wrapped her arms tight across her chest. "This was a mistake."

His heart faltered, roared in his ears. "Amelia—"

"Please… don't call me that. You can't protect me from myself, Hiro. Or you. That's why I must go to Lhasa alone."

"I can't let you—"

"We have no choice."

He was going to pass out. He clutched the edge of the table for support, forced himself to take a breath. "Duty."

She nodded miserably and rushed out of the room.

CHAPTER 119

Hiro beat his fists against the wall, rested his forehead against the cool plaster. His body throbbed, insistent. Urgent. He bolted from the room and into the night, heading for the one place where he could fix at least one thing wrong with him.

His feet found the Street of Red Lanterns without any trouble. No Dollhouses but a triple-story business with golden lights strung between the lanterns that boasted healthy and refined-looking girls. He pressed a doros into the madame's hand.

Her fingers snapped over the gold coin like a snare over a bird. Her prettiest ladies appeared, a flutter of pink chiffon and long legs. He chose one for her eyes, and she took his hand with a coy smile.

She led him into an empty room, leaned against the door until it clicked into place. "Alone at last." She splayed her fingers across his chest, lips pushed into an appreciative pout. "Gods above, I'm actually going to enjoy my work tonight."

The whore brushed the pink chiffon off her shoulders and guided his hand to a swell of toned flesh.

His fingers trembled. Heart thundered a competing staccato to the throbbing in his groin. He squeezed his eyes shut, clenched his pounding head. She had Calliope's height, Lakshmi's black hair, Azelie's elfin nose, Mercedes' curves, *her* eyes.

Lips on his neck, fingers tugging at his belt.

He retreated from the assault of women, backed away until his legs bumped into a couch and collapsed under him. They pounced as he fell, straddled his lap, and pushed full breasts into his face.

He swept the phantoms aside, tried to focus on the real woman in front of him. His hand glided from her hip up into her hair, clenched. Her lips left a wet mark on his neck as he tugged her head back. Even in his carnal haze he could tell something was wrong with her eyes. The cold blue of a winter sky, not the cerulean of the summer ocean. Not *hers* at all.

This wasn't her touch, her voice thickened with passion. This wasn't their bed, her hips grinding against his as her mouth trailed along his skin. There was no trace of jasmine, just incense to force this mirage—

"I can be whoever you want me to be." The whore's teeth nibbled on his ear as she thrust a hand between his legs. "Even *her*—"

Her touch was electric. He launched to his feet, spilling the whore onto the carpet.

Her wrong-colored eyes flashed resentfully. Then her mouth quirked up into a knowing smile, and she rolled onto her hands and knees. "Is that how you want it, big man?" She arched her back, glanced over a slim shoulder. "Rough?"

Hiro bolted out of the room. Ignored the madame's calls to see if there was anything else they could do to make his visit more pleasurable. He did not stop running until he was back in the rock garden of the White Lotus Hotel. Pushed through the juniper bushes and slumped against the wall. The stones were cold, yet they did nothing to quench the fire that still throbbed in his groin. If *she* wasn't the one to touch him, no one else would.

Facing the wall, he undid his trousers and spent himself against the stones. His carnal ache satiated, he staggered to one of the lotus ponds. He washed himself under the mocking glare of the gibbous moon. It was already tinged with orange. Yueshu was coming.

She's an idiot if she thinks she's going to Lhasa without me. He stuffed himself into his clothes, headed back to the room. *It doesn't matter what we said, she has to—*

"Sanu, open up." He pounded on her door. It swung open, unlocked. "We need to talk—"

His foot tripped over a lump on the floor. Hiro shot out a hand to grab the edge of the table he knew was there, but his hand never found it. He crashed onto the floor. Floundered around, bumped into furniture that'd been moved, stumbled to the window, and pushed open the shutters.

A bright lance of moonlight cleaved the gloom.

There'd been a fight. The upturned edge of the rug, scattered fragments of broken porcelain, blood. Someone had been looking for something, something he didn't find in her strewn belongings, something she hadn't hidden in the mattress or the pillows. The goose down of the murdered bedding covered everything in feathery snow. He followed the dark smear along the floorboards to the lump by the door.

Kale.

Hog-tied and gagged. A wound on his head bled down the side of his face. His hazel eyes were like chips of glass in the moonlight, bright. Frantic.

Hiro yanked the gag out of the boy's mouth, sliced through the ropes. Fingers probed the wound: shallow, beginning to clot. Recent. While he was out in the garden behind the juniper bushes. Clenching his jaw, he resolved to hate himself later. *"Which way?"*

"I don't know," the boy coughed. "They just left. Hiro—"

But he was already out the door.

She'd been taken. And so had Isen. The blind fool had probably been clubbed over the head and dragged along with her.

He ran into the hall, descended the stairs three at a time until he was in the lobby.

Kale thundered down the stairs. "Hiro, *wait.*"

The clerk was nowhere to be found; Hiro didn't waste any time looking for him. Wild, he ran out into the street. Searched for any sign, any hint of the direction they'd gone.

When he'd returned from the pleasure house, he'd come up from the southeast. He would've seen something if they'd come out the back of the hotel. Which meant they left through the front exit. North. There was nothing but mountains to the north – mountains would slow them down – but there were docks to the west of the hotel. Escaping by boat would be quicker.

The greatsword sang as it cleared its sheath, joined the rhythm of his feet pounding against the street. Kale chased after him.

Hiro pulled up short in the middle of a deserted intersection as something glinted in the cobbles ahead of him. Panting, he dropped down to one knee and plucked the gleaming object from the stones. It was a gold bead, finial-shaped, the same kind found on the Sanu's sari.

As he pocketed the bead, a muffled cry carried in from the west. Followed by a louder curse. Hiro sprang after them, slashing the night air with his sword.

"Wait, Hiro—"

He was not going to wait. He was going to kill them all.

The street emptied into a small square lined with squat merchant houses and lit by the glaring gibbous moon. An obelisk sprouted from its center, the engraving on its face hardly visible from years of weathering. An open palm with a blooming lily encircled by suns.

On the other side of the square, a dark mass shuffled around Isen and the Sanu. Herding. Black clothes, black cloths obscuring the lower halves of their faces, eyes lined with kohl.

The Shadow Army.

"Amelia!" His voice echoed loudly across the quiet square.

The drones stopped their scuffling. As one, they looked back at him.

Isen seized the momentary pause, grabbed the Sanu and shoved her forward. The mass rippled away from them like a stone dropped into a pond.

The Sanu flung out a hand, straining for him.

Thank the gods—

Isen dropped his staff, drew a knife from his sash. He wrenched the Sanu back a step and pressed the curved blade against her throat.

An opium sickle.

Hiro's world stopped. There was nothing. No thoughts, no pulse, no breath. Just the moonlight catching on the steel digging into the Sanu's skin.

Kale skidded to a halt by his side, doubled over as he caught his breath. "I've been *trying* to tell you," the boy panted. "Isen's the one who took her!"

CHAPTER 120

The night was silent.

The insects had ceased their droning hum, and the wind teasing the water by the docks dared not whisper between them. Overhead, the stars were just glittering pinpricks of light. Cold. Indifferent.

Hiro fought to breathe.

"The Shadow Army... you're with *them?*"

"More like they're with me." The priest's voice was calm, matter-of-fact. His head cocked in that birdlike way. "How's your head, Kale?"

Hiro grabbed the boy's collar as he lunged.

"You shoulda hit me harder!" Kale shouted.

"Apparently."

"Isen, *what* are you doing?" Hiro took a cautious step forward, eyes on the knife. Even from across the square he could see its vibrating glint as the priestess trembled. Pale, slick with sweat, caught in the throes of a panic attack.

"Stay where you are, Ishida."

With great care, Hiro sheathed his greatsword. He spread his hands out to his sides and continued to advance. One slow step at a time. Flexed his wrists until the knives hidden in his sleeves slunk into his palms. "Isen, let her go."

"Not a chance. I've worked too long, too hard, to see this opportunity snatched away. Lhasa will be *mine* this time."

"This time? Isen, you're a priest. You can go to Lhasa anytime you want. Let her go."

"Stop *moving*, Ishida." The blind priest wrenched the priestess's arm behind her back, settled the knife more firmly against her throat. Her whimper cut him more keenly than any blade.

Hiro clenched his jaw, stopped where he was. He'd crossed half of the square. Close enough.

Moonlight flashed on whirling steel.

Blood sprayed from Isen's neck. Snarling, his grip on the Şanu faltered as he clamped a hand against the wound. The second knife buried into his shoulder, and the priestess wrenched free.

Isen snatched a handful of her hair, gave it a vicious yank. Shrieking, the Sanu clawed at his hand. Ignoring the knife in his shoulder, he gave the Sanu another shake. Ordered her into submission.

Hiro skidded to a halt just a few yards away as Isen replaced the opium sickle across her throat. The wound on Isen's neck had already healed.

"That's close enough, Ishida. My, you're as troublesome as your bitch of a mother. It's starting to rub off on sweet Amelia here."

"How would you—"

"I know all about the great General Bethsaida Ishida," Isen snarled. "She'd decimated my troops for days. Then, *finally*, on the banks of the Hotun River, *I cut her down.*"

Hiro shook his head. "No. That's impossible."

"Is it? I remember every second of it. My greatest victory yet of my entire campaign: the fearsome Ishida Dragon, cut down by my sword and opening the Jewel of the East for the taking." The priest's mouth twisted into a bitter smile. "Only the thing they don't teach you in the history books is that with her dying breath, she called upon the name of the Crown Prince of Heaven. Not to save herself, not to save her family, but to intercede on behalf of Eurasia itself. And a call as selfless as that could not go unanswered.

"And *he* came. As the Guards engaged my army, we battled by the riverbank over her corpse. I was about to slay my first god when the tricky *hundan* pivoted. My sword lodged in his breastplate. When I yanked it free, the blast of light that exploded from his armor threw me into the river. When I woke days later, I was in the body of my twenty-five-year-old self. I've not aged a day since. I've been given a second chance to unite the provinces under one rule and bring them to paradise.

"But my chances lower if you continue to interfere. So it's come to this."

Isen rammed the sickle into her belly.

"*AMELIA!*"

The priestess screamed. She sagged against the priest, stared at the hilt protruding from her flesh with bulging eyes.

With a roar, Hiro drew his greatsword.

"Take another step and I pull the knife," Isen bellowed. "I'll find another way to claim Lhasa, and she'll bleed out in *minutes*. It'll be agony, Ishida. She won't survive. But let us go, unmolested, and the knife stays put until a surgeon stitches her back up. That's the choice, Ishida. Kill me or save the woman you love."

Seething, Hiro lowered his blade.

"I thought so. Now, Amelia, sweet girl—"

The priestess moaned a prayer in Latan. Kale strained forward, lips moving in a silent translation.

"That's *enough*."

The Sanu choked on a sob. Her shaking hands reached for the knife protruding from her belly.

"Uh-uh." Isen's hand slid around her abdomen like he was caressing their unborn child. "We don't want that knife wiggling free. I know what you're thinking. You'll sacrifice yourself so I won't gain access to Lhasa. It's not that simple, sweet girl. Yueshu, remember? Or do you want Earth to be forever separated from Heaven? That's not what your precious Crown Prince died for, is it?"

The priestess sobbed harder, secured the hilt with her hands.

"Good girl. Now off we go." He pulled the Sanu back a step. The drones swarmed, engulfing them in a sea of darkness. They made no sound as they left the square, smothered even the Sanu's whimpers.

Hiro trailed at a distance, heart in his throat.

At the end of the wharf, the drones piled into a sloop like plague rats. The sail unfurled, and a traitorous wind filled it to bursting.

Hiro sprinted to the very edge. He caught the piling with one hand to prevent him from pitching over and strained out over the water. "I'll find you, Amelia! *I'll find you!*"

He shouted until his throat was hoarse.

The sloop rounded a bend into the open sea, disappeared.

Hiro sank to his knees. He beat his hands against the salt-crusted planks until they were numb.

Kale moved silently up to his side, curled a hand over his shoulder. "Those that wear the golden crown light the path through Heaven's Wall."

He shook his head, not understanding.

Kale squeezed Hiro's shoulder reassuringly. "I know where we need to go."

CHAPTER 121

AMELIA DIDN'T STRUGGLE AS THE MAN IN BLACK WITH THE EMPTY, soulless eyes undid the ropes tying her wrists together. He freed her with mechanical efficiency, clamped a hand on each shoulder, and hauled her to her feet.

The man was silent, and Amelia didn't waste her breath trying to talk to him. She'd screamed and pleaded herself hoarse last night, but no one came. The crew ignored her, Hiro couldn't help her, and the silver dragon was gone.

Gone.

Not curled into a coil with a head hidden under its wing. Not reduced to a smoldering ember. Just *gone.*

Pale silver light, empty of life, was all that remained in its place.

Remember the water.

She pressed a hand against her chest, willing the fire to return, until the man in black yanked her outside.

Purple clouds with pink underbellies streaked the pale blue sky. The night peeled away from dawn, the stars winking out of existence as the sun crept over the horizon. She was not granted any time to perform the Dance of the Morning – not that she had expected any – and was herded up the stairs to the quarterdeck. The man in black pushed her into a chair and shoved her snuggly against the table. The teacups rattled in their saucers. A long-fingered hand reached out to steady them.

Sitting across from her was Isen.

"Good morning." He said it quietly, like he didn't want to startle her.

Amelia ripped out of her chair.

He shot out a hand, snatching her wrist. His face hardened into granite for only an instant before smoothing into his self-deprecating smile. It was like putting on a mask. Amelia was frozen half out of her seat. She didn't know whether he was going to break her arm or release her.

"You have nothing to fear, sweet girl," he assured her. "Please, sit down."

"*What did you do to me?* I can't..." She flexed her fingers, but no silver fire sprang from their tips. "It won't..."

Her chest heaved as she fought for breath. A cold sweat washed over her skin. She braced her free hand against the table and squeezed her eyes shut. *The panic, it's coming again—*

"Calm down, Amelia. Taijitu. What can be unleashed can be confined once again. The process is irreversible, I'm afraid. I couldn't very well have you burning me to a crisp, could I?"

She wrenched her arm, but he held her fast. His grip was impossibly strong. Even if she wanted to run, a ship full of his men would seize before she'd gone three steps. Trembling, she eased herself back into her chair, and he released her wrist.

His priestly white robes and turquoise sash were gone, replaced by a black shirt and a form-fitting tunic of silk brocade. Swirling designs in cyan and violet rippled over his torso. A new strip of black linen covered his eyes, and his hair framed his face in curled waves of gold.

He looked devastatingly handsome.

Amelia wanted to lunge across the table and throttle him.

She hadn't seen him since *that* night.

Delirious, she'd caught only fragments since the square. The rocking of waves against the hull of the sloop; soulless eyes glowing like moonstones in the torchlight; ropes cutting into her shoulders as she was hoisted on board; Isen yanking apart the folds of his robes to extract the pendant he'd kept hidden there all this time.

In one swift motion, he plucked the sickle from her gut and pressed the knotwork amulet against her wound. She threw her head back with a howl. White light burst from the amulet, searing the backs of her eyelids.

The pain had been excruciating. When she'd woken sometime during the night, she'd discovered her wound was completely healed. A scar, thin and white, was all that remained.

Amelia pressed a hand against her abdomen, forcing the phantom pain aside.

Isen gestured to the table. "Please, eat."

There was yogurt spiced with cardamom, boiled eggs, fruit, cheese, and a stack of griddle-fried flatbread still steaming. She reached for an egg.

Isen hefted the teapot and poured an amber stream into her cup.

It was jasmine. Her favorite.

She'd traveled with Kogusanji, the Tybetan Monster, for months without once suspecting he was more than a priest. Not once in the million moments they'd shared. He knew her ways intimately, and she was just beginning to understand that she knew nothing about him. Even his sea-sickeness has been a lie.

"I'm glad you've chosen to be sensible instead of trying to starve yourself. You need to regain your strength."

She couldn't look at him. *"Break bread with enemies and friends alike, for all are Men under Heaven."*

"That's what I like about you, Amelia. You're practical."

"And you're a monster, Isen. Or should I even call you that?"

"I've become rather fond of that name now."

Amelia noticed that he picked up a wedge of cheese as if he knew exactly where it was. Before, his fingers had always fluttered in the air until they landed like little birds on whatever he'd been searching for. "Are you even blind?"

He lifted one side of the black linen, revealing a ghastly mangled and burned eye socket. "Quite. But I can still see. Marvelous, isn't it?"

"Does it have anything to do with the amulet you wear around your neck?"

The corner of Isen's mouth quirked up into a smile. "Do you want to see it?"

He slowly undid the buttons at his collar and pulled his shirt apart. The amulet dangled on the end of a chain, nestling in the valley of his chest. The knotwork design made her head hurt. The myriad threads of golden wire seemed to writhe, like a storm cloud trapped in a bottle. "I'm sure you'll recognize it. It's the same design of the silver inlay on the Raion Chest."

Amelia ventured another look.

The Tybetan Monster was in possession of the centerpiece of the Crown Prince's breastplate. It could heal with a touch and give sight to the blind. What other power this relic possessed was inconceivable.

She stole a final glance at the amulet as Isen rearranged his clothes. It bulged only slightly, as it if was melded against his skin. Becoming as much as a part of him as—

"That's a piece of the Gate," she breathed.

Isen's fingers paused over one mother-of-pearl button. "*Very* good, Amelia."

"Is that how you're controlling all those men?"

He finished buttoning his shirt with a shrug. "Well, most of them. Some are not enthralled."

"It's why they're acting like drones in a hive. *You have their souls.*"

"Practical *and* clever. I'll admit, I didn't think you'd figure it out. It does seem rather far-fetched."

"But... how?"

He leaned forward with a conspiratorial grin on his face. "This amulet is part of the breastplate of the Crown Prince of Heaven. When he sacrificed himself to create the Gate, it was forged from his armor as a sign of peace. When he took human form to engage me by the Hotun River, he was in his armor – the Gate – and it had become vulnerable.

"When my sword pried out the amulet, the Gate broke, but *this* still worked. How do you think the souls have been passing into paradise since then? *Through this amulet.* The soul energy gives it power." He smoothed a hand over the bulge beneath his shirt. "I've worn it so long I can even sense it when it's not around my neck. It... hums.

"The souls of my men are tied to it, fueling it, freely given in exchange for paradise when I break down the Gate. None of these souls will be refused entry and forced to be reincarnated. It's a one-way trip to Heaven. All they needed to do was submit their bodies for my purpose."

"You've turned them into slaves."

"They're better than slaves," he scoffed. "Slaves you have to beat into submission and constantly threaten with death to quell any notion of rebellion. With these men, I merely think it and they do it."

She shook her head. "Isen, you've *murdered* them."

The Tybetan Monster leaned back in his chair with a dismissive snort. "Hardly. I've set them free. At least, they will be after I destroy the Gate. Well, after *you* destroy the Gate."

"I'll do no such thing—"

"Oh yes you will. You're not *pure.* Your heart cannot have two masters. And what do you see in that brute, anyway? *I* am your intellectual equal, and I know you think I'm handsome. We were friends, once. How is it you didn't lose your heart to *me?*"

She looked away angrily. "I don't know what you're talking about."

Isen laughed. "I *know* you, Amelia. Even now you're trying to convince yourself otherwise. You'll do it too, because you can't accept that you, *a Sanu*, have fallen so far from grace. You'll perform Yueshu just to prove me wrong. You think your little dance will mend the Gate and reseal it.

"But not only will you destroy the Gate, you'll tear a rip in the space between realms. My army will walk right into Heaven. You, sweet girl, are the unwitting harbinger of the greatest destruction our world has ever seen. The apocalypse. Who knew you'd be so beautiful?"

CHAPTER 122

"Why did you do it?" Amelia whispered. "Any of it?"

Her hands on either side of her plate clutched fistfuls of the table-cloth. Below her, the waves rocked the ship as it sailed along the coast; overhead, the seagulls cawed their undulating cry. She felt and heard none of it. Her focus had narrowed only on his voice. His beautiful, golden voice.

"I was born *harijan* in Balasore. A 'child of the gods.' A person so low only the gods could be bothered to look after my welfare. But they didn't. I didn't care so much until some opium domo who likes little girls abducted my eight-year-old sister. He took her when I was out diving for aeris to feed us. He raped her to death, Amelia, and no one lifted a finger.

"Sanctisum says that we are caught in a cycle of reincarnation until we choose the narrow path, accept the sacrifice of the Crown Prince. So that domo has done those despicable things in countless lifetimes, to countless versions of my little sister—"

She shook her head violently. "That's not how it—"

He made a cutting motion with his hand, silencing her. "Tell me, what kind of benevolent god can allow an innocent to live in the slums, hoping for a better life with each aeris her brother brings from the ocean, only to be raped and murdered in every single one of them? All while the wicked are reborn into power again and again?

"Rectifying this infernal loop is my life's pursuit, Amelia. What *wouldn't* I do?"

"But… you *can't*." She bit her lip, refusing to cry. A few tears slipped down her cheeks anyway.

Isen leaned forward, drawing a handkerchief from his pocket. Gently, he dabbed the tears away. Amelia fought to remain still; the tender gesture sickened her. When he was done, he folded the cloth into a square and placed it by her hand. "Yes, I can," he told her gently. "And I will. I was hoping you'd join me, Amelia."

"How can you ask that of me?" she whispered.

"Because I love you."

She snorted. "You *stabbed* me. Just yesterday. People just don't go about stabbing others as a profession of undying love. You don't know the *meaning*—"

"If I didn't love you, I would've killed you long ago. That *had* been the original plan." He leaned back in his chair. "I thought myself a genius for infiltrating the temple at Bastogne to learn more about how I'd failed the first time. That's where I learned about the Raion Chest. The ability to summon the Crown Prince of Heaven by his true name. And with his throat under my knife, I would ransom him for Heaven. The Most Holies might not care about us, but they love their son. And the only ones who could interfere were the peace-loving Sanu and their rituals."

"So you sent that sorcerer to kill us."

"But you survived. Tareq told me one had escaped, so I waited at that crossroad to meet the Sanu who could thwart demons. I even let that skein scar my face to sell the story. And with the Raion Chest destroyed, I needed you. I needed your failure. So I called off the hunt."

"But the erebus—"

Isen winced. "Tareq was out of line. And he paid for it. He is *manabudh* now."

Amelia crossed her arms over her chest. "I'm not sorry. And love is not using someone for personal gain, by the way."

"You're right. But then Ishida came into our lives, and I understood what you meant to me. I suppose I always knew, I just was never aware of it until then." He let out a long sigh. "But I guess it was for the best. You needed to be *tainted* for Yueshu to be a failure, and my attempts at subtle seduction were being ignored. He cracked you like an egg."

"Jealous?"

"Of course. I want what I want. And the son of my most hated rival was stealing you away from me."

"I suppose you tried to kill Hiro, too?"

"Several times. The wasteland bandits, Tareq's men... it never seemed to take. And never directly, you understand. I couldn't have him or you suspecting me. It was subtle, using his own drive to return home against him. He never would've risked the Wasteland Fork without my nudge."

"And Kale?"

"No. I'm rather fond of the boy, actually."

"So just Hiro and me."

"Like I said: I'm very sorry."

"You must be out of your mind to think that I, a *Sanu*, could ever be with a man, much less a man who up until a few months ago was set on *murdering* me!"

"Perhaps you'll change your mind when the Gate's destroyed and you're no longer bound by a Sanu's laws. There'll be no need for them then."

"How can you claim to love me, yet are set against everything I believe in?"

"A man might love a whore but hate her profession."

Speechless, she just stared at him for a long moment. "Isen, you're insane."

He chuckled once. "Funny how the line between insanity and enlightenment is such a fine one. You don't seem to understand that it's out of the love I have for my fellow man that I intend to bring down the Gate. That way all can enjoy paradise. Like we were created to."

"There's a reason Heaven and Earth were divided. Mortals chose greed. You think the Gate was made to prevent *us* from entering Heaven? Have you ever thought that the Gate was meant to protect *us* from their wrath?"

"So the Most Holies are wrathful? I couldn't ask for a better reason to overthrow them."

"You'd be wrathful too, if your creation rose up against you. And we're still offered a way out of this endless cycle—"

"Oh, it's not endless, Amelia. I've cheated death, remember? I was afforded a glimpse of my lifeline, and I saw each reincarnation strung upon it like a pearl on a necklace. But that necklace has an end, Amelia, and mine is coming. Apparently reincarnation has an expiration date, too.

"Which is why I must act. To save myself, and to save the thousands if not millions of others who don't know their time is up. I'm saving *innocents*, Amelia, not just myself. My work will be undone with my death, so I *must* march on Heaven."

She shook her head vehemently. "You'll just taint it. It won't be pure—"

"Feh. There's nothing *pure* about Heaven. Gods above, the Crown Prince wields a *sword*—"

"To protect those he loves."

"Protect them from *what*? The citizens of Heaven only know love and peace, remember?"

"There are more realms than just Heaven, and there is evil in them. I'm looking at it right now."

Isen sighed and picked up a grape. "I'm not evil, Amelia."

"Debatable."

He plopped the grape into his mouth and rapped his knuckles on the table.

A thrall seized her arms and wrenched them behind her back.

Amelia thrashed, but the thrall held her fast. "Let. Me. *Go*."

Isen slipped his hand below the table and drew something from his lap. He placed the Raion Chest on his plate.

"*No!*" Amelia kicked away from the table, toppling backward. The thrall collapsed against the deck, stunned, pinned under her chair. She stumbled away from his pawing hands and sprinted for the taffrail. She could swim. She had no idea where she was in the ocean, but she could swim—

Hands plucked her from the air and yanked her off the railing. They dragged her, screeching, back to the table.

"No, Isen, *please—*"

"Shh, sweet girl." He swept the hair out of her face and trailed his fingers down her neck. She wrenched away, but his fingers only tightened in the V of her collar. "I don't want to do this like some sort of animal, Amelia, but I will rip your clothes off if I have to. If I've learned anything, it's to have multiple contingency plans. Now that the Raion Chest is back in my possession, I'd be a fool not to open it. You might not have to perform Yueshu after all."

Tears stung her eyes. "Don't do it, Isen. *Please*, if you love me at all, don't do this."

"That's exactly why I'm doing this."

He pulled her tunic down until the tops of her breasts were exposed. His sightless gaze lingered for only a heartbeat, just long enough for his breath to hitch. The chest hovered over her skin. He laid the silver inlay against her tattoo just as he pressed his mouth against hers. His lips were gentle, deceptively sweet.

The golden lily flared, and the hidden tumbler clicked into place. A breath of cool air puffed against her skin.

She spat him away.

Undeterred, Isen leaned forward and kissed her forehead. "Thank you, sweet girl. Now, do you want to know the most powerful name in all creation?"

He held the chest off to the side so they both could see. The knotwork design unraveled into myriad threads of quicksilver and soaked in the rosewood lid. They dripped into a pool at the bottom of the box, writhing like a nest of snakes. With a muted flash, they condensed, hardening into a name.

Kiran.

Isen clutched the box to his chest. *"Finally.* You will not escape me—"

The silver flashed again.

He frowned, peering into the box. "Arjun? No, wait, it's... Ibrahim? Phil? *What is this?"*

Amelia began to laugh as the chest continued to flash. It was just supposed to be a giggle of disbelief, but the laughter grew into something hysterical. "Did you think you could force a Sanu to open it under duress without consequence?" She laughed even harder, giddy with relief.

Isen snapped the lid shut. The silver threaded itself into the knotwork design, and the chest sealed with a click. *"Fix this."*

"Fix a *relic?"* she tittered. "How's that been going for me so far? That chest is *useless* now."

With a screech, the Tybetan Monster threw the Raion Chest over the side. The silver inlay caught the sun in one last piercing lance of light and disappeared beneath the waves.

Amelia doubled over, howling with laughter.

Isen silenced her with a backhand that slung an arc of red from her lip.

"Don't crow yet." He pinched her cheeks hard between thumb and fingers. "I still have *you,* remember?"

CHAPTER 123

AMELIA WAITED UNTIL SHE HEARD THE KEY SCRAPE IN THE LOCK AND the footfalls of the thrall recede into silence before she breathed. She gulped in a shuddering breath and bolted for the bed. They hadn't bound her wrists this time. Her back to the door, she slid her hands down her sari until they mounded over the hidden lion hilt. It purred under her hands.

He hadn't found it.

He must've seen the bulge of the Raion Chest in her pocket when he'd hauled her, delirious, onto the ship. Had Isen peeled apart her clothes to put his amulet against her bare flesh, he would've discovered the hilt. And then he'd have two pieces of the Gate.

The horror of that night was still fresh in her mind.

After she'd left Hiro's room, she'd sought solace in the rock garden. Sprawling junipers and clumps of shivering bamboo shone silvery-green in the moonlight. Koi slipped between the roots of the lotus flowers, rising to the surface at her shadow. Their gaping mouths churned the water as they pleaded for food.

Just like the ones on Mount Taru.

Tears springing to her eyes, she splashed the water. The fish scattered, taking the memories of her dead sisters with them. One family lost. Another forbidden.

Heartsick, she returned to her room to gather her things. She couldn't stay a moment longer. Pushing open the door, she was greeted with the sound of tearing fabric.

Kale – trussed up like a fertility festival pig all ready for roasting – muffled a warning behind his gag. Behind him, Isen ripped apart her bed and pillow with a curved knife that looked vaguely familiar.

An opium sickle.

Feathers floated in the air like dandelion fluff, covering everything in a powdery snow. The contents of her pack were strewn across the table. Clearly he hadn't found what he was looking for and assumed she'd hidden it in the bedding.

"*ISEN!*"

The priest whipped around, his sickle glinting in the candlelight.

She shook her head in disbelief. "What are you—"

I'm not seeing this. This has to be a mistake. Not Isen—

Faster than she could blink, he lunged forward and grabbed Kale by the hair, pressing the curved knife against the boy's throat.

Silver fire snapped over her fists. "Let him go!"

"Cage that creature, or so help me I'll slit his throat."

Squirming, Kale muffled an angry protest.

Isen silenced him with a vicious shake. "Do it *now*, Amelia."

The silver fire snuffed out.

"What did the druid give you?"

"It's n-nothing, just a lump of—"

"*Show it to me.*"

Amelia stuck her hand into her pocket. Her fingers slid past the Raion Chest and curled over the gemstone. She hestitated, suddenly loath to give up the only momento she had of a father she'd never known.

Her fingers tightened. Her real father lay buried under the roots of the sacred peach tree on Mount Taru. She withdrew the lump and tossed it over.

Isen caught it midair, as if he could see it coming. The gemstone flared in his palm. "Do you have any idea what this is?"

She shook her head. "Garnet?" Her tattoo blazed against her flesh, hot as a branding iron.

"Phoenix Tear quartz. It can heal anything." He stuffed the gemstone into his robes. "You have no idea the treasure you held."

"Isen, just let Kale go—"

"Did he give you anything else? *Did he?*"

"No." She forced herself to remain still as the golden lily burned her skin again.

"*I don't believe you!*"

"Isen, *please,* why are you doing this?"

He knocked Kale hard in the back of the head, grabbed her by the arm, and jabbed the sickle into the small of her back. "Don't even try it, Amelia. I'll sheath this knife into your flesh before you can burn me. And then Yueshu will fail."

"You'll die too, Isen. The apocalypse—"

"I have an exit strategy already in place, sweet girl. Now *move.*"

And he had taken her into the night.

CHAPTER 124

"GODS ABOVE," HIRO WHISPERED.

Stretched across the sea were hundreds of langskip warships. Black hulls, red sails, the bleached skulls of their enemies lashed to the gunwales. Twenty oars on each side helped propel the warships across the Bengal Sea. One by one they entered the narrow channel east of the plateau, their boats narrow enough and shallow enough to maneuver the waters. Maut – Death, in the native tongue – was a voracious spur of the Brahma Rush that sliced through the land like a knife and came closer to Lhasa than any other waterway. There was only one people whose warriors were fearless enough to dare its waters.

Baltic Raiders.

Hiro yanked on the mainsheet, cut their little sailboat to the west and out of sight. Kale hung onto a rope at the mast, mouth agape.

The Sanu had been taken from them last night, and it had gone against every instinct not to pursue her. Kale was adamant they abandon the horses and sail north up the Bengal Sea. They'd left his mare and the Sarabi stallion with Domo Khan's resupply caravan, acquired a trimaran, and had been sailing ever since.

The Gull practically flew over the water.

"I thought Baltic Raiders never went too far from the Scandinavian Archipelago." Kale kept his voice low, as if the wind would carry it to the langskips. "What are they *doing* here?"

"Sjávar Ulfur."

"'*Sea Wolf?*'"

"That's what they called me."

He'd left none alive in Red Ellick's clan. He'd been thorough. He'd been sure. But news of their decimation had reached the ears of the other clans, and they'd lived in fear of Biscay Bay ever since. But now Isen had lured them away from their traditional hunting grounds with Hiro's identity. The man who slew the infamous Sjávar Ulfur would be a legend.

"They're so many. Do you think they'll all make it up the Maut?"

"They'll try. What I'm most worried about is getting to the cliff unseen, and once we're there, scaling it."

"Amelia wouldn't have told us to come here unless she was sure."

Ever the optimist.

Isen had betrayed them. The Sanu had been kidnapped. The Shadow Army pinched Lhasa from two sides and flooded into his homeland. He teetered on the knife's edge of despair, the boy's fortitude the only thing steadying his balance.

"How much longer?" Kale asked.

"We'll get there by nightfall."

"Good, then—"

"We're not going to scale a thousand-foot cliff by moonlight," Hiro interrupted firmly. "We'll start in the morning."

"But—"

"We're no use to her if we're dead, Kale."

The boy huffed out a sigh. "Fine. But won't they see us?"

"I doubt it. The mouth of the channel is farther down the coast. They'd only see us with a spyglass, and only if they had reason to look."

Hiro tightened the mainsheet, propelled them ever onwards across the sea to the Chehara Cliff. Centuries ago the white expanse of rock had been known as Heaven's Wall. The only known access point to the Lhasa Plateau before roads were cut in. Most of those who dared to scale it lost their footing and fell to their deaths; those who succeeded created a place dedicated to peace on top of the bones of an ancient city. Often shrouded in clouds, it became known as the sole place where Heaven touched Earth.

It took all of his willpower to follow his own words. He wanted to throw himself at that cliff, race to the top and cut a bloody path through the Shadow Army. Reclaim *her*. Instead, he threw the anchor over the side and watched the Baltic Raiders disappear into the Maut.

With the dawn, the cliff was a blinding white. Hiro shaded his eyes. "So *how* are we supposed to do this?"

"She said 'those that wear the golden crown light the path through Heaven's Wall.' We just need to find – There!" The boy's hand shot out as he pointed to a yellowish smudge near the base of the cliff.

It was moving.

Seconds later, another yellowish smudge launched itself from the sea. Followed by another and another. Then by hundreds.

"Those are crown gannets. They have golden heads," Kale shouted above the wind. "Get us closer."

Hiro was already tightening up the sail. The wind skipped them over the white-capped waves, rushed them headlong toward the cliff. As they neared, Hiro slackened the line, let the wind escape. The tide had them now. *The Gull* soared toward the rock.

The water erupted as scores of the giant seabirds sprouted from the water, gray beaks full of fish. They landed on a ledge not too far above the crashing waves. If they jumped for it, they could make it.

Probably.

CHAPTER 125

THE BOAT SPUN SIDEWAYS, CAUGHT IN THE GRIP OF A WAVE. HIRO grabbed Kale by the collar and hurled him from the boat. The boy landed with a grunt among the agitated seabirds. Squawking, they flared their black-tipped wings and hopped out the way. Hiro hit the ledge with his chest. His hands scrabbled against the rock, looking for purchase.

Their trimaran bashed against the rocks below him, the waves breaking it into smaller and smaller pieces like a child shredding tissue paper into confetti. Kale grabbed his arm, helped get his hand onto a knot of rock.

Hiro fought his way onto the ledge, the waves crashing just below his feet. Rolling onto his back, he took a moment to breathe.

The smell was vile.

Larger than albatrosses, the crown gannets left even larger piles of sticky white droppings. The odorous remnants of their fishy meals would've knocked him off his feet if he wasn't already on his back.

Hiro gagged, forced himself to stand. The crown gannet nearest to him lowered its golden head, hissed. He stomped his boot. "*Shoo.*"

The bird squawked and waddled away.

Hiro eased onto his feet, wiped the grit from his hands. "I guess we just follow him."

"*He's* a girl."

Rolling his eyes, he produced a rope from the boy's pack and secured it around their waists. Followed the birds. They went slow, Kale in the lead and gently scooting around the gannets. Hiro made them move.

The gannets nested on a series of switchbacks and crumbled ledges. Scree skittered underfoot, and bird droppings alone kept the rock spackled together. Kale scrambled up the cliff as nimbly as a mountain goat; Hiro made sure every foothold and handhold was secure before shifting his weight. There was nothing but the white stone before him, the blue sky above, the churning sea below.

Sweat dribbled into his eyes. Stung. He shook the hair out of his face, fought against the memories of the crucible-like room where Lakshmi had held him captive.

They paused on the wider ledges only to drink, and the water went fast. Hiro plucked the waterskin from Kale's greedy lips and strapped it back to his thigh. Motioned with a hand for the boy to get going.

The rock crumbled into sand beneath the boy's foot. Kale let out a strangled cry as he vanished through the hole.

Hiro snatched the rope, cursed as it bit into his palms. Gritting his teeth, he gave the rope a mighty jerk. Halted the boy's fall even as his own feet skidded forward a few inches in the dust.

Wrapping the rope securely around his forearm, Hiro ventured a look over the side. "Kale?"

The boy clung to the rope, eyes wide and face as white as the rock face.

Hiro sucked in a shuddering breath. "Just stay still."

Each foot of rope he coiled beside him sapped his already dwindling energy. Kale scrambled onto the other side of the hole, clung to the cliff like a spider. Hiro stomped along the hole's edge, allowed the treacherous rock to fall away without claiming another victim. The gannets below shrieked at the pebbly assault.

The birds were just as thickly settled up here as they were down by the waves. The endless jabbering and whistling and squawking almost drove him mad. He forced himself to drown out the cacophony, focused on putting one foot in front of the other.

The Chehara Cliff was pitiless. The ease of switchbacks disappeared into suspended ledges. Hiro slumped against the rock while Kale scaled the cliff to the next ledge, blinked back the exhaustion. He dug his foot into a crevice and lunged for a handhold. His fingers caught the lip of the rock, the rough edge biting into his palms. The grit caked the sweat of his hand into sludge. Started to slip.

He braced his foot against the cliff face, scrambled for a handhold. The rock against his chest shifted, crumbled away.

The boy jerked forward. *"Hiro!"*

CHAPTER 126

THE ROCK FELL AWAY.

There was a moment when he felt weightless. Nothing but the hot air swallowing him whole.

Then his hand caught a shallow lip. His fingers clenched. Sank into the stone like a hawk's talons into rodent flesh. The nails of three fingers tore free, and blood gushed from his slashed palm.

Hiro grabbed the lip with his other hand, scraped his boots against the cliff face until they found purchase. A foothold and a toehold. Good enough.

Breath gusting against the rock, he risked an upward glance.

There was a jut of stone large enough to curl his hand around. And a ledge not too far above the handhold. He'd just have to jump.

He shifted his grip, wiped his bloody hand on his greatcoat. The jostling freed the pebbles under his boot, slid his foot off its hold.

Hiro leapt into the air.

BLOOD SPLATTERED AGAINST WHITE STONE.

It dripped freely from his torn hands. Made an ugly trail on the otherwise pristine bricks.

Kale tugged on his sleeve, pointed to a tiny fountain nestled in an alcove. A fish-shaped spout bubbled water into a basin full of little black-and-blue striped minnows.

Gingerly, Hiro lowered his hands into the water. It was eerie to feel their silken bodies bumping against his fingers, whispering over this skin. Their tiny mouths cleaned the debris out of his wounds, nibbled the dead flesh away. One fish even cleaned the grit out of the crevices of his signet ring.

It'd been an easy walk through the orchards after they'd reached the top of the cliff. There wasn't any time to rest. Kale gathered the last of the summer lychees as they trudged to the city, alternatively storing them in his shirt and ripping through the prickly red skins with nimble fingers. They'd passed through the seaward moon gate unmolested – what were two sentries armed only with horns going to do? – and headed for the golden dome.

Hiro wiggled his fingers, alerted the fish he was done. They were only one of the marvels Lhasa had to offer. Mother had told him so many stories of this place: the sibyl and her sibylline, the catacombs, the cleaner minnows, the temple's doors that if closed could never be forced open.

There was a peace here that gnawed at his purpose, threatened to distract him with the quiet warbling of tropical birds and bubbling fountains. Even the air – warm with the scent of sea roses – dulled his senses.

The horns were silent, the city's inhabitants performing their everyday routines with oblivious tranquility. The Shadow Army was nowhere in sight.

But it would be, and soon.

He shook his head clear of the haze, clenched his hands. Let the pain narrow his focus.

Amelia.

The temple doors were open. Wincing, he grabbed one of the iron rings and rammed it against the wood repeatedly. He wasn't interested in squandering what precious time they had left by hunting down a clergy member.

"Yes?" A young priestess hurried up to the door, leaned against the red cedar as she caught her breath. "The doors *are* open now, you *can* come in—"

"I am Prince Hiro Ishida, son of Bethany Cavill, and I must speak to the High Sister immediately."

"*The* Bethany Cavill?" The priestess looked him up and down. "Please, follow me."

She kept glancing over her shoulder as she ushered them through the temple. Like they'd get lost. Or she didn't believe she was escorting the son of *the* Bethany Cavill.

Hiro ignored her. Gazed up at the statues that towered over them instead. Shafts of sunlight bathed the white stone in a honeyed glow.

Kale slowed to a halt in front of Lady Bosetsanu, mouth open as he craned his head back to look into her gentle face. The light burned his auburn locks into a mane of reddish-gold curls. Dust motes like fallen stars drifted around his head like a halo.

"Kale. Keep up."

He scurried after them.

They twisted through a maze of hallways until they came to a door embellished with carvings. Lilies and swallowtail butterflies – the first creatures of Creation – seemed to come to life in the cinnamon-colored wood.

The priestess rapped her knuckles on the door once. Again after a lengthy pause.

"I heard you the *first* time. These old bones don't get to the door as fast as they used to!"

The door wrenched open. An old Sanuset blocked the doorway. Dove-gray eyes, face seamed like a topographical map, lemony yellow silks that hung from a stick-like frame. "*Yes*, Sister Penelope?" The old woman addressed the young priestess, but never took her eyes off him. She watched him like she would a wild dog, not sure if he'd bite her.

The young priestess bowed hastily. "High Sister Rosara, this is—"

"Trouble. Just look at those shoulders. My, the flames didn't do you justice."

"P-prince Hiro Ishida," Sister Penelope stammered, flushing, "son of Bethany Cavill. He—"

"Did he show any identification?"

"N-no—"

"Did you *ask* to see any to verify his claim?"

Sister Penelope's cheeks reddened. She looked at the floor.

"After what we've just been through, I expected you to show more *sense*, child. You cannot be swayed by celebrity status and a handsome face. No matter how devastatingly handsome that face is."

It was Hiro's turn to raise an eyebrow.

"This man could be an assassin," the High Sister said. "Couldn't you?"

"Once," Hiro replied darkly. "And one time more."

Sister Penelope shrank away from him.

"I've not come for you, High Sister," Hiro said. "I must speak with you at once."

"Yes. But what's wrong with the boy?" She pointed a twig-like finger at Kale's midsection. "He looks... lumpy."

Kale grinned sheepishly, tugged his shirt out of his trousers. Lychees bounced and scattered across the floor.

"Ah. That's much better. Now that I know he's not infected with some boil-related pestilence, we can get down to business. What can I do for you, Prince?"

"Amelia's been taken."

The High Sister straightened as if she'd been prodded with a branding iron. "Sister Penelope," she said through tight lips, "bring Sister Ophelia here at once."

She dismissed the young priestess with an urgent flick of her hand. Taking a step back, she opened the door as wide as it could go. Gestured them inside. "I think you'd best come in."

CHAPTER 127

"Why don't you take a seat, Prince? Boy, there's water over there."

Kale darted to the sideboard, sloshed water into the available glasses. Despite his thirst, he offered the first to his hostess. She declined with a gentle shake of her head. Kale shoved the second glass into Hiro's hand and guzzled from the rejected cup.

Hiro fell into the proffered seat, exhausted. It hurt to hold the glass. The fish had cleaned his wounds, but nails were still missing and gashes had yet to close.

The High Sister's old eyes missed nothing. She shuffled to the desk opposite the hearth. Rooted around in a drawer and extracted a jar and a roll of cloth. Like an impatient grandmother, she snapped her twig-like fingers at him. "You're ruining my Pirsan rug."

"We have more important things to worry about than my hands and your rug."

"We're waiting for Ophelia. Now give me your hand."

She slapped ointment on his palms and ruined nailbeds like it was spackling paste. Grimacing, he turned his attention to the map above the hearth. Meh-teh peeked out from behind the mountains, sirens from the sea.

Yawning, Kale set his glass on the table and collapsed in front of the hearth. He stretched once like a cat, curled up into a ball with his back to the little fire, and fell asleep.

Something hard nudged Hiro's thigh. He glanced from the map, found the High Sister poking him in the leg with his signet ring. He hadn't even felt her take it off.

"How did you—"

"Light fingers." She smiled thinly. "I had another life before the white flame chose me. Sometimes I like to practice. Besides, it was getting in my way."

Hiro stuffed the ring into his pocket, next to the Sanu's bead, let the priestess finish bandaging his hand.

The High Sister had one hand wrapped and had moved on to the second when another priestess hurried into the room. The same dove-gray eyes, willowy limbs, a face whose wrinkles seemed to smooth and disappear as he watched. The sibylline blinked in surprise. "Y-you're Hiro Ishida. Why aren't you with Amelia? The last time I saw you—"

The High Sister cut her off. "Amelia's been taken, Ophelia."

"By Kogusanji."

The sibyl and the sibylline looked at him with unblinking, stoic faces. Skeptical.

"Kogusanji's been dead for twenty years," the High Sister said slowly. Like she was speaking to a child.

Hiro snatched his hand away. "I don't have time to explain to you how it's true, but it is. And he has Amelia."

The High Sister leaned back in her chair. "The Tybetan Monster has never breached these walls."

"He already has. You know him as the Delphian priest Isen."

"The traitor," the sibylline whispered. "Brother Michael! Sweet mercy, we've got to tell Captain Julian—"

The High Sister passed a trembling hand over her eyes. "The Militum Dei have already carried out the sentence. Brother Michael is dead."

Hiro shifted in his seat impatiently. "I'm sorry about this Brother

Michael, but we need to focus on stopping Kogusanji. Before he can kill anyone else. You sent Amelia on a mission to retrieve an artifact. Something to fix the Gate."

"H-how did you—"

"I'm not an idiot," he snapped. "I knew something was off. And… she told me. But I don't know how successful she was. I-I think she can lie."

The sibylline shook her head vehemently. "That's impossible. She's—"

"Sanu. I know. Better than you'd think."

The High Sister's gaze narrowed. "Whether Amelia can lie or not is irrelevant now. Is she still *pure*, Prince?"

Hiro shifted in his seat. "Yes."

"You know what's at stake—"

"*I said yes.*"

She let out a short sigh. "Good."

"Can Yueshu still work with a broken Gate?"

The sibyl and sibylline shared a look.

"We don't know. The white flame cannot provide an answer to that question." The High Sister smoothed a wrinkle from her yellow silks. "All could be lost."

Hiro leaned forward. "What about Kogusanji? He's got an army with him – the largest I've ever seen – and hundreds of langskips have entered the Maut. He's convinced he can use Amelia to, I don't know, he said something about uniting the Provinces under one rule and bringing them into paradise? I think he's going to use her to destroy the Gate."

"An incomplete ritual or a tainted Sanu will cause a rip between the realms," Sister Ophelia whispered. "*The Lady will hide her face, and the moon shall become red as blood. Her Lord will lower his shield, and the Abyss shall rise and cover the world in eternal night.*"

"Don't get hysterical, Ophelia. Kogusanji or Isen or whatever you call him will never get close enough to the Gate to destroy it," the High Sister said confidently. "Perhaps with a broken Gate, Yueshu won't even be required. Who knows? The sacred texts teach us that since the creation of the Gate, the Most Holies vowed to never again abandon those that trust in them. Something *will* happen, and Amelia would rather die than be used against Heaven. Besides, if Isen had an army with him and was marching on this holy city as we speak, we'd know about it."

Off in the distance, the undulating blast of a sentry horn sounded. It was joined by a second horn, then a third. The horns melded into a reverberating sound not heard in decades.

Kale sprang from the rug, ran for the window. Ophelia peered out over his head.

The horns sounded again.

The High Sister turned her wide eyes from the window to face him. She was completely ashen.

"Consider yourself informed," Hiro said bitingly.

The sibyl rocketed to her feet. "Ophelia," she hissed. "*Decedo!*"

The sibylline balked, looked like she was going to disobey. Pale eyes glistening, she took up the sibyl's hand and pressed the knuckles against her forehead. Then she bolted out of the room.

When she was gone, the High Sister turned back to Hiro. Seemed shocked that he was still in the room with her. "You have to *go*." She shooed them toward the door.

"If Isen is bringing Amelia here, I will *not* abandon her," Hiro snarled.

"Bless that child. I don't know how she resisted you." The sibyl took his face in both of her withered hands. Yanked his head down to eye-level. "Do as I say, and you might have a chance."

CHAPTER 128

THEY TOOK THE CITY IN AN HOUR.

Amelia had watched from the top of a southeastern rise as the Shadow Army poured across the land like a plague of blood flies. They swarmed up the sides of the Lhasa Plateau like the surf breaking upon a rocky shore, finally cresting the edge and spilling over into the farmland beyond.

And not a sound was made except for the thundering of their feet against the sod.

Isen and Amelia followed behind on a pair of white horses, riding through the eastern gate like the city's long-lost king and queen.

What little resistance they met from the sentries was snuffed out after one of the thralls buried a sword into the man's gut. The sentry's clothing parted as his intestines bulged forth and spilled over the rent in his abdomen. He staggered back, clutching his ruined belly and screaming.

Amelia turned her head to the side and retched.

After that, the submission of the city had been unanimous.

The thralls swarmed through the streets and rounded up everyone they could find. They corralled the citizens into community buildings, courtyards, even in the picketed pastureland like chattel. When the streets were deserted, the thralls marched into Lhasa's heart and laid siege to the temple.

The destruction was everywhere. No matter where Amelia looked, there were doors torn from their hinges, trampled flower beds, and fountains that spurted their water into cracked basins to dribble into the streets. Glass from shattered windows crunched underfoot, pulverized into glittering dust to be kicked up by the wind.

The Shadow Army divided like mackerel for a shark, allowing just enough room for her and Isen to pass on their horses. The gap closed behind them as the thralls rippled back into place.

The temple's great golden dome burned like a torch, reflecting the afternoon sun with a blinding ferocity as if it was some last defense against evil. Though untouched by the thralls' destruction, the temple seemed dead. Its pearlescent luster was gone, replaced by the bleakness of bleached bone. Amelia dragged her palm against the carving of a lily as her horse passed by and shivered. It was like touching a corpse.

Some invisible force spurred four thralls to break from their ranks. They rammed their shoulders into the great cedar doors, but the wood didn't even creak. The iron rings rattled faintly with each blow. After the fourth attempt, there was a sickening crack. Right arm dangling out of its socket, the thrall switched directions and continued the assault with his left shoulder.

Amelia kept the satisfied smile off of her face.

Isen wheeled his horse around angrily. "Bring the rams!"

Amelia calmly turned her horse and retreated to a spot well out of the way. The army undulated like a wave as it parted to make room for the battering rams. Great trunks of felled hopea trees were suspended on chains from iron chassis, their faces bristling with metal shards and nails as thick as her arm.

Boom. Boom. Boom.

It was the drum beat of giants. Fine white dust sprinkled their hair with each concussive blast, and the debris littering the streets jumped like gleeful frogs. The mound of red splinters continued to grow.

But the doors to the temple remained shut.

The warning blasts the sentries had managed to sound before they were cut down had given Rosara enough time to fortify the temple.

It was a ruse of course, for the real Gate lay beyond, unguarded, deep in the heart of the banyan forest. But the doors would protect the clergy as Rosara enacted *decedo*. The Militum Dei would oversee the evacuation, guiding the priests and priestesses out of the city through the catacombs. Then they would round up what civilians they could find and lead them on game trails to safety in Nargarze.

That's if the whole of the Shadow Army was accounted for in the Xinjiang Plains and on the Lhasa Plateau. Minus the thralls who'd entered the Cave of Lights. Only their captain, a man whose soul wasn't bound to the amulet, had returned screaming of great hairy white beasts.

"*Again*," Isen ordered.

After the fifth round, the spent thralls were exchanged for fresh ones. Amelia took the liberty of dismounting and finding herself a spot in the shade. A few thralls followed her. She was never without them. The constant watch made escape impossible, but in in the smallest of silver linings, she wanted for nothing.

"I'd like a cushion and something cool to drink, please," she told them. "And some water for the horses."

Two thralls vanished into the ranks.

The one carrying her cushion and a tankard of fruit juice returned first. Pale orange and faintly floral, she forced herself to choke it down. She hated persimmon juice. At least the fat cushion provided some relief.

When she lowered the tankard, Isen stood only a foot away from her, looming. His visage blotted out the sun like an eclipse, the residual rays burning around his head in a tasteless parody of a halo.

She hadn't heard him coming.

"Something I should know?" he asked her, voice hard.

"Dehydration's a nasty way to go—"

"*About the doors!*"

Amelia jumped, spilling the rest of the juice. She set the tankard aside, flapped the juice from her sari, and forced the trembling in her fingers to subside. "They're guarding the holiest place in the world. Did you really think entry would be easy?"

"Open the doors, Amelia," he ordered softly.

The hair on her arms stood on end, but she turned her gaze resolutely away. "Not a chance, Isen."

Seething, the Tybetan Monster spun around on his heel. "Keep at it!" He snapped his fingers at the nearest thralls.

Four disappeared into the ranks. They returned shortly with a chair and a child.

"Isen, what are you—"

The blind priest dropped into the chair, crossed one leg over the other, and hauled the child onto his lap.

The young boy was no more than three, with coffee-colored skin and eyes like golden honey. His face was splotchy from crying, but he wasn't crying now. He was silent, his honey eyes wild as Isen's hand lazily caressed his head.

He was petrified.

"Open the doors, Amelia."

She slowly got to her feet, wiping her hands on her thighs to rid them of the sweat that had suddenly appeared. "Isen, please—"

"The *door*, Amelia," he bellowed, yanking the boy's head back violently.

The child squealed.

Isen pressed his opium sickle against the squalling jugular. "Make me ask you again, and I will spray this boy's blood all over you."

"*Alright*," she shrieked. "Let him go, Isen. Let him go, and I'll do it!"

Isen took the blade away and dumped the child into the street as he stood. The boy hit the bricks with the same grace as a sack of potatoes and started crying again.

Amelia lunged forward and snatched him up. She murmured soothing nonsense into his ear and checked his throat for any damage. Beside the scraped knees, he was physically fine. When Isen's stance made it evident he was glaring at her, she set the boy down on his feet. "I need you to be brave now." She smoothed his hair out of his face. "I need you to run to your mother as fast as you can. Do you know where she is?"

The boy nodded between his sobs, rubbing his tiny fists into his wet eyes.

"Then go. *Now.*" She gave him a little push, and the child was off, worming his way through the stoic thralls. They made no move to stop or steady him.

Isen cleared his throat.

Glowering, Amelia marched up to the doors. *Only the gentle may enter my house.'* Her hand hovered inches away from the red cedar. *The Blessed Lady forgive me.* She tapped her index finger on the seam.

The doors swung open, and the thralls flooded into the temple like a dark tide.

CHAPTER 129

A HAND PRESSED INTO THE SMALL OF HER BACK, URGING HER FORWARD. Amelia resisted for as long as she could before reluctantly putting one foot in front of the other. As she passed under the doorway, she looked wildly around, hoping all of them had escaped.

They had, except one.

Seated in a chair in the middle of the recessed pool, High Sister Rosara watched silently as the thralls swarmed the rotunda. Above her, the late afternoon sun shone through the oculus in a slanted beam of yellow light. Hands clasped in her lap, braid draped over one shoulder, she was a picture of serene composure.

Amelia knew better.

Kogusanji, the Tybetan Monster, had just conquered her home.

His thralls packed into the sanctuary like vultures on a fresh carcass. Hundreds of pairs of kohl-lined eyes focused on the sibyl in the center of the room, unblinking.

Isen stopped at the edge of the pool, just outside the sunlight. "So nice of you to save me the trouble of hunting you down."

"How did you do it, Monster?" she barked. "How did you trick the flame and pollute my home? An innocent man was put to death because of you."

"Oh, he wasn't innocent. None of them were. Your clergy is riddled with varying degrees of debauchery."

Rosara's eyes narrowed into slits.

"Michael was just the unfortunate *hundan* to stand next to me." Isen tapped a finger on the amulet under his clothes. "A little concentration and a little divine intervention and you have yourselves a traitor. There was no reason to test me after he was taken away."

The High Sister fixed Amelia with a pained expression. "And you opened the doors to this monster even after he put one of your brothers to death?"

Amelia lurched away from Isen and knelt in the shallow water before the Sanuset priestess. "He took a child, Rosara. He was going to kill him."

"One child's life is not worth the souls of millions!" Rosara roared, lunging out of her chair. The old woman's twig-like fingers went for Amelia's throat. With a startled cry, Amelia fell onto her back, the sibyl's hands scrabbling for her neck. "You've doomed us all, you wretched girl!"

Rosara smashed Amelia's head into the pool, grinding it into the shallow water. Terrified, Amelia bit the hand closest to her mouth as she tried to wiggle out from under the old woman. She coughed up a lungful of water as the High Sister yanked her head free of the pool by her collar.

Thin runnels of blood dribbled down the withered hand and disappeared into a sopping wet sleeve. Rosara yanked her close, close enough to whisper, "Get to the north wall of the garden," before Isen clobbered her over the head.

He grabbed fistfuls of the old woman's clothes and dragged her off of Amelia. Rosara thrashed, pawing at his shirt and clawing at his face. Shrieking as her nails made fleshy ribbons of his cheek, Isen threw her aside.

The Sanuset hit the water hard, sliding through the shallows until she shored up against the chair. The impact snapped her head back, and the water bubbled at her mouth as she gasped for breath.

Isen sloshed across the pool and snatched the High Sister by her hair. Hauling her upright by her braid, he threw her into the chair and slapped her hard across the face.

"*No.*" Amelia ran to the old woman's side. "Please, Isen, *don't.*"

Isen sniffed but took a step back. "Ever the forgiving Sanu."

A thrall immediately stepped forward with a cloth. Isen wiped off his face and tossed the cloth aside, the black linen strip across his eyes appraising the High Sister. Slack-mouthed and panting, her head lolled to one side as water dripped from the wisps torn free of her braid.

Amelia picked up the discarded cloth, wrung out the water, and bound the bite wound on Rosara's hand. "I'm sorry."

"You are too good, Amelia." Isen motioned for her to back away. He leaned forward, clamping one hand on each arm rest, pinning Rosara into her chair.

She lifted her weary gaze to meet his.

A smile slowly spread across his face. "My men are already flooding the catacombs."

Amelia felt her heart drop like a stone into her toes.

"While you were busy interviewing this sweet girl, I found myself with plenty of time on my hands. No one thinks about what they tell a blind man. I learned quite a lot during my stay here. Fascinating history this place has."

"You murdered those priests in Bastogne," Rosara spat. "You slipped up, didn't you? They found out who you were. That's why they blinded you. You're not so clever as you thought you were, *Kogusanji.*"

Isen straightened with a sour expression. "My name is Isen. Kogusanji was a failure, and I will not fail again. And those priests were hypocrites. I had taken my vows, just like all the others, but when my sins were flushed out into the light, instead of being forgiven, I was punished."

"Only the Most Holies can truly forgive. Humans have to work at it. We're prone to hold grudges against genocidal murderers."

"Then there should be something written in fine print to that effect when you sign up for the Sanctisum clergy."

"You never had a change of heart. You were *never* a priest."

"It's true. But it proves that I'm right." He leaned down to sneer into her face. "Tomorrow, this fallible religion you mindlessly cling to will no longer burden this world. You're nothing but frauds, peddling an archaic system that enables the depraved and ignores the weak. Tomorrow you hypocrites will answer to me, and I will judge you by your actions, not by your flimsy professions of faith in some anachronistic sacrifice."

Rosara spat into his face.

Isen straightened, wiping the glob of spittle from his cheek. The amulet had already healed the gashes left by her fingernails.

"You'll never be a *god*, Kogusanji," she snarled. "You'll never take Heaven."

"We'll see."

His thralls swarmed around him and wrested the High Sister from her chair.

She fought until Isen sank his fist into her stomach. Pacified, she sagged in their grip, her bare feet scraping against the stone as they dragged her away. Isen took Amelia's hand and followed.

Amelia yanked her fingers free with a chastising glare and quickened her step. She might be his hostage, but she refused to make it easy for him.

The Garden of the Gate sprawled peacefully within its rose-covered walls, untouched, oblivious to the destruction happening on the other side of the climbing roses. Even the air was void of smoke and the stench of blood. As sacrilegious as he was, even Isen treaded softly here.

But the birds were quiet, and the dragonflies were gone. The crunching of gravel became a thunderous roar as hundreds of feet marched down the path.

The foliage parted, and the Gate appeared.

CHAPTER 130

THE GATE OF HEAVEN GLITTERED IN THE EVENING SUN, AN ARCH OF black diamond against an orange sky. Impossibly smooth, it caught the failing light and threw it back in a blinding lance. The water trickling in its trough shimmered like crushed pearl.

Beside her, Isen clicked his tongue against his teeth in disappointment. "You know, I thought the Most Holies would've made it more garish. Something more visually appealing."

Amelia sputtered. "It's made entirely of black diamond. It's *priceless*."

"It's impressive, just... simple."

"If all it needs is a carving or two to keep you from destroying it, I'll get a chisel right now."

"Ha, ha, Amelia."

Trailing his fingers in the sacred water, Isen prowled a circle around the Gate. Amelia followed him with her eyes until the arch blocked him from sight, then flicked her attention to the north wall. In her absence, one of the climbing roses had grown nearly to its top. Orange blooms the size of muskmelons clung to thick and woody vines. Sturdy enough to support the weight of a full-grown adult.

Maybe not Hiro, but any normal——

Amelia dropped her eyes to the grass as Isen reappeared. She shuddered as his long fingers curled around her elbow. *"Hands."*

It was a familiar touch now repulsive. He wasn't the endearing priest she'd met at the crossroads; this was Kogusanji, the Tybetan Monster, determined to sacrifice the world to the End Times just to satisfy a personal vendetta.

She dropped into the grass beside the glowering sibyl, pulling her knees up to her chest. Wrapping her trembling arms around her legs, she hid her face and pleaded to the dragon. *Come back. I can't do this without you.*

The void remained, just shapeless silver light. The way was shut.

"What am I still doing here, Kogusanji?" Rosara demanded angrily. "You have the Sanu, you have the Gate, and your army is almost done conquering Eurasia. What more can you want?"

"To see the horror on your face when my life's pursuit is fulfilled. You're here to witness the Heaven you so desperately yearn for brought under my heel."

"My faith is one that feeds the hungry, clothes the naked, and promises a joyous release from an endless cycle of drudgery. *Yours* is one of domination and greed. I pity those who follow you."

He smiled, the black cloth crinkling at his eyes. "And yet there are millions. Why bet on faith when you can have a sure thing?"

"You don't know that."

"Oh, but I do. I've met the Crown Prince. I know *they* exist. And I know that cycle of reincarnation is only meant to punish us, not refine us like Sanctisum claims. You preach of their love, but then why are we constantly reprimanded for the sins of our ancestors? How can we break free of that oppression? *I* am the key to our immortality!"

The anger in the High Sister's face was slowly replaced with pity. Her voice was quiet. "I will pray for your soul, Kogusanji."

"Feh. As much I enjoy these little conversations, I'm going to go take a bath. Battle makes me *filthy*. I saw a large pool behind the heliconias—"

"*No!* That's the Pool of Heavenly Tears. It's *sacred.*"

"Good," the Tybetan Monster sneered. "One more desecration to urge those gods out of hiding. I *want* them to be angry. I *want* them to send their Crown Prince to challenge me again. Because when I'm done bathing my sword in his blood, theirs is next."

CHAPTER 131

Amelia and Rosara sat on opposite sides of the table. Amelia picked at her food, but Rosara ate with the gusto of a woman determined to extract one last moment of pleasure from this world before she died tomorrow. Isen slouched comfortably in his seat, sipping from a long-stemmed glass as he watched the High Sister gorge herself.

They dined under a pavilion just out of sight of the Gate. The thralls had confiscated it from the city, along with the fire bowls of fragrant oil from the temple. Their aromatic smoke clashed with the flowers' perfume, overwhelming the evening air with a cloying haze.

Unable to stomach more than one grain of rice at a time, Amelia watched under lowered lashes as Rosara stuffed food into her mouth by the fistful.

When she tore off a leg from the peacock centerpiece, Amelia made a small squeak of protest. Rosara merely glared at her and started stripping flesh from bone. Grease dripped from her twig-like fingers onto her plate, where it splattered softly into the congealing sauce.

Isen's upper lip curled in disgust. "I thought the Sanctisum clergy were vegetarians."

"You're destroying the world tomorrow, aren't you?" Rosara swallowed noisily, smacking her lips. She washed it all down with a glass of wine, tipping her head back until red streaks dribbled over her chin and down her neck. "Why not indulge a little? I've missed meat *so much*. Truly, I should be thanking you for this opportunity."

"It's like dining with an ogre." Isen tucked a napkin into his collar to protect his clothes from wayward flecks. "You'd think you'd have better table manners."

"If I'm offending you, by all means, please feel free to see yourself out of my house," she replied with a savage smile.

Isen snorted.

The High Sister shrugged, picked up a sausage in each hand, and started gnawing.

Amelia cringed.

"When do we get to see dessert?" Rosara asked through a mouthful of masticated pork.

"When the bird is eaten."

"Will there be mango custard?"

"Of course."

Rosara dropped the half-eaten sausages and wiped her hands on a soiled napkin. She leaned out of her chair and yanked the platter with the roasted peacock closer. Amelia clamped a hand onto the purple tablecloth as the other dishes jumped, sloshing brothy noodles and braised vegetables. The last of the summer lychees rolled away like spilled marbles.

The High Sister rubbed her sticky hands together as she surveyed the challenge. She was just about to rip off a wing when she paused, fingers hovering over the bird. "Forgive me. Would you two care to join me?"

"I honestly couldn't eat another bite," Isen said.

Amelia just shook her head, too appalled to speak.

"Goody for me." The High Sister focused on her devouring with renewed fervor.

"Isen, *please*," Amelia implored, "don't instigate—"

"She's doing it to herself." He leaned forward and plucked a tiny dumpling between his thumb and index finger. He gave it a little swirl in a sauce bowl before plopping it whole into his mouth. "I had thought to enlist some entertainment from the locals, but the High Sister here is all the amusement I need."

"Glad I could assist you—"

Then it happened.

Rosara stopped chewing as her eyes bulged wide. She twisted out of her chair. Pawing at Isen's chest, she yanked the napkin out of his collar and lurched away. She got only a few steps before her vomit sprayed over the flowers.

Amelia jumped to her feet. Immediately the thralls swarmed around her.

"Isen," she snapped. "Sweet mercy, give us some privacy, won't you?"

The Tybetan Monster scowled, but he waved his hand in irritated consent. "Take her farther in," Isen barked. "I don't want to smell her filth."

Amelia pushed through the thralls to the retching sibyl. She swept the High Sister's braid out of the way and took hold of her elbow. They staggered to the Gate, the High Sister scrambling to support herself against the trough. Hands clamped on its diamond rim, she heaved into the grass, just barely missing the sacred waters.

"Rosara, what were you thinking?" Amelia hissed, rubbing the old woman's back. "I don't want to call you an idiot, but—"

The cloth napkin fluttered into the grass. The High Sister slapped something warm and round into Amelia's hand and spat the filth from her mouth.

Amelia lifted the object into the failing light. It hummed in her hand.

The knotwork amulet.

Mouth agape, Amelia shoved the relic into her sari. "You little *thief*—"

Rosara grinned, then doubled over again. Still retching, she jabbed a finger toward the north wall and its ladder of orange roses.

Amelia kissed the top of the sibyl's head and raced across the lawn, the thick grass muffling the sound of her feet. She sprang into the arms of the vining rose and began to climb.

CHAPTER 132

THORNS PRICKED HER FLESH.

Amelia gritted her teeth. Her sandals were thick enough to withstand their incessant stabbing, but blood coated her hands in a crimson sheen. The roses clawed at her clothes, tearing rents in the silk. She didn't slow.

Behind her, Rosara continued to vomit into the grass. Loudly.

Twilight had them now, the western horizon just a streak of turquoise. The moon hid behind the mountains, unwilling to rise and reveal her escape. Only the stars observed from the sky, their frantic twinkling urging her to *hurry hurry hurry.*

Amelia was nearing the top when the roses began to thin. The central vine had lost its thickness, and the myriad little fingers it dug into the stone to keep it anchored started to snap under her weight. She was going to run out of vine.

There's got to be a crack, just something large enough to get my fingers in—

She brushed the tender new growth out of the way, leaving streaks of red on the pale green leaves. The stone was flawlessly smooth. Heart in her throat, she shimmied up the wall one inch at a time, praying the vine beneath her feet remained strong. She only needed a tiny bit of leverage so she could kick off and—

Rosara let out an enraged shout.

Amelia whipped her head around. A thrall had encircled the High Sister with a pair of burly arms, and she thrashed and kicked at the others struggling to seize her legs. She tore into the thrall's arms with her nails, biting and shrieking like a harpy. Someone managed to dodge her flailing limbs and crack her across the face with a vicious backhand.

"*Amelia!*" Isen bellowed.

The vine shook violently as half a dozen thralls seized the rose. Orange petals rained against her face and fluttered down to the grass only to be trampled by churning feet. They were beginning to climb.

"I will *kill* her."

She winced, but she kept her attention on the rose bush. The tenuous grip it had on the wall was weakening with every jerk. It started to peel away from the stone.

There was a squelching sound of steel sheathing itself in flesh, and Rosara screamed.

Amelia wedged her foot against the last of the central vine and shoved off, scrambling with her right hand. Her fingers skimmed the top of the wall and fell short.

A scream tore from her throat as the wall began to fall away.

Rosara had died for nothing—

Isen would destroy the Gate—

Heaven would fall—

From the darkness, a gloved hand clamped down on her wrist. She hit the side of the wall with a *thump* and cried out as the leather pinched her skin.

"Gotcha."

Amelia grabbed the arm hauling her up and scrabbled her feet against the wall. A mane of auburn curls and a face she knew as well as her own popped into view.

"Hi!" said Kale.

She sputtered for only a moment before hooking her elbow over the edge. She helped hoist herself up, and with a yelp, tumbled over the lip and into a trough.

The aqueduct.

Panting, she lay belly-down on the cool stone and looked into a pair of seal-brown eyes. "Hiro," she breathed, scrambling to her feet. She wanted to leap into his arms.

"*ISHIDA!*" Isen screamed.

"Time to go. And no, I'm not going to ask for permission."

Hiro grabbed her hand and jumped.

CHAPTER 133

THEY PLUMMETED INTO AN OVERSTUFFED WAGON THIRTY FEET BELOW. The straw spat her into the street with grass sticking out of her hair like some forest sprite. Kale hopped into the depression she'd just vacated and rolled more gracefully to his feet. He rooted around in the straw, extracting Hiro's bow and quiver. Instead of handing them to his master, the boy strung them both over his shoulder.

Hiro yanked her upright. "Don't gawk, Sanu. It's time to *move*."

The world exploded around them.

Alarm trumpets blasted the night air; fiery arrows took to the sky, exploding in brief pockets of light and fizzling into showers of red sparks. The feet of a thousand thralls pounded the streets with one quarry in mind.

Them.

Hiro tightened his hand around Amelia's so hard it hurt. Blood seeped from the cuts left by the thorns. She didn't care. She just focused on keeping up with his long legs as he guided them through the warren of streets. Their feet splashed through the pitiful streams of broken fountains, crunched over shattered glass, scrambled up a stacked tower of wooden crates, and ran along the residential rooftops.

Behind them, Kale knocked over the crates so the others couldn't follow. In seconds, the boy was by their side, running for all he was worth with the biggest grin on his face.

It didn't take long before the thralls figured out where their prey had gone. Arrows whizzed by their heads like deadly flies. Hiro never stopped. He just dodged, yanking her with him. They were nearing the edge of the city when he barked Kale's name.

The boy diverted to the right, bumping into everything he possibly could. Large clay pots rolled over the side and shattered rainwater against the bricks. Clotheslines snapped and ensnared the thralls with their shirts and sheets. The arrows diverted their course, but they never caught him. The boy was a shadow as he raced along the roofs, jumping and tumbling like a kitten with a ball of yarn. It was like he was having *fun*.

Hiro tugged on her hand, jerking her attention forward. "Jump!"

The slate shingles crumbled under the impact. Their hands ripped apart. Amelia fought for a handhold as she slid down the roof. The shingles sliced deeper into her torn palms, leaving a dark smear in her wake. She felt air over her feet, her legs, her hips—

Her fingers dug into the eaves. She wrenched to a stop, shoulders popping. Amelia yelped, fighting to find purchase with her feet. Anything to alleviate the agony in her arms.

"Sanu." His voice was impossibly close beside her. "Just let go."

"Are you *crazy*?"

She glanced down. The ground waited only a hand's breadth under her dangling feet. She was clinging to the roof of a pig pen. Its occupants were corralled inside for the night, snoring and grunting in their sleep. The stench was incredible.

"Sanu, we don't have *time*." Hiro held out his hands. "I'll catch you if you'd like."

Amelia dropped the remaining inches, stumbling into him as her feet twisted in the soft earth. He steadied her, his hand lingering on her arm even after he's pushed her away.

An arrow exploded above them.

Hiro vaulted over the sty's fence, Amelia scrambling after him.

Her legs were limp noodles as they ran across the farmland to the western wall. Thick enough to support two sentries on horseback, it stalled the encroaching growth of the banyan forest. Her heart faltered in its looming shadow. She didn't have the strength to climb another wall.

Sensing her apprehension, Hiro squeezed her fingers. He was relentless as the tide, the determination in his eyes cold and uncompromising. They flicked to the left.

He saw them before she did.

The *shiing* of his greatsword clearing its sheath rang with challenge. Amelia shied away as Hiro plowed to the western gate. The thralls abandoned their post, swarming across the dew-soaked grass like a cloud of plague flies.

He caught the first one with a straight arm, immediately shifting his weight to the opposite foot. The greatsword sprouted through the rear of the second thrall's skull before the first had even finished flipping onto his back. Hiro pierced the first through the chest with a vicious jab and spun, clearing his blade and cleaving the third's head from her shoulders. Black spurted from the empty neck like a geyser of crude oil.

Hiro lifted the rippling steel to shoulder height. A syrupy drop oozed off its tip, winking once in the moonlight, before the thralls engulfed him.

There was a whistle, and the night erupted into fire.

Yellow flames raced across the ground like a pack of frolicsome hellhounds. The thralls thrashed in the conflagration, a thin scream like steam escaping from a kettle piercing the roar of the inferno.

She couldn't see Hiro.

A shadow darted across the light, and Kale took hold of her hand. They leapt through a gap in the fiery gore. Kale hooked the bow under a thrall's foot and yanked, clearing the last obstacle between them and the moon gate. On the other side of the wall, the boy dropped to one knee and lit another arrow with a rasp of flint against steel. He drew the fletching back to his lips and waited.

Hiro stumbled through the archway a moment later, clutching his side and coughing.

Kale loosed the arrow.

The moon gate shattered as the stone exploded, crumbling the archway into a heap of rubble. The blast launched Hiro into the air. He landed in a crumpled heap, his greatsword sticking out of the grass a few feet from his hand. Amelia wormed under one of his muscled arms as Kale tugged the blade out of the sod. Hissing, Hiro pressed a hand against the wound in his side and staggered upright. His fingers dug into her shoulder, her hand twisted into his greatcoat, and they disappeared into the shelter of the banyan forest.

Enveloped in darkness, Amelia risked a glance behind her. There were no thralls, no pursuit, just the black billowing smoke that blotted out the stars. Only the moon cut through the ashy haze, glaring bale-fully at the carnage below with one great white eye. Tomorrow, it would be as orange as the cinders that swirled into its sky.

Under the weight of Hiro's arm, Amelia squared her shoulders.

Tomorrow she would dance and destroy the Tybetan Monster, or the world, forever.

CHAPTER 134

AMELIA SAT ON THE FOREST FLOOR, LEGS DRAWN UP TO HER CHEST AND chin resting on the tops of her knees. Sighing, she idly stirred the coals of the dying fire with a stick. Hiro rested in the leaf litter nearby, the stripe of cauterized flesh flashing like the shiny underbelly of a snake with each breath. He was pale, but alive; the wound deep, but not fatal.

Twigs and dead leaves sprinkled the ground from above. Kale was in the arms of the nearest banyan tree, watching the way they had come. So far, he hadn't raised the alarm.

She stabbed at the coals angrily. The silver dragon was gone; Isen's betrayal had locked it away. They'd been forced to heat Hiro's dagger to glowing before pressing it against his flesh. The wood had splintered between his teeth, his howl startling the sleeping myna birds into flight.

Isen.

Amelia slipped her bandaged hands into the shreds of her sari. The hilt and the amulet hummed against her fingers. They were still there. A sigh of relief shuddered past her lips.

"I'll be ready to move shortly," Hiro said, his eyes still closed. "You can stop sighing."

"It's not you," she said quickly. "Please, take your time. Well, don't take *too* much time, obviously. Just enough for you to get back on your feet. And then we can—"

He cracked open an eye and shut it again. "You're rambling. You only do that when you're flustered."

"Hiro, what are you *doing* here? I mean, I'm thrilled, but how—"

"Kale translated what you'd said in Dhaka after Isen... took you. So we sailed up the Bengal Sea and climbed the Chehara Cliff. *Don't* ask me to do it again. We managed to warn the High Sister just before the Shadow Army was spotted. She told us about the Gate – the *true* Gate – and then tried to evacuate the city.

"After that, Kale and I had about an hour to secure our escape. He went to the aviary while I rigged the western moon gate. We did what we could before we had to hide in the aqueduct by the roses. Then it was all a matter of waiting for you."

Amelia smeared the tears from her cheeks. "Thank you."

"Hn. I had a vow to fulfill." He smiled, his face brightening for a fleeting moment before twisting into a grimace.

She tentatively touched the flesh around his wound. "How're you feeling?"

"It... hurts." He flinched and pulled her hand away. His fingers curled over hers, keeping them pressed over his heart. "How come you couldn't heal me the normal way?"

She barked a laugh. "My glowing hands are *normal* now?"

"I've grown used to it."

Amelia slipped her fingers free and stirred the coals again. "Isen... did something to me. I don't know what exactly—"

"He broke your taijitu." Kale thrust his head out from the branches. "When he betrayed you. Twice. First when he kidnapped you, and second when he stabbed you. You've got two fish warring in the pond now."

"I'm going to pretend to know what you're talking about, boy."

"Amelia knows. Isen breaks everything. Family, *hearts*..." He disappeared sourly behind the screen of leaves, still listing. "... trust... rituals..."

Amelia sat bolt upright in alarm. "My fans, the water! I can't perform Yueshan without—"

"What do you think is in there?" Hiro asked, pointing to the pack Kale had left at the base of the tree.

She snatched the pack and yanked the ties apart. Mixed in with traveling supplies were all of her belongings, the ceremonial items wrapped in their square of orange silk, even the Bethany Journal. She smoothed a hand over its worn cover, her bandage snagging on the braided reeds. "Your adventures have gotten me into a lot of trouble," she muttered.

"*Hiro.*" Kale dropped to the ground with a loud thud. "They're coming. They've cleared the western gate and are starting for the forest."

Grimacing, the prince tugged his gi into place over his wounded ribs. Amelia covered the smoldering coals with dirt and concealed the bare spot with leaf litter. Kale shrugged the pack over his shoulders as Hiro strapped on his greatsword. They melted deeper into the forest in a matter of minutes.

It wasn't easy.

The banyan trees sprouted from the ground like fat javelins, their broad branches weaving together into an impenetrable net. The moonlight was rarely strong enough to spear through the canopy. Thin beams of celestial light sliced through the gloom, and more than once Amelia was convinced she'd seen *yakshini* lifting their heads from their sinuous embrace with their trees.

The last thing we need are sultry tree-women distracting us. Or seducing—

A mental image of a beguiled Hiro stumbling after a voluptuous dryad set her blood to boiling. She banished the thought, wincing as her nails dug into her tender palms.

With the silver dragon lost, she had to rely on memory to guide them to the Gate. She knew it was east of them, but there was no spectral butterfly to follow this time. The Gate of Heaven could be anywhere in the miles of forest that stretched across the plateau.

She was sidling between two close-growing trunks when something tickled her stomach. Yelping, she pawed at her sari. The relics vibrated at her touch.

"What is it?" Hiro smacked her hands away. "Did you get cut—"

"No, I-I'm fine." She pulled away. "It must've been a... bug." Amelia tried to keep a straight face as the tattoo seared against her flesh. She wanted to tell them about the relics, but she couldn't risk it. If she couldn't fix the Gate, at least Hiro and Kale could live their last moments knowing they'd done everything they could.

"A bug." Hiro crossed his arms over his chest. "Let's hope a *denki mushi* didn't find its way into your clothes. They sting like electric eels."

Amelia slapped at her silks just in case. Snorting, Hiro disappeared into the trees. She waited until he was out of sight before she pressed her hands against her sari. The relics purred against her skin. They practically jumped when she turned east. "This way," she called.

Once felt, their hum was impossible to ignore. They knew which way was home.

Orange leaves that had turned copper in the moonlight crunched softly underfoot. The air was heavy, almost viscous, thick with the scent of arboreal rot. Sweat squeezed from every pore, and sometime after moon-set she stopped trying to peel her clothes away from her skin.

It was well after dawn when Hiro sagged against a trunk. "We have to stop," he panted. "*Where* are you getting all this energy?"

Kale slumped into the embrace of a banyan's roots, already half-asleep.

Amelia walked right past them. The relics were buzzing like a beehive. She couldn't stop now.

"Sanu?"

The trees were beginning to thin. They were older here, spaced farther apart. The air lightened, and something pale rose from the forest floor.

Amelia leaned her forehead against the white stone, tasting salt on the back of her tongue. The relics quieted to a gentle purr, finally content.

"We're here."

CHAPTER 135

THE DEAD BODHI TREE SCRATCHED AT THE PALE BLUE SKY.

Biting her lower lip, Amelia pressed her palm against the trunk of the sacred tree and felt its smooth, lifeless bark cold beneath her fingertips. It had the same aura as a deserted house that had once been filled with a loving family. She took her hand away.

When she turned around, Kale's solemn face was drinking in the sight of the cracked white stone and the dead Bodhi tree. Not even the wind blew here.

Tears welled up in his hazel eyes. "I *hate* Isen," he whispered.

Amelia reached out and pulled him into her arms. He wrapped his around her and cried into her sari. She looked over his head as she stroked his hair.

Summer was failing, and autumn had already sunk its claws into the north. The trees beyond the banyans were tipped in orange, and the Bhutan Steppes were beginning to yellow. In the east, the Himalayas were forever in the clutches of winter. South of them, the Bengal Sea twinkled in a line of sapphire.

And smoke boiled from the holy city.

Punishment for her escape.

It felt as if an invisible hand had reached inside her chest and squeezed.

Kale peeled himself away, wiping his eyes with the back of his sleeve. "I'm gonna go sharpen Hiro's sword."

His feet crunched on the latticework of the broken mesa. Fine powder – salt dust – rose in a thin plume behind him. In the shade of the Bodhi tree, Kale carefully extracted the greatsword from his master's sleeping form.

The prince was exhausted.

His head lolled against a shoulder, the worries he carried no longer creasing his face. The golden cuff of his rank gleamed like a star on his ear. Sweat crusted in his hair, and only his nose poked out of the Bodhi tree's shade.It was rosy with sunburn.

Amelia threaded her fingers into his hair and gently rolled his head to his other shoulder, out of the sun. He moaned softly. She let her hand slip from his face, shivering as the stubble on his cheeks tickled her fingers.

Her hand fell empty to her side, and their connection winked out of existence.

THE HEAT of the last day of summer lulled her into a state between waking and dreaming.

Amelia sat on the honeycombed mesa away from the others, hands resting open in her lap. Only the repetitive rasping of the greatsword against the whetstone punctuated the silence.

It was the unmistakable call to duty.

Fear is the hungry mouth that devours all you give it. Give nothing. Fear nothing.

But she was afraid.

Afraid that something – some*one* – now had her devotion besides the Blessed Lady. Because it was true.

Hiro.

She shoved the thought away.

Distance yourself, for your heart's sake, echoed the sacred white flame. *There will come a time when you will have to give them up.*

But what if I can't? I'll be alone. Again. Even the dragon is gone.

The panic was coming back. Already her heart was thumping like a terrified rabbit against her ribs. Without the dragon, it would consume her.

Remember the water.

Silver light was all that remained of that place. Yet something eddied, shifting light and shadow. Something only glimpsed from the corner of her eye.

Maybe it wasn't gone. Maybe it was just lost.

You must be a true bridge between realms, and attachments only tie you down to one side. The Gate cannot work without a bridge.

Amelia hugged her legs up to her chest, miserable. She could see them now, the myriad links of the chain that imprisoned her heart. And they each had names.

Shame.

Yuki – the best friend she'd abandoned to the skein because she'd been afraid.

Aunt Saoirse, Revered Onu Jocasta, the novices, even stern Sister Matilde, she'd deserted them all.

Rosara – the rebellious sibyl who'd sacrificed herself so Amelia could escape.

Anger.

The Sorcerer, Lady Cosette, Lakshmi, Ellaria; their links were heavy, forged from lead.

Hate.

Isen – the Tybetan Monster. The Deceiver. She'd trusted him with everything, even a piece of her heart. His link was forged of pain, the same white-hot agony that lanced into her heart every time she lied.

'Hatred is never healed with hatred, but by compassion alone. They will take everything from you, but forgive, and they can never take away your joy.'

It was time to let it go. She might not have forged the links, but she'd let herself be imprisoned.

It was agonizingly slow. She was forced to confront the emotion buried in each link, forced to relive the circumstances of their creation. It was pain she had buried away, hidden under another name. But the chain melted, one link at a time, until only two remained. The last two holding her back. They were feathery-light, fine as spider silk but as strong as dragon scales.

Kale.

The boy was the child she could never have. He'd made her laugh instead of cry, helped her, defended her, loved her. She could picture his shining hazel eyes and his impish grin as vividly as if he was standing right in front of her. But the reality was Sanu could not have children. Kale and his smiling face became mist and wafted away.

Hiro.

His mirage stood before her in his battle armor, his greatsword sheathed on his back. His seal-brown eyes were focused somewhere on the honeycombed mesa near her feet.

"You need to let me go." His rough voice was soft but firm.

Amelia surged to her feet. "But... I love you."

Hiro lifted his eyes. The misery she saw in them mirrored her own. *"Attachment interferes with duty."*

She looked away, smearing her tears from her cheeks. "I know."

He cocked his head, hearing something in the distance that she did not. He drew his greatsword and let the point rest on the salty ground.

"Save me." It was plea not for him, but for her.

She felt like her heart was crumbling into ash.

"Go," she breathed.

And like the wind, he was gone.

CHAPTER 136

It was almost sunset when she opened her eyes.

Overhead, black storm clouds boiled with their swollen bellies bathed purple by the dying light. Threads of white lightning crackled between them with thunder growling soon after, threatening the earth with a deluge.

Hiro and Kale were gone.

She felt a pang of loneliness, but it didn't hurt as much as she thought it would. Amelia traced the golden lily tattoo on her sternum; it had always sustained her.

Retrieving the pack from the shade of the Bodhi tree, Amelia carefully extracted the bundle of orange silk. She smoothed it over the cracked earth and laid out her fans, the jade flask of sacred water, and the bottle of golden henna. The knotwork amulet and the lion hilt joined them, along with Kale's blue opal she'd extracted from her pocket. She'd quite forgotten about it.

She stripped out of her shredded uniform, bathed in the meager remains of the water canteen, and painted her skin with the henna. Swirls and dots spread from her hands to her arms, rooted on the tops of her feet and coiled up her legs. It was a mandala, blooming from the tattoo in the center of her chest.

The thunder snarled above her, but the clouds didn't break. They stewed in the sky like slavering beasts, restrained by some unseen hand.

Eying the storm, Amelia dressed briskly. She slipped the knotwork amulet over her neck along with the strand of pearls, and the relic hummed against her tattoo. She'd tried pressing the amulet and the hilt together, against the Bodhi tree, against the salt mesa, and nothing. They'd remained stubbornly separate, purring like insolent kittens.

Stuffing the rest into her sari, she set off for the center of the Gate. Her sandals crunched against the salt, the ground glowing red as the sun sank deeper into the western sky.

The relics trembled.

Twilight came, streaking the heavens with violet, and Amelia quenched the rising tide of butterflies in her stomach. It was all wrong. The Gate was cracked, its broken pieces refused to cooperate, a cold sweat threatened to ruin her henna work, and the silver dragon—

Amelia clenched her fists, squeezed the tears from her eyes.

Fear is the hungry mouth that devours all you give it. Give nothing. Fear nothing.

She yanked the flask and the fans from her sari, soaking the silk with the water until it was fully saturated. Heart beating wildly, Amelia waited until the Harvest Moon rose impossibly large and orange over the horizon.

Taking a deep breath, she lifted the fans high over her head and began to dance.

HIRO BRACED his foot against the thrall's chest, kicked the corpse off his sword.

More were coming.

They displaced every shadow between the trees, crawled through the branches like crow *tengu*.

"*Kale.*"

There was a snap, a loud *twang*, and the boy wormed his way through a gap in the trees. "That was the last trap," he panted. "They're *everywhere.*"

"Fall back to the Gate."

The thralls gave chase. The ground trembled under their thundering feet, tore the leaves from their canopy into an arboreal hailstorm.

Hiro squinted against the assault, batted the leathery leaves out of his way. He snatched Kale by the back of his shirt and launched him at the mesa. The boy scrambled up the stone like a spider. Hiro climbed after him, smashed the face of the thrall clawing at his leg with his boot heel.

The sky snarled. It roiled like the ocean caught in a maelstrom, the clouds building and crashing like tempestuous waves. Lightning, white and crackling, lanced across the boiling black. Goaded the thunder into a deafening roar.

In the distance, the Sanu danced under the furious sky, her silks snapping like flames.

And beyond, the thralls sluiced over the mesa. Flood waters released from a broken dam. They were a torrent headed straight for her, a little island of light in a sea of darkness. To crash upon her shores. Swallow her. Yet she continued to dance, fearless. Faithful.

Then suddenly, they just stopped. Rows upon rows of motionless shapes, packed so thick he couldn't see where one left off and another began.

"H-Hiro?" the boy quavered.

The thralls rippled apart, and the Tybetan Monster sauntered to the front of their ranks.

Hiro gave the boy a little shove. "Get out of here, Kale."

The boy backed away, turned, and sprinted for the Sanu.

Isen's staff was gone, and a pair of hook swords dangled from his hip. He'd exchanged his priestly robes for clothes befitting a lord. A rich one. Silk shirt, sleeveless tunic of cyan-and-violet brocade, polished boots.

Isen stopped a few yards away, shoved his thumbs into his belt. "You were always doomed to fail, Ishida." He said it calmly, like he was stating a simple fact. "I've worn that amulet for the last twenty years. I can sense it even when it's not around my neck."

"Don't *do* this, Isen. When are you going to get it? If she doesn't seal that Gate, Heaven will close its doors and the Abyss will flood the earth!"

The blind man smiled faintly. "Yueshu is *lost*. When that moon leaves the sky, the gateway between Heaven and Earth will rip apart, and I will lead my troops to immortality. Now get out of my way."

Hiro rooted his feet. He hefted his greatsword, wiped the gore and salt away on his sleeve. He wanted to know when he drew Isen's blood.

"A futile gesture. Even if you kill me now, I'll just be reincarnated. I'll have another life to try again."

"Then I will hunt you down and kill you in all of them!"

Hiro launched into the air, sliced his greatsword down in a mighty arc.

The Tybetan Monster flung up his swords to block, the impact driving him down onto one knee. Golden threads fluttered to the ground. Isen shoved the greatsword aside, rolled away onto his feet. His long fingers combed through his shortened hair.

Snarling, Isen linked his swords at the hooked ends. He raked them against the earth, filled the air with salt.

Hiro stumbled away from the cloud as a flash of silver sliced across his eyes. He fell away from the blinding strike, the blade catching only the bridge of his nose. A bead of crimson splashed against the white salt, exploding in silent fury. He flipped onto his feet as Isen swung again.

The greatsword caught the crescent guard and yanked. Isen stumbled forward right into Hiro's fist. Blood erupted from his mouth, sprayed the air with a rosy mist. Hiro pivoted, rammed his shoulder into Isen's side, and slashed the rippling steel in an upward arc.

Screeching, the Tybetan Monster staggered away. His ruined

clothes sloughed off his shoulders like burned skin. He ripped them free, cast them aside with a hiss.

Hiro stood dumbfounded, unable to tear his gaze from Isen's back.

The rampant lion dominated the vast expanse of skin. A line, from hip to opposite shoulder, bloomed red from where Hiro had cut him. The blasphemous cat rippled as Isen rolled his shoulders.

Lightning tore across the sky; thunder shook the earth. The storm clouds roiled black and copper under the baleful eye of the orange moon.

Isen smirked, pointed to the sky. "Someone's insulted."

Hiro lunged.

Three sharp cuts, and one of Isen's swords bounced against the salt. Hiro batted the oncoming swing aside as he would a fly, rammed his forehead into Isen's nose. The bone crunched, and wet splashed across his face. Isen stumbled back, collapsed with a grunt.

Seething, Hiro yanked the greatsword to shoulder height and summoned the strength for the final strike.

Movement.

The thralls jostled, hastily parted for a figure storming to the front.

The Bowman drew the green fletching back to his mouth and fired.

CHAPTER 137

THE SACRED WATER SPRINKLED THE AIR WITH EVERY WAVE OF HER FANS. Amelia kept her mind clear, focused only on the sequence and not on how the Gate should've been covered in water and mirroring the night sky. It wasn't perfect, but she hoped it would be enough.

Something sounded in the distance. It was thunder, or waves, but the ground shook—

No.

She couldn't be distracted. Yueshan was performed once a century. She threw the fans out behind her as she leapt, curling them close as she plunged into a twirl.

A metallic clang—

Not her problem.

She dropped down on her left knee and arched her back, the fans facing Heaven.

The storm clouds roiled above, furious.

Somebody shouted—

Amelia twisted on her knee and came up into another twirl.

She danced the om, her footsteps glowing faintly behind her. The stone carving on the pagoda wall seemed to come to life in her mind's eye. She focused on it, lingered on its curves as she sprang into the air, arms and legs stretched in a dynamic leap.

Something hit her in the chest.

What?

Amelia collapsed onto the salt, the fans clattering from her hands. She blinked sluggishly at the arrow protruding from her right breast. Her body went numb as her thoughts turned to mush.

The dim sounds of pounding feet rattled her teeth as they approached.

Amelia blinked again, trying to recognize them. *Yueshan.* She had to warn them! Her mouth opened, but only a croak came out. Her body was getting colder, stiffer, like it was going to sleep without her permission. When she blinked again, her eyes rolled back into her head.

"AMELIA!"

Hiro sprinted past Kale, breath tearing through his lungs in fiery gasps. *Almost there. Just hold on—*

He stumbled forward, pain exploding from his left shoulder blade. A hornet's stinger burrowed into his flesh. A branding iron stamped a seal on his bone. Witchfire danced in his blood.

Howling, Hiro twisted around and pawed at his back. His fingers tightened around something, yanked. The ivory knife, slick with scarlet, slipped from his hand.

"*Hiro,*" the boy screamed. "Behind—"

Snick.

Hiro dropped to one knee, clamped a hand over the rent in the back of his leg.

Snick.

The fingers in his right hand went numb as the muscle in his arm was split to the bone.

A foot rammed into his sternum, sent him sprawling onto his back. Hiro choked on a wheezing gasp, fought for air like a drowning man. Barely raised the greatsword to block the steel slicing for his heart.

The hooks buried into his shoulder and ripped away.

He only grunted as something hot and syrupy pooled against his cheek.

"*Hiro.*" Kale struggled against the Bowman's fist in his hair, tears dripping from his cheeks.

"Yet another Ishida Dragon slain," Isen crowed, lifting his arms to the sky. "Congratulations for lasting longer than your bitch of a mother. And she had some tenacity. You can let the boy go now, Tareq. He's nothing."

Kale shoved away, ran to his side. He tore the gi off his skinny frame and stuffed it into the hole in Hiro's shoulder. "*No, no, no—*"

"Ah!" Isen clapped his hands. "Look who's awake. Amelia, sweet girl, I think you have something of mine."

The Sanu was on her feet. Ashen skin, sharpened teeth, she stared at them with glowing green eyes.

Hiro's heart thumped loudly once against his ribs, then stopped.

Henge.

"No," Hiro moaned.

She smoothed a hand up her sari, curled her fingers around the shaft protruding from her breast. She plucked it like a flower from a garden, tossed it aside. The green runes on the ivory barb flickered once and snuffed out. Without so much as a glance in their direction, she sauntered to her master.

"Brilliant thinking, Tareq. This is even better. Now the Most Holies can witness their most devout servant betray them." Isen took her hand and pressed a kiss against her palm. "And you, sweet girl, will have a new body in Heaven. I promise you that."

The Sanu bowed her head, and the Tybetan Monster removed a chain from around her neck. Settled it over his own.

"Thank you. Now pick up your fans and complete the ritual. Only this time, dance the sequence out of order. Come on, Tareq, we'll watch from over here. Ishida's starting to stink."

"*No,*" Kale screeched. "Amelia, *don't.*" He tugged on her arm, but she just swatted him aside.

She retrieved her fans, snapped them open with a flick of her wrists. Her green eyes stared into the distance as she lifted them above her head.

"Sanu."

It came out only as a hoarse whisper, but her face turned. She'd heard him.

Isen gestured impatiently. "Any time now, sweet girl."

"Amelia."

Her name was a caress leaving his tongue. She straightened.

"Come to me."

Her sandals rasped against the cracked earth. Hiro steeled himself, focused all of his strength into his numb fingers—

"Sweet girl, what are you...?"

—and plunged his greatsword into her stomach.

CHAPTER 138

HER OCEAN-BLUE EYES FLUTTERED AS THE BLOOD LEFT HER BODY IN A rush.

"*AMELIA!*" Isen screamed. He sprinted across the mesa.

She fell to the side, the blade sliding slickly from her belly.

Hiro managed to push himself upright, pulled her across his lap. Cradling her head in the crook of his elbow, he pressed a hand weakly against the severed flesh. "I'm sorry, I'm so sorry. Amelia—"

Kale scrambled to unwind her sari and plug up the hole.

"Just... leave it," she rasped. Her fingers pushed weakly at his fumbling hands.

"*No, no, no,*" the boy kept muttering, the tears rolling off his cheeks and splattering on her gushing abdomen.

Something metallic fell from the orange silk and bounced against the ground. Startled, the boy held it up into the moonlight. It was a hilt, shaped like a roaring lion. Its golden mane flowed away from the open maw to form the grip, and rubies studded its eyes.

Kale slowly stood, the hilt cradled in his palms. "It's... *perfect.*" He rolled it into his right hand and tightened his fingers around the grip.

Angelfire sprouted from the hilt. Rippling white and crackling, the sword blazed like a silver sun. The boy turned his wrathful hazel gaze toward Isen. The Tybetan Monster screeched to a halt. The Bowman took one look at him and ran.

"*My turn,*" the boy hissed.

He leapt over the Sanu's body with a roar. The ripping white fire slashed through the air, left tendrils of light in its wake. It shattered one of Isen's swords into shimmering splinters.

Hiro weakly pulled the sari over the Sanu's wound, fingers trembling. They just wouldn't work properly.

"No," she whispered.

"I can't let you die." He swallowed to keep his voice from shaking.

"He made the bridge... with his life. I can... honor it... with mine."

"Amelia, *please.*"

The moon shone on her sallow face, made the tears on her cheeks glisten like crushed crystal. His own tears sprinkled her with diamond dust. Her eyes, once blue as the summer ocean, seemed as colorless as glass. Her pale lips parted as if she was going to say something, but no sound came out.

He waited, heart in his throat, not daring to breathe. "Amelia? *Amelia.*"

He jostled his arm, trying to rouse her, but she remained still. The blood was barely oozing from her wound now.

"*Amelia.*" He took his hand away from her abdomen to slap at her cheeks.

Red mingled with the diamonds and turned them into rubies. Red on white, like winterberries against the snow.

"*Kale!*" he screamed. "Kale, she's – Gods above, she's—"

Behind him, Isen shrieked. He was covered in blood from a dozen cuts, pinned to the ground with Kale's foot jammed into his gut.

"This. Is. *Mine.*" The boy ripped the amulet from the Tybetan Monster's neck.

Isen clawed at the air after it. "*No!*"

Kale stepped away, slammed the amulet against the center of his chest. It vibrated against his skin, glowed hot like the heart of a forge. With a thunderous *whoosh,* the amulet burst into a million fragments of golden light. They swirled around the boy like cinders in an updraft, then condensed on his skin as if sucked there by a magnet. His stature grew, thickened into the golden armor. The light ebbed, and he took one stalking step forward.

His hair had lengthened until the reddish-gold mane brushed his shoulders. His hazel eyes had cleared to amber, as warm as summer sunlight, but his mouth still had that impish grin. He was now the height and breadth of a young man in the power of his prime, and he bore the breastplate on strong shoulders.

Overhead, the storm clouds unleashed their fury upon the earth. Rain flooded the mesa, poured over the sides to drown the banyan forest. The water smoothed the honeycombed surface of the Gate, transformed it into the world's largest mirror. A perfect reflection of the night sky.

Hiro curled himself over the Sanu, shielded her as much as he could from the deluge. The roar of the rain muted any other sound, but he heard his heart break when the last of the Sanu's blood swirled into the water.

As suddenly as the downpour began, it stopped. The clouds dissipated, dissolving into mist and wafting away. Hiro blinked the water from his eyes and peered through the misty haze.

The Crown Prince of Heaven, the Lion Before the Storm, shook the rain from his reddish-gold curls and winked at him. "I look pretty good, don't I?"

Hiro could only nod.

His voice was deeper, yet still familiar. He stuck his blazing sword into the ground, took hold of his neck, and cracked it to either side. Yawned a mouthful of white teeth. "Sweet mercy, it's been a while."

"Kale," Hiro breathed.

"Naming me after a vegetable was *not* your finest moment, Hiro," the Crown Prince said dryly. His amber eyes flicked to the priestess's slack face. "Hold onto her for me." Then he snatched up his sword and marched toward Isen.

The Tybetan Monster sidled away, hand grasping for his one remaining blade.

"I remember you now. It's like I've been in a dream, and now everything has finally fallen into place. You've been *very* bad. Mother and Father are very disappointed in you."

Isen screeched and swung at him.

The Crown Prince ducked and dodged as deftly as if Isen was a child at his first fencing lesson.

"I'll not have you steal away my victory," Isen bellowed. "I've not lived two lifetimes to be stopped now!"

"I've lived a million of your lifetimes," the Crown Prince said, "and I will never be stopped." He batted Isen's sword aside, clamped a gauntleted fist around his throat.

A strangled cry as Isen was lifted off his feet. He dropped his sword and scrabbled at the fist. Sliced his fingers on the spiked tips of the armored scales.

"There are more realms than just Heaven and Earth, and there is evil in them. Go, and join your brothers."

And the Crown Prince rammed his blazing sword into the Tybetan Monster's chest.

CHAPTER 139

THE ANGELFIRE CONSUMED ISEN FROM THE INSIDE OUT, SEEPED OUT OF his wounds in great slashes of white and shone from his pores in countless pinpricks of light. It streamed from his screaming mouth, glowed from his burned eye sockets, until it blasted him apart.

The tens of thousands of thralls that had impassively watched the events like silent statues collapsed where they stood. Puppets whose master had just severed their strings.

The gray flakes of Isen's confetti-like existence floated in the air until the Crown Prince blew a long sigh. The confetti swirled one instance and compressed the next, tightened into a ball no bigger than a sycamore seed. It shook as if enraged, glowing redder and redder until it vanished with a *pop!*

Shoulders slumped, the Crown Prince walked back to them. The angelfire vanished; he replaced the hilt on a hook on his belt. Curling a hand over Hiro's shoulder, he knelt in the water beside him. His amber eyes were wet with unshed tears. "Oh, Amelia."

Hiro bent over her, sobbing as he clutched her closer. "Please. Take me instead. My life for hers. Please. *Please.*"

"You'd die for her?" the Crown Prince inquired softly.

"Yes. A thousand times, *yes.* I... I love her."

"And I love her too much to have a life without you in it." With a gentle smile, he smoothed the caramel hair away from her face. "Oh, my darling, you needn't die for them. I did that already. I appreciate the gesture, but I'd much prefer watching you dance."

He bent over, kissed her tenderly on the forehead.

When he straightened, her eyes were open.

Hiro choked back a sob of relief.

"Kale?" she murmured. "You look... different."

The Crown Prince of Heaven smiled at her. "And you, Amelia, have some dancing to do," he told her with mock sternness. "The sacrifice has been honored, but I will not be deprived of such a beautiful display of devotion."

She nodded, and the Crown Prince helped her to her feet. The Sanu retrieved her fans from the water and lifted them above her head.

"Just a minute, Amelia." The Crown Prince turned his attention back to Hiro. "Aren't you forgetting to ask me something?"

"What?" Hiro asked dumbly.

The Crown Prince raised an eyebrow and gestured to all of him. "Did you want to bleed out, or did you want to me help you with that?"

Hiro glanced down at himself, took mute stock of his wounds and gaping flesh. He'd gone numb from the pain and shock. "Oh, yes. Please."

The Crown Prince smiled his impish grin and winked.

The strength of a good night's sleep seeped into his body. Restored him. He pulled at the tattered shreds of his gi, examined his arm and leg. Stuck his fingers though the gap by his shoulder, found no wound or torn flesh. There wasn't even scar tissue.

He scrambled to his knees, pressed his fist into his palm and bowed. "Thank you, my lord."

The Crown Prince smothered a smile. "That's... ironic. You're welcome. Now pick up anything you don't want destroyed and come over here and enjoy this."

Hiro snatched the ivory knife, now clean of his blood, and stuffed it into his boot. He stuffed the Sanu's things into her pack and slung it over his shoulder.

The Crown Prince encircled his arm around Hiro's shoulders and gestured to the Sanu. "Amelia, please continue."

She nodded, began to dance.

Clothes in tatters, matted with blood, hair a disheveled mess. The water mirrored every sweep of her arm, every leap of her strong legs. Her fans stroked the sky and bathed the stars.

Hiro couldn't take his eyes off her.

Yueshu was beautiful.

CHAPTER 140

BLUE LIGHT TRAILED AFTER HER FOOTSTEPS.

The om shimmered in the water, light bubbling up from the salt below. It swelled across the Gate, veined into the Bodhi tree, and popped new buds like rubies from its branches.

The water frothed, boiled.

Yueshu ended as the orange moon disappeared behind the mountains. Head bowed, the Sanu folded the fans over her chest.

Light erupted from the Gate.

The bodies of the thralls were incinerated; not even ash remained. The light disappeared into the heavens, dissipating among the stars.

When it was over, the Sanu closed her fans. She sloshed through the shallows, head bowed shyly.

The Crown Prince yanked her into his arms. The Sanu laughed, flung her arms around his neck. A gauntleted hand grabbed the front of Hiro's gi and yanked him into their embrace. "Thank you, Amelia," the Crown Prince said after a long time. He broke free of them gently. "That was beautiful."

"Thank you," she breathed, "for... everything."

He grinned. "My pleasure. Souls like you make everything worth the effort. And now, my friends, I wish to go home. I've been away too long—"

"Why didn't you tell me who you were?" Hiro blurted.

The Crown Prince reached up, placed a hand on each of his shoulders. Hiro sank to his knees, unable to stand. "I didn't know at the time. Pieces of me were missing. I just knew that I was lost. And you gave me a home."

Hiro shut his eyes, turned his face away. "I should've been better," he whispered. "You deserved better."

"You were just as you needed to be." The Crown Prince passed a hand over Hiro's hair. "There was so much hurt in your heart, but you still showed me the best version of you. Don't dwell on the past, Hiro. You're free of it now."

"Yes, sir," he mumbled.

The Crown Prince laughed. "I don't know if I'm ever going to get used to that coming from you." He turned to the Sanu. "Amelia?"

"What is your name?" she asked.

His smile was as radiant as the sun. He leaned forward, whispered it into her ear. Her face brightened at its sound. Kissing her forehead, he slipped the hilt from its hook and retreated a few steps. "May you both be blessed."

Angelfire erupted from the hilt. When the blaze faded, he was gone.

Hiro tore his gaze from the stars, looked at the Sanu. "Amelia—"

His greatsword clattered to the ground as she leapt into his arms. Hiro crushed her against him, knotting his hands into her caramel hair. He encircled her with all of his strength, arms threatening to burst. She was alive, pink-fleshed, and eyes as blue as the ocean deep. He buried his face into her shoulder and wept. Her arms tightened around his neck, and he felt her own tears trickling down into his shirt.

After a long time, they parted awkwardly from each other. Cheeks red, the Sanu busied herself by rewrapping her sari. Something blue rolled down her trouser leg, splashed into the shallow water. Hiro bent, retrieved the chicken egg-sized lump.

"Kale's opal," the Sanu breathed. "I forgot—"

"If he needed it, he would've said something. Why don't you keep it for now? Something to remember him by." He held it out, curled his fingers over hers when she reached for it.

Her blush deepened. "Hands."

Hiro flinched.

But her grip only tightened. "No," she said. "May I hold your hand?"

Swallowing thickly, he removed his glove, entwined the fingers of his burned hand in hers.

Together they walked across the Gate of Heaven, its water-soaked plains a perfect reflection of the night sky.

CHAPTER 141

LHASA GREETED THEM WITH ALL THE HOSPITALITY AND WARMTH OF A graveyard.

Despite the rain, the city continued to smoke, its white stone stained with soot. Ash mingled with oil and water and slithered down the rubble-strewn bricks. The husks of the thralls, deep in the throes of decay, littered the streets outside the temple. Swarms of flies rippled over their bodies, flicking their iridescent wings in a macabre parody of a rainbow.

The red cedar doors, scorched but not destroyed, hung open on steady hinges. Sunlight glowed on the empty chair, turning the pool in to a vat of liquid gold. Rising from the gloom, the great statues of Lady Bosetsanu and her Lord Delphi beckoned them.

Amelia ran.

Startled, Hiro shouted for her to wait, but she ignored him.

Gravel sprayed as she skidded to a stop.

She squinted against the bright-green light. Red-crowned cranes skittered in the shadows of the bamboo stalks. Jacarandas showered the paths with their purple blossoms, and the grass undulated like waves in the breeze. It smelled fresh here, like a winter forest awoken by spring.

The garden was untouched, oblivious to the destruction on the opposite side of its walls. It grew with quiet tenacity, a pocket of resilient life.

Hiro's boots came to a crunching halt behind her. His hand melded against her shoulder. Even with the heat of his palm soaking through the silk and into her skin, she felt overwhelmingly alone.

Alone, because she could not reciprocate its warmth.

Alone, because the sisters of Mount Taru and their sororal love were dead.

Alone, for the woman who could've given her immediate comfort and guidance lay dead in a crumpled heap at the end of the winding path.

The High Sister curled around the wound in her chest, her twig-like fingers splayed in eternal shock. Her face was strained, her eyes staring at something far away. The mischievous spirit that had enflamed this body with life was gone.

Amelia leaned away from Hiro's hand. "I need to take care of Rosara."

"Stay here," he said gently. "I'll go."

"No."

"Then we'll do it together."

Amelia fashioned a crown of flowers for the sibyl's head, studding her braid with buds and berries. Hiro pried the ring of office off her stiff finger and collected the other jewelry that would be passed on to the sibylline. When he was done, he wrapped the purple tablecloth around Rosara's body, folding it in such a way that the edging of gold-and-scarlet thread coiled around her in a protective embrace.

Fighting back tears, Amelia arranged the High Sister's hair over her shoulder and down her chest so it hid her hands. Hiro laid her on the pyre he'd built from the pavilion and pulled a flap of the tablecloth over her head.

"May Delphi the Protector guard your steps and the grace of the Blessed Lady be upon you always," she whispered.

She turned away as Hiro reached for the torch.

CHAPTER 142

Hiro left the Sanu to mourn in private.

He retreated to the forgotten feast on the table, brushed a cluster of green-back flies from the peacock carcass, and fed. So long as it smelled acceptable, it went down the gullet. He was fishing the last of the dumplings out, skins leathery but still juicy inside, when feet grated against the gravel paths.

Hiro ripped away from the table.

Four familiar faces and a host of others greeted him.

"*Boss.*"

The Si Tanin swarmed him like a pack of gleeful hounds. School-children eagerly telling their father about their studies. Shin's hand squeezing his shoulder, Azelie's infectious smile. Takāto's crushing embrace, Calliope's stoic nod.

"… got out through the catacombs—"

"… Militum Dei are *tough*—"

Tatako's joyous laughter—

"… all dropped dead—"

"… just got back—"

"… saw the smoke here—"

"*Report.*" Hiro's voice cut through the thick of it. "Casualties?"

Shrugs.

"Nobody lost anything they didn't already have two of."

Calliope was missing an eye. A thick wad of bandage strained red packed into her left socket.

"The clergy?" Hiro asked.

The Si Tanin parted as the sibylline rushed between them, face flushed. Apprehensive. "The Sanu Maitre...?"

"She's at the Gate..."

Relief.

"...by the pyre."

Horror. "R-Rosara?"

Hiro placed the Sanuset Seat's ring and the sibyl's other jewelry into her palm. "I'm sorry. She... passed, ensuring the Sanu could escape."

Sister Ophelia closed her fingers over the sparkling mound, drew it against her chest. "I-I see. Please, excuse me." She disappeared behind the bend, the rest of the haggard clergy shuffling behind her like lambs.

"Mmm." Takāto rubbed his hands together, nosed the air. "Something smells like... food. Sort of. You cook, boss?"

Hiro rolled his eyes, gestured to the table.

The Four Little Dragons pounced.

Shin silently slurped cold noodles as Azelie skewered sausages with her knives. Calliope's chopsticks plucked braised vegetables from their broth like a stork striking after fish. A stork with horrible depth perception. Hiro snagged one last morsel from the peacock as Takāto dragged the platter up against his gut.

A drumstick sticking out of his mouth, Hiro mounded rice onto a plate for the Sanu, scrounged up a pair of clean chopsticks—

Boom. Boom. Boom-boom-boom.

The plate slipped from his hand.

Boom. Boom. Boom-boom-boom.

The drumstick bounced across the grass, slung a trail of saliva in its wake.

Hiro ran.

He ripped out of the temple, scrambled up the rubble onto a partially collapsed roof.

They streamed from the east, from the Brahma Rush. Blue woad on their faces, pelts draped over their shoulders, they beat the heinous rhythm on drums made from the skins of their enemies. Many clans, united under one cause.

Sjávar Ulfur. *Him.*

"Boss?"

Boom. Boom. Boom-boom-boom.

He slid down the rubble, stumbled into the street. "Baltic Raiders."

"*Goushi.*"

"We need to get to the river."

The Si Tanin didn't hesitate.

"We'll take the catacombs, boss," Calliope said. "We can sneak around their flanks."

"Go."

Hiro followed the Si Tanin into the temple. Takāto slammed the heel of his hand against one of the stars on Lord Delphi's plinth, stepped back as a section of tile dropped into a hidden compartment beneath the floor. He disappeared down the ramp into the catacombs, Azelie right on his heels.

Hiro backed away from the mouth of the tunnel. "I can't. Not without—"

Calliope tugged on his arm. "She'll understand, boss."

"No." He shook her off. "I just need—"

"Hiro?" Her voice drifted from the hallway, her sandals echoing on the stone. "What's that noise? Are those drums?"

Thank the gods. He whirled away from Lord Delphi's statue, running the rest of the way to the Sanu. Confusion creased her forehead, turned her eyes dark as a storm-swept sea. His hands itched to yank her close, but the knot of clergy hurrying in her wake made that impossible. "Amelia, I have to go."

"What? Why?"

Hiro swallowed thickly. "I... I slipped up. Those drums – those are Baltic Raiders, Sanu."

Her eyes widened. Of course she'd heard of them. Her mountain was on the western coast – their hunting grounds. No doubt the survivors of the towns they ravaged would go to her temple to find some measure of peace. "B-but what are they doing here?"

He shook his head. "Isen must've rallied them to his cause with the promise of meeting me in battle. They're searching for Sjávar Ulfur. For *me*."

"I don't understand."

He grasped her shoulders, squeezing. The High Sister choked on an outraged gasp, but the Sanu's attention was only on him. "Amelia, they pillage and rape and kill until they have what they want. They'll take this city to find me. I can't let them take you, too."

"I thought we were done," she whispered, tears brimming in her eyes. "No more fighting, just picking up the pieces—"

He smeared away the tear that slipped down her cheek with the back of his hand. "Me too."

Boom. Boom. Boom-boom-boom.

"*Boss*," Calliope barked.

Hiro released her, backing away. "I have to go. I'm sorry, Sanu, but they won't have you."

He lingered at the mouth of the tunnel, just one heartbeat more, then dropped into the catacombs.

Amelia jumped when a hand curled over her shoulder.

"We've got to get you out of here," Ophelia said.

"Wait, what?" She turned away from the statues, away from the stone that hid the entrance to the catacombs. Hiro had disappeared into the gloom, the stone grating back into place like the lid of a tomb.

"He's not the only one who's had experience with the Baltic Raiders." The High Sister yanked up her sleeve, revealing a thick gash that hadn't healed right. The scar was the ugly purple of a bruise, sewing the flesh of her forearm together like a shiny satin ribbon.

"They have no regard for religion. You'll just be another ripe fruit to pluck when he fails."

Amelia wiggled out of her grasp. "*When* he fails? *That* is Hiro Ishida."

"You are the last Sanu, Amelia. We can't take that risk. Captain Ursula. Boris."

A wiry woman with her brown hair slicked back from her face and a monk the size of a mountain marched up from the rear of the clergy. Their robes were black, a red sun embroidered on their chests. Militum Dei.

"You'll take my lady back to her home. Back to Mount Taru," the High Sister ordered.

Amelia's hands clenched into fists, but no silver fire came to her call. "You can't make me leave!"

Ophelia's dove-gray eyes glistened. "Forgive me, Amelia. But yes, I can."

With a snap of her fingers, the Militum Dei seized her.

Hiro swept the screen of leaves aside with a cautious hand.

The langskips formed a jagged line along the riverbank. Red sails stirred in the autumn breeze; flies buzzed the slack-mouthed faces of the severed heads that adorned the gunwales. The sentries were minimal; no Baltic Raider found glory guarding a boat.

The Si Tanin stirred restlessly behind him.

"Take them."

He knew they'd come for him.

Flames devoured their ships and one canoe, blotted out the sun with smoke darker than coal. The heads of their sentries smoldered in a pile beside him, their flesh sloughing from their skulls like melting wax.

He waited, the shaggy pelt of the sea wolf draped over his shoulders.

The whetstone rasped against the greatsword. Summoning.

"Sjávar Ulfur!"

A champion emerged from the forest, raced across the field. Big, scarred, blue woad smeared in a slash across his face. Berserker. A hatchet sprouted from each fist, chopped the air with each stride. The whites of his eyes shone like ivory rings, screaming teeth like stumps of rotted wood.

Hiro stood, swept to the side, and cleaved the Raider open from hip to opposite shoulder. One hack removed the champion's head. He heaved the body onto the pile of smoldering skulls, placed the head in the grass in front of his stool and sat. One.

The collection of champions' heads fleshed out into a crescent, then a ring.

The Baltic Raiders streamed out of the forest like deer from a fire, eager for the chance to slay the legend. Until they saw the collection of heads, and the man in the wolf pelt sharpening his sword with their langskips burning behind him. Their bravest had already faced Sjávar Ulfur and lost. It cowed the rest of them into superstitious uncertainty.

Hiro fought to appear cool, unconcerned. But his pulse was like lightning in his veins. He wanted to gasp, wipe the sweat out of his eyes, guzzle water, but he couldn't look weak. There were thousands left, held at bay by their belief that he was the great Sea Wolf. The man imbued with an indomitable, vengeful spirit.

Arm trembling, he rasped the whetstone against his greatsword. Taunting.

Weapons clinked, pelts rustled, and the Raiders hastily parted.

Yellow eyes, skin a lacework of black runes, an ugly scar roped around his throat. Their conjurer stalked through the long grass.

Hiro remained seated, nonchalant, even as every fiber of his being screamed one word. *Run.*

The conjurer stopped a few feet away from the ring of heads.

Hiro gestured to the burning ships with a wave of his whetstone. "I see you all got my message."

"Are these theatrics supposed to scare me?"

Howling in the forest. White shapes raced in the trees. Cries of alarm, then gurgling screams. The Baltic Raiders in the field shifted nervously.

"Hold your gr—" The command cut off with a squelch.

"*Draugur!*"

"He commands the spirits—"

The Si Tanin, covered in ash and howling like wolves, melted in and out of the shadows. Slew the unwary and scattered their dismembered bodies to be stumbled upon by their clansmen. The shrieks were building to a fevered pitch.

"Well... it seems to be working on them."

The conjurer crossed his wiry arms over his bare chest. "Hiro. Ishida. The Sea Wolf."

"And who are you? I thought I'd killed you."

He traced the scar at his throat with a pointed nail. "You didn't cut deep enough. I was able to heal this vessel."

Gooseflesh rippled up Hiro's arms, sent a shiver into his toes. *Run!*

Hiro cleared his throat with difficulty. "You've been quiet these past years."

"It took a long time to heal. That sword... weakened me. Robbed me. But the rise of the orange moon is auspicious to my kind, too." The conjurer lifted a hand, splayed his fingers to mime an explosion. The fire of the langskips yowled, twisted and danced to every flick of his fingers.

Hiro hissed, phantom pain seizing his burned hand.

"Your fear... it's *intoxicating.*" Inhaling deeply, the conjurer's eyelids fluttered shut as the runes on his skin flared to life.

RUN!

Hiro didn't hesitate.

Yellow eyes, doors to the sulfurous Abyss, snapped open. Lips peeled back into a snarl. The eyes lowered to the rippling steel sheathed between his ribs.

Panting, Hiro twisted the blade. Felt it pulse with the rhythm of the conjurer's heart sawing itself apart on its edge.

The conjurer slumped onto his knees, a blade of grass submitting to the wind. Gasped a meager breath as Hiro tugged the greatsword free. His head rolled back, lips parted. Amber vapor, sinuous as a snake, wafted from his mouth. *"Ese, ese, ese—"*

The rippling steel scattered the vapor into a cloud of hellish fire-flies. A shrill cry, an insect roasting alive in its shell, and the sparks fizzled into nothingness. Hiro rested the tip of the scorched blade on the conjurer's corpse, glared at the Raiders staring mutely from across the field.

They wouldn't stop even if only one was left breathing. But he had to give them the chance. He couldn't be the Beast any longer.

"Twice, I have defeated your conjurer. Twice, I have bathed my sword in Baltic blood. But a wolf does not take more than its share. The ships downriver have not been touched. Go, and I will feast no more." Hiro pulled the skull of the sea wolf over his head, assumed the full authority of the avenging spirit. "Stay, and I will gorge upon body and soul. You will never see the halls of your ancestors. Stay, and not even the wind will remember your name."

A pause, where even the ships burned without sound.

A berserker bellowed a challenge, thrust a studded mace above his head—

And was silenced.

The chieftain of the Frostrunners smacked the back of his hand flat against his berserker's chest. Shook his head once. Whistled. His tribe followed him to the south. The Corpse Crows left next, then the Nighthunters. The Horned Men lingered, antler headdresses clicking as they mulled, until the Sickle Moons drove them forward with their scythes.

Hiro watched until the last of the langskips shoved off from the shore.

Legs buckling, he sagged into the grass. The greatsword rolled out of his hand. He peeled the pelt off his shoulders, ran his fingers through the shaggy fur. Pressed the sea wolf's muzzle against his forehead in the ancient gesture of connection.

"Good-bye, old friend."

And he threw the skin into the fire.

PART IV

CHAPTER 143

MOSS-COVERED COBBLES SNAKED AWAY FROM THE TORII GATE, disappearing into the pine trees. The lichen had claimed more of the pillars, encasing them in downy blue almost to the crossbar.

Amelia paused at the marker and curled her hand over Bosetsanu's sigil. Worn from weather and grief, the lily left only a faint imprint against her palm.

"Eridani? You don't have to—"

"Yes, I do, Aurelio." She faced the sea gypsy with a brave smile. "Thank you, for seeing me this far. I know you're loath to be so long away from the sea."

She'd only had a moment to collect her things before the Militum Dei had hustled her out of the city. There was a loose stone by the Pool of Sacred Tears that revealed a tunnel that emptied out somewhere near Nagarze. It was pure dumb luck that at the docks she recognized the chips of sea glass in his hair, the leather trousers that clung too embarrassingly to his hips, the red scarf that looped several times around his neck. The Militum Dei had had no choice but to follow her on board the *Siren's Call*.

Aurelio waved the comment aside, those chips of sea glass clicking in his hair. "It was an honor. You are most welcome at Valencia anytime. You will *always* have a home there."

Home.

Her eyes traced the winding cobbled path that would bring her back to the only home she'd ever known. The home she had abandoned.

She fished the mariner's ring out of her pocket, blushed faintly at the sight of the voluptuous mermaid curled around the fat emerald. Held it out to him. "Before I forget."

The Atlantican's hand curled around her fingers, enclosing them around the ring. Captain Ursula cleared her throat warningly. Ignoring her, Aurelio pressed her knuckles first against his lips, then against his forehead in the ancient gesture of respect. "Keep it. In case you need me again. May the horizon stretch before you."

"And the wind be ever at your back."

His sea-green eyes sparkled. "Ciao, Eridani."

"Ciao, Aurelio." She turned to the Militum Dei. They both looked exhausted. They'd spent countless days and nights keeping watch, making sure she got home safely. "Well, our time together certainly didn't start out very cordially, but I've come to view you both as friends. Thank you, for your help."

Boris bowed, a smile tugging at the corners of his mouth. It'd only taken a week after leaving Lhasa before they were playing backgammon at night instead of him standing guard over her as she slept, worried she'd try to sneak off.

Trust had taken longer with the Siberian captain. The wiry woman was shorter than Amelia, with pale blue eyes more piercing than Lord Ishida's. She'd been aloof, detached, even aggressive, until one night on Valencia when Aurelio had managed to get her to relax with a cocktail of puréed pineapple, coconut milk, and rum. A few drinks, some songs, even a dance, and Amelia was there with a cool cloth when the captain spent the rest of the evening vomiting into the bushes. After that, all pretenses were gone.

Ursula leaned forward, touching her forehead against Amelia's. "*Pax vobis*, my lady."

Amelia smiled, but it didn't reach her eyes.

The moss muffled her footsteps. One step at a time, her feet took her over the cobbles, up the one thousand steps of worn stone, out of the arboreal gloom and into the light of the azaleas.

Pink and orange flowers shook off the dregs of evening dew and blazed in the morning sun. Color blanketed the mountainside, bright as wildfire. Bumblebees droned between the blooms, and the delicate scent of peach blossoms wafted from the orchards.

Nature had completely restored what the demon had destroyed.

Not everything.

Feet heavy, Amelia stepped over the threshold.

Singing greeted her.

Novices swept out the Hall of Lilies, laughing as they herded a wayward cricket back into the crepe myrtle. Two young girls, yellow sleeves rolled up to their elbows, weeded the jasmine by the sanctuary. Others lacquered new shutters for the library, and someone hauled a bucket of kitchen scraps from the dining hall to feed the chickens.

The singing faded into the mountain air as the novices gradually noticed her.

A jet-haired woman stumbled down the sanctuary steps. *"Amelia?"* She bolted across the courtyard, scattering the peacocks and halting just a few steps away. Her chest heaved from the sprint, or with anger, disbelief, or any one of the million emotions flickering across her face. Tears turned her tawny-brown eyes into muddy puddles.

"Yuki." Amelia sank to her knees. The strand of multicolored pearls clacked against the flagstones. She stifled a sob and forced herself to look at her friend. "H-how're you alive? The demon... it should've killed every Sanu, every priestess marked with a golden lily on her hand."

"Mine's not golden."

"What?"

With a watery smile, Yuki tugged down her sleeve. "You did something to me, when we were hidden in the jasmine. You turned my tattoo silver, and the demon passed me by. You saved me."

671

Amelia shook her head, slinging tears onto the flagstones. "No, I ran. Yuki, I can never earn your forgiveness, but if you can just *try*—"

Yuki knelt and crushed her sister against her. "Welcome home."

IT WAS twilight when Yuki crested the spire. Her sandals scuffed against the bare rock, stopping in front of the moon peach tree. She crouched on the opposite side of the low table, setting the basket on its surface with a faint *thud*. The candle flame wavered.

Silk fans, a jade flask, food, and a bottle of peach-honey wine peeked out from the whicker rim. Glancing up into Yuki's frowning face, Amelia set the writing stylus aside.

"*Amelia.* It's been a week now. Tonight, we are going to drink this bottle of wine and you are going to finish that journal. Tomorrow morning, you're going to come down from this spire, *take a bath*, and resume your normal duties."

Yuki tossed a white tassel onto the table. The mark of the Revered Onu.

Amelia ran a hand down the strand of multicolored pearls and blanched. "I'm not ready for that responsibility—"

"Something for you to think about, then. You and I are the *only* Sanu left until the flame selects more from the novices. We have a duty to keep our sect alive. Yueshu comes again in another hundred years, and *you* are the only one who knows the ritual. That knowledge *must* be passed on. Is any of this unclear?"

Amelia shook her head quickly.

"Good." Yuki folded her legs under her and popped the cork.

The peach-honey wine was like liquid summer on her tongue. Amelia took a long swallow before passing it back.

"I thought giving you time to unburden yourself in these journals would've made you happier than you look."

Amelia rolled the writing stylus from one side of the page to the other, not looking at her. "When I thought you and the others were gone... I had a family again, however dysfunctional. And now it's torn apart. Even though I'm back with you – and I've missed you so much, Yuki – I feel… adrift. I don't know why."

"Then we'll figure it out together. We'll drink, you'll talk, and I'll listen."

The moon was low in the sky when they finished the bottle of wine.

Yuki's hand slid across the table and curled around hers. "You're heartsick, Amelia."

"Don't be ridiculous—"

"You didn't get to say good-bye. Not a real one, anyway. He could be dead for all you know. No wonder you're crying."

Amelia pressed her fingertips to her cheeks; they came back soaked.

"And this Isen… yeesh."

Her dearest brother and her greatest enemy.

"Well, at least he's dead," Yuki sniffed. "Good riddance."

"Yuki, you're Sanu. *'Honor all life, for all has value.'*"

"I'm sure there's some fine print somewhere in the sacred texts."

She gave a watery chuckle and smeared the wet from her cheeks. "Well I'm never going to finish this journal if I keep blubbering so—"

"Amelia." Yuki's hand tightened. "Your heart cannot have two masters. You *must* decide. If you don't, and you're not Released, that lily will burn a hole through your heart. I just got you back. I-I can't lose you again. Not like that."

Amelia nodded solemnly.

Yuki brushed the grit from her silks and blotted her eyes with her sleeve. "I'll see you in the morning."

It only took a few minutes to finish the final journal. Amelia pinched out the candle flame with wet fingers and drew her legs up to her chest. She pulled the blue opal from her pocket and set it on the stack of books. Its freckled surface sparkled in the starlight.

Sanu were not allowed to have material attachments. Hers was a life of dedication to Bosetsanu, a life of detachment so that she might be a pure vessel of love for her Blessed Lady. Tomorrow, she'd put the opal in the library with the other artifacts that had survived the fire and rejoin her sisters.

But tonight was for her. Tonight was for good-byes.

Amelia lifted her hand to the starlight, and the little scar glinted like a sliver of silver. A memento of when *he* had sucked a splinter from her palm that first night they'd met. She curled her fingers around the scar and tucked it against her chest. The lily tattoo seared her fist.

Gasping, she clutched her heart as it thumped hard against her ribs. It was worse than when the tattoo caught her in a lie. Her heart strained, ready to burst like a summer fruit too full of juice. To explode.

Desperate, Amelia pushed the thought of *him* aside. Buried it. The pain ebbed, and she sagged against the smooth bark.

Under the fluttering leaves of the sacred tree, her heart mended for the last time.

CHAPTER 144

AMELIA TRUDGED DOWN THE SPIRE, THE JOURNALS TUCKED UNDER ONE arm and the basket slung around the other. The morning mist sloshed in the jade flask. Two moon peaches nestled between the fans, their ripe flesh wafting a trail of sweet perfume behind her.

At the temple threshold, she set the basket and her stack of journals on the opposite side of the stone block, but she did not enter. Grime caked under her fingernails and dust coated the backs of her hands. She'd retreated into the pages of the journal, revealing her innermost thoughts to something which could neither condone nor condemn, at the expense of personal hygiene.

Repulsed, Amelia diverted to the spring by the orchards. The sun had not yet penetrated the shadows on the southern slopes, but the honeybees were already hard at work. She bathed to their droning wings, scrubbing her hair and flesh until it tingled.

Singing drifted from the temple as her sisters performed their morning devotions. Amelia hummed, dressing in fresh silks as if layering on armor. Draping the sari diagonally across her chest, she wound it around her waist and tucked in the end so the fringe slapped against her thighs as she walked. The golden beads clicked softly like leaves rustling against stone.

Retrieving her journals, she shouldered open the new doors to the library. Though faint, the stench of smoke still lingered on the stones. One lone bookshelf stood off-center in the vacant space, newly crafted and reeking of cedar. Stripes of sunlight from the eastern shutters glinted on its dusty shelves.

Amelia slid the books onto the center shelf, trailing her fingers down their spines. Three new additions to their library; a Sanu's tales of adventure, loss, victory, redemption and regret. Now that they were out of her heart, it was easy to let them go.

I can come back now. She looked inside to that silver place, and a shadow eddied under the light. *And so can you.*

Smiling for the first time in days, Amelia went to rejoin her sisters.

They were waiting for her, lined under the eaves of the sanctuary. But they weren't looking at her.

On the flagstones, a few feet away from the sanctuary's stairs, knelt a hulking figure. Yuki sat on a stool in front of him, engrossed in an inaudible conversation. From the dampness of his clothes and hair, it appeared he'd been there since last night. The pilgrim's head was bowed, his hands resting on his thighs. A folded coat covered the flagstones in front of him. Two small scrolls lay on the fabric, white on black like oracle bones ready to foretell the future.

Catching sight of her, Yuki ceased her conversation and rose from the stool. She stepped aside, gesturing for Amelia to take her place.

Tension seized her shoulders. The last pilgrim had nearly destroyed them. But Yuki's face was calm, sorrowful even. Amelia sank into the seat as the pilgrim raised his head.

Seal-brown eyes bored into hers.

Hiro.

It took her a minute to find her voice.

Clearing her throat, Amelia crossed one leg over the other and linked her hands over her knees. "I see you're *alive.*"

"I am."

"Any new scars?"

"A few. Want to see?"

"No, I do not want to *see*," she exploded, hopping to her feet. "I am Sanu! And what are you doing here? After all this time, you think you can just show up—"

"I did not just 'show up,'" Hiro replied testily. "I've been here, kneeling on these forsaken flagstones, since sundown."

"You could've gotten up," she said sourly.

"Not if I wanted to be proven worthy."

"Worthy of what?"

A faint smile was her only answer.

Amelia huffed and returned to the stool, smoothing the wrinkles out of her sari with shaking hands. "I thought you were dead," she whispered. "I sent eagles to Lhasa, to Kolkata, Arashiyama, even left word in Nagarze—"

"Wait. When where you in Nagarze?"

"The High Sister had the Militum Dei forcibly remove me from Lhasa after you left. She wasn't confident that you'd succeed."

"Hn." He sat back on his heels. "That'd explain a few things."

"We were in Nagarze maybe a day after, and Aurelio just happened to be there with his ship. We left immediately."

"I'm glad you did. Some of Isen's followers weren't enthralled. Those damn Hadi Centers exploded with loyalists, taking entire cities hostage. Nagarze became overrun. You must've just missed it. I didn't know if they were going to march on Lhasa or just be content to destroy their own city. And I didn't know you weren't in Lhasa anymore. After the Baltic Raiders were dealt with, we took a langskip to intercept."

"And after?"

He gave a helpless shrug. "Domo Khan's men finally arrived from Kolkata, and I led them north. By some miracle, Toshiro was still alive and had received the eagles Kale had sent. The Siber Guard had joined forces with him just before the Shadow Army had invaded Jianshu. With most of the army dead after Yueshu, we pinched together to... incapacitate the rest of them."

"I understand how that might have kept you busy—"

"*Might have?*"

"—but your hands seem fine. You couldn't write a letter and send an eagle?"

The hands in question balled into fists. Hiro's eyes blazed, his jaw clenching at he fought to remain calm. Amelia knew she was being difficult, but he'd wounded her. Deeply. It'd been months since Yueshu and not one scrap of news from him.

He took a purging breath. "I was in prison."

Amelia blinked in surprise.

"I had to stand trial for *dimittere*. To make sure I hadn't deserted. With witnesses scattered across the continent, my trial took longer than expected. I wasn't allowed outside communication with anyone, not even my own family. Imagine my surprise when I was released and discovered you had vanished."

Blushing, Amelia lowered her gaze to her hands. They were worrying the beads of her fringe into a tangled mess.

"Everyone knew you were going west to Mount Taru, but no one knew your travel route. Imagine how terrified I was when I couldn't find you and there were still thousands of the Shadow Army unaccounted for. Even that sorcerer *hundan* hasn't been found. I did the only thing I could do to help keep your path safe. I returned to the Councilary Army."

"We'd gone south to the coast," she said in a small voice. "Aurelio took us to the Andalusian Islands, to Valencia."

His eyebrows pierced the sky. "So while I was searching the continent for you, you were spending your winter on the beach drinking rum?"

"And sending every eagle I could get my hands on," she said hotly. "They're in short supply in the islands. And it's not my fault they hardly reached you, with you moving about as much as you were."

"So you were drinking rum." There was a hint of a smile on his lips, a teasing glint in his eye.

Amelia laughed once, smearing the tears from her eyes and letting the tension drain from her shoulders. "So much rum."

He huffed a relieved sigh, raking a hand through his hair. The obsidian mane now swept past his shoulders. "The day I learned the Ciel Pass was open, I left. For you, Amelia."

Her name rolled off his tongue like a caress. A shiver tingled into her toes, startling a cloud of butterflies into flight in her stomach. Flushing, she jerked her chin toward the scrolls on top of the great-coat. Anything to keep her mind off the hammering of her heart. "So what are those?"

His seal-brown eyes softened.

With great care, Hiro gathered the scrolls in one hand, picked up the edge of his coat, and peeled it back.

Lilies, all in various states of desiccation, made a neat row upon the black cloth. There was a pink-and-white stargazer, a speckled tiger lily, a maroon, a white Madonna, a lemon, and a purple one almost as dark as his coat.

Mouth agape, Amelia tore her gaze from the flowers. Hiro held a scroll in each hand.

"These are messages for General Vasilios. The one in my left hand says I'll be headed to Arashiyama to marry the love of my life. The one in my right hand says I'll rejoin the campaign without delay. I need you to pick one, Amelia."

CHAPTER 145

Hiro was nothing but patient. He knelt, seemingly impervious to the flagstones, with his hands outstretched, offering the scrolls.

"Why do they look like that?" Amelia blurted, pointing at the lilies.

It clearly wasn't the response he was expecting. "I-I wasn't sure what kind you liked, so I raided every greenhouse I could find. It took some time to amass this many. It was the middle of winter, you know."

"Yes, I know," she whispered.

Her mind wouldn't work. Thoughts fluttered by like butterflies, and she had no net to catch them.

"Amelia." His rough voice was soft as a summertime breeze. "I was lost for so long, wrapped up in so much hate and anger. You were relentless... showing me kindness I didn't deserve. You penetrated the gloom that was my life—"

"Hiro, please *st*—"

"—and now that I can see the way out, I don't ever want to go back. When I'm with you, I actually like *me* again. I love you, Amelia. I'll love you for eternity. You'll never understand the extent of what you did for me."

She buried her face into her hands. "Sweet mercy, why couldn't you have stayed dead?"

"W-what?"

"I gave you *up*, Hiro," she sobbed. "Twice. My heart can't break a third time."

"It doesn't have to." He reached for her.

She ripped away from his touch, knocking over the stool. "Don't you see? I'm the only one who knows Yueshan. I'm the only one who can prepare the next generation for the ritual." She glanced back at the line of novices under the sanctuary eaves. They stood rigid, hardly daring to breathe, watching with fearful eyes. Yuki's head was bowed, staring at the floorboards at her feet. "I abandoned them once. I can't do it again."

"*Duty.*" He spat the word out like it was something sour. "I see."

Nodding numbly, he rolled onto his feet and swept the greatcoat around his shoulders. The lilies plummeted to the ground, petals breaking free as their floral heads dashed against the flagstones.

"Hiro, please—"

He stopped, broad shoulders rising and falling in deep, shuddering breaths. Raising his chin, he held out his hand. It was the first time he'd ever asked permission.

Tentatively, Amelia slid her hand into his.

His fingers curled over her wrist, gently twisting until her palm faced upward. The scar from the splinter he'd sucked out of her palm glinted like a crescent of moonlight.

Squeezing his eyes shut against unshed tears, he lifted her palm to his lips. His mouth was warm, soft, promising a tenderness reserved only for her. Her fingers curled against his cheek, desperate to cherish one more forbidden touch. Her heart paused between one beat and the next, crashing against her ribs when he broke the kiss. He raised those seal-brown eyes and forced a brave smile. "Maybe we'll get our chance in another life."

He guided her hand back to her side instead of letting it drop. He bowed, a short snap from the waist, and backed away. "I have to go," he whispered. "Good-bye, Amelia."

Amelia chased after him, stumbling through the blinding tears. "*Hiro—*"

But he was already stepping over the threshold, out of the temple and out of her life.

She sagged against the torii gate, legs buckling under her.

"May Delphi the Protector guard your steps—" She choked on a sob, unable to finish the blessing.

The words had turned to ashes in her mouth.

End of Book I

APPENDIX

abn haram: bastard, in Sarabi

aeris: copper piece

biaozi: bitch, in Old Imperial

decedo: flee, abandon, evacuate, in Latan

dimittere: release of military service on religious grounds

Domo/Doma: a title of respect given to those in great authority, below a Prince/Princess in hierarchy

Dongxue Shandian: literally Cave Lightning, but more commonly translated to Cave of Lights, in Old Imperial. Another name for Matha Gupha (Moth Cave).

doros: gold piece

draugur: spirits, in the Baltic tongue

Ese ese esejen – *rise, rise, rise again*, an incantation to transfer the spirit into another vessel

henge: changed being, in Old Imperial

hundan: bastard, asshole, in Old Imperial

goushi: dog shit, in Old Imperial

itoko: bullshit, in Old Imperial

khadim: servant, in Sarabi

Lord/Lady: governor of a Province

Master/Mistress: title of respect given to those of elevated status, below Domo/Doma

ma petite: literally, my small (one), in Atlantican; a term of endearment.

manabudh: Forsaken One, in Sarabi

notué: meaning 'no kill', a martial art that uses an opponent's momentum against him.

pax vobis: peace to you, in a Latan

Prince/Princess: children of a Lord or Lady, or a Lord/Lady's siblings, as immediate
family members may also inherit under the tanist principle

raffiné: refined. Used to describe someone with a generous, kind heart, excellent manners, preferring to diffuse situations through conversation than physical violence, someone slow to anger, compassionate, gentle. A term of highest respect.

ryushutsu: no official translation; a term of immense disrespect with the insinuation of being ill-bred, in Old Imperial

sadiq: friend, in Sarabi

shrub aleasl: a fortified fermented drink made from honey and spiced with cardamom and cinnamon and sometimes orange, in Sarabi

takrim: honored one, used to address someone held in the highest regard, in Sarabi

Tilk Alnidal: meaning 'those that struggle'; a religion prevalent amongst the Bédu tribes of Pirsa and parts of Tybet that stresses the betterment of humanity through struggle. Caste systems are often a result within practicing communities; they believe it encourages the members to 'struggle' to improve their lives and social standing.

yaoguai: a malicious spirit, in Old Imperial

Yueshan: bridge – another term for Yueshu

Yueshu: the Blessing of the Gate; a ceremony performed by a Sanu priestess once every century to reseal the Gate between Heaven and Earth. Ensures access to the afterlife.

zaeim: a political leader in the Cedonia Province, especially among the Bédu tribes. They wear gold, fingerless gloves as a sign of their station.

THANK YOU

Congratulations! You've reached the end of Book I of The Paradise War! Thank you for your tenacity. I don't have any cake as a reward – if someone told you there was cake, they lied – so I hope the story was enough.

If you liked what you read, please leave a review on Amazon.com. And if you REALLY liked what you read, please leave reviews on Goodreads, Bookbub, and any other social media site that strikes your fancy. Your support enables me to keep on writing!

For those of you upon whose hearts I've danced a merry Irish jig at the end of this novel, FEAR NOT! Amelia and Hiro will be back in Book II, The Phoenix Tomb.

Sign up for The Paradise War Newsletter
AND receive your FREE gift!

https://www.subscribepage.com/theparadisewarsignup

ACKNOWLEDGMENTS

Heb 12:11 *No discipline seems pleasant at the time, but painful. Later on, however, it produces a harvest of righteousness and peace for those who have been trained by it.*

Rom 5:3-4 *... because we know that suffering produces perseverance; perseverance, character; and character, hope.*

God: for giving me the energy to keep chipping away at this project without having to resort to illegal substances or copious amounts of caffeine and/or alcohol.

My parents: who taught me the rewards of that discipline and perseverance. Without it, I could've never traveled to the places whose cultures inspired this book.

The hubby: thanks for doing the little things I sometimes didn't find time to help with – cleaning up after dinner, doing the laundry, walking the dog. Sorry he didn't listen to you very well. At least the dishes and the laundry didn't give you any sass.

My twin, Liz: I know the fantasy genre isn't your thing, but thanks for supporting me in all those other ways, including buying this book. (Even though we both know it's destined to wind up unread on your bookshelf... collecting dust... for all eternity.)

My beta readers, Sarah and Erin: I'm so sorry for that beastly first draft, but thanks for slogging through it!

Self-Publishing School: for teaching me what I didn't know.

My mentor, Ramy Vance: your honesty enabled me to write the best version of this book possible.

My editor, Shavonne Clarke: thank you for handling my work gently but being firm about its flaws.

My cover artist Thea N.: you made Amelia come to life!

To those who supported me, your encouragement means more than you know. And to those who were skeptical, thank for you for your doubt. It made me want it even more.

Let your success be the laughter in the faces of those who thought you would fail.

ACKNOWLEDGMENTS

Heb 12:11 *No discipline seems pleasant at the time, but painful. Later on, however, it produces a harvest of righteousness and peace for those who have been trained by it.*

Rom 5:3-4 ... *because we know that suffering produces perseverance; perseverance, character; and character, hope.*

God: for giving me the energy to keep chipping away at this project without having to resort to illegal substances or copious amounts of caffeine and/or alcohol.

My parents: who taught me the rewards of that discipline and perseverance. Without it, I could've never traveled to the places whose cultures inspired this book.

The hubby: thanks for doing the little things I sometimes didn't find time to help with – cleaning up after dinner, doing the laundry, walking the dog. Sorry he didn't listen to you very well. At least the dishes and the laundry didn't give you any sass.

My twin, Liz: I know the fantasy genre isn't your thing, but thanks for supporting me in all those other ways, including buying this book. (Even though we both know it's destined to wind up unread on your bookshelf... collecting dust... for all eternity.)

My beta readers, Sarah and Erin: I'm so sorry for that beastly first draft, but thanks for slogging through it!

Self-Publishing School: for teaching me what I didn't know.

My mentor, Ramy Vance: your honesty enabled me to write the best version of this book possible.

My editor, Shavonne Clarke: thank you for handling my work gently but being firm about its flaws.

My cover artist Thea N.: you made Amelia come to life!

To those who supported me, your encouragement means more than you know. And to those who were skeptical, thank for you for your doubt. It made me want it even more.

Let your success be the laughter in the faces of those who thought you would fail.

ABOUT THE AUTHOR

Kat Lapatovich Healy is a displaced Yankee living in the middle of the Midwest heartland. A biochemist-turned-aspiring author, she loves all fantasy, science fiction, basically anything with some sassy wit, cool tech, and action-movie heroics. You'll find that in her work, along with characters struggling to connect with not only others, but themselves as well.

When she's not glued to her computer, she daydreams about when she'll be able to go snorkeling again, bakes way too many pastries, and tries to grow things in her garden. She's pretty bad at it, but she's hopeful. The plants aren't.

Facebook: @KattasticReads

Made in the USA
Middletown, DE
23 April 2021